THE DEVIL'S PAWN

A Retelling of the Faust Legend, Book Two

OTHER TITLES BY OLIVER PÖTZSCH

The Faust Series

The Master's Apprentice

The Hangman's Daughter Series

The Hangman's Daughter

The Dark Monk

The Beggar King

The Poisoned Pilgrim

The Werewolf of Bamberg

The Play of Death

The Council of Twelve

The Black Musketeers Series

Book of the Night

Sword of Power

Knight Kyle and the Magic Silver Lance

Holy Rage

THE DEVIL'S PAWN

Translated *by* Lisa Reinhardt

Oliver Pötzsch

AMAZON **CROSSING**

Text copyright © 2019 by Oliver Pötzsch

Translation copyright © 2021 by Lisa Reinhardt

Previously published as *Der Lehrmeister: Die Geschichte des Johann Georg Faustus II* by Ullstein Buchverlage GmbH in Germany in 2019. Translated from German by Lisa Reinhardt. First published in English by Amazon Crossing in 2021.

Published by Amazon Crossing, Seattle

www.apub.com

Amazon, the Amazon logo, and Amazon Crossing are trademarks of Amazon.com, Inc., or its affiliates.

ISBN-13: 9781542014595

ISBN-10: 154201459X

Cover design by M.S. Corley

Printed in the United States of America

For my children, Niklas and Lily.
To love sometimes means to let go.

Prologue

THE HOLY FATHER FOLLOWED THE SCREAMS THAT DIRECTED him through the catacombs. The shrill sound told Pope Leo X that the time had come.

Hunched over, he hurried through the low passages, his red velvet cap brushing against the dirty ceiling from time to time. Leo panted, trembling with anticipation as he always did when he came down here to conduct the final interrogation. Built on the banks of the Tiber River more than a thousand years ago as a mausoleum for Roman emperors, Castel Sant'Angelo, the castle of the holy angel, was a maze of cells, grand halls, and corridors, filled with escape tunnels, hidden doors, and burial chambers. The castle was the grave of many known and unknown prisoners, while also serving as papal fortress and refuge—Sant'Angelo was considered impregnable.

The pope's chambers, in the upper stories, were lordly rooms, every inch of the walls covered with oil paintings by the most famous artists. Bronze taps spouted cold or warm water on demand; servants carried trays of candied fruit and ice, which had been carved from the distant mountains north of the Apennines and sweetened with outrageously expensive sugar that was shipped from the newly discovered lands beyond the sea and was as precious as gold. The upstairs halls smelled of violets and perfume, forcing out the stink of the Roman gutters, and the stone walls breathed the spirit of God.

But deep down in the catacombs, death and perdition reigned.

Pope Leo X paused when another scream rang out, even shriller this time, almost as if from a child. He was definitely on the right track. His heart thumping with excitement, he walked faster and turned right, to where another set of steps led even farther down. Leo was fat, weighing more than two hundred pounds; he'd been putting on weight since the day he'd ascended the throne. He was troubled by shortness of breath and recurring, painful fistulas in his behind. He dreaded climbing all those stairs back up, but his growing sense of anticipation spurred him on.

Perhaps I will learn the truth today!

Smoking torches illuminated a narrow, soot-stained corridor. The pope occasionally passed a Swiss guard, each one bowing low before the pontiff. Leo didn't deign to look at them. He didn't like being seen down here, but every now and then it was simply unavoidable.

Especially when a secret must not make its way to the surface.

More stairs went even deeper down into the darkness. At the bottom, two guards became visible in the gloom of the corridor, positioned to the left and right of a heavily reinforced door with a small, barred window at eye level. That was where the screams were coming from, growing louder once more, as if the person behind the door wanted to give the Holy Father a special welcome.

Leo scowled; the howling was barely tolerable. Thankfully, it ended as abruptly as it had begun.

The pope, out of breath, signaled for the guards to open the heavy door. The room on the other side was dimly lit by a torch, and a sweetish, smoky smell oozed into the corridor. Glowing braziers stood in the corners of the almost perfectly square chamber built from rough-hewn blocks of stone. Leaning against the walls were pincers and other utensils whose purpose Leo merely guessed at, though he had seen some of them before—in Florence, for example, where he came from. Leo nodded appreciatively. He bore the plump face and stubborn temperament of a peasant, but his wit was that of a scholar. And he was as ruthless and cunning as everyone in his family.

We hid the truth well, he thought. *In the lowest spot of Rome.*

Giovanni (as he was named at birth) was a descendant of the Medici family, the same wealthy dynasty that had been ruling the fate of Florence—of all northern Italy, even—for more than a hundred years. His father was Lorenzo de' Medici, called *il Magnifico*, the Magnificent. As second-born son, Giovanni had been destined for a career within the church; at the age of seven he was named canon of Florence, then cardinal at fourteen. Following the death of his elder brother, Piero, he became ruler of Tuscany. All things considered, it took surprisingly long before Giovanni's ambition, his hunger for power, and, most of all, his family's influence made him pope. For five years now he had been holding the position that he and his family had been longing for since his childhood.

He was the most powerful and richest man in Christendom.

Leo intended to enjoy every single day of his hopefully very long tenure. He wanted to enter the history books as the pope who led Rome into a new golden era by completing the enormous Saint Peter's Basilica. The monuments celebrating him would be forged from gold and silver.

In pursuit of his goals, Leo had resorted to measures that brought sweat to his forehead at night and robbed him of his sleep. He had done things so unspeakably cruel that he hoped God would look the other way and condone them tacitly.

It's all for the benefit of the church! For the church's benefit and my own, of course. But is there even a difference?

The pope wrinkled his nose in preparation for the foul smell and entered the dungeon, gathering up his red robe so it wouldn't drag across the ashes and blood on the stone floor. The stench in the chamber nearly knocked him off his feet; it was the fetid reek of blood, feces, and vomit.

The stench of fear—of fear and of the truth.

Leo's eyes turned to the rack in the center of the room. Lying on top was a seemingly lifeless, scrawny man clad in nothing but a torn loincloth. His arms and legs were covered in burn marks from the previous interrogations, and his bearded face was twisted in a grimace of pain. Images of the suffering of Christ came to Leo's mind, but he quickly forced the thought aside.

"So?" he asked the beefy, bullnecked man with the bloodstained apron standing next to the rack with a poker in his hand. "Did you get anything out of him?" Leo tried to suppress his excitement.

"Unfortunately not, Holy Father," the jailer said, shaking his head.

Leo knew the jailer from other tortures; he came from the Marches, where he'd served the infamous Cesare Borgia. The man was considered one of the best in his field and was as silent as the grave, but it would appear that even he was at his wit's end.

"He only jabbers and doesn't make any sense," the torturer explained with a shrug. "To be honest, I don't believe he ever knew anything of value. He's a fraud, just like all the others."

"A fraud, you say? Nothing but a filthy fraud?"

The pope strained to hide his disappointment. He took a step closer and studied the prisoner's bruised face, covered with festering wounds. The man's teeth had been pulled out, one by one, just like the nails on his fingers and toes. He no longer bore any resemblance to the imperious, loudmouthed fellow who until recently had advertised his skills on the squares of Rome. With trembling lips he started to garble something, a thin rivulet of bloody saliva running from a corner of his mouth.

"For . . . forgive me, Father," he struggled to say. "Forgive me . . ."

Leo turned away with disgust. He would have liked to kick the pathetic creature, but that would have been inappropriate for the most powerful man in the Christian world. He should have known that this attempt would be nothing but a dead end, just like so many others before. But the sources had been promising, and he'd wanted to make sure. He had to follow any possible lead.

Leo breathed deeply, trying to ignore the stench. Well, at least there was hope. Only a few days ago a new path had opened, and it was a particularly promising one. Despite the defeat just now, Leo felt deep in his heart that he was very close to his goal. It was as if God had spoken to him in his dreams. Yes, soon he would learn the secret—he had it on very good authority, after all. And now that this last path had turned out to be an error, there was no other option left. Leo could only hope that no one else would beat him to finding the man he so desperately sought.

The man who was probably the only person on earth to know the well-guarded secret.

Only a little longer, the pope thought wistfully. *The Lord is testing my patience.*

"Get *that* away from here," ordered Leo, gesturing at the quivering bundle on the rack. "And make sure no one ever finds him."

"Mercy!" screamed the prisoner, yanking at his chains. He tried to sit up and cried out with pain. "Mercy! I . . . I know it! By God, I swear I know it! Please—"

"You had your chance," muttered Leo as he walked away. At the same time, he thought that he couldn't afford to take any risks, not even the smallest. This was too important—to him, to the Holy Mother church, to the entire world. As he passed the guards, he beckoned to one of them.

Leo gave a small nod in the direction of the burly jailer, who was just placing the poker back into one of the braziers.

"His service is finished," he said quietly to the soldier. "For good. Take care of it and you shall be handsomely rewarded. Throw his body into the Tiber together with the other one, understood? Sewn into a sack with stones. It must be as if he never existed."

The guard nodded silently, and Leo placed a shiny gold coin into his hand. Then the father climbed the many stairs, panting and sweating, to where bright lights, the beguiling scent of violets, and God's grace awaited him.

Oh yes, there was much left to do.

Act I

The Beast's Breath

1

THE FLAMING ARROW SHOT INTO THE EVENING SKY, WHIS-
tling as it released its orange-yellow load. Accompanied by the cries of the audience, it dragged a tail of fire across the clouds, like the handwriting of an angry
god. Up high, way above the roofs of the town and the spire of the church, the
arrow exploded with a deafening crack, glittering sparks raining down like falling
stars. The citizens of Bretten moaned with fright and pleasant horror.

Greta watched the faces of the spectators from her hiding place behind the
stage. She estimated that a few hundred people had gathered around the well
on the Bretten market square. Gaping in disbelief at the spectacle above, some
of them even covered their eyes with their hands. Greta couldn't help but smile.
The flaming arrow was a sensation every time; it marked the beginning of their
evening show and instantly caught everyone's attention. The doctor built each
of the arrows by hand, and not even Greta knew the precise ingredients used
to fill the tubes made of glue and cloth. She guessed it was blackpowder mixed
with various secret concoctions. These so-called rockets were the latest craze at
the courts of nobility throughout the empire as well as in Italy and France; few
were privy to the details of their manufacture, which allegedly stemmed from
a country far to the east. It was marvels like these that made the doctor's shows
so successful that even counts and bishops begged to see them. Along with the
wealthy citizens of Bretten. Everyone in the audience now turned back to the

stage beside the well, watching amid reverent murmurs as a lone figure stepped out from behind the curtain.

"That's him," whispered an excited elderly woman in a bonnet, clasping her hand to her mouth. "God protect us! They say his black dog is the devil himself. The doctor charmed him with a pentagram, and now Satan must serve him!"

"How creepy that man looks!" groaned a girl next to her, shuddering. "Almost as if he were a demon, too. In Erfurt he made the beautiful Helen appear, and then the students all ran after her, right out into the street. And he turned the hunchbacked old deacon young again."

"I wish he'd do that to my Hans," sighed the older woman, fidgeting with her blouse. She turned her gaze back to the man, who had just reached the front of the stage.

The doctor was tall and haggard, wearing a black-and-blue cape embroidered with stars that glistened in the light of the torches. He was no longer young, his pronounced cheekbones shaded by a floppy hat. Two piercing black eyes shone from the dark, the left one especially menacing. His hands were covered in smooth leather gloves, making them look somewhat clawlike. Now the man raised both arms, like a priest during the holy Communion. A loud voice that didn't belong to him rang out from somewhere in the background.

"Watch and be amazed, honorable citizens, because no lesser man than the world-famous Doctor Johann Georg Faustus has arrived!" declared the speaker. "He traveled the hot lands on the other side of the vast ocean, studied with Avicenna and the great Albertus Magnus, escaped the hellish breath of the Sphinx, and was graced with the honor of foretelling our beloved emperor Maximilian a long and healthy life. And now he is here in Bretten to share with you his skills. If anyone would like to know their fate, please step forward. The doctor will cast your horoscope for just two hellers! Upon my soul—the stars don't lie!"

On the signal, Greta struck a piece of tin with one hand, creating a loud thunderclap, and with the other hand she swung a ratchet. The stage consisted of several crates pushed together; panels of dark-blue fabric adorned with pentagrams and mythical creatures formed the backdrop on three sides.

For almost a whole week they had been staying in Bretten, about thirty miles south of Heidelberg, and each of their shows had filled the market square to capacity. No one saw Greta behind the walls of fabric as she used tin, ratchet, cymbals, and a bagpipe to provide the sound effects for the speech delivered by Karl Wagner, Faust's young assistant.

"Step forward, brave men and women!" Karl continued, moving out onto the stage. "He who hesitates will regret his mistake!"

The doctor's loyal assistant was in his midtwenties, with straight hair that reached down to his shoulders. He was shaved smoothly and was so handsome that several young women in the audience were starting to whisper. Perhaps they could smell the perfume made from essence of violets that Karl always used a little too heavy-handedly.

"The first brave candidates receive a bottle of Doctor Faustus's Original Theriac for free, and a glowing prophecy on top of that," shouted Karl, winking at the blushing ladies. "Who knows—maybe one or two of you will meet your future husband before the year's out."

Some spectators now climbed the stage and had their palms read by the famous Doctor Faustus, who was sitting on a stool.

Greta set down the sheet of tin and the ratchet and prepared for her act. She smoothed her skirt, which was sewn together from colored patches of fabric, as was typical for jugglers; then she laced up her tight bodice and tied back her stubborn blonde hair with a scarf. Her costume was like armor to her, shielding what was inside. Just last spring she had turned twenty. Sometimes, when no one was watching, Greta studied her reflection in the polished piece of tin and wondered what to think of that young woman in front of her. She couldn't stand the freckles that covered her skin like specks of muck, especially in the summer, but she liked the curve of her lips and her small nose. The bodice she wore for the shows made her look more feminine than she felt. The doctor often told her that he loved her laughter, and then he'd gaze into the distance as if remembering something from a long time ago.

"I see a significant change approaching in your life," Faust was just telling a trembling girl, clutching her hand tightly in his clawlike grip. "Stay away from the wrong fellows. The right one will come, and soon!" He drew her close to him. "Try to avoid the barns in the fields—their walls are thinner than you think." Faust gave her a wink, and the girl shrank back as if she'd been caught red handed.

Greta had known the doctor for more than six years now, ever since he'd rescued her from the prison in Nuremberg when she was still a little girl, an orphan who didn't know who her mother and father were. Ever since then, she'd traveled the country with the famous Doctor Faustus. To Greta, the frightening man whom many believed to be in league with the devil had become a sort of father; she called him Uncle Johann. She'd learned much from him during the last few years and had turned into a clever trickster and nimble acrobat. She knew how to play the bagpipe, the lute, and the flute. The audience loved her pert manner, her graceful dancing, and her talent for balancing on even the thinnest rope. But they didn't know who she truly was—and Greta didn't really know herself. There was so much she didn't understand, like her uncanny gift; she still didn't know whether it was a blessing or a curse.

In the last few weeks it had seemed to her more like a curse.

Those large black wings . . .

Greta shook off the gloomy thoughts and stepped out from behind the canvas. A glance up at the heavy clouds in the autumn sky told her that it would rain soon. They'd be lucky if they finished the show without getting wet. The doctor was reading the palm of a colorfully clad and visibly intimidated patrician.

"Your Fate line shows a turning point in your business this very year," Faust said in his trademark croaky voice, and the bystanders watched in reverent silence. "And the stars agree. It's too soon to tell whether this turning point will bring good fortune or ill luck. I see"—he closed his eyes—"a city with golden roofs."

"Venice," breathed the patrician. "Dear God, my precious cloth delivery that's on its way to Venice! I wonder if the prices have dropped?" He rushed off after giving Faust a few silver coins.

Greta held her head high as she mingled with the crowd in front of the stage. She loved this atmosphere—it was where she felt at home. As soon as she stepped outside the curtain, she was no longer the introverted, occasionally melancholy girl but Greta the cheeky juggler, the young companion of the famous Doctor Faustus.

The spectators regarded her with a mix of respect and repulsion. Greta knew the look that upstanding citizens always held in store for people like her—musicians, jugglers, dancers, relic traders, bear tamers, and other traveling folk: shunned and yet admired. They were dishonorable and untouchable; here today, gone tomorrow; neither past nor future—and that was just what Greta loved about this life.

She smiled as she approached a farmer's boy in the front row and hinted at a bow. "In the mood for a game of dice, young sir?" Greta had noticed the boy before the show, and she'd liked the looks he'd given her. She felt herself strangely drawn to his mischievous, shrewd-looking face, his full brown hair, and the well-proportioned muscles showing under his clothes.

Greta showed him her empty hands before reaching behind her right ear and producing a die carved of cow bone. Then she picked a coin out of her left ear. The young man gave a startled laugh.

"How can I play the dice with you if you can make them vanish at any moment?"

"Don't worry, my friend, you're the master of your own fortune." Greta's voice had the praising, almost bewitching pitch so typical for jugglers. She winked. "You roll the die, and I guess your number. If I get it right, you pay me a heller—and if I'm wrong, you get a kiss from me. Shall we?" She held out the die.

The boy rocked his head from side to side, his eyes traveling down to her small breasts, which were pushed up by the tightly laced bodice. Greta knew she had most men eating out of the palm of her hand in this outfit, and she used the knowledge to her advantage.

"A fair offer, meseems," said the young man with a grin. Then he raised one finger and gave Greta a serious look. "But first I want to roll the die a few times to make sure it isn't rigged."

Greta nodded. Some jugglers used dice that contained small pieces of iron so they always landed on the same side. The boy rolled the die a few times, and then he covered it with his hand.

"Now guess," he said to her.

"Hmm, it isn't one, is it?" began Greta, scratching her head. "Two, perhaps? No. Three?" Suddenly her face brightened. "Well, I believe it's a six."

The young man lifted his upper hand. It was indeed a six.

"Just a lucky guess!" He handed her a coin. "I want to try again."

Greta started in on her game once more, and again she guessed correctly. When she guessed right the third time, the boy eyed her suspiciously.

"That's witchcraft," he grumbled. "You dishonorable jugglers are all the same—spawn of the devil. Give me back my money, you cheat!"

Greta's smile vanished. She had been looking forward to this harmless encounter, but now things were developing in a way she didn't like at all.

"No, I think I'd better donate it at church tomorrow and say thirty Lord's Prayers for the salvation of your soul. God bless you." She slipped the coins into a pocket, gave him a nod, and walked off.

There were many people who believed jugglers to be the spawn of the devil. Some church scholars claimed they were descendants of fallen angels who now wreaked havoc on earth. How could Greta explain to a dumb farmer's boy that what she was doing had to do not with witchcraft but with intuition and practice. Greta observed her victims carefully, studying every small change in their facial expressions and gestures. That was how she guessed the numbers right almost every time. She and Karl often used this technique during their shows. Greta would guess what people carried in their pockets while Karl would give her secret clues.

Sometimes, however, there was also something else. Something she hadn't wanted to admit to herself for a long time: sometimes she actually saw the numbers before her.

Greta walked behind the stage, where they'd set up a small tent next to their wagon. The tent contained crates and chests and served as a changing room. Colorfully striped clothing with bells and tassels lay strewn across the floor. Even though it was mid-October, it was hot and muggy inside the tent; a thunderstorm had been brewing for hours. Greta could hear the people of Bretten clapping—the show must have come to an end.

She struggled to breathe in the tight bodice and loosened it. She was still pulling out the strings when she heard a noise behind her. She turned around and cursed her carelessness. The boy who'd lost in their game of dice stood in front of her with his arms folded. He was smiling, but his eyes looked hungry, greedy, and his handsome face now seemed crude and shifty.

"If you won't give me back my money, I'll take something else from you," he growled. "You won't get away this easily, you hussy."

Greta took a step back. It was always the same. Men encountered her role as a cocky, playful juggler and confused her act with reality. They believed she truly was a loose woman.

The fellow came closer, reached for her breasts, and tried to drag her onto one of the chests. But Greta was prepared. She jerked up her knee and hit him hard right between the legs. It wasn't the first time she'd been forced to defend herself against a pushy man, and often a knee where it hurt the most was enough to put those men back in their place. Greta was a small woman, but she was athletic and strong from years of practice with the rope, skittles, and balls.

The young man groaned loudly but stayed put. Evidently, he was tougher than she'd thought.

"Just you wait, whore—I'll take you even harder for that!" He wiped the sweat off his forehead and spread his strong, hairy arms.

He threw himself on her like a bear and managed to pull her to the ground. Greta wanted to scream, but he pressed his hand to her mouth. She smelled stables and muck. As he pushed up her skirts, she desperately felt for the small knife she always carried under her bodice. There it was! But the boy forced her hand to the side, and the blade slipped from her grasp. Meanwhile he had pulled down his trousers to his knees, and she could feel his erection between her legs like a cudgel. Greta turned and twisted until she managed to free one of her hands. Immediately she grabbed the knife.

"I promised you a kiss," she hissed. "Here it is!"

With one quick movement she swiped the blade across her attacker's cheek and nose. The boy howled with pain.

"You . . . you goddamn witch!"

He let go of her and held his nose with both hands, blood spurting from his face. The blood was everywhere—in his face, on his hands, on his jerkin. The tent looked like they'd just butchered a pig.

Greta watched with gratification.

"Looks like it isn't your lucky day," she said as she got to her feet. "Now get out of here and find yourself some peasant wench before—"

She paused as she heard a low, menacing growl. She looked to the entrance of the tent and saw the black dog that was almost the size of a calf. It was the doctor's dog, a monster of an animal, with mighty wolf fangs and glowing red eyes. Some people really believed the dog was the devil, which was why the doctor called him Little Satan.

Little Satan's effect wasn't lost on the profusely bleeding lad.

"Jesus Christ," he gasped. "What in God's name?"

Trembling hard, the young man took his hands from his face and hastily tied up his trousers. He tried to run but tripped and fell.

"What are you doing here?" said a voice as deep and dangerous as if it came straight from hell. "Speak up before my dog tears you apart like a hare."

The doctor had entered the tent behind Little Satan, followed closely by Karl, who was carrying corked bottles of theriac.

"I . . . I . . . ," stammered the fellow. Blood still dripped from the long cut on his nose and cheek.

Greta hoped he'd carry a scar as a memento.

"You are soiling my tent." Faust pointed at the floor. "And blood drives the dog mad. Mad and hungry, as you can see." On cue, Little Satan pulled up his jowls and bared his sharp yellow teeth, each one the size of a small knife.

One look at Greta told the doctor what had been going on. He turned as white as a sheet, and blind rage took over his cool composure.

"By the dark forces and the pale light of the moon," whispered Faust, his eyes flashing like small, hot stars, his voice trembling with anger. "If you touched as much as a hair on her body, I—"

"It never came to that, Uncle," Greta said, almost feeling sorry for the young fellow. "He's been punished enough. Let him go."

The doctor took a deep breath. For a brief moment it seemed he would set the dog on the boy, but then he gave a soft whistle, and Little Satan lay down.

"I give you precisely three blinks of an eye to leave this tent," said Faust quietly, his voice as cold as the north wind. "And another three blinks to go hide in a very deep hole. Believe me—if I ever see you out there again, Little Satan is going to swallow you whole. But not before I've turned you into a rat. Because that is all you are: a rat on two legs. Now get out of here!"

The last words echoed like thunder. It never ceased to amaze Greta how the doctor could rock the entire world with his voice.

Whimpering and bleeding, the boy staggered past Faust, Karl, and the growling dog. They heard his hasty footsteps rushing off.

Then Faust turned to Greta, still trembling with fury.

"How many times do I have to tell you to stop making eyes at the boys! Now you see where it gets you. One minute later and that fellow would have mounted you like a billy goat."

"I was handling it," replied Greta, sounding surer than she felt. She laced up her bloodstained bodice. "I am quite capable of defending myself, you know. The two of you have taught me a fair bit in the last few years."

Karl grinned. "Indeed we have. That fellow looked as if he'd been in a brawl against three men at once. He won't be back anytime soon." Unlike the doctor,

Karl wore a plain black coat that made his slim stature seem even skinnier. The intelligent eyes in his feminine, clean-shaven face told of a keen mind. During the last few years, Karl had become Greta's closest and only friend and confidant. He was like a big brother to her. And with Karl she could be sure that he wasn't interested in her as a woman—because he wasn't attracted to women at all, at least not sexually.

Karl's expression soon turned serious again. "But I fear the scoundrel could cause trouble for us. He's bound to have a few friends in town. Or he might report us as sorcerers." He looked at the doctor. "Perhaps threatening to turn him into a rat wasn't the best idea."

"It would be a wasted effort, because he already is one." Faust gave a shrug. "Besides, we won't stay in Bretten for much longer."

"How come?" asked Karl, raising an eyebrow.

"Well, I received an invitation that I shouldn't turn down. The letter came by messenger a few days ago, but I didn't tell you about it because I wasn't sure what I was going to do." Faust gave a laugh. "But it's more of an order than an invitation."

"Who are you talking about?" asked Greta.

The doctor sighed. "It's an invitation from the venerable prince-bishop of Bamberg, asking me to cast him a horoscope. He writes of a royal salary, but I detest the idea. Something like that will raise far too much dust, and that's the last thing we need at the moment." He gestured to the outside. "Did you hear the people whisper? My reputation in these climes isn't the best, and even here in Bretten there are some who call me a necromancer and my dog the devil himself. And now Greta starts a fight with an idiot!"

"Hey!" exclaimed Greta in protest. "You make it sound like I asked the guy to rape me."

"I'm only saying you need to take better care. I can't always bail you out."

"And I don't want you to," replied Greta coolly.

Faust waved dismissively. "Perhaps Bamberg isn't the worst place to go. We need winter quarters, after all. And there are worse places to spend a winter than Altenburg Castle, where the prince-bishop resides."

Greta bit her lip. Her limbs still ached from the struggle, and red streaks showed on her skin. But hurting the most was the shame she'd so nearly suffered.

Men were like animals—maybe that was why she had never let any of them go all the way, even if Uncle Johann thought otherwise.

"When are you thinking of leaving for Bamberg?" she asked. "I thought we wanted to stay until the next market day." She didn't want to admit it—especially since she thought the prince-bishop's invitation a little strange—but after what had just happened, she was glad to be leaving Bretten sooner rather than later.

"First thing tomorrow morning," replied Faust. "There is just one more thing I need to do here." His expression darkened. "Something I should have done a long time ago." He left the tent without another word.

Greta gave Karl a puzzled look, but he only rolled his eyes.

"I've known the doctor for so long," he said with a sigh. "But at the end of the day I don't know him at all."

Once more Greta realized that she felt the same way. After all those years, she still couldn't say what kind of a person Faust really was. The doctor could appear gentle and considerate one moment and cold and forbidding the next. His sharp wit overshadowed everything else, and his arrogance was the stuff of legend. Whenever Greta tried to ask him about himself or about her own past, he changed the topic. No one knew what really went on behind Faust's dark eyes.

Greta reached for Karl's hand and squeezed it tightly. He could probably tell that she was still shaken. But that was all right—Karl was the only person she trusted completely.

"Johann Georg Faustus will probably remain a closed book to us forever," she muttered, gazing into the overcast night sky through the opening in the tent.

Deep down inside, Greta felt she'd just described herself, too.

~

Thunder rumbled in the distance; to the west the clouds piled up in dark clumps. They didn't seem to agree on when they would release their heavy burden. Not even the slightest breeze stirred in the trees, as if Mother Nature were holding her breath.

His head bent low over the horse's neck, Johann galloped toward the small town of Knittlingen, which stood just a few miles from Bretten. He had set off with Little Satan right after his conversation with Greta and Karl, out through the Weisshofer Gate and along the Weissach River. He closed his eyes and tried to blank out the memories from long ago, but he failed.

Swimming in the river, low-hanging willow branches . . . I pull myself up and jump back into the water. Look, Margarethe, watch—I'm an evil water sprite.

Soon he could make out the Knittlingen town wall in the muggy haze, and the gentle slopes full of vines beyond, as if time had stood still for all those years. The western gate was still open, and the sole watchman let the strange rider pass without asking questions, glad to stay inside his shelter in view of the impending rain. Or perhaps he didn't want to approach the large black dog trotting alongside its master.

Johann kept his head down until he realized that he was the only person in the street. He guessed most Knittlingers were still at work in the fields, trying to get as many grapes to safety as they could before the storm broke. Johann darted a glance into the courtyard of the prefecture with the wine presses, then at the market square and the small Saint Leonhard's Church. He could also see the Gerlachs' house beside the church—the house he was born in, an eternity ago. The two-story building was freshly whitewashed and the shutters had been painted a different color, but other than that, nothing had changed.

So many memories.

Johann felt a stab in his chest. He hadn't been back in Knittlingen for almost a quarter century. He had avoided the place because it reminded him of how everything had begun. Neither Karl nor Greta knew that this was where he came from; really, they knew nothing about him. No one did. He had grown up just a stone's throw away, with three brothers—of which the elder two had been blockheaded peasants—and a stepfather who had always hated him. Johann still didn't know who his real father was. Just like Greta had no idea who her father was.

I must tell her before it's too late.

The old familiar Lion Inn appeared to his left, muffled voices humming inside. A handful of horses were tied to the hitching rail outside the door, and an old cart was parked in an open shed next to the building.

Johann involuntarily stopped his own horse and listened. Knittlingen sat on the post road that led from the Netherlands all the way to Innsbruck in the Alps and beyond. The elderly emperor Maximilian had had it built in his younger years so that he could better control his huge empire. Because of this road, travelers from faraway countries frequently stayed at the Lion. Countless times as a small boy Johann had sat underneath the tables, listening to their tales. Afterward, back at home, he would tell those tales to his sick mother.

The Lion Inn had been his window to the world—a world he would see far more than he'd ever imagined. Johann had sworn to himself that he wouldn't return until he was a learned and successful man. And that was what he had become—although in a completely different way than expected.

Little loudmouthed Johann Gerlach from Knittlingen had become the famous Doctor Johann Georg Faustus, the greatest magician in the empire, an astrologer, chiromancer, and alchemist, much admired and much scorned.

Johann hesitated before climbing off his horse and tying it beside the others. He had come to Knittlingen for something else, but the inn drew him in almost magically, like a sweet, nostalgic call from the past.

"You wait outside. Sit!" he commanded Little Satan, who obeyed instantly. Johann's heart beat wildly as he entered the tavern. He pulled his fur-lined cap down over his face, even though he thought it highly unlikely that anyone would recognize him after all these years. Johann knew that his brothers and stepfather had died of a fever years ago. His family no longer existed; the house had been sold. Johann hadn't felt any grief.

Because I've always been a stranger.

The moment Johann entered the familiar taproom, all conversation stopped. He guessed the men at the tables were a mix of travelers and Knittlingers, but he knew none of them, and no one seemed to recognize him. People soon turned back to their cups of wine. He was just another traveler. The young innkeeper came to his table.

"What can I get you, sir?" asked the man, bowing his head. Instead of his famous star cape, Johann was wearing a wide coat made of silk and fustian, along with a fur-lined cap in the style of wealthy merchants and patricians.

"Is old Hans Harschauber still around?" asked Johann with a foreign accent to avoid any unnecessary risks. "The old innkeeper. I came through this town years ago and met him. A good man. Knew much of the world."

"Oh, him." The innkeeper gave an apologetic wave. "He died a long time ago. There was a nasty fever."

Johann nodded. It was probably the same fever that had taken his family. He had liked old Harschauber, one of the few people in the village who had treated Johann with respect even though Johann had always been a little different from other Knittlingers. But it was probably for the best. The fewer people who knew him from back then, the smaller the chances of being recognized.

"Bring wine," he said. "But not the swill from the local vineyards. I want something better."

The innkeeper scurried off and soon returned with a jug of red wine. Johann filled his mug, trying to suppress the shaking that rolled through his body like a wave. It had become worse again recently, and sometimes he thought he'd lose control over it—the shaking and the stiffness in his joints that came over him like a thief in the night. He sincerely hoped no one had noticed yet. Slowly, he set the mug back down and took a deep breath.

Whenever the shaking grew particularly bad, he retreated into his wagon, telling Karl and Greta that he was plagued by terrible headaches. It wasn't even a lie—the expensive glass eye he'd had a Venetian glassmaker produce for him sometimes pinched and stung. Johann had lost his left eye and a finger on his right hand during those eerie events in Nuremberg six years ago. But he knew that wasn't the source of the shaking.

He suspected a different cause, something far worse. If only he could—

"I . . . I . . . know you . . ."

Johann was so lost in thought that he hadn't noticed the man approaching his table. He was very old, with white hair and a bent back as if he'd spent his entire life carrying heavy baskets full of ripe grapes. He looked emaciated, as from a long illness, and his fingers trembled as he pointed at Johann.

"I . . . know you," he repeated quietly.

Johann gave a strained smile. "That may well be. I've come through this town before, so perhaps—"

"Johann," whispered the old man, and the small eyes flashed between the wrinkles. "Little Johann, it's you, isn't it? Of course it's you!"

Johann flinched. Could this old man really have recognized him? He studied the eyes—and then he recognized the man. His eyes hadn't changed; they held an unspeakable sadness, a pain originating from over twenty years ago. A wrong that couldn't be righted. Johann thought of a dark forest, a devil's face on a rock, and whispering unseen voices.

Who's afraid of the boogeyman?

He suddenly felt as cold as if he were in an ice cellar.

My God.

"What did you do to my Margarethe back then?" asked the old man softly. "My daughter . . . the apple of my eye."

"I . . . You're confusing me with someone else." Johann rose abruptly. Coming here had been a mistake. He dropped a coin on the table and turned to leave. "I don't know you."

The old man's trembling hand grasped him by the shoulder. "What did you do to my daughter?" he repeated, louder this time. A few patrons turned their heads. "What devil did you see in the woods back then?"

"I really don't know what you're talking about," replied Johann. "Now let go of me. My horse needs to be fed."

He rushed to the door, the old man's voice echoing through his head.

What did you do to my daughter? What devil did you see in the woods back then?

Outside, he looked behind him once more and thought he could see the lined face through the crown-glass window. It was the face of the old Knittlingen prefect, the man whose heart he'd broken all those years ago. The last twenty years had not been kind to him, Margarethe's father.

What did you do to my daughter?

The face behind the window vanished, and in the same instant a mighty thunderclap crashed.

One moment later, the rain set in.

Johann didn't look up again until he arrived at the cemetery. In a daze he had untied his horse and galloped off. The rain was so heavy that he could hardly see the houses anymore.

He never should have entered the inn. Of all Knittlingers still living, the old prefect had been the one he'd been most afraid to see. Terrible things had happened back then. In the Schillingswald Forest, not far from Knittlingen, Johann had lost his innocence—but moreover, he'd also lost his little brother, Martin, and the girl that he loved more than anything. That he still loved today.

Margarethe.

He had tried to forget what happened that day, but it wasn't possible. The past always came back to haunt him in his dreams.

What devil did you see in the woods?

It was a question that tortured him to this day, too—although he suspected he knew the answer. The devil had entered his life back then, had brought him money and fame, had turned him into what he was today. But at what cost?

Johann held his face into the rain, letting the drops wash away the memories, including those of the old prefect. The cold wetness felt good, extinguishing the flames inside him. The cemetery had been the reason for his visit to Knittlingen; he'd been wanting to return here for many years.

He tied his horse to the gate and walked into the graveyard, where several crooked tombstones stood in the darkness. There wasn't another soul here at this hour. The rain beat down relentlessly, sounding like pebbles on a drum.

Johann impatiently spun around to the large black wolfhound following him at a distance.

"Come on now, Little Satan! I must say farewell to someone. I promise it won't take long."

The dog hesitated, as if he could smell that death was at home here. Then he trotted after his master. Johann's coat was drenched by now, and water ran in streams from the brim of his hat. His fine leather boots were covered in muck. But Johann didn't notice any of it. He strode across the graveyard with his head down and stopped eventually in front of a small, unremarkable tombstone right beside the cemetery wall. The stone was crooked and overgrown with moss and ivy. No one had cared for the grave in a long time. Johann bent down and scraped away dirt and branches until the inscription was legible: *Elisabeth Gerlach, died on 12 July in the year of the Lord 1494.*

Twenty-four years.

Johann could hardly believe how much had come to pass since then. He had been a boy of sixteen back then, his head full of nonsense, full of hopes and dreams, the pride of his mother. He had come to say goodbye to her one last time. He used to love a girl from Knittlingen and play with his brother in the vineyards west of town. And now? The girl and the brother were just as dead as his mother, and his hopes and dreams blown away like leaves in the fall. His beloved mother, lying here in front of him, had foretold him a great future—a future someone once read in the stars for her. She had also been the first to call him Faustus.

Faustus, the lucky one.

Johann gave a sad laugh as he gazed upon his mother's grave. He had paid a heavy price for his luck.

And for a few months now he thought the price might become much heavier yet.

"For thine is the kingdom and the power and the glory, forever, amen."

Johann struggled to his feet. Praying had never come easily to him—he didn't really believe in it. And the accursed shaking was returning. But he felt better nonetheless; the visit had done him good.

The dog's growling roused Johann from his thoughts.

"Hush, Little Satan!" He looked around suspiciously and noticed movement behind one of the gravestones a little farther away. He could discern the outline of a figure and thought he could hear a scraping noise over the sound of the rain. After a few moments he recognized the noise as a shovel scraping over soil and rocks.

"Who is there?" he shouted into the wind. "Whoever you are—I've got a dog with me. A very large dog who doesn't like surprises!"

A man straightened up behind the gravestone. He was holding a small, flickering lantern, so Johann could see his thin outline against the dark background. The man wore a floppy hat with a red rooster's feather, his face remaining in the shadow below the brim. A shovel leaned against the gravestone beside him.

Just the grave digger, thought Johann with relief. *People die in any weather.*

"Greetings," he said and raised his hand.

The man did nothing for a moment, then he started to walk toward Johann with the lantern. He was as skinny as a scarecrow and walked slightly hunched over, as if he had a crooked back. A filthy eye patch covered the right side of his face.

"Not a good time for a visit to the graveyard," the man said. His voice was soft and pleasant, and Johann noticed that he didn't have a Kraichgau accent.

"A . . . an old friend of mine is buried here," replied Johann, gesturing vaguely to the gravestones in front of him. "I was passing through town and stopped to say a quick prayer."

The man nodded without looking at the stones, scrutinizing Johann instead.

"You're not from around here, then," he said eventually.

"That's right." Johann shrugged. "But I used to . . ." He paused. "I used to know a few people in Knittlingen."

Once more he saw the wrinkled face of the prefect in his mind's eye and heard his voice.

What did you do to my daughter? What devil did you see in the woods back then?

Oh yes, he had laden a profound guilt upon himself.

"Are you all right, sir?" The grave digger took another step toward him, and Little Satan growled like he always did when strangers approached his master.

But then something strange happened: the grave digger leaned down to Little Satan and patted his head as if he were a cute lapdog, and to Johann's astonishment, the dog didn't seem to mind. Johann had never before seen Little Satan tolerate the touch of anyone but himself or Greta.

"This . . . old friend of yours—you must have been very close?" asked the man as he scratched the dog behind an ear.

"Closer than anyone else," Johann said reluctantly.

The man issued a quick laugh and grinned, showing his surprisingly white and complete set of teeth. "And yet he's nothing but a pile of rotting bones now. Isn't it sad what becomes of us? God created us in His image, and at the end we're nothing but stinking bags of maggots. No matter if we're the emperor, the pope, or a beggar." The grave digger sighed and straightened back up. He truly did look frightfully gaunt—not much more than a pile of bones himself.

"I've lowered so many people into the hole—old ones, young ones, grand-parents, and children. Children are the worst." He shrugged. "I mean, why does God allow it? Why hasn't He shown us how to stop death? From the day we are born we start to rot and die. Can you feel it, too? We're dying all the time—a little more every day."

Johann said nothing and studied the man. He was no longer certain the man with the eye patch was the Knittlingen grave digger. He spoke far too well—more like a priest, even though a man of God would never have spoken about the Lord thus. The man came a little closer and Johann thought he could smell a faint whiff of sulfur.

"Do you know what?" whispered the stranger into Johann's ear, his breath as damp and sticky as a dirty rag. "I think death is the price we all have to pay. The price for living. Everything has its price, and everyone must pay someday. Someday—but pay they must. Do you understand what I mean?"

"I . . . I think I do," said Johann hoarsely. He shuddered. This conversation was becoming stranger by the moment. Johann nervously looked around for

Little Satan and saw that he was hiding behind a gravestone, seeming afraid. What the hell was going on with the dog?

The man took a step back and smiled. His teeth looked pointed and reminded Johann of a wolf.

"Ha! I knew it. There aren't many who understand me. Not many who are willing to go further than the others, who want to see more, who never rest." He lowered his voice. "Are you finally ready to pay your price, Doctor Faustus? Are you ready?"

Without waiting for a reply, the man turned away and trudged off through the rain with the lantern in his hand.

Johann was too astounded to say anything for a few moments. Then he shouted, "Hey! How do you know my name? Who . . . who are you?"

But right then, the light of the lantern went out, and the stranger disappeared as suddenly as he had arrived. Johann listened. Through the rain he thought he heard a faint melody. The sound of a flute drifted over to him from beyond the cemetery wall; perhaps it came from the inn. It was the tune of a children's song.

Susie, dear Susie, what's rustling in the straw? 'Tis the little goslings, they don't have any shoes.

Johann stood, frozen, at his mother's grave. After a few moments he startled as if waking from a bad dream and hurried toward the gate. He jumped on his horse and rode through the storm, dashing past the stunned watchman at the gate as if the devil were after him. The dog raced behind him. Only much later did Johann realize that he couldn't remember the man's face.

It was as if the rain had washed it away.

~

High up between hail clouds and billows of rain, three birds glided in circles. They were two crows and a large old raven with tattered feathers and a scuffed beak. When they heard the soft tune somewhere below, they cawed and returned to their master. The skinny man was still standing between the gravestones at the farthest edge of the cemetery, as far away from the church as possible. He didn't like churches. With his long, insect-like fingers he played the gentle tune his raven and the crows had been forced to follow for so many years.

"He's changed, hasn't he?" said the master as the birds searched for worms and maggots on a fresh, steaming grave mound. "To me he's still the same impertinent brat, even if everyone craps their pants nowadays when they talk about the great, oh-so-famous Doctor Faustus. Shuddering is man's best quality." He chuckled. "My little Faustus! When will you finally learn that the die has long been cast? The stars don't lie."

He put the flute in his pocket, took off the floppy hat that had been keeping his face in the dark, removed the eye patch, and started to wipe away the makeup. He had played so many roles by now—magician, juggler, mercenary, quack, count, baron, and beggar. And now grave digger. It was a role that suited him.

He who takes my hand will be dragged belowground. Sooner or later. And someday I will knock on your door, Johann.

The master licked his pale lips.

The devil is always that which you fear the most.

"Azazel, Baphomet, Belial," called the master to his three servants. "Quit picking for worms—let's go find something better."

~

That night, Johann stayed up for a long time, bent over his books by the light of a candle. He, Greta, and Karl were renting three spacious rooms at the Bretten Crown Inn at the market square. It was the best house in town; even the emperor had stayed there. The walls in Johann's chamber were hung with soft rugs and furs, and the room had its own fireplace and a four-poster bed strewn with fragrant lavender. The landlord had been happy to give his best room to the widely known astrologer, who had shown his appreciation with an especially favorable horoscope. But no amount of luxury could restore Johann's inner peace. He couldn't stop thinking about the strange grave digger.

The way the man had spoken, the softness in his voice, had sounded as if he came from west of the Rhine. The haggard stature, the wolfish teeth that looked like they'd been sharpened. And he had called Johann by his name, even though he hadn't introduced himself.

Are you finally ready to pay your price, Doctor Faustus?

It could have been coincidence. Word of Johann's shows in Bretten must have gotten around, and he was no longer a complete stranger around here.

The fellow might have been a little odd, but he was a grave digger, after all—a dishonorable person who lived on the outskirts of society. People like that sometimes were odd.

And yet Johann felt almost certain, even though everything inside him tried to fight the thought: the man at the cemetery had been Tonio del Moravia, his former master.

More than twenty years ago, Tonio had picked up Johann on the road after his stepfather had thrown him out. He had traveled the empire at Tonio's side and learned much from him. But then the man had revealed his true face.

To this day Johann didn't know the real identity of his former master. Tonio was an expert in deception, a Satanist, and possibly something worse—yes, maybe he was the devil himself. He never seemed to age, unlike Johann, who felt every single one of his years in his bones.

Another bout of shaking overcame him; it shot into his hand and from there spread through the entire left side of his body. Beads of sweat formed on his forehead as he tried to gain control over his body. It had been going like this for six months now. At first, it had been nothing but a slight twitching of his fingers. Johann had suspected it was a late aftereffect of the amputation back in Nuremberg, when Tonio had cut off Johann's little finger of his right hand and then taken out his eye. But the trembling had become worse, spreading inside Johann like a fever or paralysis. Sometimes, at night, his body became as hard as a shell and he struggled to breathe.

This must be what it feels like to be buried alive.

He dug his fingers into the tabletop and the shaking subsided, slunk back into its hiding hole like an old reptile waiting to pounce on him again another day.

"Damned disease! What . . . what are you?" gasped Johann.

The grave digger had spoken about a price that every man had to pay. Could this disease be the price he meant?

During the last few months, Johann had reached the conclusion that it wasn't so much an illness as a curse—yet another part of the pact he had entered with Tonio all those years ago, a handshake on the highway between Maulbronn and Ulm. He had succeeded at much in life since then, had gained glory and wealth, but everything had its price. And now Tonio—or whoever the master was—was reaching out for him and demanding his share.

How much time had he left?

At that moment there was a knock on the door, and Johann started. Had the devil arrived to fetch him already? But then he heard Greta's voice and breathed a sigh of relief.

"I can see light under your door, Uncle. May I come in?"

Johann closed his eyes for a moment, trying to calm down. Then, attempting to sound preoccupied and impatient at once, as if she had disturbed him in deep thought, he called out, "Well, if it's important. I'm still at work."

The door opened and Greta came in. As always upon seeing her, Johann felt as though someone had lit a light in the darkness. Greta's merry face brightened his darkest hours, and when she laughed, all was well. But he knew that even she could be melancholy at times, that even for her the world was framed in black.

Just like it was for her mother, may she rest in peace. A peace that I'm not granted.

Sometimes when he secretly observed Greta, he almost thought he was looking at Margarethe. The same poise, the same movements, the same ringing laughter. Several times he had reached out to stroke Greta lovingly just to pull back his hand as if he'd been bitten by a snake, and Greta would look at him with surprise.

"Karl and I were worried about you," Greta said reproachfully as she walked to his table. "Where have you been? What was it that you needed to do so urgently before we leave for Bamberg?"

"An . . . an old story," he replied. "Something from before your time. Nothing important."

How could he explain to her that he had paid a visit to his past in Knittlingen?

A past that includes your mother, my darling.

Johann was Greta's father. Her mother was Margarethe, his first and only love, who had been strangled and burned at the stake as a witch because of him. His guilt ran so deeply that he couldn't bring himself to tell Greta the truth about her origins. He'd been waiting for the right moment for more than six years now, but it never seemed to arrive. Several times he had come very close to telling her, but something always happened. By now he believed that he'd never be able to tell her—perhaps it was simply too late.

Everything was fine the way it was.

Greta watched him closely. For a brief moment, Johann thought he saw fear flashing in her eyes—a fear he couldn't explain. Greta was hardly ever afraid of anything. Sometimes he wished she were a little more cautious. The incident that afternoon was typical for the forward demeanor she displayed during her performances. Men truly believed in the act she put on—while Johann still saw the small, timid girl he'd rescued from the Nuremberg catacombs when she was still playing with dolls, even if he knew that she had grown up.

"Something is wrong, isn't it?" asked Greta. "You're as pale as a corpse." She paused for a moment. "Karl is worried, too. You've been getting gloomier for months, and a few times you didn't even turn up for a show. You're always hiding in the wagon with your books." She gestured at the open tomes in front of him. "What are you doing with them? It's like those books have put you—the great magician—under a spell."

"I have my reasons."

"Is that so? Reasons?" Greta folded her arms on her chest and glared at him. "You might be a powerful magician to the people, but I think we ought to drop the secrecy behind closed doors. You never told us about the letter from Bamberg! I am twenty years old—sometimes I feel like you forget that."

"I don't forget it, because I can see what's happening. Earlier, in the tent—"

"I was handling it," said Greta, cutting him off. "I know how to defend myself." She smiled grimly. "That fellow is going to remember me for the rest of his life whenever he sees his reflection."

"That may be, but I still don't like the way you flirt with the boys." Johann sighed. "What about that dandyish fop you met at the fair in Frankfurt? You were gone for two nights. Anything could have happened to you."

"And what if! It's none of your business. Just because you live like a monk doesn't mean I must live as a nun."

"Insolent brat!" Johann rose angrily. "Watch your fresh mouth. You forget who pulled you out of the gutter!"

He raised his hand but lowered it again immediately. Greta was right. She was old enough to make her own decisions. She was a grown woman who would probably soon go her own way. A woman who turned men's heads. Whenever she got talking with good-looking minstrels or jugglers, Johann would glower and snarl. No one had been good enough for him so far, and he was glad Greta hadn't found the one for her yet. But he expected that sometime soon Greta would leave him and Karl, that she would meet a man who measured up to her and she'd join a different troupe.

That day will be the saddest of my life.

He himself hadn't loved another woman since his decisions had cost Margarethe her life back in Heidelberg. He had visited whores a few times, but even that he'd gradually given up. He loved his daughter and his books—he didn't need anything else.

And I'm probably going to lose one of those two things soon.

"Let's not argue," he said. "You're right. I should have told you as soon as I received the letter from Bamberg. It's time we found winter quarters. The rain earlier on was the first messenger—from now on it is only going to get colder." He tapped on a map of the German Empire that lay rolled up between the books. It was one of the best that had ever been drawn, part of the map of Europe by the well-known cartographer Martin Waldseemüller and worth as much as three destriers. The map went from the North and Baltic Seas down to Italy, and from the lands east of the Elbe River all the way to Burgundy and Brabant. They had traveled many of those regions together in recent years. They had been at home everywhere and nowhere at once.

"I am looking for a safe route to Bamberg," Johann explained. "Just like I've always done. You know how dangerous the roads are at the moment." He attempted a smile. "Even for the famous Doctor Faustus."

Greta suddenly stepped up to him and gave him a kiss on the cheek. "I love you, Uncle," she said softly. "Whatever happens. I just wanted you to know that."

"I . . . I love you, too," he replied, surprised by Greta's sudden show of affection. He liked it when she called him Uncle, but this time the word had sounded anxious.

"I love you more than anything, Greta. I would never forgive myself if anything happened to you."

The last words had just slipped out, but they came from the bottom of Johann's heart. He had a feeling that Tonio had returned in order to drag him into the abyss with him—for good this time. This accursed disease had a firm grip on Johann, and he sensed that the good life on the road was coming to an end. He hadn't much time left. But most of all, he was afraid for Greta. If evil had come back to his life, it wouldn't shy away from his daughter. The grave digger and his wolfish grin took shape in Johann's mind.

Are you finally ready to pay your price, Doctor Faustus?

"And I wouldn't forgive myself if anything were to happen to you." Greta squeezed his hand. "Good night, Uncle." She gave him one last nod and left the chamber.

The room immediately seemed much darker. The candle flickered, and then a gust of wind blew it out. The redoubtable Doctor Johann Georg Faustus was alone with his books and his fears.

2

THE MAN FLAILED HIS ARMS AS HE TUMBLED. FOR A BRIEF
moment he seemed to be suspended in the air, then he screamed as he fell off the
scaffolding onto the cobblestones, where he shattered like a puppet. The dozens
of Roman citizens who'd gathered among the blocks of stone and sacks of lime
on Saint Peter's Square groaned and whispered among themselves. It wasn't long
before a handful of guards appeared to take away the lifeless body, and so people
turned their attention to more exciting things. Only a puddle of blood remained,
which soon dried in the late-autumn sun.

Pope Leo X turned away with disgust. Such accidents reflected badly on
the construction of Saint Peter's Basilica, especially on the day he visited the
site personally. Servants had set down his litter opposite the cathedral so that
he might watch the progress. Standing to his right was his personal architect
and painter, the young master builder Raffaello Santi, who had just launched
into a monologue about his new plans for the barrel vault. The laborer's fatal
accident—he appeared to have slipped and tumbled to his demise—had cut
Raffaello off midsentence.

"An unfortunate accident," muttered Raffaello. "The fellow was probably
drunk."

"Not the first accident of its kind," Leo remarked smugly. He was in a bad
mood because he had been in pain for days. Not even the plentiful silk cushions
and fur rugs could change the fact that he was once more tortured by his old
familiar affliction, which sometimes drove him to the brink of madness. Leo
restlessly shuffled his broad rear end back and forth in an attempt to find a more
comfortable sitting position; the inflamed fistulas flared up like the fires of hell.
"By the devil! You truly ought to pick your workers more carefully, Raffaello."

The master builder, a fine-boned, somewhat feminine-looking man, was considered the best painter in Rome, if not in the whole world—but even he wasn't safe from Leo's fits of temper. Raffaello had already decorated the papal apartments for Leo's predecessor, Julius II, and created unforgettable master-pieces. He was one of the few people who dared to contradict Leo publicly.

"With all due respect, Holy Father," he said coolly, "we have to work our men extremely hard if we want to complete the construction within the time frame. And now that payments are in arrears again, morale is down."

"You'll get your money," hissed Leo. "Don't you worry about that. You've been paid well so far, haven't you, Master Raffaello? So you'd better focus on speeding up this building!"

The rebuilding of Saint Peter's Basilica was Leo's most ambitious project. The previous pope had started it, and construction had already been going for fifteen years. The dome was going to be the biggest and most beautiful in Christendom, no matter the cost. After all, the disciple Saint Peter himself had been buried here, following his martyr's death head-down on the cross—the first pope in a long succession whose most recent member was now Leo.

And I will be the one who leads the church back to its former glory. A second Saint Peter!

Every year, thousands of pilgrims from all over the world came to Saint Peter's. To finance the construction, money from sales of indulgences was brought to Rome, collected by Leo's loyal assistant Johann Tetzel and many other helpers, from Naples in the south up to the Hanse region in the north. Basically, it was a trade from which everyone benefited. The good Christians shortened their time in purgatory, and the church shone in a new, brighter light. The trade in indulgences financed not only the rebuilding of Saint Peter's but also the wealth of paintings, altars, and frescoes that prettied the face of the old whore that was Rome. Leo thought back to the day he had ascended the papal throne. The procession alone had cost a hundred thousand ducats—a seventh of the pope's possessions. But it had been worth it.

The pope sat up in his litter, with its red velvet canopy, and gritted his teeth as another wave of pain rolled through him. His plan was to enter history as the regenerator of the church, and now, of all times, some silly little monk from a German backwater had to pop up and interfere with his life, railing against the letters of indulgence, writing provocative theses, and nailing them most theatrically onto a church door. The last part was probably nothing but gossip to make the story sound more interesting. Whatever the case, the stream of money was becoming noticeably thinner, and maybe someday soon it would dry up altogether. It was enough to drive a man up the wall!

But hopefully all that would soon come to an end—very soon.

"Tell me about the progress with the southern columns," he said to Raffaello.

The master builder nodded dutifully and started another monologue, allowing Leo to let his thoughts drift. Why had he even agreed to this boring site visit? What he needed was distraction! But his favorite jester was ill at the moment, and his cardinals tortured him with irritating reports from the German province, where, on top of everything else, the peasants were growing increasingly discontented. The smell of uprising and change was everywhere—it was as if a powerful autumn wind were blowing through the country, rattling it to the core.

Where are these times going to lead us? To paradise ahead or back into the darkness?

He would ensure that the church, at least, was on the right track. But to do so, he urgently needed the one man he'd been waiting for so desperately. The only man who, after all these setbacks, actually knew the secret that would solve all of Leo's problems.

". . . particularly spectacular are the crossing pillars, which, with the aid of a new roof construction . . . ," said Raffaello, and Leo heard it as if through fog as his gaze traveled across the many scaffolds.

It's all been taking too long.

And then the pain in his backside—he could hardly bear it.

He was greatly relieved when a messenger appeared next to his litter, bowing low. Leo's heart beat faster when he saw that the man carried a letter. The pope had demanded to stay informed about certain occurrences in the empire at all times. Raffaello ceased his explanations once more, unable to suppress a scowl. Leo took the letter and broke the seal, trying to stop his hands from trembling. His eyes darted across the lines. They'd been written by one of his best men—the only man he could trust with this mission and the only one who possessed the necessary discretion.

Leo's mouth twisted into a smile when he finished the letter.

Lord in heaven, praised be thy goodness.

Everything was ready. All he had to do now was wait.

He would pass the time with a few interesting experiments, deep down below Castel Sant'Angelo.

"Thank you for your illuminating updates, Master," he said, turning to the dumbfounded Raffaello. "Important commitments force me to take my leave. I expect you will ensure that your men work more and fall off the scaffold less. If you complete the barrel vaults this year, I will pay your weight in gold. If you don't . . ." He paused and studied dainty Raffaello as if studying a pretty, shimmering bug. "Well, the dungeons of Castel Sant'Angelo are in need of some renovations. If you know what I mean."

He clapped his hands, and the four litter carriers rose. Swaying like a fat old camel, Pope Leo X hovered away above the heads of his flock.

~

It took Johann, Greta, and Karl ten days to travel to Bamberg, and unlike normally, they spent the nights not at warm inns but in the drafty wagon. The people of Franconia were particularly superstitious and fond of beer, and following the incident in Bretten, Faust was more wary than usual of the danger of drunken mobs. Besides, they traveled faster that way.

Greta sat next to Faust on the box seat and enjoyed the gentle swaying that was always part of their journey. She held the reins loosely; the horse knew how to find its way. The road wound endlessly through the Franconian hills, which were speckled with tufts of autumnal fog. Their wagon was in fact a carriage, a terribly expensive vehicle invented in the kingdom of Hungary. On this new type of transport, the compartment was suspended, making for a much smoother ride. The inside of their wagon was a chaos of chests, crates, and colorful clothes that hung from the ceiling alongside fragrant bunches of dried herbs. It smelled of mint, chamomile, and the cheap, potent theriac brandy. The small clay bottles jingled like little bells when the carriage moved. At nights, the wind swept through the thin timber walls.

A book in his hands, his legs wrapped up in a thick woolen blanket, Karl sat leaning against a chest in the back of the wagon while Faust and Greta watched the world go by in silence. Little Satan was jogging alongside the carriage, as he did so often. Greta loved these moments of peace, when nothing seemed to exist but the present. But she knew these times couldn't last forever. She had often toyed with the idea of leaving their little group. She was good enough to join another troupe of jugglers, and she hoped she might one day find the right man for her and leave behind the gloomy past that connected her to Faust. But her friendship with Karl kept her put.

And an insight she hadn't shared with anyone yet—not even with Karl.

The black wings.

Greta shivered. They hadn't spent this many nights in their wagon for a long time. Over the last several years, the doctor had preferred expensive inns and the chambers of castles and abbeys. Greta felt certain that Bamberg's Altenburg Castle would suit Faust's extravagant tastes. Prince-Bishop Georg Schenk von Limpurg was one of the most powerful men in the empire, his influence extending far beyond the walls of Bamberg. As far as Greta knew, he was answerable only to the pope. Not even the emperor could order him around. Greta suddenly thought that such a high-profile meeting wasn't without danger.

"Have you been to Bamberg before, Uncle?" she asked.

Her voice startled Faust. Evidently, he had been deep in thought.

"Oh yes, and so have you," he replied with a smile. "But that was a few years ago now. I guess that's why you don't remember. It's a beautiful town, with a large cathedral and excellent smoked beer. But sadly, we won't see much of Bamberg itself, as the bishop resides at Altenburg Castle, which lies some way outside of town."

"I think a little peace and quiet will do us good," said Greta. "You especially."

She gave him an inscrutable look, and Faust frowned. "Are you trying to tell me something?"

Greta looked away. As much as the matter tormented her, she couldn't bring herself to open up to Faust. He was a man of reason—he was bound to shrug off her fears as nonsense.

And what if he doesn't?

That thought was even worse. The possibility alone that she might be right made her quiver.

"Karl and I are going to use the winter months to change a few of the backdrops," she said instead and flicked the reins, spurring the horse into a trot.

"I need Karl to help me with the horoscope," he said with a shrug. "A horoscope for a bishop has to be about as thick as the Bible. I hear the coming year is going to be a decisive one for the people in power. Something like that requires solid, irrevocable horoscopes."

From conversations they'd overheard at taverns along the way, they gathered that the prince-bishop had played an important role during the Augsburg diet, which had only just come to an end. Apparently, the main reason for Emperor Maximilian to call every elector, prince, and representative of the free imperial cities to said diet was the securing of his grandson Charles as his successor. Maximilian sensed that his life was coming to an end; for years he had been traveling the country with a coffin in tow. But contrary to his expectations, all anyone had talked about in Augsburg had been that Augustinian monk Martin Luther. In the course of just one year, the little monk from Wittenberg in Saxony had become so influential that bishops, princes, and even the emperor himself were forced to take him seriously. These were strange times indeed.

"Jugglers are always needed," said Greta. "No matter the times—people want to be amused."

"The bishop doesn't like buffoons, so you can forget your usual tricks. We'll have to play it careful." Faust shook his head. "No dancing on the rope, no juggling, and no knife throwing. Most of all, no flirting with any guards or servants—understood?"

Greta rolled her eyes. Since the incident in Bretten, Faust was even sterner with her. But how could he know that she'd never slept with a man? She had tried a few times; there had been plenty of opportunities. But every time it came close, she had shied back as if from a wall of fire. She hadn't yet sufficiently trusted any man—only Karl, and he was out of the question. Sometimes she wondered whether she was a normal woman. Women bore children and started families, while she crisscrossed the German lands at the side of an aging magician and his sodomite assistant. This way of life would soon have to come to an end.

"I think I am quite old enough to decide with whom I flirt," she said sharply. "You're not my father—you can't order me."

Greta expected Faust to launch into another tirade, but—strangely—he remained silent.

"Your . . . your mother would have agreed with me," he said haltingly after a while. "I'm sure of it."

"You . . . you knew my mother?" Greta froze, her heart skipping a beat. She stared at Faust with wide eyes. "Is . . . is it true? Tell me! Why do I only find out about this now?"

The doctor had never told her anything about her family. As far as she knew, she was an orphan who had grown up with a distant relative named Valentin. Following a series of events she never fully understood, she had ended up under arrest in Nuremberg as a young girl. People claimed she was a witch, and they had locked her up in a prison below the city hall. Her uncle Valentin and Faust had freed her back then. She had no memory whatsoever about how exactly they'd escaped from the underground passages, but whenever she thought of it, she broke out in a sweat. It was as if an evil beast she mustn't wake slumbered in the depths of her consciousness. Uncle Valentin had died in the course of her liberation, and ever since then she had been with Faust, who claimed to be a friend of her uncle's. No one had ever mentioned her parents.

"What do you know of my mother?" she pressed him now. "Why have you never told me that you knew her? In all these years!" She shook her head in disbelief. Dozens of questions raced through her mind.

"Well, I . . . I didn't really know her," said Faust, looking straight ahead. "I only saw her once or twice, when your uncle Valentin was a young lad. We . . . we studied together in Heidelberg, as you know. And she turned up one day to visit him. That's all."

"What did she look like?"

Faust swallowed hard. "She . . . she looked like you. Exactly like you."

"And what was her name?" asked Greta.

"Margarethe. Uncle Valentin named you after her. Apparently she was the daughter of a prefect and died of a fever when you were just a babe, and so did your father. That's all I know."

"But—"

"Get a move on, you bloody old nag!"

Faust snatched the reins from her hands and flicked them angrily.

"We'd better try to get as far as we can before the rain starts again," he grumbled. "And now quit badgering me with your questions. I must focus on the task ahead. It's not every day I cast a horoscope for a prince-bishop."

Around noon on the tenth day, they finally arrived at Bamberg. The city was built on seven hills, which was why it was also called the German Rome. In its center stood the cathedral with its four towers, and beneath that flowed the lazy blue ribbon of the Regnitz River. A line of merchants' carts stood outside the city gate, noisily waiting to be let in. It was market day. Before they reached the city wall, Johann steered their carriage to the left and followed a smaller road around the town, where Altenburg Castle sat enthroned on one of the seven hills. For many years the castle had been the seat of the Bamberg prince-bishops, whose realm included large cities like Bayreuth and Rothenburg.

Johann cursed himself for telling Greta about her mother. It had just slipped out, and for a moment he'd been tempted to tell her more. But, like so often, he had changed his mind for fear of the consequences. After all, he was to blame for the death of Greta's mother—and how could he have explained that he was her father? That would have raised too many other questions, including questions leading to Tonio del Moravia, and to the black core of his own soul. And so he had lied, as he had so many times before in his life. Greta had made a few other attempts to get more out of him during the remainder of their journey; she'd even asked Karl about her origins. But Johann had threatened Karl a long time ago, vowing to kick him out if he told Greta the truth. So far, Karl had kept his word, perhaps not least because he didn't want to upset Greta with the truth.

The road wound its way up the wooded hill in tight serpentines. Soon, between the dripping branches of the forest they could make out the castle, a bulky construction with several smaller keeps and one massive donjon. A drawbridge led to a heavily guarded outer ward. Johann told the men his name and they opened the gate. The wagon, squeaking and creaking, rattled into the cobbled courtyard.

When he saw the hive of activity in front of them, Johann froze. All his worries about Greta were forced into the background, at least temporarily.

What on earth?

Even from his box seat it was plain to see that something very big was going on at Altenburg Castle. The courtyard was full of vehicles, all of them magnificent carriages with shiny horses, velvet upholstery, and elaborately engraved compartments. Some of the servants shot disparaging glances at the colorful jugglers' wagon. In the background, dandified heralds with trumpets seemed to be expecting important guests. The air was full of whinnying and babbling voices.

Johann climbed down, stretched his legs, and looked around. The yard was encircled by several buildings, the most notable being the tall donjon, the castle's hulking inner tower. Not far from it stood the *palas*—the imposing great hall and living quarters—where the bishop resided. Johann could see servants at work behind the crown-glass windows; evidently, the castle was preparing for a large banquet.

Johann noticed that the first onlookers had begun to whisper. With his black-and-blue star cape and the huge black dog at his side, he was easily recognized; peddlers throughout the empire sold printed images of him along with some hair-raising stories. From the corner of his eye he saw one of the servants rush to the entrance of the palas.

Karl and Greta also looked around with awe. No sooner had they unhitched the horse and handed it to one of the stable boys than the sound of marching steps approached. A delegation of soldiers wearing the typical colorful, slit jerkins and carrying pikes and halberds was heading straight for them. Then they opened their ranks, and the Bamberg prince-bishop stepped forward.

Johann recognized him from a copperplate print he'd seen in a book about the lords of the empire not long ago. The bishop was rather short, and his chubby face and portly stomach made him look jovial, almost grandfatherly. This impression was underlined by the warm coat and plain cap, but the many gold rings on his fingers and the thick gold chain around his neck gave away his high rank.

"The honorable Doctor Johann Georg Faustus, if I'm not mistaken," he declared with a friendly smile. Limpurg's eyes were reddened, as if he spent a lot of time reading in poor light—a typical ailment of scholars. "I am so pleased that you found your way to us, Doctor."

"And it looks as though I'm not the only one," replied Johann. He knelt down and kissed the fleshy, perfumed hand of the bishop. "I gathered from your invitation that you'd like me to compile your horoscope? I did not realize that various other powerful gentlemen were planning on making use of my services."

The bishop chuckled softly, and it sounded like the ringing of small bells. "It is indeed possible that I'm not the only one requiring a good horoscope these days." His expression turned serious. "Especially now, in these turbulent times."

"I beg your pardon?" asked Johann, still kneeling.

"Well, my dear doctor, if you had been at the Imperial Diet in Augsburg, you would know what I'm speaking of." Limpurg sighed. "That little monk from Wittenberg caused serious upheaval among most of the noble lords, when there were more important matters to discuss. For example, the succession of our venerable emperor, who is lying on his sickbed in Innsbruck and must soon enter the kingdom of heaven." The bishop shook his head. "Therefore I deemed it necessary to call another meeting of the high-ranking representatives here in Bamberg—for the well-being of the empire. We need to discuss how we are going to react to Luther's theses." He closed his eyes for a moment, batting his astonishingly long eyelashes. "What we need is unity, not division! There are those who consider Luther's theses to be as dangerous as blackpowder."

Johann said nothing. Now he understood the meaning of all these carriages, horses, and self-important heralds and servants. The bishop was sounding the attack on the little Augustinian monk, and what he needed was a nice horoscope that supported his honorable intentions. What on earth had Johann gotten himself into!

"Don't you think it commendable to question the excessive nature of today's trade with indulgences?" suggested Johann, trying to gain some time. "Luther isn't the only one who believes that the vending of divine grace has taken on rather unheavenly proportions. If I understand his theses correctly, he believes that one cannot buy God's grace; it is bestowed upon us."

"A heretic thought paving a speedy way to the pyre," a voice said from farther back. "Sadly, Luther declined the invitation of the Holy Father to visit him in Rome and elaborate this thought. He will rue the day."

Johann looked up to see the source of the foreign, slightly nasal voice. A man stepped out from among the soldiers. He was wearing a snow-white robe in the manner of Dominican monks, with a wide leather belt from which dangled an ostentatiously large rosary. He seemed to be around Johann's age, although his formerly black hair was mostly gray and cut into a tonsure. His bushy eyebrows were raised as if he was deeply alarmed about something. But his most notable feature was his nose, sticking out from the beardless face like a mighty beak.

"Ah! May I introduce you to a very special guest, my dear doctor?" said the bishop. He only seemed to notice now that Johann was still on his knees and waved impatiently for him to get up. Then he gestured at the clergyman beside him. "This is Viktor von Lahnstein, papal representative. He was at Augsburg with Cardinal Cajetan, trying to convince Luther to abandon his heretical theses."

Lahnstein nodded gravely. "For three days the cardinal tried, imploring Luther like a stubborn mule. In the end, the conceited monk evaded further discussions by running away. Luther appears to believe he can hide behind the Saxon elector Friedrich, but he won't succeed. Rome's arm reaches far—very far!" Johann felt as though Lahnstein was looking at him especially hard during those last words.

"His Reverence came straight from Augsburg with me," Limpurg explained. "The meeting at Altenburg Castle was his idea." He smirked. "And it was also he who suggested I ask you for a horoscope."

Johann's expression froze. His eyes turned to Viktor von Lahnstein, who smiled ominously. If calling him to Altenburg Castle had been Lahnstein's idea, Johann had to expect the worst. Someone might have reported him as a sorcerer in Rome, and now he was in danger of landing on the pyre, just like that Luther. What was it Lahnstein just said?

Rome's arm reaches far—very far.

Johann involuntarily looked around for Karl and Greta but couldn't see them anywhere.

"Oh, if you're looking for your retinue, the assistant and the girl, they have already been taken to their chambers," said Limpurg, guessing the meaning of his searching glance. "For you, Doctor, we have prepared a very special room." With a smile he pointed upward, to the top of the donjon. "The tower room of Altenburg. You'll be entirely undisturbed up there, and it offers the best view of the stars—and I assume you're going to need those for the horoscope. I wish you all the best for your work, Doctor Faustus."

With the unpleasant feeling of having walked straight into a trap, Johann allowed two soldiers to walk him to the tower. And with every step he took, he thought he could feel the eyes of the papal representative on his back.

∼

With his head held high and slow, measured steps, Karl Wagner strode through the rooms and halls of Altenburg Castle and studied the delegates whispering to each other in the window bays and by the many fireplaces. They all wore warm, precious fur coats over beautifully dyed clothes made of fustian. There were a few handsome young men among them. Karl had also donned his best clothes, a tight-fitting black tunic and a slightly stained but still reasonably good coat, giving him the air of a young, ambitious cleric.

I could almost be one of them. A delegate from some small bishopric, a talented theologian who could make it all the way to cardinal in Rome.

He wondered how his life would have passed if he had completed his studies at Leipzig. Perhaps he would be a doctor or an advocate by now, working in an elevated position as adviser for a baron or count. Karl knew that he was intelligent and educated, blessed with more knowledge than most men in this room. But he also knew where this knowledge had come from. No university on earth could have taught him as much as the nearly ten years he'd spent with Doctor Johann Georg Faustus. But still, the sight of all these elegant, beautifully dressed men who laughed together, drank wine from paper-thin Venetian glasses, and debated politics filled him with longing. These men led a life not granted to Karl. He was an outcast, twice over: first as assistant to a magician and astrologer, and second as a clandestine sodomite.

Karl loved men. He knew it was a deadly sin, but he couldn't change it. Years ago, the doctor had saved him from execution at the very last moment, and since then Karl had traveled the empire with Johann. He had tried to subdue his affliction, but unsuccessfully. He'd been discovered more than once and narrowly escaped arrest, leaving the doctor furious each time because Karl had put all their lives in danger.

Occasionally Karl wondered whether Faust even knew why he stayed despite the temper tantrums, despite Faust's frequently condescending ways, and despite their differing opinions in scientific matters. Sometimes the doctor treated Karl as if he was still the same naive young student from Leipzig he had been ten years ago. But Karl hadn't even told Greta the real reason; his shame ran too deeply.

Because I love someone who will never return my love.

Karl missed Greta acutely just then, thinking she must have stayed in her room. They had grown very close in recent years, almost like brother and sister. Greta had become Karl's closest confidante, even if he couldn't reveal all his secrets to her. It pained him that he wasn't permitted to tell Greta more about the incidents back in Nuremberg, but the doctor had made his wishes very clear. Still, perhaps it was for the best. Whatever had happened in the underground passages of that city had been so profoundly evil that Greta's consciousness had good reason to suppress the memories.

The bishop's servants had assigned them two drafty, damp rooms in an adjoining building where the footmen of the delegates were housed. Karl hadn't tarried long before leaving that hole to mingle with the higher-ranking guests. No one had stopped him at the door to the palas—possibly thanks to his pompous demeanor.

"Apparently there's even a delegate from England," said a corpulent gentleman in a fur coat to another man. "And also a representative from the house of Fugger, probably to gauge the mood among the German princes." He sighed. "Ever since that Luther printed his confounded 'Sermon on Indulgences and God's Grace' in German, even the peasants want to have their say in it. I heard that someone reads it out to them, and then those donkeys debate the matter in the stable as if they were lords!"

"I'm sure young King Henry is interested in more important matters than German leaflets," replied the other man. He was skinny and old and he leaned on a cane, warming his gouty back by the chimney. He chuckled softly and glanced about the room. "They are sharing out the bear's skin before the beast is killed. And those French frog eaters—" He noticed Karl in an alcove nearby and broke off. Karl quickly averted his gaze and walked away.

He crossed two further grand rooms decorated with several paintings. They were impressive if slightly lugubrious images of the Madonna and the savior, portraits of influential clergymen, paintings of former popes and also one of the current pope, Leo X, whose burly stature reminded Karl more of an innkeeper or a butcher. Portraits were very fashionable these days, partly because of the growing number of wealthy, confident burghers, but also because of the church, which liked to invest its riches in frescoes and paintings, not only in Rome.

Karl, too, was a passionate artist, even if he couldn't afford the expensive oil paints that had been used for the works in front of him.

Beneath the artworks sat the delegates, snacking on sweet pastries and candied fruit plucked from glass bowls. Karl could tell by the robes that among them were at least two bishops, several abbots of various orders, and a handful of imperial delegates who looked more nervous than anyone else. This truly was a meeting of the most powerful men in the empire!

Karl had learned by now that the official meeting wouldn't commence for a few days yet, when the last delegates from faraway lands arrived. He tried to estimate how many barrels of expensive French wine the men would have drained by then, and how many honey-glazed pigs would have made it to their stomachs. This Bamberg prince-bishop must have been incredibly rich—he probably made a profit from dealing in indulgences.

"A fitting sight, *n'est-ce pas?*" said a voice from right behind him. "Each day to this small folk is a feast of fun."

Startled, Karl spun around. A gaunt man stood in front of him, wearing plain, dark clothes and holding himself slightly hunched over, with an apparent crooked back. The only color in his appearance was his red cap and the rooster's feather attached to it. His face was deathly pale, as if he had rubbed chalk on it, and he spoke with the soft rhythm of the Western countries. The man was gesturing at the feasting delegates reaching out for more candied fruit.

"*Voilà!* The common people give the little money they own to shorten their time in purgatory, and the high and mighty use said money to stuff their faces. This way, everyone wins, everyone is happy. What a show—one could almost turn it into a play!" The stranger smiled, and Karl didn't know if he was jesting or serious. He decided to say nothing.

"How rude of me. May I introduce myself?" The man gave a small bow. "Louis Cifre, one of the French delegates." He eyed Karl curiously. "And you are . . . ?"

"Um, Karl Wagner, assistant to Doctor Johann Georg Faustus. He's one of the bishop's advisers, employed to write up a horoscope for him." Karl had considered lying to the man and making up some random name and position, but he'd judged it too dangerous among all these high-ranking nobles.

"Ah, that's how I know the learned man." The French delegate raised an eyebrow. "I have heard much about Doctor Faustus. He is a clever man, *c'est vrai.* The bishop can consider himself lucky to have him at his side. It is not easy to tell friend from foe in these times. A prophet can only be of use."

"How do you mean?" asked Karl, reaching for one of the wineglasses lackeys were proffering on silver trays.

"Now, I'm sure you're aware that we're all here to figure out what to do next with this Luther and his theses. But that is only half the truth, *mon ami.*" The man lowered his voice. "In truth, we're here because a powerful man is dying."

"You're talking about Emperor Maximilian," said Karl.

The man nodded, and as if by magic he now also held a glass of wine in his hand. "The physicians are saying His Imperial Highness has only months left— weeks, perhaps. A growth in his intestines—nasty business, they say. Not even prayers will help." He sighed deeply. "Maximilian himself wants to be sure his grandson Charles follows him onto the throne, but that is not what the German electors want—and it's they who choose the new king. Charles—Carlos—is a Spaniard, not a German. His mother is Joanna of Aragon, known as 'Joanna the Mad,' and his father, Philip the Handsome, was the king of Castile himself until his early death. The pope isn't the only one fearing an imbalance of power in Europe if Charles ascends the throne. The new German king would rule an empire that reaches from Castile all the way to the North Sea, and in the west even unto the distant lands beyond the sea. *Compris?*"

Karl sipped his red wine and tried to appear as serene as possible. He'd only understood about half of what the delegate had told him, but he didn't want to make a fool of himself. Politics appeared to be almost as complicated as painting.

"A rather intricate affair indeed," he said.

"*C'est vrai.*" The delegate shook his head slowly and continued. "Well, Elector Friedrich the Wise of Saxony wouldn't make a bad German king at all." He gave a malicious smile. "Not to mention my lord and ruler."

"Your—?" Karl choked on his wine and coughed. "The . . . the French king as German emperor? Are you serious?"

Louis Cifre shrugged. "Why not? Francis is young and ambitious, and the German electors like him. And the German Empire is as brittle as an old clay jug because of all the constant disturbances—especially now with this Luther." Cifre took a sip of his wine, and small red droplets rolled off his lips. Karl noticed that the man had astonishingly pointy white teeth.

"It's not like Francis is the only European ruler who has expressed an interest," Cifre went on. "The English king Henry might put up his hand, too. Like I said—exciting times ahead! And one would do well to consider on whose side one stands." He raised his glass and winked at Karl. "Whose side are you on, Master Wagner?"

Karl's head was spinning with all the names and political stratagems. What could he say that wouldn't embarrass himself or offend his conversational partner? "I stand on the side of my master, Doctor Faustus," he declared eventually. "If you're on the side of a prophet, you're always right, are you not?"

"Well said!" Monsieur Cifre laughed and clinked his glass against Karl's. "How is the doctor doing, by the way? I haven't seen him yet. Is he well?"

"He is."

"So this is where you're loafing about!" Karl winced at the sound of Greta's ringing voice. "I've been looking everywhere for you. Didn't we say we'd meet by the wagon to take a look at the torn backdrops?"

Greta was wearing a red dress with green slits that perfectly suited a juggler lass, but—so Karl thought—it looked garish in these halls, especially since her bodice was laced rather sloppily. Several older gentlemen had turned to gape at Greta and her feminine shape beneath the dress. Karl was embarrassed by Greta's flippant demeanor.

"Er . . . a maidservant of the doctor," he said quietly to the French delegate, hoping Greta wouldn't hear. But Greta had ears like a fox.

"*Maidservant?* Are you in your right mind?" Greta stormed up to him, noticing the man next to Karl only at the last moment. The man grinned, baring his sharp white teeth.

"A pretty maidservant indeed. And with a quick tongue."

Greta wrinkled her nose as she eyed Monsieur Cifre. Then she pulled Karl by his arm. "You'll excuse us. The *maidservant* has something important to discuss with this noble lord."

She dragged Karl along until they came to a quiet bay window that overlooked the forest all the way down to Bamberg.

"Are you crazy?" snarled Karl. "That was the French delegate! Your behavior could cost us our heads."

"I didn't like him. He smelled weird," replied Greta. "Didn't you notice? If it was perfume like those frog eaters use, he'd better leave it off. I like yours much better."

In fact, Karl had noticed the strange smell, almost like sulfur, but he hadn't thought anything of it. He had been much too enraptured discussing high politics with the French delegate.

"Monsieur Cifre is a very interesting conversationalist," he said bitterly. "I would have liked to speak with him for longer."

"Karl, what are you doing?" Greta looked at him sharply. "You and I—we don't belong here! To me it looked more like the fellow was trying to sound you out."

"Sound me out?" Karl laughed. "And why should he do that? We talked about politics. And yes, he wanted to hear about the doctor, too, but who doesn't? Doctor Faustus is renowned right across the empire, after all." He gave her an angry look. "You might not like it here, but I love it. For once we don't have to travel the lands like dishonorable jugglers. For once—"

"Karl, stop it." Greta sighed. "Do you think I don't see how you're growing further and further apart from us? I understand. You are no juggler, no minstrel— at the bottom of your heart, you're a scientist. You should go back to your old university, become a magister—a doctor, even . . ."

"You forget that I was forced to leave Leipzig as a wanted sodomite," Karl replied coldly.

"Then don't go to Leipzig. Although it's been so long, I doubt you'd have anything to worry about."

Karl crossed his arms on his chest and gazed out at the city below. Dusk was spreading over the houses; the first lights had already been lit. "Sounds almost like you want me to leave you," he muttered.

He couldn't tell Greta the real reason he was staying, why he couldn't get away from the doctor.

Because I love him. Even if he'll never return my love.

"And speaking of our little troupe," he said, turning back to Greta. "I could say the same thing about you. You're young and beautiful, Greta, no longer a timid little girl like when you first joined us. And you're a talented juggler and trickster."

"Do you think I've never thought about leaving?" replied Greta softly. "I even came close to doing it a few times. This winter would be a good time, I've been thinking. Especially since the doctor is becoming grumpier and more withdrawn by the day. He doesn't want to tell me anything, neither about my parents nor about himself. But then—" She broke off.

"Then what?" asked Karl.

Greta swallowed. "It's . . ." She hesitated. Then she dropped onto a cushioned stool and buried her face in her hands. Her shoulders shook, and when she straightened back up, Karl saw by her reddened eyes that she'd been crying.

"I wanted to tell you some other time," she said. "I've been waiting for the right moment. But there is no right moment for something like this."

"What are you talking about?" asked Karl anxiously. "What are you trying to tell me? Speak up!"

Greta took his hand and held it tightly.

"Karl, I'm so sorry. But I know for certain that the doctor is going to die very soon."

~

Johann paced back and forth in the tower room of the donjon, restless like a beast of prey in its cage. He paused and looked out through the small, barred window at Altenburg Castle in the evening light, and Bamberg beyond, and then forests and fields as far as the eye could see. In the distance, a ridgeline disappeared into the haze. The view was spectacular, but Johann felt like a prisoner nonetheless.

The soldiers had been forced to carry his luggage up the many stairs, complaining loudly about the doctor's heavy gear. His crates were filled with various apparatuses, including the strange stargazing tube Johann had taken from Tonio all those years ago, which allowed him to see the heavens closely, as with divine eye glasses. And, of course, there were the countless books he loved so dearly.

Johann remembered exploring the Maulbronn library like an exotic garden as a child, each volume a priceless treasure. Later on he'd invested much of his fortune in books, which protected him to some extent against theft. Not many gallows' birds knew that—for example—the illustrated *Schedelsche Weltchronik* was worth more than three good horses. And, thankfully, neither thieves nor soldiers knew anything about the false bottoms in his chests, which were filled with gold and silver coins of various currencies. They were Johann's insurance in case he was ever wanted as a heretic and sorcerer and needed to disappear.

He walked over to one of the chests and opened it. Then he carefully lifted out something wrapped in oiled cloth. It was a book and his dearest and most precious possession.

Johann gently folded back the cloth and ran his fingers over the cover, as if he was about to open a treasure chest. The volume was leather bound and about as thick as a hand, with pages made from the finest goat vellum. The drawings inside showed many different perspectives of the inside of the human body, limbs, and organs. The illustrations were so perfectly done that Johann always thought he was looking at real muscles, sinews, and innards. He could practically smell the blood.

The Italian title of the book was *De Figura Umana*, which Johann translated as "About the human form." It was written and drawn by the great painter and inventor Leonardo da Vinci, whose work Johann had been admiring for many years. He had first heard about Leonardo back in Venice as a young juggler. Johann had bought the book two years ago for a horrendous amount of money from the bishop of Speyer, who in turn had received it as a gift from the Duke of Milan.

Basically, it was just a collection of loose pages, and some bookbinder had done a rather rough-and-ready job of sewing them together. The pages were all different sizes. Johann guessed da Vinci hadn't allowed his drawings into print because the dissection of corpses was forbidden, bar a few exceptions. The artist must have conducted a large number of dissections himself, or he never would have been able to draw with so much detail. He described many diseases, including the white and the black plagues, the falling sickness, Saint Anthony's fire, cataract, and the extremely painful stone sickness that only the best physicians could treat. The text, like many of da Vinci's other works, was written in mirror writing, making deciphering it rather arduous. Johann had hoped to find a clue about his own mysterious disease in this book, but, so far, in vain.

On cue, his left hand started to tremble. Johann set the book aside and reached into the crate with the theriac. Alcohol was the only way to get the shaking somewhat under control. He pulled the cork out of a bottle and took a long sip, and the shaking eased. He only hoped Karl and Greta hadn't noticed how fast the theriac was vanishing.

Absentmindedly he gazed down into the courtyard, where another carriage was just arriving. He heard whinnying and the clatter of hooves, and the loud voice of a herald announcing some delegate or another. With a sigh, Johann set the book down on the table and started to unpack.

In the course of their journey, Johann had made peace with the idea of the bishop's invitation—at least their stay would give him ample time to research his strange illness. But the brief conversation with the papal representative earlier had changed everything. Lahnstein himself had advised the bishop to invite Johann. There could be only one explanation: Rome had taken notice of the famous Doctor Faustus. He had to expect the worst.

Johann was just opening another chest of books when he heard footsteps coming up the tower. As soon as he'd closed the lid, someone knocked on the door.

"Who is it?" asked Johann.

Instead of a reply, the heavy, reinforced door creaked open. Standing outside were Viktor von Lahnstein and the biggest man Johann had ever seen. He was so tall that he had to double over in the narrow corridor. The giant wore a blue, yellow, and red jerkin and matching trousers, as well as a scratched cuirass with shoulder plates and a helmet with a comb that hid about half of his bearded, pockmarked face. On his back he carried a two-handed sword so long and heavy that Johann doubted he could lift it, let alone fight with it. Lahnstein noticed Johann's puzzled look and smiled.

"Impressive, isn't he? Hagen is a Swiss mercenary and a member of the new palace guard the current pope's predecessor, Julius II, introduced. Each one of those Swiss mercenaries is an experienced soldier and loyal unto death to the Holy Father. His Holiness has lent me Hagen as my personal bodyguard. The journey through the empire isn't without dangers."

"You don't have to tell me," muttered Johann.

The mercenary gazed at him blankly, and Johann wondered whether it had been a mistake to leave Little Satan with Greta down in the yard where he had more space to run about.

"May I come in?" asked Viktor von Lahnstein. Hagen waited outside the door while the papal representative entered the chamber. Lahnstein saw the books on the table and nodded. "I see you're making yourself at home." His eyes fell on *Figura Umana*, and his expression hardened. "Look at that, the work of that godless Milanese inventor. Did you know that until a few years ago, Leonardo worked for the Holy Father in Rome? Pope Leo never liked him much, although admittedly he's an ingenious artist—devilishly good, one might say." Lahnstein shuddered with disgust. "The Holy Father must have sensed that at the bottom of his soul, Leonardo is a heretic. They say he dissected bodies, but no one could ever prove it."

Johann pushed the book beneath some of the others, hoping Lahnstein wouldn't get the idea to leaf through it. "I'm sure you didn't come to chat about Leonardo da Vinci," he said.

"Indeed I didn't." Lahnstein took a step forward and gazed out the window, his hands crossed behind his back. "You're a smart man, Doctor, just like me.

That is why we don't need to play games. When I told the bishop to ask you here, I had my own agenda." He spun around brusquely and looked Johann in the eye. "I want you to accompany me to Rome."

Johann groaned inwardly. His worst fears were coming true. But he merely smiled thinly. "Does the pope want a horoscope, too? One at a time—the bishop asked first."

"Don't mock His Holiness," snarled Lahnstein. "Pope Leo X is after something else." He lowered his voice. "Something much bigger."

"I think you overestimate my abilities, Your Eminence. I'm a simple astrologer and doctor. Not much good as an Antichrist, I'm afraid—you'd be better off taking that Luther. So if you want to accuse me of heresy—"

"Balderdash!" Lahnstein cut him off with a wave of his hand. "Heresy? Nonsense! The pope knows very well that you're not much more than a fraud and a quack. But he also heard that there is something you know, something"— Lahnstein hesitated—"very particular. Something few people know. And it is a knowledge the pope is highly interested in. Consider it an invitation to a conversation among the like-minded."

Johann frowned. This encounter had taken a sudden and unexpected turn, and he didn't know whether he liked it.

"What sort of knowledge?" he asked after a while.

Lahnstein looked back out the window. He said nothing for a long moment, and when he spoke, he spoke quietly as his eyes traveled across the dark forests beyond Bamberg. Night had fallen outside.

"It is the knowledge of a man who was born a long time ago," said Lahnstein. "A very powerful and profoundly evil man. His name is Gilles de Rais."

Johann shivered as if winter had just arrived.

Gilles de Rais.

Would this nightmare never end?

"I . . . I don't know what you're talking about," replied Johann eventually.

"Oh yes, you do." Lahnstein turned back to him. He pointed his index finger straight at Johann, his beak-like nose making him look like a gigantic bird of prey in the dim light. "There is a secret that surrounds Gilles de Rais, and you know that secret, Doctor Faustus! We have it on good authority." He gestured toward the window. "Whatever you're doing out there, whatever swill you sell and how you fool the common people—Rome doesn't care. Rome is only interested in *true* arcane knowledge—knowledge that you share with Gilles de Rais. And do you know why?" He lowered his face, his voice nothing but a whisper. "Because he told it to you himself."

"You know very well that the man you're speaking of has been dead these eighty years. How should he be able to tell me anything?"

"Is he really? Dead? I wouldn't be so sure." Lahnstein smiled thinly. "Why so modest all of a sudden, Doctor Faustus? I heard wizards like you could speak with the dead. Isn't that what you claim in your shows?"

The papal representative slowly walked to the door while the shadows of night spread through the chamber. "Compile your pretty horoscope, Doctor, just as the bishop wishes. And then travel to Rome with me. Pope Leo X can't wait to make your acquaintance. Yours and that of your many secrets. He wants to talk to you about Gilles de Rais and his arcane knowledge before other powerful men do. You're in demand, Johann Georg Faustus, and these are tumultuous times."

At the door, Lahnstein turned back to Johann once more.

"Oh, and one more thing. I am going to inform the bishop that your work is taking up so much of your time that you don't want to leave this lovely chamber. Your meals will be brought to you, and if you need anything else, your servants can see to it. You're the bishop's guest, after all. For your own safety, Hagen will keep watch outside your chamber. God bless you."

With these words, the papal representative left the room. Before the door slammed shut, Johann caught a glance of the Swiss mercenary, still eyeing him as blankly as if he were a bug.

Then the bolt was pushed across and Johann was alone.

The shaking came over him shortly after Lahnstein had left. It was much more severe than before—more severe than ever—and Johann had to sit down on the chair so he wouldn't fall. His left arm jerked like a twitching snake, sweat ran down his forehead, and he forced himself to breathe calmly. Each passing moment felt like an eternity while thoughts flashed through his mind like lightning.

Gilles de Rais. Gilles de Rais. Gilles de Rais.

For the first time, Johann felt certain that his ailment was indeed a curse. How else was it possible that the mention of that unhappy name triggered a fit? First Tonio del Moravia, his former master, had entered his life again, and now Gilles de Rais!

Who are you? And what does it have to do with me?

To this day, Johann didn't know how Gilles and Tonio were connected. They were two pieces of a mosaic that he still couldn't see in its entirety. Gilles de Rais had been a powerful French knight, an extravagant marshal who had lived nearly a hundred years ago and become a slave to sorcery and Satanism. He used to catch children like hares and murder them—not one or two, but hundreds, all of them victims who served to invoke the devil during gruesome rituals. De Rais's deeds were still told as ghost stories by the people of his region, even though he'd been hanged at Nantes many years ago. He was executed as the most godless heretic and cruelest murderer that had ever lived. Lahnstein's question from earlier came to Johann's mind.

Is he really? Dead? I wouldn't be so sure.

The shaking was growing stronger. Johann reached for the books on the table as if they were his lifeline, but he couldn't grasp them and they crashed to the floor. The books couldn't help him now; not even they could tell him more about the insane knight with the eyes of an angel, which had once gazed at him from a basin filled with blood. That had been in Nuremberg, when Tonio had tried to sacrifice him for some kind of dark offering.

Johann closed his eyes and felt cold sweat on his forehead. He heard loud crashing and breaking, and it took him a while to realize that he was lying on the wooden floorboards and that it had been his body crashing to the ground. He must have tried to brace himself against the table and had gone down—table, chair, books, and all. Johann opened his mouth, saliva dribbling from his lips like a rabid dog. The words came haltingly.

"Gilles . . . Tonio . . . cursed . . . pact . . ."

Johann thought of the bright young boy who'd shook the hand of a magician long ago. A boy who'd gained glory in the course of his life, and knowledge and wealth, but who now, many years on, had to pay for it.

There was no escape.

With this final thought, he blacked out.

~

"What?" Karl gaped at Greta. "The doctor is going to die? How . . . how do you know?"

Greta was trembling, trying with all her might to compose herself. She had always known that this day would come—she couldn't carry this terrible secret around with her forever.

"I don't mean to frighten you, Karl," she said. "Maybe I'm mistaken. But I don't think I am. I saw it clearly."

Karl gave a desperate laugh. "What do you mean, you saw it? In your dreams? I don't believe in dreams—I am certain they are nothing but illusions."

"I saw it in the palm of his hand. Do you understand?"

"Do you . . . do you mean you can read in someone's hand if they're going to die?" Karl turned pale. "I always thought that was nothing but hocus-pocus. You simply tell people what they want to hear. And besides—you haven't read anyone's palm in years."

Greta sighed. "And now you know why. Because it is just too awful sometimes."

She'd been carrying this dark secret around with her for a long time now. She had been young when Johann had introduced her to chiromancy, the art of reading palms. The long, forked Life line that ends above the thumb, the mysterious Fate line, the Heart line, the Mount of Venus, the so-called simian crease, and more. In the beginning she had enjoyed it, but one day three winters ago, something had happened.

She had seen a person's imminent death in their palm.

It had felt like steady pulsations, and for the briefest moment the Life line had glowed; then something had covered the hand, something like the black wing of a bird. And Greta knew with certainty that this person would soon die.

At first she had told herself that she'd only imagined it, that it was part of the melancholy that befell her from time to time. But then they spent the winter in Erfurt, in Thuringia. A young woman had asked to have her palm read, and Greta had obliged; the black wing had appeared once more. One week later, the woman had fallen ill with a fever and died.

The black wings.

"The doctor has become more and more sullen in recent months," she said slowly. "You must have noticed that something is bothering him. And then there's the strange shaking that he's trying to hide from us."

Karl nodded. "Perhaps it's the alcohol. He's been drinking a lot lately, mostly in secret."

"Whatever it is—he won't talk to us. So I went to his bed one night to look at his palm. He only ever takes off his gloves when he sleeps." She looked at Karl closely. "You never told me why he's missing the little finger on his right hand, and his left eye."

Karl didn't reply, and Greta continued.

"When I picked up his hand, I felt something. It was something dark, evil! And do you know what else was strange? His lines were barely recognizable, as if they had faded, as if . . . as if they were gradually disappearing. I have never seen anything like it before." Greta pressed her lips together. "And then it happened. The Life line lit up in a dark purple, and then a black shadow—like the wing of a bird—swept across it. And I felt the same throbbing as with the others before. And they all died a short while later." She closed her eyes. "I should never have done it, but now it's too late."

"I . . . I think you're mistaken," Karl replied weakly.

But Greta could tell that he was keeping something from her. Terrible things had happened back in Nuremberg—so terrible that her consciousness had suppressed most memories of that night. The few recollections that remained were blurred, as if she were looking through a dull lens. Sometimes, in her dreams, she saw herself lying naked on a stone altar. A choir of voices chanted a sinister litany; a knife flashed in the darkness.

O Mephistopheles, O Satanas.

"Karl, you have to tell me what happened back in Nuremberg," urged Greta. "The doctor said someone gave me a potion that made me pass out. What kind of a potion? It's almost like my whole childhood has been erased. Johann is keeping something from me, I'm certain. And so are you! Karl, please talk to me." She squeezed his hands. "Who are my parents?"

"It's better if you don't know," replied Karl glumly. "Trust me. We oughtn't speak about the time in Nuremberg."

"Yes, that is what the doctor and you are best at," said Greta bitterly. "Not speaking about things. And even now you don't want to see the truth: the doctor is in grave danger and I think he's going to die. Something indescribably evil is reaching for him—I can feel it!"

"And I say that nothing is proven," Karl retorted. "I am a scientist, Greta—I don't believe in witches, sorcery, and the devil's handiwork, nor that one can foresee someone's death in the palm of their hand. Not as long as—"

He broke off when a shadow fell on them both. They looked up and saw a huge, armored mercenary with a sword on his back gazing down at them.

"Are you the servants of Doctor Faustus?" asked the giant. He spoke with the harsh accent of the Swiss confederates.

Greta nodded.

"Then follow me, quickly. Your master needs you." The huge man let out a growl that made him sound like a bear. "If it isn't too late, damn it."

Greta hurried after Karl and the soldier through the corridors of Altenburg Castle.

She feared the worst had already happened.

They ran up the stairs to the tower room as fast as they could. When they arrived at the top, breathing hard, Greta saw to her surprise that the door was barred from the outside.

"You locked the doctor in?" she asked the soldier as she struggled to catch her breath. "Why?"

The giant man didn't reply and unlocked the door. The room on the other side was dim, the only light coming from a few candles on a sideboard. Faust was lying on the floor among his books, some of them torn to shreds. He was twitching and squirming as if a hundred invisible devils were tugging at him. Saliva and vomit trickled from his mouth as he slurred incomprehensible sounds.

"Jesus!" cried Greta, rushing to the doctor's side. "What happened?"

"How should I know? I found him like that." The soldier gave a shrug as he eyed the doctor like a squashed beetle. "If you ask me, I'd say your master is possessed by the devil or some sort of demon. But one thing I know for certain: if he kicks the bucket now, my master, the papal representative, won't be pleased at all. And he'll take it out on all of us. So do something!"

"He'll choke on his vomit if we don't help him soon." Karl knelt down and held Faust while Greta cleaned out his mouth, muttering softly as if soothing a child. Johann was still shaking, his head jerking from side to side. But the twitching gradually eased, and his head came to rest.

"At first I thought he was just putting it on when I heard the racket," grumbled the big man. "But then it got worse. So I thought I better fetch help."

"What is all this about?" demanded Karl, pointing at the exit. "Who are you and why was the door locked?"

"It's . . . it's all right," said the doctor feebly. "I . . . I'm better now." He was lying on his back, his face deathly white. The fit seemed to have passed. He looked at the mercenary. "Please leave us now, Hagen."

The giant hesitated for a moment, then he walked out and closed the door behind him, the bolt crashing shut loudly. Karl moved as if to protest, but Faust held him back. "Leave it. I . . . I can explain everything. Please help me sit up."

Together they lifted Faust like an old man and sat him on a stool. It was strange for Greta to see the doctor weakened like this. She had only ever known him strong and resilient in both body and mind. Nothing could stop him—whatever he wanted to achieve, he would achieve. And now he sat slumped on the stool like a puppet whose strings had been cut. At least his eyes looked a little livelier; his strength seemed to return.

Greta shuddered. Faust truly had looked as if he were possessed by the devil. Could it be possible? She thought about the shaking she had observed in recent weeks, and also about the dark, evil something she'd seen in his hand. She decided not to mention her nightly palm reading—she was much too afraid there was indeed an evil force that had grabbed hold of the doctor.

It was freezing cold in the doctor's chamber, and Greta thought once more she could smell sulfur, like earlier on with that strange French ambassador. She shivered as she looked to the window and the dark night beyond. A black shadow drifted past, like the wings of a gigantic, monstrous bird.

Now you're seeing ghosts.

"What happened?" she asked gently while Karl took the doctor's pulse and patted dry his forehead. "It wasn't the first time, was it?"

Johann moaned. "I should have known that you'd notice." He tried to smile. "Can't hide anything from a woman."

"I noticed, too," said Karl. "The shaking, worse at nights. At first I thought it was the booze, but this . . ." He shook his head. "Hmm, it could be the falling sickness, or Saint Anthony's fire, or—"

"Don't you think I haven't tried to figure out what's ailing me, damn it?" snarled Johann. "I read through dozens of books, but my symptoms don't match anything I could find in the usual works."

"And how long has this been going on?" asked Greta.

"About half a year."

Once more Greta got the feeling that he was keeping something from her.

Johann closed his eyes and took a deep breath. "But that's not the worst part."

"Not the worst part?" Karl gave a desperate chuckle. "I can't imagine what might be worse than what we just witnessed."

"I am to be taken to the pope as a sorcerer," said Faust. "That's why the giant is standing outside the door, and that's why the door is locked. It's an order by Viktor von Lahnstein. As soon as I've completed the bishop's horoscope, Lahnstein is going to escort me to Rome in chains." He snorted. "I don't know which I'd prefer: for this mysterious illness to kill me beforehand or to be drawn, quartered, and burned on the papal scaffold."

Karl groaned. "That explains it. The horoscope was just an excuse. I always feared this would happen one day. Doctor Faustus is known through-out the empire, so why not in Rome? Perhaps the Bamberg prince-bishop could—"

Faust waved impatiently. "He's got better things to do than stick up for a quack suspected of meddling in black magic and necromancy." He counted on his fingers. "There's Luther, an emperor on his deathbed, rebellious peasants . . . There's trouble brewing in every corner of the empire. No, we're on our own, damn it."

He fell silent and bit his lips. Greta knew her uncle was thinking hard when he looked like that.

"We'd have to escape," he mumbled. "If only I could get out of here, I know someone who could help me. If not he, who else?"

"But how do you propose to get out of here?" asked Greta, looking around. "This is a tower room high above the ground." She nodded at the narrow, barred window; deep down below a few torches flickered in the courtyard. "The door is bolted from the outside, and that awful fellow in front of it ensures you can't leave your chamber. You'll definitely remain locked up until you've finished the horoscope and then—"

"Say that again!" Faust grabbed Greta by the hand and she started with alarm. Was he having another fit? She gave the doctor a close look.

"What do you mean?" she asked cautiously.

Faust had a grim smile on his face, and his eyes flashed with renewed determination. "Ha! You said I'll remain locked up in here until the horoscope is finished. That is correct. But at some stage I am going to have to present the horoscope to the bishop, even if it's just for pretense. The bishop is vain, I could tell, and so he expects something grandiose from me. I'm certain the presentation won't take place in this barren tower room but most likely in the palas, in front of all those noblemen. The bishop won't pass up the opportunity to put on a show."

"That doesn't help us," said Karl dejectedly. "I'm afraid they will continue to guard you closely, especially in the palas. How can we escape with all those papal mercenaries at Lahnstein's disposal?"

"By distracting them." Faust nodded. "By distracting them with a very particular apparatus." He rose to his feet, still shaking a little, and walked over to some books on the floor. There he knelt down and started to rummage. "Darn it, it has to be somewhere. I saw it earlier . . . Here!" He held up a book triumphantly and placed it on the table that Greta and Karl had stood back on its legs.

"We are going to build a new *laterna magica*!" he declared.

"The laterna." Karl sighed. "I thought we'd never use that devilish machine again. Do you really think that—?"

"Oh yes, I do." Faust grinned and gestured at the window. "The entire German Empire is gathered down there, and I think it's time I did my reputation justice." He opened the book and leafed until he found the page he was looking for—the page with the drawing of a box, a tube, and the outline of a devilish creature against a wall. He tapped his finger on it and jutted out his chin like he always did when he wanted to prove something to the world.

"One thing is for certain," he growled. "The bishop and the delegates are going to witness the greatest and most breathtaking spectacle the empire has ever seen. No one toys with Doctor Faustus!"

~

The idea had come to Johann the moment he spotted the book on the floor. Just like Leonardo da Vinci, he jotted down his thoughts and ideas on pieces of parchment that he later had bound. Some of his notes dated back to his student days in Heidelberg. Back then he had constructed a laterna magica with his friend Valentin. He had been blind with ambition, and in the end the apparatus had led to the arrest and execution of his one true love. The thought of it made him tremble, and he breathed deeply.

Margarethe, my everything.

Nonetheless, he had used the laterna magica again during his early shows with Karl, until it was destroyed in the underground passages beneath Nuremberg. The apparatus could transfer images painted on glass plates so that they were displayed against a wall, where they appeared larger than life. It created a true spectacle, and Johann and Karl used to fill rooms and halls across the empire. Johann had kept the plans. It might take a while and cost a fair bit to get all the parts together, but they were guests of the Bamberg prince-bishop, after all. He was working on the horoscope of Georg III Schenk von Limpurg, and the bishop wouldn't expect it to come cheap.

As soon as he'd finished explaining his plan to Karl and Greta, Johann had begun to put it into action. It was the morning of the following day now, and he had worked through the night, spending only the smallest part on the actual horoscope. He was sitting at the table, fine-tuning drawings and calculations like he always used to do. They would need a hollow mirror and lenses—he could borrow the ones from the stargazing tube—but most importantly, they needed glass plates for Karl to paint on, as he had before. Johann still thought the young man was very talented. Karl had soon overcome his initial reservations and liked the idea more and more; it would allow him to paint, and something more challenging than the pictures they had used for their shows.

Johann nodded with determination as he added more details to the drawing on the table. The delegates would never forget these images.

Johann had explained his idea to the bishop first thing in the morning. Georg von Limpurg had climbed all the way up to his tower room, apparently curious to see what sort of books the learned Doctor Faustus carried with him. Following a stimulating conversation about Aristotle, Roger Bacon, and Albertus Magnus, Johann broached the topic he really wanted to discuss.

"Your Excellency, I am planning on presenting your horoscope in a very special manner," he said, after gifting to the bishop a poem by Dante handwritten by the artist himself.

The bishop lowered the pince-nez he had used to check the poem's authenticity. "And what manner is that?"

"I've discovered a way to make my presentation of horoscopes a little more . . . entertaining. I use an apparatus that conjures up colorful images that everyone can understand." Johann rocked his head from side to side. "Reading out horoscopes is tedious business, a bunch of complicated numbers and tables. With my method, many people can take part in the presentation. Everyone will enjoy hearing firsthand what the stars hold in store for you and your church—and also for that Luther monk," Johann added ominously.

"Colorful images, you say." The bishop smiled and put down his pince-nez. He studied Johann with amusement from his small, reddened eyes. "Times are changing faster than I ever could have imagined as a young man. You're not wrong, Doctor—those monk's theses aren't all bad, but they're coming at a very inconvenient time. The empire can't afford any more unrest, and so we're going to have to take drastic measures. It would be helpful if your horoscope hinted at something like that." He raised one finger. "But I can only allow your presentation if it doesn't involve any kind of sorcery. If the horoscope predicts what I need, I would be willing to pay more. I hope you understand what I mean."

"My current calculations indeed suggest an epochal event," Johann replied earnestly. "And I can assure you that my apparatus has nothing to do with sorcery and is purely mechanical."

"I'm so glad we understand each other." The bishop rose with a soft groan; he was no longer the youngest. "You shall have everything you need, Doctor, no matter the cost." He paused. "If, however, you were hoping I could spare you from your trip to Rome, I must disappoint you. The papal representative has made the pontiff's wishes clear. The Holy Father is determined to make your acquaintance, and, as you know, I'm answerable to no one except . . ." He gave an apologetic shrug.

"The pope," said Johann. "Yes, I know. Well, my conscience is clear, and therefore I have nothing to fear."

Georg patted Johann's shoulder with his fleshy fingers. "Spoken like our savior himself. I'm pleased to hear it."

The bishop made sure Johann received glass, the hollow mirror, and everything else he needed. He worked in the tower room for five days and five nights while Karl and Greta started on the images. The screwing, filing, and fiddling on the copper housing, the tube, and the oil lamp helped Johann calm his mind. He was following a clear goal: he would get out of here with one last big bang. He wanted the empire to remember him for a long time.

And he knew exactly where he would go once he made it out.

Johann felt relief at not having to hide his illness from Greta and Karl any longer. He wouldn't have been able to for much longer, anyhow. He still started to shake every now and then while bending over the lenses or the hollow mirror in the dull candlelight, but it was never as bad again as the night Viktor von Lahnstein had spoken to him about Gilles de Rais. Johann had been racking his brains ever since, wondering what the pope could mean by his claim that Johann shared a secret with the insane knight. Why might the church be interested in a heretic and mass murderer like Gilles de Rais? And what did Viktor von Lahnstein mean when he said that others were also interested in Johann's knowledge?

But there was one question that bothered him more than any other.

How did the pope know about his connection to Gilles de Rais in the first place? Johann had never told anyone about it, not even Greta and Karl.

Viktor von Lahnstein had visited him twice since then. The papal representative wasn't overly thrilled that Johann was taking so long to compile the horoscope; he seemed to sense that something was up. But Lahnstein didn't dare to defy the bishop's wishes, and Hagen the mercenary remained at his post outside the door.

Until the sixth day, when the laterna magica was completed and the show ready to begin.

3

KARL PEEKED THROUGH THE CURTAIN AT THE CROWD waiting in rows of chairs in the darkened great hall of the palas. At the end of the long room a small stage had been set up, divided in half by a damask tapestry suspended from the ceiling. The three of them waited together in the darkness behind the curtain for the last of the bishop's guests to arrive. The doctor was perfectly calm as he stood next to Greta, who was holding Little Satan by a leash, waiting for the signal they had agreed upon.

Karl could not understand for the life of him how the other two managed to be so composed, while his own heart seemed to be beating in his throat. He guessed it was the poise of jugglers, which he would always lack. He still couldn't bring himself to believe their plan might actually work. But if it didn't, they would probably all get boiled alive and broken on the wheel—the usual punishment for black magicians and necromancers.

I never should have agreed to this, thought Karl. But he hadn't been able to resist the temptation of once more putting on a great show with the laterna magica, featuring images painted by him. He liked this kind of magic—magic that had a scientific explanation. And painting was Karl's passion.

Once upon a time, he'd dreamed of becoming a painter like the famous Albrecht Dürer, but his father had intended a medical career for Karl—and then he'd been forced to quit his studies. Since then, Karl was painting not holy virgins or saints but backdrops and canvases. Sometimes he secretly drew pictures of naked young men, but when he was finished he burned them immediately.

Most of the powerful men of the Holy Roman Empire, along with several delegates from foreign countries and men of the church, seemed to be gathered in this great hall decorated with expensive damask and shining armor. Karl recognized the magnificent regalia of abbots and canons, saw representatives and patricians who had traveled a long way from the free imperial cities, clad in velvet jerkins and fur-collared coats. In among them sat aging swashbucklers and knights in polished cuirasses with swords on their belts, like emblems of a bygone era. But Karl couldn't spot the French delegate Louis Cifre anywhere. The Bamberg prince-bishop was sitting in the first row on a wooden throne, surrounded by guards who were holding a kind of canopy above the clergy-man's head. Beside the bishop, in an equally imposing chair, sat the papal rep-resentative Viktor von Lahnstein with a sullen expression. The enormous Swiss mercenary stood behind him like a statue, his hands leaning on the hilt of his two-handed sword.

Karl's excited anticipation caused him to sweat, and he struggled to breathe. They had given so many shows before, including performances in front of counts, barons, and bishops, but this here was something else. All delegates had arrived at Altenburg Castle by now, and deliberations had begun. The bishop had invited his guests into the great hall this evening as part of the entertain-ment, featuring the famous Doctor Faustus presenting the horoscope. Georg Schenk von Limpurg had promised a surprise, and so every pair of eyes in the room stared expectantly toward the stage. A few torches along the walls and one big chandelier dangling from the center of the ceiling illuminated the hall suf-ficiently for the audience to see.

"Are you ready?" whispered Johann to his companions. Karl and Greta nodded.

The murmuring stopped abruptly when Doctor Faustus pushed the tapestry curtain aside and strode to the front of the stage with his head held high. At the doors, Karl noticed, were posted additional guards, evidently belonging to Lahnstein's men. He felt certain that it would take only a wave of Lahnstein's hand to stop the show if even the faintest suspicion of escape arose. Karl entered the stage, pushing a table on wheels holding a copper box with a tube protruding from its front. Another tube stuck out the top of the strange apparatus.

Faust scanned the audience slowly. Karl knew that the dark, piercing eyes of the doctor always did the trick. And horoscopes were the latest fashion—even the pope had had one compiled, and allegedly, it wasn't entirely in his favor.

"Your Eminent Highness the prince-bishop, Honorable Excellencies, ven-erable papal representative, it is a great honor to be received in such illustrious circles at Altenburg Castle," began Johann loudly, his voice sounding much deeper and more menacing than usual. "My name is Doctor Faustus, and I presume one or two of you have heard of me before." The audience whispered excitedly, and several church dignitaries made the sign of the cross. Karl tried to suppress a grin; the doctor knew what the audience expected of him.

"We all look with eager anticipation toward the coming year of 1519—a year that the great Albertus Magnus and the omniscient Hermes Trismegistus described as a fateful one. A year that will decide where God leads humanity. And it is my honor to tell you that the scholars were right! At the behest of the highly venerable prince-bishop, I compiled an extremely interesting horoscope." With a theatrical gesture, he produced the horoscope from underneath his black-and-blue star cape.

Karl had earlier copied it in blood-red ink onto a scroll of parchment.

"Jupiter and Saturn are in the third house together, and Venus, too, inclines to the east, which suggests the occurrence of fateful events," explained Johann with a grim voice. Then he listed a number of star constellations and Latin terms, which mainly served to impress the audience.

Meanwhile, Karl had pushed the laterna magica to the edge of the stage and placed it so that the tube at the front was aimed at the curtain. Faust pointed upward, and the eyes of the audience followed.

"Until now, the only way to see looming events was in the stars. We received the answers hidden inside complicated formulas and tables, wherefore the interpretation of the stars remained a mystery to laymen." With a sweeping gesture, Johann pointed at the copper casing next to him, which glinted like a thing of magic in the light of the torches and chandelier. "With the help of this apparatus I've manufactured, it is now finally possible to display future events in a way that everyone can understand. We are bringing the stars down to earth!"

With those words, Johann tossed a handful of sulfur and a pinch of black-powder into the brazier at the edge of the stage. There was puffing, cracking, and smoking, eliciting murmurs and cries of excitement from the audience. Hidden behind the fumes, Karl inserted the first glass plate and lit the oil lamp concealed inside the casing. They used to perform shows like this all the time, and each movement felt as familiar to Karl as if the last show had been only the day before. On Faust's signal, the guards put out the torches in the hall, leaving the chandelier as the only source of light.

"Let the stars speak!"

A murmur went through the crowd when, as if by magic, a flickering image appeared on the tapestry behind the doctor, pale and translucent as if from another world. The image showed four riders on scrawny horses. The first one was a tottery old man, two carried swords and bows, and the fourth carried scales. Karl had copied Dürer's horsemen of the apocalypse only the day before. He loved this image and would have liked to have created it himself, but he'd accepted the fact that he was a better copyist than painter.

"See here the four plagues that will befall the empire next year if we don't rise up to fight them," intoned Johann. Standing in a cloud of sulfur smoke with his star-spangled cape, his long black hair streaked with gray and his arms spread wide, he looked like a true wizard. The performance achieved the desired effect: the guests gasped and moaned, and the prince-bishop and Viktor von Lahnstein couldn't take their eyes off the image hovering on the tapestry. Karl grinned to himself. The apparatus was really quite simple. Bundled light streaming through a tube, making images appear larger than life against a wall. But, as always, someone had to come up with the idea first.

"War, pestilence, famine, and death!" shouted Johann. "That is what's in store for us if we don't gain control of the unrest in the empire. But we oughtn't requite blood with blood and war with war. The stars promise unity if it is achieved peacefully." He raised an admonishing finger. "If we *all* come together under the protective roof of the holy Roman church. 'Unity and not separation' must be our motto!"

The bishop nodded enthusiastically, and Karl swallowed back another grin. The doctor had his audience hooked now.

"Our enemy is not the peasants, but one man who stirs them up with his heretical speeches. He calls himself a Christian and a monk—when in truth he is nothing but a pig wallowing in the troughs of the church."

The doctor signaled to Karl, who inserted a new glass plate. The four riders were replaced by the monk Luther, wearing the robe of the Augustinians, but he was adorned with a pig's snout and a pig's tail, his face twisted into a grimace of hatred and greed.

The effect was powerful. The guests—most of them passionate opponents of Luther—cried out with hatred, clapped, and cheered. Karl was proud of his drawing, which he had made using a cheap printed leaflet from the Augsburg imperial diet. The picture had turned out rather well, especially the pig's snout.

Johann raised his hand. "This Luther stirred up the peasants, even if he says he didn't. I foresee great unrest in matters of faith for the coming year. Only if we put aside that argument will we be able to vanquish the four horsemen of the apocalypse. And the stars tell us who will lead our way." He paused for effect. "See for yourself!"

The image changed again, and a portrait of Pope Leo X appeared. The chubby, peasant-like face, the bags under the eyes, the red velvet skull cap, the ermine-collared coat—Karl had made a good likeness of the pope, even if he hadn't had much time and the image was almost too realistic. He glanced over to Lahnstein, who shifted restlessly in his chair. It seemed the papal representative wasn't sure what to make of all this gushing praise. He probably suspected some sort of ruse.

And damned right you are, thought Karl. *You're in for the shock of your life.*

"Beneath the strong hand of our Holy Father we will succeed in uniting the church once more and defeat the apocalyptic riders!" exclaimed Johann loudly. "The stars don't lie, and that is why they show you the truth—the whole truth." He paused again before continuing. "Even the truth about who is going to rule in Rome if we don't succeed in unifying the church. Lo and behold the fearsome creature awaiting us all!"

With another sweeping gesture, the doctor again tossed a load of powder into the glowing embers. But this time, there was a deafening explosion, followed by thick smoke. On cue, Karl changed the image again, and this time a terrible beast appeared—so terrible that every member of the audience screamed out with horror.

It was a huge dragon with a fiery tail, its horned head looking straight at the crowd. The monster took up the entire curtain, its tooth-studded mouth wide open, its eyes glowing, smoke seeping from its nostrils. Karl gazed at his work with pride. He thought his painting was on par with Dürer's horsemen, if not better. At least, it was just as terrifying. Another explosion followed, and this time a large ball of fire rose from the brazier. To the audience it looked as if the dragon was spitting fire.

"And I saw a beast rise up out of the sea, and it had seven heads and ten horns, and upon its horns ten crowns, and upon its heads the name of blasphemy," shouted

Johann against the noise. "The apocalypse of John. Yes, be afraid, because the end is nigh."

Only then did Greta emerge from behind the curtain. She still held Little Satan's leash in her left hand, while with her right she swung a small throwing knife which she now—sheltered by the smoke and unrest—hurled with one swift movement toward the chandelier. The knife sliced through one of the ropes holding the chandelier to the ceiling. The metal construct, weighing several tons, gave a jerk before swooshing to the ground and burying some screaming delegates. At the same moment, the hall turned pitch black except for the stage, where the flames of the brazier continued to flicker as wafts of sulfur and biting smoke spread through the room.

"Behold and fear the apocalypse! The beast is nigh . . . ," shouted Johann with outstretched arms, truly looking like a sorcerer. The rest of his speech was drowned out by the screams of the guests, who all sprang to their feet and rushed to the exit. Chairs crashed to the ground, and someone prayed loudly to Archangel Michael; meanwhile, the fire from the brazier had caught the curtain, which in moments was in full flame. From there the fire soon spread to the tapestries along the walls and even the canopy of the prince-bishop, who had rushed to the door with the rest of the guests. Only Viktor von Lahnstein and his mercenary, Hagen, remained still amid the uproar. Hagen raised his mighty sword while Lahnstein furiously pointed to the front.

"Apocalypse my ass! This is nothing but a cheap trick!" he called out. "Guards, arrest this heretic! He is only trying to . . ."

Just then a black shadow emerged from the mist, accompanied by a sinister growling.

Greta had let Little Satan off the leash.

Like a dark angel the wolfhound leaped out of the smoke at Hagen, who was climbing the stage with his sword raised. Little Satan aimed for Hagen's throat but the man dodged him, lunged forward, and, one moment later, stood in front of Faust with his sword against the doctor's chest. The dog disappeared into the darkness behind Hagen.

"You're going nowhere, Doctor," snarled the mercenary. "Stay right where you are."

Karl swore. They hadn't reckoned on the huge Swiss soldier. A single man was enough to foil their elaborate plan. He shot a panicked glance at Greta, who was just picking up a fire poker from beside the brazier, holding it like a sword. Karl doubted that Greta—or the three of them together, for that matter—could do anything against the hulk with the longsword. As if he had read their minds, Hagen grinned and pressed the point of his sword harder against Johann's chest. The fabric of his shirt tore and a bloodstain appeared on it.

"One wrong movement, sweetheart," Hagen said in Greta's direction without taking his eyes off Faust. "If you as much as blink, I will skewer your doctor like a rabbit. You'll see how—"

He was cut off by a piercing scream behind him. In the light of the spreading fire, Karl saw that Little Satan had attacked Lahnstein in front of the stage. The calf-sized hound was pinning the mortally frightened, squirming man to the floor with paws as large as the palm of a hand.

"Off, off!" shouted Lahnstein over and over. "Goddamned mutt! Hagen, help me, why won't you help—"

Lahnstein's pleading gave way to panicked screams as Little Satan's mouth came closer to his face. Hagen hesitated one more moment before lowering his sword with a curse, turning away from Faust, and leaping off the stage to help his master.

"You will burn for this, Faustus!" screeched Lahnstein, grappling with the dog. "You will burn alive for this!"

"Maybe," said Johann, panting and wiping the sweat from his brow. "But not here and not today."

As Lahnstein continued to rant and rave behind them, Faust, Karl, and Greta hurried through the biting smoke to a small side door near the stage. A tiny wedge Greta had installed the night before had prevented it from falling shut. During the same nighttime visit, Greta had managed to climb up to the chandelier and cut into the ropes just enough that one well-aimed throw had been sufficient to send the whole thing flying.

A dark, smoky corridor led them out into the courtyard, where chaos reigned. Guards were running back and forth with buckets of water, black smoke came pouring out of the palas, and delegates coughed as they staggered toward their chambers to save their belongings before the fire spread. The castle gate stood wide open as throngs of people fled out onto the road.

The troupe's wagon was in the stable and the horse already hitched. Karl was climbing up when the wolfhound appeared from a cloud of haze, trotting toward them as if nothing had happened. His snout was red with blood.

"Little Satan!" exclaimed Johann joyously. "And I thought that Hagen finished you off." He knelt down to greet the dog and stopped short. "Hey, what is that? Drop it, Satan! Drop it now." With visible disgust, he pulled something from the dog's mouth. Karl had to look twice before he recognized what it was, and when he did, he felt sick.

It was a human nose, or rather, what was left of it. A pale lump of cartilage with a scrap of skin.

"If I'm not mistaken, that is the beak of that papal representative," said Greta from the box seat. "Yuck, Satan! You have bad taste."

"It was much too big anyhow." Faust tossed the bloody piece of meat far away from him. "But I fear we may have just made an enemy for life. High time for us to leave."

He jumped up onto the wagon next to Karl, and Greta moved to the back. The gray horse whinnied and started trotting toward the open gate, while behind them, Altenburg Castle was ablaze.

Just like the doctor had prophesied, the apocalypse had arrived.

~

A solitary man stood among the smoldering, crackling chairs in the great hall and uttered a quiet curse. Guards ran past him; guests wailed, prayed, and shouted; someone was sounding the bells. But the man didn't seem to notice any of it. He was staring outside through one of the barred windows, watching the doctor fleeing through the gate with his wagon. *How ironic,* he thought. Faustus had invoked the devil and thus managed to escape from him. The man took off his cap with the red feather and hurled it into the flames. He had been too impatient, and now he needed a new plan.

"*Merde!*" said the master angrily in the language of his childhood, from the time before he became an eternal traveler, forever hungry, forever on the search for something, much like the doctor.

"*Dieu, je te maudis!*"

Not far from him a burning beam fell from the ceiling, burying a guard. One of the guests, a fat abbot, ran past him with his robe on fire, looking like a torch with legs. The fire crept up the stairs and hungrily devoured the second floor of the palas.

The master nodded approvingly. Young Johann had truly learned much in the last decades, more than any university could have taught—yes, more than he himself could have taught him. Life had allowed little Johann Georg Faustus to mature like good wine. And perhaps it was for the best that he got away once more. So far, everything had turned out for the best.

There was a time for everything.

A time to grow, a time to die.

With slow strides, humming a tune, the master headed for the exit while chaos consumed the world around him. He loved chaos—it was his elixir of life.

For all things that exist deserve to perish, and would not be missed.

Everything would fall into place—if not today, then in the near future.

Up in the sky, concealed by thick plumes of smoke, three birds followed him.

~

The wagon sped toward Bamberg groaning and creaking. Johann whipped the horse like a man possessed, and the animal raced along the road at a wild gallop. Several times the carriage almost toppled rounding the sharp corners; Little Satan followed them, his tongue hanging from the side of his mouth. Johann knew they didn't have long. Even if Viktor von Lahnstein had died following the dog's attack, there were still Hagen and the bishop of Bamberg. By now, half an army could be close at their heels. If they caught him, Johann dreaded to imagine what punishment they might expect.

In spite of their desperate situation, he couldn't help but grin. The show they'd put on had been truly worthy of Doctor Faustus. An invocation of the beast of the apocalypse of John—and in front of all delegates, the bishop of Bamberg, and the papal nuncio. The tale of tonight's events would spread through the empire like wildfire.

And then we won't be safe anywhere in the empire.

When they reached the foot of the hill, they continued on a little longer, the axle groaning awfully. Eventually Johann allowed the horse to stop. The gray's fur was saturated and the animal gasped dreadfully; Johann guessed it wouldn't have made it much farther.

"What's your plan?" asked Karl, who had been sitting next to his master, chalk-faced and silent. Greta, cowering behind them, also looked nervous.

Something in her eyes irritated Johann—he had expected her to handle the situation more confidently, or at least better than Karl. Or was there something else on her mind?

"Help me get the horse and the wagon into the woods," ordered Johann briskly. "We must get off the road."

Together they dragged the exhausted horse and the wagon through the hawthorn bushes at the edge of the forest. On the other side, they paused beneath the sparsely leafed canopy of the autumnal oaks. It wasn't long before they heard the rumble of many galloping horses from the road. All three of them held their breath, but the sound soon faded. The soldiers had ridden past them.

"I'll tell you what we're going to do," said Johann quietly but decisively. "We will only take what we absolutely need. If we walk north from here, we'll come to Hallstadt, a town just a few miles away. If we're lucky, none of the soldiers will have been there yet and we'll get fresh horses at the inn. And then we can get a good amount of distance in a short amount of time between us and Bamberg."

"And what about the wagon?" asked Greta.

"Stays here, just like the old horse."

"But . . . but my backdrops!" said Karl. "The theater, my notebooks, the scientific research—"

"Everyone only packs one bag," said Johann. "Not more—" He winced as the sword wound Hagen had given him stung, though thankfully it was just a superficial injury. "Our most valuable belongings are in the tower of Altenburg Castle, anyhow. The stargazing tube and most of my wonderful books." He sighed as he pulled out a handful of tattered leather-bound volumes from under his coat. "At least I managed to take Leonardo's *Figura Umana* and a few of my own notes. And I have enough money."

He had sewn as many gold ducats into his coat as he could manage, but all his books apart from *Figura Umana* had remained in the tower room with the larger part of his fortune; he had lost almost everything. Johann gave the others a look of determination. What he had to say next pained him, but he knew there was no way back.

"Listen, you don't have to come with me. From now on I'm a wanted man from one end of the empire to the other. The power of the Bamberg prince-bishop reaches far, not to mention that of the papal representative. If Lahnstein is still alive, he and the entire Roman curia are going to be looking for me—most of all that giant of a bodyguard. I'm afraid our happy times as a troupe of jugglers are over, once and for all. We have fallen a long way, and I don't know if we'll ever be able to rise back up again." Johann paused before saying quietly: "Perhaps this is the moment we should go our separate ways."

In truth, he had been considering leaving Karl and Greta for a while. As long as his daughter was by his side, she was in danger. He had wanted to protect her, but instead he had dragged her further and further down with him. During the previous night Johann had seen clearly that he needed to go this path alone, at least the last part. This here was between him and Tonio. His former master had sent him this disease. That much Johann had figured out by now.

And there was only one person who could help him in his battle against Tonio.

Karl and Greta gazed at him for a long while before Karl said, "I will not abandon you, Doctor. I stayed with you back in Nuremberg, down in the underground passages, and I'm going to stay with you today. You . . . you're my mentor, now and always."

"Thank you." Johann swallowed. "You know I have nothing to give but blood, sweat, and tears."

Karl smiled. "That's more than my own father and the professors at Leipzig ever had for me. I accept the challenge. It is an honor to travel alongside the famous Doctor Faustus." He gave Johann an affectionate look. "And besides, you need someone to take care of you when that accursed illness returns."

Johann swiftly wiped his eyes with the back of his hand, hoping the others wouldn't notice. How many times had he been gruff with his assistant; how often had he been impatient and stern? Karl's words touched him more deeply than he cared to admit. And Karl would always be of use to him, with his clever mind and many talents, even if Johann would never say so. Then he slowly turned to Greta.

"And . . . what about you?"

Greta sighed, then she stepped toward him and hugged him tightly. Johann felt certain that this was a hug goodbye, the farewell from his daughter whom he'd always tried to protect from all the evil in the world. And whom he still hadn't told the truth. They remained standing like this for a long moment while the rain pattered onto the few leaves left in the trees. Somewhere in the darkness a nightingale called.

"I'm going with you," said Greta eventually. "But only if you share your plan with me."

Johann was shaking, and he struggled to speak. He hadn't expected Greta to stay with him. Her decision to remain by his side was almost more than he could bear. He knew she would most likely be safer without him, but he couldn't bring himself to turn down her offer. Greta was the person he loved most in the world, even more than himself.

"Thank you" was all he managed to say.

Greta loosened her embrace and looked at him expectantly. "So? Where are we going?"

"You . . . you've seen that I'm ill," Johann started slowly. "The fits, the shaking, loss of control . . . They call me a scholar, wise—omniscient, even. But I don't know what ails me or how much time I have left. And that is why I want to visit someone who might be able to help. He resides quite far from here—we'll be on the road for a long time."

Karl nodded. "I'm guessing you want to head to the university in Paris. Or to Córdoba, where even after the defeat of the Ottomans the best physicians practice. Or—"

"No. I'm afraid not even the best physicians can help me now. We are going to travel to where the most intelligent man I know lives—probably the most intelligent and educated man in the world." Johann smiled thinly. "And you know I don't say such a thing lightly. After all, I consider myself rather well read."

Then he told them the name of the man.

4

THAT DARK AND STARLESS NIGHT, THE THREE OF THEM SET off together on another new journey. They walked along narrow game paths, the only light coming from a flickering lantern. They had left the wagon behind as well as the old gray; Faust had given it a slap on the backside and it had trotted off. Greta hoped it would find a new home somewhere and not fall prey to wild animals; the aging horse had grown on her in the last few years. Little Satan sniffed at the trees and lifted a leg here and there. Greta thought how happy he seemed compared to his humans.

She still wasn't entirely sure why she had decided to stick with the doctor and Karl. She liked Johann, adored him, even, and since she'd read his palm, she worried about him. But there had also always been something about Johann that frightened her. Somewhat like fire—it warms and attracts but can also burn if you get too close. Greta had been thinking about leaving Karl and the doctor for months, and she guessed she still hadn't done it because Johann had told her about her mother. Greta wanted to find out more—she had a hunch that he was keeping something from her. If she left now, she would never find out what happened to her parents and what had gone on in Nuremberg all those years ago.

They paused to listen every time they heard a noise, and they took many detours, but they didn't see the bishop's soldiers again—not even when they reached the market town of Hallstadt early the next morning. At the inn, Faust bought three horses and plain pilgrims' clothing for far too much money. Wearing a skirt the color of ashes and a simple woolen coat, Greta looked like a girl from the country. She buried the colorful juggler's costume she had worn at Bamberg in a dunghill. The innkeeper watched them suspiciously, and Faust gave him another ducat as hush money. It was possible that the innkeeper had already heard of yesterday's events at Altenburg Castle.

They wolfed down a hasty meal before galloping off into the frosty November day. The sky hung low above the woods, the clouds heavy with rain. Faust kept his eyes on the road while Little Satan ran ahead of them, following the highway through forests and swamps. Behind him, Greta and Karl galloped on their horses, the rapid clattering of hooves the only sound on the empty road heading to the west.

Meanwhile, Johann had told them more about their journey ahead. Many years ago, before the time with Greta, he and Karl had met a learned man with whom he had become close friends. The man and Faust hadn't seen much of each other since then, but they wrote to one another regularly. It was a correspondence between two of the empire's most intelligent men, but probably also the vainest.

Heinrich Cornelius Agrippa von Nettesheim was a few years younger than Johann and, unlike him, came from a good family. At thirty-two years old, Agrippa was already one of the most famous scholars of Europe, being a doctor of medicine, theology, and jurisprudence and possessing vast, self-taught knowledge in the fields of astrology, mechanics, optics, the Jewish kabbalah, and, most of all, magic. His early work *De Occulta Philosophia* was still considered the standard reference for any form of sorcery. Following his work as an agent at the court of England, he and his family had moved to a town called Metz near the French border. But Johann hadn't yet let on why, exactly, he thought Agrippa would be able to help him.

"You really think Agrippa knows something about your mysterious disease?" asked Karl once he and Greta had caught up to the doctor. It was still raining, and the wet pilgrim's outfit hung on Greta as if she had fallen into a stream.

"If not he, who else?" replied Johann vaguely. "Heinrich Agrippa is the greatest scholar of the empire—and knows it, unfortunately, and loves to hear it repeated." He sighed. "The man is ambitious and loudmouthed and thinks very highly of himself."

"Those traits sound rather familiar to me," said Greta with a smile.

"I know. And perhaps that's why we get on the best in writing, because no one can cut the other one off midsentence." Johann turned to look at her. "Agrippa is like the lost library of Alexandria, a beacon of knowledge. Apart from that, we also need a safe place to stay for winter, outside of Rome's reach and that of the bishop of Bamberg. Metz is a free imperial city near France. The burghers of Metz have never let anyone tell them what to do—no bishop, no emperor, and no pope. We should be able to hide there for a while."

Greta hoped Johann wouldn't have another fit like the one at Altenburg Castle. They made good progress for the first few days, and the doctor was merely pained by a few headaches. Their way led them west along old imperial roads, some of which were the same ones laid by the Romans. Grass and weeds were growing between the worn-down flagstones, and occasionally they saw milestones with Latin inscriptions. The roads, passing through the heart of the German Empire, were busy with travelers and merchants. Smaller and larger villages lined up like pearls on a string, and there wasn't much left of the huge forest that once covered the entire center of Europe. Vast clearings and smoldering piles made by charcoal burners lined the roadsides; during the last few centuries, people had spread here like flies.

They gave the Episcopal city of Würzburg a wide berth so they wouldn't run into soldiers or henchmen of the pope. They never stayed longer than one night in any place. If someone asked, they said they were pilgrims of Saint James on their way to Santiago de Compostela, a city in the faraway kingdom of Castile where the grave of the apostle Saint James was located.

Beyond Würzburg they followed the Main River toward the Rhine flats, and eventually they came to Mainz, the same city in which a certain Johannes Gutenberg had started to print books nearly a hundred years earlier. Greta would have liked to stay for a while, but just like Bamberg, Mainz was an Episcopal town and it was likely that they were wanted here, too. Outside the city gates, a delegation of the bishop's soldiers had cast suspicious glances at them, and so the very same day they boarded a raft heavily laden with cackling chickens, blocks of salt, and stinking barrels of herring, taking them across the wide, lazy Rhine.

West of the river, the land became more sparsely occupied and rougher, and the few roads were so muddy that the three travelers were glad they'd left the wagon behind. They came to the Wasgau region, a seemingly endless hilly forest between the German lands and France. Derelict fortresses sat on the peaks of the hills like silent watchmen from a bygone era when the legendary emperor Barbarossa hunted these woods. The road led through shady vales, across narrow wooden bridges over roaring rivers and creeks; gnarled oak and beech trees spread their limbs in all directions. The trees were growing so closely together that hardly any sunlight reached the ground; it was forever twilight in these woods. Not many travelers were on the road in this no-man's-land, and only rarely did they pass an almost-forgotten border stone where they had to pay a toll to wild-looking keepers.

And it was here in the Wasgau that Johann suffered another fit.

It was the end of November by now. The first snow was falling in watery gray flakes onto the bare trees. The travelers' coats were permanently damp and cold, and Greta's teeth wouldn't stop chattering. Until then, Faust had only been shaking a little from time to time, but now it was growing more severe by the day. Greta and Karl looked after him, but no matter what they tried—a boiled brew of ivy with willow bark, dried Saint-John's-wort, or wet bandages drenched with sulfur water—the shaking did not abate. Johann struggled to hold a spoon in the evenings; only in the mornings did his hands steady a little, sometimes for a few hours.

They had just passed through a ravine, and the next village was still many miles off, when a group of men stepped out of the woods, blocking their way. Greta could tell at once that they were highway robbers, which were common in this mountainous region. They wore torn trousers and shirts, their beards long and straggly, their skin covered in scabs. They might have been farmers once upon a time, before poverty and hunger forced them into the woods. Now they weren't much more than wild animals.

"Your horses and your money," growled the one at the front, a one-eyed, older man with yellow pus running out from under his eye patch. He was swinging a rusty dusack, the weapon of peasants and thieves, a sword suitable for harvesting as well as murdering. "Hurry up now! Then we'll let you go."

Greta looked at Karl and Johann, who had halted their horses; riding around the men was out of the question. They all knew that in spite of the leader's words, they wouldn't leave this forest alive if they didn't fight. It wasn't the first time they'd come across bandits, but so far, they'd been protected by the doctor's reputation as a sorcerer as well as by Little Satan; the sight of the dog was enough to send anyone in their right mind running. But evidently these men were so hungry and miserable that not even the huge wolfhound deterred them. Little Satan growled with raised hackles, sensing that his master was in danger. The peasants took a step back but continued to block the road with their scythes, knives, and pikes. Johann raised his hands and smiled at them.

"We are but plain pilgrims," he said. "We have nothing to give. God protects us and punishes those who lay a hand on innocent Christians."

"To hell with your nonsense, man," replied the leader harshly. "Your God isn't my God. One look at your face and your fine hands is enough to tell me you're not one of us. We believe in the God of the poor—the pope uses your money and my money to build himself a golden outhouse! Luther is damned right: no more shoving money up the pope's ass!" He stepped forward and reached for Johann's reins. "So you might as well hand it over—it's of much more use to us."

"Take your dirty fingers off him," shouted Karl from his saddle now. He reached for the hunting dagger dangling from the side of his horse. "Do you have any idea who you're talking to? This man is the famous Doctor Faustus! If he wanted to he could turn you into a slimy toad on the spot!"

"Doctor Faustus? Hmm . . ." The man seemed rattled for a moment. He frowned and rubbed his nose. "I've heard of him. A powerful magician, they say." Then he grinned, exposing a row of black tooth stumps. "Ha! But I don't see no magician—all I see is two mollycoddled moneybags and a wench."

"A wench that is going to send you straight to hell if you don't let us pass." Greta opened her coat. She was holding the hand cannon she had taken from the wagon along with her few belongings. Now she aimed the weapon at the gang of men. "Well, who would like their head blasted off first? You or one of your stinking comrades?"

Again the men stepped back, deliberating like hungry wolves. They muttered and eyed their prey. Greta hoped the men would retreat. But then someone threw a stone, followed by more, and then a hailstorm of dirt and rocks descended upon the travelers. One of the stones hit Greta on the head and she lowered the cannon for a moment. That was all the robbers needed to pounce upon their victims.

"The woman is mine!" shouted one of them.

A hairy hand reached for Greta and dragged her off her horse; she dropped the weapon. Several men stabbed at the doctor and Karl with their pikes, while

Karl flung his hunting dagger wildly to all sides, cutting open the side of a man's throat. The peasant screamed, and blood spurted from the wound and onto the ground. Karl's horse neighed in panic and reared up, Karl desperately clinging to the reins. Meanwhile, two of the peasants had lowered their pants and held Greta down. One of them tugged at her blouse while the other pushed up her skirt. She screamed and struggled as hard as she could, but she was held firmly.

"Little Satan, attack!" called out Johann.

Like a black flash the wolfhound hurled himself onto the two robbers, sinking his teeth into the bared manhood of one of them, causing the other one to run away screaming. But not even in view of the mortal danger did the others give up—on the contrary. They had worked themselves into a frenzy, probably not having eaten anything but acorns and bark for days. Angry and drooling like animals, they tore at Johann's saddlebags. Some of the precious notebooks fell into the muck of the road, where naked feet trampled them into the dirt. The peasants rummaged through the bags in search of gold or something to eat. With a low growl, Little Satan pounced on his next victim.

At that moment, Greta saw how Johann was struck by an invisible sword.

It was as if an enormous blow wiped him off his horse. He landed on the side of the road, where he squirmed like a man possessed. Saliva ran from his mouth; he twitched uncontrollably, his limbs flying in all directions. The remaining peasants stopped what they were doing and stared at him like a ghost. Even Little Satan pricked up his ears and whimpered as he approached his master, who was making gasping sounds.

"To . . . To . . . Tonio del Moravia . . . ," Johann stuttered. "Damn . . . damned . . ."

"By God, the devil has taken ahold of him!" shouted one of the peasants, pointing at the doctor. "Look!"

Faust's face was contorted into an awful grimace that looked scarcely human. His skin was taut, as if something was pressing against it from the inside, and his tongue darted out like a slimy frog.

"It really is the unhappy Doctor Faustus!" exclaimed another robber. "God in heaven! Run before the devil takes one of us!"

The men ran into the woods, leaving behind their pikes and dusacks. They carried one of their comrades with them, while three others remained on the road, dead or severely injured. The man whose private parts Little Satan had bitten off was lying on the ground groaning and tossing from side to side. Greta, bleeding from her forehead, ran over to Johann.

"Uncle!" she said. "Jesus, Uncle, wake up!"

She caught his hand and held it tightly. His body convulsed, then turned as stiff as a plank. Greta felt his hand throb and, despite herself, shot a glance at his palm. What she saw in his hand this time was so unspeakably evil, so horrific, that she started back as if she'd been bitten by a snake.

"Tonio del Moravia," whispered Faust. "The pact is sealed. He . . . he is coming for me."

His lips trembled too strongly now for Greta to understand any more.

"Who is coming for you?" asked Greta. "Who?"

But Johann no longer spoke.

In her despair, Greta did the first thing she could think of: she knelt beside the doctor and prayed.

She had believed in the power of prayer from early childhood. Praying had given her strength when she'd spent weeks locked in the catacombs of Nuremberg, not knowing if she'd ever see the light of day again. Prayers were like rays of sunshine connecting her to her childhood. She uttered the first prayer that came to her mind. In her shaking voice, the ancient words came tumbling out.

"The Lord is my shepherd; I shall not want. He maketh me to lie down in green pastures and leadeth me beside still waters . . ."

Johann's eyes closed then, his breathing steadied, and he fell into a deep sleep.

~

When Johann woke up, he was lying beside a fire in the woods. It was the middle of the night and the stars sparkled above him. He felt cold and as exhausted as if he'd been riding for days, his limbs aching. Little by little, the memories returned, but the images were jarred and from another perspective, almost as if he hadn't been there. Greta was sitting next to him, while Karl was busy sorting torn pages of books a few yards away from him; a ripped cover was lying on the ground in front of him.

"The *Figura*," said Johann weakly as he tried to sit up.

"Is quite safe." Greta gently pushed him back down on his bed of leaves and twigs. "The pages are dirty but complete," she said with a tired smile. "Besides, you should be worrying about your own health, not that of your books. This fit was much worse than the one at Altenburg Castle."

"At least it made those scoundrels take to their heels. We survived. You—" Johann paused when a thought struck him. He cleared his throat. "You held my hand earlier. What were you doing?"

"What I was doing?" Greta hesitated before continuing. "I . . . well, I prayed for you."

"You did what?"

"I prayed for you. Is that really so strange?" Greta breathed deeply. "You did look as if you were possessed by the devil. It was the same psalm Uncle Valentin used to recite when I was a child. I . . . The words suddenly came to my mind. Believe it or not, afterward I felt better."

"You . . . you prayed for me." Johann smiled faintly.

Greta was his daughter, and he had never felt this truth more strongly than right at this moment. And she'd started remembering things from her childhood. How much longer could he keep the truth from her? But if he told her now, he would also have to tell her everything else—his terrible guilt, the death of her mother, the pact with Tonio, and everything that had happened back in Nuremberg. And all the small and big lies since then.

He couldn't bring himself to do it.

"You mentioned a name during your fit," said Greta into the silence. "I think it was . . . Tonio del Moravia or something like that. An odd name. I feel like I've heard it before. You said he was coming for you. You mentioned a pact." She paused, trying to work out where she might have heard the name before. "Who is this Tonio? Should I know him?"

Karl looked over to them, darting a questioning look at Johann. They fell silent for a while.

"He is no one of consequence," said Johann eventually. "Just an old acquaintance. I'm tired now. I want to sleep."

When he closed his eyes he heard the cawing of crows or ravens, and he wasn't sure if it was a dream or reality.

A few days later, they finally left the Wasgau region behind. The landscape became flatter as they approached the land of Lotharingia, or Lorraine, a beautiful area crossed by rivers and studded with deep-green ponds that were beginning to be covered by a thin layer of ice.

Johann remembered hearing about this country for the first time as a child. The grandsons of the most famous emperor of all time, Charlemagne, had split France into three even parts. The eldest grandson, Lothar, had received the middle part, which used to reach all the way to the North Sea; all that remained of it now was this narrow strip of land behind the Wasgau, where cities, counties, and duchies were forever arguing. Of all the tiny dominions along the western border of the German Empire, the city of Metz was the most powerful, and a wide, well-maintained trading route led straight toward it.

The free imperial city lay on the Moselle River, which had its source in the Vosges Mountains and wound its way in countless bends past steep vineyards toward Koblenz, on the Rhine. It was snowing so heavily when they arrived at Metz that the city walls were merely vague outlines. It was still afternoon, but dusk already crept across the city's roofs. With the month of December, winter had arrived—earlier than in previous years. Johann was glad they had finally reached their winter quarters. He only hoped they'd traveled far enough to be safe from the papal henchmen.

Metz was one of the biggest cities of the empire. Much of its wealth came from money-lending businesses. A ring wall several miles long enclosed twenty thousand inhabitants. Through the snow Johann could make out many towers and the rooftops of monasteries and churches, and farther in the distance the spire of Metz Cathedral, its yellow limestone glowing in the last light of day. Like so many other cathedrals, it was unfinished—an eternal building site in God's honor.

The three travelers entered the city with a caravan of merchants via a stone bridge that ended in a bulky, narrow gate flanked by two watchtowers. Throngs of people pushed in both directions, and Johann heard the soft French tongue that always reminded him of Tonio del Moravia. Others spoke German, and some spoke Lingua Franca, the mixed language used by merchants from the distant czardom to Constantinople and the Red Sea. Johann overheard conversations about banking, the final harvest before winter, and a large parade that would be taking place soon and for which visitors from other cities were expected. People mentioned a dragon, some kind of terrible beast, but Johann couldn't really figure out what the conversation was about.

Despite the cold and the falling darkness, the lanes were still busy, vendors on the squares selling bleating lambs, cackling chickens, and even fish that they kept in large wooden tubs. Money changers sat below the arcades at the edges of the squares, exchanging gold, silver, and copper coins and foreign currencies from countries like Italy, Castile, or the deep south of France. Frozen mud and feces covered the cobblestones in the lanes, and Johann wondered what the stench would be like in summer. Even now, the stink mixed with the acrid smoke from cooking fires was almost unbearable.

It didn't take Johann long to find out from a money changer where Heinrich Agrippa lived. The scholar was well known in the city, and they found the way across the river to a wealthier quarter. It was quieter here, and the lanes were cleaner—and the air smelled much better.

Heinrich Cornelius Agrippa von Nettesheim resided in a three-story stone house with a garden by the riverside. Johann knew from their correspondence that his friend had accepted a position as municipal advocate at Metz this year, a quiet post that enabled him to spend more time with his small family. Johann had announced his visit in a letter several days earlier, and so it wasn't long before the famous scholar came rushing down the wide, carpeted staircase to receive them in the vestibule, which was hung with expensive damask and furs. Evidently, the city of Metz paid well for the services of the renowned scholar.

"Johann Georg Faustus, my worthy colleague and dear friend!" exclaimed Agrippa, spreading his arms. He still spoke with the broad accent of his hometown, Cologne. "So it is true! You traveled all this way just to see me." He winked at Johann. "Or is there perhaps another reason?"

Agrippa was shorter than Johann. Even though he was at home, he wore his beret and gown as if he were lecturing at the university. As he had before, Johann particularly noticed the alert eyes and the pointed nose, giving his friend the appearance of a cunning fox. In spite of his young age, Agrippa's hair was turning gray. He gestured toward Little Satan, who looked as if he was about to pee against the elegant furniture. "Is that the same devilish beast you brought to Cologne all those years ago?"

"Her successor," said Johann, dragging the dog off the damask blanket. "His name is Little Satan."

"Very fitting indeed. What a beast. Why don't you get a small, harmless poodle for a change?" Agrippa gave him a smirk. "Now don't tell me you only came because you and your dog need a hiding place from the Bamberg prince-bishop." He wagged his finger at Johann. "Your stay here in Metz will cost you dearly, Johann Faustus. I crave stimulating conversation, so prepare for late nights."

Johann smiled. "So news of our little adventure at Bamberg has made it this far?"

"Little adventure?" Agrippa laughed out loud. "Ha! The whole empire is talking about the famous magus Doctor Faustus invoking the devil at Altenburg Castle in front of the collective German and foreign delegates."

"Well, to be precise, it was not the devil but the beast from John's apocalypse." Johann pointed at Karl and Greta, who were still standing in the door. "My two assistants kindly helped in the manufacture of a new laterna magica. You've already met Karl Wagner. He painted the image of the apocalypse. He is very talented."

"And the pretty young lady is . . . ?" asked Agrippa.

"A distant relative," replied Johann. "And a talented juggler and trickster who is going to get far in her field."

Agrippa nodded at the other two and grinned. "The laterna magica. I see. I remember highly entertaining demonstrations back in Cologne, when you visited for too short a time. But I don't understand the purpose of your performance this time. You won't be able to show your face in the empire for a considerable time."

"I realize that. There was no other way," replied Johann with a shrug. "But that's a long story."

"Oh, I love long stories." Agrippa clapped his hands together. "This town is so drab that I'm practically withering with boredom. You must tell me about the events at Altenburg Castle, and also about that Luther, who is turning everything upside down at the moment. I am truly looking forward to our nights by the fire, Doctor Faustus." He gave a wide smile. "And most of all I'm looking forward to your stories."

The following night, the two scholars sat together by the open fire in Agrippa's study on the second floor. The wind howled outside, the logs in the fire crackled, and, like in Cologne, the room smelled of rotting apples, old man, and parchment—and of something else that Johann struggled to place. He watched as Agrippa picked up a hollow wooden stick about as long as a forearm with a small pot at one end. Agrippa took a few dried leaves from a case and crumbled them carefully into the little pot. He pressed them down and held a glowing piece of fatwood against them. Smoke started to rise up, and Agrippa sucked on the end of the stem.

"I saw this pastime at a harbor down in Portugal," he explained, puffing out plumes of smoke. "A seaman freshly returned from the New World had learned the so-called smoke-drinking from the natives there. I bought a small barrel of the weed from him and had one of these sticks whittled for me. It tastes a little odd at first, but it really helps me to think."

"Well, if you say so." Johann waved the stinking smoke away from his face. "If it helps with thinking, I shan't complain."

"Now tell me about this meeting at Altenburg Castle," said Agrippa, taking a deep drag. "If I heard correctly, delegates from the entire empire had been invited. It was about that Luther monk, wasn't it?"

Johann nodded. He told his friend about the gathering and about Lahnstein's order to accompany him to Rome. Agrippa smiled knowingly.

"So that is why you had to escape. I can sympathize. So far, everyone who has handed himself in to the Roman church as a possible heretic has ended up regretting it. The Bohemian Jan Hus was burned at the Council of Constance, and I'm certain Luther would have fared similarly in Rome. By the way, I don't think his writs are too bad. I had them sent to me right away. This trade with indulgences *is* truly criminal. Money for the forgiveness of sins—that is divine corruption." He winked at Johann. "That sounds more like the realm of the worldly lords."

"Are you hinting at anything in particular?" asked Johann.

"Well, it's not exactly a secret that the German throne is going to cost a fortune. When Emperor Maximilian passes, the electors are going to choose a new king. And you don't seriously believe they're going to elect someone who won't show their gratitude?" Agrippa laughed softly and rubbed his hands together. "The Fuggers will have to part with a considerable sum if they want to see their favorite—Charles, the grandson of Maximilian—on the throne. They hope he will dance to their tune, just like his grandfather. But if the French are willing to pay more . . . Who knows what happens then?" Agrippa shrugged.

Abruptly, he leaned forward with his pipe. "Enough of the gossip, old friend. I can see that something bothers you. You didn't come here because you needed winter quarters or because we're so good at discussing politics, did you?"

Johann gazed into the rising wafts of smoke before replying. "No, indeed. I came to you in the hope that you can help me. I"—he hesitated—"well, I am suffering from a malady for which I cannot find a cure. I've tried everything." Haltingly, he described to Agrippa what had been happening to him in recent months; his friend listened in silence. When he had finished, Agrippa nodded.

"Hmm, that sounds more than a little concerning," he said pensively. "It could be the falling sickness or Saint Anthony's fire. Could you have eaten bread made from flour that contained ergot? I have heard that victims squirmed for weeks after the consumption of such bread, twitching and dancing, even."

Johann knew about ergot. It was a fungus that grew on rye and had the power to make people suffer horrendous torment, causing hallucinations so bad that some thought they were in hell. Johann thought about the terrible nightmares that plagued him. He would have preferred a fungal poisoning, but he knew it wasn't true.

"My assistant also thought it might be Saint Anthony's fire," he replied. "But the symptoms don't match entirely, and it's been going on for too long."

"The fungus could be on your clothing," Agrippa suggested. "Or it could be a spider bite. There are those who believe that the accursed Saint Vitus's dance is caused by the bite of a spider called tarantula."

Johann shook his head. "No, I think it's something else." He lowered his voice. He hadn't even told Greta and Karl what it was that he wanted from Agrippa. It was time to come clean.

"I . . . I believe it has something to do with an evil spell," he said reluctantly. "That's why I'm here, Heinrich. Because you know more about sorcery than anyone else. You wrote the *Occulta Philosophia*—there is no better work on magic."

Agrippa smiled, visibly flattered. "I'm honored to receive such high praise from the most famous sorcerer in the empire. But you do realize that I always endeavor to find scientific explanations for magic?"

"And yet there are some things between heaven and earth that can't be explained," said Johann vehemently, leaning forward. "Didn't you once tell me yourself that I oughtn't meddle with certain dark forces?"

Agrippa chewed his pipe nervously. "I am not sure I know what you're talking about."

"Oh yes, you do! I am talking about Gilles de Rais. Back in Cologne you pretended not to know of him, but in your later letters you warned me about him. You wrote that you had gained new insights."

"You should be taking my warning seriously," Agrippa replied coldly. "You are right, my friend. There are things so ancient and malevolent that they cannot be explained scientifically. Gilles de Rais is one of them. I urge you to look no further."

"But what if my disease is connected to Gilles de Rais?" persisted Johann. "What if I am certain that I can only defeat this disease by learning more about him?"

"I'm not sure I follow." Agrippa frowned and took another drag on his pipe. "How could your illness be connected to Gilles de Rais? The fellow was hanged at Nantes a long time ago. His black soul is cursed for all eternity. You are speaking in riddles, my friend."

Johann didn't reply. The smoke from Agrippa's pipe rose to the ceiling like a poisonous breath from hell. The wind howled and rattled at the shutters.

"I think it's about a pact," he finally said. "A pact I once entered into. The time has come for me to fulfill my end of the bargain." Johann gave his friend a dark look. "Heinrich, I'm more afraid than ever before in my life. The devil is coming for me—I can feel it. He is already tugging at my soul."

~

Downstairs in the sitting room, Little Satan was lying in the gap between the tiled stove and the wall, whimpering in his sleep. Greta was sitting at the table with Karl, playing cards in silence. Tarocchi was one of the most popular card games at the moment, having spread across Europe like a disease in the last few years—much to the dismay of the church. Agrippa's wife, Elsbeth, a short, rotund woman with friendly eyes, had served them some cold meat and wine before putting her four-year-old son, Paul, to bed. But Greta felt no appetite and struggled to focus. When she mixed up the king of hearts with the queen for the third time, she put down the stained cards and stared out the window, where solitary snowflakes fluttered by in the darkness.

"It's the doctor, isn't it?" asked Karl warmly before refilling their cups with wine.

Greta nodded and took a sip. "The fit in the Wasgau . . . It's getting worse." She shivered despite the heat of the stove. "And there's something else."

"You read his palm again," said Karl in a low voice. "I saw it. You leaned over him when he had the fit."

"The . . . the dark pulsating was back. An aura so evil that I thought I was having a stroke." She shook herself. "And his lines are fading, Karl. I mean— everyone has lines on their hands. Why are his vanishing?"

"You prayed for him?" said Karl.

"Yes, and then the shaking stopped. It was as if . . ." Greta paused, searching for the right words. She had the feeling that praying had not only helped Faust but also given her renewed strength. "It was as if the prayer was medicine. That's what it was like. Medicine."

"I'm afraid prayers won't help the doctor for much longer," Karl said glumly. "He needs real medicine, and soon."

Greta gazed into the distance, seeing the doctor on the ground in her mind's eye, twitching and drooling like a rabid dog. "That name he mentioned: Tonio . . . Tonio del Moravia."

A log cracked in the fire and she started with fright. Why did that name make her jumpy?

"What is it with that name?" she asked Karl, who was visibly uncomfortable. "I can see it in your face! There is something both of you are keeping from me. And it has something to do with the events in Nuremberg, am I right? Damn it!" She swiped the cards off the table. "I want to know what happened back then!"

Karl said nothing at first. "I promised the doctor . . . ," he began. Then he sighed deeply and made a gesture as if he was throwing something away. "To hell with it! Why shouldn't you find out? You have a right to know."

"To know *what*?"

"Tonio del Moravia used to be the doctor's master," explained Karl. "Apparently he took Faust under his wing when he was still very young. Later on, the doctor found out how infernally evil Tonio was and ran away from him." He lowered his voice. "Tonio sacrificed children for some sort of gruesome satanic rites. Lots of children."

"Even . . . even in Nuremberg?" asked Greta. In her mind's eye she saw the knife shooting down and heard eerie chanting.

My torn doll on the ground of a prison cell—a bitter juice running down my throat—I don't want to swallow, but I must. The tall man with the dead eyes whispers in my ear. He says I must, or else he will drag me down into his realm.

The memories came rushing over her and she felt nauseated.

Karl nodded. "Even in Nuremberg. Tonio took you as his hostage because he wanted the doctor. The potion must have erased your memory. There . . . there was a sacrificial ritual during which the doctor lost his eye and his little finger. Those people in the underground crypt . . ." He hesitated. "They were trying to summon something."

"What?" asked Greta. "*What* were they trying to summon? Speak up!"

A few moments passed, the only sound coming from the wind, howling outside like an animal, and the fire.

"The . . . the devil." Karl swallowed. "I believe they were trying to summon the devil." He lifted a hand. "Not that I think they succeeded. In my opinion, the devil is much too abstract a being to invoke. But people can pray to him, just like they can pray to God."

"You said that Tonio took me as a hostage to get to the doctor," said Greta. "That means Johann must have known me beforehand—I must have meant something to him. What about my mother? My father?"

Karl hesitated. "I think you should speak to him," he said eventually. "And soon. He is the only one who can tell you what really happened."

The logs cracked, and Little Satan whined as if something terrible was chasing him in his dreams.

~

"What sort of devilish pact is that supposed to be?" asked Heinrich Agrippa upstairs. He had just lit his pipe for the second time. "Not that I believe in such things. But I'm intrigued."

"When I was just a lad, I shook hands with a man," said Johann. "He took me on as his apprentice and spoke of a pact that only he could release me from. His name was Tonio del Moravia."

Agrippa frowned. "Go on."

"Since that day, many things have happened in my life, both terrible and wonderful. I gained wisdom, glory, and wealth. I am the most famous magician and astrologer of the empire. Now, in hindsight, I realize how many obstacles suddenly evaporated right before my eyes. Random strangers would tip me off so I could escape from superstitious city guards at the last moment. Enemies and competitors died of mysterious diseases. Towns that had mistreated me fell victim to massive fires." Johann shrugged. "They could all be coincidences. But I don't really believe in coincidences any longer. I think it was the pact between me and Tonio—a pact that made this life possible. And now I must pay the price."

"And what does any of that have to do with Gilles de Rais?" Agrippa asked and took a long drag on his pipe.

"Well, I . . . I believe Tonio del Moravia and Gilles de Rais are one and the same." Johann paused. "I know, it sounds crazy. Gilles de Rais was hanged at Nantes eighty years ago, and yet I'm convinced by now that he is following me. I don't know how he does it and what kind of magic he uses. Perhaps it has something to do with all those child murders. Gilles sacrificed hundreds of children in horrific ways, and Tonio did, too. Sometimes I think he is the devil himself." Johann leaned forward and gave Agrippa an intent look. "I can no longer close my eyes to it, Heinrich! There is a pact between me and Tonio, between me and Gilles de Rais." He hesitated. "And there is something else. The papal representative also spoke of Gilles de Rais. He said there was a secret that Gilles de Rais shared with me."

Agrippa's face turned ashen. "Rome knows about your connection to that villain?"

Johann nodded. "The pope appears to be under the impression that I am privy to certain knowledge. To some great secret. That's the reason I was supposed to travel to Rome. But, by God, I haven't the faintest idea what the secret's supposed to be." He gave Agrippa a pleading look. "So if there's anything else you know, please tell me. I believe it is the only chance I've got to stop this terrible disease. Speak before it kills me and this unholy pact drags me straight to hell—me and everyone who's dear to me!"

Agrippa said nothing for a long while. The pipe went out, but he didn't seem to notice.

"I am certain that if I tell you what I know, it will be your undoing, Doctor," he said eventually. "I'm still struggling to believe what you're telling me—perhaps

I don't *want* to believe it. Especially the church's involvement—it would be just . . ." He shook his head. "Give me a little more time to think it over, my friend." With a sigh he set down his pipe. "And now let us speak of something else. I loathe having to discuss such unfathomably malevolent things when I'm trying so hard to eliminate evil in scientific ways."

"What do you mean?" asked Johann.

Agrippa rolled his eyes. "Barely a year I've been in Metz and already I am dying of boredom. Insignificant trials, neighbor disputes, speeches at some irrelevant receptions. I promised Elsbeth peace and quiet, but I'm so pleased that's going to be over for a while." He leaned forward. "It's about a witch trial I am to be part of as a lawyer for the city. The suspect is a woman from Woippy, a village not far from here. Apparently the neighbors have an eye on her property and decided to accuse her of witchcraft. And the fool bishop of Metz has nothing better to do than lock her up without any sort of proof. During her first hearing alone, so many procedural mistakes were made that any student of jurisprudence would turn away in horror."

"That won't help the poor woman," said Johann, hoping Agrippa might soon return to his own case.

"Presumably." Agrippa nodded. "As you know—once you've been arrested by the Inquisition, you don't walk free. When it's blindingly obvious that anyone would confess anything if tortured long enough! That method is a shame, yes, a grave moral error of our time. At the time of Thomas Aquinas you would have been executed for saying witches and sorcerers *existed*—and now this."

"You don't believe in witchcraft and yet you wrote the best work on the matter," Johann remarked with a thin smile.

"I merely wrote down everything that humanity has come up with on the subject. And I'm not denying that some sort of magic could exist. But not in such a ridiculous manner. Flying broomsticks, hail spells, and mouse plagues— give me a break!" Agrippa shook his head. "The city wants me to supervise the trial as a lawyer and sign off on the execution like a dumb lamb. But they have underestimated Heinrich Cornelius Agrippa von Nettesheim." He laughed grimly. "I've decided to get this woman out of jail, and by juridical means alone."

"Impossible," said Johann.

"Just as impossible as a French murderer still walking the face of the earth a hundred years on—with the knowledge of the church." Agrippa tapped out the contents of his cold pipe. "I have a suggestion for you, Doctor. You help me to free this woman, and in return I will tell you what I know about Gilles de Rais. That is my final word. *D'accord?*"

He held out his hand to Johann.

"Agreed," said Johann slowly. "Even though I doubt we'll succeed."

When he clasped the hand of his friend, he thought back to the handshake with Tonio, when he was still a young boy with dreams and ideals, before he became the famous Doctor Johann Georg Faustus.

The same man who was probably possessed by an incurable curse.

~

On the following morning, about two hundred miles from Metz, a small troop of soldiers marched through the snowy German forest. It was led by half a dozen horsemen serving as the vanguard, and they were followed by foot soldiers armed with pikes and halberds and dressed in the yellow, red, and blue of the Swiss guard. In the center of the train, a carriage rattled along the boggy highway, pulled by four noble black horses, each of which was worth as much as a tavern. The doors and windows of the carriage were closed, and each hatch hung with black velvet.

Inside, seated on soft cushions, was the papal representative Viktor von Lahnstein, praying to God to send him a sign. The bandage covering most of his face itched and chafed. The skin underneath—or rather, what remained of it—burned, but it was nothing compared to the fire of hatred burning inside him.

An eye for an eye, a tooth for a tooth, thought Lahnstein. He had always felt closer to the Old Testament than the New Testament, which lacked the necessary sharpness in several places. He believed in a God of retribution, not in a God of mercy. As the second-born son of a German knight, Lahnstein had always suffered under the fact that his father didn't see the future heir in him, even though he was the more talented one. Lahnstein had taken revenge by carving out a career with the church. By the time his impoverished father had lain on his deathbed and his elder brother had brought the estate to the brink of ruin, he was already in Rome as a close confidant of the pope. He hadn't shed a single tear for his father. Lahnstein owed everything to the church, and he would do anything to strengthen it.

But right now that task seemed unbearably hard to him. God was testing him like never before.

Every morning, Lahnstein had the bandage taken off to clean the wound. So far he had avoided looking in the mirror, but the horrified expressions on the faces of his servants told him more than a thousand words. Lahnstein's fingers sought the spot on the bandage where his nose used to be. Now there was only a bony stump. That damned black hound from hell had turned his face into a bloody mess—Faust's accursed hound from hell!

Viktor von Lahnstein closed his eyes and visualized Doctor Faustus on a pyre in Rome. He could hear Faust's screams and smell his burning flesh. The image eased his own pain a little, if only for a short while. Because Lahnstein knew very well that the pope hadn't sent him out to drag the doctor onto a pyre. In fact, it was more likely he who was going to burn or rot miserably in the dungeons of Castel Sant'Angelo if he didn't find the doctor. The Holy Father had made it very clear that he expected to see Faust in Rome before others took notice of him and the precious secret he suspected Faust of harboring.

Lahnstein had no illusions. If he returned to Rome without Faust, he might as well garrote himself and climb into the fire. Especially since the Holy Father had told him what kind of secret Faust knew about—the kind of secret that would change the course of the world. He himself was an accessory, and accessories were discarded when they were no longer needed—or when they failed.

Where the hell are you, Faustus?

The rattling of the carriage was wearing Lahnstein down. For more than two weeks he'd been in the grip of a fever at Altenburg Castle, persecuted by strange dreams and visions, images of hell and a fiery-tailed Satan—probably aftereffects of the doctor's diabolical performance at the great hall. Everyone had fallen for Faust's charade—even the bishop! Everyone except Lahnstein.

After many days of unconsciousness and pain, Lahnstein had departed abruptly. He had sent out messengers in all directions, and the Bamberg prince-bishop, realizing his error, assured Lahnstein of his uncompromising support. Georg Schenk von Limpurg craved revenge, too, considering that damnable magician had made a fool of him in front of the whole empire. At every inn Lahnstein and his troops passed, people talked about how the famous Doctor Johann Faustus had pulled one over on the assembled delegates of the empire.

The carriage jerked, then stopped abruptly. Viktor von Lahnstein sat up and listened. He could hear voices and the neighing of a horse. What was going on out there? Was his well-armed papal delegation being attacked by highwaymen? Lahnstein nervously reached for the small dagger he always carried, knowing full well that it wouldn't be much use to him.

Then someone knocked on the shutter.

"Yes?" asked Lahnstein grudgingly.

The window opened, and on the other side stood a man so large that he filled the entire frame.

"Hagen!" exclaimed Lahnstein with relief. "I thought you'd never come back."

"Been on the road a lot," grumbled the huge mercenary in his harsh Swiss accent. "Been asking around at taverns here and there, in the whole of Franconia and beyond. A few times I had to . . . jog people's memory." Hagen's eyes gleamed coldly, and the papal representative felt a shiver run down his spine. He thought the giant was creepy, but Hagen was also the best soldier he'd ever seen, a killing machine as precise as one of those new clocks that adorned city halls throughout the empire.

"And?" Lahnstein asked, struggling to curb his excitement. "Do you have good news for me?"

"Oh yes." Hagen grinned, which made his pockmarked face look as though a monstrous whale were trying to smile. "I found him. Or rather, I know he headed for France via the Wasgau. He and his two companions are dressed as plain pilgrims, but they have been recognized. No one forgets that black dog."

"Tell me about it," muttered Lahnstein. "Alert my soldiers that we're turning west. Five gold ducats for the man who brings me the doctor and his hound. And the two companions, too. I want them alive. Got it?"

Lahnstein closed his eyes and uttered a prayer of thanks. It was such a pity that he had to deliver the doctor to Rome unscathed. But the secret was worth it. The pope had promised him ample reward and the post of a cardinal. And then there were also that young man and the girl who had helped Faust. Who was she? A juggler or perhaps even a witch? Whatever the case, he would find out.

He had ways. And he had Hagen.

Viktor von Lahnstein reclined into his cushions. For the first time in days he was all but pain-free.

Revenge is a sweet medicine.

Clattering and clanking, the carriage moved on.

5

JOHANN SPENT THE FOLLOWING DAYS STUDYING THE FILES of the Corbin case and working on a defense strategy with Agrippa. Sitting in the upstairs study, Agrippa smoked so much of this newfangled tobacco as they talked that Johann sometimes grew dizzy. He had come to terms with the fact that Agrippa would only tell him more about Gilles de Rais if he helped with this basically hopeless case.

Josette Corbin was a simple peasant woman whose entire misfortune was owed to the fact that her neighbors liked her property. They had accused her of so-called *maleficium*—witchcraft intended to cause harm to others. According to various inhabitants of their village, Josette Corbin had conjured up a hailstorm, curdled milk, and summoned thousands of mice to lay waste to the fields. Additionally, a dead calf with two heads had been born in the vicinity. The local judge, Jean Leonard, had at first left the poor woman at the mercy of the superstitious peasants, who—without any official warrants—tortured her brutally. But Josette Corbin did not confess.

Up until then Agrippa hadn't managed to visit the accused at the Hôtel de la Bulette, a gloomy prison on the highest hill in Metz. The bishop and the cathedral chapter were irritated by the city's involvement, and so Faust and Agrippa didn't see the accused until she was dragged in chains into the hearing room at the Palais des Treize, the city hall of Metz, one week later. Josette Corbin was probably around thirty years old, but in her torn dress and with her skinny arms and legs covered in bruises, she seemed as frail as a child. They had cut off her long blonde hair, and her haggard face showed both fear and pride.

Johann nodded approvingly. He didn't know how clever this woman was, but she was definitely as stubborn as her cows or she wouldn't have lasted this long.

And yet you will confess sooner or later, he thought. *No one can withstand the torture of the Inquisition.*

Karl and Greta stood among the many spectators staring at the accused from behind a barrier. Guards had been posted at the windows and doors, ushering back the curious onlookers with imperious gestures. Seated at a long table were the representatives of the prosecution as well as the defense, and in between sat the mayor and two councilmen. Johann knew that Josette Corbin had to confess to something in order to be convicted. The longer the trial dragged on, the more she would get tortured. It was just a question of time. Even now she could barely stand upright; two city guards had to occasionally steady her when she started to sway.

The trial itself was a farce, conducted partly in French, partly in German and Latin. The Inquisition was represented by a Dominican named Savini who was notorious throughout the region. He was a bony fellow with long, clawlike fingers, which he kept extending toward the accused.

"We have statements from eight upstanding men that this woman is a witch," he declaimed. "Eight men who attest that Josette Corbin devastated the fields all around Woippy with hail and thunder and that she killed livestock. And still she lies! I propose we continue torture right this day."

Savini had uttered the last sentence in French, looking directly at the accused. Josette Corbin groaned and fell to her knees, praying quietly, but she didn't confess.

"Your Honor, I would like to point out to you that four of these so-called upstanding witnesses have already retracted their statements," said Agrippa, waving a piece of paper at the mayor of Metz. "All of them are known to be right drunkards and braggarts in the village and cannot be considered credible. In addition, their statements were not—as is customary—taken by the cathedral chapter, but by the local judge." Agrippa gestured toward a portly, older man with a red nose and a stained vest who was sitting at the right-hand side of the table. Johann could smell the alcohol on the man's breath from where he was sitting. "Judge Jean Leonard clearly overstepped his competency."

"I granted the proceedings retroactively," said Savini arrogantly. "Everything is perfectly aboveboard, my dear colleague."

The greater part of the trial that day was held in Latin, which enabled Johann to follow it well. His Latin was almost as good as his German, and even his rusty French was coming back to him. Once the prosecution had finished presenting their case, he raised his hand.

Savini studied him from small, suspicious eyes.

"It is not customary for anyone except the lawyer to speak for the accused," he said.

"As you've already been told, Doctor Lamberti is an old friend from the university in Cologne," explained Agrippa coolly. "I obtained permission to employ him as my assistant yesterday." He smiled. "As you can see, it is all aboveboard, my dear colleague."

Johann and Agrippa had agreed to keep Johann's real identity a secret. Metz was a free imperial city far away from Bamberg or Nuremberg, but it was likely that the legendary Doctor Faustus didn't enjoy the best reputation even here—especially not as a lawyer. Johann feared, however, that they wouldn't be able to keep up this charade for long. He was simply too well known in the empire.

Johann rapped his knuckles on the table and cleared his throat. "You spoke of maleficium witchcraft," he said, addressing Savini. "Harmful spells that were cast over the village, according to you. Forgive me, but I spent my childhood in a wine-growing region. The grapes froze from time to time, hailstorms would damage the harvest every other year, but no one ever blamed it on witchcraft. If our livestock died then, it was either old or ate something it shouldn't have." He put on an expression of innocence. "Or was it witches all along and I didn't know?"

"Of course there are natural causes occasionally," allowed Savini. "But not in this case."

"And how do you know for certain?" persisted Johann. "And another question: If this poor woman here truly is a witch, then why doesn't she conjure meat upon her table or make roast pigeons fly in through her window? Why does she content herself with childish weather spells that simultaneously destroy the fruits of her own garden?"

Murmurs and even laughter rose from the audience. Johann glanced at Agrippa, who gave him a furtive wink. At least they were making Savini sweat.

The unrest in the room grew louder, until the mayor brought down his gavel on the table. "Quiet!" he shouted. "Or I'll have the room cleared."

Evidently, not everyone in the audience wished the accused woman harm, and now they jeered and stamped their feet.

"Hey, Josette," one called out. "Where are our roast pigeons? Or do they all fly to Judge Leonard, the old drunk?"

The others laughed and clapped their hands.

"Quiet, damn it!" repeated the mayor.

Once order had been restored, Savini turned to Johann, his face flushed with anger.

"You come from faraway and might find all this amusing. But believe me, for the people here it is anything but. Just this morning I heard that children went missing from around Metz. How much longer should we wait before passing this witch into the purging flames?"

"How long have the children been missing?" asked Agrippa.

Savini frowned. "They are children of travelers. I only learned of it today, so I assume it happened within the last few days."

"Then the accused can hardly have anything to do with it," Agrippa said pointedly. "Josette Corbin has been in jail for much longer."

"She may have helpers." The inquisitor's gaze traveled across the audience. "Perhaps even in this room."

People began to mutter, and the mayor knocked his gavel on the table again. "Please don't digress, Your Honor! We are dealing with the case of Corbin. So long as the accused doesn't name any helpers, we will leave it at that. It is bad enough as it is."

"As you wish, monsieur," replied Savini with pinched lips. He seemed to realize that the mood was turning against him.

When Johann and Agrippa walked past the accused late in the afternoon, she cast them a hopeful glance. Josette Corbin probably hadn't caught much of what the gentlemen had discussed at the table, but she must have sensed that these two men were her only hope of escaping the pyre.

"Not a bad move," said Agrippa once they were back at his house with their books. He gave a chuckle. "Childish weather spells. How did you come up with that?" He lit a pipe and inhaled the smoke hungrily.

"I'm merely stalling," said Johann soberly. "You said it yourself: once the Inquisition has sunk their teeth into someone, they don't let go. I'm afraid we won't be able to help this woman." He lowered his voice. "And then there are those missing children Savini mentioned. Did you know about that?"

"I've heard of it, yes." Agrippa shrugged indifferently. "But I don't think they'll have an impact on our trial. We're talking two or three children of traveling folks—scissor sharpeners, peddlers, gypsies. My guess is they moved on, or they ran away from their parents in search of a better life. And Savini knows it, too—that is why he's putting his money on the witness statements."

Johann shuddered. Missing children always reminded him of Tonio and the tower near the Alps where he had found blood and a pile of children's clothes. And of the horrific night near Nördlingen.

Small, whimpering bundles in the trees.

"I know what we'll do—we change tack." Agrippa's loud voice brought Johann back to the present. The scholar rummaged between his books on the table until he found the one he wanted, picking it up gingerly with an expression of disgust. "The accursed *Hexenhammer*—the hammer of witches—by Heinrich Kramer, from which the Inquisition loves to quote. The author, a German Dominican, tried to present their bloody deeds in a scholarly light." Agrippa grinned. "And therein lies our chance."

"What do you mean?" asked Johann with a frown.

"Well, we should beat those white-robes at their own game. I am well aware that whoever denies sorcery runs in danger of being named a sorcerer. But we can prove that the Inquisition made procedural mistakes. This is a court trial, after all, and held according to the Roman laws. The judge is an old drunkard and Savini not nearly as clever as the two of us." He nodded with determination. "We are going to drive them to where we want them with judicial finesse. You'll see, my friend: this trial is going to make history. No one picks a quarrel with Heinrich Cornelius Agrippa and Doctor Faustus!"

They used the next few days of the trial to pick apart the reasons for Josette Corbin's arrest. Whatever issue Savini raised, Johann and Agrippa had an answer. When the Dominican cited Bible passages in Latin, they produced the correct translations from the Hebrew. When Savini quoted the witness statements, they pointed out to the mayor that those statements had been unlawfully obtained. Savini was growing more insecure by the day, and Judge Leonard, too, struggled with the perpetual probing.

"So what you're saying is that after the accused was arrested and taken to Metz, you handed her back to the peasants?" asked Agrippa. "On what legal basis?"

The judge groaned and rubbed his hands nervously; it was obvious he was longing for a drink. "On . . . the basis of . . . ," he mumbled. "Of . . ."

"Of money? Were you perhaps offered money?" said Agrippa. "Money from the farmers who want Josette Corbin's property for themselves?"

The spectators whistled and cheered, and several of the witnesses blushed. Not for the first time, the mayor had the room cleared.

Johann gave a little smile. He was glad Agrippa's judicial games were distracting him from his own worries. His friend might not have given him a cure for his curse yet, but at least he allowed him to forget his disease for a while.

The weeks passed, and December turned to January. Ankle-deep snow in the lanes covered the worst of the city muck. The old emperor, Maximilian, had died during one of his many arduous journeys. People were saying that he put on his own burial gown beforehand and ordered his men to flog him once he was dead, cut off his hair, and break out his teeth as a sign of penitence. Everyone speculated about who the new emperor was going to be—Maximilian's grandson Charles, who resided in Spain, or perhaps the French king Francis?

Johann didn't hear much of the gossip, and he didn't have time to visit the many churches and palaces of Metz, some of which dated back to Roman times. On most days, he saw Karl and Greta only for supper, and even then he was bent over books. He slurped the soup Agrippa's wife, Elsbeth, had cooked while his thoughts were far away in the world of Thomas Aquinas, Albertus Magnus, and other theologians, forever on the search for a passage that might help them at the trial. Greta watched him thoughtfully.

"When you told us we'd be spending the winter here in Metz, you didn't mention that you would live only on books and parchment," she said one evening when she and Johann were alone at the table in the dining room. "Karl and I would like to know if you've learned anything about your disease yet."

"Not yet." Johann shook his head and chewed absentmindedly on a piece of bread. "But the strange thing is that ever since I started focusing on this case, the fits have stopped, apart from some weak trembling."

"And yet they will return—you know that," Greta said, squeezing his hand. "By the way, Karl told me what happened in Nuremberg."

Johann straightened up. "What did he tell you?"

"Well, I know that there was a pact between you and this Tonio del Moravia, who used to be your master. Karl told me that Tonio tried to invoke the devil in Nuremberg and that you believe this pact is the reason for your illness."

Johann sighed. His assistant had kept his word and told Greta neither that he was her father nor any precise details about what happened at Nuremberg. Still, Greta knew more than he wanted her to. He sensed that he couldn't string her along for much longer.

Deep in thought, he used the bread to soak up the last of Elsbeth's soup.

"It's true," he said eventually. "There are things you . . . things you should know. Soon. Let me see this trial through first, all right? And then we'll have time to talk." He rose abruptly. "And now excuse me. Agrippa and I must study some files."

~

A few weeks later, Karl and Greta sat in a tavern near the Moselle over a jug of wine, gazing out through the dirty crown-glass windows. It was late afternoon and darkness was falling, even though it was already early February, the month of carnival. Josette Corbin still hadn't confessed. The woman had been through ten days of trial and as many tortures now, and while she grew weaker each time, she still held up.

In the beginning, Karl and Greta had joined the doctor at court, but when proceedings began to drag on and turned into a series of legal battles, they stayed away and chose to explore the city instead. Karl had also been painting, while Greta practiced her juggling tricks and often felt bored to death.

Elsbeth, Agrippa's wife, treated her very kindly, almost like a sister. But Greta had soon realized that she would never have a real connection with the plump, cheerful woman. Elsbeth had her child, and she cooked, did the washing, and looked after her forgetful husband, while Greta was a traveling juggler, destination unknown. Greta sometimes wondered whether the path Elsbeth had chosen—that so many women chose—wasn't the better one.

The snow had given way to a cold dampness, a frosty fog that crept into the clothes and made one shiver as with a fever. From the tavern they could hear shouting and music outside, the monotonous thud of a drum, several bagpipes, and flutes playing a melancholy tune, followed by the footsteps of a crowd marching past.

Slightly tipsy from the strong wine, Greta set down her cup and looked around the taproom. She and Karl were just about the only patrons. Everyone else was outside to watch the annual Graoully procession. The Graoully was a mythical creature that had allegedly inhabited Metz a long time ago. The burghers of Metz had fetched the huge wooden puppet from a storeroom in the cathedral, renewed some of the scales of the dragon, and polished its red glass eyes. Now people followed the beast through the lanes in their best clothes, laughing and singing to the beat of the musicians. The monstrous dragon puppet moved past the tavern window, and Greta involuntarily shrank back from the glass.

"I wonder for how much longer we must stay in this rotten city," she muttered and refilled both their cups. For some time now they had seen Johann only briefly, for dinner. He hadn't yet fulfilled his promise of telling Greta more about her past and her mother.

Karl shrugged. "I think we could be doing worse. Those windows in the cathedral are stunning—they practically glow. Elsbeth is an excellent cook, and the wine here is much better than in Bamberg." He smiled, but then his expression turned serious. "But you're right, of course. The doctor hasn't come an inch closer to his goal of learning more about his mysterious illness. Agrippa is holding out on him."

Greta drained her cup and wiped her mouth. "If only I hadn't seen the throbbing in his hand again—I'd be long gone!" The words had slipped out because she had drunk too much, like so often in the last few weeks. She drank to forget her woes, but they always returned and continued to grow.

"And what about you?" she asked Karl. "The doctor doesn't even look at you these days. And still you run after him like a pup."

"You don't understand." Karl lowered his gaze. "I . . . I can't help it. The doctor and I . . ."

Suddenly Greta understood, and she was filled with sympathy, regretting her harsh words.

"Dear God—you're in love with him, aren't you?" she said gently. "Of course! That is why you're staying." She smiled sadly, feeling much more sober now. "I should have noticed sooner. All those years . . . You poor thing." She shook her head. "How awful it must be to love someone, unable to confess your love and without hope of ever being loved back."

"It eats you up. It's like the candlewick that forever flickers but never goes out." Karl's handsome face was fine boned and serious. Greta thought about how many girls Karl could have had—dozens had run after him. But the one person he pined for was unattainable.

He tried to smile. "And yet it's not as bad as you might think. I'm with him, at least, and when his illness returns he's going to need me. I will always be there for him."

And I? thought Greta. *Am I going to be there for him when his illness returns?*

The procession with the dragon and its followers had gone; suddenly, it was very quiet.

"There is something else we need to discuss," said Karl into the silence. "Something more important than my personal problems. I heard it at the market this morning. It's about the missing children from the country—you remember? Savini mentioned them during the trial." He swallowed. "Now children have also gone missing here in the city. In the beginning I thought it was coincidence, but I'm no longer certain."

Greta gasped. "You don't think—?"

Karl raised a hand. "I don't think anything. I'm a scientist. I merely observe. We've been talking about Tonio del Moravia, and children go missing. Just like in Nuremberg, and also beforehand, when the doctor traveled the empire with his master. If nothing else, it is at least . . . strange, I would say. Tonio wasn't vanquished back then, and I'm sure his followers still exist. They might have gone into hiding, but they're still around, just like their master."

"You're scaring me." Greta stood up slowly. "I've had too much to drink for ghost stories today."

She walked to the door, and Karl followed once he'd paid the tavern keeper. It was icy cold outside, their breath coming out in small clouds. They could hear the music and the cheers of the crowd in the distance; the procession had probably arrived at the cathedral by now. Damp mist rose from the river and covered the alleyways like a shroud. The bell of the Saint Livier

Church chimed nearby; the outline of several mills emerged in the haze of the river, their wheels creaking in the current.

An eerie feeling overcame Greta. Hastily she turned west toward the Pont des Morts, the bridge leading across the river to Agrippa's quarter. She shuddered. Why did the people of Metz have to give their bridges such awful names? *Bridge of the dead.*

She was about to cross the bridge when Greta saw something strange in the shadow of the stone arches beneath the far side of the bridge. It kind of looked as if an additional pillar jutted out from the bridge. Greta blinked, then froze.

The pillar was moving, like the probing leg of a monstrous spider.

Greta stayed on the first steps of the bridge as if paralyzed. She suddenly felt stone-cold sober.

"What is it?" asked Karl.

She pointed across to the other side of the river. Now it was clearly visible: a man had stepped out from the darkness beneath the bridge. He was dragging something that Greta had first thought was a sack, but then, to her horror, she recognized what it really was.

A lifeless child.

They hurried across the bridge together, Greta's mind whirling. A memory rose to the surface. She had suppressed it for a long time, but it had been haunting her nightmares for years. It had happened back in Nuremberg. Someone whose face she couldn't remember had lured her beneath a bridge, to where a child had lain.

A child whose throat had been ripped open as if by a wolf.

Only moments later, the city guards had caught her right there and locked her up. They found a magical talisman in her pocket that someone must have slipped her.

The man with no face.

Greta remembered it clearly for the first time.

If Faust doesn't come to me, then I'll just take you, my dear. And when you've come of age I will mate with you on Blocksberg Mountain.

The words flashed through her mind like lightning bolts, long-forgotten memories. Greta's heart beat wildly. Deep down she knew that below the bridge walked the same creature as back in Nuremberg—the monster that had done terrible things to her, things she had kept buried deep within her. Things that were now reemerging, like maggots.

Kiss my scaly skin. Feel the closeness of the beast.

She and Karl were the only people on the bridge; everyone else seemed to be at that confounded procession. Steps beside the bridge led down to the slimy, algae-covered bank of the Moselle. The steps were icy and slippery, but Greta still took several at once.

The man—or whatever it was—wore a black coat with the collar up so that they couldn't make out his face. He was bent over the child now, looking as if he was caressing it. Greta stopped and watched, fear of the monster rooting her to the spot. Old memories wafted around her like poisonous fog, buzzed around her like angry hornets. It was almost more than she could bear, and her knees grew weak as the scenes of the past swept over her.

Kiss my scaly skin . . . if Faust doesn't come to me . . . on Blocksberg Mountain, on Blocksberg Mountain, on—

"Get away from the child, you monster!" yelled Greta.

Fury and hatred gave her renewed strength. She drew the dagger she always carried and leaped at the man with the coat, but the strange figure slipped away as fast as a snake and disappeared beneath the arches of the bridge. The lifeless child remained on the rocky shore.

Greta glanced at it and shrank back with shock.

The girl was about five years old; she stared into the fog above with empty, dead eyes. Her throat had been bitten through, her pale skin ripped as if attacked by a wolf. Fresh blood oozed onto the stones, bright red against the gray and black surroundings.

Bridge of the dead.

"There he is!" called out Karl above her. "He's running away!"

Greta hesitated only for a brief moment, then she turned from the bloodied child and raced back up the steps. The man had run up the stairs on the other side of the bridge and was heading toward the cathedral, which rose up into the dusk not far from them. Karl and Greta set off in pursuit. The music grew louder the closer they came to the square in front of the cathedral, where most of Metz appeared to have gathered. The fog had arrived here, too, and even though it wasn't fully dark yet, torches had been lit to illuminate the gloomy scene in front of the church. Swaying in the center of the square was the tall dragon, held up with long poles by a handful of young men. Low murmuring lay over the crowd as the people strode toward the entrance of the cathedral with bowed heads. Inside, the beast was going to be sprinkled with holy water.

The man had almost reached the throng of people now. His black coat billowed behind him like the wings of a bat. All of a sudden he spun around, and Greta saw his face for the first time.

He was deathly pale as if he wore makeup, only his lips gleaming blood-red, and Greta thought the teeth behind those lips were pointed like the fangs of a wolf. The man wore a red cap with a rooster's feather, which until then had been concealed by the tall collar. The most frightening part was his eyes. They were black holes—ancient, deep craters—and evil gleamed from within their depths like oil in a puddle.

He raised one hand and waved, his mouth twisting into a malicious smile.

Then he turned back around and disappeared in the crowd.

Who are you? wondered Greta. *A man or something else? No matter what you are—I'm going to hunt you. You won't drag me down again!*

"After him!" she shouted to Karl. "He can't get away!"

But Karl just stood there, gaping, and only started following her after a few long moments. They elbowed aside men and women who swore and elbowed them back; they pushed forward as fast as they could until they stood directly beneath the huge dragon puppet, whose red eyes glowered down at them. But it was all for nothing.

The man had vanished.

"Damn, if you hadn't frozen back there, we might have caught him!" gasped Greta. She made her way through the crowd and slumped down on one of the steps along the side of the cathedral. "What was the matter with you?"

Karl was still deathly pale. He shook his head slowly. "That man," he murmured. "I knew him, but . . . but that's impossible."

"You knew him?" Greta grasped Karl's trembling hands. "Then tell me! Who was it? Damn it, Karl, that monster killed a child, and most likely not just the one. Who or what is he?"

Karl cleared his throat. "Didn't you recognize him? It was the French delegate from Altenburg Castle. Louis Cifre."

Greta closed her eyes. She remembered the man well, even though she'd seen him only briefly at Bamberg. She could almost smell the sulfur she had smelled then. She hadn't recognized him in the foggy twilight. To her it seemed that it was Louis Cifre and at the same time it wasn't, like a fat larva that had just emerged from its cocoon, revealing its true face.

Somewhere not far away they could hear the soft melody of a flute.

It played an old children's song.

～

"That Savini is cleverer than I thought, but still not as clever as us."

Agrippa puffed another plume of smoke into the room, making Johann's eyes water. It felt like they'd been sitting in Agrippa's study for weeks, breathing in stuffy fumes. Elsbeth would occasionally bring up some cold meat or cheese, which they'd eat without much enthusiasm and wash down with a glass of thinned wine. Then they'd carry on working. At some point Little Satan would help himself to the leftover meat and chew loudly under the table. Then he liked to curl up by the fireplace, yelping softly in his sleep.

The two scholars left the house only on trial days, and it wouldn't be long until the next one. During the last one, Savini had pulled an unexpected card from his sleeve. He had declared triumphantly that Josette Corbin's mother had been accused of witchcraft and that he had proof—an old document that had unexpectedly resurfaced. Therefore, according to Savini, witchcraft ran in the family, a kind of original sin that could only be extinguished by the flames. Following this revelation, Agrippa had asked for another adjournment of the trial, well aware that Josette Corbin was at the end of her strength. The hangman of Metz, who was also responsible for torture, was a master of his craft.

"That document must be falsified," said Johann, reaching for the jug of wine.

The sound of music and crowds could be heard in the distance; it was growing dark outside. Agrippa had told Johann about the dragon procession, but they hadn't spoken of it again. They had more important work to do.

"Even if it is, that won't help us," Agrippa replied with a sigh. "The mayor wants to get the trial over and done with, and to that end he'll accept any absurd piece of evidence."

"You're probably right."

Johann gave a tired nod; he, too, was exhausted from this trial. He wasn't sleeping much at night, leafing through theological books or combing Agrippa's library for volumes on medicine. He still hadn't learned anything new about his disease, but it hadn't been bothering him much lately. Could he be healed? Perhaps he was so distracted by the trial that the healing had happened all by itself? Johann thought about the time back in Heidelberg, when he had constructed the very first laterna magica with his friend Valentin. Then, too, he had been driven by a single thought, by an unstoppable determination. Science, studying—the perpetual search for something new had pushed aside everything else.

And in the end, the girl he loved the most had died.

And it was my fault.

". . . might be more suitable to build a theological argumentation on . . ."

Johann heard the voice of Agrippa, who, as usual, was thinking out loud. Johann listened for a moment, but then he remembered Greta. When had he seen her and Karl last? What if the curse had now transferred to her because she was his daughter? Just as Josette Corbin was accused of witchcraft because her mother had been tainted with the curse?

"She is innocent," he muttered. "Nothing but an innocent child . . ."

"Beg your pardon?" Agrippa gave him an irritated look. "What did you say?" Then his expression brightened. "Of course, you're right! Josette Corbin was baptized as a child, and so she can't carry evil inside her even if her mother was accused of witchcraft. Otherwise baptism—the holy sacrament of the church— would be ineffective. Any child that is baptized is innocent. Ha!" He patted Johann on the shoulder. "Didn't I tell you, old friend? Together we can—"

The door crashed open. Little Satan growled but calmed down as soon as he saw who was entering. Karl and Greta were standing in the hallway, the young woman's eyes flashing angrily. Both of them were breathing heavily as if they'd been running.

"We have to talk," said Greta between breaths. "I am sick and tired of this game."

"What do you mean?" asked Johann with surprise. Despite the raucous entrance, he suddenly felt very glad to see his daughter.

"I want to know what's really at the bottom of this accursed disease and our escape," said Greta, entering the study, followed by Karl. With a trembling hand, she pointed at Johann. "Children are getting murdered out there by some kind of monster that *you* most likely lured to Metz. A monster that I saw back in Nuremberg and that followed us here. And you two sit here on your backsides poring over dusty old files!"

"What are you talking about, girl?" asked Agrippa. "What murdered children?"

"Children have been going missing," explained Karl.

Agrippa raised his hands. "But we already know that. Like I said—"

"Listen to me, damn it!" said Greta, cutting him off. "While you two sit here congratulating each other on your cleverness, more and more children are vanishing out there. My guess is they're all dead. As dead as the child we just found—and we saw her murderer."

As quickly as she could, Greta told the two scholars what she and Karl had witnessed. Johann listened in silence, his hands and feet turning cold as ice.

"What exactly did the man look like?" he asked with trepidation.

"Pale, almost like a woman with makeup," said Karl. "He was skinny and wore a red cap with a rooster's feather. His whole appearance was somewhat . . ." He searched for the right words. "Like a spider."

Johann groaned. "It's Tonio. He followed us. When is this horror going to end?"

"Enough of the secrecy!" Greta abruptly sat down on a stool next to Johann. With one sweeping movement she cleared the table of books and files and gave the doctor a serious look. "You've always been my teacher and my role model, Uncle. But if I am to trust you from here on in, then we must tell each other the truth. I haven't been entirely honest with you, either. I . . ." She took his hand in hers and gave him a sad look. "I read your palm—you know I'm good at it. And I saw something terrible in it. It was in the Wasgau."

Johann had had a hunch but had never asked. He didn't *want* to know.

She inherited it from me. I should have known.

"That is why I stayed with you—to protect you," continued Greta. "And I will keep on doing so, but only if you're honest with me. Can you do that for me? No more lies. Promise?"

Johann nodded, still shaken by what Greta had just told him.

She has foreseen my death. The pact is coming full circle, just like it did for Peter, the red-haired fiddler.

"Tonio is at my heels," he said quietly, more to himself. "Somehow I've always known."

"But how can that be?" asked Greta. "The man we saw under the bridge wasn't that old. Tonio would have to be much, much older by now!"

"Oh, he is," said Johann with a sad smile. "Trust me, I know. He doesn't look it. But I suspect Tonio is even older than you can begin to imagine." He looked at her intently. "I believe that in truth he is the godforsaken Gilles de Rais, the most cruel and insane murderer there ever was—a man who lived during the first half of the last century. The devil on earth!"

In the distance, the bells of the cathedral rang out, and then the dull thudding of a drum set in. The crowd was now moving from the cathedral toward the other side of the river, toward the quarter where Agrippa's house stood.

Johann turned to Agrippa. "I believe the time has come when you must tell me what you know about Gilles de Rais."

Agrippa set down his pipe, which had gone out. Johann noticed that his friend looked rather pale and thought that it probably wasn't sleep deprivation.

"The children, the dead girl," muttered Agrippa. "Dear God, Faustus! If that is true, then you really did lure the monster to Metz."

"What monster?" asked Karl skeptically. "What exactly do you mean? Are we talking about a man or a ghost?"

By now they were all sitting around the fire. The books lay scattered on the ground, tossed aside as if all the knowledge in the world couldn't help them now. The huge dog slumbered among them.

"When I advised you in my letters to steer clear of the subject of Gilles de Rais, I did it with the best of intentions. I was hoping to save your life—your soul, even," started Agrippa. "But now it would seem we have wakened the beast. It has picked up your scent." He hesitated before continuing. "I've been preoccupied with Gilles de Rais and his horrible deeds for a long time, for years. As you all know, the popular French marshal tried to invoke the devil in order to gain power and wealth. The great war that raged between England and France released something inside him that had been hidden until then. Gilles lived extravagantly. When he ran out of money, he tried to gain gold with the aid of the devil. But instead, the devil came for him. Never before and never thereafter was there a person as profoundly evil as Gilles de Rais."

"How do you know all that?" asked Karl. "That happened a hundred years ago."

"The documents from his trial survive to this day—that is how we know so much about his crimes. Gilles's first victim was a peasant boy he strangled before cutting off the boy's hands. Then he ripped out his heart and used the blood as ink to pen the words required to invoke the devil. Apparently, a former priest named Prelati helped him do it. From then on Gilles de Rais murdered hundreds of children with the aid of his henchmen. He tortured them, hanged them, slit them open, and violated them. He enjoyed it more and more. And in doing so he, well . . ." Agrippa faltered. The great scholar struggled to find the words. "I can't prove it, but I fear that in doing so the marshal became the devil himself."

"You . . . you're saying Gilles de Rais is *the* devil?" asked Karl with disbelief. "You can't be serious."

"He was, he is, and yet he isn't," replied Agrippa.

Karl frowned. "You speak in riddles."

"Admittedly, it goes beyond our human intellect, and I'm not even sure if I fully grasp it or if it isn't a silly ghost story after all. The devil appears in all kinds of shapes, in every culture and region on earth. He is one and yet he is many, and he is always that which we fear the most."

"A child-murdering monster," whispered Greta. "Children are what we hold dearest."

Agrippa nodded. "It is possible that the devil used Gilles de Rais like a shell—like a costume one can put on. I'm guessing Satan needs a human form in order to walk on earth. He may be vulnerable in that state, but he can also lead people astray. He's been doing so since ancient times—descriptions of him can be found in the oldest writings ever found, in the Jewish Talmud, in Persia, Babylon, and of course in the Bible. The Greeks called him Diabolos, the bringer of chaos. He seeks out people who are susceptible to him—magicians, sorcerers, demon conjurers . . ."

"People like Gilles de Rais," said Johann softly. "Like Tonio del Moravia."

"Like Tonio del Moravia." Agrippa looked at his friend. "When Gilles de Rais died on the scaffold at Nantes, the devil probably needed a new shell. I'd been looking for information on Tonio del Moravia, and at last I found something. What I dug up in the old scriptures is as surprising as it is frightening. It would appear that Tonio was a juggler and magician who grew up in the area of Constantinople, in the time before the Ottomans conquered the city. At first he was just one of the many traveling quacks who had also read up on Babylonian sorcery—probably in an attempt to impress the common people. But then he must have begun to study the subject more seriously. It is possible that Tonio summoned the devil with some sort of old Babylonian rites, and Satan truly appeared. Tonio was tried in Constantinople and condemned to burn, but he managed to escape as if by magic. Ever since then his name pops up right across Europe, and always then when children are reported missing or killed. A malicious fellow and, well"—Agrippa sighed—"possibly the devil's new coat. It seems as if Satan depends on the blood of innocent children in order to walk on earth. Only the devil knows how many different human shells he has already used to live among us. Tonio del Moravia is just one of many—there'll be more after him."

"Hang on a moment." Karl cast a skeptical glance around the small group. "I do believe in the devil—I even believe that he's in every one of us. But it's the person who brings evil into the world. Gilles de Rais was an evil person. And back in Nuremberg, it was the people who murdered those poor children for some kind of horrific ritual. I've never seen *the* one devil. And why should he walk the earth? He leads people astray using what they already carry within them, with their own needs and cravings and thoughts. The rest is nothing but fiction."

"These people never smell the old rat, even when he has them by the collar," muttered Johann.

Agrippa raised his hands. "Like I said—pure theory. I can't prove anything. Sometimes I pray that I'm wrong."

There was noise outside the window now, shouts, marching footsteps, but no one paid it any attention.

"Back in Nuremberg, Tonio spoke of a coat," said Johann pensively. "He said I was that coat." He closed his eyes and tried to remember the words. "*And when the day arrives and the great beast awakens, give it a coat.* Those were his words. You spoke of a shell. Am I . . . ?"

"The devil's new shell?" Agrippa rocked his head from side to side. "To be honest, I don't know, my friend. You said yourself that your master taught you much. He would have had great hopes for you and must be feeling deeply disappointed now. But perhaps it's something entirely different."

"If the doctor wasn't supposed to serve as a shell," asked Greta, "then what had they intended for him? What could be worse than giving one's body to Satan?"

Agrippa frowned. "Well, I think even worse would be if the devil had more than one body. So far he is just one single person. One who doesn't age and is very powerful, but vulnerable nonetheless. Nothing that can truly throw the world into chaos." Agrippa reached for the cold pipe and tapped gray ashes onto the table.

"But what if the world no longer belonged to God but to the devil? What if the ritual back in Nuremberg was part of a greater plan? The plan to achieve the state that Saint John describes in his apocalypse. The state of the world that Tonio's dark followers long for. What if he is still trying today to create this devilish empire?"

Agrippa paused before continuing. "His followers await the eternal rule of evil—the devil in his true form. Let us all pray that they are mistaken, that I am mistaken. That the beast stays deep down below in hell and doesn't return to earth, subduing us all as his slaves. The return of the beast is the return of chaos. It is the spirit of perpetual negation."

There was a shattering noise. Johann ducked instinctively and saw a stone flying through the broken window. Angry shouts could be heard from the street. Something warm ran down his cheek. He touched it and saw that it was blood.

The return of the beast, echoed Agrippa's voice through Johann's mind. *The eternal rule of evil.*

Then the great nothing spread its black wings over him.

~

"Watch out!" Greta dived under the table when two more stones were hurled through the window. She saw the doctor fall—was he hit? And what was going on outside?

Hunched over, she scuffled to the window and cast a cautious glance outside. About twenty men and women were standing in front of the house, all of them dressed in plain, worn-out clothes. Some were holding cudgels, others torches, and others again were picking up more stones. It was clear from their staggering movements that most of them were drunk—they'd probably come straight from the Graoully procession. When they caught sight of Greta in the window, they started to shake their fists angrily and shout.

"Send out the witch doctor!" demanded a broad-shouldered, bearded man swinging a heavy club. Greta recognized the landlord from the tavern she and Karl had been drinking at not long ago. "Give us the doctor or we'll come and get him!"

At first she thought they were talking about her uncle and that word must have gotten around about Agrippa's new assistant. But then Agrippa stepped to the window beside her, and instantaneously the shouts grew louder and angrier.

"Agrippa, black sorcerer!" cried the people. "You're in cahoots with that witch!"

"What are you talking about?" asked Agrippa harshly. He didn't seem frightened in the least. "I am a lawyer employed by the city, not a sorcerer. How dare you, you rabble? Get away from here before I call the city guards!"

In the twilight below, Greta thought she could make out some guards among the crowd. They didn't intervene, however. On the contrary—they seemed to be part of the angry mob. Greta decided to keep quiet for now.

"And as a lawyer you ensure that the witch doesn't burn as she should but continues to wreak havoc and murder!" shouted the broad-shouldered leader. "What did she give you for your services? A love potion? A mandrake that fulfills your every wish? Spit it out, advocate of the devil!"

More stones were flung and Agrippa ducked.

"The fellow once lost a trial against me as lawyer for the city," Agrippa whispered to Greta as they waited below the windowsill for the onslaught to ease. "Perhaps he thinks he can take his revenge this way." When things calmed down a little, Agrippa rose cautiously and addressed the crowd once more.

"And who is the witch supposed to have murdered?"

"Our children!" cried a younger woman now, tears in her eyes. "They just found my little Marie dead by the Pont des Morts with her throat ripped open. And two other children from town have gone missing, just like the children from the country a few weeks back. It was the witch, that accursed Corbin, and you defend her. May God punish you for it!"

Greta swore under her breath. The people had found the dead girl and come straight here. And another mob had most likely rushed to the prison at

Place Sainte Croix, throwing rocks and demanding the guards hand over Josette Corbin.

Agrippa lifted his hands with the palms up. "And how is she supposed to murder children from her prison cell?"

The people said nothing, some muttering under their breath.

"She's a witch," yelled a skinny old man with a scythe, looking like Death himself. "Witches can do such things. She uses magic to get out of prison for each murder."

"Hmm, if what you say is true, then I'm sure she's not in her cell right now," replied Agrippa. "And that means I can't have her handed over to you. She'll have used magic to get over the hill and far away—she's probably on Blocksberg Mountain by now, dancing with the other witches."

It was too much logic for the plain people, most of them illiterate day laborers, and tired and drunk to boot. The uproar subsided as quickly as it had begun. The crowd muttered and cursed for a while longer, then the first people turned to leave. That was when Karl touched Greta by the shoulder.

"I need your help," he said. "The doctor."

Greta turned around and saw to her horror that her uncle was lying on the floor, twitching wildly. Clearly, he was having another fit. Just like last time, saliva ran from his mouth, and his arms and legs were completely rigid one moment and thrashing about wildly the next. He made slurred sounds alternating with groans and piercing screams. Little Satan stood next to his master and barked as if trying to rouse the dead.

"What's going on up there?" demanded the leader of the mob. He raised his cudgel once more.

"You woke my boy," replied Agrippa frostily. "He often has nightmares—and no wonder, with the spectacle you've been putting on. Time to go home now—tomorrow is another trial day, and everything will be resolved. Even the murder of your children. I promise you, if Corbin is a witch, then—"

Another long, mournful cry rang out behind him, followed by the mad barking of the dog. Greta had meanwhile rushed to Johann's side and tried to pin him to the ground. But the doctor still squirmed and jerked like a fish on dry land. The crowd downstairs grew angry again.

"We must do something," hissed Karl. "Or they'll storm the house!"

Greta nodded. She leaned over Johann, held his hand, and murmured soothingly.

"It's going to be all right, Uncle," she whispered. "You have nothing to fear."

He thrashed about once more and struck Greta on the head. She was hurled aside, and the people on the street began shouting again.

"Did you hear that? The devil's up there!" cried the younger woman. "I bet it's that other doctor and he's invoking the devil right now. Just think of his big black dog! The fellow's in league with Satan."

Stones and lumps of ice came flying through the window again; someone rattled the front door, and Greta heard Elsbeth cry out in fear. She was downstairs with the boy and must have been frightened to death. A burning torch was flung onto the roof, but it slid down the wet shingles and dropped into the lane without causing any harm. Still, one of the men was ready to throw the next torch.

In her desperation, Greta threw herself on Johann and held him down with her whole body. Then she started doing what she'd done in the Wasgau: she prayed. She muttered the verses she'd learned from her uncle Valentin and which now appeared like gleaming seashells at low tide.

"From the rear and the front you encompassed me, and you placed your pressure upon me," she murmured, haltingly at first and then more and more steadily. "Even darkness will not obscure anything from you, and the night will light up like day, as darkness so is the light."

And the miracle happened once more.

The doctor calmed down. With each word of the ancient psalm, Johann became quieter, his rapid twitching slowing until he finally passed out with exhaustion.

". . . and see whether there is any vexatious way about me, and lead me in the way of the world," concluded Greta with a trembling voice. "Amen."

Suddenly Johann opened his eyes again. He looked at Greta with perfect clarity for a brief moment. Then he reached out his hand and stroked her hair.

"My daughter," he whispered so quietly that only Greta could hear. "Apple of my eye, don't leave me. My only, my beloved daughter . . . stay with me . . ."

Then his eyes fell shut again. Greta sat beside him as if she had turned to stone. She couldn't believe what she had just heard. Had the doctor spoken in a fever—had he been confused? And yet so much that had happened in the last few years would suddenly make sense if it were true. But she found the thought incredibly difficult to accept.

My daughter.

Greta felt myriad puzzle pieces fall into place in an instant. Soundlessly and with shaking lips, she repeated Johann's words.

My daughter. My only, my beloved daughter.

"As you can hear, my son went back to sleep despite the racket you've been making," said Agrippa to the drunken mob. "Go home now before I am forced to report this incident to the city. If you leave now you have nothing to fear."

He slammed the shutters closed and listened. It seemed like the people were indeed leaving. Agrippa gazed at Greta, who was still on her knees, bent over Johann. She was sweating and shaking as if from heavy labor. But neither Karl nor Agrippa had heard Faust's whispered words.

My only, my beloved daughter. Apple of my eye.

"I owe you my gratitude, girl," said Agrippa.

Greta barely heard him. When she finally turned to look at him, she noticed that the scholar was also shaking, his earlier composure gone. "You saved my family. If I hadn't seen it with my own eyes and heard it with my own ears, I wouldn't believe it." He shook his head. "You called upon God, and God helped! The devil had taken hold of Faust's body, but you banished him and saved your uncle. Divine miracles really exist."

Agrippa didn't know that another miracle had just happened to Greta.

Or was it a curse?

⁓ .

Johann dreamed.

He stood on a wide, barren plain, the wind whistling and howling like a thousand wild ghosts. Suddenly he could make out another sound, very faintly at first, then louder and louder. It was the galloping of horses. Now he could see three black dots on the horizon, rapidly approaching.

Three horsemen headed straight for Johann. Pouring rain set in, scourging him.

The first horseman was pale, chalk-faced, and he wore a red cap with a rooster's feather. The second rider was a knight with blond hair and the beautiful face of an angel.

The third horseman had no face.

Where the face should have been were curling wafts of black smoke, and in the place of hair writhed worms and snakes. In his right hand the third horseman held a long sword that he now raised up and swung above his head. Then it swooshed down.

The devil is on earth and he walks among the mortals.

With a hoarse cry, Johann woke up.

Agrippa leaned over him and wiped the sweat off his brow with a cloth. When he saw that Johann had opened his eyes, he smiled.

"Welcome back to the realm of the living, my friend. I thought you'd never wake up."

"I . . . I had another fit?" asked Johann.

Agrippa nodded. "The very moment the mob approached my house. But all went well."

"How . . . how long was I asleep?" Johann's head ached as if the sword really had struck him.

Agrippa cocked his head to one side and studied him with the professional gaze of a physician. "Two whole days. How are you feeling?"

Johann shot up. "But the trial—"

"Didn't take place." Agrippa gently pushed his friend back into bed. "You didn't miss anything. Well, at least not the trial."

They were in one of the many bedrooms of the Agrippas' grand house. There was a brazier in the room and furs and rugs on the floor. Johann was lying in a four-poster bed with beautifully carved pillars. The carvings showed scenes from Judgment Day. Flying at the top were the angelic hosts, while down on the bed's feet, hairy devils tore the flesh off sinners.

No wonder I had nightmares, thought Johann.

"What about the trial?" he asked. "Why—?"

But then Elsbeth came in, carrying a tray with steaming-hot spiced wine and a bowl of soup. She set it down on a small table beside the bed and gave Johann an encouraging smile.

"Ah, you come at just the right time, Elsbeth," said Agrippa. "Our patient has just awoken and must be hungry. Tell me, has our son returned from his friend's house?"

Johann thought he could hear concern in Agrippa's voice.

Elsbeth nodded. "Over an hour ago. It is past noon already."

"That's good. Now leave us again for now—I'll be down soon."

Elsbeth closed the door softly, and the men sat in silence for a while.

"How are you feeling?" asked Agrippa again.

"I feel like I was caught in a landslide," said Johann, stretching. "And I'm exhausted, as if I've been battling a fever. But aside from that, I feel fine." His face darkened. "The things you told me before I passed out . . . about Gilles de Rais and Tonio."

"I hoped you'd forget," Agrippa said with a sigh. "Listen, it was pure speculation. Silly theories of a scholar who spends too much time in his study. I got carried away by a flood of thoughts. I'm sure you know what I mean."

Agrippa winked at him, and yet Johann couldn't shake the feeling that his friend was keeping something from him.

"Of course," he murmured. After a while he asked, "Why didn't the trial take place? It would hardly have been because the lawyer's assistant fell ill."

"No, indeed." Agrippa hesitated. "It was because, well . . . strange things happened."

"What sort of strange things?"

"Well . . . where do I start?" Heinrich Agrippa rose and began to pace the room. "I was about to leave for the Palais des Treize the next morning when a delegation of guards arrived and asked me to follow them to the house of Judge Leonard. The judge lay dead in his bed—apoplexy, it would appear. Much more surprising, however, was the letter on his nightstand, which he evidently wrote just before he died. In his letter Leonard admits to accepting bribes and says there is no truth to the accusations against Corbin. The neighbors lied and he supported them."

Johann sat up abruptly. "He admitted to his lies and died shortly thereafter?"

"Yes—strange, isn't it?" Agrippa shrugged. "The city scrapped the trial and released Josette Corbin. She withstood severe injuries during torture, but she'll probably recover. They now suspect a bunch of gypsies to be responsible for the murder of the girl and the missing children, but they've already left town." He sighed. "We won, old friend. Even though it wasn't the way I would have liked to win."

"And the judge really died of natural causes?"

"As the physician who examined him, I couldn't detect anything to the contrary. Apoplexy is not unusual for a prolific drunk."

Agrippa held Johann's gaze, but for a brief moment the scholar's eyes flickered.

"There is something else I need to tell you," Agrippa said quickly. "I came across it yesterday and thought it might be of use to you."

"Go on," said Johann without taking his eyes off Agrippa.

"There is a man who complains of symptoms similar to yours," continued Agrippa, sitting back down on the stool beside the bed. "I saw it while browsing through some old letters yesterday. I should have remembered sooner, but there was the trial and—"

"Who is this man?" asked Johann impatiently, his head still hurting as if someone had struck him with a hammer.

"Leonardo da Vinci."

"Leonardo . . ." Johann's jaw dropped. He straightened up. "You . . . you and Leonardo da Vinci write to one another? And you never told me?"

"I correspond with many great men of Europe," Agrippa said evasively. "With kings, scholars, bishops." He laughed. "With you, too. And occasionally with Leonardo da Vinci. He truly is a genius, an expert in many fields, a bright light, even if he's no longer the youngest. Sadly, painting is a talent I wasn't endowed with. Perhaps I should—"

"What did da Vinci write about the disease?"

"Not much," replied Agrippa with a shrug. "He writes of a trembling in his hand that he can't get under control. And from time to time he is plagued by fits very similar to yours. Paralysis, grimacing. Leonardo, too, was at a loss, but in his last letter he hinted that he might know what lies at the bottom of his ailment."

"Last I heard, he worked in Rome for the pope," Johann said thoughtfully, his heart beating faster. "But that was quite a while ago. I don't know where he is now."

"You're right." Agrippa cleared his throat. "He hasn't been in Rome for two years. Apparently, the French king made him an offer he couldn't refuse.

Francis I gave Leonardo a castle where he might enjoy the autumn of his life. He is rather old and—"

"Where is that castle?" asked Johann.

"Ha! I knew you would want to know." Agrippa chuckled. "It's in the Loire Valley, west of Orléans. The town is called Amboise. An exceptionally picturesque area the king likes to visit often. There are magnificent castles and good wine and—"

"Do you have horses?" asked Johann, cutting him off again.

He felt his strength returning. Strength, and also hope. He should have thought of Leonardo much sooner. He was the best observer of the human body, of that wonderful apparatus called man. And now he was plagued by a condition similar to Johann's. Could it be possible that the famous inventor was also possessed by a curse? Whatever the case, Leonardo would have made observations—observations that might help Johann.

All is not lost yet.

Agrippa eyed Johann with curiosity. "You intend to travel to the Loire Valley?"

"Why not? I must use any chance I get—any! Even if I have to climb down into the depths of hell." Johann was about to get up when Agrippa held him back.

"Perhaps you should speak with your two companions first—especially with the young lady." He passed the bowl of soup to Johann. "She has been waiting outside the door for quite some time. I think she has something important to discuss with you. I told her you would awake soon." He smiled. "That young woman is an extraordinary person, by the way. Not at all a simple juggler. Did you know that her prayers alone brought you back from hell?"

Johann winced. A vague memory surfaced in his mind. During his fit he had stroked Greta's hair and said . . .

Had he told her that she was his daughter? Or had he only dreamed it?

Apple of my eye.

Suddenly Johann felt certain that he had told Greta the truth. How had she reacted? At least she was still here, despite the lifelong lie. She was waiting outside his door. His mouth felt very dry.

"She . . . she wants to talk to me?"

Agrippa laughed. "Why else would she be waiting outside the door? May I call her in now?"

"No. I mean . . . wait, please." Johann started to sweat.

All those times he put it off, all those lies were finally catching up with him. No test at Heidelberg University had ever been as difficult as the one he was facing now.

"Are you feeling worse?" asked Agrippa with concern.

"I . . . I'm all right," Johann said and ran his hand through his hair. "You can ask her in now. I believe I need to speak with her."

Agrippa nodded. "I think so, too. I was going to make her wait until tomorrow, but when I saw her look of determination, I knew: that girl is very strong-minded—almost like you."

When Greta entered the room a few moments later, Johann could tell right away that he wasn't mistaken: she knew—it was written all over her face. Her eyes studied him as if she was seeing him for the first time. Agrippa had left them alone, and Greta now stood in front of his bed with a straight, rigid back, like a traveler about to depart. No one spoke for a while.

"I told you, didn't I?" said Johann eventually. "During my fit. You know that I . . . that I . . ."

"That you are my father," said Greta, completing the sentence for him. "I still struggle to say it out loud." Her voice sounded bitter. "And I struggle to believe it."

"It's the truth, Greta," he said softly. "You are my daughter."

"Why didn't you say anything in all these years? Why did you—you and Karl—lie to me the whole time? All those years! It is just . . . disgusting!" She looked down on him with contempt, no warmth in her eyes at all. "I only came to hear it from your mouth one more time. Do you know how I feel? As if my whole life up until now wasn't real. You robbed me of my real life!"

"I . . . I had reasons," said Johann weakly.

"What sort of reasons could someone have to deny their daughter?" Greta waved dismissively. "I don't even want to hear them. Maybe it would be better if I continued to believe that you're just some distant relative who happened to save me. Or maybe it's not even true, who knows? You're just as great a liar as you are a magician."

"I am your father."

"Prove it. How can I be certain that you're telling the truth for once?"

Johann could have told her about all the little ways in which she reminded him of himself—the looks, the gestures—or he could have shown her the heart-shaped birthmark they both carried on their right shoulders, or pointed out their shared tendency for melancholy. But then he remembered something else.

"You foresaw my death," he said. "Did you not? You foresaw my death in my hand."

Greta froze. "How do you know?"

"Because it is an ability you inherited from me, Greta. I, too, can see a person's death in their hand. It's a terrible gift. I wasn't yet eighteen when I felt it for the first time."

"Me . . . me too." Greta sat down on the stool by the bed.

"It's like a throbbing, right? Then the lines begin to glow, and an awful premonition hits you like a blow." Johann reached for her hand. "A long time ago I saw it in the hand of someone dear to me—Peter, a fiddle player and the leader of our troupe of jugglers. And I, too, didn't dare tell him the truth—just like you didn't want to tell me. Isn't that so?"

Greta nodded silently.

"Do you believe me now? I am your father. And I would understand if you walked out that door right now and never wanted to see me again. But then I wouldn't be able to set things right."

Greta looked up. "How do you think you can ever set things right?"

"By telling you all, Greta. I promise you there won't be any more secrets between us." The words came gushing out. Johann knew that it would be better for them to go their separate ways. He was a danger to Greta—to everyone who traveled with him. But he couldn't bring himself to send her away. He loved Greta more than anything else.

"I must travel to France. I will explain the reason shortly," he continued. "If you come with me, I will tell you everything. We have a long journey ahead of us, and we'll have plenty of time to talk. About Tonio, too, and . . . and about your mother."

"About my mother?" Greta looked at him darkly and with crossed arms, clearly torn. But there was real interest in her eyes now, mixed with fear of the truth.

"You better start right now," she said eventually.

~

Around the same time, Agrippa walked through the hallways of his house toward the dining room. His face was pale and sunken, as if he had aged by years in the last few days.

And maybe I have, he thought. *Everyone must pay their price.*

He didn't know what the girl wanted from Johann. But it had cost him a great deal of energy to keep up appearances in front of his friend. He wasn't fooling himself: the doctor was no idiot, and he was bound to draw his own conclusions.

Agrippa corresponded with many great men in Europe—with the king of England, with the learned abbot and student of magic Johannes Trithemius up until his death, and nowadays even with Luther—but not with Leonardo da Vinci. It was a circumstance that had always vexed him a little, but the old master simply didn't seem to care for Agrippa's scholarly discourse. It was a pity, but there was nothing he could do about it.

I hope he never finds out what I've done.

Agrippa had told Johann precisely what the man with the red cap and the rooster's feather had told him to say. During the night of Johann's fit, someone had knocked on Agrippa's door. An ice-cold breeze and the smell of sulfur had wafted into his house along with the man. He had promised that Agrippa would win the trial if he gave Johann this one piece of information.

There is a man who complains of symptoms similar to yours. His name is Leonardo da Vinci.

Agrippa knew neither whether this information was true nor what the man hoped to achieve by having it shared with Johann. And he didn't want to know why Judge Leonard was found with a broken neck the following morning, or why his wide-open eyes had looked as if he had seen the devil himself. He knew only one thing: two nights ago, evil had come to his house. He had smelled its breath and had been enormously relieved when the man left again.

All his theories had turned out to be correct. But this time the scholar couldn't find any joy in the fact. At least he had won the trial. And his renown would grow—perhaps they would still speak of him in several hundred years as one of the most intelligent men of his time.

We are more alike than you think, Johann Georg Faustus.

He paused outside the door to the dining room, his hand resting on the doorknob. He raised the hand and sniffed at his fingers, as if he could still smell the sulfur. For hours after he'd shaken hands with the man, Agrippa's hand had hurt as if it was burned.

We have a pact, Heinrich Agrippa. Never forget.

He truly liked the doctor. There was no one he could engage in more interesting conversations with. And together they had saved a woman accused of witchcraft from the pyre—the first lawyers to ever achieve such a thing. Well, with a little help. Agrippa winced as if a cold breeze had come over him. Suddenly the expression *advocatus diaboli* took on a whole new meaning.

But despite their similarities, there was one decisive difference between him and the doctor. Johann had no family. And Agrippa's family was sacred to him.

The man with the rooster's feather had made it very clear which child might next be found beneath a bridge with his throat ripped.

Agrippa opened the door and smiled when he saw his wife and the small, only just four-year-old Paul sitting at the table. What good was all the wisdom, all the knowledge, in the world if there was no one to love and no one who loved you back?

"Papa," called the boy, holding out his arms.

"Let us eat, Elsbeth," Agrippa said softly and joined his family at the table. "I am starving."

He folded his hands in prayer and asked his son to say the daily psalm from the Old Testament. Despite his young age, the boy recited the lines with a clear, sometimes halting voice, and the great scholar Heinrich Cornelius Agrippa von Nettesheim had tears in his eyes.

Act II

The River of Kings

6

GRETA LIVED THROUGH THE FOLLOWING DAYS AND WEEKS as if she'd been reborn. She came to view the last few years of her life in a different light. Her childhood, which had been nothing more than faint recollections overshadowed by blank nothingness, now seemed to her like a deep, shady valley waiting to be explored.

She rode beside the man who for years used to be her teacher, friend, and protector. But he was also her father, and the man responsible for her mother's death. He was so familiar to her, and yet she felt like she hardly knew him at all—perhaps less than ever.

"So many wasted opportunities to tell me the truth," she said to Johann one day as they rode side by side, Karl straggling behind. "Many times I saw in your eyes that you were keeping something from me. I thought it was to protect me from . . . from the terrible things that happened at Nuremberg."

"And that's the truth," Johann said. "You were just fourteen, Greta. You were deeply disturbed for weeks. Karl and I thought it better not to stir up your memories."

"I'm twenty years old now! How long were you planning to wait? I think you were just too gutless."

Greta tried hard to understand why he had kept the truth from her for so long. She thought he probably had meant to protect her, at least in the beginning. But she couldn't forgive him the long silence entirely, not him and not Karl, who had known all along. And yet she traveled to France with them.

She knew her reasons for that decision: she went because her father might die soon, and he was all the family she had, and because Karl was her only friend. And most of all because Johann was making good on his promise to tell her more about her mother, her childhood, Valentin, and also more about herself. Johann was a good storyteller who knew how to save part of the tale for the next day, and the next, and so on.

Their journey led them west toward France, where Johann hoped to learn more about his disease and the curse. They were on their way to a man Greta had heard much about. Leonardo da Vinci was even more famous than her father. Karl had told her about Leonardo's paintings, which were celebrated throughout Europe. Most impressive of all was Leonardo's reputation as an inventor. He was considered a genius, an expert in medicine and anatomy, and he had served at various courts. It was quite possible, then, that he knew something about Faust's mysterious disease.

The meltwater rushing down the mountains in March made the roads muddy and at times impassable, forcing them to take detours and sometimes travel along narrow game paths. Agrippa had organized fast horses for them and instructed them on the route to the Loire Valley. The city where Leonardo lived was called Amboise, and there was also a castle belonging to the king. They still needed to be careful of being followed, and so they traveled under false names and wore the plain pilgrims' garb they'd used on their way to Metz. They avoided hostels and thus went without warm nights and the Lorraine region's seductive-smelling food.

Greta usually sat with Faust and Karl in forest clearings in the evenings, listening to her father's tales while Karl turned the spit with a hare he had caught himself and stuffed with wild onion and herbs. There was so much she wanted to know, and Faust told her everything, even about the horrible events at Nuremberg, when Tonio del Moravia had used the fourteen-year-old Greta as bait to lure her father underground. Sometimes, as she stared into the crackling flames, images appeared before her mind's eye, pale at first but growing clearer as Johann told her more.

A high-ceilinged room like a church, chanting that rises and ebbs, a cross hanging upside down behind the altar, a girl tied down on the altar.
Me.

Since the encounter in Metz, Tonio had returned to Greta's life. And even if she didn't like to admit it, she wanted to learn more about the man with the black eyes as deep as ancient craters. Tonio had lodged himself like a thorn in

Greta's and her father's lives, and she wouldn't have a good night's sleep again until that thorn was removed.

And Greta heard everything about her mother, beautiful Margarethe.

Her father had known Margarethe since childhood. But his ambition and unscrupulousness had been the ruin of them both. It was Johann's fault that Margarethe had to burn at the stake at Worms after she gave birth to Greta in the bishop's dungeons.

"Your mother was the person I loved most in this world," muttered Johann, staring into the flames as if he could still see Margarethe there. "Her laughter was the medicine that saved me, the only remedy that had the power to rouse me from my never-ending pondering. It was her laughter that protected me many times." He looked up and smiled at Greta. "You are very much like her."

"And I'm like you, too," said Greta. "Even though I find it hard to admit."

"Well, I'm not all bad, am I?"

Her anger with her father and Karl gradually evaporated; she had known them for far too long. Only a very small, smoldering part remained. Some days, things were almost the way they used to be—but only almost.

"This gift of foreseeing someone's death in the palm of their hand—this gift I inherited from you," said Greta hesitantly. "It is a curse nearly as great as the one torturing you now."

"But death doesn't always have to follow. I've experienced that a few times— not often, to be honest, but occasionally I ran into the person again later on. They were marked by great suffering, but they lived." Johann took her hand in his, struggling with the movement because of the paralysis growing in his left arm. "Perhaps it is the same with me. If only I can succeed in stopping this accursed illness."

Greta could feel his whole body shaking, as it often did in the evenings.

"We ought to seek out Leonardo da Vinci as quickly as we can so we can learn more about your disease," said Karl from his place by the fire, leafing through his notes.

Karl had purchased a pair of those newfangled eye glasses in Metz. They were increasingly popular at monasteries and universities, and they gave him the air of a learned Adonis.

Greta surmised that his love for the doctor had prevented Karl from telling her the truth. She had reproached him bitterly at the start of their trip, and now their relationship had cooled off noticeably. But Karl was still the only friend she had.

"Although I still think Córdoba would have been better," continued Karl. "There are excellent physicians there, and Leonardo da Vinci, as much as I admire him, is no physician. He's an inventor and a painter."

"But he appears to have the same disease as me," said Johann. "Agrippa said that Leonardo knows something about it. Maybe even something"—he paused for a moment—"something about the curse."

"So you still believe it is a curse?" asked Karl skeptically.

"Oh yes, I do."

It wasn't the first time Johann and Karl had had this conversation since their departure from Metz.

Karl set down his quill. "I still struggle to believe what Agrippa told us. Tonio is the devil himself? Where is the proof? If he really is the devil, then why doesn't he just take you right here and now?"

"Even the devil must follow ancient rules," said Johann quietly. "And Tonio aside, France offers us safety from the papal sleuths."

"What secret might you have learned from Tonio or Gilles de Rais?" said Greta, staring into the fire, where blue flames danced like will-o'-the-wisps. "It must be something very special for the pope to take an interest."

Karl nodded. "An interesting question indeed."

"Whatever it is—I don't know the secret," said Johann glumly. "But either way, I'd rather have as many miles as possible between us and Lahnstein and his men."

Greta jumped when a few branches cracked in the pitch-black forest behind them; something snorted. Little Satan, who was lying next to them chewing on a bone, pricked up his ears. He had heard it, too. Some larger animal was probably making its way through the woods, like a stag or a boar.

Or something else, thought Greta, moving closer to the fire.

Days and weeks went by. They rode through Nancy, the magnificent capital of the duchy of Lotharingia, an outpost of the German Empire. Then they came to the large, vibrant market town of Bar-sur-Aube in the county of Champagne, its lanes full of bleating lambs, goats, and calves. They had crossed the border into France without even noticing. For a while now, people had been speaking the soft, poetic language Greta knew from a few songs, so different from the harsh-sounding German. Communication was arduous at first, but Greta soon found that she had a knack for learning languages. She listened when her father negotiated their quarters or bought supplies in the small towns along their route, and soon she could lead halting conversations herself.

Greta noticed that her father often gazed into the sky, growing visibly restless as soon as a swarm of birds circled above them. Ravens especially seemed to make him nervous. But when Greta asked him about it, he just waved it off.

"An old habit," he said. "I've never liked those beasts."

They swiftly trotted and cantered through the green lands of the duchy of Burgundy, the formerly large realm that used to stretch across half of Europe and which now belonged to France. If anyone asked, they were pilgrims on their way to the abbey in Fontevrault. The abbey was situated in the county of Anjou, not far from the Loire Valley, and was one of the biggest and best-known abbeys in France. It had been Johann's idea to tell people that they were a deeply religious goldsmith family from Metz, the father with his son and younger daughter. The daughter would, so their story went, remain at the abbey as a nun to fulfill a family pledge.

"The pilgrims' clothes suit you," said Karl with a wink, riding next to Greta. The two of them had become closer again. "Although I can't really picture you as a nun. A life without juggling, music, and colors—how sad!"

Greta snorted. She wore a plain brown woolen coat and a wide-brimmed hat typical for pilgrims. "Johann would love that, locking me up in a nunnery." She hardly ever called him "Father"; she found it hard to say the word. "Ever since he told me that I'm his daughter, he is even more jealous."

"You can't blame him." Karl smirked. "You're his greatest treasure."

"That is precisely how I feel. A treasure, not a person. A treasure that must be guarded. And I've got enough on my mind without a French love affair."

Greta kicked her heels into the horse's sides and galloped off.

At Gien, a pretty little town with colorful half-timbered houses and a newly erected castle, they finally reached the Loire River. They let their horses graze on the top of a hill and gazed down onto the glittering green ribbon below. Now, in spring, the river was even mightier than usual, its rippling current twirling branches, leaves, and logs. It was wider than most rivers Greta knew—almost as wide as the Rhine.

"The Loire is the biggest river in France," Johann said and raised his hand toward the south. "Its spring lies deep in the mountains, and its mouth beyond Nantes on the shores of the Atlantic Ocean. Some say the Loire is the country's main artery. In any case, it divides this vast kingdom into north and south, which might be one reason for the French kings' preference for the Loire Valley. During the long war against the Englishmen, when Paris was in the hands of the enemy, they even ruled from here." He grinned. "Even now, it is said, Francis I likes to spend more time at his beautiful castles along the Loire than in stinking old Paris. He is a passionate hunter."

"How do you know all that?" asked Greta.

Johann shrugged. "I read a lot, including those new leaflets called newspapers. Granted, there's much nonsense in them about earthquakes, falling stars, and the wrath of God. But also the odd interesting bit. At the moment it's all about the election of the new German king, since Maximilian has passed away. The French want to stay informed because their king is part of the game."

He gazed down the wide river until it disappeared behind a bend. "There really is only one way to travel the Loire Valley."

"Which is?"

"By boat, of course." Johann winked at his two companions. "And I know just where to find one. I expect you two will love the lively city. It's called Orléans. *Allez!*"

He gave his horse a slap on the hindquarters and, followed by Little Satan, rode down the hill toward the road that led west.

Johann hadn't exaggerated—Orléans was indeed a city to Greta's taste. It was not gloomy like Metz but spacious and bright, as if a different sun shone in the south.

The Loire was navigable from Orléans, and so the northern bank was crowded with moored boats and rafts of all shapes and sizes. A large bridge with an island in the middle led across the water. Greta saw with amazement how some of the ships folded down their masts to pass beneath the bridge. Behind the defensive walls of the city stood the towers of a cathedral that seemed to be unfinished. The riverside by the ships was as bustling as a fairground. The air was full of the shouting of the skippers on their vessels and the laborers carting the freight off the barges into town.

They had crossed the river at Gien, so that now they approached Orléans via the great bridge. A solid gate tower formed the entrance to the city; it was marked by soot, shot holes, and gashes that looked like wounds.

"The Englishmen tried to take Orléans several times during the war," explained Johann as they passed through the gate. "The city was an important bridgehead to gain control of the south. The fact that the English didn't succeed comes down to a single woman. Her name was Joan, daughter of the farmer Jacques d'Arc. In France, she is revered like a saint. They call her Jeanne d'Arc."

Greta remembered that in the course of their journey through Lorraine and Burgundy, she'd occasionally seen small clay figurines along the roadside. She'd assumed they were statues of Saint Mary, but now she realized they had all been dedicated to this famous Joan. Now they passed yet another memorial of her on the bridge.

"What happened to Joan?" asked Greta, gazing at the statue of the kneeling woman with armor and long hair. The statue prayed, alongside the French king, to a pietà.

"She suffered the same fate as your mother," replied Johann curtly. "The Maid of Orléans was burned on the pyre as a heretic. By the English, who thereby turned her into a martyr."

The island in the middle of the bridge was overgrown with grass and bushes and grazed by a handful of sheep. It held a hospital for pilgrims, which also contained an inn, and that was where they stayed. The rooms were plain, the pillows filled with flea-ridden straw, the windows drafty—no comparison to the lodgings the doctor usually preferred. But Johann didn't want to draw attention; it wasn't impossible that tales of him had even made it to France. They took care of their horses, left their few belongings with the landlord, and headed for the city. It was late afternoon by now, but the north bank of the river still sounded busy.

"We need to find passage on a ship that can take us all the way to Amboise," said Johann as they walked across the bridge toward the bustling port to their right. "I don't think it's far—two, three days, perhaps."

Soon they arrived at the port, where the ground was slippery from fish blood and the murky water sloshing over the bank. The smell was of spilled wine, smoke, and pungent spices that had arrived from faraway countries. Sweating day laborers lugged crates to the various boats, dodging tired-looking wagon drivers who had come from the north—some even all the way from Paris—to offload their freight here. Men gesticulated loudly, some argued, and there was noise and shouting like at a cattle market. Built directly against the city wall were numerous taverns and storehouses where barrels, crates, and bales of cloth piled up. Even though they were many miles away from the Atlantic coast, Greta felt like she was at a teeming sea harbor.

After a while they decided to split up and look separately for a ship passage. Now in spring, at the end of the long winter break, the ships were filled to capacity with freight, with no room left for passengers—or if there were any spots, they came at outrageous prices. Johann and Greta were about to head for the last few small barges west of the bridge when Karl came rushing toward them, visibly excited. At his side walked a young man whose wavy fiery-red hair stood out from the crowd. He had no hat and wore a tight-fitting leather jerkin and equally tight leather trousers. His clean-shaven face was covered in freckles. Karl introduced him to the others.

"This is John Reed, a merchant from Scotland. He's willing to take us to Amboise."

"To the end of the world if you can pay," said Reed with a wide grin, exposing two complete rows of white teeth. He spoke German with a faint British accent. "John Reed at your service. Reed as in red—you can probably guess why."

"We don't have a lot of money," said Johann, ignoring Reed's chatter. "And as far as Amboise will do. How much do you charge?"

"Your companion said you come from Metz and are on your way to Fontevrault Abbey?" said the young merchant. "Then why do you want to go to Amboise? You'd be better off traveling to Tours or all the way to Angers. I could—"

"Let that be our concern," said Johann.

John Reed eyed the travelers with curiosity, especially Greta. She noticed that the young man with the bright, mischievous eyes was of rather athletic build, his shape accentuated by the tight-fitting clothes. He was wiry and not very tall. A knife that could pass for a short sword dangled from his belt.

"My son and daughter and I are on pilgrimage," said Johann with a dignified expression, intuiting that Reed expected some sort of explanation. "My beloved wife—God rest her soul—passed away a few months ago. She asked us to atone for her and our sins at the grave of the learned Eleanor of Aquitaine at Fontevrault. But first we're going to visit relatives at Amboise. My daughter will remain at the abbey as a nun."

"What a shame," said John Reed, his eyes again scanning Greta's body. He grinned, and she noticed that his nose was slightly crooked, like from an old injury. "The world in general and men in particular will lose a veritable gem. Who knows—perhaps you'll find a wealthy gentleman at the court of the king in Amboise to wed this beauty before the doors of the abbey close forever."

Greta could feel herself blush and cursed herself for it. The fellow had that very particular kind of charming cockiness that both repulsed and attracted her. And she had to admit that he was rather easy on the eye, even if he wasn't classically handsome. The red hair and the crooked nose gave him a rakish look. Now it dawned on her why Karl had been so excited. He, too, liked the young man.

"I can pay fourteen livres for the passage," said Johann, ignoring the flattery of his daughter. "Four for each of us and two for the dog. He is a rather large animal, as you can see."

"Bloody large." John Reed scratched his red head of hair as he watched Little Satan lick his private parts. "Fourteen livres isn't much indeed, considering I'd have to leave profitable freight behind to allow for you. What the hell! I'll do it." He winked at Greta and gave a small bow. "The sight of your lovely face will more than make up for it."

"Better keep your eyes on the river so we don't have any accidents," she replied coldly. The fellow was beginning to annoy her.

"In any case," he said, still smiling, "I'll see you tomorrow at sunrise. My boat is moored near the bridge. It's the *Étoile de Mer*, you can't miss it." Reed held out his hand. "You pay half now, and the other half when we arrive at Amboise."

"You will get the first half once we're aboard tomorrow, and not a minute sooner," replied Johann. "I may be a landlubber but I'm not stupid. Good evening to you, Master Reed. We must retire to our prayers."

"Prayers, of course." John Reed grinned once more. "Then don't forget to include Saint Nepomuk in your prayers, the patron saint of skippers and raftsmen, and ask him to keep us safe on our journey. God bless you!"

For some reason Greta had the feeling that the young merchant wasn't buying their pilgrimage story. But before she could give him another look, he vanished in the crowd with one last nod.

~

That evening, Karl and Johann sat bent over a chessboard in the taproom of their lodgings. Greta decided to take a stroll through the city. Her father hadn't been particularly thrilled at the thought, but he accepted the fact that he couldn't order her around. And so he had said a grumbling farewell and asked her not to be home too late.

Orléans was a large, vibrant city, and Karl understood Greta's desire to see faces other than his and Johann's. He regretted now that he had kept the truth from Greta for so long.

As for him, he had enjoyed the journey from Metz to France, especially because there was a chance they would meet the great Leonardo da Vinci at the end of it. Karl had been fortunate enough to admire some of the master's paintings in person, including a mural at a monastery in Milan that showed Jesus and his disciples at the Last Supper. Karl revered Leonardo's technique, especially the way in which he seemed to create light as if he knew how to fetch the sun from the sky. But Karl doubted the man's abilities as a physician.

The sun had gone down by now, and smelly tallow candles were placed on the tables in the taproom. Johann and Karl had chosen a table off to the side where other patrons wouldn't disturb them, although the large black wolfhound chewing on a ham bone under the table already ensured their privacy.

Johann loved playing chess, and Karl, too, had grown to enjoy the game over the years. These days he even won every now and then, which caused the doctor to quibble and complain. Karl felt proud when he beat Faust at a game considered to be one of cool intellect and known as the game of kings. In those moments he felt closer than ever to the doctor; it was like a game of love that was carried out with pawns instead of kisses—the only form of passion Faust allowed between the two of them. They were two men completely unlike one another who got on best during a round of chess and their scientific discussions of anatomy and Leonardo's *Figura Umana*.

"Check," said Karl, sliding one of his bishops diagonally.

Johann smirked as if he had already anticipated the move. He pushed his pawn forward by one square, forcing Karl to think hard. He hadn't expected this move; the pawn was completely unprotected. He adjusted his eye glasses and leaned over the chessboard.

"This Reed," said Johann after a while, interrupting Karl's train of thought. "What do you think of him?"

"What?" Karl looked startled. "He's a handsome, bright fellow. A little loud-mouthed perhaps, but—"

Johann waved impatiently. "I want to know what you think of him, not whether you want to hop in bed with him. I saw you admiring him. Don't you go do anything stupid!" He lowered his voice. "I've told you a hundred times that your escapades will be our downfall someday. Don't forget—sodomites end up in the seventh circle of Dante's hell, together with blasphemers and usurers."

"You don't need to remind me," replied Karl, hurt by Johann's caustic reproach. "I know the Bamberg penal code as well as you. And Dante's *Inferno*."

"I'm sorry. I didn't mean to be nasty." Johann sighed and fiddled with one of the chess pieces that was already off the board. "What I meant was, Do you think Reed is trustworthy?"

Karl shrugged. "Why not? He's just a Scottish merchant who wants to earn a little extra."

"A Scottish merchant with remarkably good German," said Johann somberly. "The sum I offered is laughably low, and yet he didn't negotiate, not even a little. He agreed immediately."

"Maybe because he likes the look of Greta?" suggested Karl. "It was rather obvious that he was interested in her."

Karl hoped the doctor didn't hear the frustrated note in his voice. It wasn't the first time that Karl had an eye on a man just to watch him fuss over Greta.

"How did you meet him by the river?"

"Well, he . . . he approached me and . . ." Karl paused. He realized now that it wasn't he who had found Reed but the other way around. John Reed had asked *him* if he required passage. The smile of the handsome young man had won Karl over instantly.

"I think we ought to at least be careful," Johann said, staring at the chessboard as if their onward journey was drawn on it. "Who is to say Tonio hasn't followed us to Orléans?"

"You . . . you're saying John might actually be Tonio?" asked Karl with disbelief. "Then he would be incredibly well disguised. I mean, Reed is much younger, his hair is red, and—"

"And he's making sheep's eyes at my daughter." Johann gave a little laugh. "You're right, I'm seeing ghosts. I'm probably just jealous. Still . . ." He turned serious again. "Did the French delegate look like the same Tonio you met at Nuremberg? He might have changed his guise again, and he's a master of masquerade. Trust me, I know."

Karl said nothing. He was no longer certain whether the figure at Metz really had been the French delegate Louis Cifre. All this talk about the devil and his many faces seemed so fantastical to him—he believed in science. A new age was dawning, and what they talked about here sounded like old-fashioned superstition.

"Have you ever considered that all those stories might be the result of your own fears?" said Karl as he made his next move. "You're plagued by a terrible illness and you're looking for someone to blame. It's understandable. And now you've found the devil. But what if it is nothing but a disease? There's no evidence that Tonio is following us, and none at all that he is responsible for everything. Not one scrap!"

"He is," grumbled Johann.

"And the proof? Where is the proof? We would do better to ask ourselves why the pope is after you. Now that is a real danger, not some random ghost story about the devil."

Karl shook his head. He still couldn't understand how his master, normally the most rational person in the world, could become so entangled with the occult.

"And why should Tonio be following us in the first place?" asked Karl more gently. "Let us assume for the moment that he really did send you this curse, perhaps as a kind of reminder of your pact. Then why should he be sniffing after you like a dog? It doesn't make sense."

"Because it is not me he is after, but *her.*" Johann moved his white queen forward, close to the black king. "He is after Greta. Back then in Nuremberg, Tonio said that he could also perform the ritual with her. That he would beget a child with her. A child of the devil."

"You can't be serious," Karl hissed.

"He who dances with the devil must be ready for anything," said Johann. "I've been watching the birds in the sky. Tonio always used to send out his birds as scouts. Two crows and an old raven. I think I saw them again. And where the birds are, Tonio is never far." His gaze went into the distance. "Now make your next move."

Karl moved his rook into a new position without really thinking about it. His mind was on other things now. The doctor was slipping away from him, living more and more in his own world—a circumstance that Karl found incredibly painful. Faust was moving beyond his grasp. And Karl would have so much liked to take care of him.

"I spoke to a few people earlier about the great war that took place around here a hundred years ago," said Johann, his eyes now fixed on the chessboard. "The war is still very much in people's minds in these parts, and especially Jeanne d'Arc. Did you know that was precisely the time when Gilles de Rais was marshal of France? He was at Joan's side when she rode against the English—he was her champion."

Karl looked up. "Gilles de Rais and that martyr woman knew each other?"

"Oh yes, and more. Agrippa showed me the old records. The villain was always at her side. Later, too, during the battles of Jargeau and Patay. Her loyal liege and bodyguard. There were people who claimed the two were a couple. At the very least, Gilles was devoted to her until the day she was burned at the stake in Rouen."

"By the devil and all the saints." Karl shook his head. "Reality is sometimes more bizarre than any ghost story. I'm only glad—"

He faltered when he noticed the doctor's trembling. Johann's left hand hovered about a finger's breadth above the table, trying desperately to reach one of the chess pieces. But he couldn't do it. His arm was completely stiff.

"Your arm is paralyzed," called out Karl, loudly enough for some of the patrons to turn their heads.

"Damn," uttered Johann through clenched teeth and dropped the hand back down. Beads of sweat stood on his forehead. "Yes, in God's name, it is paralyzed. It's been coming and going for weeks. Usually it is worse in the evenings. Greta noticed a long time ago."

He fell silent, and Karl knew what they were both thinking. If the paralysis continued to spread, the doctor would soon be nothing but a stiff puppet.

"All the more reason to travel as fast as we can," gasped Johann, leaning back in his chair, his face as white as chalk. "Order wine for me."

"I don't think you should—"

"Get me wine, I said! If I can't play chess, at least I want to get drunk."

Karl was about to stand up and signal to the tavern keeper when he saw a movement behind the window. It was Greta, wildly knocking on the window with an expression of horror on her face. She looked as though she'd just seen a ghost.

~

Two hours earlier, Greta had felt free for the first time in a long while.

After saying goodbye to Karl and her father, she had strolled through the lanes of Orléans, crossed lively little squares, and walked past the many taverns and colorfully painted half-timbered houses, the sounds of city life streaming through open windows. She drank wine, drifted with the crowd, and caught scraps of French conversations. Her father was right. News of the German emperor's death had made it to France. The French king had cut short one of his many hunting parties for consultations at court—after all, he was a possible candidate for the German throne. Apparently Francis I had already paid an incredible sum of money in bribes to the German electors—money that France needed badly, and more than a few people grumbled about it.

Much of what was discussed at the taverns Greta couldn't understand, and she didn't want to eavesdrop too conspicuously. Nor did she want to engage in any sort of flirtation. Johann had asked her to take Little Satan along, but she'd said no. She would have been the center of attention with the enormous black dog by her side, and she didn't want that.

When the city gates closed, she felt like meandering along the river for a while. The setting sun painted red reflections on the current of the Loire. Greta dreamily gazed out at the mighty river, which was almost three hundred paces wide in this spot. Ships and smaller barges drifted past. Some of the young boatmen cast lascivious glances at her, and some even whistled, but Greta had only a thin smile for them. Most of those boys were younger than her and acted as if they were tough men. It was always the same—either men were still wet behind the ears or they were old and fat and overly proud of their well-filled purses. Most likely, the right man for her didn't exist. Greta thought of Agrippa's Elsbeth, his friendly, content wife and a mother. Would Greta ever have a family of her own? She felt a twinge of pain in her heart.

Perhaps I'm more like my father than I knew, and I will always be alone.

Greta was so lost in thought that she didn't notice as the houses grew more sparse. The shouts of the port workers became quieter; the moorings ended. Not far past the city, the muddy riverbank turned into marshland with reeds and cattails as tall as a man. A few startled herons took off. Dusk spread over the water and turned its rich green color first to gray and then to black.

Greta was about to turn back when she spotted something moving in the reeds. She saw a flash of red and heard furtive footsteps. She gave a little jump but told herself to relax. It was likely just that John Reed following her. He probably thought his cheeky manners and a few compliments would suffice to seduce her among the reeds. The impertinent fellow wouldn't be the first to get nothing but a bloody nose from her.

"Why don't you come on out, you coward?" she called, bracing her hands on her hips. "I know it's you, John Redhead. Didn't my father tell you that I'm going to the nunnery? You're wasting your time. But you're welcome to join me for a rosary!"

There was more rustling in the reeds nearby, the brown seed heads of the cattails swaying gently in the wind.

Then Greta realized that there was no wind. The reeds swayed because someone was moving them. Maybe there was even more than one. She began to feel a little concerned, reaching for her knife and looking all around her.

"If you think you can frighten me, you're mistaken!" she shouted into the darkness. "All you'll get from me is a bloody nose."

But all remained silent. In the distance, she could hear the noises of the port—soft laughter, shouts, and even a faint melody. Someone was playing the flute. Greta recognized the tune, surprised that someone would play an old children's song.

Susie, dear Susie, what's rustling in the straw?

Greta listened. Did the melody actually come from the port? The sound was so faint, played on a willow whistle like the type shepherds sometimes used. Suddenly she felt certain that the melody wasn't coming from the port.

But from the reeds.

Susie, dear Susie what's—

The melody broke off as abruptly as if the flute player had his throat cut. Greta kept her eyes peeled, listening. There! Another glimpse of something red among the rushes. It had to be a shock of hair, but it vanished in an instant. The reeds swayed again and a whirring sound arose, a swooshing and rushing as if a storm was swiftly approaching.

Greta suddenly wasn't so sure whether it was John Reed lurking in the reeds or . . . something else.

She started to run. She ran back along the same narrow dirt track she had followed here, the first lights of the harbor only about fifty paces away, and yet the distance seemed to stretch forever. The cattails rushed and whispered beside her as if they were talking to her.

Greta . . . Greta . . . ssstay . . . ssstay with ussss . . .

As she continued to race along in panic, she realized the reeds were moving with her! Something or someone was running alongside her, very closely, concealed by the rushes.

Ssstay with usss . . .

And there was another sound she now heard.

Panting.

Greta ran as if the devil were after her. Reeds hit her face, then suddenly she felt gravel underneath her feet followed by the slippery timber of planks. She had reached the moorings. But she didn't stop—she ran and ran and ran until she came to the first brightly illuminated tavern. Only then did she stop, doubling over and gasping for breath. Her heart was beating in her throat, almost drowning out the noise from inside the tavern. She turned around and looked at the reeds, which stood out as a black silhouette against the night sky. She thought she could still see some of the rushes move, like waving hands.

Farewell, Greta.

Greta shook herself. What was the matter with her? She wasn't usually easily frightened. But what if—

A hand grasped her by the shoulder. Greta screamed.

"Can I help you? You look like you've seen a ghost."

She spun around and saw the face of John Reed. The flickering lantern above the tavern door shone on his red hair, making it look like flames. He must have just come from the narrow alley next to the building.

Or he had been very close behind her.

Greta's hands moved to the dagger at her side.

"Thanks, I'm fine," she said, carefully glancing about. A merry group of men walked past, gawking at her. Now she was glad of it, because at least she wasn't alone with the creepy Scotsman.

John's face darkened. "Listen, lass, I don't know what you think of me, but I'll tell you one thing: I'm not one of those men who helps themselves to a woman like a cow or a sheep." He gave a smirk. "And you're not *that* pretty. Don't flatter yourself, princess." He saw the knife in her hand and frowned. "Christ, how suspicious can ye be? I should be glad you didn't cut me down like a common thief."

The door to the tavern opened and a young, slightly drunken man looked about searchingly. When he saw John with Greta, he grinned.

"Ah, that's what's been keeping you," he said with a laugh. "We thought you must have fallen down the outhouse hole." He winked at the two of them. "You two going to be much longer? Then I'll just roll the dice for you, John."

"No, the two of us are quite done," said John brusquely, giving Greta a nod. "See you in the morning, princess. Better put that letter opener away before you hurt yourself." Then he followed the other man back into the tavern.

Greta stood as if rooted to the spot. She felt terribly stupid. She'd immediately assumed that it had been John Reed hiding by the river, when all this time he had been playing dice at the tavern. Or had he gone outside a while ago and followed her? But then his friends would have come looking for him sooner. Greta sighed. She no longer knew what to believe.

As she slowly walked back to the inn where her father and Karl waited, she continuously had the feeling that she was being followed. But every time she spun around there was nothing. No man, nothing red.

Red.

Greta held her breath and stopped.

Just as she arrived at the inn and saw the outlines of Karl and her father sitting at a table behind the windows, she realized who else the red head might have belonged to.

Kiss my scaly hand . . . farewell, Greta.

And then she remembered how she knew the melody that she'd heard by the reeds.

"It was Tonio! I saw Tonio!"

Greta stared at the two men, her eyes flickering. Johann hadn't seen his daughter this terrified in a long time—not since she'd been locked up in a jail below Nuremberg as a fourteen-year-old girl. With trembling hands she clutched a cup of wine.

Greta had stormed into the taproom moments after knocking on the window. Now she was sitting at their table, white-faced, her dress drenched in sweat despite the cold night. Johann gathered from her hasty words that someone had followed her. It seemed that his worst fears were coming true.

Tonio was reaching out for his daughter! The shock was so profound that it suppressed another fit.

"I told you it was too dangerous to walk about by yourself," groused Johann, trying not to show how afraid he was. "And no one said you could hang about the harbor. Why didn't you at least take the dog?"

"Don't talk to me as if I'm a child," she retorted. "You can't order me around."

Johann was about to reply but stopped himself. At least Greta was still defiant, despite the bad fright.

"I know it was a mistake to go into the wetlands," she admitted. "But I couldn't know—"

"What makes you think it was Tonio?" asked Karl.

"It was his red cap. The same cap he wore as a French delegate and later in Metz. Remember, Karl? At first I thought it was that John Reed following me, but then . . ." She shuddered.

"What is it?" asked Johann.

"I heard a song in the rushes, very softly," she whispered. "Someone played it on a flute. It was a children's song, and suddenly I remembered."

"Remembered *what*?" asked Karl with growing frustration.

Greta just clutched the cup with the steaming spiced wine.

Johann thumped his fist on the table impatiently, causing a few people at the other tables to turn their heads. "Speak up! What did you remember?"

"Back in Nuremberg," Greta said. "You know how someone lured me underneath the bridge near the Hospital of the Holy Ghost, to the dead child? Where the guards found me with the talisman in my pocket and arrested me. There was a man by the river . . . and he played a flute. He played the same song." Greta looked up and locked eyes with Johann. "It was Tonio, both times. I had forgotten the encounter at Nuremberg. I *wanted* to forget. But I recognized him by the song. And he hummed it later, too, in the prison cell, when he made me drink the potion. He said that if Faust didn't come, then . . ."

"Then he'd take you in my stead," muttered Johann. "That goddamn pied piper."

"And you're completely certain that you didn't imagine it all?" asked Karl. "I mean, the rushing in the reeds, whispering and whistling. It could have been the wind. The howling of the wind sometimes sounds just like a willow whistle. And our own fears do the rest."

Johann shook his head. "No, I believe it truly was Tonio. That evil creature followed us. For some reason he wants to prevent us from visiting Leonardo da Vinci. But he won't stop us. Not if we—" He went to squeeze Greta's hand, when he realized that he couldn't move his arm.

"What is it?" asked Greta, worried.

"The paralysis," whispered Karl. "It's progressing."

Johann said nothing. He had sworn to Greta that he wouldn't lie to her again—and yet he had done it. He had told her that sometimes a person whose death he'd foreseen didn't end up dying. He had said it to lend courage to his daughter, to leave her with some hope. But it wasn't the truth.

The lines of the palm always showed the future.

He would die.

The only glimmer of hope he had left was Leonardo da Vinci. If Agrippa was right and the great artist was grappling with the same disease, he might be able to help.

Maybe Leonardo also entered a pact with Tonio. Maybe he knows how we might beat the devil.

"We don't have much time left," said Johann with a glance at his left arm, hanging limply at his side like a dead piece of meat. "Let's hope that John Reed has a fast boat. The game begins. *Rien ne va plus.*"

With one jerking move he swiped all the chess pieces off the table.

∼

In the shadow of a wall stood a man, licking his lips. The dampness of the nocturnal fog had made his makeup run, revealing wrinkly skin, sunken features, and two maliciously gleaming eyes like glowing pieces of coal inside a skull. The man's palate was dry; his tongue felt like a withered old root. Perhaps that was what it had been for years. Nothing but an old root. The man was waiting for news from his winged messengers. He looked up once more and finally spotted three black dots moving toward him in the sky.

"Azazel, Baphomet, Belial!" called out the master. "There you are! Why did you take so long?"

The birds cawed and landed on the outstretched arm of the master. Their beaks clattered as if they were speaking to him. The master closed his eyes and nodded.

"Very well," he said after a while. "Everything is going to plan. Everything— what is it?" The birds flapped their wings restlessly and the master laughed. "Of course, you're hungry. How thoughtless of me. We all need something to eat and to drink—hunger is chewing through my innards, too."

Almost lovingly he set down the raven and the two crows, who instantly started bickering over a rotten fish. The master watched them with amusement.

"We need better meat. Much better. And younger."

He pursed his lips and whistled a song.

Susie, dear Susie, what's rustling in the straw?

"Let us go hunting." Like a phantom he peeled from the shadows and started moving down the lane where the houses huddled closely. Lights still burned behind many of the widows. "Mmmh, I can smell them in their soft little beds. Can you smell them, too?"

The birds cawed, and the master chuckled with relish. "The sky is heavy with fresh grapes. How do they say? *Vivre comme Dieu en France!*"

7

THE GOBLET MADE OF THE FINEST VENETIAN GLASS WENT flying through the air and landed precisely on the breasts of the dainty, half-naked dancer, shattering into a thousand pieces. Red streaks ran down her skin, a mix of blood and wine. Shaking and crying, the woman cowered on the ground, shielding her head with her arms for fear of further attacks.

"That isn't dancing, that is just wild leaping about! The monkeys in my menagerie can do better."

Pope Leo X had risen from his throne and was looking around for other missiles. Thankfully, the servants had swiftly removed all other drinking vessels. The pontiff's outbursts were legendary, but they always fizzled out as quickly as they arrived. The assembled Vatican court held its breath; servants, courtiers, and even the musicians had taken a few steps back, isolating the young woman on the floor as if she had a contagious disease. Even Leo's jester was silent, which didn't happen often. Next to the pope, the Spanish ambassador Don Arturo de Acuña cleared his throat. He seemed to be the only person brave enough to stand up to the most powerful ruler in Christendom.

"Holy Father, I beg you," he said. "Please consider your heart."

"Get that wench out of my sight before I feed her to my panthers," growled Leo, already a little calmer. His throne with the silken baldachin was standing in one of the many courtyards of the Cortile del Belvedere, where the pope received important foreign guests like the Spanish ambassador, who was seated next to him, albeit a little lower.

Leo reached for a bowl with chilled candied fruit and leaned back into his cushions adorned with peacock feathers. His throne was surrounded by cages filled with screeching parrots, dozing lions and leopards, monkeys baring their teeth, one mangy bear, and one so-called giraffe, which looked like a spotted donkey with a ridiculously long neck.

Leo was enormously proud of his menagerie. Many of the animals were gifts of noblemen, cardinals, and prince-bishops—from rulers far and wide who wanted to demonstrate their devotion to the pope and incidentally secure their living. Leo adored each one of his animals. His favorite used to be the elephant Hanno, a gift from the Portuguese king Emanuel I. Sadly, the white giant died of constipation a few years ago, after the physicians administered a laxative enriched with gold. The rhinoceros that had been sent as a replacement had gone down with the ship on its way to Rome, much to the pope's dismay.

He preferred animals to people, as the latter only ever tried to betray him or fawn and curry favor. This de Acuña was no exception. In an attempt to make the pope well disposed toward him, the Spanish ambassador had presented him with five precious parrots from the New World. The birds paid homage to him in five different languages—not a bad idea from the Spanish Habsburgs. But Leo knew the real reason for de Acuña's visit.

"To be honest, I am glad we finally get some time to engage in a proper conversation," said the ambassador in a honeyed voice. "As much as I love your shows. ¡Por Dios! They are like perfect works of art."

"Well, art is long! And life is short and fleeting," replied Leo. "If you have something to say—out with it."

De Acuña lowered his gaze. "As always, you are right, venerable father." He wore a tight, bodice-like tunic with a ruff on his neck, as was fashionable among the Spaniards. His decorative épée would at the most be useful for killing a rat. "Have you put any more thought into the matter of the imminent election of the German king?"

Leo smiled thinly. "Since when does the pope get a vote in that election?"

"Perhaps not a vote as such, but your word carries a lot of weight," replied de Acuña cautiously. "The prince-bishops especially look to you for guidance."

"You know my opinion," said Leo curtly, watching as some Swiss guards finally dragged the bawling dancer away. De Acuña was right. Following Emperor Maximilian's death back in January, it was time to choose a new king of the Germans. The king was elected by the seven electors—the most powerful men in the country—and three of those were bishops, allies of the pope. But Leo had indicated a long time ago that he favored the French king Francis I instead of Maximilian's grandson Charles. With a Habsburg emperor on the throne who ruled Spain and the German lands as well as northern Italy, Rome would be in a dangerous position.

"Perhaps His Holiness would consider more gifts—" started de Acuña.

"More parrots?" Leo laughed out loud. "Let's not fool ourselves, dear de Acuña. Young Charles needs all the money in the world right now if he wants to sway the election in his favor. And as far as I have heard, the Fuggers are divided over the question of advancing any more funds to the Habsburgs."

The pope nibbled on grapes and signaled for the musicians to play on, allowing him to close his eyes and think. There were things that were more important to him than the imperial election. Only that morning a messenger had arrived with a new letter from his representative, reporting that Viktor von Lahnstein was still looking for Johann Georg Faustus and that they were following a lead west. Leo still struggled to believe how that crafty doctor had managed to escape at Altenburg Castle—in front of half the empire! Faust had thumbed his nose at all of them. Since then, Lahnstein was in pursuit of the doctor, who seemed to have gone into hiding in France, of all places. Leo's time was running out. And instead of the distraction he so direly needed, he was forced to listen to de Acuña's greasy flattery.

"Have you heard of the events at Bamberg?" asked Don de Acuña now. He tried to sound casual, but Leo heard the glee. "This Doctor Faustus everyone is talking about, he made a right fool of you. The beast from the apocalypse will soon rule in Rome." He chuckled. "The nerve of it!"

"This doctor will receive his just punishment," hissed Leo. "Don't you worry about that."

"Are you sure? I hear he has vanished without a trace—just like a real magician. And apparently that isn't the only skill he has mastered," added the Spaniard ominously.

"What . . . what do you mean?" Leo's head spun around; the music and the laughter of the others suddenly seemed far away.

What do you know?

Don de Acuña shrugged his shoulders innocently. "Faust is a magician, an astrologer, and an alchemist, too. Someone like that is difficult to catch. His skills are manifold." He rose and bowed low. "Please excuse me. It's been a long day."

Leo held out his fleshy fingers, and de Acuña kissed his ring. As the Spanish ambassador walked away past the silver lion cages and aviaries, the pope's gaze followed him.

What do you know? What do the Habsburgs know?

Damn, it was high time for Lahnstein to find that doctor before someone else did. Time was running out. He needed the doctor here in Rome—now!

Leo fell back into his cushions with a sigh. He craved diversion, and something better than that silly dance. The tune had sounded rather heathen—not to mention the way she had twisted her body. Though he had to admit that the girl had a pretty figure. Those small, firm breasts, almost like lemons.

"Why do you throw a tantrum when such a cute little thing dances just for you?" said a voice behind him. "Is your formerly proud manhood waning? Are you angry because nothing stirred underneath the papal gown but hot air?"

"How dare you!" Outraged, Leo turned around only to realize it was his jester, Luvio, who had sneaked up to him from behind and now waved his tambourine.

The jester bowed low, making his absurdly large hunchback and the ridiculously garish costume stand out even more. "Always at your service, Your Holiness, with jest and foolishness."

Leo smiled for the first time that day. At least good old Luvio had recovered. He'd been worried the wart-covered ugly fool would die from that marsh fever that had brought half of Rome to a standstill over the winter. There had been hundreds of deaths, and Luvio had spent several weeks in the hospital. But his jester always bounced back.

Just like me.

The pope took a deep breath and listened to the music, a cheerful rondo played with flutes, harps, and violins, and much more familiar than those shrill tunes from earlier. The gentle notes soothed him. His fate was prescribed—he would enter history as the pope who led Rome back to its former glory. And neither Habsburg nor France could change that. Surely, he had been mistaken. Don de Acuña knew nothing. How could he?

He leaned down to Luvio. "You're right, my fool," he said quietly. "I was overpowered by anger."

Luvio grinned. "Fools always speak the truth, Your Holiness. Just like whores."

"Make sure that little whore is brought to my bedchamber tonight. I will prove to you and her that a mighty storm still rages beneath my gown. You will hear her screams right through Castel Sant'Angelo."

The jester jingled his bells and bowed once more. "Oh, I don't doubt it."

The music ended with one last beat of the drum.

~

Holding a well-used deck of cards, Greta sat on a chest at the rear of the boat and let the cards slide through her fingers. She only ever moved one card, and the rest seemed to follow as if by magic. Then Greta picked up the entire deck, bent it, and let it go so that the cards went flying through the air with a hissing sound. She cleverly caught the deck with her other hand.

"Not bad. I used to be able to do that. I believe I was one of the first. I used to perform it for your mother. There weren't many printed playing cards around then, but the church screamed bloody murder, calling it the devil's game."

Greta looked up. Johann had come over soundlessly and now stood there smiling at her. She still struggled to view him as her father. To her, he was one of the smartest and most learned men in the world, famous and notorious, the hero of many tales both true and false. But her father? How much did they have in common? She feared it was more than she cared to admit.

"I've been practicing this trick for a long time," said Greta, putting the cards away. "I'm surprised you only noticed now."

They stood together in silence, gazing out at the river that rolled lazily through the landscape like a huge snake, past woods, gentle hills, villages, and distant castles. It was almost noon; they'd been traveling for a few hours since their departure from Orléans. The Loire Valley was as lovely as if God had put in a special effort during its creation, but Greta struggled to see its beauty. Her mind was still preoccupied with last night's eerie encounter. Had it really been Tonio stalking her in the reeds? After she'd gone to bed she dreamed of a creature with eyes as deep as craters reaching out for her with its scaly hand. The face of the creature had changed all of a sudden, turning into that of her father, who dragged her into the abyss.

Kiss my scaly hand, my dear. We are going to change the world.

She had woken with a scream, drenched with sweat and the bitter taste of ash in her throat. At the same time she had felt strangely excited and aroused. What was this Tonio doing to her?

Johann's left arm still hung limply at his side. When he noticed Greta's look, his smile died.

"It hasn't gotten worse, if that's what you're wondering. But not better, either. I entreated Reed to go faster—I even offered him more money—but he doesn't want to. Reckons we have to spend the night at Blois anyhow, because he's picking up more freight. Maybe we should have taken the horses." Johann sighed. "Too late now."

They had sold the horses at Orléans because they couldn't bring them aboard the *Étoile de Mer*, as Reed had named his boat ostentatiously. It was nothing more than a shallow, single-masted barge, ten paces long; it had seen better days. There were patched-up holes and the timber was worm-eaten, and the crew consisted of three somber-looking fellows who treated Karl, Johann, and Greta as if they were only more crates and cloth bales. They did respect Little Satan, though, and tried to avoid him—not an easy feat on a small boat. The young man John had played dice with the night before wasn't part of the crew. These men seemed more like grim soldiers than boatmen.

John wasn't nearly as jovial as the day before, and he hadn't looked at Greta once. Most of the time he stood at the prow with a long pole, checking for shallow patches. Greta was sorry about how she had treated John the previous night. She had acted like a stupid little girl.

But none of that mattered. What mattered was what lay ahead.

"What do you intend to do once we reach Amboise?" she asked her father. "It's not going to be easy to meet Leonardo da Vinci in person. He is a famous, busy man."

Johann shrugged; the gesture came out looking rather helpless with the limp arm. "I am famous and busy, too. We'll see who people are still talking about in a hundred years." He smiled thinly. "I just hope the great Leonardo will grant me an audience. I've been keeping an ear out. They say the French king is crazy about him. Francis I brought Leonardo from Rome to the Loire a few years ago and gave him the magnificent manor house where the king spent his own childhood. It is called Château du Cloux, even though it isn't a real castle."

Johann gazed at the opposite bank. Greta wondered if he scanned the reedy edge for possible threats.

"When the king resides at Amboise, he sees Leonardo almost every day," continued Johann. "Francis treats Leonardo as if the artist were his father. You're right, it won't be easy to get an audience." He clenched his teeth and held on to the railing with his right hand. "But I must try. This book Leonardo wrote . . ."

"The *Figura Umana*?"

Johann nodded. "It proves that Leonardo has studied the human body intensively, probably more than most scientists. He is a true genius. I browsed through it again last night. Believe me, if there's anyone who can tell me what this accursed disease is about and whether there's anything we can do against Tonio, it is Leonardo da Vinci. I should have sought him out much sooner."

Johann's eyes turned to the sky, where clouds collided like huge dragons. "No birds," he said with relief. "Maybe we managed to shake him."

Instead of explaining, her father gently touched Greta with his hand. "I'm going to sit down for a while. I'm tired. I think we should reach Blois in about two hours. Let's hope Reed hurries up."

He gave her an encouraging smile and walked over to Karl.

Greta's eyes followed him. She thought her father had aged in the last few years, not so much on the outside, but inwardly. He looked as though something was consuming him from the inside, some sort of parasite that grew stronger as he grew weaker. Greta thought of the lines in Faust's hand that faded more and more, and of the throbbing she had felt and the dark aura she had seen in his palm.

Who are you really, Father? And what is your connection with Tonio?

To take her mind off things, she walked past the many chests, bales, and crates to the front of the boat where John Reed was sitting. His strong arms held the pole he used to detect shoals. She watched him for a while before clearing her throat.

"I want to apologize," she said.

He said nothing at first, staring into the water as if something extremely fascinating was floating by. Then, without looking up, he asked, "What for?"

"For acting like a fool last night. You aren't a common thief or one of those men who prey upon young girls in the night."

"Oh, now you're doing me another injustice. I'm definitely a rascal." John looked up and Greta saw the mischief in his grin. "I think it's in my blood. The Scottish are a small, stubborn people, forever careful to keep our bigger neighbor at bay with wit and cunning. But I know just how you can make it up to me." He put down the pole and stood up.

Greta hesitated. "And how is that?"

"First, don't talk to me like I'm some sort of fop—I'm John, plain and simple, John. Got it?" He held out his hand and smiled, showing his white teeth again. "Second, you and I are going out for a cup of wine in Blois. I know a cozy little pub where they cook a stew almost as good as in the Scottish Highlands. Simple, soggy, and salty—no frills, unlike most grub you get in this land of frog eaters and oyster slurpers."

"All right," replied Greta, laughing. "On one condition." She gestured toward Johann, who was just throwing a piece of meat to Little Satan, who caught it and swallowed it with one big gulp. "The dog comes along. Little Satan will make sure no harm befalls me."

John's eyebrows shot up. "The dog is called Little Satan?" He laughed out loud. "The devil watches over the nun. For heaven's sake. Well, I'm sure we'll both be very safe."

They arrived at Blois in the early evening. After one last bend in the river, the hills suddenly opened up, and Greta's eyes beheld a city so beautiful that she thought she was dreaming. If Orléans had been stunning, then Blois was the definition of royal pomp. Sitting enthroned above the Loire was a large, three-winged castle with oriels and little towers, its rows of glass windows reflecting the sunlight. The castle was surrounded by gardens landscaped in terraces. The houses down by the river were tiled with slate, and several flights of wide steps led to a large church and more houses. Through the evening haze Greta could make out palatial buildings that probably belonged to noblemen or court officials. There seemed to be nothing ugly in this city—no poverty, no malice, and no dirt.

Karl, too, appeared to be impressed.

"Think about the holes we call castles and towns back home," he muttered as the boat navigated toward the other vessels in the harbor. Many of them had hoisted the flag of the French king, depicting a fire-spitting salamander. "All those dirt-poor German knights in their drafty keeps. The nobility here truly knows how to live. *Savoir-vivre*—that's what they say about the French."

"Not bad, huh?" John grinned. He was standing at the prow with a rope in his hand, ready to dock when the boat reached the moorings. "You'll see more of those castles in the coming days. The valley is full of them. But Château de Blois certainly is one of the most beautiful. Blois was the main residence of the previous king, Louis XII. Francis I also comes to stay a lot, but I think he prefers Amboise. His wife, Claude, spent her childhood at Blois."

"Spare us your commentary," said Johann abruptly. "All I want to know is how long we're going to stay here."

"At least until midday tomorrow. I have business to take care of. You can attend early mass at Saint Nicolas Church and touch the relics of Saint Laudomar, considering you're a pious pilgrim. The saint was said to be a grumpy hermit—just to your taste." John winked at the doctor, who ignored the jest.

Greta had told her father that she was going to a tavern with John that evening. Johann hadn't been thrilled, but when she assured him that she would take the dog, he had given his consent—he knew he couldn't stop her, anyway.

"You'll do it whether or not I say you can," he'd answered. "But please be careful."

The crew tossed the ropes ashore, where a handful of laborers caught them and pulled the boat parallel against the dock. A plank was extended, and the ostensible pilgrim family went ashore. They left their few belongings on the boat, where the crew would also be staying. They were immediately assailed by enterprising locals trying to sell them a room at an inn, but John fobbed them all off.

"You're staying at the Hotel Tambour," he said decisively. "It's the best you'll get if you don't want to spend too much. Follow me."

A few royal soldiers hung about the port and unenthusiastically checked the newly arrived wares. The harbormaster sat at a table and noted down the freight. The unshaved man with his red-and-blue officer's cap had nothing but a tired glance for the three travelers. Karl and Johann were walking ahead when Greta noticed a crowd of people down by the shore a little off to the side, close to the fishing vessels. She could hear loud wailing and crying, and then a woman screamed out. Greta stopped and listened.

"What is going on there?" she asked.

"Hmm, an accident, perhaps?" John squinted but couldn't make out much in the evening light. He walked down to the group and returned a short while later with a sad expression on his face.

"They fished a dead child out of the water," he explained. "A little boy. Apparently he's from a village up the river. It looks as though the poor lad got caught in a net and drowned. His mother just arrived."

Another scream rang out, and Greta shuddered. The woman cried and wailed, and now they could make out words between the sobs.

"*L'ogre!*" she lamented. "*Mon Dieu, l'ogre mange nos enfants! L'ogre!*"

Greta's French was good enough by then to understand the gist of what the woman was saying.

"'The ogre eats our children'?" She turned to John. "What is that supposed to mean?"

John shrugged. "I'm a Scotsman, not French. Probably an expression for when the Loire claims a child. It happens from time to time—children play by the river, run about while their mothers do the washing . . ." He turned away and started to walk up toward the city gate. "Enough of the ghost stories. Blois is a royal residence, remember? Sadness is prohibited under penalty of death."

As they followed John, they heard the mother cry out once more, a high-pitched, shrill scream like from a dying animal.

Not much later, Greta and John sat in a tavern with an earthen bowl between them, the brown, viscous contents of which John hungrily devoured. Under the table, Little Satan waited for the occasional spoonful. The meal had an unpronounceable name, but its main ingredients appeared to be tough ram, offal, pearl barley, and turnips, all simmered over the fire for several hours. Not even the many herbs—Greta thought she tasted a little mint—could overpower the dish's musty smell.

John had been so excited about this meal, but she struggled to like it. She stirred her spoon around the bowl, not feeling any appetite, and nibbled on some hard barley bread. She didn't say much, which wasn't John's fault—the young merchant tried very hard to please her, and not entirely unsuccessfully. He was charming, talkative without being obtrusive, and, despite his crooked nose and the freckles, rather handsome. If Greta was entirely honest with herself, she had grown fond of the young swashbuckler, even if she'd never tell him that. John thought much too highly of himself as it was.

The tavern was located amid a maze of small, steep lanes near a church on one of the hills Blois had been built upon. John had pointed out the carvings on the front of the house as they'd entered, including the figures of jugglers and musicians. The tavern was called Le Coq Rouge and appeared to be popular among the locals; there was much laughter and even music. But Greta couldn't get in the mood, because every time the flute player started a new song, she was reminded of the song from the reeds the previous night.

Susie, dear Susie, what's rustling in the straw?

And there was something else she couldn't stop thinking about.

"This dead boy," she said, cutting off John as he once more praised the smelly stew. "I can't stop thinking about the mother's words. 'The ogre eats our children.' You know what it means, right? I could see it in your face."

"*Touché.*" John sighed and put down his spoon. "I didn't want to frighten you with old tales. I thought it wouldn't be a good start for a merry evening together. But, very well, if you really want to know: the ogre is an ancient mythical creature. They say he eats little children. He makes jewelry from their bones and wears their skulls around his neck. Parents in the Loire Valley use his tale to frighten their children." He raised a finger and made his voice sound low and menacing. "If you're not good and don't eat up your salty stew, the ogre will come and swallow you whole."

"That's not a joking matter," said Greta. "Do . . ." She hesitated. "Do children often die in this area?"

"How do you mean?" John looked confused. "Well, no more than elsewhere, I guess. But now that you mention it . . ."

Greta felt the hair on her neck stand on end. "Yes?"

"I remember hearing some horror stories—a little farther southwest, though. Toward Brittany. I heard merchants talking about missing children being found with their throats slit open. They said that there wasn't a drop of blood left in their bodies, as if someone had sucked them out like an oyster." John shook his head. "That's nonsense, of course. Most likely, those children fell victim to some scoundrels. The woods are full of bad fellows, madmen and lepers. Or they were taken by slave traders. It happens—the Atlantic Ocean isn't far."

"How long has that been going on?" asked Greta.

"How should I know? I've been going up and down the Loire for years. You hear all sorts of things." John frowned. "Why are you so interested?"

"You're probably right—not a good topic of conversation for our evening together. Especially not with oversalted, tough ram stew." Greta tried to smile, but it came out a little crooked. "Please don't be offended if I'm not raving about your meal, in spite of your enthusiasm."

John laughed. "The look on your face when the bowl hit the table said enough. Scottish cuisine is perhaps a little peculiar. But you can make it up to me by not talking about such awful matters anymore."

"Agreed." Greta nodded. But her mind continued to churn. Could those gruesome incidents be connected with Tonio? She thought about the missing children at Metz, the dead girl under the bridge, and the monster drinking her blood. But the murders John told her about seemed to have happened a while ago. If Tonio had been following them to France all this time, it couldn't have been him. She decided not to mention anything to Johann for now. Maybe Karl was right and she was seeing ghosts where there were none. Karl was the only sensible one among them.

He and John.

She pushed the bowl of cold stew aside. "I'm full. If you don't mind, I could really do with some fresh air."

"Not at all. I don't like the dessert here, anyhow. Beer sweetened with honey." John grinned and picked a piece of meat out from between his teeth. "I don't think you'd like it. And I admit that the stew has been better. They didn't put enough kidney in, and the ram was probably older than the lambs of Abraham." He stood up. "Let's go outside. I want to show you a place that you'll never forget. It'll take your mind off things."

He took her by the hand and led her outside, the dog trailing quietly. Greta was surprised how willingly she followed John. Just last night she'd feared that he might pounce on her like a common thief, and now she walked with him through the dark alleys of Blois. But she felt safe at his side. The encounter in the reeds near Orléans had shown her that Tonio and her nightmares could haunt her anywhere. She saw the glowing windows of the castle in the distance, dozens of them, and Greta wondered how many candles were burning inside.

As many as there are stars in the sky, she thought. *What a wondrous valley this is—divine and devilish at once.*

"Where are we going?" she asked John, but he merely smiled enigmatically.

"It's a surprise. You will like it."

They were headed straight toward the castle on the opposite hill. When they reached the lower walls, John turned and walked along the wall until they came to an ivy-covered older part. John pushed the ivy aside, and Greta saw there was a gap behind it, just wide enough for a person to slip through.

With a grin, John held up a half-chewed bone he'd been hiding in his pocket. "If the old ram isn't much good for anything else, at least it'll keep the dog occupied for a little while."

He tossed the bone into the air, and Little Satan caught it nimbly. He immediately settled down to chew on it. Meanwhile, John slipped through the gap, and a moment later Greta heard his voice from the other side.

"Your turn."

Greta felt like she was ten years old again. A faded memory came to her mind. She had lived with Valentin in Nuremberg at the Order of the Teutonic Knights, and sometimes a boy her age, the son of a girdle maker, visited her by climbing over the wall of the commandery. Together they had roamed the lanes of Nuremberg by night—the dirty yards, the bridges, the deserted cemeteries. At John's side she felt like a little girl again.

And just like back then, you're doing foolish things.

She followed John though the gap and found him waiting on the other side. They were standing among boxwood bushes looking like fantastic beasts in the light of the moon. Further on, Greta could see rosebushes bearing the first buds. The air smelled of flowers and spring. A chilly breeze swept through the bushes, but Greta wasn't cold.

"The royal garden," explained John in a whisper. "I found the hole in the wall not long ago."

"And how many girls have you brought here since?" jeered Greta, trying, unsuccessfully, to sound confident. She allowed John to lead her past the rosebushes and freshly raked flower beds to a brick wall as high as her hips. On the other side, the land dropped steeply, and the Loire gleamed below them like a ribbon of black silk. Above the garden, the stars and the moon seemed to compete with the sparkling lights of the castle. John looked at her.

"Did I promise too much?"

He grasped her hands and pulled her close. Greta hesitated. How dare he? Did he believe she'd let him take her like some sort of hussy? But then she just let go. So many awful things had happened in the last few weeks, so much death and suffering, but this park here seemed to be a different world—a better, safer world, where she was protected by John Reed, this red-haired braggart of a Scotsman with his crooked nose and flashing eyes. He gave her the feeling that there was a normal life beyond all the horrible things that had been going on. She smelled his sweat and it reminded her of a young fox. Then her lips found his.

"I . . . I'm not one of those, you know . . . ," said Greta between kisses.

John chuckled softly. "Neither am I. That's one thing we have in common."

His tongue was wet and demanding, toying with her, and she let herself fall. It was as if John was taking away all her fears from the last few days and weeks. In his arms she could forget everything—Tonio del Moravia, her father, the horrible things she'd seen, and her fear of the future.

If she really had to, there would be plenty of time tomorrow to regret her weakness.

8

THEY HAD ONLY ABOUT TWENTY MILES TO GO UNTIL Amboise, but Johann felt like it was an eternity. Every single mile stretched as if they were fighting their way through muddy swamps. Fog covered the river, bathing the landscape in a milky white that seemed to swallow everything.

Shortly after their departure from Blois, Johann had walked to the boat's prow and gazed ahead, as if he could somehow speed up their journey. Once he thought he saw an old raven with ruffled feathers in a willow tree, but he could have been mistaken. Back then, many years ago, Tonio had him followed by his crows and the raven, and it wasn't impossible that he was doing so again.

Hundreds of doubts and worries raced through Johann's mind. What if Leonardo wasn't currently at Amboise? What if he didn't want to receive Johann? And even if he managed to get through to the old genius, who was to say that Leonardo knew anything about this accursed disease—if he was still sick at all? Maybe da Vinci's illness had passed by now like an upset stomach, and the whole journey was for nothing.

And Johann's strength waned with every day, with every hour.

How much time do I have left? Who is going to look after Greta when I'm no longer around? Karl? I'll have to talk to him.

Johann hated depending on others. He had always been free and made his own decisions. But now he needed help. His paralysis had become worse overnight. His left arm was nothing but a dead piece of meat, and he felt as though his facial expressions sometimes froze for brief moments. He hoped Greta hadn't yet noticed how poorly he was doing. It wouldn't do any good if she worried even more. Although she appeared to be preoccupied with something else.

Or rather someone else.

Johann now and then glanced to the back, where Greta stood beside John, flirting. Johann had noticed that their demeanor had changed since the previous night, even though they tried to hide it. There were certain moments between them, smiles, furtive touches. At least Amboise was near, and therewith the end of their journey on the *Étoile de Mer*.

Farewell forever, John Reed.

"If looks could kill, our John would long be floating in the river. But I guess that's the difference between you and a real sorcerer."

Karl had stepped beside Johann. The younger man smiled thinly. "I was afraid Greta might like the boy. I know her taste. He's got that little something. He may not be a Greek god, but he makes up for it with wit and charm."

"Only yesterday you thought he was rather handsome, didn't you?" said Johann grumpily. "To be honest, I would rather the fellow were dallying with you, not with my daughter. I told you I don't trust the guy farther than I can spit. I never should have left them alone last night."

"You forget once more that Greta is no longer a child," said Karl with a twinkle in his eye. "And you kept the secret of your paternity from her for too long to have any say in her life. Besides, I think you're too suspicious. John might be a flirt, but—"

"Well, we won't have to worry about him for much longer," said Johann, turning away brusquely.

It was true, he mistrusted Reed. But the truth was, he was also consumed by jealousy. While he slowly rotted alive, his daughter amused herself with this ginger fop. He had never before felt this helpless. A cripple without a plan. What had become of the famous Doctor Faustus and his great mind always devising a solution?

A fanfare tore him from his daydreams. It had come from somewhere in the fog in front of them. A second fanfare followed, and emerging from the fog on the left bank was another castle, the biggest one so far. It stood on a terrace-like elevation and looked splendid with its towers, crenellations, and large windows, just like Blois and other castles they'd seen along the way. The buildings seemed familiar to Johann. Evidently, the French kings had sent for architects from Italy but also added their own twists, something dreamy that went well with the swamps and the milky sun under which the Loire ran its course. Fairy-tale castles—beautiful and eerie at once.

Amboise, thought Johann, his heart beating faster.

The harbor was just as bustling as the ones at Orléans and Blois. Johann could hardly wait for the boat to be tied up. When they finally stopped moving, he picked up his bundle and handed Reed a few coins.

"I thank you. We will no longer require your services."

John looked astonished. "So fast? Why don't you at least wait until—"

"I'm afraid we can't put off the visit to our relatives any longer. I hope your business will continue to go well."

Johann briefly raised his pilgrim's hat and walked ashore, hastily followed by Karl. Greta stood next to John for another moment, then she ran after her father.

"Hey, what are you doing?" she asked angrily and tugged at his sleeve. "We've been traveling for weeks and now we're suddenly out of time?"

She turned to look at John, who was still standing at the railing, staring after them. He waved, and Greta waved back.

"It's because of him, isn't it?" she said bitterly. "You don't like that I went with him. You don't want me to go with anyone."

"I freely admit that I don't like the fellow. But you seem to like it when the next-best harbor rat courts you. In your disguise as a future nun you ought to—"

"You'd like that, wouldn't you. That I become a nun with you as my only god. Do you have any idea how self-absorbed and bullheaded you are, you . . . you sick old man!"

Greta clearly regretted her harsh words the moment she'd said them. She stopped and gave her father a sad look.

"By God, I just don't know what's going to happen. To me, to us, to . . ." She looked back toward John. "Everything is about as clear as this damned fog. I just need a bit of a diversion from all the creepy things that have been happening."

"And you shall have it," replied Johann. "We're visiting the most famous painter and inventor in the world, remember?" He closed the gap between them and touched her gently. "I'm sorry for being so abrupt. I'm sure your John will stay here for the day. You can call on him later, all right?"

Greta hesitated for a moment and glanced back at John. "Give me a minute," she said to Johann.

She walked back to John and they exchanged a few words. Johann saw that their hands touched for longer than was proper. Then Greta returned.

"All right." She nodded. "John has to take care of the freight, anyway. It's not like I don't want to meet this famous man, this genius the whole world talks about. It isn't every day that I meet someone who is even more famous and smarter than my father."

"And he is probably only half as self-absorbed as me," said Johann with a smile.

Amboise clearly owed its prosperity to the castle, towering like a huge shadow directly above the town, and a wide bridge that led across the Loire. It was the first bridge since Orléans, and the road was accordingly busy. Carts clattered across the timber planks, and horses and donkeys laden with sacks and bales were led toward the market.

The town itself was wedged between the Loire and a smaller river. It was narrow in shape and consisted mainly of a few parallel lanes lined by half-timbered houses and a few more significant stone houses, which probably accommodated court officials. The fog had lifted. As the small group with the dog passed through the city gate, Johann noticed a bell tower above them with a clock that had a minute hand. Only the wealthiest cities could afford such clocks. The burghers they passed were dressed in fine garments with bright colors. They all seemed to be in a hurry and kept their eyes straight ahead, as if every one of them fulfilled a particularly important task.

It wasn't difficult to find the house of Leonardo da Vinci. The first passerby they asked told them the way. They left town through the back gate and walked past several houses made of volcanic tuff that were built into the rock like caves. The dusty road led along the same terrace where the royal castle was located. After about a quarter mile they reached a wall surrounding a two-storied house built with red roof tiles and gray tuff, and several smaller outbuildings. In contrast to the castle, which they could still see in the background, the house seemed modest, more appropriate for a higher administrator than for one of the greatest minds of Christendom.

Johann could tell by the crowd gathered outside the gate that they were at the right place. The people seemed to wait as reverently as the disciples of a messiah. Most of them, with their dusty clothes and creased hats, looked like they had traveled far to be here. Several court officials in livery were among the crowd, accompanied by a handful of soldiers. The men armed with halberds paced the rows of supplicants and appeared to question each one about their business. Johann noticed that people spoke in hushed voices, like at a funeral.

"Is it always this busy?" asked Karl, looking around. "I mean, Leonardo is a famous painter and inventor, but this . . ." He tapped the onlooker closest to him, an older man who looked like a scribe with his black garb and slightly inflamed eyes. "Are all those people here to see Leonardo da Vinci?"

"Well, only very few will actually get to see him," the man said with a shrug. "But everyone wants to pay their respects to the great artist before it's too late."

"What do you mean?" asked Johann.

The man looked at him with wonder. "Haven't you heard? Leonardo da Vinci is seriously ill. The physicians say he won't be with us for much longer. The king has already been to say farewell. Apparently his majesty would have liked to stay longer—he loves Leonardo like a father, after all—but the election in the German Empire forced him—"

"I must see him," said Johann, trying to hide his shock. At the same time he felt strangely empty.

It can't be! Please, God, tell me it isn't true!

"See Leonardo da Vinci?" The man gave a low chuckle. "Look around you!" He gestured at the crowd of others waiting outside the gate. "Everyone here feels somehow connected to Leonardo. And many have come a long way to be here. The master worked in Rome as well as Florence and Milan. I myself have traveled from Romorantin, where we still hope for a canal system thought up by the great Leonardo that will drain our swamps. I am the second mayor there." He made a sweeping gesture at everyone around them. "These people are patricians, officials, and some commoners who want to thank the master for a small sketch or a painting in a church. Others are here to seek his advice, or they hope to gain access to his famous notebooks where he recorded many of his inventions. There is so much the master knows, and it would be a pity if it were forgotten after his death."

"Indeed," replied Johann faintly.

He felt very old all of a sudden. He had traveled all the way from the snowy, cold German Empire, from Bamberg to Metz and on to France, just to end up in front of closed gates. The man he had pinned all his hopes on was dying, perhaps from the same affliction Johann suffered. How much time had he left? Days, weeks? He and Leonardo were similar in this respect, too—death was reaching out for them. How could he have believed the great Leonardo da Vinci would receive him just like that—a goddamned nobody?

A nobody.

He looked at the mayor from Romorantin.

"Who must I speak with if I want an audience?"

The mayor pointed at a young man with long blond hair, a very broad nose, and a self-important expression on his face. He was holding a scroll and occasionally noted down a name. Then he continued to pace the rows. So far he hadn't let a single person through the gate. "That is Francesco Melzi, sort of the steward at Château du Cloux. But don't waste your efforts—the fellow can't be bribed and is generally a real toad. He decides who is allowed to see the great master, like Cerberus, the hellhound."

"Thank you." Johann turned away and started heading toward the steward.

"What are you doing?" asked Greta in a whisper as she and Karl tried to keep up with him. "Are you going to threaten the flunky?"

"I hope that won't be necessary." Johann pulled the *Figura Umana* from his bundle. The pages were tattered and dirty from the long journey, and the binding was coming loose in places. "Tear it in half," he ordered Karl. "I don't have the strength."

"The *Figura*?" Karl stared at him with shock. "You can't be serious!"

"Perfectly serious. If we want to see Leonardo da Vinci, we have to make sacrifices. My left hand is paralyzed—I need your help. Tear it in half."

Karl sighed deeply. Then, wearing a pained expression, he took the book and ripped it in two.

Johann thanked Karl, took the two halves, and coughed noisily until the steward finally looked at him with irritation.

"What do you want?" barked Francesco Melzi, already turning his attention back to his scroll. "You can see yourself that there is a long line. If you have a present for the master, you can hand it to one of the servants. Other than that, come back tomorrow. Or better yet, next week."

"I do have a present indeed. But I will only give it to the master in person," Johann said before handing Melzi one half of the *Figura Umana.*

"This is original work by Leonardo da Vinci," explained Johann. "He wrote it himself. Take him the book and tell him that the second half is in the possession of an equally famous man who is waiting outside."

Melzi frowned, his eyes shifting from the ripped pages in his hand to Johann and back. "And who is this famous man supposed to be?"

"Doctor Johann Georg Faustus, come especially all the way from the German Empire to pay my respects." Johann bowed. "I think the master knows me. And he will recognize his own work."

"Doctor Faustus? *You* are supposed to be the famous Doctor Faustus?" Francesco Melzi looked him up and down, his voice thick with mockery. "Since when does a magician and astrologer travel like an impoverished pilgrim?" He eyed Faust's lifeless arm. "And since when is he a—pardon the expression—a cripple?"

"Since when is an underling employed to ask stupid questions, wasting the precious time of his master?" retorted Johann harshly. "Now hurry—or do I have to speak with the king first?"

Melzi gave all three of them a long, hard look before scrutinizing the large black dog. Then he leafed through his half of the *Figura Umana*, turned around, and walked to the gate, knocking profusely until someone opened it.

"I thought we didn't want to be recognized?" whispered Karl after a while, noticing some of the onlookers starting to whisper and point. "After that performance, the whole world will soon know that the famous Doctor Faustus is in France. And then the pope might find out—Leo and the French king most likely keep in contact."

"There was no other way," said Johann. "We can only hope that we've managed to shake our pursuers. This meeting is too important."

"And you really believe Leonardo da Vinci will receive you?" asked Greta.

Johann's neck was crooked from the paralysis; now he tilted his head even farther to the side with thought. "If he's anything like I think he is, then Leonardo possesses a very particular trait we both share."

"Which is?" asked Karl.

Johann smiled. "Curiosity. Who can resist a visiting magician?"

Just then the gates opened and the steward waved at them impatiently.

"Come in," ordered Francesco Melzi unhappily. "I don't understand why, but the master really wants to see you."

~

Karl followed the doctor with a thumping heart. He hadn't expected Leonardo da Vinci to receive them. The news of Leonardo's imminent death had shaken Karl almost as badly as his master. Leonardo da Vinci was—along with the much younger Raffaello, who was currently making a name for himself in Rome, and the eccentric Michelangelo, who had decorated the Sistine Chapel a few years ago—one of the greatest painters of the Christian world. To Karl, who would have liked to become a famous painter himself, meeting Leonardo came equal to an audience with the pope. And now this man, whose works of art had already made him immortal, was apparently dying?

No one is immortal, thought Karl wistfully. *Not Leonardo, not I, and not even the doctor.*

He looked over at Greta, who didn't seem too upset. Her thoughts were probably still with John. The way the two of them had touched down by the harbor had been more than friendly. Karl felt a twinge of jealousy, and he cursed himself for being glad that she'd had to part with Reed.

Behind the walls, they walked through huge, parklike gardens. The manor house was much more magnificent from this side than from the front, consisting of a two-winged main building crowned with gables and an octagonal tower. Several steps led up to a portal, and an old servant wearing a threadbare, dirty linen frock waited outside. The man looked more like a gardener than a footman, leaning tiredly on a stick that served him as a walking aid.

"Our dear Battista will lead you to the reception room," said Francesco Melzi tightly. "I have given instructions that the conversation cannot last longer than a quarter of an hour. Not a minute longer. The master is extremely weak. The devil knows why he wants to see you at all. A sorcerer, ha! Not even that can save him now." Shaking his head, he turned back toward the gate.

The old servant bowed and limped ahead of the travelers. The rooms they passed were plain and clean, no pomp or pageantry. It smelled of pickled cabbage and wood fire.

"I wouldn't have thought your reputation reached this far," whispered Karl to the doctor. "I wonder if Leonardo would show us some paintings? I heard he brought some of the most beautiful ones to France. I would love to know how this sfumato—"

"I didn't come here for advice on shading and brushwork," growled Faust.

"I know," said Karl with a sigh. "But I still fear the great Leonardo knows more about painting than about medicine."

"We shall see."

They entered a long room with an open fire crackling at one end. The room was dominated by a table that took up almost the entire length, atop which stood vases filled with fresh flowers. Late-afternoon light fell through the tall windows. The servant, who clearly struggled to stand for long, sat down on a stool in the corner. Karl sensed that Battista was secretly observing Johann, but every time he turned to look at the old man, his gaze was lowered.

Thus they waited for a long while. Just as Karl decided he would ask the servant, a door creaked open and a stooping old man came in. Karl took off his pilgrim's hat, his knees shaking as if he were a young maid before her wedding. Seeing the famous master face to face was more than he could ever dream of.

Leonardo da Vinci wore a knee-length rose-colored tunic and a yellow cap—bright, garish colors one would expect to see on a woman. The most notable features were his beard and the white hair that reached to his shoulders and framed his wrinkled face. Sparkling beneath the extremely bushy eyebrows was a pair of alert, youthful eyes that didn't seem to match the face of an old man at all. Strangely, they reminded Karl of the doctor's eyes, radiating spirit and wit and studying everything with childlike curiosity. But while Faust's eyes were dark, almost black, this man's eyes were pale blue, like the sky on a beautiful day in March. The old man spread his arms and gave a little laugh.

"Three dusty travelers and a large black dog," he said to the doctor, who took a low bow. Karl and Greta followed his example. "I've heard about the dog, but I always imagined its master differently. Somewhat more"—he smirked—"imposing, scarier, well . . . more magical."

"We tried to avoid causing a stir," replied Johann, holding the old man's gaze.

"Even though you're much admired?"

"Much admired and much scorned."

Da Vinci stepped forward, the two men standing face to face. Karl studied his two idols. It seemed to him like the meeting of two equal forces, two poles, simultaneously attracting and repelling each other.

"I see. A Doctor Faustus who doesn't want to cause a stir," said Leonardo into the silence. "What a shame. I thought you always arrive amid lightning, thunder, and smoke. That's what I've been told, at least. I heard you sent the collective delegates of the empire running with a dragon at Bamberg."

"That's a slight exaggeration." Johann smiled. The ice seemed broken, or at least there was a truce. "And by the way, I can't fly, in case you've heard that, too. Not on a broomstick or a dragon."

"Then it is all the more surprising that you took this long journey upon yourself just to visit an old man who is waiting for the end," replied Leonardo. His voice was bright, somewhat feminine. He spoke Italian with the doctor, a language Karl knew almost as well as Latin. Greta, on the other hand, probably struggled to follow the conversation. She bent down and patted Little Satan, who had started to growl at the old servant.

"So it's true what they say outside?" asked Johann with a worried expression. "Your life is coming to an end. You don't look overly frail to me, though, if I may say so."

Leonardo gave a dismissive wave. "I am not as feeble as they think or as the doctors try to tell me. Still, I feel that my time is nearly over. I . . . have my reasons."

Karl looked more closely at Leonardo. As far as he knew, the great artist was in his late sixties, but he looked much older, drawn, as if some sort of demonic force had sucked out his strength before his time. Karl suddenly noticed that Leonardo's right hand was hanging down limply, and his whole right side seemed a little stiff. The doctor noticed, too.

"Does your condition have anything to do with this paralysis?" asked Faust, nodding at Leonardo's arm. "I've heard of it." He cleared his throat and gestured at his own lifeless hand. Then he said in a low voice, "I think we have something in common, Master Leonardo. And neither of us has much time left." Karl heard the anxiousness in his master's voice. "Could it . . . could it be possible that we suffer from the same ailment?"

Leonardo said nothing for a long while. Outside, a blackbird chirped; time seemed to stand still. The head of the old servant had slumped onto his chest; he'd probably gone to sleep.

"Maybe," said Leonardo eventually, looking at Johann very closely. "My ailment is very rare. Only very few share my affliction. To be honest, you would be the first one I've met in my life. Is that the reason you came here? Your paralysis?"

"I admit I had hoped to find an explanation here for this strange disease. Perhaps even the prospect of a remedy."

"The ways of man are finite, and we can't explore every path, Doctor Faustus. At least not with the usual methods and the brief time we're granted."

Leonardo pulled the torn half of the *Figura Umana* from a pocket in his tunic and held it out to Johann. His long, delicate fingers were studded with gemstone rings. "I never thought I'd see those pages again. I was in financial difficulties back then, and the Duke of Milan was kind enough to help. I always assumed he would burn the work."

"It is an honor to return it to you," said Johann. "What I want to know isn't in these pages."

"Some things oughtn't to be written down. They are too awful—too . . ." Leonardo hesitated. "Too outlandish. People would never believe them." He gently placed the ripped manuscript on the table between them.

"Then tell me about those things." Faust carefully added the other half of the book so that it looked like it had never been torn apart. "Sometimes thoughts must complement one another to form a whole."

"True indeed." A mischievous smile spread across Leonardo's wrinkly face. "I think the two of us can learn from each other, Doctor Faustus. Brothers in spirit." He paused and gazed at Faust's limp arm. "And maybe even more than that."

～

Not long thereafter, Greta hurried back to the port of Amboise.

Her heart was beating fast, and not just because she was running. The meeting with Leonardo da Vinci had been impressive, but she hadn't been nearly as moved as Karl. The men had conversed in fast Italian, and she had felt excluded. She'd soon realized that Leonardo wasn't interested in her. Faust had introduced her as his daughter, but Leonardo had merely given her a nod. The conversation had soon shifted to scientific subjects and painting. Greta had understood that all three of them were welcome to stay at Château du Cloux, much to the dismay of Francesco Melzi. The quiet old servant had shown her to her room, and an equally old maid had brought her hot water. As soon as Greta had washed the dust from her face, she slipped back out the gate past an astounded Melzi.

Now she was heading down to the port, where John was waiting for her.

John.

She couldn't get the red-haired, freckled, eternally grinning lad out of her mind. He buzzed through her thoughts like a fly. She was attracted by his charm and his wit, and most of all the ease with which he viewed the world. It was an ease both she and her father lacked.

Greta's shoes sounded loud on the cobbled street. Now that it was evening, the lanes were quieter. Business was finished for the day, and the hordes of officials and courtiers were sitting in the castle or in their villas with a glass of wine. Since their hasty goodbye earlier that day, Greta had thought about the previous night again and again. It had been wonderful—more than wonderful. She and John had made love in the royal gardens of Blois for hours on end. She hadn't felt the cold or the stones or the wet grass beneath her. In John's arm's Greta had slept well for the first time in a long while, without nightmares of dead children and a chalk-faced man beneath a bridge.

If he had noticed that it was her first time, he hadn't let on. Greta was confused. She barely knew John, and yet he felt so familiar. She thought of his touch and his kisses and walked faster. Her mind was spinning. She couldn't bear the thought of losing him so soon after they'd met. She wanted to learn more about him, wanted to make love to him again, wanted to make love to him many more times. And now she would stay here at Château du Cloux with her father and Karl, and he would carry on his journey toward the Atlantic.

The Atlantic.

Greta stopped in the middle of the street. She had been unsure for so long, but now she believed she knew what she had to do. If John would have her, she would go with him! She could work just as hard as any man, and the boat would carry her far away—far away from all the horror and dark memories. John would take her to a better world. What did she have to lose? Her father had reached his destination; maybe Leonardo da Vinci would truly be able to help him. Karl would be fine without her. The two of them would understand. They had always known that it would come to this one day.

It was time to say farewell. Her life was heading in a new direction.

Greta arrived at the harbor with a spring in her step. Sweating laborers carried crates past her; the air smelled both of stale water and of the great, wide world. Greta counted the vessels; there were more than this morning, a confusing maze of masts and sails. She walked toward where the *Étoile de Mer* had been.

And stopped dead in her tracks.

The boat was gone.

Greta looked around. She had to be mistaken. Perhaps it had been moved? But search as she might, the *Étoile de Mer* was gone. Finally she stopped one of the laborers and asked him in broken French about the boat. The man gave her a quizzical look at first, then his face brightened.

*"Ah, l'*Étoile de Mer*!"* he said. *"Elle a quitté le port, il y a deux heures."*

Greta tried to clarify several times, but the man insisted.

The *Étoile de Mer* left port two hours ago.

Greta suddenly felt exhausted, as if she'd been walking for days. She dropped onto one of the bollards and stared out over the river, where vessels drifted past in the light of the early evening. She didn't know whether to laugh or cry. She felt so stupid, so ridiculously simple and naive, like a young girl from the country. She had made a mistake that she'd never made before.

She had trusted a man.

And she had been terribly disappointed.

9

IN THE WEEKS AND MONTHS TO COME, JOHANN WOULD often think back to the time he had spent at Château du Cloux with Leonardo da Vinci. He relished every minute, and every word uttered by the famous artist seemed to give him strength. Leonardo also flourished, despite his age and illness. It was as if two halves that had used to be a whole had found one another: on the one side there was Johann's analytical, crystal-clear reason and his ambition, and on the other was Leonardo's creative, chaotic way of thinking, as if he viewed everything through the eyes of a child and saw coherences where no one else had ever noticed any. Leonardo da Vinci was Johann's new teacher, and Johann drank in each of the old man's words.

Together they often strolled through Leonardo's garden, which had the dimensions of a park. A few years ago all this had been swampland, but then it was drained with the creation of canals. Now cheerful brooks bubbled through a shady wood, lambs grazed by their mothers, and there was a vegetable garden, a glass house in which Leonardo cultivated rare plants, an atelier bathed in light thanks to hundreds of small panes of glass, and an herb garden with both kitchen herbs and poisonous and medicinal plants that Leonardo used for experiments.

Leonardo had invited Johann, Karl, and Greta to stay at Château du Cloux on the very first evening they arrived, and days had turned into weeks. Their walks were often interrupted because the great artist would observe something new in the garden: the cumbersome flight of a bumblebee, water cascading into a pond, the movements of the clouds above, the complex structure of a beehive. On such occasions, Leonardo pulled out the little notebook that always dangled from his belt and wrote a few lines or drafted some sketches. Since he was left-handed, his paralysis didn't bother him much. There were times when Leonardo seemed perfectly healthy, but then a trembling would overcome him and he'd have to sit down, illness and death written in his face.

"See the dragonfly over there?" he asked Johann one time when they discussed the possibilities of a water clock consisting of twenty-four individual vessels that filled and emptied every hour. "It flies with four wings. Each time the front pair of wings lifts, the back one drops, like a small apparatus designed by God. Astounding, isn't it?"

Johann blinked. "I can't see much, to be honest. How can you make out individual movements in all that whirring?"

"I just see them." Leonardo gave a shrug. "It would seem my eyes pick up more than those of others." He paused in his tracks. "Hmm. If a dragonfly gains so much uplift with four wings, then accordingly larger wings on a person . . . Oh, just look at that sunlight breaking in the small waterfall over there! The water acts like a filter that separates the individual colors. Highly interesting!" He gathered up his coat and hurried toward the waterfall, like a small boy on the hunt for dragonflies. He whipped out his notebook and immersed himself in a series of sketches with his charcoal stylus.

Johann looked at his host's back with wonder. It happened all the time—Leonardo was interested in so many things at once that he struggled to focus on any one thing for more than a few hours. Spending the days with him was like wandering through a forest of ideas without ever stopping. Johann had met many great scholars, the most intelligent of which was probably Agrippa; but even Agrippa was a man of the mind, piecing together the world in his head. Leonardo, on the other hand, studied the life that was directly in front of him, smelling it, tasting it, touching it. He took an interest in everything Johann described to him, be it simple juggling tricks, astrological problems, nifty sleight of hand, the possibilities of alchemy, or the foul-smelling flaming arrows Johann produced for his shows.

"In Milan, I developed a machine that can loose hundreds of arrows at once," said Leonardo thoughtfully during a stroll one mild April evening. Karl had joined them, while Greta preferred roaming the streets of town, as she had been doing for days. She seemed quiet, even sullen. She hadn't mentioned John Reed again—evidently the fling hadn't been as serious as Johann had feared.

Leonardo hardly seemed to notice Greta's absence, but he often inquired about Karl, who was more than happy to join them on their walks. With his ring-studded left hand, Leonardo picked up a stone and threw it into the pond. Little Satan, who walked with the men when he wasn't with Greta, barked and leaped after the rock.

"All arrows follow the same elliptical path," Leonardo went on. "The same goes for cannonballs, which are being used increasingly. The person who figures out how to predict their course exactly has the power to decide a war."

"Have you ever offered your knowledge to one of Europe's leading rulers?" asked Karl. "Especially now, with the advance of the Ottomans, I'd imagine people would pay anything for inventions like the arrow-shooting machine."

Leonardo took his time and weighed each word carefully. "I used to think that to preserve the greatest gift of all—freedom—any means were permissible. But I've changed my mind. Some thoughts oughtn't be recorded—yes, not even spoken out loud. They are too dangerous."

"But shouldn't all thinking be free?" asked Johann.

"It is a dilemma indeed." Leonardo sighed. "I'm afraid this subject will occupy humanity more and more in the future. Thoughts, inventions, and countless possibilities grow faster all the time on the trees of our imagination." He gave Johann a long and searching look. "How can we ensure that our ideas don't turn out to be our undoing? I see a gloomy picture up ahead. Mankind is going to subjugate the earth, and there will be nothing left on land or in the water that we don't persecute, rout out, and destroy."

In those moments Leonardo grew as depressed as Johann had grown in his own darkest hours.

The days became a blur. Johann saw Greta only at nights or in the morning, and then he and Karl would continue their scientific discussions with Leonardo. He didn't know what his daughter got up to during the day. It was like in Metz when he and Agrippa were working on the witch trial, or like at Heidelberg when he had built the laterna magica with his friend Valentin. The discussions, the work, and the countless new inspirations gave wings to his spirit. And he forgot everything else around him, even the people he loved.

But one thing was strange: when Johann mentioned Heinrich Agrippa to Leonardo, the old man said that while he'd heard the name before, he didn't know of any letters the two of them had supposedly exchanged. Johann suspected Leonardo had simply forgotten his correspondence with Agrippa. Thousands of letters, notes, and scraps of paper were piled up in Leonardo's library, some of which had even been used twice in order to save paper. Sometimes the great master had an ingenious thought one day just to forget it by the next because he'd had three more since.

But there was one thing they never discussed during these first weeks: their illness. Whenever Johann broached the subject, the old man avoided the question or gave vague replies.

"The church says there is a time for everything in life," said Leonardo once as they sat together over dinner. "A time to grow, a time to die, a time to take, and a time to pay." The cook, Matturina, silently placed stew on the table and sat down in a corner, where she awaited further instructions. She and the old servant, Battista, always hovered near Leonardo, apparently ready to help him should the old man fall or struggle with his paralysis.

"Maybe now is the time to pay," continued Leonardo. He trembled as he spooned up the stew with his left hand; he grew weaker by the day now. A silver chain with a pendant, one of the many chains Leonardo wore around his neck, almost dangled into his food. "What about you, Doctor? Have you got any outstanding scores? An account to settle with someone more powerful than yourself?" Johann felt that the old man was studying him closely once more. In the course of the last few weeks, Johann had become increasingly convinced that Leonardo da Vinci had also made a pact.

Your extreme giftedness, the intellect, the luck. Where does it all come from, old man? Is it God-given or did the devil make you an offer you couldn't refuse?

He was almost ready to mention the matter to Leonardo, but lurking behind them was always the cook, who seemed to listen to their every word.

"As you know, I studied your *Figura Umana*," said Johann instead. "Your sketches suggest to me that the human body is a type of machine, like a complex clockwork. Maybe all we need to do is replace a small spring or screw."

"We both have a loose screw?" Leonardo grinned, childlike mischief glinting in his eyes. "I like the image. And I agree with you in general, Doctor Faustus. But maybe there are some diseases that can't be cured because . . ." He hesitated. "Because the bill can only be paid a certain way."

Johann's hand paused above his plate. "How do you mean?"

But instead of giving a reply, Leonardo da Vinci ate his stew in silence.

Francesco Melzi, the steward, who had looked at Johann with derision in the beginning, occasionally crossed paths with them on the huge estate. Johann knew now that Melzi was a young Italian painter who had been a loyal friend of Leonardo's for years and who had followed him to France. Leonardo liked to surround himself with handsome men, including another young painter with the nickname Salai, meaning "little devil," who currently traveled around Italy. Melzi's main task was to sort through the countless notes Leonardo had made over the last several decades. The steward hadn't had a chance to paint in a long while.

Melzi was visibly annoyed that his patron accommodated Johann and his friends as guests—Karl especially was a thorn in his side. Melzi seemed to be jealous of Karl because Leonardo looked at him a certain way. Johann had soon realized that Leonardo, too, was secretly a sodomite. Was that why he'd suddenly left Rome a few years ago?

From time to time Francesco Melzi allowed people in for an audience, including men of nobility for whom Leonardo had built automatons for their courtly celebrations. But the king never visited. They said he was residing farther north, where he led negotiations about the German election. He sent letters sealed with gold leaf and inquired about Leonardo's health several times a week.

In all their time with Leonardo, Johann came no closer to finding answers to his own questions. He was permitted to study Leonardo's books and notes in the library but found no clues about his disease or about Tonio. But at least his paralysis wasn't getting worse. He was increasingly using theriac, however, for the worst of the pain. He always kept a bottle under his bed where Karl couldn't see it.

One evening, when Leonardo was still painting in his atelier, Johann was sitting in the library next door. Reading and studying here by candlelight was like a journey with an uncertain destination. The books weren't sorted—not by author nor by subject or title. The tomes piled up on shelves and tables like dusty mountains of knowledge; in between lay scrolls of parchment and crumpled scraps of paper—part of Leonardo's famous collection of notes. The great master seemed to document everything he saw. With wonder Johann gazed at the sketch for a type of umbrella from which hung a man, evidently gliding to the ground with it. On a different drawing Johann saw a crossbow the size of a ship. There were men with bird wings, cogwheels, war chariots, movable bridges, dozens of cannons in a row, men who looked like monsters and appeared to breathe underwater, but also drawings Johann didn't understand, like gruesome war scenes full of the dead and injured.

Johann came upon one especially shocking sketch: it was of a castle that sat enthroned on a mountain of bones and skulls. The longer he stared at the drawing, the more he thought the castle itself was one huge human skull. A single word was written at the top.

Seguaffit.

Johann didn't understand; he'd never heard the word before. But for some reason it seemed just as terrible to him as the castle of skulls.

Seguaffit. What in God's name?

"You shouldn't be reading this late. You'll ruin your eyes."

Johann gave a start. When he turned around, Leonardo was standing in the door. It seemed to Johann that the old man had been watching him for a while. Leonardo held a brush in his left hand, the drawing hand, while his right hung down limply.

"The same goes for the painter next door," said Johann with a smile. He pushed the paper with the strange drawing aside, feeling as though Leonardo had caught him reading something forbidden.

"You're right. I was about to finish up, anyhow. Melzi just gave me some bad news."

Johann turned serious. "What has happened?"

"My young stable boy, Silvio, had a riding accident. Apparently, there was a branch he missed in the light of dusk. Sadly, he fell in such a way that he broke his neck." Leonardo sighed. "I never thought that Silvio would depart this life before me. The funeral is in two days, and until then, his body is over in the shed and . . ." He paused and looked at Faust.

"You said once that man is like a machine," he continued eventually. "A rather heretical thought indeed, especially since it could only be proven if we looked inside the human body . . . which is forbidden by the church."

"The church forbids many things," replied Johann cautiously. "But not all of it makes sense in my eyes."

"I, too, prefer independent thinking to religion. I guess I will soon find out whether that was a mistake. Ask me again when I'm on the other side." Leonardo gave a grunt. "I would like to show you something, Doctor."

"What is it?" asked Johann.

"Come to the shed tomorrow night with your assistant, at midnight, when everyone's asleep," said Leonardo. "Perhaps then we'll finally find an answer to the question that has been torturing us for the longest time. Is our illness merely a loose screw or a"—he hesitated—"an incurable curse? I am tired. Let us go to bed."

Leonardo waited until Johann had left the library. When Johann wanted to take another look at the drawings the following day, including the terrifying sketch with the mysterious word *Seguaffit* scrawled on it, he found the library door locked.

It would remain locked to Johann for many weeks.

~

The following morning, Greta, along with many other believers, headed for the small Saint Denis Church above town.

The church stood a little outside of Amboise on a wide road that led from the Loire up a hill. It was Sunday, and Greta had left Château du Cloux before breakfast to roam the streets of town, like she had done for nearly two weeks. On several occasions she'd had the feeling of being followed, but she thought she was probably mistaken. For safety, she usually brought along Little Satan, who was better than three highly trained bodyguards.

Greta found it very hard to get over John's betrayal. She had truly believed the night at Blois had been special for him, too. But she guessed she was just one of many girls he picked up along the Loire each week. A fun adventure, a brief bit of pleasure, nothing more. She had been so embarrassed about the rebuff and her naive longings that she hadn't even told Karl about it. The two men were always busy with Leonardo; no one cared about Greta at Château du Cloux. It was high time to leave all this behind.

But where should she go? Greta wasn't fooling herself. A single young woman in a foreign country was fair game, and her French wasn't good enough to join a troupe of jugglers. She had given herself a few days to consider her options.

To take her mind off John and all the other gloomy thoughts, she and Little Satan had been exploring Amboise, the port, the nearby tuff caves, and the castle, even though she never got farther than the upper gates.

When mist rose from the Loire like a white sheet in the mornings, the castle appeared to hover above the town. A paved lane led up the inside of a tower in serpentines, wide enough to fit carts and carriages. Courtiers and officials came and went, but the king hadn't returned. He was still somewhere north, trying to sway the election of the German king in his favor.

In one of the caves at the foot of the hill, Greta had discovered a small chapel. She liked to pray in it, and it soon became her favorite spot, her refuge. Since she had helped her father twice with the power of prayer, her belief had grown strong again. Memories returned from church visits with Valentin back in Nuremberg. The prayers gave Greta strength and dispelled her fears and doubts. That was also the reason she was going to church today. She had left the dog at Cloux; he wasn't an appropriate churchgoer.

When the bells rang, Greta followed the other believers into the cool building and sat in a pew at the back. No one paid her any special attention. The smell of incense wafting through the vaulted room soothed her instantly. The citizens of Amboise started to sing a simple hymn that sounded like a children's song. Greta hummed along softly.

"Mon Dieu, protégez nos enfants."

Lord, protect our children.

Just as in Blois, farther upstream, here in Amboise people told stories of a child-eating monster. Several times Greta had heard the word *ogre* in taverns, and people had seemed anxious and downcast. And there was another word she'd heard repeatedly in connection with this ogre.

Tiffauges.

Greta didn't know what it meant—was it another monster, or the name of a place or a person? She had considered asking Karl, but he was so preoccupied with Leonardo that she'd dropped the thought.

The chanting of the believers rose, and Greta joined in.

"Je crois, je crois, je crois."

She was kneeling down to pray with the others when she sensed that some-one was watching her. It was the same vague feeling she'd had a few times lately, like an itchy spot on the back that you couldn't scratch. Carefully, she looked around. She was kneeling in the pews of the women, all wearing scarves around their heads and some even veils. Greta looked to the rows of men to her right. They, too, were kneeling with their heads bowed, but one of those heads, so Greta thought, had only just turned away. The man was sitting on the far side of the church; she couldn't make out more than a shadow in the dim light.

Greta's heart beat faster until the end of the service. Here inside the church she felt safe, untouchable. Evil couldn't harm her here. When the priest spoke the final blessing with his arms wide open, she stood up and followed the other women outside. But unlike the others, she turned right and hid around the corner of the building. The chiming bells and the murmuring of the crowd gave her courage. If anything happened to her here, she could call out for help.

After a while she heard footsteps; someone was approaching her hiding place. Greta gathered all her courage and stepped forward.

She almost collided with the man.

When Greta recognized him, she was lost for words at first.

"John?" she asked, puzzled. She took a step back and looked at him. He was unshaven and pale, as if he'd been sleeping poorly. But other than that, he was just the same. Greta was so surprised that she forgot to be angry.

John, too, looked confused at first, but then he gave a tired smile. "Look at that, the little princess. And I thought you lived at your castle with that old codger and your father, the dragon."

"And I thought you were somewhere on the Atlantic with your boat, en route to God-knows-where." Greta crossed her arms. "After our abrupt good-bye two weeks ago, I came back to the harbor like we'd agreed. But you weren't there."

"We . . . we must have missed each other," he said evasively. "I had to be somewhere. Business has been going poorly."

"So poorly that you take off without a word? I haven't seen your boat any-where. And now you're here at a church service. Are you praying for better weather?"

"My men and I, we . . ." John hesitated. "We had differing views of where business was going from here. And so we went our separate ways."

"The crew took your ship and left you behind? You can tell that to your hussies and whores at the port. How dumb do you think I am?"

"How dumb do you think *I* am?" John glowered at her. "You told me you were simple pilgrims on your way to Fontevrault Abbey. And then I find out that in truth, the man claiming to be your father is a magician, astrologer, and alchemist famous far beyond the borders of the German Empire. And then you take up lodgings at Leonardo da Vinci's."

"I see you've been busy." Greta took a step toward John and gave him a hard look. Apparently John didn't know that she really was Johann's daughter; her father had told no one but Leonardo. But he seemed well informed about everything else. "You've been watching me—admit it! What are you up to? Why are you spying on me?"

John opened his mouth, about to say something, but then he dropped his arms. "What the hell. I'll just tell you. It would have come out sooner or later."

Greta stepped even closer to him. Strangely enough, she wasn't afraid; not of John. "Tell me."

He gestured toward the weathered stone steps in front of the church. Most churchgoers were on their way back to town; only a few older women still stood near the entrance, leading hushed conversations. No one took any notice of the young couple. Greta hesitated briefly, then she shuffled away from John and sat down on the cool, hard stone.

John began awkwardly. "We . . . we never intended to take you all the way to Amboise."

"What is that supposed to mean?"

"Well, you must understand that we're not merchants as such, but . . . but . . ." John kneaded his hands. "Well, people who don't take the burden of taxation too seriously."

"You are *smugglers*?" asked Greta, astonished.

"A harsh term." John lifted his hands, seeming almost offended. "All we do is bypass the staple right. By law, all ships must offer their wares for sale at each larger town along the Loire and also pay taxes. Our wares, however, go straight to the Atlantic and are therefore much cheaper." He winked at Greta. "Our cozy little *Étoile de Mer* is larger than she looks. She has a pretty fat belly."

"Then why did you take us?"

"When I saw the three of you at Orléans, I thought you could be milked. Do you understand? Simple pilgrims, ha!" John gave a laugh. "I never believed you for a moment but thought instead that you were rich merchants with some kind of highly precious freight sewn into your garments, like jewels or pearls, something like that. We were going to clean you out at Blois and set off before dawn, but then . . ." He broke off.

"What happened then?" asked Greta.

"That night with you, damn it . . . Nothing like it ever happened to me before. I plead guilty, Greta." John paused and looked down. "Guilty of falling in love with you."

She flushed and her heart began to race.

John edged a little closer, and Greta suddenly felt hot. She should be angry with him—she should have slapped the faithless bastard and walked away. But she couldn't. Greta smelled smoke, wine, and tangy sweat as if he hadn't washed in a while. But, strangely, that didn't bother her. On the contrary.

"Yes, I've fallen head over heels in love with you," he continued softly. "I still can't believe it. Up in the castle gardens at Blois I felt like I was struck by lightning. And then . . . and then everything changed. I asked my men to hold off on the robbery. I needed time—time to figure out how it would go with . . . with the two of us. But then your father up and departed with no warning and you left me standing in the port like a dumb ox. We argued. My men were angry because they hadn't received their fair share. I went and got as drunk as a lord while those goddamn bastards took off with the ship and left me behind. Since then I've been stuck at Amboise. And . . . and . . ."

"You've been following me, haven't you?" said Greta. "That's how you know where we're staying."

John lifted a hand. "Guilty as charged," he said again. A little embarrassed, he ran his hand through his tousled red hair. "Although that part wasn't hard to find out. Half the town is talking about the famous Doctor Faustus lodging at Leonardo da Vinci's. Several times I came close to speaking to you, but I was afraid you would send me away. Because you found out what a piece of scum I am." Suddenly he looked up and spoke with a firm voice. "No more lies, Greta. I stand before you as a smuggler, a thief, and a fool who is hopelessly in love with you."

"Things would have been a little easier if you'd told me all of this sooner," she replied gruffly. But she felt her wall crumble. This was like a dream that was too good to be true—Greta only hoped no one would wake her.

"By the way, you looked gorgeous at mass just then. Like an angel fresh from heaven."

John gave a big smile, and this slightly crooked, sheepish grin finally won her over. The space outside church was deserted now; it was just the two of them.

Greta gave a little sigh and hoped John wouldn't hear it. She remembered that not long ago she'd demanded of her father to always tell the truth. How could she judge John for doing just that? It felt so good to have him near her again. There was something familiar about him—it felt like they'd known each other for a long time. And there was something romantic about smugglers.

"You . . . you selfish, dumb—" she began.

The rest of the sentence drowned in a long kiss. Greta tried to resist at first, but then she returned John's kiss with passion. John had kindled a fire inside her that had continued to smolder after his disappearance, and now it was flaring back up. But this time, she wouldn't be the weak girl who was getting seduced. She turned her face away abruptly and stood up.

"What are you doing?" asked John in surprise.

Greta smiled. "There might not be anyone watching, but this here behind us is still a church. I know an overgrown orchard nearby. It's not as magnificent as the royal gardens at Blois, but it's at least as beautiful." She pulled John up and led him by his sleeve, and he followed without protest. Arm in arm they walked down the narrow lane that led to the vineyards and gardens outside of town.

That was why Greta didn't see the old raven perched on the walls of the church, staring down at her with hateful red eyes.

~

When Greta hurried back toward Château du Cloux with a spring in her step that evening, two other shadows followed her progress from one of the caverns in the tuff rock along the way. In the darkness of the cave, only the outlines of their bodies and the whites of their eyes showed, the one shadow towering above the other like a mountain.

"There she is!" hissed Viktor von Lahnstein. "The doctor's wench."

"Do you want me to grab her so we can question her?" asked Hagen, adjusting the long, bloodstained sword on his back. "It's a good opportunity. For once she isn't with that mutt." He pulled the blade from its scabbard with a swooshing noise. At his feet lay the dead beggar who had been unfortunate enough to sleep off the booze inside this cavern. At least he hadn't felt much.

Lahnstein considered, then shook his head. "No. We'd have to get rid of her afterward, just like this poor devil. And who knows if she'd spill anything at all. If she goes missing, questions will be asked—and the doctor would disappear. There must be another solution."

"We could take her as a hostage," suggested Hagen. His Swiss accent sounded hard and gnarled, like creaking timber.

"Blockhead!" snarled Lahnstein. Speaking was still difficult. A patch made of red silk covered the gash where his nose used to be. The wound still wept, and the patch was always a little wet. The pain nearly drove him insane, especially at night. Lahnstein had decided that all this must be a test from God. Whenever hatred threatened to get the better of him, he reached for the rosary hanging around his neck. Oh yes, God would reward him for resisting revenge for the good of the church.

"Faust is a clever, ruthless fellow. The life of this girl probably isn't worth more to him than that of a fly. She's a nobody—just a servant, or perhaps his plaything. Besides, I doubt a stupid girl like her will know much." Lahnstein adjusted his nose patch so that his speech was a little clearer. "No, let us wait a little longer. I want to know what the bastard is doing at Leonardo da Vinci's. Leonardo, of all people—it can't be coincidence!"

Viktor von Lahnstein clenched his teeth and thought hard as darkness descended over the valley. It had taken them almost two months to locate the doctor. They had nearly caught him at Metz, but the papal soldiers had no sway in the free imperial city. Lahnstein had been forced to conduct secret negotiations with the authorities. And then Faust had vanished all of a sudden, just when Lahnstein had finally secured the permission for his arrest. It was enough to drive a man insane!

They had picked up his scent again here in the Loire Valley. A traveling merchant had told them at Orléans that the famous Doctor Faustus had asked for an audience with the mortally ill Leonardo da Vinci. Lahnstein could hardly believe it at first—Leonardo da Vinci, the old heretic! Only a few years ago,

Leonardo had been a guest of the pope, but the Holy Father's dislike for the painter and inventor had eventually driven the man into the arms of the French king. There had been rumors of blasphemous dissections of corpses and similar heinous crimes. In addition, Leonardo was considered to be a sodomite.

What in God's name could Faust want from this shady old man?

They had headed for Amboise as if the devil was after them, and Lahnstein had made inquiries. The girl had been the final clue that they had truly found the doctor.

A cool breeze brushed Lahnstein's cheek. Now, in April, it probably carried the scents of meadows and fields, but Lahnstein couldn't tell because he had lost his sense of smell. In its stead was nothing but pain.

And you will pay for it, Doctor! A thousandfold. But not now. The welfare of the church—of the whole of Christendom—is more important than my own.

"We wait," Lahnstein said eventually and retreated into the darkness of the cave. He turned to Hagen, who sheathed his sword with a grunt and dragged the body of the beggar to the back, where beasts of prey would soon find it and chew it down to the bones. No one could know about their presence here, least of all the French king.

"I will write to the Holy Father. The letter must leave for Rome today. We need new instructions." Lahnstein smiled grimly, which, together with his distorted face and the silk patch, made him look like a rare predatory fish from the deepest depths of the ocean. "I think Leo will be more than astonished to learn that Doctor Faustus is residing with Leonardo da Vinci, of all people. He will draw conclusions, just like I am."

10

WHEN THE BELLS OF THE NEARBY VILLAGE CHURCH CHIMED midnight, three figures clad in black stood around a corpse by the light of a torch.

Karl reached for the scalpel with a steady hand. He placed it between the collarbones and cut down the sternum all the way to the pubic bone, slicing through skin and flesh until he had exposed the rib cage. He put aside the scalpel, picked up a saw, and cut through the ribs. Gleaming below them were two pink flaps, which until recently rose and fell with every breath. Karl was once again wearing his eye glasses, which helped him greatly in the poor light.

"The lungs look fresh," explained Leonardo as he bent over the open torso, his necklace swinging like a pendulum. "Excellent blood flow. It is easy to tell that this body belongs to a young man. I remember dissecting an old man once, almost a hundred years old, at the Santa Maria Nuova hospital in Florence. The artery that feeds the heart and other body parts was all dried up, shriveled and withered like the brittle stem of a plant."

Johann, standing next to Leonardo, nodded pensively. "Age probably dries up the arteries in other places, too. It is possible that such dehydration leads to paralysis. What do you think?"

But instead of replying, Leonardo addressed Karl. "Let us take a look at the heart now. *Scalpellum minimum.*"

Johann handed Karl another one of those sharp knives that Leonardo had brought for the dissection and which had been laid out on a stool next to the body. Karl carefully cut out the lungs and put them aside.

"Gently, please," said Johann. "We want as little damage as possible."

"This isn't my first dissection," replied Karl. "I know what I'm doing." He tried to sound calm and composed but couldn't entirely hide his excitement. He hoped that in the light of the torch the doctor didn't see the sweat running down his forehead.

This might not have been Karl's first dissection, but it was the first he conducted all by himself, and he was watched by the two men he admired the most. Because of their paralysis, neither Johann nor Leonardo was able to hold a scalpel steadily, so they acted as his assistants. The three of them were standing in the shed behind Leonardo's mansion, the body of the stable boy on a wooden block covered with a wax cloth between them. Karl studied the corpse's face, which looked as if it was made of wax. Until very recently this young, handsome lad had breathed, laughed, loved, eaten, and drunk, and now he was nothing but a shell, the shed skin of a larva.

It was the middle of the night. Dressed in dark garments, the three had sneaked out of their bedchambers like thieves and met here. Groaning with effort, Karl had lifted the cold body out of the casket and onto the wooden block. They didn't have much time; the grave diggers would arrive at first light to take the plain wooden crate to Saint Amboise Cemetery. The body already smelled strongly, forcing Karl to press his hand to his mouth and nose from time to time. Leonardo hadn't yet told them why he wanted to dissect this body.

Karl suppressed the urge to gag and cleared his throat. "How many dissections have you performed, master?" he asked Leonardo as he severed muscles and veins.

"Oh, I don't recall. Several dozen," replied Leonardo, gazing into the distance. "Most of them at Florence, because people there are very open to this method of research. I believe dissections are as important for students of medicine and painting as the Latin roots of words are for grammarians." He paused. "However, they didn't like this way of thinking in Rome."

"What happened?" asked Johann.

"It seemed I had a traitor in my own workshop. The pope found out that I skinned three corpses."

"So he sent you away?"

"There was more than one point of conflict. I was asked to do . . . things that I wasn't prepared to do. Thankfully the French king was kind enough to grant me asylum. I fled through the mountains in a simple cart." Leonardo smiled.

"And I've been here ever since. I was able to take my favorite paintings, including my beloved *Gioconda*. It wasn't easy to get the girl across the Alps. The king lets me do as I please, more or less. To him I am like a jester who builds him a funny automaton or sets up fireworks. But he probably wouldn't approve of this dissection. The king doesn't want to offend the church."

Karl nodded. He and the doctor had also performed the occasional dissection. The bodies had mostly been those of executed men that no one claimed and who wouldn't be buried in consecrated ground. The church considered the dissection of dead bodies a sin, and exceptions were only occasionally granted at universities. God alone created man, and His work oughtn't be destroyed. The human body was a representation of the entire universe. But how should they understand God's work if they couldn't take it apart and study it? How should they find out what causes illness, suffering, and death?

Leonardo leaned over the body again. "Now let us take a look at his heart."

"I very much hope we will get closer to an answer to our question," muttered Johann.

"It is just as Socrates once said," replied Leonardo with a smile. "Teachers are often but the midwives of our answers. We must birth them ourselves."

With the doctor's help, Karl gently placed the lung flaps into a tub. It was important that they didn't leave any marks of their activity behind. Even a man as respected as Leonardo da Vinci wasn't immune against a trial if it was about disturbing the dead. And Karl and Johann would definitely burn.

Now they could see the heart in the stable boy's opened torso. It was a muscle the size of a man's fist and didn't look much different from the heart of a pig. As Karl took a rag and wiped off the clotted blood, he could feel Leonardo's eyes on him. It wasn't the first time that Karl suspected that he and Leonardo had something very special in common. The colorful garments, the feminine gestures, Leonardo's preference for young painters. They were brothers in spirit, without a doubt, but neither of them would say it out loud. Karl wondered if and when he would ever find the courage to confess his love to the doctor.

Probably never.

"There are two chambers here," said Leonardo, pointing his knife to the inside of the heart, which was now exposed. Karl was grateful that the dissection distracted him from the feelings that washed over him like a flood. The old man's fine voice soothed him.

"The great Avicenna wrote that the blood runs first into one chamber and then into the other."

"What a shame we can't observe the heart while it pumps blood," said Johann. "It would be interesting to see how it works." With his gloved right hand he pointed at the opened corpse. "The Greek physician Herophilos experimented on live humans—prisoners, mostly. That would be the only way to gain insight."

"I think there could be other ways," replied Leonardo. "If it were possible to build a model made of glass, we could see inside. I prepared sketches to that effect a while ago." He stretched his back, aching from being hunched over. "But you're right. We'll probably never find out what exactly drives the heart."

"Or man in general," said Johann with a glum expression. "I have yet to discover a soul inside a heap of bloody meat." He looked at Leonardo. "As much as it pleases me to conduct a dissection with you—I'd quite like to know the reason for our clandestine meeting." He gave the old man a pleading look. "We haven't got much time left—either of us."

Leonardo continued to gaze at the corpse.

"When I was young, I, too, thought man was a machine," he said eventually. "I searched for the general principle that ruled the universe, and also for the seat of the soul."

"I believe the soul doesn't remain in the body after death," said Johann. "It seeps out like air."

"Yes, but where does it fly to? To heaven or to hell? What about your soul, Doctor? And mine? Where do they go after death?" With the tip of his knife, Leonardo lifted a white band that had been concealed in the flesh. "Just look at the sinews! They always remind me of strings, like the ones puppets are suspended from. But who moves the strings—who is the puppet master wriggling us about?"

"I . . . I think it is God," remarked Karl hesitantly.

"If we believe in the principle of God, then we must also believe in the devil, grappling with God for this world, right?" replied Leonardo with a bitter smile. He caressed his pendant on its thin silver chain with bloodstained fingers. Karl realized only now that it was a tiny globe. A strange thought struck him.

The whole world hangs around Leonardo's neck.

"So you also believe that the . . . the devil sent us this disease?" asked Johann in a defeated voice.

"Concerning yourself, you are the best person to answer that question. One thing is for certain: he who dances with the devil needs good shoes." With three well-placed cuts Leonardo lifted the edge of the skin on the man's face and pulled it off, turning the head into a red grimace that stared at them from eyes like milky marbles.

"The devil is a good businessman," he murmured and gazed at the grotesque face. "He always returns for his share. But by God, you can cheat him good."

"I'm afraid I don't understand," said Johann.

"What you don't feel, you'll never catch by hunting." Leonardo turned away without another word and washed his hands in a tub, the blood mixing with the water like small, deadly clouds.

~

In the following days, Greta hurried to a long island in the Loire early every morning, closely followed by Little Satan.

The Île d'Or, as the locals called it—the island of gold—lay between the two parts of the bridge connecting the banks of the Loire. Few houses had been built upon it, and one of the buildings was a hospice for lepers who were banished here to protect the other citizens of Amboise—and to spare the king the sight of them on his occasional visits. Behind the hospice lay nothing but swampy pasture; a few dirt paths wound their way through weeds, bushes, and islands of cattails.

Greta left the bridge and was instantly surrounded by the monotonous buzzing of thousands of mosquitoes. She and the big black dog leaped across swampy puddles and made their way to the outermost tip of the island. There stood a small, solid, forgotten church. It was an old building that seemed as impregnable as a fortress. Greta's heart beat wildly with anticipation and her knees grew weak. This was where they could be together undisturbed.

This was their love nest.

To Greta, the last few days had been the most wonderful in years. Her encounter with John outside the church of Saint Denis had changed everything, and they had been meeting here every day since. Something had developed between them, something Greta had thought impossible: true love.

Greta's love for John had hit her like a landslide. When she was with him, a thousand butterflies fluttered in her stomach, and when she was apart from him, she felt terribly empty and lonely. He was the air she needed to breathe, and he seemed to feel the same way about her. They lived together in their own world; everything else had receded. Tonio, the curse, worry about her father. All those thoughts were still with her, like dark shadows outside the window, but when Greta was with John, she was inside a warm, bright house and evil stayed outside.

When she arrived at the small, ivy-covered church, Greta looked around but couldn't see John anywhere. He had found the old building a few days before their reunion. It formed the perfect hideout for the two of them, also offering shelter from the area's frequent April cloudbursts. Of course, Greta didn't tell her father about where she was going and who she was meeting, and neither had she told Karl. She was afraid that they would advise her not to go.

She entered the quiet church, with its plain stone altar and the cross carved from cherrywood. Sunlight streamed through the broken windows.

Someone gave a cough very close to her, and Little Satan barked wildly.

"My fair young lady," said a familiar voice.

Greta spun around with fright and looked into John's smiling face. It wasn't the first time he'd played this game with her. His ability to sneak up on her was uncanny. Not even the dog had noticed him at first.

"Oh, John!" She rolled her eyes. "Didn't I tell you not to frighten me so? Like a thief in the night."

"I *am* a thief, remember?" He winked at her and raised his arms apologetically. "But all right—I won't do it again. Promise."

"Why is it that promises from your mouth never sound very convincing?" She laughed and fell into his arms as if they hadn't seen each other in weeks, though they'd only been apart for one night.

Greta unfolded the cloth she had used to wrap up a loaf of bread and some cheese. John helped himself hungrily. He had almost used up all his money. She sometimes wondered how he could still be so cheerful. He had lost his crew and his boat, but he seemed unafraid of the future.

"What is the news from the big, wide world?" he asked between mouthfuls, wiping his lips. "What is the master painting? Any new inventions? How about some sort of flying machine that can take us away from here?"

She gave a sad smile. "You know that Leonardo doesn't really see me. To him, I'm just some young thing. He probably thinks I'm Johann's maid."

Greta hadn't explained the real reason for their visit to Amboise. She had told John that Johann simply wanted to see the famous Leonardo da Vinci—two great men meeting as equals. She hadn't told John that she was his daughter, either. He assumed that she was some distant niece.

"A maid? Ha!" John opened his eyes wide. "You're a princess." He bowed to her. "Your Highness, will you please allow me to whisk you away to someplace where we can start together afresh?"

She laughed. "With pleasure!"

"Then why don't we? Your uncle can look after himself, and there's always his handsome assistant. If he doesn't want to give his permission, you just go without it. What's stopping you?"

"You . . . you don't understand." Greta didn't fully understand it herself. She wanted to leave but couldn't bring herself to do it. She had been traveling with Johann and Karl for so many years, and even after she learned that he'd lied to her for the longest time and that he was to blame for her mother's death, she found that she couldn't now abandon her father. She felt with certainty that if she left him now, she would never see him again.

Because he will probably die soon if Leonardo da Vinci doesn't find a solution, she thought. *And a solution doesn't seem likely.*

"Then explain it to me," demanded John. "Why don't you?"

"Another time." She kissed him, and Little Satan watched with interest as they sank onto the stone floor of the church. Greta wondered for a moment whether it was a sin to make love beneath a cross, but then she pushed her thoughts aside and focused on John's lips.

Still, deep down she knew that soon she would have to tell John the real reason for their visit to Amboise.

Her father had made a pact with the devil.

~

During the following days, Leonardo da Vinci's health worsened noticeably. He grew weaker and slept much. Now he spent hardly any time in his atelier, where a number of his paintings remained unfinished. Among the paintings in the room was also the one of the beautiful woman with the strangely wistful, knowing smile. Johann sometimes wondered if it wasn't Leonardo himself smiling on that canvas, as if he was guarding a secret that no one else knew.

Following the dissection in the shed, they had closed the body, carefully sewing it up, and placed it back in the coffin. No matter how much Johann had asked and urged, Leonardo hadn't uttered another word about the devil or the disease, and Johann still puzzled over the old man's hints.

The devil is a good businessman. He always returns for his share.

Evidently, Satan sometimes made deals with people. He allowed them to achieve extraordinary things—but at some point they had to pay the price. Just like Johann, and like Leonardo. And yet the old man seemed relaxed, at peace, toward the end of his life. Had it something to do with his final remark?

But by God, you can cheat him good.

What did Leonardo mean by that? Was there a way out after all? Years ago, at Nuremberg, Johann had cheated Tonio. Johann's best friend, Valentin, had sacrificed himself for him and Greta. Had Leonardo managed to arrange something similar?

And would Johann manage to do it again?

His hopes waned by the day. The library doors remained locked and the walks in the garden gradually ceased. Johann wondered whether he had disappointed Leonardo. Why did the old man always speak in riddles? To test his wit? Leonardo's comments during the dissection had been almost as mysterious as the word *Seguaffit* that Johann had found on the note in the library.

Francesco Melzi took all this as a welcome sign that Johann had fallen out of favor with the master. One day at lunch he took the doctor aside.

"I think you can see for yourself that the time for your departure has come," Melzi whispered to Johann as Leonardo ate his soup with a trembling hand.

The face of the great painter was gray and sunken, and his beard was dirty with the remains of the barley porridge from breakfast. The great Leonardo da Vinci had aged by years in the last few weeks. His pale blue eyes flickered tiredly, the light in them slowly dying out like embers in a stove. Little Satan lay under the table, looking like the black devil waiting for the soul that was promised to him.

"The master needs rest now," continued Melzi with a self-important expression. "He told me himself that he can't bear your continuous badgering any longer."

Johann thought that was probably a lie but said nothing. It pained him to watch as Leonardo withered like a flower in fall. And he suspected that it was indeed time to say farewell.

What are you trying to tell me, old man? Is it fear that prevents you from speaking? Who or what are you afraid of?

"Pack your things," ordered Melzi abruptly. "Battista will help you. I don't want to see you here tomorrow."

"I want to speak with him one last time," said Johann, glancing at Leonardo, but the artist just gazed listlessly into space. "You can't deny me this one request."

"Very well. If you promise that you're gone by the morning." Melzi sighed. "You may visit him at his bedside later. But refrain from asking all those nosy questions—they agitate him. I will ask Battista to keep an eye on you."

That evening, Johann climbed the stairs to the bedroom of the great painter and inventor one last time. Breathing hard, he pulled himself up on the banister. The paralysis that had slowed down during the last few weeks had spread to Johann's left leg. Climbing stairs was becoming difficult for him, and he moved like a very old man. Leonardo was his last chance. If this great man couldn't help him, he saw no way out.

What are you trying to tell me?

Like the other rooms in the mansion, Leonardo's bedroom was modestly furnished. There was a fireplace with a large desk in front of it, and on the other side of the room a four-poster bed adorned with carvings. In the bed, buried amid cushions, blankets, and furs, lay the great Leonardo. He seemed tiny in the huge bed, reminding Johann of a mummified chick. His eyes were closed; the rising and falling of his scrawny chest was accompanied by an ugly rattling sound.

There will never be another like him, thought Johann. *Not in a thousand years.*

The old footman Battista, with his bloodshot eyes, sat on a stool in the corner, leaning on his cane. Johann merely glanced at him. Why did the fellow always have to hang around the sick old man? And the cook, too?

Johann cautiously approached the bed. Just as he reached its side, Leonardo opened his eyes as if he'd been expecting him.

"Ah, Doctor Faustus," he said with a tired smile. "It looks as though I will soon find out whether religion is preferable to philosophy after all. What a pity we can't write letters from the other side. Or can we?" His voice sounded as brittle as a cracked bell.

"We must leave first thing in the morning," said Johann without responding to Leonardo's strange question. "I just came to tell you that it has been a huge honor—"

Leonardo shook his head impatiently. "Spare yourself the praises, I don't have time for those. I heard the king himself will arrive soon to say goodbye, and I must finish my will." He laughed and coughed at the same time. "I never knew that dying was this exhausting."

"Your enormous store of knowledge should belong to everyone." Johann bowed. "To the whole world. And your paintings and notes, too."

"Francesco Melzi inherits my writs," replied Leonardo. "I know you don't like him very much. The feeling is mutual, by the way, but you'll have noticed that by now." He gave a dry laugh. "Don't let it get you down. Francesco is a good man, just terribly jealous. He will ensure that my writings fall into the right hands. And don't worry about me—I want a simple funeral, no spectacle fit for a king."

Johann cleared his throat. The moment had come—the very last opportunity to learn something after all.

"You . . . you said a while ago that you were able to answer my question," he began. "But you still haven't. My disease is a curse, isn't it?"

"Indeed, a curse. And we both know what's behind it." Leonardo closed his eyes and nodded. His fingers were cramped around the tiny silver globe hanging from the chain around his neck. "You can't cut out a curse like a wart. It stays. Trust me, I tried—I tried everything!" He coughed again, then suddenly broke out in a smile. "Ha! But I played a trick on him. Not even the devil is all-powerful. He can be outwitted. He doesn't get everything he wants."

Leonardo signaled for Johann to come closer.

"Do you remember our conversation in the garden?" whispered Leonardo. "When we spoke about war machines?"

Johann thought. "You said some thoughts oughtn't be written down or even spoken out loud. Is that what you mean?"

Leonardo nodded. "Such thoughts must be taken into the grave. That is where they are safe. *In the grave.*" He coughed again. "Sometimes danger lurks on the side where we least expect it. The devil likes to play."

Suddenly the old man pulled Johann so close that his lips tickled Johann's ear. "The night we were in the shed with the dead body. We gazed into the innermost—that was what I wanted to show you. The greatest secrets lie at the innermost core. Do you understand? The *innermost*."

"I . . . I don't know if I . . . ," replied Johann. The dying man seemed to talk feverishly. Johann was going to say something else, but Leonardo pushed him away.

"Some thoughts must be burned," he said more loudly. "They must never come to light! I think there will be a big fire before I die, and I am going to warm my gout-ridden fingers on my many ideas one last time. I want to be alone now. Fare thee well, Doctor. And give my regards to your handsome assistant. What a shame I couldn't have met him in my younger days." He raised his trembling hand in farewell. "I consider you my brother in spirit. Walk the rest of your path with care."

He sank back into his pillows and closed his eyes. Battista shuffled toward Johann and gestured at the door.

"Thank you. I can find my own way out," muttered Johann.

He gave one last nod in the direction of Leonardo da Vinci, the greatest genius the world had ever seen, and walked out into the hallway. The door creaked shut behind him.

And with the closing door vanished the last glimmer of hope that Johann could still escape his fate.

There was no way out.

He was lost.

～

When Greta hurried to the Île d'Or the following evening, the rushes and the swamp looked creepy to her, like hostile beings. The evening sun cast a red glow over the trees, and the shadows on the muddy ground were long. The magic she had always felt on the island had vanished. The bad news she'd received earlier awakened old fears, like a scab that was ripped off.

This time John waited for her outside the church, his face wrought with worry.

"Where have you been all day?" he asked, walking toward her. "I thought God-knows-what happened!"

"Something has happened," said Greta quietly. John hugged her, waiting for her to continue. But she took a few moments; she was too upset.

They had left Château du Cloux very early that morning, at Melzi's request. Leonardo da Vinci was on his deathbed; for all she knew, he might have already died. The news had hit Karl hard, since Leonardo was one of his idols. But her father was even worse. He had spent the whole day staring at the ceiling of an attic room at an inn below the castle. He murmured strange things while Karl sat watching over him. It was as if her father had given up, as if he waited for death in that bed—or for that which came after. His state probably wasn't helped by the large amounts of theriac he consumed.

Greta had taken another look at the lines in her father's hand before she left. They had become even paler, like the trails of fireflies fading in the night.

He is going to die, she thought. *There is no way out.*

"What's happened?" asked John. He gently led her into the church, where some candles had been lit on the altar. Greta gazed at their shared hideout, knowing that the time had come: she needed to make a decision. She felt in her heart that she'd already made it: she would go with John, the man she loved.

Why was it so incredibly difficult to take this step?

My father's story is also my story.

"My news isn't very good," she began. Then she told John haltingly what had happened in the last few hours. "I knew it would end like this," she said bitterly. "I just didn't want to accept it. This whole journey was doomed from the beginning. Maybe all we're chasing is a phantom. I should never have followed my father."

"Your *father*?" John gaped at her. "The famous Doctor Faustus is your father?"

"Yes, he is. That and more . . ." Greta was shaking, unable to go on.

"I think it's time for you to tell me the real reason for your journey," said John, taking her hand in his. "No more excuses, Greta. And no lies. We made a promise to each other, remember? I am a smuggler, but who are you, Greta? I know nothing about you."

She hesitated for another moment, then she spoke. "Back in Blois, at the tavern. You told me that people around here speak of a child-eating ogre."

John rolled his eyes. "Not that again! Don't tell me your father believes those fairy tales and is too scared to leave the house. I mean, he is Doctor Faustus. He should—"

"What if those ogres are real?" asked Greta, cutting him off. "What if my father has been cursed by such an ogre?"

"Cursed?" John looked stupefied. "What in God's name are you talking about?"

Haltingly at first, Greta began to tell John about Tonio and the pact her father had made with him a long time ago. Her voice grew steadier as she told him about Johann's illness and the suspicion that Tonio was some kind of ancient creature, perhaps even the devil himself. In the end, the words came gushing out of her as if she confided in John in the hope of finding solace and absolution. He listened silently. When she had finished, he shook his head.

"It all sounds very strange. I honestly don't know what to think. This Tonio—an old pact with the devil?"

"You don't have to believe it. I don't know myself how much of it is true. But at least now you know why we visited Leonardo da Vinci. My father suspects that Leonardo, too, made such a pact with the devil, and that he might know what can be done about it. But Leonardo revealed nothing, and now Melzi has thrown us out." Her voice trembled. "I saw it in my father's hands. He . . . he is dying. I could come to terms with that, but not if the devil swoops in to fetch him!"

"And you could really foretell his death by his hand? You can actually do that?" John held out his right. "Do you want to—?"

"No!" Greta almost screamed and recoiled as if his hand were a poisonous adder. "I will never read anyone's palm again. It is . . . Afterward, nothing is the way it was before. I don't want to know when your end is near, John. I just want to be with you. But I also want to help my father, even if he lied to me for years. Damn it!"

Tears overcame her then and she was racked by sobs. She who was always so strong suddenly lost her footing as the events of the last few months seemed to come crashing down on her. John wrapped his arms around Greta and held her tightly. She felt his warmth, but now his closeness didn't offer protection.

"All is going to be well, Greta," he whispered. "All will be well with my help and with that of God."

"With God's help?" Greta gave a desperate chuckle. "Where is God? All I can see is evil, evil in human form! In the shape of Tonio del Moravia, evil walks upon this earth—just like that awful villain before him, Gilles de Rais, and others before him. It is always there."

"Gilles de Rais?" John frowned. "Hang on a moment. What does Gilles de Rais have to do with all this?"

"You . . . you know of him?" Greta swallowed, realizing she hadn't yet mentioned Gilles de Rais to John. She had spoken about Tonio and the devil, but not about Agrippa's and Johann's suspicion that Tonio and the former French marshal were in fact the same person.

"Everyone in the Loire Valley knows of Gilles de Rais—the bastard murdered children in this area, too. There are those who believe that Gilles de Rais is the child-eating ogre you've heard of. And some even believe that he is still taking children today. His former castle isn't too far from here. It's to the southwest, down in Brittany."

Greta stared at him, her mouth open. She took a few moments to let the meaning of John's words sink in.

His old castle isn't too far from here.

John shrugged. "To be honest, I always thought it was just another scary story to frighten children."

Greta was thunderstruck. Everything made sense to her all of a sudden. The pursuit in Orléans, the constant menace. Tonio hadn't followed them.

He lived here.

A stone clattered somewhere and Greta gave a start. A raven cawed in the rafters. Little Satan growled and pricked up his ears, but nothing happened. Greta soon calmed down. The church was very old; it was probably just a loose roof tile. The spire was partially collapsed, which was why they hadn't dared go up there, even if the view was probably spectacular. Across the island and the Loire, over to the castle and beyond . . . Tonio's homeland.

"What is the name of the castle?" she asked.

"It's more of a fortress. It is called Tiffauges and lies in the barony of Retz. People say it is cursed, even after all these years."

Greta closed her eyes.

Tiffauges.

She remembered people talking about it at the taverns. She'd heard the name but hadn't known what it meant. Now she did.

And she also knew what needed to be done.

Greta grabbed John's hand with determination and dragged him to the door.

"Hey! What are you doing?" asked John. "You owe me at least one kiss."

"I want you to come with me," replied Greta firmly. "Whether my father likes you or not. But this news will rouse him." She glanced back at the cross above the altar.

"Tiffauges," she murmured almost inaudibly. The word tasted sour, like milk that had turned, or like a foul-smelling subterranean stream that had suddenly burst to the surface. And yet it offered her a solution.

It was as if God had shown her a new path.

~

Upstairs in the derelict spire, Viktor von Lahnstein ran his tongue over his cracked lips. He signaled Hagen to remain quiet. The coarse giant had almost given them away—then they never would have heard what they just had. Or only with much greater effort and accompanied by irritating screams and wailing.

This way had been much easier.

When they could no longer hear any footsteps, the papal representative rose from the dusty floor, which was covered in mouse droppings, dead flies, and mummified birds. He adjusted his coat and went to the window, where he watched the two lovers walk away. His plan had worked. When Faust had retreated to an inn, they had stuck to the heels of the girl, and now she turned out to be the doctor's daughter. A pretty lass who would certainly come in handy.

Won't you look at that—the doctor isn't as prim as he pretends to be. What is it they say? He who has children also has worries.

Lahnstein smiled underneath his silken bandage, but only briefly, as any movement of his facial muscles still caused him pain. Lucky he had one homing pigeon left. The knowledge he possessed now would guarantee him the post of cardinal.

Because one thing was clear: the secret the Holy Father so desperately longed to learn was hiding at Tiffauges.

Lahnstein had always assumed he would have to take Faust to Rome, but now the doctor would lead him to the secret like a witless donkey with a carrot in front of its nose. And the best part was: afterward, Doctor Faustus would no longer be needed. He would be superfluous, like a weed ripped out by the roots. There would be no memories left of him. His name would be erased from the chronicles. Yes, God was just! After all his trials, he, Viktor von Lahnstein, God's most loyal servant, would finally get the revenge he craved.

An eye for an eye.

The papal representative stared into the growing darkness for a long time. Lahnstein would have liked to hum a song, but it hurt too much. His facial muscles would never be the same again. But he could think of countless things they could do to the doctor, his daughter, and that young assistant.

"Gather our men," he said to Hagen. "Our journey will soon come to an end."

Oh yes, those three would experience hell right here on earth.

~

Johann imagined he was floating in warm water, his body drifting on the surface like a cork, without feelings, without pain. Every now and then someone wiped the sweat off his forehead. He guessed it was Karl but couldn't say for certain, because that would have required opening his eyes, and he'd rather not. He would rather have another drink.

"Theriac," he muttered. "Just one more sip."

"You've had enough theriac to last you a lifetime," said a voice that was probably Karl's. "Do you think I haven't noticed the increase of your daily dose over the last few weeks?"

"Good Karl." Johann smiled. "Can't hide anything from you. You'd have made an excellent physician if you didn't have to travel the lands with that accursed Faustus. I wonder if people will tell your story in years to come, too?"

In an attempt to fight his shaking, Johann had indeed consumed more and more of his medicine, which contained henbane, thorn apple, and poppy juice. It wasn't the cheap, harmless swill he sold to his patients but his very own mixture that had become a constant companion. In the beginning he had only taken a few drops in the evening, but now he mixed three or four spoonfuls with a glass of brandy, several times a day. Today he had drained the whole bottle. It eased the pain and the shaking, but most of all it helped him forget.

He would go to hell, and then Tonio would fetch his daughter.

We will mate with her on Blocksberg Mountain, my little Faust. Through her, evil will receive its new coat.

Something pulled at him. At first Johann thought it was the jagged beak of a raven. Earlier that day he had seen an old raven on the opposite roof as if the beast was waiting for him. Johann growled like an angry wolf, but the pulling didn't stop.

"Go away, you damned creature!" he shouted. "Tell your master that I won't go with him! Not yet."

Then he opened his eyes.

There was no raven. Leaning over him was Greta, and behind her stood another figure who looked like it was trying to remain in the background. The figure had hair like fiery flames. Had the devil come in person to take him?

"Greta," he whispered. "Forgive me . . . I wanted to protect you . . ."

"Jesus Christ, wake up, Father!"

Cold water hit his face, followed by a slap across his cheek. He started up and beheld the face of John Reed with his flaming red hair, his hand raised for another slap.

A wave of anger overcame Johann. He felt so furious that he even sobered up a little.

"How dare you!" he snarled. "And what are you doing here? You have no business being here—you can forget about my daughter!"

John grinned at Greta and Karl beside him. "Didn't I tell you? Anger can be an excellent medicine. I'd be happy to slap him again if—"

"I think that's enough, John," said Greta. She looked at her father intently. "Now can you listen to what I have to say?"

"I am neither senile nor a fool," said Johann. "Say what you must say and then leave me in peace."

"Tonio is nearby," started Greta.

Johann groaned. "I know that. I've been saying all along—"

"He's always been around here, because his castle isn't far from here. It's in Brittany," she said. "It is the castle of Gilles de Rais!" She took Johann's hand.

"Do you understand, Father? He didn't follow us. We traveled to his realm without even knowing!"

"What are you saying?" Johann shot up as if struck by lightning. Little Satan, who had been lying next to the stove, pricked up his ears and gave a low growl.

"It's just as your daughter says," piped up John. "This Gilles de Rais used to live at Tiffauges in the barony of Retz. Folks tell a lot of scary stories about that castle. When Gilles was on trial, they found the bones of hundreds of children in the cellars, and large stoves where his helpers supposedly burned the small bodies. To this day it is a place people avoid."

Johann's head was thumping and he struggled to concentrate. He tried to remember what the great scholar Conrad Celtis had told him about Gilles de Rais many years ago. Celtis, too, had mentioned castles of the dark marshal, but Johann never knew the names of the castles.

"What is the name of the place again?" asked Johann. Something had rung a bell in Johann's mind.

"Tiffauges," repeated John. "It lies in Brittany and—"

"*Seguaffit!*" exclaimed Johann. "Of course, *Seguaffit!*"

"I'm afraid you have a fever." Greta tried to feel his forehead, but Johann swiped her hand aside.

"Leonardo wrote that word on one of his notes in his library," he explained. "Below it was the drawing of a castle upon a mountain of skulls and bones. I couldn't make head nor tail of the word, but I didn't consider the fact that Leonardo often writes in mirror writing. Only this time he wrote the letters correctly but the word back to front. That's why I didn't see it! Seguaffit is Tiffauges—Leonardo knows of the place. And that means he also knows of Gilles de Rais."

Johann remembered that Leonardo had watched him in the library for a while. He probably saw what Johann was looking at, and afterward the room had remained locked. Because Leonardo didn't want him to find out more? It was too late to ask him about it, but it showed that they were on the right track.

"How far is Tiffauges from here?" asked Karl.

John rubbed his nose. "Hmm, a little over a hundred miles, perhaps. Not a good area down there. I've heard new stories of missing or dead children.

Although I guess people talk a lot, and most of it is probably superstitious nonsense."

Trembling, Johann rose from his foul-smelling cot. The news had sobered him up greatly. He swayed a little but managed to sit down at the table.

"Bring me a bowl of water," he ordered. "I want to wash. And a clean shirt!"

Karl threw up his hands in horror. "You don't want to go to that castle, do you? In your condition?"

"It is my last chance, and I should have grasped it much sooner." Johann tried to laugh, but it came out as a hoarse cough. And yet he could feel his strength returning, slowly but steadily. "I am called Magister, Doctor, indeed, and still I can't see the forest for the trees. Tonio, alias Gilles de Rais, is sitting in his web like a fat spider, and the center of the web is called Tiffauges! We've been nearing his home without knowing."

"Even if Tiffauges used to be the home of Gilles de Rais—why should we go there?" asked Karl. "What are you hoping to find there?"

"Haven't you been listening?" snapped Johann. "The bastard is still there, even if he's called Tonio now. The missing children prove it. And there's something else." He thought of the old raven on the rooftop and the black birds that had been following him for weeks. They, too, had been harbingers. "I must defeat Tonio. I should have tried a long time ago. I've been running from him for far too long." Johann nodded with grim determination. "He used to be my master, but at the end of the day he was always my archenemy, my nemesis. I must rise to the challenge once and for all. That is the only way to break this curse."

"But that's madness!" said Karl. "You're sick. You need a physician. In Córdoba—"

"Stop going on about your goddamned Córdoba!" Johann wiped the empty bottle of theriac off the table with his good hand, and it shattered on the ground. "I visited the most learned scholar and then the greatest inventor in the known world, and neither one was able to help me. And why? Because only I can help *myself*! I must challenge Tonio at Tiffauges and vanquish him!"

"You . . . you want to vanquish the devil?" asked Greta incredulously. "Are you serious? That is impossible."

"I like people who strive for the impossible," replied Johann with a smile.

He knew his plan was madness. But what other choice did he have?

"The devil is a good businessman. He always returns for his share," he said, repeating Leonardo's words. "But by God, you can cheat him good. I've done it once before, down in the crypt below Nuremberg. Why shouldn't I do it again?" He gave Karl a challenging look. "The only question is whether I'm going on my own."

No one spoke for a few moments. Then Karl stepped forward.

"I will come with you, Doctor," he said quietly. "I've long traveled by your side, and if it is your belief that you must run straight into perdition, then I'll just have to run with you."

Johann saw John and Greta exchange furtive glances. Then the red-haired fellow jutted out his chin.

"Whoever is murdering those children in Brittany, be it devil or man, they are dangerous. Too dangerous for two weak bookworms. The least I can do is serve as your bodyguard."

Greta seemed surprised; clearly she'd expected something else.

"John, are you sure you want to do this?" she asked.

"He's your father, isn't he? You can wait here in Amboise until it's over. I'm sure it won't take too—"

"You've got to be kidding me!" Greta's eyes were flashing in a way Johann had always feared in his daughter. "How come you men always think you can make decisions for us? First my father and now you! If you feel like you have to act the hero, very well. But I'm certainly not going to sit here and wait for you."

John frowned. "That means you . . . ?"

Johann groaned. He'd known Greta long enough to know that she would do as she pleased, no matter what. "Won't you listen to reason, dear?" he said nonetheless. "It is my disease, and I made this pact with Tonio, not you. Go home and—"

"Home? And where is that supposed to be? I am your *daughter*, remember?" burst out Greta. "The daughter of the forever roaming Doctor Johann Georg Faustus! I have no home. And Tonio is part of my story, too. You could even say he is also my curse."

Johann shook his head hard. "I don't want you to come with me. It was a mistake to bring you here. It's much too dangerous. Tonio knows that you're my daughter. If I fail, he will take his revenge on you. Worse: he will use you for his evil goals. You're still young, Greta! I have lived my life, and what a life it's been." He lowered his voice. "You've seen the lines in my hand. You know what they mean."

"Didn't you say yourself that they don't necessarily have to mean death? And besides, I'm not leaving John." Greta squeezed John's hand. "We are together, and we're just as inseparable as you and Karl. Where John goes, I go, too."

Johann studied Greta's companion coldly. "I don't want you or your beloved John to come," he said harshly.

John glared at him defiantly, his bright-red hair hanging into his eyes.

"Now listen to me, Herr Doctor, I am well aware of the fact that you don't like me. But know that the barony of Retz is a dangerous corner. There aren't just stories about an ogre, there are also other dangers. Huge wolves coming from the mountains, false tracks in the swamps, bands of robbers who live in the woods. The whole area hasn't fully recovered from the long war against the English." John continued in a lower voice. "I've heard stories about Tiffauges Castle. The current owner is in Italy, fighting for the king. And the steward who's in charge in his absence, well . . ." He paused. "I don't know any details, and I'm not a superstitious person. But it seems there really are strange things happening at that castle."

"Tonio," growled Johann. "It's all connected to Tonio, I'm sure of it."

John gave a dismissive wave. "Tonio or not—you need help. I know the area and I know how to defend myself. The dog alone won't save you." He grinned. "And by the looks of it, you don't get a choice."

"Then so be it, damn it all. I can hardly tie you both down." Johann wagged a finger. "But don't you think for a moment that I will pay you."

John smiled with his white teeth and placed his arm firmly around Greta's shoulders. "Don't you worry, Doctor. Your daughter's love is payment enough."

Act III

The Ogre's Cave

11

A SMALL GROUP OF TRAVELERS MOVED STEADILY TO THE
southwest through dark oak and chestnut forests.

Walking at the front was a handsome young man who, despite his plain
pilgrim's garb, appeared learned, like a student or a magister of the liberal arts.
He leafed through a book as he walked, balancing some newfangled eye glasses
on his nose. Following one step behind was a young woman, her hair modestly
hidden beneath a bonnet except for the few unruly strands that insisted on falling into her face. At first glance she appeared to be a pious pilgrim, but a closer
inspection revealed a powerful, muscular body and a proud bearing resembling
that of a countess. Riding on a donkey behind them was a stooped older man,
evidently the father of the two unlike siblings. A strongly built red-haired fellow
formed the rear guard, a long knife and a sack dangling from his belt. He seemed
to be the family's hired guard. A huge black dog darted through the thicket.

A soft whistle rang out. Greta looked back and saw that John was asking the
group to stop. The Scotsman pointed at Little Satan, who was emerging from the
underbrush with a fat pheasant in his mouth; the dog placed it on the ground
in front of John. The bird still flapped a little, so John picked it up and wrung
its neck with a swift movement.

"My compliments on your dog. He hunts better than any terrier." John
laughed as he stuffed the pheasant into the full sack. "Three rabbits and now
this in one day—the black devil truly is an outstanding huntsman." He winked

at Greta. "Better than our young scholar, who's more likely to stumble over a rabbit while he studies his books." He gave Karl a mocking grin. "Is that perhaps because of those round things in front of your eyes?"

"These round things, as you call them, help me to excel in other areas," retorted Karl. "Not everyone is a born hunter. And since we are supposed to be a group of pilgrims, it probably doesn't hurt if at least one of us makes a contemplative impression instead of murdering animals all day long."

Greta smirked. John and Karl taunting each other had become a normal part of their daily routine. Greta suspected that they liked each other well enough, even if Karl was possibly a little envious. John was everything Karl was not: manly, loud, and hands-on, while Karl possessed a higher education and tact, which John lacked. Greta loved them both, but John was the man she desired.

She still didn't fully understand why John had offered to accompany her father. She thought it must be his sense of honor that forbade him from letting a sick old man who happened to be the father of his beloved walk into the wilderness by himself. And she, too, had realized that she wasn't ready to leave Johann.

I also want to find out the truth about Tonio. Because Tonio is part of my life, too.

Greta groaned and pushed her hands into her lower back; they'd been walking all day. "Do we have to camp in the woods again tonight?" she asked tiredly.

"We'll see." John moved his head from side to side. "There aren't a lot of inns around here. But I'm hoping we'll find one tomorrow night. There is a pilgrims' hostel at Azay-le-Rideau."

"I told you we should have gone by boat," said Johann grumpily. He swayed back and forth on his donkey like a sack of flour. "It would have been much more pleasant. And at Tours—"

"They would have already been expecting the honorable doctor," said John. "The traders, at the very least, will all know by now that the famous Doctor Faustus is visiting the beautiful Loire Valley. Perhaps you shouldn't have been quite so loudmouthed outside Leonardo's house at Amboise—especially in front of a bunch of fellow travelers. But it's too late to cry about that now. If we want to stand a chance of remaining unrecognized, then we must travel through the woods. And that is what you want—to stay unrecognized—isn't it?"

Johann said nothing, and Greta could tell by his face that he knew very well John was right, even if he didn't want to admit it. The doctor had traveled to many places before, but this area was completely new to him. Johann was well aware of the dangers lurking in the woods along the Loire, even with Little Satan at their side. John's protection was necessary.

Greta had told her father and Karl about John's real profession, which didn't particularly improve Johann's opinion of his daughter's lover. And yet the two men had formed a sort of truce, probably in part because Johann didn't want to spoil things between him and his daughter. But it was clear to see what he thought of Greta's relationship with John. Even now, on this arduous and perhaps final journey together, the doctor visibly struggled to accept that his daughter had found her love. During the evenings by the campfire, especially, he sometimes failed to swallow back a nasty comment, which had led to more than one argument between him and Greta.

They had been traveling through the forests of France for over a week now, always in the direction of Tiffauges. They spent some nights at inns and others in the woods, making rather slow progress. Johann's paralysis had worsened, spanning his entire left side and down his leg so that he now walked with a limp. He could no longer cover great distances on foot, and that was why the donkey had been the best choice; they certainly couldn't afford four horses. From time to time Johann's head tilted to one side like a puppet, and his face cramped up, making him look even grimmer than usual. At least his condition bore the advantage that everyone believed their pilgrimage story—clearly, they were on their way to Fontevrault Abbey because the sick old man on the donkey hoped for a miracle. The barony of Retz and Tiffauges Castle weren't far from there.

After another two hours of hiking, they finally made camp. John plucked the pheasant, stuffed it with wild carrots and herbs, and roasted it together with the skinned rabbits on a spit. When he divided up the delicious-smelling meat, he tossed a few lumps to Little Satan, who devoured them happily. The dog obeyed John almost as readily as he obeyed Johann, which didn't help to improve the doctor's mood.

As the branches cracked in the fire and everyone's faces were shiny with fat, John told the others what he knew about this area.

"This land was a war zone for decades, almost an entire century," he began. "When Charles IV died as the last Capetian king without a male heir, an argument over the succession of the French crown broke out. The English laid their claim and occupied the entire north of the country. The border was right here, along the Loire." John lowered his voice. "People say this region bled more than any other in France. They say the ghosts of the dead soldiers still haunt these woods."

"Cut out the ridiculous ghost stories," said Johann. "You're our guide, not a juggler or jester."

"Oh, perhaps the doctor would like to tell us his own ghost story?" jeered John. "About a knight who is over a hundred years old and still roams the Loire Valley?"

"I have to agree with John," said Karl. "What you need is real medicine, not the castle of a villain who died a hundred years ago. The whole thing is . . . absurd!" He shook his head. "You are a man of reason, of intellect, and now you're looking for the devil on earth. I had hoped fervently that Leonardo would steer you back onto the right track."

Karl still regretted deeply having left the great Leonardo behind on his deathbed. He would have liked to stay at Cloux for much longer, but instead, they were chasing a phantom.

Or Satan himself.

Greta, on the other hand, had come to believe her father. There were too many events that couldn't be explained with reason alone, as Karl insisted. She prayed every day now, thinking about her mother, who had found God toward the end of her life—and still had to burn at the stake like Jeanne d'Arc, companion of Gilles de Rais.

God and the devil always form a unity, thought Greta. *Like two sides of a coin. What side is my father on?*

The honest truth was, she didn't know.

Around noon the following day they came to a small abbey with lodgings. It had been raining heavily since morning, and they were glad to warm their limbs for a little while and dry their soaked coats by the fire. A handful of other travelers had also sought shelter in the narrow, smoky pub room. They were served steaming mutton stew, cheese, and a slightly sour but drinkable wine. Greta noticed the other guests repeatedly turning their heads to stare at her father. His paralysis was obvious now, and his crooked neck and shaking hand when he lifted the spoon to his mouth turned him into a leper, an untouchable. It seemed to her like the people sensed that the man in their midst was cursed. Johann, however, didn't deign to look at anyone in the room. After he'd finished his meal, he picked up one of his books with shaking hands and awkwardly started to read it. It was the *Figura Umana*, which Faust had stitched back together at Cloux. The tattered work was the last reminder he had of the great Leonardo da Vinci.

They dozed by the fire. Evidently, the chimney hadn't been cleaned in a while; the smoke escaped very poorly. Greta eventually decided to go outside for some fresh air. She stepped out the door and peered through the rain. Over by the stables she saw John with several men. Greta blinked. She could have been mistaken, but two of the men looked almost identical to John's former crew members. When John spotted Greta in the door, he quickly walked away from the men with a nod and hurried over to her. He hugged her tightly.

"They are carpenters from Tours who are here to put a new roof on the abbey," he explained. "They, too, have heard stories of missing or dead children, especially in the barony of Retz." John shook his head. "Hell, I'd really like to know who is behind it."

"If it isn't an ogre, then who?" asked Greta.

"My guess is that it's a gang of slave traders. They might abduct children to sell them to the Ottomans, and whoever is too weak they kill. It wouldn't be the first time—the Atlantic isn't far." John frowned. "But then again, it might actually be connected with Tiffauges. Those carpenters reckon the steward allowed some strange people into the castle, and since then nothing is the way it used to be."

"Those men from Tours do seem to know a lot," said Greta.

John laughed dismissively. "I'm sure much of it is just talk. But one thing is true: there are a lot of wolves in this area. They've become a real pest in recent years. We must be careful."

As if to prove his point, they suddenly heard a howling from the woods, followed shortly by the howling of a second creature.

John nodded grimly. "We'll spend the night here. I don't want to take any risks."

When they set off the next morning, the rain had stopped. The sun broke through the clouds, and it wasn't long before the forest was as muggy as a midsummer day. Damp haze rose up among the tree trunks, and the mosquitoes nearly ate them alive. Karl's blood was apparently the sweetest, as he was worst affected.

Karl asked himself for the hundredth time what he was doing here. The doctor suffered from some kind of terrible disease, and they were making their way through the wilderness in search of the castle where a ghost was supposed to live, an undying mass murderer who'd been hanged a long time ago. This was all complete madness! And still he followed the doctor because . . . because he couldn't help it.

Because I love him.

Karl would stay with Faust until his dying breath. He had sworn it to himself after Leonardo hadn't been able to help them. The great Leonardo. Karl could have learned so much from him. The brushwork alone, the play with light. A few times Karl had been lucky enough to observe while the master painted. Was Leonardo still alive? He had written his will on the eve of their departure.

From the inn they followed the road west but soon left it, turning onto a narrow, overgrown path that Karl would never have found on his own. He admired John Reed, who seemed very much at home in this wilderness and who was superior to him in many other areas, too. His admiration was tainted with a quiet jealousy. He and Greta had always been best friends, and it hurt him to watch how she moved further and further away from him now. But he understood. Greta had changed a fair bit in the last few weeks. She had become even more withdrawn and serious than before. Wearing the pilgrim's garb, she indeed looked like a future nun who would take her vows at Fontevrault Abbey.

Soon Karl's freshly dried clothes were drenched again, this time from his own sweat. The ground was marshy, and in places the track was covered in ankle-deep water. The few villages they passed in the following hours were drab backwaters inhabited by dull-eyed peasants in torn clothes who stared at them like the undead.

When they set up camp in an overgrown clearing that night, everyone was so exhausted that they soon fell asleep. Karl, who had volunteered for the first watch, struggled to keep his eyes open. After a while he heard the howling of wolves, and this time it sounded much closer than the night before. He thought he also heard a low growling not far from their clearing. It was probably Little Satan; Karl hadn't seen the dog in a while. He picked up a burning log and cautiously walked toward the black wall of trees. A pair of eyes glowed between the branches. Karl hurled the log at them and the eyes vanished. But instead he saw something else.

A man was standing among the trees.

Karl could clearly see the outline of a man half-hidden behind a tree only a few steps away from him. Before Karl could say anything, the man saw him and disappeared with lightning speed behind the tree trunks. Karl heard a rustling, but then it was as if the man had never been there. His heart racing, Karl rushed back to the camp and awakened John.

"I saw someone," he whispered urgently. "Right by the edge of the clearing!"

John was instantly awake. He picked up his long knife and stood quietly.

"You stay here," he whispered. "Wake the others. I'm going to take a look."

A moment later John had vanished into the woods. Again the wolves howled, and there was a rustling and cracking in the undergrowth. Karl listened. Was it John or someone else?

Or something else, thought Karl. Then he called himself a fool. All this talk of an undead knight was messing with his mind.

He sneaked over to Greta and shook her awake, and then he woke Johann. Together they sat and listened but couldn't hear anything apart from the howling of the wolves. They sat this way for a long while, listening in silence, but John didn't return. The minutes seemed to stretch forever.

"What could have happened to him?" asked Greta, her face pale, her hair tousled. "Why isn't he coming back?"

"I don't know, damn it!" said Karl. "I only know that someone was in the forest—some man."

"Tonio?" asked Johann. "Do you think it might have been Tonio?"

"It was too dark. And besides . . ." Karl fell silent when they heard footsteps. Branches snapped. Karl was about to call out to John with relief, but then he stopped. What they heard were clearly the sounds of several people. Karl realized that the dog still hadn't returned.

"John?" shouted Greta. "Christ, John, where are you?"

There was no reply.

Karl's hand moved to the hand cannon he was keeping under his blanket. He cursed under his breath when he remembered that he hadn't loaded it. What good was an unloaded pistol?

Well, at least potential attackers wouldn't know that it isn't loaded, he thought.

He rose abruptly, clutching his weapon. "I'm going to take a look myself. I'll be back soon."

"I don't think we should all split up, God damn it," said Johann. "We must stick together and . . ."

But Karl had already disappeared among the trees. As soon as he left the clearing with the campfire, everything around him became pitch black. Again he heard furtive steps sneaking through the woods and another growl, and this time Karl thought he could make out Little Satan.

"Satan," he hissed. "Come here!"

Karl thought saying this unholy name out loud in the dark of night sounded like a bad omen. He clutched the handle of the hand cannon tightly, holding it out in front of him like a protective amulet. He listened for a while longer. When nothing happened, he walked back to the clearing.

And froze.

"What the devil?" he gasped.

Greta and the doctor had vanished.

Their furs and blankets were still by the fire, and one of the books lay on Johann's bed, the pages moving in the breeze. It looked as though the two of them had just left for a moment, but Karl knew they weren't coming back.

Someone or something had taken them.

Just then Karl heard a noise behind him, a soft hissing as from a snake. A leather string was thrown around his neck and tightened, suffocating him.

Then everything went black.

~

Johann slowed his breathing.

Panic welled up inside him in tall waves, each new surge making it harder to breathe. He thought he would suffocate, mostly due to the dirty rag someone had stuffed into his mouth. Another rag had been tied around his eyes and nose, so that Johann was gliding through a sea of darkness. But worst of all, he couldn't move.

This is what it's going to be like, he thought. *Very soon. As if I'm buried alive.*

He jerked back and forth wildly, like a fish on dry land. Someone hit him over the head. He was almost grateful for the blow, because it reminded him that he wasn't wholly paralyzed but merely bound and gagged. He was tied belly down to the back of a horse, and the steady rocking and occasional snorting calmed him down. His breathing was becoming more regular. The rag over his nose didn't let much air through, but enough to prevent him from passing out. How long had they been riding? Minutes, hours? He had lost any sense of time.

The last thing he remembered was the sound of a branch snapping behind him. He had just risen to fetch Karl back from the forest when someone placed a strap around his neck and pulled tight with brutal force, and then he must have lost consciousness. Whoever was behind this abduction knew what they were doing. They didn't want to kill him, just immobilize him. He had awoken on the back of the horse, tied up like a bale of cloth.

He heard soft whimpering from beside him and breathed a sigh of relief. It sounded like Greta. They'd probably done the same thing to her. Johann thought frantically about who their abductors might be. The most likely candidate was Viktor von Lahnstein. Was he planning on taking him all the way to Rome like this? Or could it be Tonio and his henchmen? But somehow this attack didn't feel like Tonio's handiwork. It had been too rough and, at the same time, not malicious enough.

Johann occasionally heard the muffled voices of men. They conversed in French, but Johann couldn't make out much. He hung across the animal's back like a sack of flour with his head down, the blood collecting in his legs, which grew increasingly numb. It felt like the paralysis was finally spreading through the rest of his body. Johann was overcome by profound fear. He felt like a dead lump of wood with eyes and a mouth, rigid and lifeless yet conscious.

That's how it's going to be soon.

He tried to think of something nice. Of his daughter, the most precious thing on earth to him, even if she had taken to that braggart of a Scotsman. Was John Reed still alive? Or had their kidnappers gotten rid of him, and Karl, too? To his horror, Johann realized that he wasn't feeling grief at the thought.

My heart is also turning numb. Or has it always been that way?

After what felt like an eternity the sounds changed, the clatter of the hooves becoming brighter, as if the horses were walking on cobblestones now, then timber. Then they stopped. Someone shouted something, there was a creaking and rattling, and they moved on. A chilly wind tugged at Johann's clothes. His back ached as if someone had hit him with a cudgel.

Finally his horse stopped again. Men laughed as they dismounted, then someone grabbed him and dragged him off the saddle. He caught a brief glimpse through a slit in the rag covering his eyes and made out a dark courtyard lit by torches. The chilly breeze gave him the impression they were atop a hill. Someone cut the ropes around his feet, pulled him up, and gave him a slap on the back, as if encouraging an old mule to walk. Johann's legs caved in, so the men carried him up many steps, cursing profusely in French. His hands were still tied and he couldn't see.

After a while they seemed to arrive at a chamber. It was cold and echoey. They sat Johann down on a stone bench, and then nothing happened for a while. He could tell by the groaning to his left and right that he wasn't the only prisoner. He thought he could make out at least two other people and prayed that they were Greta and Karl.

Finally a door opened somewhere and footsteps approached.

"Retirez-lui le bandeau des yeux," ordered a soft voice.

Rough fingers removed his gag and ripped the cloth off his eyes. The light from the torches blinded his good eye like the sun so that Johann couldn't make out much for a while. Men clad in polished armor walked away and a door slammed shut. Johann blinked and rubbed his eye. A figure as large as a bear blocked his field of vision. He lifted his head and blinked again to make sure he wasn't dreaming. But it was no dream.

Standing in front of Johann was the king of France.

12

THERE COULD BE NO DOUBT.

Johann knew King Francis I from countless paintings. The young French ruler had an interesting face with a particularly large nose, which the ladies considered an expression of his manliness. His black beard was cropped short, according to the latest fashion, and his eyes looked somewhat sleepy underneath heavy lids. Francis was a giant of more than six feet, with a mighty chest and a muscular build. And then there was the royal garment he wore, made from the finest green silk, and the silver-plated cuirass displaying the fire-spitting salamander of the royal crest.

"Welcome to Chinon Castle, my dear doctor," said the king. His French was soft and melodious, like that of a bard. "I hope your journey here wasn't too uncomfortable."

"The suspension of the carriage didn't seem to be the latest model," croaked Johann. He looked to his left and right on the stone ledge and saw Greta and Karl perched there as well. There was no sign of John Reed. Johann felt profound relief washing over him but tried not to show it. Greta and Karl also appeared to have recognized the man in front of them and stared at him with a mixture of surprise, fear, and respect. It wasn't every day that they had an audience with one of the most powerful rulers in the world.

"At least I traveled in good company," said Johann now. "I despise going anywhere without my daughter and my assistant."

Francis smiled. "I'm glad you haven't lost your sense of humor, Doctor. Your French is excellent, by the way."

"I learned your language by reading the books of your wonderful poets," said Johann. "Jean Molinet, François Villon . . ."

"Je suis Françoys, dont il me poise," recited Francis I with a nod. "Villon is one of my favorite poets, too. *Né de Paris emprès Pontoise, et de la corde d'une toise,"* he went on in a soft rhythm. "Villon was put in jail repeatedly and only narrowly escaped death a few times. Apparently, he was quite the swindler and charlatan, but also a genius. Does that sound familiar to you, Doctor?"

Instead of replying, Johann tried to make out more of their surroundings. There were three narrow arrow slits but no windows and no furnishings. The three of them were tied up on a stone bench that jutted out from the wall. The king in front of them was illuminated by torches in rusty brackets. Astonishingly, there were no guards in the room. Francis interpreted Johann's look correctly.

"This conversation isn't for everyone's ears—there are too many eavesdroppers already." He wrinkled his royal forehead. "That was also why I had to bring you here in such an uncomfortable manner. Please accept my apologies."

"Where is John?" asked Greta now. "What have you done to him?" Leaves and twigs were tangled in her hair, and her dirty face made her look like a charcoal burner, but she seemed unhurt and hadn't lost her pride.

"Who?" Francis looked at the young woman with irritation, unaccustomed to being addressed this disrespectfully. "If you are speaking of the large dog, we have taken him into custody. He resides in the royal kennels. Truly an exceptionally—"

"Not the dog, the third man in our group," said Greta, her eyes flashing at the king. "Where is he? Where is John?"

"Oh, you mean Jean!" The king laughed as if Greta had told a funny joke. "I have been told that the handsome lad has his eye on you—and vice versa, as I see now." He gave a wave. "Don't worry, he is fine. You shall see him again soon. But first I want to speak with the doctor. I want to talk about a friend we have in common." He turned back to Johann. "I believe you know who I mean."

"Leonardo da Vinci," said Johann quietly.

Francis's expression darkened. "He died in my arms three days ago. Leonardo was like a father to me, and more. Someone like him will never come again."

"I will miss him, too," replied Johann, slumping. The news of Leonardo's death pained him, even if he'd known that this moment would come. Now one of the greatest men of mankind had become history.

And one or two secrets have gone with him, I'd say, thought Johann.

"You might be pleased to hear that Leonardo mentioned your name toward the end. And that of your fetching assistant, too." He winked at Karl. "It appears he liked him a great deal, and now I can see why. Do you know what he said just before he died?"

The king leaned closer to Johann. "He said that Doctor Faustus knows the secret. Strange, isn't it? Those were his final words. *Doctor Faustus knows the secret.*" From one moment to the next, Francis seemed anything but sleepy, eyeing Johann closely. "I wonder what kind of secret that is, Doctor. Can you tell me? My scholars sifted through Leonardo's writings, page by page, but they found nothing."

Johann froze.

"What kind of secret?" repeated Francis.

"Toward the end people often speak in riddles," replied Johann awkwardly.

"And yet they always tell the truth." Francis's face was very close to his now, and Johann could smell the strong perfume of which one vial probably cost more than a good horse. "What secret do you share with Leonardo, Doctor Faustus? I am not daft. My men have been watching you ever since Lahnstein and his bloodhound started nipping at your heels."

"You . . . you know about the papal representative?" Johann's thoughts raced. Did the king also know about their search for Gilles de Rais? What sort of game was being played here?

"Of course." Francis straightened up with a smile. "Rome and France might be allies in the fight against the powerful Habsburg empire right now, but that can change very quickly. In Italy, everyone plays by their own rules. And just like the pope has his spies, I have mine. That is how I know that fat Leo has been interested in you for a long time. He wanted to have you taken to Rome, am I not right? You managed to slip through his fingers at Bamberg. I wondered for a long time why you fled to France thereafter. Why not England, Spain, the Netherlands?"

The king squared his shoulders.

"But when you went to Amboise, it became clear. What reason might the famous Doctor Faustus have to visit the equally famous inventor Leonardo da Vinci? I believe it was to learn the secret that the pope assumed you already knew. But you didn't! Or at least not the whole secret—there were a few last questions, weren't there? And so you asked Leonardo. And now that he is dead, you are the only person in the world who possesses the knowledge of the secret."

"And . . . and what is that secret supposed to be?" asked Johann. He had a hunch that he would finally learn why Lahnstein wanted to take him to Rome—and why he was now in this castle in front of the French king.

"Well, what do you think?" The king grinned. "Don't play the fool, Doctor. It is the secret the whole world is burning to know, first and foremost the pope, that greedy pig, who is looking for you. Now you'll just tell me instead. The fate of the world might depend on it."

Francis leaned down once more and breathed into his ear: "It is the secret of the *lapis philosophorum.*"

$$\sim$$

Hundreds of miles away, Pope Leo X climbed down narrow stairs into his inner sanctum, directly beneath his chambers in Castel Sant'Angelo. This room was better hidden and protected than the papal coffers. To get to the secret chamber, he had to go behind one of the tapestries and locate a particular stone in the wall that didn't look any different from the stones surrounding it. When it was pushed, part of the wall slid to the side, revealing a staircase that led to an iron door that was barred with three locks. The locksmith who had made them was no longer alive, and neither was the builder of the secret chamber. Aside from Leo, there was only one other person who knew of the room.

Leo pulled out his keys and opened the locks one by one. Then he pushed against the heavy door, which creaked open. The stench of sulfur and quicksilver hit his nose. To Leo it was a pleasant smell, more tantalizing than any perfume. He entered the small, square room; its walls were lined with tables and shelves full of crucibles, retorts, and vials. In the center of the room, a stone table stained by various corrosive substances held a still made of glass, and next to it glowed the remains of a fire. Between mummified salamanders and dried seahorses that were rotting away in an old mortar lay numerous books bound in yellowed leather. Leo had read them all and knew large sections by heart.

Grind the dried bezoar of a goat and mix it with the poison of an adder . . . Vaporize some quicksilver until a cloud rises to the sky . . . Mix a quart of mouse blood with wine from burgundy and the urine of a unicorn.

Years before he ascended the papal throne, Leo had discovered his passion for alchemy. He was an intelligent man, a scholar, no charlatan, and therefore he approached the subject in a serious and scientific manner. He had learned to discern lies from the truth just as he could skim the dross off iron. Alchemy was much too important a field to leave to lunatics and sorcerers. Great men had studied the subject—Democritus, Avicenna, Albertus Magnus, Nicolas Flamel, Roger Bacon. They all had tried their hands at transmutation, the complex craft of turning one element into another. This wasn't about heretical black magic, but about white magic—or that which was nowadays called science. There even were highly venerable men of the church who practiced alchemy. No one had fully achieved transmutation yet, although minor milestones had been accomplished here and there. But no one had recognized the bigger picture yet, because everyone was only mucking out their own stables.

Leo stepped beside the glowing embers in the fireplace. An iron pan was suspended above it, and inside the pan was a reddish powder. Leo picked up a pair of bellows and pumped air into the embers until beads of sweat formed on his forehead. He breathed heavily, the quicksilver fumes making him dizzy and sharpening his senses at the same time. Everything seemed so easy, the solution was probably right before his eyes. But why couldn't he see it? Why?

There was one person who did know it. Someone who was dead and yet alive.

In old documents deep down in the Vatican archives, the pope had stumbled across Gilles de Rais, a French marshal who had lived the high life a hundred years ago until he ran out of money. The marshal had turned to alchemy in his despair, and the documents showed Leo that Gilles had indeed solved the mystery toward the end.

Albeit using the aid of rather cruel methods.

With the future of the church at stake, however, Leo couldn't afford to be squeamish.

He continued to pump air into the embers, which were now bright red. The pope was panting, his fat body quivering as if from convulsions of lust. It was an urge, a kind of flagellation that sometimes overcame him at night, and he would go downstairs to pore over books, stir, pump, weigh, grind, burn, and cook until the concoction foamed and bubbled. Sometimes the *other one* was down here with him, he whose wisdom was so much greater than Leo's and who knew how to hide it well. It had been he who had brought the notes about the dark marshal to Leo's attention. Leo was certain that God spoke through the mouth of the *other one*. He had told the pope about Gilles de Rais and that Doctor Faustus, the famous sorcerer and necromancer, had summoned the Frenchman's soul.

And that was when Gilles de Rais had revealed his secret to the doctor!

Leo pumped faster, and the red powder in the iron pan dissolved, turning sticky at first and then liquid. Fumes rose into the air and then the *other one* was with him, placing his hand on Leo's shoulder, whispering in his ear.

Do you know Faust, the doctor, my servant? Bring him to me.

Leo had questioned so many alchemists, on the rack, in chains; he'd had their limbs crushed and torn in his quest to learn the truth. But they had all been charlatans—the doctor was his last hope. And the *other one* had told him that Faust held the answer.

As Leo gazed at the bubbling liquid in the pan, he thought of the last letter from his personal representative, which had arrived three days ago. Faust had been staying with Leonardo da Vinci. And now he was on his way to Tiffauges. Leo was sure that Faust would invoke the dark marshal at the castle once more in the hope of learning more secrets. The *other one* had been right—the doctor was indeed the person who would serve him and the whole world.

But first he had to get Faust here, to Rome.

Leo dreaded to imagine what would happen if the French king or that young Habsburg prince found out about this. The scales of destiny would suddenly tilt to the other side. This couldn't happen, ever. The continuity of the Christian world was at stake: monuments had to be built and new churches erected to demonstrate God's glory to the rabble. Now especially, in these uncertain times when so many renounced the true faith.

It cannot happen.

With each word, Leo pumped another gust of air into the fire, the whispering in his ear as hot as the orange embers.

Bring me Faust. The doctor. My servant.

With one last gasp the Holy Father collapsed in front of the fireplace.

In the acrid fumes above him rose a creature that was larger, older, and more malevolent than anything men had ever imagined in their worst nightmares.

∼

"The *lapis philosophorum*—the philosopher's stone?"

Johann now understood what the French king wanted from him. It cost him a considerable effort not to break out in hysterical laughter.

"You . . . you believe I can produce gold?"

"The philosopher's stone, the red lion, the elixir of life, panacea—call it what you will." King Francis I didn't bat an eyelid. "Since the days of the great Hermes Trismegistus the alchemists have been searching for the substance that can turn base metals into gold. If there can be a divine soul substance that suffuses everything and that can take an endless number of shapes, then such a transmutation must also be possible. Isn't that what you've been claiming in your lectures again and again?"

Johann groaned inwardly. The philosopher's stone was part of alchemy just like horoscopes were part of astrology, and it was true that he'd been telling people for years that he knew its secret. But that was a lie. He didn't rule out the possibility that such a substance existed, even if Avicenna and other great scholars had voiced their doubts. But he hadn't identified the substance, and knew of no one who had.

He remembered what Agrippa had told him, that Gilles de Rais had also dabbled in alchemy. That was why Viktor von Lahnstein had mentioned his name back at Altenburg Castle. Someone had told the pope of Johann's connection to the dead French marshal, and now Leo thought Johann had learned the secret of the *lapis philosophorum* from Gilles de Rais. It was absurd! Admittedly, Johann had done everything in his power to feed his reputation as a mysterious alchemist. It seemed that now he was paying the price for his foolishness.

"So that is why they wanted to take the doctor to Rome?" asked Karl incredulously. "Because the pope believes he can make gold?"

King Francis nodded. "Leo is in dire straits financially. His court devours horrendous amounts of money—a hundred thousand ducats a year, which is more than twice as much as his predecessors spent. Leo wants to expand the Roman church with any pomp and circumstance he can think of. The construction of the enormous Saint Peter's Basilica is just the beginning. He is convinced that people need huge Christian monuments to solidify their belief. And just when things were starting to become difficult for him, this little German monk comes along and pees on his parade." The king gave a chuckle. "At first the Holy Father didn't take Luther seriously, but now he's running short of money, and his trade with indulgences is dwindling. If things carry on this way, Leo will get buried in a pauper's gown."

"I wouldn't have thought you were in any danger of sharing this fate," said Johann mockingly.

"You are right. Generally speaking, I can't complain. But right now I need more money than you can imagine." Francis paused for effect. "Almost one million guilders, to be precise."

"One *million* guilders?" Karl's jaw dropped with astonishment. "But . . . but . . . I mean . . . why?"

"I think I know why," said Greta, her gaze fixed on the king. Her French was good enough by now to follow the conversation. "It was all over town, back in Orléans. His Majesty may be the king of France, but he's not king of the world yet. For that he needs the German kingship—and, of course, the title of emperor."

Francis smirked and looked at Johann. "Your daughter, isn't she? A clever child indeed. I've always said that women would go far in politics if only they were allowed to participate. My Claude, for example—"

"You want to buy the German throne?" asked Johann, cutting him off but too confused to notice the impudence. Then he nodded thoughtfully. "Of course . . . the old German emperor Maximilian is dead, and a new king must be elected. It is between you and the Habsburg Charles. But you need the votes of the seven German electors."

"Four would suffice. The elector of Brandenburg is the greediest. I promised him a French princess, but apparently he is too ugly for her. She eloped into the arms of the Duke of Savoy." Francis sighed and played with the rings on his finger. "Young and ambitious Charles from the house of Habsburg doesn't have much money to buy votes, either, but he does have the powerful Fuggers, the dynasty of merchants who financed his grandfather. And the Fuggers want Charles as their puppet so that their old notes of debt to the Habsburgs don't expire, and so they give him the money. Even if old Jakob Fugger and Charles share a profound dislike of one another."

Johann wondered whether the Habsburgs also believed in the fairy tale that he could turn something worthless into gold. It looked as though he had become a pawn in the hands of the powerful, a victim of his own bragging and of a pope obsessed by a ludicrous idea—an idea the French king shared. It was utter nonsense and yet logical, a consequence of his countless claims and tricks over the years.

Doctor Johann Georg Faustus, the greatest magician and alchemist on earth.

Johann cleared his throat.

"Your Majesty. I am sorry to spoil your plans, but I'm not the one you take me for. I am not a bad astrologer—if you need a horoscope, I'm your man. And I know a fair bit about medicine and alchemy. But the philosopher's stone—"

"Taisez-vous!" hissed Francis. He gave an impatient wave. "My spies overheard several conversations in the papal chambers, so there's no need to tell lies. You are no simple charlatan but the great Doctor Johann Georg Faustus. Your deeds are known even here in France."

"But they're just stories, tales—lies and exaggerations."

"And why, then, did you visit Leonardo da Vinci? What reason could there be for the most famous sorcerer of the empire to seek out the most famous inventor of our time if it isn't to learn about a secret?" Francis's eyes were narrow slits now. *"Doctor Faustus knows the secret*—those were Leonardo's last words. Are you telling me he was lying? Don't play me for a fool, Doctor. I am no dumb peasant but the king of France!"

Johann said nothing. He didn't want to tell the king the real reason for his journey. Evidently Francis hadn't noticed yet that his left side was paralyzed. He probably ascribed Johann's crouched posture and the pain in his face to the fetters and the long ride. And Johann had no idea what Leonardo da Vinci had meant with his last words.

What damned secret was he supposed to know?

"Chinon Castle has a long history, by the way," said King Francis, changing the subject. "It used to belong to the king of England, who had many possessions in France. You could say that this castle is the starting point of the long, unhappy war between our two countries. The famous Richard the Lionheart came and went here, and it was here that Jeanne d'Arc met Charles VII, dauphin of France. The maiden persuaded him to take up the fight against the Englishmen once more. Chinon is considered impregnable." Francis spread his arms. "This truly is a formidable place steeped in history. But it is also a sinister place. Here in Coudray Tower the Knights Templar were incarcerated with their grand master Jacques de Molay before they were taken to Paris for their execution. Did you know that? I hope it won't come to that for you, Doctor. I will give you time in this dungeon to think about what Leonardo might have meant about the secret. Oh, and before I forget . . ." Francis smiled. "For one of you there is a little surprise waiting behind this door." He walked to the door and knocked three times. *"Mettez-les au cachot!"*

The door opened and several guards stepped into the room. Now that Johann's eye had adjusted to the light, he could make out their uniforms. They were green like the robe of the king. The uniformed guard at the front was of athletic build though not particularly tall, and he avoided Johann's gaze. But Johann recognized him anyway.

The man's hair was bright red.

"John!"

Greta jumped up despite her tied ankles, tripped, and fell hard on her knee. She realized immediately what John's appearance meant but didn't want to accept it. She felt like she was falling into an endlessly deep hole, and as if she suddenly stood naked before the whole world. Maybe there was some sort of convincing explanation—there had to be an explanation!

When she scrambled back to her feet, John was standing in front of her. He looked at her with sad eyes.

"Tell me this isn't true!" shouted Greta. "You . . . you . . ."

"I know—Jean can be very charming when he wants to," said the king from behind John Reed, smirking. "One of the reasons I made him the leader of my household guard at Amboise, in spite of his youth. Quite apart from that, he is a capable combatant who would fight to the death for his king. Like everyone else here." He gestured at the heavily armed men in the room. "All of them Scotsmen like Jean. The Scottish have always been our close friends, and they hate the English as much as we do."

Greta stared at John. It was as if she'd been slapped in the face. Everything she had felt for him, for the only man she'd ever really loved, suddenly crumbled to dust.

Before her stood a traitor.

At first she was overwhelmed by grief, but then an even more powerful emotion took over: anger. Anger and hatred. How could she have been so blind?

"I'm sorry, Greta," muttered John. "Believe me, I didn't want this to happen. But my assignment—"

"I spit on your assignment," snapped Greta. "So that's what I was to you—an *assignment*! How could I have been so dumb? I feel like whipping myself for my stupidity!"

Beside her, Karl sighed quietly. "Your father was right after all. We never should have trusted him."

"That is my first and foremost rule," said the king, giving Greta an almost pitying look. "I never trust anyone, and I fare quite well with that rule. Take it as a lesson, girl. Life is often nothing but deception and trickery—something you ought to know as a juggler." He gave a little laugh. "You see, Jean told me about you. When my spies alerted me that the legendary Doctor Faustus resides in France, I immediately sent my best man after you."

Greta now recognized some of the soldiers behind John. They were the crew from the *Étoile de Mer*, staring at her sternly. It was as if a veil had been pulled from in front of her eyes. Everything made sense now. The coincidental meeting at the port of Orléans, their rendezvous in the gardens of Blois, John's strange disappearance at Amboise, and the way he watched her in church. That he stayed close to her without a boat and a crew.

"That night at Orléans when someone followed me in the reeds—that was you, wasn't it?" she asked John. "I thought it was someone else, someone with a red cap, but it was your red hair all along." Greta recalled her escape through the wetland and the eerie song that had probably been a product of her fears. She had been convinced that Tonio was after her.

John nodded. His face was stony, with no trace of triumph. "I wanted to find out where you were going," he said quietly. "But then you spotted me and I was forced to run. I made it back to the tavern just in time. My men covered for me. Believe me, Greta, I didn't mean for this to happen."

"Enough," said the king. "Take them to the dungeon." He turned to Johann once more. "Think, Doctor. I promise you one thing: the German throne weighs more than any life. Including yours. The grand master Jacques de Molay was mistaken to believe that he was irreplaceable. He burned for a long time, and then there was nothing left of him but ashes in the wind. Don't make the same mistake."

He snapped his fingers, and the soldiers grabbed the three prisoners, dragging them off the bench. They did not resist, like cattle on the way to slaughter.

~

On the sheer cliff below the castle, a figure pulled himself slowly but steadily upward. He inched forward like a monstrous spider, using a small hole for his hand here and a narrow ledge there. Tied to his muscular back was a leather scabbard holding a mighty sword.

Hagen paused for a moment on the wall and took a deep breath. He avoided looking down. It was the middle of the night, and clouds had moved in front of the pale moon. How many feet had he climbed? One hundred, two hundred? His eyes darted to the left, where more figures clad in black were clinging to the rock face. There were about a dozen of them, handpicked by Hagen for this mission. Miraculously, not one of them had fallen—yet.

When Viktor von Lahnstein had given him the order to break into Chinon Castle a few hours ago, Hagen had thought at first that it was a bad joke. The castle was situated on a long elevation consisting of three rocky outcrops connected by bridges. On the side where the Vienne River lazily flowed toward the Loire, the walls of the fortress rose steeply and impregnably behind the town. The north side looked a little better, with vineyards that gradually gave way to an increasingly steep slope. But even here there was still the problem of a tall wall with numerous towers filled with watchmen, making sure there was no attack from that side. The whole affair was complete madness, but Lahnstein had insisted. And so, after some deliberation, they had decided on the north side.

Hagen clenched his teeth and climbed on. The stones were wet and slippery. He tried his best to keep three of his four limbs attached to the wall at all times, just as he had done on many other walls before. But this one was particularly difficult to scale. As he reached up with his right hand, his legs slipped out from under him.

Damn!

Hanging on the rock with just one hand, Hagen dangled above the abyss. He forced himself to remain calm as he searched for a crack or some small ledge that might serve as a foothold. During his many years on the battlefields of Europe he had learned that rushing things often led to death. Hagen came from a poor peasant family near Bern that fell victim to a troop of mercenaries from Burgundy. His father and mother had been hanged from the rafters, while his sister had been allowed to stay alive a little longer as several men raped her before their leader slit her throat. The mercenaries had taken the small but strong boy with them and taught him to fight. At twelve years old, Hagen had at last grown bigger than the leader of their troop. He had rammed his sword into the filthy pig's stomach and looked him in the eye as he whispered the name of his sister. Since then, Hagen had only worked for himself, a mercenary of death and the best at his game. He was always loyal to whoever paid him the most.

Even if that sometimes led to suicide missions like this one.

Cold sweat stood on his forehead when he finally discovered a gap that fitted his fingers. In an almost superhuman effort, Hagen heaved his more than two hundred pounds upward until his toes found a narrow ledge to stand on. He paused to catch his breath. He only hoped that the goddamned Doctor Faustus was worth all this. Or, rather, the secret he harbored.

The secret of how to make gold.

Hagen's size, his beastly strength, and his taciturn way led people to believe that he was as dumb as an ox. But that was not at all the case. If he were dumb, he never would have made it into the uppermost ranks of the Swiss guard, serving the pope as a personal bodyguard. If he were dumb, he would be dead by now or inside the dungeons of Castel Sant'Angelo, which was much worse. Hagen was clever, his mind sharpened by the many political intrigues during which he had assisted the high and mighty. That was why he had grasped very quickly why the doctor was so valuable. And why he mustn't land in the hands of the enemies.

Hagen had warned Lahnstein that it was a mistake to observe the doctor for this long—they should have struck a long time ago. But Lahnstein had wanted to wait and see what the doctor intended to do at Tiffauges Castle. And now those damned frog eaters had snatched him away.

A harsh Swiss curse on his lips, Hagen climbed on. He was high enough now that he could make out individual soldiers in the watchtowers. They laughed and warmed their hands over braziers, unaware of the almost invisible shapes crawling up the wall like lizards.

Two more times Hagen almost fell but found a hold in the last moment. Then he finally reached the battlements and pulled himself over the top, soundlessly jumping into the courtyard on the other side. A large building towered in front of him—the palas of the main castle, he guessed—and to his left, the track led across a bridge. To his right, another bridge led to the third rocky outcrop that held several squat towers.

Where are you, little doctor?

Meanwhile, the other Swiss mercenaries had also jumped over the battlements. All of them were experienced warriors, armed with long knives and crossbows; only Hagen had brought his German longsword, despite the additional weight. Most of them knew each other from wars; they were hardened soldiers who spoke the same language and who could communicate by gestures alone if need be. The Swiss guard was considered an elite troop, and these men were the best of the best. Hagen signaled to the men, and together they moved along the battlements to the west.

Hagen grinned when he saw that the moon was completely covered by clouds now. The heavens were on their side. At least Lahnstein had done his homework and, for a few coins down in the village, had found that the dungeons were situated inside Coudray Tower, which was immediately beyond the second bridge. In the light of the torches, Hagen could make out several heavily armed guards and an external staircase that led to the tower's second story and a door. The door was additionally secured by a small walled balcony from which the guards could stymie any advance without exposing themselves. Hagen counted five or six men downstairs, while his own group was twice as strong. If they were swift and silent, and nothing unexpected happened, they would eliminate the enemy before anyone could sound the alarm.

Hagen was about to give the signal when he noticed movement below the bridge. He squinted into the darkness.

Someone was there!

Hagen saw the figure clearly now, hunched amid the bridge's beams like a giant bat. Then Hagen saw other men clad in black beneath the bridge—they were about to climb up.

What the hell?

Hagen's thoughts raced. They certainly weren't Frenchmen. Why should they climb their own bridge in a secret mission? And obviously, it wasn't his own men. They were standing behind him awaiting his orders.

Who are you?

When the first mysterious intruders climbed over the bridge railing and headed toward the guards' chamber, Hagen realized that he didn't have much time. Hunched over, he started to run as soundlessly as possible in his heavy leather armor. Just as he reached the bridge, another figure climbed over the railing. He was entirely clad in black and, like the others, wore a black mask over his face. Hagen only saw the gleaming whites of the eyes. The man seemed just as surprised as Hagen, but he committed a crucial mistake.

He spoke to Hagen.

"*¿Amigo o enemigo?*" whispered the stranger.

Those words told Hagen enough. He shoved the man hard on his chest, and the man screamed as he fell into the depths.

A moment later, chaos broke loose on the bridge.

Men roared commands and ran at each other with swords and knives. Crossbow bolts whirred through the air, and some hit their targets. The soldiers from the guards' chamber ran onto the bridge. Hagen heard shouts in Spanish, French, and Swiss German, and he spun around when another masked man stormed toward him with his short sword raised. In one fluid movement, Hagen stepped to the side, drew his sword, and turned sideways. When the man's sword struck thin air, the huge Swiss mercenary lunged and decapitated his opponent with one single stroke. The headless torso ran for a few more yards until it finally collapsed.

A bolt shot into Hagen's muscular thigh. He clenched his teeth and fended off another attack with his two-handed sword. This was where he felt most at home—in battle. His blood was rushing in his ears, and he felt a greater thrill than he ever did with women.

This is my world!

In the darkness of the night he couldn't tell for sure whether he was fighting Frenchmen or Spaniards at any given moment. As he parried the enemies' strokes with fluid movements, he considered what had just happened. Evidently, the Habsburgs had also learned of Faust's secret and sent their Spanish soldiers. Just like Hagen and his men, they must have been watching the doctor for a while, and once the French had locked him up at Chinon Castle, they decided to break him out.

Hagen swung the four-foot-long sword above his head, giving himself a short breather. All around him men screamed and died, and now he could hear the sound of horns and cries of alarm from the other towers.

Hagen's senses were heightened, as always in such situations. He saw, heard, and smelled more than others, which had saved his life on more than one occasion. But this time their situation seemed hopeless. Very soon, every single soldier at the castle would arrive here, and then it would be only a matter of time before they were all dead. What angered Hagen the most was that Viktor von Lahnstein would be spared—when it had been the damned priest in the first place who put them in this position with his reluctance to act.

Lahnstein was probably sitting at a tavern with a jug of wine, while they would all have their heads chopped off. Yes, they would all die. Unless . . .

Unless we have a valuable hostage.

With an angry scream, the giant hurled himself at his enemies. He cut down the first one with two mighty strokes and tossed the next one off the bridge.

Then Hagen stormed toward the tower that most likely contained the doctor.

~

Down in the dungeon, Greta stared at the slimy green mold on the opposite wall, breathing in the smell of feces and rot. Karl had tried to speak with her several times since they were brought down here, but Greta had put up an invisible wall around herself. She still couldn't believe she could have been so wrong. The man she had loved and desired was a traitor. He had only used her to get his hands on her father. All his love, charm, and wit, all his affection, had been nothing but an act. She felt incredibly stupid and at the same time awfully empty. It was as if someone had ripped out her heart. How could she have trusted John? She should have known in the port of Amboise, when he disappeared so suddenly. But her stupid feelings had been stronger.

The three of them cowered on bug-ridden straw inside a circular shaft below Coudray Tower. Countless notches and scratched sketches served as reminders of the hundreds of prisoners who had been detained here over the centuries, including powerful men like the former grand master of the Templars of France. Well above their heads there was a door in the wall. The ladder they had climbed down—Johann with his one good arm and Karl's help—had been taken away by the guards. It was damp in the tower and as icy as the deepest winter, but Greta didn't feel the cold. Anger burned hotly inside her.

Next to her, Karl coughed. He was sitting opposite her father, who also hadn't spoken since they had been brought down here. He kept his eyes closed, like he often did when he was concentrating.

"Believe me, Greta, I trusted him, too," said Karl with a sad smile. His voice echoed through the shaft as if they were sitting at the bottom of a deep well. "He was so handsome and charismatic. No need to beat yourself up. I honestly thought—"

Greta shut him up with a wave of her hand.

"It won't help if you—" tried Karl once more.

"Leave her be," said Johann tiredly. "It will take some time for her to recover from this. No amount of talking is going to help. And besides, I should have been more careful, too. At least now I understand why the dog didn't sound the alarm in the woods—John lured him away. The fellow struck me as suspicious from the start. But for my daughter it had to be true love."

"Oh, shut up, Father," snapped Greta. "What do you know of love? The only woman you ever loved died at the stake because of you. Don't you dare talk to me about love."

Johann was about to reply but then changed his mind. Greta wondered if she'd gone too far. Her father suddenly looked terribly old and tired.

"Let's not talk about it anymore," he said at last, his face ashen, his head tilted to one side. "We should be thinking about the king's demand. I have no idea what to do. I can't make gold—that's utter nonsense!"

"And yet on his deathbed Leonardo da Vinci spoke of a secret that you know," said Karl. "What did he mean?"

"How many more times do I have to say it, damn it? I don't know!" Faust slammed his fist against the mold-covered wall. "The last time I was with him, he seemed confused, muttering as if he were in the grip of a fever. He said the greatest secrets were hidden at the innermost core. The *innermost*—that's what he stressed several times. But I haven't got the faintest clue what he meant by that." He sighed. "Even if Leonardo intended to give me a message with those words, I have no idea what he was trying to tell me. And besides, I wouldn't know why he would do such a thing."

"Because he considered you his equal," said Karl. "Perhaps he mentioned you in his will?"

"I don't think in the usual sense, or else the king would know." Johann pressed his lips together. "I've been racking my brain over Leonardo's words, but I can't figure them out. And as long as I don't, we will rot down here. The king made himself very clear. The only good news is that I'll probably spoil Francis's fun by croaking beforehand."

"Has the paralysis grown worse?" asked Greta. She wanted to think of something other than John's treason. She did have other problems, after all. The lines in her father's palm suggested that his death wasn't far off.

Perhaps the time has come, she thought.

"I'm no longer thinking of myself, Greta," said her father in a low and depressed voice. "I'm thinking of you."

"How . . . how do you mean?"

Before Johann could answer, they heard a noise from upstairs. Greta listened. Were the guards coming already to fetch her father for torture? But the noise sounded different. She frowned.

They could hear men shouting, weapons clanking, and a dull thumping. The noise grew louder, and moments later the door above them creaked open. When Greta looked up, she beheld the face of the man she despised the most.

It was the face of John Reed.

He was breathless and sweaty, blood dripping from the sword in his hand.

"You need to get out of here, quickly," he gasped, pushing the wooden ladder down to them.

"What's this about?" asked Greta coldly. "If you think I will follow you anywhere—"

"There's no time for explanations, damn it!" shouted John. "All hell has broken loose out here. If you three want to survive the next few minutes, you must do exactly as I tell you!"

The ladder hit the floor and Karl reached for it, casting a suspicious glance at John. "Is this just another one of your tricks?"

"I swear by God and my dead mother, this is gravely serious! Someone is attacking Coudray Tower. I'm guessing they're mercenaries who have come for the doctor."

"Lahnstein's men," said Johann.

"Everyone is fighting everyone out there!" said John hastily. "We can use the confusion and escape. I know a secret passage on the northern side—"

"*We* can escape?" jeered Greta. "You can't be serious! Why don't you just wait until your men have sorted out everything? This is just another ruse designed to put pressure on my father."

John gave her a pleading look and held out his hand to her. "Believe it or not, I didn't want any of this. I . . . I love you, Greta. That's why I'm helping you get out of here. I'm not going to let you rot in this hole. There won't be another chance to flee like this. This is your only opportunity—your last opportunity."

"What other choice do we have?" Johann stood up and started to scale the ladder with John's help. He could only use one arm to climb. "We have nothing to lose, so we might as well follow this swindler."

Behind him, Karl climbed up the slippery rungs. Only Greta stayed where she was.

"I won't go," she declared. "Not with that—"

"Christ, there is no other way! Don't you see that?" snarled Johann. "Let's get out of here and you can scratch out his eyes afterward."

Greta clenched her fists and, a few moments later, stood up. At least her fury gave her renewed strength. When she reached the top, she glowered at John with hatred. "Don't you think for one moment that I will fall for you again."

"I don't care what you do later, but I want you to stay alive." John led the way. "Stay close to me," he called over his shoulder. "It's chaos out there. No matter what happens—follow me."

Soon they had climbed the inside steps to the first floor and found themselves in the same chamber where the king had met them a few hours ago. The noise was very loud now, coming from behind the door that led outside.

"Are you ready?" asked John, clutching the hilt of his sword. The others nodded in silence. "Then let's go!"

He opened the door.

Several dozen men were fighting in the dark courtyard. Some of them were covered in black, while others wore the king's green uniform; cries came from all directions. There were dead and injured men on the ground, and someone was screaming with pain. Greta heard weapons clashing and blades swiping, then someone gasped for breath. To her horror, she saw that on the steps below them, two men were locked in a deadly fight, each with his knife lodged in the stomach of the other. John rushed toward them and kicked them until, arm in arm, they flew off the stairs and into the moat. The path to the courtyard was clear.

Greta took in the battle scenes from the corner of her eye. To her left, more men were fighting outside a guards' chamber. Most of them bore swords, axes, or knives, but there was also a handful of crossbow shooters on the towers around them, firing deadly shots. The scent of fresh death, excrement, and fear filled the air like an exotic perfume. Greta staggered more than she walked, closely following John, who forced his way through with his sword. Behind them, Karl helped the doctor, who could barely walk.

"This way!" shouted John over the noise.

Several times one of the darkly clad men blocked his way, but John was a nimble fighter who dodged every stroke and lunged to his left and right as he hurried along, avoiding getting caught up in longer duels. A crossbow bolt zoomed past Greta's face, then she caught a glimpse of a terrified pair of eyes that vanished a moment later. It was like being stuck in a nightmare. Bent low, Karl and her father hobbled along beside her, swerving around dead bodies and fighting men. They had almost reached the back of the courtyard when a harsh voice rolled across the square like thunder.

"The doctor! He can't get away!"

Greta looked back and, to her horror, saw the giant of a man who had accompanied the papal representative in Bamberg. Back then he had also tried to hinder their escape, and this time it looked like he'd rather walk through hell than let them get away.

The enormous soldier ran toward their small group across the field of dead and dying men. Wielding his longsword, he looked like an avenging angel, like the black silhouette of Saint Michael. His harness was spattered with blood, and he was baring his teeth like a wolf. And even though he was limping, Greta knew that they wouldn't get away from this giant.

John, too, had seen Hagen. He hesitated for a moment, then he faced their opponent. Without turning his head, he told Greta quietly and urgently: "Go to the westernmost end of the wall. There is a small postern that leads to a tunnel that will take you to the vineyards." He fumbled for a key under his coat and gave it to her. "Don't wait for me."

Greta opened her mouth to say something, but John pressed his bloodied fingers to her lips. "I've made so many mistakes," he whispered. "Allow me to do something right for once."

Then he turned around and raised his sword in preparation. Greta gazed at the two unequal opponents: John, short and athletic, looking like a dancing fire sprite with his red hair, and the dark giant who roared as he stormed toward John. Greta saw John hold his sword with both hands as the blade of the giant smashed against it, the impact hurling John backward. He caught himself, feinted to the right, and attacked on the left, which the giant deflected as if he were a wall. But John continued to buzz around him like a fly looping around the nose of an angry bull.

"Run, Greta!" he shouted at her. "Run! It's your only chance!"

Greta's hand clutched the small key tightly, and she ran toward the outermost corner of the wall with Karl and her father.

Behind her, she could still hear the screams and noises of battle. In spite of herself she listened for John's voice, but she couldn't hear him.

After searching for a while they found a narrow, rusty gate in the northern wall. Greta trembled as she pushed the key into the lock. It fit. The door swung outward, and on the other side was a low corridor that reeked of blackpowder and had an arrow slit every few yards. The three of them hurried along the tunnel until it ended by a trapdoor in the ground. Karl opened the bolt, pulled up the door, and gazed at the iron rungs leading down a black shaft. A cold wind howled toward them.

"We're supposed to go down there?" asked Karl, holding up Johann by the arm. "Your father is never going to make it."

"Don't worry about me," growled Johann. "If I don't make it, I'll be dead one way or the other."

He signaled to Greta and she started to climb down the shaft. Her fingers clung to the rusty metal, and she felt her way through the darkness. Every other rung was missing, and her feet searched the walls for any footholds. Above her she heard Karl and her father follow. Johann panted and groaned, but he seemed to manage despite his paralysis.

To her horror, Greta realized that in their rush they hadn't locked the escape door behind them. Once the giant mercenary killed John—which she assumed would happen—he would run after them and find the open gate. Greta felt grief overcome her at the thought. As much as she hated John, her love hadn't fully died yet. She listened hard but couldn't make out anything apart from her own breathing and the sounds of Karl and her father.

After what felt like an eternity, the shaft ended in a natural grotto that was blocked with very old iron bars. On the other side, Greta could discern the sloping vineyards on the north side of the castle. When she pushed against the bars, they simply fell outward. The sudden noise echoed in the grotto like musket fire. But nothing happened, and so Greta stepped outside. She was standing at the foot of the cliff, the outlines of vines in front of her, a warm May breeze caressing her cheeks. There was not a noise to be heard from the chaos raging above them.

The sound of coughing made Greta spin around. It was her father, leaning on Karl. Johann was deathly pale and shaking all over, his left arm hanging down stiffly. Greta wondered how much willpower it had taken him to climb down the shaft. For a while no one spoke. A nightingale chirped in a nearby bush.

"What the devil was going on up there?" asked Karl eventually. He shook himself. "I heard men shouting in Swiss German, Spanish, and French."

Johann stared into the night without saying anything.

"I think I would recognize Hagen anywhere," went on Karl. "A hellish apparition like the grim reaper from a painting. That means Lahnstein and his men really did follow us. But the Spanish? Do you think there are other rulers who are after the secret Leonardo supposedly shared with you?"

"If Francis has spies everywhere, then Charles will, too," said Johann, struggling to bring his shaking under control. "It seems like the whole world is after me. Lahnstein, the French, the Habsburgs . . . And all because of a bloody secret that I just don't know!" He shook his head. "Who put the idea in the pope's head? It's almost as if—"

A bloodcurdling howl rang out, followed by barking. A large black shadow came darting up the vineyard toward them. Johann was the first to recognize it.

"Little Satan!" he exclaimed happily. "He must have found a different way out of the castle and his nose led him to us. I only wonder who let him out of the kennel. It's all right, boy. I'm here now." He patted the dog and studied his fur, which was speckled with blood. There was blood on his snout, too. "Hmm, whoever tried to block your way must be regretting it."

"Shh!" Greta raised a hand. "Do you hear that?"

The others, too, heard the scraping noises, a soft scratching that was coming closer. Little Satan pricked up his ears and growled as the others listened.

Someone was climbing down the shaft.

"Damn, it must be the giant!" uttered Johann. "Let's get out of here."

Greta's mouth was bone dry and her limbs ached from the long climb; she didn't know if she could run away again—not from this monster. Together with the others she hurried over to the vines, which looked like gnarled dwarfs in the darkness. Only Little Satan stayed where he was, panting and wagging his tail.

"The damned mutt will give us all away," whispered Karl. "Come here, Satan, sit!"

But the dog didn't listen. Instead, he started to yelp almost joyfully. Greta wondered if Hagen could smell them, like a predator that had picked up the scent of its prey, just as Little Satan had smelled them.

And she thought of John. If Hagen was after them, then John was probably dead by now. Again she felt a stab of pain in her heart. She couldn't let him go—not yet. Why had he turned up once more and rescued them? It had been so much easier to hate him wholeheartedly, truly thinking he was a traitorous scoundrel.

Little Satan had walked back to the grotto by now. The scraping became louder, and then someone jumped the last few yards to the bottom of the shaft. Their pursuer groaned and coughed, and then he emerged from the cave, staggering like a drunk.

It was not Hagen but John Reed.

Wagging his tail, the dog jumped up on him, and John toppled like a sack.

"John!" exclaimed Greta, cursing herself for the relief that flooded her. Her feelings hadn't disappeared, not in such a short space of time.

John was clearly wounded, if not dead; he didn't stir. Greta made to go to him, but her father held her back with his good hand.

"What are you doing?" he said between clenched teeth. "Have you still not had enough of him?"

"He saved us," said Karl.

"It's just another trap," hissed Johann. "Who's to say that this wasn't another plot by the king?"

"He . . . he is hurt or even . . . dead." Greta was torn by her emotions. She would have liked to wish John to hell, or at least to the moon, and yet she longed to hold him, to take care of his wounds and wash the blood off his face.

"If he's dead, he doesn't need your help anymore," said Johann. "And if he's just injured—hey!"

Greta pulled her arm free and rushed over to John. She pushed aside Little Satan, who had begun to lick the blood off John's face; evidently the animal viewed him as his new playmate, or as his dinner. John's coat was ripped and covered in dark bloodstains, but he was breathing. Greta spotted a deep gash on his right thigh that bled profusely.

"He's going to bleed to death!" she called to Karl and her father, who were still standing among the vines.

"Let him," grumbled Johann. "He is a traitor. You could say he's getting away lightly. Usually, traitors are boiled in seething oil."

Karl looked at his master with a mix of bewilderment and quiet rebellion. "A long time ago I studied medicine," he said. "And there I learned that every life is precious, even that of a traitor."

"We don't have time. It's highly likely that Hagen or someone else is at our heels. If we don't get away from here as fast as we can, we're done for!"

"He's bleeding to death, damn it," shouted Greta. Frightened, she gazed into John's pale face. His eyes were closed but it seemed he could hear her.

"Greta," he whispered. "Is this paradise?"

"Paradise for a fraud like you?" she hissed, gripped by an overwhelming sense of relief at finding him conscious. "Forget it! For every kiss you stole from me you shall burn a hundred years in hell." In spite of her harsh words, she started to tear strips off her dress for a bandage.

"Let me," Karl said, kneeling beside her. "It's been a while since my days at the university, but I think I remember a few things." He leaned over John and felt for his heartbeat. Confidently he started to bandage John's leg and brace it with a stick. "His heart is beating weakly," he said. "We must stanch the bleeding as fast as we can."

Johann still stood among the vines, a little crooked, like a tough old oak tree in the wind. The paralyzed side seemed to push him down.

"Damned love," he cursed.

Then he limped over to the others.

13

A FEW HOURS LATER, THE FOUR ESCAPEES COWERED BENEATH a rocky overhang inside a wet hollow filled with rotting foliage. It had started to drizzle, and Greta shivered despite the mild temperatures. They had waded through several streams to shake off the dogs that were bound to be at their heels. Greta's clothes were dripping wet, and twigs and leaves stuck in her hair. Karl and her father didn't look much better.

But worst of all was John. He had stopped bleeding, but he was barely conscious. The wound on his thigh wasn't the only injury he had carried away. Karl and Greta had braced him between them during their escape, and Karl had carried him through the streams. One time Karl broke down under the heavy burden, and they'd had to drag the injured man out of the bog.

Greta leaned over John and wiped the mud from his pale face. He opened his eyes for an instant and smiled at her.

"You are so beautiful," he breathed.

"Liar!" snapped Greta. "I look like a scarecrow. Spare me your compliments."

For the hundredth time she wondered how long it would take the king's soldiers to find them. They couldn't have covered more than two or three miles in the last few hours. Little Satan was standing guard outside their hiding place, and Greta hoped that the dog would bark if anyone approached. But then what? They didn't stand a chance with one man seriously injured and the other one sick.

"At least I gave it to that hulk," moaned John in one of his lucid moments. "What . . . what did he want from you? He was a Swiss guard, so probably one of the men the pope sent after you. But the others were Habsburgs."

"You ask a lot of questions for a wounded man," said Johann, leaning back against the rock. "No one asked you to help us."

"You don't have to like him, Father. I no longer trust him, either," said Greta. "But without John we'd still be in the dungeon. That's a fact."

"It's also a fact that we'll soon be back inside the dungeon along with him." Johann gave a desperate laugh. "The king of France isn't going to stand by and watch as we simply walk away. I'm guessing half an army is searching for us right now. And we are stuck in this filthy hole. I say we leave the traitor behind and—"

"No way," said Greta. "On his own, John is as good as dead. And you aren't particularly suited for an escape yourself. Look at you! A bitter old man who limps and stumbles more than he walks."

Karl cleared his throat. He had just renewed John's bandage and inspected the wound. Now he looked at Faust sternly through his eye glasses, which, miraculously, had survived their escape. "We would be no faster even if we left John behind. And our chances are next to nil either way. We have no horses, no provisions, no money—nothing! Not to mention your physical condition. How do you propose to travel to Tiffauges in your state?"

"We must. We have no other option."

"Jesus, why do you have to be so pigheaded?" shouted Greta at her father. "We have a badly wounded man here, you can barely walk, hundreds of soldiers are searching for us, but you don't care! You are the oh-so-famous Doctor Faustus—you can fly away if need be, or conjure up a demon that will fight back the enemy. Wake up, Father! Your mission is over."

"Why do you think I'm doing all this? For myself? It's for *you*, Greta!" Johann gave her a pleading look. "I must find Tonio and face him. If he wants to take me—fine, so be it. But I will do everything in my power to protect you!"

"Is that the bargain you want to offer him?" asked Greta softly. Suddenly she regretted having yelled at her father. "Your life for mine?"

Johann was about to reply when he noticed that John was repeatedly uttering a word. Greta hadn't understood him until then, but now his voice was loud and clear.

"Seuilly," he said, trying to lift his head. "Seuilly . . . We have to go to Seuilly . . ."

"What do you mean?" asked Greta. "What in God's name is Seuilly?"

"It's a . . . a tavern in the woods. By a crossroads. The . . . the tavern keeper will help us . . ."

"How far?" asked Karl.

"Seven, eight miles from here." John groaned in pain. "I . . . I know the way."

"Eight miles?" Johann shook his head. "Impossible. Not with him."

"He is the only one who can guide us," said Greta. "And I'll say it one more time: I am not leaving John behind." She gave a thin smile. "Besides—since when is anything impossible to Doctor Faustus?"

Johann sighed. "Very well. Let's give it a try. I admit that our options are somewhat limited at the moment." He gave John a hard look. "I only hope that this isn't another trick. I wouldn't put anything past him, even in his current state."

They left their hiding place and continued to make their way through the dark forest, Karl holding up John while Greta helped her father. They scarcely spoke, and not just because of the exertion. Greta had the feeling that any further conversation would only end in argument. She couldn't understand how her father could be so heartless. Yes, John had betrayed them—her, first and foremost. He had delivered them into the hands of the French king, but then he had risked his life to help them escape. His love for her was stronger than his love for the king.

Or was he just playing another game? Greta had realized that she still loved John despite everything that had happened. Why did feelings have to be so complicated?

Hour after hour they trudged through the deep woods, arduously following narrow game paths and streams, step for step. Thankfully the moon had emerged from behind the clouds and they could make out the shapes of bushes and trees. Karl had fashioned a torch from a stick, some dry moss, and scraps of clothing and managed to light it with John's tinderbox. The pathetic little flame was supposed to serve as protection against wild animals rather than a light source. Every now and then a stag or a wild boar would move in the underbrush nearby, but aside from that and the occasional hooting of an owl, all was silent. John needed to rest frequently. Then he would gaze into the starry sky or touch the moss on the trees before continuing on their way.

"Seuilly lies east of the castle," he muttered. "I used to go hunting with the king at Chinon, so I know this area almost as well as the Scottish Highlands." He tried to smile, but it turned into a grimace of pain. "The . . . the next time we come to a creek we must follow it. It will lead straight to the tavern."

"How can you be sure that the tavern keeper won't deliver us to the king?" asked Karl.

John again attempted a grin but failed. "Let's say . . . we've known each other for a while."

Little Satan stayed close to John's side; he appeared to have taken a true liking to the red-haired bodyguard. Every now and then the dog paused and pricked up his ears. When they crossed an old, overgrown clearing, he suddenly started to growl. At first Greta thought he had caught a whiff of their pursuers, but then a loud howling rang out, followed by the howling of a second beast.

"Wolves," breathed Karl. "That's the last thing we need. And they're close!"

Greta remembered people at the inns along their way speaking of a veritable wolf infestation, even though it wasn't even winter. The animals came from the west—from Brittany, where the forests were sparsely populated and wild. Another high-pitched, long howling rose up, much closer this time.

"They picked up our scent," said John. "We have to find the stream."

He tried to walk a few steps by himself and fell. Karl helped him up.

"This is madness," groaned Karl. The trials of the last few hours were showing in his face. "We don't even have weapons to defend ourselves. Everything we owned is at Chinon!"

Little Satan sniffed, barked, and leaped into the bushes at the edge of the clearing. Greta thought she could see several pairs of eyes in the darkness. There was a loud bark followed by a yelp. Greta guessed Little Satan had bravely attacked the pack of wolves. Now she could make out the outlines of the bodies behind the pairs of eyes. They were large beasts, almost as big as Little Satan, and they prowled around the clearing waiting for their chance. The biggest of them broke through the undergrowth and stalked toward Greta, growling. His fur was black and shaggy, and he was holding his ears flat and his jowls raised, exposing two rows of long, pointed teeth.

"Up the trees!" commanded Karl, pointing at several oaks at the edge of the clearing. "We have to climb up the trees!"

"How?" snarled Faust. "The traitor can barely walk, and I won't even make it to the first branches without help. If only . . ." He fumbled in his pockets, and suddenly his expression brightened. "Stand back!" he shouted. From one of his many coat pockets, Faust produced a small bottle and pulled out the cork with his teeth. He carefully poured a black powder onto the ground. Then he took a few steps back.

"What are you doing?" asked Karl.

"When the beasts get closer, throw your torch. The torch must land on the powder. Can you do that?"

Karl nodded. Moments later, half a dozen wolves emerged from the trees, while Little Satan continued to growl, bark, and yelp somewhere in the darkness beyond, probably fighting the rest of the pack. The six beasts in front of them were enough to make Greta's blood run cold. They were almost as big as their leader, and their eyes glinted voraciously.

When they had reached the spot with the powder, Johann shouted, "Now!"

Karl threw the torch. For a moment Greta thought the flame would be extinguished on the wet forest floor, but then a hissing broke out, followed by a deafening explosion and a red flash that lit up the clearing for a split second. The wolves yowled and scattered; two of them lay dead in the clearing.

"Blackpowder," whispered Johann, "with a pinch of cinnabar for effect. I always carry a small bottle on me—this lot was from our show at Bamberg." He grinned. "You never know when you might need it."

"I'm afraid it won't keep the wolves away for long." Karl pointed at John, who had collapsed once more and was lying on the ground not far from the wolves. "We can't keep carrying him. He's too heavy."

Greta saw her father's look. "Don't you dare think about it," she said coldly. "I stay with John. He might be a rascal and a swindler, but he saved our lives. I'm not going to throw him to the wolves."

On cue, there was movement between the trees again. Greta reached for a fallen branch with a grim expression on her face.

Come and get me, you mongrels! she thought. *My life won't come cheap—nor that of the red-haired scoundrel.*

But then she dropped the branch. It was only Little Satan limping toward them. The huge wolfhound was bleeding from several wounds. There was a hole where his right eye used to be, his fur was torn like an old cloth, and he was dragging one of his back feet.

"Little Satan," exclaimed Johann. He dropped to his knees and stroked the dog's blood-smeared head, the left ear hanging down in shreds. "My God, you poor thing . . ." His voice was shaking.

It hurt Greta to see how much more Johann cared for the dog than for John, but she knew that Little Satan was his favorite companion. She thought her father probably loved the dog more than he loved most people.

The dog, who had been so strong just a short while ago, whimpered in pain. He tried to stand up but couldn't, and a shudder went through his body. Greta saw that he was dying. Johann continued to stroke him as if he were a small child. Tears stood in his eyes.

"It's going to be all right," he murmured. "It's going to be all right, my darling."

Johann didn't even move when the wolves' reddish eyes gleamed at them again from the bushes.

Greta uttered a curse and hurled a branch at them. "Haven't you had enough?" she screamed. "Then come if you dare, you damned beasts! I will rip out your throats myself!"

It was courage born out of despair, out of hopelessness. At her feet lay John Reed, the man who had betrayed her but whom she loved nonetheless. Her father had buried his face in the bloodied fur of his dying dog; only Karl, her old friend, still stood beside her. He, too, had picked up a branch and waited for the wolves to attack. He looked over to Johann with a sad smile.

"I wonder if he'd care for me thus if I lay dying?" he said to Greta. "I guess I'll never find out."

So this is how it ends, thought Greta.

Karl was about to launch his club at one of the wolves when a loud thunderclap cracked through the air. At first Greta thought some of her father's blackpowder hadn't exploded the first time, but then there was another loud crack. The wolves pricked up their ears, put their tails between their legs, and ran off. Greta heard the rustle of leaves for a few more moments, and then the creatures had vanished like ghosts in the night. Soon she could hear the shouting of several men and saw torches in the darkness.

The king's soldiers, she thought immediately. *They found us.*

But the men who stepped into the clearing were no soldiers. They looked like simple workers, armed with crossbows and hand cannons. In their midst, one man was riding on a horse. He was so fat that Greta wondered why the horse wasn't collapsing. The luscious hair streaming out from beneath his black gugel was almost as bright red as John's. Some of the other men also had red hair. The fat one studied the small group in front of him from keen eyes. When his gaze fell on the unconscious John, his bushy eyebrows shot up.

"What's the lad done now?" he asked. "If only he'd stayed in the Highlands. When I told his mother I'd look after him, I didnae ken how much bother he would cause me."

"Who . . . who are you?" asked Karl.

"Who am I?" The big man straightened up in his saddle, a mountain of flesh with small red eyes that flashed at Karl, Greta, and Johann. "I am Albert MacSully of the old line of MacSullys. My family traces back to the glorious days of William Wallace. And the only reason you're still alive is because there's a MacSully among ye." Suddenly the fat man gave a roaring laugh. "Bugger me! I set out to catch wolves and instead I catch my nephew. Blood runs thicker than water, ye ken."

He turned to his men. "If I know my pigheaded nephew at all, he's a long way off joining our ancestors. Take him to Seuilly." Albert MacSully looked at the filthy band in front of him. "And don't forget the others. They all look like they need a cup of wine and a bucket of water to wash. And I can't wait to hear what sort of a hair-raising tale they'll serve us for breakfast. It better be good!"

Greta looked up at the sky. The first red glow of dawn showed above the treetops. It seemed they had escaped death for now.

But no one knew what the next day would bring.

"Bloody hell, sounds like you had more luck than brains. Crossing the woods at night without any weapons, with all those wolves about. If we hadn't come past by chance, you'd be wolf food by now—although the beasts would have spat my nephew back out, tough bastard that he is."

The big man laughed and refilled his mug from a large jug of brown ale. It was about eight in the morning, and Greta wondered how anyone could drink so much this early in the day.

Probably a matter of practice, she thought as she looked at the enormous body of the man opposite her. Albert MacSully was indeed John's uncle, and it would seem that John had saved them once more by leading them close to his uncle's tavern at Seuilly.

Albert MacSully had taken the six-year-old John with him from Scotland when the boy's mother had died of the spotted fever. Albert had taken on the tavern at Seuilly and raised John there. At fourteen, John had joined the king's household troops and, with the help of his dexterity, his strength, and especially his charm, had swiftly moved up the ranks—not exactly to the joy of his uncle, who didn't overly love the French. Greta had learned all this from Albert in the last couple of hours while he devoured a whole loaf of bread with an omelet made from twelve eggs.

"Hunting wolves is hungry work," Albert grunted and washed his meal down with a long swig of ale. Then he burped noisily.

Together with Karl and her father, Greta was sitting in the tavern's taproom. The settlement in the middle of the forest consisted of the sturdy, stone-built inn, a small chapel, and a few sheds and stables. All the buildings were surrounded by a stone wall. Two trading routes crossed in this place, one of them leading south from the Loire, the other one west toward Fontevrault Abbey, which wasn't far from here. Seuilly was more like a small fortification than a village, and for good reason. Here in the woods south of the Loire, the law of war still reigned, even with Chinon Castle nearby.

Greta had washed the worst of the dirt from her face and hair. Karl and her father looked a little cleaner, too, especially since Albert had lent them some fresh clothes. Johann had scarcely spoken; the death of his beloved dog had hit him hard. He looked older and more drained than Greta had ever seen him before, although that could also have been due to his illness. John was lying in a chamber next door, where Albert's wife looked after him.

"The boy will live," said the fat tavern keeper. "He's got proper Scottish Highland blood running through his veins—the sword wound is but a scratch for him. Though I'd love to know who gave it to him. John rarely loses a fight." He eyed the three travelers sharply. "But I think I can work it out myself. John asked me to send any French soldier within a mile of the tavern packing. Sounds to me like you're up to your necks in shit."

John hadn't told his uncle what exactly had happened, but he'd made it clear that they were on the run and that Albert ought to claim he hadn't seen them if asked. Greta doubted this plan would work for long. The king most likely knew where John had spent his childhood and would send out people to look for him there.

The big man sighed and reached for a lump of cheese. "I told the lad years ago not to join those bleeding frog eaters. But he didnae want to listen. A proper man doesna like the French, aye—but he likes to drink their wine. And the cheese isn't bad." He went on with his mouth full. "Maybe it was for the best that John left when he did. Here at the tavern he turned the head of every lass and drove my workers crazy."

Greta nodded, her lips a thin line. "Sounds just like John."

"Better watch out for that one, lassie. No woman can tame our John!" Albert wiped his greasy hands on his leather pants. "Not that it's any of my business, but the boy reckoned you want to travel to the barony of Retz. If I were you, I'd reconsider."

"Why?" asked Johann, who finally looked a little healthier after a hearty breakfast. Aside from his left shoulder sagging down, he looked almost normal.

"Not a good area down there," replied Albert. "I'm surprised the king hasn't done anything about it, to be honest. But I hear he's too busy trying to become the ruler of the world." He gave a laugh. "And besides, officially, Brittany belongs to his wife and not to France at all—although you cannae say that out loud."

Albert lowered his voice. "I've heard from travelers that the Duke of Brittany, Louis de Vendôme, has been fighting for France in Italy for years. His steward rules Retz in his stead, but he's a right drunkard. Apparently, someone else pulls all the strings in the background."

"And who would that be?" asked Karl, leaning forward.

"I don't know anything for certain, but there's been this new priest at Tiffauges Castle for a few years—"

"Did you say Tiffauges?" asked Johann, cutting him off, the muscles in his face twitching uncontrollably.

Albert shot him an irritated look. "Yes, it's the duke's main residence. Folks are saying that things have never been right at that castle. I dinnae ken if ye've heard of a certain Gilles de Rais—a right scumbag if there ever was one."

"Indeed we have," said Johann, exchanging glances with Karl and Greta.

"Terrible story, even though all that was years ago. But now folks are saying that since this priest is at the castle, children are vanishing again." Albert shrugged his broad shoulders. "I don't usually buy into such gossip, but I must admit that several different travelers have told me about it. And other strange people came into the castle along with this priest. Even those damned wolves seem to come from that area. Ye ken, Brittany has always been a wild and eerie place, and the people speak a terrible gibberish, but this . . ." He shook his head, then watched Johann, who was struggling to gain control of his muscles. "What sort of disease do you have?"

"I don't know, unfortunately. The physicians say there is no cure. That is why I'm on a pilgrimage to Fontevrault with my family."

"I thought you were going to Retz?"

"Um, yes, after our pilgrimage," said Johann evasively. "We have some . . . family matters to settle there."

"Family matters, I see. With the king's army at your heels? What a strange journey." Albert winked at him. "Like I said, none of my business. But you do seem familiar, like I've seen you before—maybe on one of those leaflets." He grinned broadly. "No, you're not just a simple pilgrim if my nephew gives up his post in the household troops to follow you. But John doesna want to say a word, and that's all right. There are three things us Highland folks can do better than anyone else in the world: drink, fight, and keep our traps shut."

Albert took another long gulp, let out another burp, and said, "If John reckons ye need to get to Fontevrault and then to the barony of Retz, then I'll be damned if I don't help ye get there. We MacSullys stick like the mud on our boots."

Three times the king's soldiers came to Seuilly in the following days, but Albert managed to send them on every time. One of those times, they searched the tavern and its outbuildings, but the MacSullys had seen it coming. There was a cellar that was accessed via a trapdoor hidden underneath a large bearskin, and that was where the four wanted fugitives hid until the soldiers had gone. After the first morning, they never showed their faces at the tavern again but stayed at the family's living quarters, hoping to avoid the attention of any nosy travelers.

Albert hugely enjoyed the game of misleading the "frog and snail eaters," as he liked to call the French. Whenever he spoke with soldiers, he pretended that his French was very poor. He claimed he hadn't seen his nephew, "the bleedin' bastard," for years. Albert was enthusiastically helped in this game by his many sons, who each had a red shock of hair like their father. Greta kept mixing them up and struggled with the complicated Scottish names.

She soon recovered from the tribulations of their escape, and John, too, became better by the day. Greta often visited his bedside, which she had to share with MacSully's wife, who didn't like to leave her beloved nephew and who was doing her best to shore him up with various meaty meals.

With every visit, Greta and John grew closer. Greta soon realized she couldn't stay mad at him, even if a certain distance remained. But it was jinxed—she loved this fellow and couldn't do anything about it. Not even the most sensible arguments helped. Who was to say that John was truly on their side now and this wasn't just another ploy by the king? But when John smiled at her, Greta's doubts melted like snow in the sunshine. And there was something else that tied her to him more than ever.

"I had a dream," said John when they were alone for a moment while Albert's wife fetched fresh water to clean his wounds. "I dreamed that you looked after me when I was lying injured in the woods. You gently stroked the hair from my face."

"You must have indeed been dreaming. Why should I do that? I mean, for a rotten traitor like yourself." Greta looked at him sternly, but then smiled. "Admittedly, a rather good-looking traitor."

"Please, Greta, try to understand." John took her hand. "I just didn't know what to do. It's true that the king sent me to catch you, and at first that was exactly what I was trying to do—use you to get to the doctor."

"And you did rather well," said Greta bitterly.

"Yes, but then I noticed that for the first time I had real feelings for a girl— for you, Greta. And yet I was bound by my loyalty to the king. I wanted to tell you, honestly, but I kept putting it off until—" He fell silent.

"Until it was too late," said Greta for him. "Back in the tower at Chinon I wanted to tear you into a thousand pieces. I was filled with hatred."

"Love and hatred are poles of the same magnet," said John. "A wise man once said that. They attract and repulse one another, but they're based on one single force."

"I much prefer love to hatred," replied Greta. "And . . ." She faltered.

"What is it?"

Greta shook her head. "Nothing. It's nothing."

She had briefly considered telling John that she hadn't bled in weeks. They had always been careful, but back then, during their first night at Blois, passion had swept them away. Greta decided to hold off telling John a little longer; she wanted to be sure. Perhaps her monthly bleedings had only stopped because of their exhausting journey. And she had plenty of other things to worry about.

"I . . . I merely wondered whether you really want to come to Tiffauges with us," said Greta. "What your uncle told us—"

"Makes me all the more determined." John squeezed her hand. "I go where you go, Greta. And if you think you must go with your father, then I will even follow you to that cursed castle. But is it what you really want, Greta? Is it?"

He looked at her closely and she averted her gaze.

She had dreamed of Tonio. He had waved to her, and she had followed him willingly. Willingly! That was what disturbed her the most: that that creature had somehow put a spell on her. As if he wasn't just Faust's master but hers as well. That was why she wanted to see him with her own eyes—to face up to him.

"If you had asked me a few weeks ago, I would have said no." Greta rose and wrung out the cloth she had used to cool John's forehead. "But I want to know what's going on at Tiffauges. I want to know if my father is right. And I can't abandon him now that . . . now that he's so sick. I no longer dare to look at the lines in his hands, but I fear they're still vanishing."

"Then I'll be by your side. Even if I struggle to believe that your father will defeat his illness at the castle, let alone confront Gilles de Rais."

"Whatever the case—something seems to be not quite right in the barony of Retz," said Greta. "And we need to help my father get to the bottom of it. Also, the French aren't the only ones in pursuit of us—perhaps it isn't the worst idea to head for a wild territory and cover our tracks."

"You're right." John nodded. "I, too, should get as many miles as possible between me and the king. Francis seems like a charming ruler at first glance, but he is rather vindictive." He gave a grim laugh. "And he won't rest until your

father tells him how to make gold. The election of the German king is soon—
Francis is running out of time. If he is to stand any chance against Habsburg
Charles and his Fuggers, then he needs your father's help."

"My father who doesn't even know how to make gold." Greta rolled her eyes.
"How many more times do I have to tell you?"

"Are you absolutely certain?" John looked at her searchingly. "How well do
you know your father, Greta?"

Once more she sensed that she didn't know Johann Georg Faustus well at
all. Worse still, as their journey went on, he was becoming more and more of an
enigma. Sometimes she wondered what side her father was on. Was he still on
the side of light, or had he long moved into the realm of shadows?

"And how well do I know you?" she asked, avoiding John's eyes. "Now hold
still before your wound breaks open again."

She placed a fresh, cold cloth on his forehead, pleased she didn't have to
keep talking.

On the tenth day after their arrival, John was well enough to travel. His leg was
still a little stiff, but he no longer required crutches. The royal soldiers hadn't
returned; they had probably widened their search and weren't looking near the
castle anymore.

"Their guess will be that you're traveling on the Loire," said Albert, who was
standing in the courtyard alongside his family to say farewell.

For the journey, the plump tavern keeper had given them one of his horses—
a big, stoical draft horse that carried Johann as if he was made of straw—as well
as a donkey for their luggage, a hand cannon with powder and lead, knives, and
two short swords for John and Karl. The whole party was clad in light, incon-
spicuous clothing in muted colors. There were no other guests around on this
rainy day in May, so they could speak freely.

"Sell the animals once you've arrived—wherever that'll be," said Albert.
"Coins will be easier for John to carry when he's in the area next to pay me back."

They all knew this wasn't going to happen. John would never return to
Seuilly, because it would be far too dangerous. And Albert had a hunch that the
crippled man on the horse was no plain pilgrim, but he stuck to the Scottish
rule of never asking nosy questions.

"I promised your mother on her deathbed that I'd look after ye until ye go your own path," said the big man to John. "I think the time has come. I always knew ye wouldn't stay with the frog eaters forever. Perhaps ye should go back to Scotland, to our clan. They could do with a warrior like yourself." He winked at Greta. "And also with a bonny, clever lass at your side to give bairns to the clan of MacSully. No matter if they're red haired or not."

John smiled. "We'll see, Uncle. Thank you for everything you've done for us."

Albert waved him off. Then he turned back to John. "For heaven's sake—I almost forgot." He said something to one of his many red-haired sons, who ran back inside the house, returning a few moments later with a bundle. Albert handed it to Johann, who accepted it with a puzzled look.

"You took your dog's death very hard," the tavern keeper said. "I understand. It was a beautiful beast, and frightening, too. I asked my men to find it and skin it. It's my parting gift to you, mysterious traveler. May it warm you on your cold nights in the wilderness."

Johann unwrapped the bundle and stared down at Little Satan's black fur. At first he looked as if he was going to throw it far away, but then he buried his nose in it, smiling.

"Thank you very much," said Johann. "The dog meant a lot to me. He wasn't my first, and we shall see whether he will be the last."

He draped the warm fur around his shoulders. Then he flicked the reins, and the large horse headed toward the gate at a leisurely pace.

~

From Seuilly, they followed the trading route that led toward Fontevrault Abbey. Fontevrault was one of the largest monasteries in France, led by nuns and answerable only to the king. Several famous personalities lay buried there, including King Richard the Lionheart. The abbey was situated south of the river Vienne in a dip in the land, and its white towers could be seen from far away.

As they passed the abbey with its busy outbuildings, hostels, and stables, Johann thought about what it would be like to leave everything behind and live here as a monk in quiet seclusion, far away from all desires and passions. He had always been a driven man, even in his youth. Johann remembered the kind Father Antonius who lent him books at Maulbronn Monastery. Back then Johann had wanted to become a librarian, but life had other plans for him. And now he would once more tempt fate—maybe for the last time.

From Fontevrault they followed the road west. The forests became sparser, and fresh clearings and charcoal piles showed that here, too, people were wresting the land from the wilderness. Ears of grain swayed in the gentle breeze of early summer, and they traveled past several inns and small villages. Almost hourly now they passed someone on the road, a group of pilgrims or a merchant who would doff their hat to Johann and his companions. Only sometimes, when they looked closer, would people notice that something was wrong with the older man on the big horse. They would eye Johann furtively and make the sign of the cross. Johann knew that paralyzed people and those stricken by the falling sickness were sometimes considered to be specially chosen by God—or specially cursed. Judging by the looks passing travelers were giving him, they considered him to be the latter. At least no soldiers seemed to be following them, and Lahnstein and that huge Swiss mercenary also appeared to have lost their prey.

After three more days they came to a large crossroads where a weathered old border stone indicated that they were entering Brittany. Slowly, scarcely noticeable at first, the landscape changed. The trees seemed to be older here, gnarled oaks with moss hanging down like beards of giant trolls. Several times they passed huge rocks with etchings, ancient symbols that no one knew how to decipher. Sometimes those boulders were arranged in a circle, and others seemed to form tables for giants.

"There are even more of those rocks farther north, on the Breton Peninsula," explained John, who was completely recovered and often whistled a merry tune despite the eerie goal of their journey. His good mood increasingly irritated Johann. "They're called menhirs. No one knows what they were used for. Apparently they were made by an ancient tribe that used to live here. Later on, migrants from the British coasts settled here, having fled from hostilities in their homeland. They brought with them their throaty language and some strange customs."

A howling rang out, and the four of them exchanged dubious looks. The woods weren't far—the road headed straight into them. Fiery red, the sun disappeared behind the trees in the west.

"Our friends are back," said Karl bitterly. "Albert said the wolves came from Brittany. I'm glad he gave us a hand cannon."

Since they'd entered Brittany, the woods had started to become thicker. Swampy landscapes interspersed with deeply rutted roads and infested with mosquitoes took turns with a densely vegetated wilderness that made it hard not to lose orientation. They met few travelers now. Occasionally they'd pass a solitary farmer pulling a plow, with a bent back and casting dark glances at the group. Compared to the lovely Loire Valley, this area seemed harsh and forbidding, as if it didn't want people to settle here. Greta prayed both morning and night now, and even Johann stopped mocking her for it.

"Brittany is a wild old land," said John, swatting a fat mosquito sucking blood from his hairy forearm. "The current French king's mother-in-law, Anne of Brittany, has always fought for the region's independence. That has changed since her daughter, Claude, became the queen. But the Bretons don't consider themselves French and will probably always speak their own language. The area farther to the west is called Finistère—the end of the world. The name is very fitting. You could also call it the ass of the world." John laughed. "My Breton isn't very good, but hopefully it'll suffice to order a roast hare and a jug of wine."

He gestured at a light in the dusk ahead, indicating an inn. The travelers were glad to find a roof over their heads for the night instead of sleeping out in the woods.

"Gilles de Rais chose his home well," remarked Johann glumly, looking up at some crows circling in the sky. "I couldn't imagine a more eerie place. Brittany truly is the land of the devil."

As if to lend support to his comment, wolves began howling from several directions, and a cool wind brought the first drops of rain.

As the rain beat against the sooty parchment in the windows, the group heard firsthand reports of missing or murdered children. They were no longer rumors of things that occurred somewhere faraway—they were gruesome facts. The other patrons led hushed conversations, huddled closely together as they eyed the strangers distrustfully. The atmosphere was muted, as if a dark cloud hung over the country, smothering all happiness.

The four travelers learned that Duke Louis de Vendôme, who ruled over vast parts of Brittany including Tiffauges, still resided in Italy. No one wanted to comment on the steward who reigned over the castle in the duke's absence. Whenever the steward was mentioned, people made the sign of the cross and turned away. John returned from the tavern keeper with a sad look on his face, carrying a jug of sour wine.

"It's true what we've heard," he said, sitting down. "Two children got killed at once in the last few days. They were siblings, a boy and a girl, no older than eight, from a village not far from here. Something sucked the blood out of them to the last drop. Their bodies were found in a clearing in the woods along with a dried toad. And they certainly weren't the only murdered children in recent years."

"Just like in Nuremberg," whispered Johann, exchanging a look with Karl. "Remember?"

Karl nodded. "Tonio was leading an order then. Those people wanted to use the children's blood to invoke the devil. Perhaps there are similar madmen in this area, too."

"Madmen?" Johann gave a laugh. "I wish they were. But I'm afraid they are disciples who truly believe in the return of Satan. Don't forget what Agrippa told us. Tonio, alias Gilles de Rais, is just a shell. The true devil is still waiting to take over the world."

Karl sighed and raised both hands. "I've long given up trying to talk you out of this theory."

"Come to Tiffauges with me and I'll show you that I'm right," replied Johann.

Suddenly he felt cold despite the blazing fire, and he tightened Little Satan's fur around his shoulders. The musty and slightly rancid smell reminded him of happier times.

"I feel certain that Gilles de Rais resides at the castle again, just like he used to. He is probably the priest Albert MacSully spoke about." Johann nodded toward the window. "I saw the old raven again and the crows. They're his messengers, just like the wolves. Gilles, or Tonio, knows that we're coming." He paused. "I should go there by myself. This is between Tonio and me alone."

"We all go," said Greta decisively. "Then we'll finally gain certainty."

She looked first at John and then at her father, but Johann avoided her gaze. He still wasn't sure if he could trust John Reed. His daughter, on the other hand, seemed head over heels in love with the Scotsman. The small gestures and touches between the young couple pained Johann more than he cared to admit.

A tight bond had grown between Greta and John, much tighter than the one he himself had managed to build with his daughter over the last few years.

Two days later they came across the first dead children.

It was in the same village the folks at the tavern had spoken of. They could hear chanting from far away, which turned out to be a Breton chorale from ancient times. It blew over to them from the cemetery that, together with a small derelict church, stood on the outskirts of the village. A low drystone wall surrounded the patch of crooked tombstones. The road led right past it.

From atop his horse, Johann watched a group of about two dozen peasants carrying two small coffins, not much bigger than dowry chests. Even though the coffins must have been very light, the pallbearers' shoulders were bent as if their burdens were unbearably heavy. At the front, right behind the priest, walked a woman and a man who clung to each other. The woman let out mournful wails from time to time, shook her fist at the heavens, and screamed incomprehensible words. She couldn't have been very old, yet her hair was gray and her face seemed to have aged before her time. The man, too—presumably the father of the dead children—was marked by grief, stiffly placing one foot in front of the other. At the end of the congregation limped an old woman with a cane. She was the only one to notice the travelers behind the wall. She stopped to look at them, and when her gaze caught Johann's, she made the sign of the cross.

"*An diaoul!*" she shouted, waving her cane at Johann. "*Ha prest out evit ober un taol gouren gant an diaoul?*"

The other funeral guests also stopped, and the procession came to a halt. Everyone was looking at the strangers now.

"*Diaoul!*" shouted the old woman again.

"What's she saying?" asked Johann, who didn't know a word of Breton.

"I'm not sure." John frowned. "If I understand correctly, she thinks you're the devil. Perhaps because of your paralysis."

Lately, Johann's spine had become a little bent, making him look hunchbacked. Johann had to agree with John—he truly could be mistaken for the devil.

The people in the cemetery stared at him as if he were an evil foreign being. The priest addressed the funeral party in an annoyed tone, whereupon the mourners reluctantly turned away from Johann. The pallbearers with the two small coffins started to move again toward a hole in the center of the cemetery, the women cried and wailed, and the church bells tolled. Only the old woman stayed where she was and pointed at Johann.

"Diaoul!" she called out again. *"C'hwi zo o c'h en em bilet gant an diaoul!"*

Johann was about to urge his horse onward when something strange happened. The old woman limped to a small gate in the cemetery wall, hobbled out onto the road, and, in a childlike gesture, dropped to her knees before Johann and the horse.

"What is she doing?" asked Johann, astounded.

John raised an eyebrow. "I don't know." He walked over to the woman and lifted her by her arms; tears stood in her eyes, which were framed by deep wrinkles. She started to speak very fast to John, pointing at Johann again and again.

"I'm not understanding much," said John eventually when the old woman paused for a moment. "But I think I was wrong. She thinks the doctor is not the devil but the one who can vanquish the devil. This woman is the village midwife. She . . ." John frowned and looked at Johann. "She said she dreamed of you. Of your arrival. *Sorceles* . . . yes, that's the word." John nodded. *"Sorceles.* She believes you're a wizard."

Johann smiled. "She isn't the only one." He hesitated briefly before he continued. "Tell her to lead us to her house. I'd like to speak with her—without the priest and half the village watching."

The old woman hobbled ahead. She turned off the road onto a narrow path that led through marshland and a grove of birch trees before ending outside a tiny hut surrounded by reeds. They could still hear the church bells in the distance; a flock of birds traveled across the hazy sky. The crooked hut was built of mud and branches in the way people used to build in older times. It was so low that Johann almost knocked his head when he entered.

"What are we doing here?" asked Karl skeptically. "Do you really believe this woman can help us in any way? If you ask me, she's nothing but a befuddled old hag who—"

"She saw me in her dreams," said Johann. "And now I'm standing in front of her. I find that warrants at least listening to her."

The walls inside the hut were so blackened by smoke that Johann felt like he was entering hell. The room stank of soot, feces, and sulfur, the only vent being a tiny hole in the middle of the roof. The red embers of a small fire below were the only source of light. There was no table and no chair but a wealth of crucibles, old sacks, and colorful wooden boxes stacked along the walls. Some pelts on the hard dirt floor served as a seating and sleeping place. The old woman signaled for them to sit down on the skins. Johann saw how hordes of lice crawled through her matted hair. Her entire appearance was so delicate and wrinkled that he couldn't help but think of an ancient earth fairy.

"I only hope she doesn't offer us anything to eat or drink," muttered John. "Brr! I shudder to think what's in those jars." His eyes went from dried bunches of herbs to snakeskins and finally to a mummified newt dangling from the ceiling on a leather string.

The old woman looked around warily, as if she was afraid someone invisible was in the room. She walked to the entrance and used her cane to draw a pentagram onto the dirt floor, then she sat down among them. She started to speak in her throaty language again, and John listened intently, his expression growing darker the longer she spoke.

"What's she saying?" asked Greta, who sat beside John with her legs crossed, holding his hand.

"My Breton really isn't very good," said John. "But she seems to believe that the devil is haunting these lands again, like he did a long time ago."

"Gilles de Rais," whispered Johann.

John nodded. "It sounds unbelievable, but apparently this woman is the daughter of a girl who, at just ten years of age, managed to escape from the clutches of Gilles de Rais and his henchmen. The name of that girl was Marie, and this woman's name is Étienne. Marie often told her daughter about the terrible events from back then so they wouldn't be forgotten."

"Gilles de Rais died in the year of the Lord 1440 at Nantes—about eighty years ago," said Karl. "That means Étienne here would have to be very old for this story to be true."

"But it's possible." Increasingly agitated, Johann turned back to John. "What else is she saying?"

"Étienne's mother, Marie, watched some of Gilles's helpers back then, and the midwife believes that those helpers—just like Gilles de Rais—never died." John lowered his voice. "The devil made them live on—the devil and the children's blood they've been drinking. They lived in the woods with the wolves for several decades, but for a few years now they've been more active again in this part of Brittany. Étienne calls them 'the wild hunt.'"

"*Chasseal loened gouez!*" said the old woman, nodding vigorously. "*Chasseal loened gouez!*"

"The wild hunt." Johann shuddered. He rubbed his eyes, reddened from the smokiness of the hut. "It's a term that often appears in myths. Ancient, evil gods who chase through the air or the woods hunting humans. They say that he who beholds them is doomed to die." A thought struck him. "Does she know the names of any of the helpers?"

John turned to Étienne, who listened and nodded. With her face twisted into a grimace of disgust, she counted the names on her fingers.

"Poitou, Henriet, La Meffraye, and Prelati, the priest," translated John. "She said everyone around here knows those names. They are like monsters, like the ogres folks use to frighten small children. Although Poitou hasn't been seen in a long time."

"Poitou?" Johann flinched. "I know him!" He looked at Karl. "Do you remember the big fellow in Nuremberg, Tonio's helper? I met him at Nördlingen for the first time when I was still traveling with Tonio. He made me drink the black potion back then!"

"Poitou . . . yes, I suppose you're right." Karl nodded slowly as he remembered. "You killed him in Nuremberg. You really think she's talking about the same man?"

"Apparently, La Meffraye is the worst of that sinister bunch," said John, concentrating to understand the old woman's words. "No one knows what her real name is. Her nickname stems from *l'effraie*, the barn owl. She would use sweets to lure small children into the woods, where Poitou and Henriet would capture them with nets and take them to Tiffauges and other castles in the area— Champtocé and Machecoul." John shuddered. "The most gruesome scenes must have unfolded there. I'm glad I don't understand everything. And it seems like it's all starting again from the beginning."

"What about that priest?" asked Johann. "That Prelati?"

The old woman made the sign of the cross when she heard the name. Then she continued to talk.

"He . . . he must have helped Gilles de Rais invoke the devil at Tiffauges," said John after he listened for a while. "The two of them were something like a . . ." He shook his head in disgust. "A couple. Étienne believes that Prelati is back there now."

"The steward's new priest," breathed Greta. "Albert spoke of a priest."

"And Gilles de Rais?" Johann's voice was trembling now, his facial muscles twitching uncontrollably. "Does she know if Gilles de Rais is also at Tiffauges?"

The old woman nodded as if she'd understood the question. *"An diaoul zo e pep lec'h ha neblec'h,"* she said intently. *"Lec'h ha neblec'h!"*

"The devil is everywhere and nowhere," translated John with a shrug. "No idea what that's supposed to mean. But she believes that you are the only one who can put a stop to the devil. She saw it in her dreams, and her mother, too, once said that a great wizard would come someday to vanquish evil." He grinned. "It's possible she's getting you mixed up with tousled old Merlin. He is considered a powerful wizard around here and used to serve a king named Arthur. Good old Merlin is a few hundred years old, however, and is buried in Brocéliande Forest."

Johann said nothing. He wondered what was meant by those words: *The devil is everywhere and nowhere.*

The old woman leaned forward and brushed her hand over Johann's hair as if he were a child. She uttered soothing words in Breton.

"She wants to give you a cream," said John. "She says she can't stop your disease but she can slow it down."

Karl rolled his eyes. "How? Ground snails mixed with crumbled wood lice?" He stood up. "Let's go before she gives you something that worsens your illness."

"Tell her I will gladly accept her cream," said Johann to John.

The old woman understood. She opened one of the small wooden boxes and reached inside with her gouty fingers. When she pulled them out, on the tip of her index finger sat a viscous, resinous lump that didn't smell bad at first—somewhat sweet, like beeswax—but beneath it lay the scent of decay.

Karl wrinkled his nose. "You can't be serious. This defies any sort of science. Don't do it—the salve might be poisonous."

"I'm afraid science can't help me any longer," replied Johann.

He didn't resist when the old woman leaned over him, took off his shirt, and rubbed his back, arms, and legs with the pungent ointment. She sang and murmured something that sounded like a nursery rhyme. When she was finished, a smile spread across her face, and for a brief moment Johann could imagine what she must have looked like as a young girl.

"Bennozh warnoc'h," she said, squeezing Johann's hand. *"Bennozh warnoc'h!"*

"She blesses you and wishes you good luck," said John.

"Thank you." Johann bowed. "God knows I can use this blessing."

He was about to head for the exit when the old woman signaled for him to wait. She opened another small box and retrieved a pendant attached to a simple leather string. It was a small winged angel, whittled from a piece of alabaster, and it looked very old. She spoke to John.

"She says it's a protective amulet," he translated. "Apparently it helped her mother back then when the henchmen of the dark marshal were after her, and she wants—" He broke off in surprise. Then he looked at Greta. "She wants you to wear it. No idea why."

"My own little guardian angel." Greta smiled and allowed the old woman to put the necklace over her head. "Thank you. I appreciate this gift. *Merci.*"

The old woman nodded and squeezed her hand. When the woman smiled, Greta could see her last two remaining teeth.

"Bennozh warnoc'h!"

Johann stepped through the cloth covering the entrance. On a crippled birch nearby sat an old raven that seemed to be watching him. It flapped its wings and then took off, cawing.

"Tell your master I'm on my way," said Johann softly, his gaze following the bird.

14

ABOUT THREE WEEKS AFTER THEIR DEPARTURE FROM
Seuilly, the group finally reached Tiffauges.

The noontime sky was blue and cloudless, and a pleasant breeze carried the
salty air of the Atlantic, even though the sea was forty miles away. It was as if
the devil tried to mock Johann by painting the site of his gruesome doings in
the brightest colors God's earth had to offer. During the last few days they had
passed through several villages that were clearly affected by the horrors of this
area, their streets deserted, with no sign of any children. Johann had felt eyes
staring at them from dark windows. In one of the villages, the inhabitants had
thrown rocks at them and shouted angry words in Breton. The inns had been
boarded up; no one wanted to accommodate strangers who might make off with
the most precious thing these people had.

Their children.

The village of Tiffauges was situated on a small rise above a dammed-up
river. Along with a smaller tributary, this long lake served as a protective moat
to the castle that lay opposite the small town on the other side of the road. From
afar, Château de Tiffauges looked like any other castle, albeit a rather large one.
A bastion at the front protected the entrance, and the defensive fortifications
stretched across a plateau upon which sat the burly keep, numerous outbuildings, and a manor house. Farther back, Johann could make out two large towers that secured the northern wing. He reminded himself that Tiffauges used
to belong to a marshal of France and close friend to the French king. Gilles de
Rais used to host extravagant feasts here until he ran out of money and turned
to alchemy and, finally, devil worship.

The road led out of an oak forest full of rooting boars and through a deep valley, and eventually toward the small town and the castle. The landscape was scattered with sweet-smelling gorse hedges. Johann stopped his horse behind a crumbling watchman's hut and waited for Karl to help him dismount. The old midwife had been right. The cream eased the trembling and convulsions, and some of his muscles seemed revived. But Johann feared this relief wouldn't last long. Supported by Karl, he sat down on a low stone wall.

"What now?" asked Greta, scooping water from a stream with both hands to wash her sweaty face. The little angel the midwife had gifted to her dangled from her neck. She shook her hair and gave her father an intent look. "What is your plan?"

Johann said nothing. He'd been racking his brain for days about how to proceed from here. After traveling so far, they were finally at their destination—only a stone's throw away resided the devil, or at least the man who was responsible for Johann's curse. Tonio, whom he'd finally have to face. But Johann hadn't come up with any plan about what to do next—not even the first spark of an idea.

The learned Doctor Faustus had reached his wit's end.

"It is possible that someone followed us," said John into the silence. "The French, that Swiss giant, or perhaps the Habsburgs. It's not inconceivable that they learned of our destination and are lying in wait here, ready to snatch the doctor." He nodded at Karl. "The young scholar and I will go into town with our ears peeled. I think the two of us are the least conspicuous."

Johann nodded reluctantly. It was a sensible suggestion. Viktor von Lahnstein might have a hunch where Johann was headed. Just like the French king, the papal delegate assumed that Johann knew how to make gold and that he had learned the secret from Gilles de Rais. Johann scanned the sky for any sign of the old raven but saw nothing.

Either way, the master knows I'm coming.

"Be careful," he said to John and Karl. "At the slightest sign that someone might be following you, you must throw them off the scent and return here. We can't take any risks."

"Don't worry, old man." John grinned. "This isn't the first time I'm scouting."

Johann inhaled sharply and glowered at John in silence.

I'm only glad he doesn't call me father-in-law yet.

Once John and Karl had left, father and daughter sat down in a meadow that was humming with bees. Greta chewed on a blade of straw and gazed at the castle towering above them.

"Doesn't look very evil," she said after a while.

Johann smiled. "The castle isn't evil, but the man living inside it is. Maybe those old walls will see better times one day."

"After everything that happened there?" Greta shook her head. "I wouldn't think so. Those walls are drenched with the blood of many innocent children. And now . . ." She broke off. "Well, what now? I still don't understand what exactly you intend on doing. If Tonio really is the devil, then you can't defeat him. The devil is invincible."

Johann nodded. "That is true. But you can barter with him, or perhaps even play a trick on him. Maybe a healthy Doctor Faustus is much more useful to him than a mortally ill one. Maybe there is a secret that I know and that he is interested in."

"Well, we know it's not the secret of how to make gold." Greta gave a little laugh. "I wonder who fed the pope such nonsense?"

"I'd love to know that, too."

No one said anything for a while, and Johann moved a little closer to Greta. The sun shone down warmly on his cold limbs, but something else warmed him from the inside. Greta was his daughter, and he sensed it and smelled it with every breath. She was the only creature in the world he truly loved. Of course, he used to love Little Satan's company, and also that of Karl, who had been at his side for many years. But those feelings were nothing compared to the love he felt for his daughter. He had never read her palms. Too great was his fear of foreseeing her death in them, the fear she might die before him and leave him behind. Johann opened his own creased hands and stared at them. He had done so repeatedly in the last few weeks, but to no avail. He couldn't make out anything in his own palms.

Only Greta could read them.

"I haven't looked at them in a long time," she said gently, as if she had heard his thoughts. "I no longer want to know. God alone should know when a person's end arrives."

"God or the devil."

He looked up and studied his daughter's face. She was so beautiful. He remembered the first time he saw her, back in the prison below Nuremberg. She had only been fourteen then, still a child, so dainty and fragile. And now she would go her own way, and he would be left behind. Whether dead or alive—he would be left behind.

"I should never have brought you here," he said. "It was pure selfishness. I wasn't ready to say goodbye. I wanted to hang on to you until the last moment."

"What are you talking about?" Greta gave a sad smile. "You're Doctor Faustus, remember? You've cheated the devil once before and you will do so again. And then the four of us will go back to the German Empire. You, me, Karl—"

"And John." Johann sighed. "You really do love him."

"More than that." Greta's face turned serious. "He is the man I will . . ." She gave a wave as if she'd changed her mind. "One thing after the other. First we confront whoever is living inside that castle."

When Johann looked at the castle again, he noticed that the fortress wasn't as imposing as he'd first thought. Some of the battlements had crumbled like rotten teeth, some of the windows were boarded shut, and ivy and gorse climbed up the walls like poisonous snakes. A cloud pushed in front of the sun, and the air grew chilly.

Up in one of the towers, a light flared up. To Johann it looked like a huge, watchful eye that gazed down at him hungrily.

~

Meanwhile, Karl and John were walking through a ghost town.

It had taken Karl a while to figure out what it was that gave Tiffauges such an eerie atmosphere. It was a small place with no wall or gates, and so they had been able to walk into town without causing a stir. Low half-timbered houses huddled along the edges of the few shady lanes. There were two churches, one enclosed market hall, and a square where several aging market wives sat behind their stalls like brooding hens. Some skinny dogs roamed the alleys, and everything was much like in any other French town. Yet something was different.

It was the quiet, Karl realized. And then it dawned on him.

There were no children.

In any village or town, small boys and girls raced through the lanes, shouting, making a racket, playing with their spinning tops and marbles, jumping in puddles, and rattling the nerves of the grown-ups. But not here. Just like at the other villages they had passed through in recent days, it looked as though the earth had swallowed up any and all children. As if some kind of creepy pied piper had lured them away, stolen them and left behind only the old folks. Where were they all? Karl looked around searchingly. He couldn't believe that every single child had been snatched and killed by Tonio. He thought it was more likely that parents no longer allowed their children out of the house.

Because they knew what could happen.

Karl still didn't believe that the devil himself lived in Tiffauges. But he had to admit—the place was creepy. His and John's footfalls sounded too loud, and soon Karl could feel eyes on his back, following their progress from behind dark windows. John felt them, too.

"I wouldn't say we're particularly welcome here." John pointed at the many shutters that were closed despite the fine weather.

The houses seemed to Karl as if they were sick, their paint weathered or flaked off, their beams black and rotting. During their short round of the village, they didn't encounter anyone except the market women and a group of old men who had glowered at them from bench perches.

"The tavern's open," John said, pointing at a tin sign with a wild boar painted on it that swayed above the entrance with an awful screeching sound.

John was about to head toward it when Karl held him back. "We don't know if Lahnstein or someone else has taken up lodgings there. Let's look through the window first."

John nodded. They entered a narrow alleyway beside the building, but all the windows were barred with heavy shutters. John pulled out his knife and levered at one of the shutters until it opened a tiny crack. Karl kept his eyes out for passersby.

As John peered through the gap, Karl scrutinized his companion from the corner of his eye. He could understand why Greta liked that red-haired Scotsman so much. John was funny and smart, even if he wasn't particularly learned, and he was handsome and would one day make an excellent father. Once again Karl grew painfully aware that he would never be blessed with such fortune. In the last few days he had often thought that it was time to leave the doctor and try his luck elsewhere, just like Greta was bound to do soon. But he just couldn't do it. He still loved Faust, even if the doctor was becoming stranger by the week.

Meanwhile, John had turned away from the shutter again. "I think it's the back room," he said in a low voice. "Some men are sitting there by candlelight even though it's the middle of the day. They're drinking and playing dice, as if they're waiting for something. I can't make them out very well, but I think some of them are wearing the colorful garb of soldiers."

"Which colors?" asked Karl.

"I think it was blue, yellow, and . . ." John paused and cast another glance through the crack. "And red."

"The Swiss guard," hissed Karl. "That means some of them made it out of Chinon alive. But how the hell do they know we're here?"

"They might have eavesdropped on us somewhere." John shrugged. "Maybe as far back as Amboise. Or that Lahnstein figured it out himself. This castle is the former residence of Gilles de Rais, after all."

"Did you see anyone who looked like the papal representative in there?" asked Karl. "You should recognize him by his face. Little Satan bit off his nose at Bamberg."

"No wonder he doesn't like you very much." John grinned and brushed his hair out of his face. "No, I would have—"

A noise made them both spin around. A long shadow darkened the alleyway, reaching for them as if with long claws.

A very large shadow.

"Jesus Christ," croaked Karl, the blood draining from his face.

Hagen stood between them and the main road.

Evidently, the Swiss mercenary had noticed that someone was watching the tavern. With a deliberately slow movement, the giant drew his longsword and started to walk toward them. Karl looked around in panic. Stacked up behind them stood rotting barrels and trash, and behind that was a wall. The alley was a dead end!

"You and I have a score to settle," said Hagen to John in his harsh Swiss accent. "I forgot to finish you off last time."

Karl instinctively took a step back. He and John had left their swords behind so they wouldn't attract attention in town. That had been a mistake. But Karl had something else—something cool and smooth inside the pocket of his vest:

the hand cannon from Albert MacSully, a brand-new wheel-lock pistol, and this time it was loaded and cocked.

Karl pulled it out and trembled as he pointed it at Hagen. "Let us pass," he said, trying to sound calmer than he felt. "Or your dumb skull is going to explode like a rotten apple."

Hagen hesitated for a moment. Then he moved with a speed that Karl would never have thought the giant capable of. He leaped toward them, dodging from side to side like a dancing dervish.

Karl pulled the trigger.

The bang was so loud that he thought he would go deaf. The recoil made him stumble backward and fall. He couldn't see if he had hit Hagen; the narrow alley was filled with powder fumes. John pulled him to his feet.

"Out of here!" John shouted and dragged Karl toward the road. Karl didn't stop to look around but ran past the tavern, where more soldiers came streaming out the door. John turned sharply and Karl followed. They ran along another narrow alleyway and came to a small square. Two old women were standing by a well and stared at them as if they were child-eating ogres. John and Karl hurried on, climbed over a low wall, crossed an overgrown orchard, and suddenly found themselves at the edge of a sheer drop.

Below them lay the dammed river.

"Jump!" called out John.

There were shouts behind them; a shot was fired and a bullet whistled past Karl. He looked back and saw Hagen storming toward them through the garden with his sword raised, more men behind him. John yanked Karl forward with a pull of his hand and then let go. Karl stumbled and saw John below him, elegantly diving into the water. Then he lost his footing and fell like a stone.

As he saw the black depths race toward him, Karl realized with horror that he'd never learned how to swim.

A few moments or an eternity later, Karl opened his eyes. He coughed and spat water, but he appeared to be alive. He saw John leaning over him, wiping his lips. Karl tasted salty saliva on his own lips and felt a pang of sweet wistfulness mix in with the mortal fear he had just experienced.

"Did you—?" he gasped.

"Kiss you awake like an enchanted prince? Indeed I did." John gave him a wink, his red hair hanging from his face like seaweed and his wet clothes clinging to his body. "But it didn't work—you're still the same slimy frog. But at least you're alive."

Shaking all over, Karl sat up. They were on the other side of the moat, not far from the spot where the derelict watchman's house stood and where Johann and Greta awaited their return. Karl looked across the black waters that stretched for several hundred feet toward the west. Some mill wheels turned slowly in the lazy current.

"'Twas a good deal of work, dragging you back up and all the way across the moat," said John. "But at least we should have some peace from our pursuers." He blinked as he squinted at the far shore. "I can't see anyone over there anymore. Perhaps they believe we've drowned."

"We . . . we must get back to the doctor," said Karl, still struggling to speak. Trembling, he scrambled to his feet. "Hagen is going to comb the entire area for us." He staggered up the slope and soon tripped on a tree root, landing on his knees.

"Slowly, slowly," said John. "The doctor isn't helped if you break your neck on the way to him."

Together they climbed up the overgrown bank that ended in a reforested patch of woods near the castle. It wasn't long before they reached the old warden's hut. Johann and Greta sat side by side on a wall and stared at the two wet figures as if they were swamp sprites.

"What the devil?" uttered Johann.

"No time for long explanations," gasped Karl. "Hagen is in town, which means Lahnstein is most likely, too. And maybe there are French soldiers, or Habsburg ones, or God knows—we can't be certain."

Greta groaned. "The whole world is after Father. When will it end?"

"Then there is no other way left." Johann stood up. "I will go to the castle right away."

"Now?" asked Karl, horrified.

"There is no point in hiding any longer. Tonio knows that I'm coming. As strange as it may sound—I'll be safest inside the castle. At least from Lahnstein, Hagen, and anyone else who might be pursuing me." Johann gave the others a long and determined look. "I am going alone. Our journey together ends here."

"And you simply leave us behind?" Greta stepped back. She crossed her arms on her chest and glared at her father. "After everything we've done for you? You honestly haven't changed at all, still only thinking of yourself."

"Greta, your father is right," said John. "If he really believes that he is cursed and that he must face up to this Tonio or whoever, then he must do so by himself. There's nothing we can do to help."

"I disagree," retorted Karl, still shivering. "The devil might live inside that castle, but so do some bad people. And I intend to protect the doctor from those bad people. Come what may." His teeth were chattering because of his wet clothes. He'd lost the pistol when he fell into the water, but thankfully his expensive eye glasses were safely stored in his luggage.

"*You* want to protect me?" Johann looked at him with pity. "How are you going to do that when you still believe that science has any place in this?"

"I stood by your side in the underground passages of Nuremberg. I followed you to Metz and then to France, and I'm not going to stop following you now." Karl squared his shoulders. "You might not believe it, but I've always remained your friend, in good times as well as bad. Maybe I am your only friend. Even if we don't always see eye to eye." He wiped away a tear and hoped that the others thought it was water. "Don't they say there's no harm in the occasional disagreement between friends? Well, I disagree with you now. I don't believe that the devil lives inside that castle. But I will follow you anyway."

No one spoke for a while, and then in a gentle voice Johann said, "Karl, believe me, I truly appreciate your offer. All those years we've spent together. But . . ." His expression changed, and he looked somewhat wistful. "But why not? I could indeed use a bit of help, even if it's just so I don't have to face the devil all by myself. Karl may come with me, but Greta stays here. That is my final word."

"And what if you die in there?" asked Greta.

"Then you won't be able to stop it from happening. You know the lines in my hand, Greta. Sooner or later, the road ends for every one of us. Maybe today, maybe tomorrow, or many years from now. But I won't allow Tonio to drag you into this."

Johann glanced over at the castle, whose walls seemed to absorb the sunlight. There was no movement on the battlements, and the windows stared down at them darkly.

"Each night that I spend in there, I will light a flame by the south wall that you can see from the forest," he said eventually. "Two long signals, two short ones, thrice repeated. If I'm in trouble, there'll be short signals only. That's how we remain in contact. Agreed?"

"And if there is no light at all?" asked Greta.

"Then my mission is over, one way or another. Don't wait for me. Greta, Tonio might reach out for you following my death. In that case you must get away from here as fast as you can." He looked at John. "I am placing my daughter's life in your hands. May God punish you if anything happens to Greta."

"I won't let anything happen to her." John gave a small bow. "You can rely on me, Doctor."

"So you'll just walk over to the castle, knock on the door, and deliver yourself to the enemy?" asked Greta. "Are you serious?"

Johann smiled. "Sometimes the simplest plans are the best. It's like with chess. Always make the move your opponent least expects."

They waited until it was dark.

Karl's clothes had dried in the meantime, and he no longer felt quite as pathetic as he had earlier in the afternoon when he'd nearly drowned in the moat. They had withdrawn into the shelter of the woods. Once or twice they heard shouting in the distance—the soldiers were probably still out looking for them. But the forests around Tiffauges were thick, and the wild gorse bushes formed a natural labyrinth. The shouting soon ebbed and didn't come closer.

They exchanged few words, afraid that talking would make saying goodbye even harder. Karl was scared; fear had grown around his heart like a layer of ice. He didn't know what awaited him in the castle, but at the same time he was relieved that the doctor had agreed to bring him along. And hadn't he even seen some affection in Faust's eyes? Karl knew that the doctor would never love him, but a bond had grown between them over the years that couldn't be broken. They would walk this path together, too—maybe it would be their last. Wasn't that what designated true love—to live through everything together until the bitter end?

And besides, Karl still hoped that maybe everything would somehow turn out well. Perhaps the steward ruling the castle would turn out to be nothing but a steward, and the new priest nothing but a priest. Maybe the death of the children could still somehow be explained by natural causes. Maybe they would leave Tiffauges Castle alive, and maybe Faust's disease was just a disease and not a curse—a malady that might be treatable, at Córdoba or wherever. But Karl had to admit that there were a lot of maybes in his considerations—more than a scientist like him could accept.

When night had descended over the woods, the four of them sneaked over to the moat, which stretched before them black and smooth. John had persuaded Johann that it would be best if he and Greta accompanied them as far as the castle. At the far end of the moat, a dam led across the river, and not far from that was the bastion forming the main entrance. The small gate, the only visible way to get into the castle, stood wide open.

Like an invitation, thought Karl.

Concealed by the darkness, they hurried across the dam and continued along the castle wall toward the five-pointed star of the bastion. When they had almost reached it, John signaled for them to stop and duck.

"What is it?" whispered Greta.

"See the bush by the moat, not far from the gate?" John pointed at the spot. "Two men are hiding there. Not castle guards, I'm guessing, but some of the same soldiers we saw in town."

Now Karl could also make out the two figures. They were about eighty paces away and barely recognizable.

"Wait here," ordered John. He drew his long hunting knife from his belt and stalked toward the bush, followed by Greta's worried gaze.

"What is he doing?" she asked. "There are two of them. If one of them screams—"

"He belongs to the king's guard," said Johann reassuringly. "I think he knows what he's doing. I still can't stand the fellow, but he certainly is a useful fighter."

Karl couldn't see John for a few moments. He wondered if more soldiers they couldn't see had been hiding, but then a shadow rose behind one of the men by the bush. The man slumped to the ground and was swallowed up by the darkness. Karl thought he heard a muffled sound, then the second man also vanished.

"Like I said—he knows what he's doing," said Johann with an approving nod.

Soon John returned, the knife back on his belt. He seemed completely composed—not at all as if he'd just slit the throats of two men. "They were Swiss mercenaries," he reported in a low voice. "I would have loved to finish off that giant, but he wasn't there. It's highly likely that he's lurking somewhere else. So better not hold any lengthy speeches when you're standing outside the inner gate."

"I'll be pleased if it opens at all," said Johann before he stood up and stretched.

His appearance was crippled and crooked as a gnarled willow, and yet he looked determined, fearless, and powerful, like a great sorcerer.

"Well, then. Let's get it over with." He hugged Greta one last time. "Don't you worry about me," he said, running his hand through her hair. "You were correct: Doctor Faustus always thinks of something." He smiled weakly. "After all, he can do magic, right?" Then he turned away abruptly and strode toward the castle gate with Karl.

15

KARL KEPT LOOKING BACK, EXPECTING OTHER MERCENARIES
to leap out of their hiding places at any moment. But nothing happened. A bridge
followed the first open gate, leading toward another gate.

The timber creaked beneath their feet as they walked across the bridge, the
dark, closed gate rising up before them. Above, stone spouts jutted out from
the wall through which hot pitch could be poured onto attackers during a siege.
Karl also noticed numerous arrow slits. Was someone watching them from the
inside? For a moment he thought he saw a flickering light behind the slits, but
it disappeared before he could be certain.

With all his remaining strength, Johann pounded his fist against the heavy
wooden door. The sound was as loud as thunder in the silence.

"Hey, open up!" commanded Johann as if it were the most normal thing in
the world to demand entrance to a castle late at night. "No lesser man than the
honorable Doctor Johann Georg Faustus requests admittance. Grant him entry
and he will compile a favorable horoscope for you. Deny him, however, and the
stars will shine on you with ill fortune!" He winked at Karl. "That ought to have
awakened whoever's inside."

"And everyone in the village, too," muttered Karl.

When nothing happened, Johann shouted, "I've traveled very far, from the
stormy climes of the North Sea, across the wooded hills of the Vosges Mountains,
all the way to Brittany. So far everyone has welcomed me and no one regretted it. Is the steward of Tiffauges going to be the first man to deny my helpful
services—the services of the great Doctor Faustus?"

Still nothing. But then there was a sound behind them. When Karl turned
around, he saw about a dozen men jogging toward them from outside the bastion.

One of them was very tall.

"Damn it, it's the Swiss guards with Hagen," exclaimed Karl.

The soldiers ran steadily toward the bastion and the bridge behind it. Karl could make out their colorful uniforms, their drawn swords and raised pikes. And at their front ran Hagen. A chill went down Karl's back. This giant appeared to be invincible. It wouldn't be long before he reached them. The only way to escape now would be if that damned gate opened—or if Karl jumped into the moat for a second time that day, the surface of the water looking oily in the light of the moon.

I'd rather get skewered, he thought.

Defiant and silent the gate stood before them, still no sound coming from the other side, while Hagen and his men got closer and closer.

Johann hammered his fist against the door as if he wanted to break it open. "Open up! Open the gate! Now!"

The first soldiers set foot on the wooden bridge. Karl thought that despite the darkness he could see Hagen smirk—when the gate finally creaked open like the gaping mouth of a huge fish.

"About time," snarled Johann.

Karl and the doctor slipped through the crack, and the wings of the gate immediately fell shut behind them. Someone banged against it from the other side, but the timber was hard as iron. A pike that had found its way through the gap lay broken on the ground. As the soldiers pounded the gate angrily, Karl looked around. They were standing inside a narrow entranceway that was separated from the moonlit courtyard by an iron gate. There wasn't a soul to be seen. But then a rattling and jangling set in, and the gate was lifted up as if by magic. The thumping behind them faded.

"A rather spooky reception," said Johann, wiping the sweat from his forehead. "But I didn't expect anything else."

He stepped out into the courtyard and scanned the buildings they could make out in the moonlight. Not far from them stood the donjon, the keep Karl had seen from outside. To their left was a small watchmen's hut, and just then two armored guards carrying swords around their waists emerged from it. Evidently they had been waiting for the two guests inside their dark room. One of the men carried a torch and shone it into Johann's face.

"So you are Doctor Faustus?" he asked in French, tilting his head, sizing up Johann. "*The* Doctor Faustus?"

"Do you want me to demonstrate on your body?"

The man said nothing at first, as if he didn't know what to think of the doctor's appearance. Then he asked, "Who are those men out there?"

"They've got nothing to do with us," replied Johann. "Now take me to your master, whoever he may be."

"'Whoever he may be.'" The soldier laughed. "Ha, that's a good one! Follow me. The *master* would like to meet you."

They followed the two guards across the courtyard, deserted and barren as if it had been forsaken by God and the world. Farther back they could see the outlines of the manor house and other buildings, but the guards led them to the right, to the donjon. Karl realized now how big and mighty this tower really was. It was surrounded by its own moat with its own drawbridge, a fortified gate, and a three-story main building—it was a castle within the castle.

As if the one who constructed it wanted to be safe from enemies not from the outside, but from the inside, thought Karl.

Now he saw another large building to the left of the donjon. It was an old church that, compared to the tower, looked weathered and crumbling. The keep's moat ran right past the church, and it looked like the church had been cut in half and the front part had simply been torn down.

The guards led them over the narrow, squeaking drawbridge, then across a courtyard and finally into a low-ceilinged hall that was illuminated by dozens of torches. Nonetheless it was dim, the large room swallowing up the light. Thick smoke wafted below the ceiling and made Karl cough. It stemmed from a great open fire at the back wall that didn't seem to draw very well. Moldy tapestries displaying battle scenes hung on the walls, like relics of a long-gone era. In the center of the room stood an enormous banquet table that easily would have seated two dozen people. Karl guessed that once upon a time roaring feasts had taken place here, but now there was just one solitary older man sitting at the table's head. He wore a surcoat that was tatty and stained; his bloated face was covered by a shaggy beard, and his right hand clutched a goblet of wine that gleamed blood-red. At his feet dozed two large black dogs that reminded Karl of Little Satan. When the dogs noticed the two strangers, they started to growl menacingly and bared their teeth.

"Arthos, Wotan, hush!" ordered the man in a similar growl. He gave the pair of guards by the door a signal. "You can leave us. I think we can handle those two on our own."

Karl was still wondering whether *we* was supposed to mean the dogs or another person when the man addressed the doctor.

"So you are the famous Doctor Faustus from the German lands," he said with a heavy tongue. He took a long gulp from his goblet and wiped his dirty shirtsleeve across his beard. His eyes were small and red, as if from years of drinking.

Johann gave a small bow. "At your service, Your Excellency."

"Tell me, how do I know that you are indeed Faust and not some kind of impostor, huh?" The man's eyes grew even smaller, and he scrutinized Johann and Karl as if they were a pair of cockroaches. "I've heard about Doctor Faustus. He is a powerful wizard, but you don't look powerful. Not to mention the fellow next to you. He looks more like a wench."

"It's him, no doubt," said another voice. "The legendary Doctor Johann Georg Faustus and his assistant, Karl Wagner. Am I right? Welcome to Tiffauges Castle!"

The voice had come from the rear of the room by the fireplace. Stepping out from the clouds of smoke was a gaunt middle-aged man clad in the black robe of a priest. His comely, beardless cheeks and chin were scarred by pockmarks that added a cruel streak to the otherwise handsome face, like cracks in a beautiful vase. His hair was raven black and long, flowing down his shoulders like pitch.

"Unlike the honorable lord steward, who is far too busy for such things, I have seen leaflets with your image at the markets," he added by way of explanation, looking at Johann. "It's a bad habit, I admit. Those leaflets often contain the most hair-raising nonsense. Oh dear!" The man gave a laugh. "Now I'm talking too much again. And I haven't even introduced myself." He gave a bow. "Father Jerome, the castle chaplain."

Johann looked at him sharply. "Is it customary in French castles for the guests to be greeted by the chaplain, not the lord of the castle?"

"You must forgive us." Father Jerome smiled. "The lord steward often feels indisposed. And in such cases he is glad when I . . . well, fulfill the occasional burdensome task for him. I'm afraid this is one such case." He gestured at the table, where the steward's head had sunk onto his chest. The old drunkard snored like a bear in hibernation, his beard hanging into his goblet.

"Yes, yes, so much work." Father Jerome gave a shrug. "Sir Albert is normally the duke's master of hunt, but the duke has been in Italy since the Battle of Marignano, and Sir Albert has been running things at Tiffauges since." He chuckled softly. "The duke probably didn't consider the fact that Albert is a better huntsman than administrator. I like to think he would be pleased to know that his humble chaplain goes over his bills and the lists of his estates. Especially since Sir Albert can barely read."

Father Jerome smiled once more, his black eyes glistening like cold crystals. He gestured at the long table covered with silver platters of cold meats, cheese, bread, and smoked fish, as well as a large wine carafe. "Why don't we sit? You must be hungry, venerable doctor, and you can tell me over dinner what brings you to Tiffauges."

They sat down and Johann helped himself to meat and wine. Karl briefly panicked at the thought that the food might be poisoned, but then he realized that there was no reason to kill them like this.

They were prisoners already.

As they ate in silence, Karl studied the priest. The man sat opposite them at the table and merely sipped on his cup of wine. If the old midwife had spoken the truth, then Father Jerome was the same man who'd called upon the devil with Gilles de Rais about a hundred years ago. Back then he called himself François Prelati and used to be something like the playmate of the dark marshal.

But maybe that was just another rumor. Karl knew from painful experience that heretics and sodomites were often lumped together. Still, he had to admit that something was gravely amiss in this castle. Clearly, the chaplain had seized control at Tiffauges—that must have been what the guards had hinted at. But that didn't mean that the man in front of them was an undying monster. In any case, he was extremely polite.

"How do you enjoy France, Doctor?" asked Father Jerome, eyeing Johann with curiosity.

"It's a beautiful country if you have an eye for castles, an ear for music, and a palate for fine food," answered Johann between mouthfuls. He seemed very calm and focused, as during a difficult game of chess.

Father Jerome laughed, causing the steward to start up briefly before falling back asleep. "You're right. But I believe you are not here because of the good food." With an expression of concern, the father gestured at Johann's lifeless arm and slumping shoulder. "I'm inclined to believe you are seriously ill. Have you traveled to France in the hope of a cure? We have excellent doctors, especially in university cities like Avignon and Paris. Brittany, however, is truly like the end of the world in that regard."

"I am indeed searching for a cure." Johann looked up from his meal. "I had hoped to meet your master here."

"Duke Louis de Vendôme? Well, like I said, he's in Milan and—"

"I meant your *other* master."

Father Jerome looked stupefied. "I'm afraid I don't understand." Then his expression brightened. "Oh, you are speaking of the uppermost lord, the ruler of us all, whom I serve as chaplain." He grinned. "Well, you didn't have to travel to Tiffauges to speak with him. You can pray to my lord from anywhere and hope to be healed."

"And yet I would like to meet him face to face. Would that be possible?"

"Hmm, he doesn't show himself to many, only to very few select people and those who serve him wholeheartedly. You should know that, Doctor. Only those who meditate and pray deeply—"

"Tell him I want to see him," interrupted Johann.

Father Jerome laughed again, and it was a soft, jingling laugh that made the dogs prick up their ears. "What makes you think that I, of all people, can get in contact with the great lord? I'm just a little priest, the chaplain of Tiffauges, nothing more."

"Oh, I know you can do it." For the first time Johann smiled, too, but his smile was as cold as ice. "You are his most faithful servant, are you not?" He rose. "I would like to retire now. It was a long day and my limbs are sore."

Father Jerome also stood up. Karl watched the two unequal men. So far, neither man had shown his true face. It was like a charade, and the audience waited to see who would first tear off the mask of the other.

"I will show you to your rooms," said Father Jerome, walking toward the door. "Let us hope that the lord in his grace hears your pleas. A bedtime prayer certainly wouldn't hurt."

Behind them, the steward snored on.

~

Johann struggled to fall asleep that night. He was lying in a musty four-poster bed covered with cobwebs on the second floor of the keep. Stretched above him was a dusty, threadbare baldachin, and the old boards of the bed creaked with every movement. The room was hot and stuffy. Johann wondered who had last slept in this bed—Gilles de Rais himself, together with Prelati the priest, who now called himself Father Jerome? Poitou, Henriet, La Meffraye? Or another one of his many hunters and bloodsuckers? Or perhaps even a child, lured here with sweets and then slaughtered like a lamb by Gilles de Rais? What had these walls witnessed?

Karl was in the chamber next to his, separated only by a thin door. Before they had gone to bed, they had given the agreed-upon signal with the torch in the window. Even if Johann was feeling afraid, he didn't think he was in any imminent danger. Not yet. Standing by the window earlier, gazing down at the lights of the small town, he had noticed a large black bird rising up from the castle's battlements. Probably a raven.

Send my greetings to your master. I am waiting for him!

Johann knew: wherever Tonio was, he would come. Father Jerome might have been a false priest, but he wouldn't make the mistake of keeping Johann's presence from his master. If Tonio wasn't at the castle, he probably wasn't far. Johann found the thought strangely reassuring. He felt as though he had been running all his life without knowing where he was headed. Now he had finally arrived.

I'm here, Tonio.

As Johann slowly nodded off, his thoughts turned to Greta. He never should have brought her this far. Maybe it really was better if John Reed was by her side, even if Johann couldn't stand the loudmouthed fellow. John would be able to protect Greta now that Johann no longer could. He would have preferred for the two of them to depart right away. Now he could only hope that nothing happened to her—after all, lurking out there were still Lahnstein, Hagen, and the mercenaries he and Karl had only just managed to get away from.

John. Greta. Margarethe.

Slowly, Johann slid into the realm of dreams where his beloved Margarethe reached out her hand for him, where his mother in Knittlingen sang a Palatinate lullaby, and where old Father Antonius at Maulbronn Monastery handed him a volume of Greek fables. His old friend Valentin stood outside the monastery and waved to him; he had forgiven Johann—they all had forgiven him.

When Johann opened his eyes, he saw a tall figure standing by his bed. Was he still dreaming? He tried to sit up but his limbs wouldn't move—not just his left arm, but his whole body. He felt as if he were buried alive. Behind the figure, a door was ajar, and it wasn't the door to Karl's chamber but a different one, one that had been hidden behind one of the tapestries. The figure bent down to him, staring at him from dead black eyes that gleamed like the eyes of a large insect. Long, clawlike fingers crawled across his body.

Cold sweat stood on Johann's forehead, and his heart raced. He wanted to move, wanted to lift at least one hand, one finger, but he couldn't. He felt a rough tongue on his face as if an ancient reptile was licking him, smelling him.

You're mine, Faustusss. You're mine, little Faustusss.

Then Johann fell into a deep unconsciousness and awoke only when it was bright daylight.

~

Greta and John also struggled to find rest that night. They had built a shelter deep in the woods, covering a hollow in the ground with branches and leaves, where they cuddled together like two young cats. The pale moon shone above them. Greta knew she should have been afraid of wild animals, or of the soldiers who might still be searching for them, but once again she felt safe at John's side—as safe as she used to feel with Johann when she was younger.

Pensively, she played with the small amulet the midwife had given her. The alabaster angel was warm, as if it were alive. A thousand thoughts went through her mind: How was her father doing right now, had he already encountered Tonio, what would happen to him and Karl behind the walls of Tiffauges? Johann had given the signal they had agreed upon, and so she guessed everything was going to plan so far. But Greta felt guilty, because her fear for Karl and her father had moved to the back of her mind. Instead she felt closer to John than ever before. They were lying on their backs beside each other, gazing up at the moon. She squeezed his hand.

"What happens to us now?" she asked hesitantly. "You've fulfilled your promise of bringing us here. My father is where he wanted to be."

"And now you think I'll disappear again?" John laughed. "Let me put your mind at rest. I won't leave you. Ever. Remember—I gave your father my word that I would look after you. That means for the rest of our lives."

"You've broken your word before."

"Those days are over, Greta. Since I met you, everything is . . ." He faltered. "Everything is different. Honestly. I want to be with you and nowhere else. Besides—there is no way back for me. If the king finds me, he'll probably have me quartered in Paris as a warning to anyone who might betray him. I am a wanted criminal, a traitor."

"And soon to be a father," said Greta, snuggling up close to him so that she could hear his heart.

He sat up and stared at her. "What did you just say?"

"I haven't bled for two months in a row now. I know that doesn't mean much, but—"

"Greta! This . . . this is . . ." John shook his head in disbelief. For the first time he seemed lost for words. Then he covered her face in kisses until she laughed and pushed him away.

Greta had been wondering if and when she should tell him. It was still too soon, really, but the moment had carried her away.

"Stop it—you're tickling me!" she giggled when his tongue played with her ear. "It must have happened back in Blois—remember?"

He grinned. "Oh yes, I remember. Let me think—I think I did this . . . and then this . . ."

He rolled on top of her, and her resistance soon died off. His lips traveled from her face to her neck, then down to her breasts, and then farther down. When he pushed up her skirts, she closed her eyes and suddenly seemed to hear and feel everything around her much more clearly. Her own breathing, the sounds of the forest, the hooting of an owl, the rustling of the leaves in the wind, the tickling of the forest floor on her naked skin.

She lived fully in the moment with no fears and no worries. And while John kissed her in the most forbidden places, she felt happier than she had in many years. John was her man, he would be the father of her children, and they would travel the lands together without a destination.

16

THE FOLLOWING DAYS WERE ONE LONG WAIT FOR JOHANN.
Tonio didn't show, but Johann knew he would come. The only question was
when.

On the morning following the first night, he had woken bathed in sweat. He
still wasn't sure if he had dreamed it or if Tonio—or someone else—had visited
his bedside. As soon as he'd risen, he had searched the walls for secret doors but
hadn't found any. There was only the door leading to Karl's room. Had it been
this door after all?

During the day he and Karl explored the vast castle complex. No one
stopped them; guards would watch Faust and Karl closely but always let them
pass as if they'd been ordered to. The castle was a huge maze of chambers, tunnels, barbicans, towers, walls, and bastions, built to withstand any siege. The
mighty donjon formed the heart of the castle and was intended as a last retreat
should the walls ever be breached. Another central building was the two-story
manor house, which sat roughly in the center of the plateau and was framed by
several storage sheds and the horse stables. Usually the duke resided here, but
he hadn't been in Tiffauges for years.

The strangest building, thought Johann, was the church next to the donjon.
It would appear that part of the nave had been torn down to give more space to
the keep. The chapel looked oddly shortened, but on the inside its former glory
was still visible. A triumphal arch separated the apse from the nave; beautifully
carved wooden statues of saints stood in the side aisles, and there were an ancient
baptismal font and paling frescoes whose color was flaking off. A service led by
the chaplain took place here every morning, and it was always accompanied by
the sound of an organ, but Johann never saw the organ or the organist.

Faust and Karl rarely encountered the steward of Tiffauges. Sir Albert spent most of his time in the donjon, drinking in the downstairs hall and staring holes into the air. He looked like a walking corpse. His dogs alone forced him to go outside from time to time. The guards greeted their master respectfully enough when he staggered past them, but they mocked him behind his back and made faces. Father Jerome, on the other hand, they met with true respect, or even fear. When the priest walked past them, they looked at the ground and muttered some words that Johann couldn't understand. Usually, he and Karl would only see the priest and Sir Albert during dinner in the hall.

They explored the castle thoroughly, including the smoky kitchen, several high-ceilinged halls, and numerous elegantly furnished chambers that appeared to be reserved for special guests. Johann even discovered a small library in one of the towers at the rear, which seemed to have been built more recently. The only building he and Karl weren't permitted to enter unaccompanied was the church. It was only open during the morning services and remained locked at all other times. When he and Karl approached the church door, two or three guards would appear immediately and position themselves outside the entrance.

"Shouldn't a house of God always be open?" Johann asked Father Jerome on the second day following their arrival, as they stood in front of the shelves in the library. Even though temperatures outside were summery and muggy, it was pleasantly cool behind the castle's thick walls. Once again the priest had appeared out of nowhere like a ghost. Johann wondered if there were secret doors in the library. This castle appeared to be one big secret.

"Parts of the church are currently under repair," explained Father Jerome with a shrug. "It is too dangerous to allow believers inside unaccompanied."

"Strange—I didn't notice any repairs during the service," replied Johann.

"They can't be seen from the nave. But the building is still . . . unsafe." Father Jerome's smile always looked somewhat predatory in his pockmarked face. "Very much so, believe me." He made a sweeping gesture at the shelves full of dusty books, folders, and parchment scrolls. "You like our humble library? Maybe you'll find something on your mysterious illness."

"I don't know about that, but I have found some very rare works. Roger Bacon's *Opus Majus*, for example, and some older writs by Albertus Magnus. As you can see, my assistant is smitten." Johann nodded in the direction of Karl, who was sitting at a desk with his glasses on his nose, engrossed in a heavy tome that was chained to the table. "All these are works, by the way, which I had the pleasure of admiring in another library, too," continued Johann evenly. "That was in Venice a long time ago, at the house of a certain Signore Barbarese. I don't suppose you know him?"

Father Jerome's smile froze. "I'm afraid I don't."

"Pity. I think you would have liked him, even if his attitude toward the church was . . . well, peculiar. He always followed his motto, *Homo Deus est.* Have you heard it before?"

"'Man is God'? I don't imagine the church would have liked that." Father Jerome frowned. "Although it is a tempting thought. What if man, not God, steered the fate of the world?"

"Or someone else," suggested Johann. "Oh, by the way, I noticed that there are no Christian works whatsoever in this library. Not even a Bible."

"They must all be in the church. It contains its own library. Would you like me to have some pious works brought to you? For prayer and reflection? I believe we own some highly edifying chapters by Saint Francis that might be of help."

Johann shook his head. "I don't believe that will be necessary. I hope your lord will speak to me when he's ready."

"We shall see." Father Jerome bowed his head and left the library.

Thus the days passed. They didn't see Hagen and his mercenaries again. Johann and the priest circled one another like two old beasts of prey, both waiting for the other to take the fatal leap. The daily routine at the castle went on, and every night Johann and Karl gave the light signals from Johann's window. On the evening of the fifth day, when they sat in the great hall with the steward and the chaplain, Father Jerome addressed Johann after their meal. He seemed to have waited for Sir Albert to fall asleep after his fourth goblet of wine. Johann thought the steward looked even more deeply asleep than usual.

"I have good news, Doctor," said Father Jerome. "I prayed at church for a long time today, and a miracle happened. The lord spoke to me!" He leaned forward, and his voice became quiet and hissing like the whisper of a snake. "And he wants to speak with you. He wants to see you."

"When?" asked Johann, pushing his plate away.

Father Jerome winked at him. "This very night. We have prepared a special mass for the occasion." He glanced at the snoring steward. "Unfortunately, Sir Albert won't be able to attend, as you can see. But there'll be other guests, and they look forward to making your acquaintance. You are a famous man, Doctor Faustus." The priest stood up. "I still have much to prepare for mass. I expect both of you in the church at midnight sharp."

A short while later, Johann paced his room restlessly. At regular intervals, the bell of the town's church chimed a quarter of a mile away, its heavy, dull sound announcing the slow passing of time. Nine o'clock, ten o'clock, eleven o'clock. The wait seemed to drag on endlessly.

Johann had asked Karl to leave him for a little while; he wanted to rest and prepare himself for what was to come. But he struggled to form any clear thoughts. He had been waiting for this moment for so long. Now he would finally face Tonio. What the two of them had begun many years ago with a pact would reach its conclusion, one way or another.

When he walked to the window and gazed into the night, he saw dots of light moving from town toward the bridge and the gate. Torches and lanterns, glowing like yellow fireflies. Johann guessed they belonged to the mysterious guests Father Jerome had invited to this mass.

The meeting with Tonio del Moravia, Johann's former master.

Every fiber of Johann's body quivered with anticipation, almost as if he were about to make love. Tonio was his enemy and more. He was Johann's alpha and omega; everything had started with him and everything would end with him. Johann felt certain: the disease Tonio had sent him was supposed to bring him to this place, to this moment in time. Strangely, he could even move his arm again a little. He couldn't tell whether that was because of the old midwife's cream or because of Tonio's proximity.

Behind him, the thin door opened and Karl entered.

"Did you manage to get some rest?" When Johann shook his head, Karl smiled. "I didn't think you would. I, too, can't stop wondering what to expect inside the church." He raised a hand. "I know, it's not yet midnight, but we should still give the light signal."

Johann gave a start. He had been so preoccupied with the thought of meeting Tonio soon that he'd almost forgotten about his promise to send the signal each night. Instead he had been staring at the dots of light signaling the arrival of the guests. He looked around for the brazier by his bed.

But it wasn't there. Only a ring of soot on the floor showed where it used to stand.

Karl followed his gaze. "Same in my chamber," he said. "I had hoped there'd be fire in your room. The torches have also been removed."

Johann looked at the rusty brackets on the wall—they were empty. Someone must have taken the torches away while they were in the hall.

"Damn it," groused Johann. "Looks as if someone noticed what we've been doing each night. Let's go—maybe we'll find a torch in the corridor that we—"

He turned to the door and stopped dead.

Father Jerome stood in front of him with a torch in his hand.

Karl hadn't heard him enter, either. The priest hadn't come in through the regular entrance; that door was still closed. Had he entered through Karl's door or . . . ?

Or through the same secret door that he used to visit me that first night, thought Johann.

He wondered how much of their conversation the chaplain had overheard. Father Jerome's face betrayed nothing. After a few moments, he hinted at a bow.

"I thought it would be polite to fetch you personally for mass," he said. "It's a little early, but the guests are growing impatient. They long to see you, Doctor. Are you ready?"

Johann would have liked to ask for more time, but he couldn't think of an excuse. How could he give the signal when he and Karl went with the priest now? Father Jerome had probably ordered the torches and braziers to be removed himself. Johann should have thought of it sooner—now it was too late. But it didn't really matter. He had only given the signal in the last few nights to put Greta's mind at ease. Tonight, everything was going to be resolved, so there was no more need for signals.

"I am ready," he said.

"Then follow me."

They stepped into the dark corridor. Here, too, any lights had been removed, making Father Jerome's torch the only source of light in the darkness of the old walls. They followed the priest down the stairs, left the donjon, and turned right toward the church. There was no sign of any of the guards, and no watch fires had been lit on the towers like usual. Johann suspected the guards had been bribed—unless the chaplain had other means of making them compliant.

Father Jerome pushed against the two-winged church portal, which swung open silently as if freshly oiled. They were greeted by a surprising brightness, and Johann was forced to squint. The nave was illuminated by dozens of torches, and, as during morning mass, the organ was playing, but it sounded incredibly low and the tune was very strange, like music meant not for mankind but for something much older. Once Johann's eye had adjusted to the brightness, he looked around searchingly. Contrary to his expectations, the church was empty. No one was sitting in the pews.

"Where are your guests?" asked Karl, who had been following Johann and the priest in silence.

Father Jerome waved dismissively. "Don't worry, everything is prepared."

He walked ahead, leading them behind the altar in the apse. Johann saw now that narrow stairs led down through an opening in the ground. During the morning services, it had been closed with a hatch that now stood open. Father Jerome pointed down below where, Johann realized, the organ music came from.

"After you."

Johann hesitated briefly, then he started to descend the slippery, moss-covered steps. If the priest and his friends wanted to kill Johann, they would do so anyway. But he didn't think they were going to—for some reason, Father Jerome treated him with something like respect.

The steps led down into a low crypt directly beneath the church. Here, too, many torches had been lit, illuminating a long room that was supported by two rows of stout columns. Farther back, a type of well was built into the ground, torchlight reflecting in the water. The organ music was so loud that it hurt Johann's ears, but he still couldn't spot the instrument.

Instead, Johann saw the guests.

There were about two dozen of them, and it was the strangest conglomeration of people Johann had ever seen. It was a mix of men and women, older ones and younger ones, although Johann couldn't see any very old people or children. It took him a few moments to figure out what was so odd about them.

It was their clothes.

Only a few of the guests wore regular garments; the rest were dressed like people in a painting.

In a very *old* painting.

Johann saw pale noblewomen with divided hennins and veils on their heads, men with pointed crakows and cloak-like upper garments that had been in fashion decades ago. The colors were garish and loud, the leggings tight fitting, accentuating the men's private parts, and some wore scarves around their heads wrapped into turbans. Silver cloak pins and jingling bells on the garments gave some of them the air of jugglers.

But on second glance, the outfits didn't seem quite as magnificent. Some were faded, others threadbare and full of mold stains, as if they'd spent many years lying in a chest.

Or in a coffin, thought Johann.

The guests nodded at him and Karl. Some of them gave an elegant bow, but no one uttered a word. Each of their movements was measured and grave. Father Jerome pointed out an older man wearing a slightly scratched silver cuirass with a faded red cape of velvet. The deafening organ music ended as if on cue.

"May I introduce you to Henri Montcourt," said Father Jerome, "the Duke of Burgundy, valued friend of the king, and one of the most feared enemies of the English. He single-handedly decapitated eight of their knights during the Battle of Compiègne."

The duke bowed low, and Johann couldn't hide his surprise. What in God's name was going on here?

"It is a great honor, sir," said Montcourt as if he were standing before the king.

"I didn't realize the English were still enemies," said Karl, who seemed just as astonished as Johann. "Hasn't King Francis I signed an agreement with Henry VIII that England drops all claims of the French crown?"

"Begging your pardon, I wasn't speaking of King Francis I but Charles VII," replied Father Jerome with a soft chuckle and slap to his forehead. "A very capable ruler who reclaimed Paris from the English eighty years ago. Duke Montcourt rode at his side back then. Yes, it's been a while." He pulled Johann and Karl along. "What you see here is old nobility, in the truest sense of the word. These people don't think in days or years, but in generations. They are the most loyal followers of our master. I am so glad that you may meet him today! Not many are granted this privilege."

"I've already had the pleasure," said Johann softly.

"I know, Doctor. I know. We all do."

They were introduced to more guests, but Johann couldn't remember the names. They were all French, and he believed he had heard of one or two of them before, in connection with a long-gone era. They were names from the Hundred Years' War, in which the French had fought the English. On the French side, Charles VII had fought with many of his followers.

Johann dared to ask a very particular question.

"I would have expected to see Jeanne d'Arc among this illustrious circle," he said casually. "I heard the maiden died a martyr, but maybe she isn't dead at all but alive and well like all the others here."

Father Jerome gave him a hateful stare. "Let me give you a piece of advice—don't ever mention this name in the presence of our lord. It makes him . . . well, rather sad. Jeanne could have had everything. The master loved her like none other, but she chose death by fire. A true shame!"

The priest shook his head as if to rid himself of an irritating thought. "But enough of the chitchat. These people traveled a long way to see you, Doctor. That is why we had to wait a few days for this mass. They all want to help you meet the lord. But I must tell you one thing—one vitally important thing." He raised an admonishing finger. "You have to say that you come willingly to him. That is the condition."

"We're not haggling," said Karl angrily, gesturing at the people around them. "What are you trying to achieve with this masquerade, anyhow? Do you really think we believe that all these people are over a hundred years old and personal friends of Gilles de Rais?"

Father Jerome gave a shrug. "You can believe what you will, Master Wagner. But if you—both of you—want to meet the master, then you must fulfill the ancient ritual. Those are the rules."

Johann remembered his encounter with Tonio at Nuremberg. Then, too, it had been important that he came to the underground crypt of his own free will.

"I come willingly," he declared loudly.

Father Jerome looked at Karl. "And you? Do you want to go with the doctor?"

"If this superstitious hocus-pocus is really necessary . . ." Karl tried a mocking smile but failed. "Very well. I come willingly."

"Good." Father Jerome nodded, then he turned to the Duke of Montcourt. "Please, monsieur, fetch the black potion."

Johann groaned when the memories returned.

The black potion.

He knew this potion. Two times already in his life he'd been made to drink it. He didn't know the exact ingredients, but he guessed the brew contained devil's trumpet, henbane, and other mind-bending herbs of the nightshade family. It made a person feel heavy and extremely light at once. Life was suddenly just an illusion and the delirium was reality; the borders between the world of dreams and real life blurred.

But mostly, it was a nightmare.

"For the journey you are about to undertake, it is crucial that you drink the black potion to the last drop," said Father Jerome seriously. "You must be pure, from the inside as well as the outside. Which is why you are going to bathe."

"What journey?" asked Karl with increasing trepidation. "And what bath, damn it?" He looked around nervously.

"You will learn the destination when you have drunk." Father Jerome watched Johann closely. "Do you want to meet the lord? Do you want your disease to be healed? Or would you prefer your life on earth to be over very soon, dying pathetically and unknowing like a sick mutt?" The voice of the father took on the tone of a snake again. "Would you prefer the master to take his pleasure with your *daughter* following your inglorious end? If you don't, then drink!"

Johann stepped toward the Duke of Montcourt, who was carrying a chalice made of black obsidian. He yanked the chalice from the duke's hand, causing a few drops to spill. Johann almost feared that they would vaporize on the floor like acid. He lifted the chalice to his nose and sniffed. The contents smelled rotten, like old fish and moldy seaweed from the depths of the ocean.

"Drink!" said Father Jerome. "It's different every time—no one can tell beforehand what the drink will show you." He gave a little laugh. "But believe me, it is always a deeply profound experience."

Memories rose up in Johann from the time he traveled to a forest near Nördlingen with Tonio and Poitou; that had been many years ago. Now he had to go through it all again.

"Then so be it."

Johann took a long sip that almost made him vomit, the liquid burning in his throat like fire. Then he went to pass the chalice to Karl but stopped short.

"You don't have to do this, Karl. You can still turn back. I am grateful for all you've done for me. No one can force you to do this."

"That is true. You must drink it willingly." Father Jerome nodded at Karl. "But when you drink, there is no way back."

Karl hesitated. He looked at Johann, and Johann thought he could detect a silent sadness in his assistant's eyes—sadness and something else. Johann was about to say something, but then Karl lifted the chalice to his lips.

And drank.

And just then, the droning bass of the invisible organ set in again.

~

The most conflicting feelings raged inside Karl when he placed the chalice to his lips. He assumed the potion was not poison but a drug. Still, his hands shook as if he was being passed a cup of hemlock. All this seemed so absurd and horrible at once. Karl knew what had happened back in Nuremberg after Faust had been given the black potion. During a gruesome sacrificial ceremony, the doctor's little finger on his right hand and his left eye had been removed. Was he facing a similar fate now?

The liquid touched his lips and then seeped down his throat. It was the most disgusting thing he'd ever drunk. His body reacted by gagging, and he struggled to keep the potion down. He could feel the eyes of the guests on him, watching him like hungry wolves. Damn—these people were at least as crazy as those Satanists below Nuremberg. Karl couldn't believe that the guests were hundred-year-olds who prolonged their life through some sorts of horrific rituals—or worse, living dead who had risen from their graves. He refused to believe it because he knew that otherwise his entire view of the world would collapse, a view that rested on reason and science and that had no room for a real devil, immortality, and all the other outrageous nonsense he had encountered over the last few months.

But still he drank. He drank for one reason in particular—a reason almost as irrational as the existence of the devil.

He did it for love.

Karl couldn't leave the doctor, not after all the years they'd spent together, and that was why he had to walk this path with him now. As painful and crazy as it was.

The liquid burned like bile as it seemed to expand in his stomach; the pain reminded Karl of a pungent, high-proof liquor. Once he overcame the initial nausea, a heat spread from the center of his body and radiated into even the smallest pores. At the same time he felt light and strangely carefree. Suddenly he had no idea how much time had passed since he'd taken the first sip. Minutes? Hours? His fear was gone, and the glow of the torches in the crypt seemed warm and homely to him, like a cozy fire on a winter's night.

Karl looked over at Johann, who was standing beside him with his eyes closed. The doctor was so handsome. Karl wanted to touch him; he reached out for Johann but grew aware that they weren't alone. The men and women inside the crypt surrounded them, but they no longer seemed crazy or evil to Karl. They were friendly, warmhearted people who beamed at him. Some laughed, others clapped their hands, and they chanted: "O lord, take them to you! Let them come to you!" And Karl laughed with them like a big, innocent child.

A hand touched him gently by the shoulder. It was Father Jerome, smiling at him.

"Follow me to the bath." Father Jerome's voice was as warm and mild as the morning sunshine in early summer. "You must wash before you can set forth on your journey."

Karl and Faust followed him submissively. Father Jerome led them to the well at the back of the crypt. The water inside gleamed black, and the well looked much larger to Karl now, almost like a basin meant for swimming.

Like an enormous baptismal font, he thought.

"Take off your clothes," said Father Jerome, not in the tone of a command-ing priest but lovingly, like a dear friend.

Hesitantly at first, then faster and faster, Karl undressed, and so did the doctor. Soon they both stood naked in front of the well, and for some reason Karl felt comfortably warm despite the chilly air inside the crypt. It was his first time seeing the doctor like this. Even though Faust was past forty now, his body still looked athletic and sinewy, without an ounce of fat on him. Strands of muscles showed beneath his skin like taut ropes, even in those places where he was paralyzed. Bushy pubic hair covered his manhood, which, Karl noticed, was rather large.

"Now enter the pool and wash," said Father Jerome. "Every part of your body! Nothing must remain untouched."

Karl didn't hesitate for long. He found the water to be surprisingly warm. When he lowered his foot into it, circles formed on the surface that grew toward the outside edge, and Karl felt magically drawn to them. He sat down on the rim and slid into the bath; it came up to his hips when standing, and it felt wonderful. He leaned down and scooped the liquid over his body. When it wet his lips, it tasted as salty as seawater. All worry and exhaustion seemed to fall away from him.

Johann climbed in next. They hadn't exchanged a word so far, and Karl wasn't even sure if the doctor was aware of him. He seemed to be entirely absorbed in his own world. Karl noticed a shine, a supernatural reddish glow that Faust exuded. What was it? Karl reached out and gently touched the doctor's cheek. Only then did Johann notice him and smile.

"Karl, my loyal Karl," he whispered. "You've always been there."

"Johann," replied Karl softly. He had never before called the doctor by his first name. "I . . . I love you . . ."

The words had come out of his mouth as if his thoughts suddenly had a voice of their own. Strangely enough, the revelation didn't seem to shock the doctor.

"I know, Karl," said Faust, smiling. "I know. And it's all right." He reached out for Karl, too.

"Now wash each other," said Father Jerome's gentle, singing voice like from another world.

With his right hand Karl stroked the doctor's hair, then his warm, salty fingers ran across the doctor's face, neck, chest, and down until they touched Faust's pubic hair. The doctor didn't seem to mind, and he, too, began washing Karl all over. With his right hand he stroked Karl and smiled at him. They were very close, their bodies touching, and Karl felt arousal rising up in him like lava inside an erupting volcano. He screamed his lust out into the world.

They embraced, standing in the pool like one being with four arms. From afar Karl could hear the chorale of the disciples, accompanying their singing with rhythmic clapping.

"Masterel, al zulath, esternis Locat, phrector! Zhooooool . . ."

Karl didn't understand the words, but they sounded very old and at the same time as if they'd only just been born. The organ music set in again, and Karl felt the drone in every fiber of his body, washing through him like a wave.

This was the most amazing moment of his life—he felt so happy!

He was completely wrapped up in his own world, his eyes closed with delight. He loved the doctor and the doctor loved him! He hoped this dream would never end.

In this state of rapture, Karl didn't see Father Jerome hand the doctor a razor-sharp dagger of polished obsidian.

~

Two hours earlier, Greta had looked up at the castle one last time. Then she turned away with a sick feeling in her stomach and walked back into the woods where John was waiting for her.

"Still nothing," she said, shaking her head. "It's long past the agreed time. So far he's always given the signal much earlier than this."

"I haven't seen any watch fires tonight, either," remarked John. "That's what I find even more strange, to be honest. A large castle like this? And there were watch fires every other night."

"Something is wrong." Greta sighed.

John came up close to her and took her hand. They were standing by the edge of the forest to the castle's west, the moat gleaming black below them. "Your father gave us clear instructions. If there are no more signals, we are to leave as fast as we can. I gave him my word that no harm would come to you, and I'm going to keep my word. I won't allow the mother of my child to put herself in danger."

"Oh, John. You, you . . ." Greta was tempted to rest her head against his wide chest, but then she pulled herself together, straightened up, and crossed her arms defiantly. "Don't talk to me as if I'm a fragile little lady sitting in a castle chamber. I've always been able to defend myself. I know very well what my father said. But that doesn't mean that I follow his orders—or yours."

"You read his lines, Greta. I am very sorry, but he hasn't got long to live. Maybe he's already gone. He chose this path—no one forced him to go. And besides . . ." John hesitated.

"What is it?"

"If we noticed that no watch fires have been lit tonight, then those mercenaries will, too. I'm guessing that papal representative isn't stupid. He has not just the giant but also some other men capable of invading an unguarded castle. You don't need an army for that. There's a good chance they'll make use of tonight."

Greta pinched her lips. John was right; she hadn't thought of the soldiers. Four days and five nights they had spent in the woods together. And even if concern for her father robbed her of sleep, it had still been an unforgettable time. John had looked after her most lovingly and built them a small, cozy camp. They had gone hunting together and purchased a few treats from nearby farmers. There John had also learned that foreign soldiers still hung around the area, including Hagen, who had been sighted. Viktor von Lahnstein had taken up residence at the tavern in town, and he was bound to observe the castle from there. It was possible that he'd decide to strike this very night. What in God's name was going on up there?

"Listen, John, I can't bear this any longer," Greta said. "I know I should keep out of it. But Karl is up there, too. And Faust . . . He is my father, after all."

"And what kind of father takes his daughter on a journey like this?" replied John hotly. "Your father is sick—not just in his body but in his head. I've always thought there's something sinister about him."

"You mustn't talk of him that way!" snapped Greta. But deep down she agreed with John. There truly was something sinister about him—malevolent, even. His wish to confront Tonio had grown stronger and stronger in recent weeks. And there was also something else—something she wasn't telling John because she didn't fully understand it herself.

If Tonio really was up there at the castle, she wanted to face him, too. Ever since those unholy days at Nuremberg, he had also become part of *her* life.

"I want to know what's going on up there," said Greta with a grim expression. "Is my father dead or alive? And what about Karl? I owe it to him, at the least, to check on them."

"And how do you propose to do that?" John shook his head and pointed at the dark outline of the castle on the other side of the moat. "Even if no fires have been lit, the gates are closed."

"I'm a juggler, remember? If there's anything I know, then it's magic and trickery, and most of all control of my body." Greta lowered her voice as if someone might be able to overhear her. But the only sound in the woods was the hooting of an owl. "Yesterday, while you were hunting, I took a look at the north side of the castle. You know—where the two newer towers are watching over the land. In the wall east of the bigger tower, numerous stones are missing and there are large cracks—I think it'll be easy to scale. Especially if there are no guards posted atop."

"You can't be serious, Greta. I promised your father—"

"Come with me or don't," she cut him off curtly. "I climb up, find out what's going on, and get out again. I'll be back in just a few hours. You can roast a hare over the fire in the meantime."

Her face remained stony. Greta didn't want John to see her inner turmoil, but she was deeply relieved when he threw up his hands in resignation.

"You're a stubborn, unruly wench, do you know that?"

Greta grinned. "That, at least, is one thing I've inherited from my father."

The northern side of the castle was the darkest.

Here, the small river Sèvre Nantaise wound its way through a valley toward the moat and the dam. The valley was so steep that scarcely any moonlight made it to the ground at the bottom. Thick undergrowth made their progress even more difficult, and Greta and John continuously got caught in thorny brambles. It was as if the castle didn't want to be approached from this side. They found a shallow spot to cross the river. On the other side, the black castle wall rose into the night sky, additionally protected by a lower second wall. Some way to their left was a gate and a narrow road leading to the river and across a bridge.

"What next?" asked John.

Greta motioned toward the right, where the larger of the towers stood, a massive construction crowned with a ring of machicolations and a covered walkway. Underneath it stood one end of the dam, which separated the moat at the castle's front from the river beyond.

"Admittedly, there was more light yesterday afternoon. But at least there are no watch fires here, either," she said. "We can climb up on those broken stones east of the tower. Also, in that spot we don't have to climb over the outer fortifications."

John looked up skeptically. The wall was at least sixty feet high. "We don't know if there'll be broken stones all the way to the top."

"I know, John! Like I said, you don't have to come. But I think it's doable. I've climbed up smoother walls than this."

It was a blatant lie. Greta could walk on any rope, and a few times she had scaled a church tower during her shows with Johann and Karl in order to reach her rope, but she had never climbed a wall like this one before. She had to convince herself that she could do it—otherwise she would falter or fall.

"All right. But at least let me climb first." John stepped up to the wall, felt along the stones, and started to climb, inch by inch. Greta watched him for a while. John was strong and athletic. He might not have been quite as flexible as an acrobat, but he was doing well—it certainly wasn't his first wall. She tied up her skirts and followed him, her fingers searching for the ledges, cracks, and crevices John had used. They climbed in silence—ten feet, fifteen, twenty, and up.

Greta avoided looking down. She focused entirely on her handholds and footholds. It still seemed endlessly far to the top, and increasingly mossy and slippery. But climbing forced her to focus entirely on the moment. There was no room for gloomy thoughts up here. Her heart thumping fast, she realized that they were doing even better than expected. They could really make it! She tried to ignore the thought that they'd probably have to leave the castle the same way.

John was climbing faster than her. He was almost twenty feet above her now, his outline just a black shadow on the wall. As he climbed like that, swift and elegant as a dancer, Greta was overcome by boundless love. This was her man, the one she had been waiting for. And she carried his child in her belly; she could sense it strongly now. It wasn't just a missed period—she was pregnant. She felt as if God had revealed to her that she would bear a child, John's child. So long as she made it back down to the ground safely, she would thank God, she would pray and donate a large candle in the next church. She would—

Her foot slipped on a slimy rock. She managed to grasp a protrusion with her left hand, a long, weathered stone, probably a pitch spout. Greta cursed under her breath. Daydreaming this far above the ground could have fatal consequences. What happened next was what she had been fearing the whole way up.

The brittle stone in her hand broke.

It fell down without a sound, the darkness below swallowing it instantly. Greta clung to the wall with only her right hand now, her fingers digging into a small hole in the rock.

"John," she managed from between clenched teeth, but it was as quiet as a small sigh. "John, oh God."

He couldn't have heard her but still he paused, looked down, and immediately grasped the gravity of the situation. He started to climb back down without a moment's hesitation. Greta knew that climbing down was much harder than climbing up, because you couldn't see where your feet were going. But John had memorized his footholds well and moved as fast as he could. Meanwhile, Greta was still dangling from the wall, her muscles aching as if they were about to tear, only three fingers between life and death. She was too weak to find a hold with the other hand, and fear seemed to paralyze her. A cold wind tugged at her dress and salty sweat ran into her eyes, blinding her. She felt her strength draining from her body; her fingers slipped, one by one.

Goodbye, John.

Just then, someone grasped her left hand and placed it on a ledge.

"Your feet," said a gentle yet firm voice.

Greta took a few moments before she understood that it was John.

"There is a ledge right next to your left foot. You can easily place both your feet there—you just have to want it. It's not hard, Greta. Do it!"

Greta's heart was beating so hard and fast that her chest ached. But somehow she managed to get her feet onto the ledge. It was another pitch spout, but this one held. She was surprised that she hadn't noticed the stone sooner. In her panic, the wall had seemed as smooth as ice. Her breathing slowed a little.

"It's not much farther to the top," said John. "Not as far as to the bottom, at least, and less dangerous. I was almost at the battlements, and I know you can do it. Can you do it, Greta?"

Greta nodded slowly, her lips pressed together tightly.

"Then say it! Say that you're a juggler and the daughter of a sorcerer. Nothing can happen to you."

"I . . . I can do it. I am a juggler and the daughter of a sorcerer. Nothing can happen to me."

Greta took one more deep breath, then she left the safety of the ledge and pulled herself up the wall again, John staying close by. This time it was much easier, because John instructed her as to the best route up. It wasn't long before her hands reached over the top. She pulled herself over the battlements and dropped into the round walk, where she remained for a long while. John was beside her, holding her hand. The crescent moon shone above them.

"Didn't I tell you?" he said softly. "Nothing can happen to you."

"Nothing can happen to *us*, John," she replied and held him tight. "Both of us, John. We are immortal. Our love is immortal."

Greta cautiously got to her feet and looked around. They were standing in the defensive corridor not far from one of the two big towers that guarded the north side. There was no sign of light anywhere—no torches, no watch fires, as if the castle had been deserted. The manor house and the donjon were completely dark, but there seemed to be a faint glow coming from the church.

"Do you hear that?" asked John.

Greta listened. Now she also made out the low sound of an organ, a sonorous buzzing that seemed to come straight from the earth. It sounded like the castle was breathing.

"Something's not right, damn it," said Greta. "Not right at all. Quick—let's go see!" She rushed toward stairs leading down to the courtyard. John followed her. When they passed the empty manor house, John signaled at a building that stood a little off to the side. The shutters were closed, but a faint glow of light came from within. They cautiously approached the house from the rear and sneaked up to the windows. One of the shutters hung crookedly on its hinges, creating a gap for Greta to peer through. She saw a high-ceilinged room with a fireplace in which the remains of a fire glowed dimly. Piled atop a long table lay chewed bones, bread crumbs, cheese rinds, and knocked-over wine cups, as if a feast had taken place. Greta started when she first saw all the men stretched out on the ground, thinking they were dead, but then she heard snoring and saw some of the men toss in their sleep as if they were having nightmares. A trickle ran from a toppled barrel on the ground.

"The guards," whispered John. "Now we know why there are no fires on the towers. Those fellows are stewed—with wine or something harder."

"Or something more poisonous," added Greta.

Somehow the men didn't seem like regular drunks to her; they appeared to be in comas. She guessed that not even a fire would have awakened them, and their dreams definitely weren't happy ones. One of them even screamed out loud now, his fingers cramping into the jerkin of his neighbor, who didn't wake up from it.

"Hmm." John nodded. "You might be right. They look like they've been knocked out. Probably with mandrake or cockle or something." He pulled her gently by the arm. "Let's go find out who is so eager to keep secret whatever's going on here."

They hurried across the deserted courtyard until they reached the church. The organ music was very loud now, and Greta could also hear a monotonous, rhythmical chanting. Awful memories rose up in her, memories from the time when she'd met Tonio del Moravia in the underground passages of Nuremberg.

I'm lying naked on a stone altar, the masked men are chanting, they are calling upon the devil in many different languages. O Satanas, O Mephistopheles.

The door wasn't fully closed, and Greta peered through the crack into an empty church that was lit up by many torches. Meanwhile, John had sneaked around the building and now returned excitedly.

"There's a small side entrance," he whispered. "I think it leads down below the church. The organ music and singing seem to come from there."

The entrance was a small but solid wooden door that was ajar, as if some late guests had just arrived. Greta hesitated briefly, then she opened the door a little further.

She froze.

"My God," she whispered. "Please, John, tell me that I'm only dreaming."

But it was no dream. Below them in the crypt, about two dozen people stood in a circle, singing in a foreign language that seemed strangely familiar to Greta. Torches burned all around them, and she could make out the old-fashioned garments of the people, who looked like they had stepped out of a fading fresco. But she had no time to puzzle over it. Her eyes caught the scene in the middle of the gathering, where a circular hole in the ground looked like a well, or a huge ancient baptismal font. Two men were standing hip-deep in water inside it. They were naked, their eyes gleaming white in the light of the torches.

"O Satanas, O Mephistopheles, O Sheitan," rose the chorus of the people surrounding the pool. "Receive your sacrifice!"

Memories from the Nuremberg crypt sprang to Greta's mind. Then, too, a group of people had chanted and invoked the devil.

But this was worse—much worse.

Standing inside the basin were Karl and her father, who was holding a black dagger in his hands.

He was raising it above his head, ready to stab Karl.

~

"The journey to the master demands a sacrifice," the priest whispered into Johann's ear. "This is the final part of the ceremony. You must free yourself from everything, including him."

Father Jerome nodded at Karl, whose eyes were closed. He was smiling, making him look like an innocent lamb before its slaughter.

"Are you ready for your great journey, Doctor Faustus? Your journey to Gilles de Rais? To Tonio del Moravia, your master and the master of us all? Then make the sacrifice."

The dagger in Johann's hand was as cold as a starless night. It felt heavy, as if he were lifting a huge rock. Father Jerome's voice echoed through his head.

The journey to the master demands a sacrifice.

What sacrifice? Was the priest talking about Karl, standing in front of him? Johann remembered that Karl had confessed his love to him a few minutes or hours ago, and Johann had told Karl that he loved him, too, because in that moment he had loved all men, had felt at one with the world. But that moment had flown away like a silly, youthful crush, and instead the sight of Karl now filled him with pity—with disgust, even. Karl's closed eyes, his slightly dumb, enraptured expression, like a mutt that drooled because someone was holding out a bone. Johann thought that for the first time he saw his assistant for who he truly was: a lesser mind, limited and incapable of rising up to the heights only few were chosen to ascend. Karl was nothing more than a creeping insect—like most people. They burrowed in the dirt, stuffed their mouths, drank, mated, but the crucial matters remained obscure to them. Knowledge, insight, eternal life, and most of all, meeting the master.

The journey to the master demands a sacrifice.

Johann had forgotten his reason for coming to Tiffauges. The monotonous organ music filled him completely. The people standing in a circle around him sang and hummed like bees; they clapped and gazed at him expectantly. Father

Jerome was still smiling, signaling toward Karl. Yes, he was the sacrifice! And what difference was there between his assistant and a dumb, bleating lamb? The fact that Karl had professed his love to him made him even less than an animal. Karl lived against nature, and it was only right that he, Johann, should kill this heretic sodomite—and therewith travel to the lord. To Tonio del Moravia, his master! How could he ever have thought of him as an enemy? He was the only one who had ever understood Johann. Johann would do anything for him. Anything!

"O Mephistopheles, receive your sacrifice," chanted the immortals. "Sheitan, Satan, Zhoool."

"Tonio, I'm coming," muttered Johann.

With a smile on his face, he brought down the dagger.

"Nooooo!"

A shrill cry rang out, made by a voice that sounded familiar to Johann, like a distant memory. The voice painfully pierced his consciousness.

"No, Father, don't do it! Oh God, don't!"

He knew this voice—it was the voice of his daughter. Did he have a daughter? Even if he did, she wasn't important now. All that mattered was his journey to the master. And yet Johann hesitated, lowering the hand holding the dagger. More screams rang out, sounding to him like the waves of a distant ocean.

Karl opened his eyes and gave him a startled look. For a brief moment, the young man's mind seemed to be alert and clear.

"What in God's name?"

Johann raised his blade again.

But then someone grabbed his arm and yanked him back. Johann cried out with indignation. Had he struck Karl? He didn't know. Because now there was this other man wrestling with him. The attacker was big and strong, and he seemed to know Johann. His hair was red and he was shouting.

"Stop it, Doctor! You're crazy! Give me the dagger!"

Johann hissed like a cat. All those dirty little worms trying to stop him from traveling to the master! But he wouldn't let them, not this close to the goal. He thought of a ruse. He paused his raging as if he had calmed down. He held his head lowered so they wouldn't see the glint in his eyes. The knife was pointing down.

"That's better, Doctor," the other man said. "It's not too late. I gave you my word that no harm would come to Greta. But I'm not going to stand by and watch as her father murders his friend."

Now Johann recognized him. It was that awful fellow who was trying to steal his daughter from him. It was John Reed, the traitor, fraud, and liar. Like a festering sore he had eaten his way into Johann's and Greta's lives, destroying everything that had ever existed between them.

John Reed, you bastard! You will never again touch my Greta with your filthy hands. You won't take her away from me.

Boundless hatred filled Johann, creeping from his heart into his fingers and the ends of his hair.

"Give me the dagger, Doctor," said John. He smiled reassuringly and held out his hand. "All will be well."

Johann stabbed him.

Not once, not twice—it was a frenzy. The blade drove deeply into the guts of this cocky, red-haired fellow, jabbing into his intestines, again and again. It felt so good! John screamed and it was music to Johann's ears. Another thrust, and another one.

When will you finally shut up! Die, vermin!

Johann was like a butcher at work. The blade rose and fell. At the end, there was just a faint wheezing. John clung to him with both hands and stared at him from wide eyes. Finally the impertinent wide grin that had tortured Johann for so long was extinguished. For good.

"Why?" gasped John. "You . . . evil . . . old . . . man . . ." A shudder went through his body and his grip loosened, but still he clung to Johann.

Greta's screams rang out again. Now Johann saw her, too. She was standing by a side entrance to the crypt, her face drained of all color. She was shivering, crying, and wailing like an injured animal. What was the matter with her? He had done her and everyone a favor. He had cut out the sore.

"Father, what have you done?" cried Greta. "For heaven's sake, what have you done? Oh God! You . . . you *murderer*! You killed John!" She tore at her hair, swayed, and finally collapsed into a tiny bundle on the doorstep.

Johann thought of Tonio del Moravia and how much they could achieve together. Johann was very close to the master now—and far, far away from everyone else.

"O lord, receive your sacrifice," said Johann.

One more time he thrust the blade into the lifeless body. John finally let go of Johann and slid into the pool amid a cloud of blood.

And somewhere deep down inside, Johann could hear Tonio laugh.

~

Greta no longer screamed. Until a few moments ago, she had thought all this was nothing but a nasty dream. That she would wake up and John would be beside her, that they would kiss and embrace to forget all this evil.

But it wasn't a dream. She was lying on the floor of the crypt and the man she loved was dead.

It was the end of the world.

When John had seen that her father was about to stab Karl, he had thrown caution to the wind. He had rushed through the crypt, past the strange people with their strange clothes, and had climbed into the basin to take the dagger from her raging father. But then everything had gone terribly wrong. John, the royal bodyguard, the seasoned elite fighter from the Scottish Highlands who had seen and done it all, had refused to believe that the father of his intended would actually attack him. In his profoundly good-natured way, he hadn't spotted the danger.

And it had cost him his life.

John's body was floating facedown in the water, his fiery-red hair streaming around his head. Johann was standing next to him, the dagger still in his hand, his face turned toward the ceiling, muttering something incomprehensible. Obviously, he had gone insane. Or had his true self finally broken to the surface? Greta was too deep in shock to hate her father in that moment. Emptiness reigned inside her, and she felt like she was tumbling through black space, incapable of feeling pain.

Next to Johann in the water stood Karl, looking like a puppet that was held upright by invisible strings. Greta closed her eyes and opened them again, but the scene was the same. It seemed like complete madness, like a painting by that creepy Dutch painter Karl had shown her—paintings of the apocalypse, and yet this was reality.

The people in the crypt had stopped singing, and the organ music had also ceased. A man with a pockmarked face and the robe of a priest looked at Greta.

"Who are you?" he hissed hatefully. "How dare you disturb our ceremony? You useless . . ." Then he seemed to see something in her, as if he recognized her. His lips twisted into a malicious grin, and then he laughed out loud. "This is good. Great, even. Who would have thought that both of you—"

Greta heard a whirring sound, and the man broke off. Surprised, his eyes turned to his belly, from which, Greta saw now, a crossbow bolt protruded. A dark bloodstain spread on the man's robe. The priest shook his head slowly as if he didn't want to believe that he was fatally wounded. He swayed, then he fell forward and remained lying there, his hands clutching the shaft of the bolt.

For a few heartbeats, the crypt was eerily silent. Then panic broke out among the guests and they began to scream and run, calling for a lord whose name Greta didn't understand.

A strong hand jerked her up by the hair.

"Devil's brood," someone grumbled behind her in a harsh voice. "About time we smoked out this nest."

Greta recognized the man even before she turned to look at him. It was Hagen, who tossed her aside like a sack of flour and stormed the crypt, followed by a bunch of soldiers. Evidently, the Swiss guard had managed to invade the unprotected castle. The wailing and screaming devil worshippers were thrown to the ground or cut down. Hagen drew his mighty longsword and leaped toward the man closest to him, an older nobleman with a silver cuirass and a cape, who glowered at the giant and muttered something in a strange language, his arms raised in a gesture of conjuring. Hagen severed the man's head from his body with one single stroke and turned to his next victim, a younger man in a feminine dress who tried to crawl away from Hagen on all fours, screaming.

"By the Virgin Mary, leave those heretics alive!" shouted Viktor von Lahnstein, who had entered the crypt after Hagen and his men. He wore a snow-white robe with a large hood that concealed the upper part of his face, but Greta recognized him immediately. His lips bore an expression of eternal triumph.

"They don't deserve such an easy death. They shall burn before entering hell to meet their master," he told the soldiers. "But first they will tell us everything they know about Gilles de Rais. By God, I want to learn every little detail, even if I have to pull off their skin in strips!"

Greta was still incapable of movement. She kept staring at John, floating facedown in his own blood. Next to him stood the man she had only recently thought to call "Father" and who had now become the murderer of her love.

"Get the doctor and his assistant out of the water," ordered Lahnstein. "By Christ, this is disgusting. Sodomy is almost as repulsive as Satanism. Thank God this farce is coming to an end now."

Soldiers dragged Johann and Karl out of the basin and over to Lahnstein. The two men still seemed caught up in their own worlds and were barely able to stand. Foam stood in the corners of their mouths as if they were rabid dogs, and their eyes were like dead caves. Lahnstein took a step back with fright.

"My God, look! The devil is possessing them! Pray that our almighty Lord—"

Suddenly, one of the guards groaned and slumped to the ground. Behind him, the pockmarked priest staggered to his feet, the bolt still in his stomach. But it would seem he hadn't given up the fight yet. He stumbled forward, grabbed Johann, and lifted the bloodied dagger to his throat—the same dagger that had been used to stab John. The priest's face was deathly pale but he stood upright, as if evil was breathing new life into him. The soldier at his feet gave one last twitch before he died.

"Get back!" shouted the pockmarked man. "Everyone, get back!"

Lahnstein made a signal, and the soldiers moved back.

"I know you need the doctor alive," said the priest with clenched teeth, holding the numbly staring Johann in front of him like a human shield. "He is of no use to you dead. So let me pass!"

Without taking the dagger off Johann's throat, he made his way through the ranks of soldiers.

"Where do you think you're going?" jeered Lahnstein. "You won't get far with your injury. You're a dead man. My men are posted by the gate. There is no way out of this castle."

"Oh yes, there is. Believe me—I know this castle well. I have had many years to study it." The priest was now walking backward with Johann in his arm until he stood at the crypt's back wall. Holding the inert doctor tightly with one arm, he reached behind himself with the other. Only then did Greta notice an embellishment in the rock, an old, weathered wolf head that was no larger than a child's fist. The priest turned the knob and a hidden door swung open behind him.

"My dear Gilles always made sure he had a way out," said the priest with a smile. "We sometimes brought children in this way before we amused ourselves with them. *Au revoir!*"

He slipped into the darkness beyond and pulled the doctor along. The heavy door slammed shut behind them.

"After him!" roared Lahnstein.

Hagen hurled himself against the door, twisting and turning the wolf head, pushing it, rattling it, but nothing happened. Swords and pikes didn't achieve anything because the slit was much too tight. Evidently, the door could be barred from the other side.

Johann and the priest had vanished, as if the stony monster of Tiffauges had swallowed them up.

And Greta was alone with her grief and her horror.

17

FOR A LONG WHILE, JOHANN WAS TRAPPED IN A STATE
between reality and insanity. Every now and then he wondered if he was still
alive or if this was hell—if Tonio had finally taken him. It was a not-entirely-
unpleasant sensation of hovering in a space without time, where memories raced
past him as colorful images.

*Bathing in the well. Father Jerome, smiling, handing me the dagger. Karl
beside me, naked like me, stroking my manhood. A red-haired scoundrel who turns
into John Reed and then back into a scoundrel. I stab him down. Greta screams.
"Murderer, murderer, murderer."*

He couldn't tell which memories were real and which were figments of his
imagination. But whatever the case, they didn't concern him. They were the
concerns of another man he didn't know.

The first thing he recognized as real was the hard stone floor he was lying
upon. And the cold. He felt so cold. He was shivering all over, moving his hands
through the darkness, feeling the dust on the ground. Then he heard heavy
breathing.

Someone was with him.

Was it Karl? John? Or perhaps . . .?

"Greta?" he whispered. "Is that you? My . . . my daughter?"

Someone chuckled. It was a man's rattling laughter that turned into a coughing fit.

"You . . . you fool," said a hoarse voice. "Your daughter is going to burn.
You might see her again soon—in hell."

The man laughed more of his creepy laughter. Johann opened his good
eye and looked at the ceiling of a square chamber built of stone. Pale morning

light streamed in through narrow slits in the wall. He turned his head and saw Father Jerome, his face white as a sheet. He was pressing his hands against his stomach, where his robe was wet with blood. A broken piece of wood stuck out from the fabric.

Johann wondered if he was responsible for the priest's injury; he didn't know.

"You don't remember what's happened, do you?" Father Jerome laughed once more with a throaty, rattling sound. "Do you want to know?"

"I . . . I am at Tiffauges," said Johann quietly as the memories returned. He realized that he was completely naked. "I wanted to find Tonio del Moravia, whom you call Gilles de Rais, your master. He cursed me with this disease and I finally wanted to face him. But he wasn't at Tiffauges."

"No, he wasn't, damn it! But we would have taken you to him. The black potion, the bath, the sacrifice—all was ready."

"The sacrifice!" Johann sat up, forgetting all about the cold. "Oh God, Karl! I was supposed to kill Karl."

"Once you'd had your fun with him, yes. Gilles would have enjoyed that." The priest giggled. "You never know what the black potion is going to do to someone—what sort of well-concealed tendencies it's going to bring out."

Johann felt ashamed when the images returned to him—the kissing, the stroking, the pleasant moans. But then he remembered how he had viewed Karl afterward, what he had thought of him, and shame about those thoughts outweighed everything else.

"You nearly traveled to the master," said Father Jerome. He, too, sat up slowly now and leaned against the stone wall. He was still pressing his hands to his wound, trying in vain to stop the bleeding. "But then that red-haired fellow appeared out of nowhere, and the ritual was cut short. You butchered the boy like a pig, then those accursed soldiers turned up and I was shot with a crossbow, and—"

"I . . . I killed John?"

"You must have rammed the dagger into him at least a dozen times—the bath was red with his blood." Father Jerome gave a cackling laugh until his face twisted into a grimace of pain. "Your eyes while you were doing it . . . reminded me of Gilles when he used to kill the little ones. But no surprise."

"I killed John," said Johann again in a flat voice. "And Greta?"

"Your daughter was there, too, yes. No idea how the two of them got in. Perhaps it was a mistake to knock out all the guards."

Johann cried out, his nails digging into the stone floor as if the stinging pain in his fingertips could erase what had happened. In his drugged stupor he had killed John Reed, and his daughter had watched. How would she ever forgive him? And Karl? How could Karl forgive him? Johann had almost stabbed him like a sacrificial lamb!

How could Johann ever forgive himself?

Father Jerome eyed him with curiosity. "Ah, I see! The young man was her sweetheart. Well, you won't be your daughter's favorite person. But who cares? She is going to burn as a witch along with all the others. Your sweet assistant will burn, too. Such a shame—I would have loved to spend a night here at the castle with him. But there'll be plenty of time for that in hell."

"You . . . you devil!" screamed Faust, attacking him.

The priest laughed as Faust pummeled him with his fists. "You honor me, but no—the devil is my master; I am but his humble servant. If anyone deserves to be called the devil, then it is you, Johann Georg Faustus. The master loves you. I wish he loved me as he loves you. He has given you so much—and how do you repay him? By running away!"

Johann paused, his arm poised to strike. With amazement he gazed at his hands. The paralysis was gone. As if the bath in the font had healed him. Cautiously, he moved his legs, his back, his shoulders—he felt reborn, as if he had never been ill at all. But the sensation brought him no joy.

He knew what price he had paid.

Father Jerome smiled thinly, almost wistfully. "See how much the master loves you? The disease was a gift from him, to remind you of him. He wants you to return to him."

"That's what I came to Tiffauges for, to face up to him."

"You fool! What made you think the master still resides here? For all the happy memories? Ha! He . . ." Father Jerome's upper body slumped forward for a moment, but then he caught himself again and straightened up. "No, the master has far greater plans. He left us here so that we would keep his legacy alive."

"Us?" asked Johann. "I know you. You're Prelati, the priest who helped the dark marshal to invoke the devil all those years ago. But where are the others?"

"You know what happened to Poitou. You sent him to hell back in Nuremberg. La Meffraye and Henriet, however." The father giggled again, and it sounded like the giggling of a nasty old woman. "Oh, you've met them. Not at this castle, however. They serve the master at another important place."

"Where?" urged Johann. "Where are they? Are they with Tonio?"

"Think, Doctor. You're so clever. The master doesn't shower many people with gifts the way he has done with you—money, fortune, wit, among other talents. But one good turn deserves another, right? When the day comes that the chosen ones must pay with their soul, they often show reluctance. But the master comes for them all. Every single one of them."

Father Jerome fell silent and closed his eyes. Johann saw that the man's end was near. But he was likely the only one who knew where to find Tonio. He couldn't die yet. The priest's words seemed to become more and more confused. Was he still making sense?

The master doesn't shower many people with gifts the way he has done with you—money, fortune, wit, among other talents.

Among other talents.

"Leonardo da Vinci!" Johann exclaimed. "His gifts, his drawing skills, his curiosity, his inventiveness . . . it all came from Tonio, didn't it?"

He had been right all along. And Leonardo must have had a hunch that he and Johann shared a dark common bond.

"I was with him," he said softly, more to himself. "I only wish I had—"

"Leonardo possessed something the master would have liked to have for himself," said Father Jerome hastily, as if he knew that his time was running out. "As a token of appreciation for all . . . all his services. But the old fool didn't want to give it to him. The master had asked him for it once before, in Rome, but Leonardo remained stubborn. So the dark marshal ordered his servants La Meffraye and Henriet to go to Cloux and search for it."

"La Meffraye and Henriet? But—"

"Oh yes. They wrote me about you. They said the old codger was crazy about you and your handsome assistant. Especially your assistant." Father Jerome gave a pained grin, waving effeminately and chuckling nastily. "Leonardo liked handsome young men—everyone knew that. La Meffraye and Henriet hoped that the senile fool would pour out his heart to at least one of you and give away his little secret. They watched you and eavesdropped on you the whole time.

But then that stupid Melzi insisted you leave. Apparently he was envious of you and your assistant."

"My God," Johann whispered, finally understanding. "How could I be so blind?"

"You aren't the first one who didn't see them," Father Jerome said. "I know. They are good at making themselves invisible. That's how they used to get the children in the villages, too. They are like shadows—no one really notices them, but they are always there."

"The servants."

Johann couldn't even recall their names, but they had always been near Leonardo. Just like Tonio's crows and the raven. They had watched him all along, him and Leonardo.

"La Meffraye and Henriet searched for that which the master has wanted for a long time, but they just couldn't find it. We thought you two might be able to help—without knowing you were, of course. We hoped he might tell you where he'd hid it. They spied on you the entire time—even at da Vinci's deathbed."

Johann's thoughts were racing. He felt as though a familiar story suddenly took on an entirely new meaning now that he knew its ending. Leonardo had tried to tell him something, and he must have had an inkling that he was being watched. Maybe he had even known that the servants who were with him day and night were in fact Tonio's, not his own. How long had La Meffraye and Henriet worked for him? Or had they somehow managed to slip into the bodies of the former servants?

But another thought was even more unsettling to Johann.

"Does that mean I only traveled to Cloux because . . . because Tonio wanted me to?" he asked, confused. "The long journey from Bamberg to France—it was his plan? That I visit Leonardo da Vinci and find something for Tonio? That I help him without even knowing?"

Johann thought about the raven and the crows. He had thought they were following him, but it had been the other way around: they had shown him the way—he had followed *them*! Once again, like in Nuremberg, Johann had walked into Tonio's trap.

"The lord is everywhere and nowhere," wheezed Father Jerome. "Everywhere and nowhere! Mark those words."

Johann remembered that the midwife they'd met on their way to Tiffauges had said something very similar.

Everywhere and nowhere.

"Where is he?" asked Johann. He grabbed Father Jerome and shook him hard until the wounded man seethed with pain. "Speak up! Where is Tonio? Where is Gilles de Rais?"

"You'll never know. The two of us are going to remain here until the devil comes to fetch us." Father Jerome laughed like a lunatic. "Ha, until the devil comes to fetch us! There is no way out. Just look around you, Doctor."

Johann let go of Father Jerome. For the first time he noticed that while the chamber possessed a few thin arrow slits, it was missing something. Something very important.

A door.

How on earth had they gotten in here?

And how was he supposed to get back out?

"I . . . I am going to leave you alone now," whispered the priest, resting his hand on his robe, thick blood seeping through his fingers. "Alone with all your questions, clever, omniscient Doctor Faustus. You must think quickly. When thirst and, later, hunger plague you, thinking is going to become harder and harder. Until your brain is dried up like an old chestnut and your nails break as you try in vain to dig your way out of here. Fare . . . well, Faustus . . . We will meet again before the master. On the other side."

With one last malicious chuckle, Father Jerome collapsed fully, twitched once more, and then was still.

Johann had never before felt so alone. Even in the underground room below Nuremberg following the gruesome ceremony, when he had woken up with one finger and one eye missing, he hadn't been this lonely. His old friend Valentin had stood by him and then Karl had, too. But now he had lost all his friends. He had been tricked into despising Karl and almost stabbed him, fueled by the drugs; he had killed John, and so Greta would now regard him as a murderer, and she would most likely burn at the stake soon. Even his dog was dead.

He had no one left.

The chamber that held him was like an allegory for his life—cold, confined, with no way out. The only company he had was a dead priest loyal to the devil. Johann was naked. The last card had been played.

Johann, stretched out on the cold ground, stared at the smooth squares of stone on the ceiling. He had been so obsessed by the thought of finding Tonio here at Tiffauges that he had been blind to everything else. As usual, he had stormed ahead without considering anyone else, raising the stakes higher and higher.

And then he had lost.

Rien ne va plus.

Tiffauges had been a dead end. Everything Johann had believed until then had collapsed like a house of cards. Could it be true that he had only ever done whatever Tonio wanted him to do? Johann had met him at the cemetery in Knittlingen, and he guessed that Tonio had also been at Altenburg Castle. Then Johann had run from Viktor von Lahnstein, who was supposed to take him to the pope because of this accursed philosopher's stone whose secret Johann didn't know. Then, in Metz, his friend Agrippa had finally told him about Leonardo da Vinci.

Agrippa, my old friend, could it be possible?

Agrippa had been the first to tell him about Leonardo's illness. In hindsight, Johann thought Agrippa's sudden flash of inspiration had seemed a little forced. His friend had always been a better scholar than actor. Had he played a part in this conspiracy? Had Tonio offered him a pact, too? Anything seemed possible. If Johann could turn murderer, then why not his friend a traitor? Only one question remained.

What was the secret Leonardo possessed and Tonio wanted so badly? Could it perhaps be the art of making gold—the philosopher's stone? The same secret the pope hoped to learn from Johann? It must have been something extremely valuable if Tonio sent him halfway across Europe for it. Where had Leonardo hidden it?

Where?

For the first time, Johann saw a tiny speck of light in the darkness. Tonio wanted something, urgently. If Johann found it before Tonio, he had something to barter with. The world had always worked this way.

You can't defeat the devil, but you can offer him a bargain.

Perhaps, if Johann presented Tonio with the secret, his former master could ensure that Greta was spared the stake. And that she forgave him—that he won back his old life.

But first he needed to get out of here.

Johann scrutinized the walls around him. He and Father Jerome had gotten in, so there had to be a way out. Only, where? Still shivering with cold, he stood up. He needed some clothes or else he would freeze before he thought of anything. Repulsed, he looked at the bent corpse of the priest in the corner. The bloodstain wasn't as big as Johann expected; evidently, Father Jerome had died of internal injuries. And so, after some hesitation, Johann undressed the dead body and slipped on the woolen robe. He tried to force aside the thought that it was the blood-soaked robe of a dead man—at least he was beginning to feel warmer.

Then he examined the walls.

There were no slits or cracks anywhere that might have suggested the existence of a hidden door. The narrow windows were high above ground and far too small to squeeze through. Johann thought with horror that this chamber had probably served as a prison for the children Poitou, Henriet, and La Meffraye hunted and caught like rabbits. Their cries had probably echoed all the way down to the township. But no one had come to help them.

After the walls, Johann examined the floor; like the ceiling, it was made of large flagstones. But he searched in vain. Increasingly desperate, he returned to the walls. He noticed that, unlike the ceiling and floor, each wall was made of one huge piece of rock. There were no individual squares. Only in the corners, where the walls met, were there lines of mortar. An idea sprouted in Johann's head, but it required scraping the mortar from the joints. How could he do it? He had no knife, not even a stick, nothing. Except . . .

Johann hesitated only briefly. He returned to the priest's body. The broken-off crossbow bolt still protruded from the wound, and Johann pulled it out with one quick movement. The bolt was a little longer than his index finger and bore a sharp metal point. A parting gift from Father Jerome.

Carefully, trying not to break the tip, Johann began scraping the old mortar out of the joints. He decided on the wall opposite the arrow slits, and indeed—behind the mortar was a gap about as wide as a finger. It was much too dark in the room to see anything in the gap. Johann knelt down, pushed the tip of the bolt into the gap, and slowly pulled it upward.

At about hip height, the tip caught on something. Johann pushed harder. Something clicked.

"Please, please," he whispered. "Not for me—for Greta."

He pushed against the wall and it swung open.

On the other side he found a small, dark room and some stairs leading down. The construction was as simple as it was ingenious. Despite his desperate situation, Johann couldn't help but admire the probably long-since-deceased architect. A metal rod had been inserted down the center of the thin stone wall, allowing the wall to swivel like a revolving door. A snap lock ensured that once it fell shut, it couldn't be moved from the inside.

Unless one removed the camouflage of mortar and pushed the bolt back up by force.

Johann left the door open so that a little light streamed into the room beyond. Cautiously, he climbed down the stairs, which ended in a corridor. The priest must have come from here. After deliberating for a few moments, Johann turned left. The corridor was low and smelled faintly of blackpowder. Soon he passed an old cannon, its rusty barrel pointed outside through an embrasure. More embrasures and cannons followed. When Johann dared a glance through one of the small windows, he saw the moat on the castle's southern side, and beyond, still shrouded in morning mist, the small town of Tiffauges. He walked faster, then started to run. Evidently he was inside the casemates, the fortified defensive corridors underneath the castle walls. He only hoped he wasn't running toward a dead end. After a while he came to a small, very sturdy-looking door. It was barred with a thick, rusty bolt that looked like it hadn't been moved in a long time. Groaning with effort, he pushed against it. The bolt broke free with a crunching sound, and the door creaked open.

Mist rose from the moat directly in front of him.

A narrow ledge led from the door along the wall toward the bridge that he and Karl had used to enter the castle a few days ago. Johann didn't see anyone, only a handful of horses grazing peacefully in the shadow of the projecting bastion. They weren't tied up, and Johann guessed they belonged to the troop of mercenaries traveling with Viktor von Lahnstein. Johann couldn't see any guards and thought that most of the soldiers were probably inside the castle they had invaded the night before.

He decided to try his luck.

He moved toward the horses, most of which were saddled. Perhaps the soldiers responsible for looking after the animals were busy catching them one by one and leading them into the castle. There was a good chance that someone would return soon.

Johann ran the last few yards as fast as he could. He decided on a young-looking mare who struck him as strong enough for a long ride. She was black, with a long mane and flashing eyes—the perfect mount for a vassal of the devil. A full saddlebag hung at her side. Without another look around, Johann jumped into the saddle and kicked his heels into the horse's sides, making it bound forward with a neigh. He raced across the bridge toward town, and no one stopped him. Then he pulled the mare hard to the right and galloped toward the woods, which were bathed in a milky fog this early in the morning.

Johann didn't know where Tonio was, but he did know that his former master wanted something particular. Something that Johann would be able to use as a pawn in exchange for the life of his daughter.

And, by God, he would find that pawn.

~

Meanwhile, Greta waited for death.

She didn't know the exact time of its arrival, but it would certainly be soon. Probably in the shape of that huge Swiss mercenary who would torture her before his men would burn her at the stake in the castle's courtyard.

Like my mother, she thought.

Contrary to her expectations, she hadn't been thrown into some dark dungeon but had been brought to a comfortable chamber in one of the northern towers. There was a green tiled stove, tapestries on the freshly plastered walls, and in the corner, beneath a barred window, stood a chair and a table with an embroidery frame holding a half-finished pattern. It was a stag surrounded by fluttering birds and small rabbits—probably the work of some dusty, long-dead noblewoman. Did those fellows seriously believe she would do some needlework while she calmly waited to be put to death?

But then again, there was nothing left worth living for. John, the father of her unborn child, was dead—murdered by her own father. The only man she had ever felt true love for and with whom she'd wanted to spend the rest of her life had been stabbed to death like an animal. Greta had no more tears left. She was empty, spent, nothing more than a shell. She didn't know where Karl was. When the guards had dragged them out of the crypt, he hadn't been in his right mind. He had only smiled a stupid smile, as if he had no idea what was going on around him—unlike the other men and women, who had been dragged away kicking and screaming. They knew what was coming for them. Greta was aware that they were heretics—worse, Satanists, who prayed to the devil. Evil people. But still she shuddered at the thought of them all burning at the stake.

Along with me.

But then she remembered something that might be worth living for. She was carrying John's child under her heart. She gently placed her hand on her belly and thought she could feel the baby growing. Pregnant women usually weren't executed, or at least not right away. They were spared until the child was born. That's how it had been with her mother when she was pregnant with Greta. Greta might die, but her child—John's child—would live! She had to tell the guards about her pregnancy and maybe they would even refrain from torturing her.

A key was slid into the lock, and Greta stood up promptly. The time had come—they were fetching her for questioning! She clenched her fists and jutted out her chin. The guards would not catch her trembling.

But no guards entered, nor Hagen the giant. It was Viktor von Lahnstein. He wore a fresh snow-white robe and, instead of the leather belt, a scapular in cardinal red that gave him a dignified look—an effect that had certainly been intended. But it stood in stark contrast to his face. Down in the crypt, Lahnstein had worn a hood. Now Greta saw for the first time what a mess Little Satan had made of the man's face back in Bamberg. In the place of a nose was a fleshy, pink stump with two gaping holes, almost like a pig's snout.

With a silent wave of his hand, the Dominican signaled for Greta to sit down. He sat opposite her and studied her, his fingers playing with the wooden rosary hanging from his neck. His mouth was half-open, and Greta could hear his labored breathing. She decided to hold his gaze, which was difficult in view of the maimed visage. After a few moments, Lahnstein began to smile, which made Greta shiver.

"The daughter of the famous Doctor Faustus," said Lahnstein. "And it looks as if she is his equal in pride. I like that. Most people can't bear to look at me. They turn away in horror." He fingered the scarcely healed scraps of meat on his face. "Strange, isn't it, how the absence of such a small part of the human body calls the whole person into question? It doesn't take much to turn a man into a monstrosity."

"What do you want from me?" asked Greta quietly. "If you're here to take me to torture—"

Lahnstein waved dismissively. "I don't need glowing pincers or a rack to make conversation. In my experience, confessions made during torture are to be taken with a grain of salt."

"What do you want, then?"

"I want to make conversation. About your father."

Greta said nothing for a while. She found it hard to even think of her father's name—it burned like acid inside her. "Trust me—I know nothing about him," she said eventually. "At the end of the day, he was always a stranger to me. Especially in the last few weeks."

"Your own father?" Lahnstein wrinkled his forehead. "And I'm supposed to believe that? How dumb do you think I am?" He leaned back. "I want to know everything, from the beginning. I have time."

Greta thought. What did she have to lose? And so she started to talk while outside the morning sun slowly rose higher. She saw no reason to hide anything. Johann might have been her father, but there was nothing left that tied her to him. He was a murderer and maybe worse. And besides, she could understand Lahnstein's motivation. Because of her father, the Dominican now looked like a monster—he had a right to learn about his enemy.

She told Lahnstein how she had met the great Faust when she was a young girl and how the two of them and Karl had traveled the German Empire and beyond as jugglers. She also told him about Faust's disease, the pact with Tonio, about their visit at Leonardo da Vinci's, and, finally, why they had come to Tiffauges. The words poured out of her like bitter bile, like poison, as if she needed to rid herself of her father once and for all.

Lahnstein listened in silence, only occasionally interrupting with brief questions. "What about the *lapis philosophorum*, the philosopher's stone?" he asked when Greta reached the end of her tale after about an hour. "Did he ever mention it to you?"

Greta shook her head. "I doubt my father is privy to that secret. And, like I said, that wasn't the reason for our journey to Tiffauges. Faust wanted to face

Tonio, his greatest enemy, who he believes to be the immortal Gilles de Rais, or even the devil himself."

"He *has to* know the secret, damn it!" Lahnstein rose and started to pace the room. The stump of his nose quivered as if he was trying to pick up a scent. "The French king is also seeking the philosopher's stone, and so are the Habsburgs. Whoever finds the formula first rules Europe, and with Europe, the world. Especially now that warfare is becoming more and more expensive. Mercenaries, equipment, provisions—it all costs horrendous amounts of money." He spun around, his eyes small and narrow. "Do you believe your father fled to King Francis to sell him the stone?"

"Certainly not."

Greta looked at the papal representative, thinking he no longer struck her as a monster but more as a haunted man. She almost felt sorry for him. The pope had become obsessed by an idea and sent his most loyal servant on an impossible mission—a mission for which Lahnstein had already paid dearly.

"The French king is only after Faust because you are chasing him," she said. "It was you who gave Francis the idea that he knew how to make gold. I'll say it again: my father doesn't know that secret."

"But we have it on good authority that Gilles de Rais personally told him during a summoning of the dead."

"Who told you that?"

"That is beside the point." Viktor von Lahnstein continued to pace the room and muttered, more to himself, "Faust has invoked Gilles de Rais before, just like he was trying to do last night in the crypt with those other heretics. The proof is irrevocable. But this time we got there early, and the whole nest of heretics will burn!"

"There . . . there is something else," said Greta reluctantly. "Something I want you to know." She raised her chin and spoke with a firm voice. "I am pregnant. By John Reed. That's the man my father killed down in the crypt."

Viktor von Lahnstein turned around, looking as if she'd interrupted his train of thought. "Indeed?" He didn't seem as surprised as Greta had expected. More like his hunch had just been confirmed. "Hmm, interesting." He rocked his head from side to side. "By that former royal household guard? Because that's what he was, right? My spies at the French court told me about John Reed's treason." He gave a devilish smile. "Faust's assistant is such a handsome young man. I would have put my money on Karl Wagner. You've known each other for a long time."

"Where is Karl?" asked Greta. "How is he doing?"

"Who knows?" Lahnstein shrugged. "He probably doesn't even know himself."

"What . . . what are you saying?"

"The devil entered his body during the ceremony, and I think we have lost him. He doesn't even flinch when glowing splinters are driven under his fingernails. Believe me, we have tried a lot in the last few hours. If you ask me, the father of your child is better off dead than insane like that poor dog."

"Oh no!" Greta gave a groan. "My God, Karl . . . my dear Karl." Greta's world became a little darker still. It seemed that the only true friend she'd ever had was gone now.

"Forget him," said Lahnstein. "We'll take him to Rome in case he comes to his senses and we can question him. But to be honest, I doubt that he'll be of any use to us." Lahnstein stepped toward Greta, scrutinizing her. "Unlike you."

"I already told you—I know nothing. I . . ." Greta faltered. Everything around her seemed black and gray, only her unborn child keeping her alive. God was as far away as a tiny, dying star. "If you torture me, I'm sure I will say many things. But they will all be lies. I'll tell you anything you want to hear, but it won't be the truth!"

"Dear child, I want to ask you a question." Lahnstein leaned down close to Greta, and she smelled something rotten—probably the poorly healed stump of his nose. "A very important question. I want you to consider your answer well." She noticed now how gaunt the Dominican was. With his disfigured face and the wide robe, he resembled a scarecrow.

"Have you ever wondered if you stand on the right side?" asked Lahnstein calmly. The rosary dangled in front of Greta's face.

"How . . . how do you mean?"

"Up until now you'd assumed we were the villains, right? We chase you, your father, and your dear friends, hunting you like animals to take you to Rome and hand you over to the pope and the Inquisition." Viktor von Lahnstein took a step back and smoothed his white robe with his hands. "Try to look at it from the other side. Your father is a heretic, a Satanist—that is proven. He summoned the devil before all the delegates of the empire and set his dog on the papal nuncio. And you saw for yourself what came to pass in the crypt last night. That was no peaceful evening mass but a devilish ritual. Faust came to Tiffauges to invoke Gilles de Rais, his master, the one he calls Tonio. And he stopped at nothing to achieve this."

The papal representative leaned down to her again and reached for the small angel the old midwife had given her. "What's that?"

"A . . . protective amulet," said Greta. "It reminds me that God is with me even in the darkest hour. That I can always pray to Him."

Lahnstein raised an eyebrow. "You pray much?"

"Daily. Even more since my father started to change. But not even God could save him." Greta's expression darkened. "His soul was probably already lost."

"True enough." Lahnstein raised a hand. "I'm guessing he told you that he wanted to face Tonio to destroy him. But you know that wasn't true, don't you? Your father is a master of deception. He deceived his assistant and even his own daughter. He is a Satanist who called upon the devil with those heretics. He betrayed you, he betrayed your beloved, he betrayed his faithful assistant—he betrayed you all. He murdered the man you loved!" He placed his cold, heavy hand on her shoulder. "Your *father* is evil, Greta. It is time that you recognize the truth."

Greta didn't reply; conflicting feelings raged inside her. Lahnstein was right. Her father had made a pact with the devil. He was a Satanist. Sure, he hadn't always been evil—not wholly, anyway, because she had seen his good side—but the devil had steadily gained more power over him. Her father had only ever done that which best served himself. In order to reach Tonio he had even murdered someone and forsaken his daughter.

A terrible thought came to her. If her father possessed such an evil side, then what about her? Hadn't she also inherited other unholy talents from him, like reading palms? Perhaps she would someday choose the dark path, too. And what were the implications for her unborn child? She had to protect her child!

"I want you to pray with me, Greta, daughter of Faust," said Lahnstein suddenly.

He led her away from the table and gently pushed her to her knees. Greta felt like she was in a trance. Lahnstein knelt down beside her and folded his hands.

"O most gracious Lord in heaven," he called out loudly, his head raised toward the ceiling. "Behold this woman who has lost the right path. Let us pray for her. For her and her father, whom the devil has taken!"

"Evil is like a disease," he said to Greta. "Like an ulcer. It must be cauterized before it spreads—even in families. Or it might be healed in time by the right faith. Maybe it isn't too late for you, Greta. For you and your child. If you decide on the right side."

Greta closed her eyes and prayed in silence. It felt good to find something to hold on to in this bleak world. Amid the horror that had been surrounding her, her faith had grown steadily. Yes, she had experienced the devil, so how could she doubt that God existed and watched over her? God would stand by her in this darkest hour.

"Are you deciding on the right side, Greta?" asked Lahnstein forcefully. He was still kneeling next to her. "There is still time to turn around."

"What do you expect of me?" she asked.

Lahnstein squeezed her hand. "I want you to accompany me to Rome. Not as a prisoner, but as a servant of good. Your father is one of the most powerful weapons of the devil. If his own daughter gives herself to God, we cause more damage to the devil than if we burn you." Lahnstein gave a thin smile. "Do you want to join our side? Do you want to serve God, Greta?"

"I . . . I do." As soon as the words were out, a pleasant warmth flooded Greta. Last night had finally opened her eyes. In her prayers and during her many church visits at Amboise, God had been calling for her, but only now had she heard Him. Lahnstein stood on the side of the pope, the leader of Christendom, while her father had joined forces with the devil. Until now she hadn't been capable of seeing that. Lahnstein offered her a return to the bosom of the church. He gave her life and the chance as a mother and believer to do penance for what she had done, for what her father had done—and for what he might still do. Her child would grow up in Rome, a place that was still a shield against all things evil, all things devilish.

And yet she couldn't agree, not while poor Karl, her last, her only friend still suffered so horribly for the sins of his master.

"I will come with you," she said to Lahnstein with a grave voice. "I will pray for my immortal soul and for the whole of Christendom. I will join the battle against the devil. But on one condition: you set Karl free. No more torture."

Lahnstein thought about it briefly, then shrugged. "All right. The poor fellow has been tortured enough. If his condition doesn't improve, I will send him to a hospital, I promise. Let the monks look after his befuddled soul. And you come to Rome with me and serve the true faith."

He held out his hand to Greta. When she grasped it, she thought of the pact her father had once made with Tonio. This was a pact, too.

But it was a pact with the good side.

Greta's grip was strong and determined. "We go to Rome," she said, more to herself. "May my child grow up in a better world than this one. May God protect this child and all who resist the devil."

~

When Viktor von Lahnstein left the room, Hagen was waiting for him. He had stood guard outside the door the entire time.

"No torture," said Lahnstein. "And no execution. She is coming to Rome with us."

The giant raised an eyebrow but said nothing. Lahnstein knew that Hagen wasn't stupid; the big man probably drew his own conclusions. They had been chasing Faust for months now. He had slipped through their fingers in the last moment at Chinon, where they had risked everything and lost a number of men. They were still in the middle of enemy territory, like a band of rogue mercenaries, perpetually expecting French soldiers who might block their way. When there were no watch fires on the towers of Tiffauges Castle, they had struck. But yet again Faust had managed to escape, and now they weren't even allowed to question his daughter.

Instead the order was to take her to Rome.

Viktor von Lahnstein clenched his teeth. It wasn't easy being the personal envoy of Pope Leo X. But there were higher goals, and that was why he had to force back his thirst for revenge, as tough as it was.

The Lord will reward me.

"Is the castle in our control?" he asked Hagen.

The tall man nodded. Hagen was the only one who didn't seem at all uneasy about Lahnstein's wound. He had probably seen worse on the battlefields. "We found the guards in a banquet hall, drunk and drugged to the brim. We picked them up like lambs. Should we . . . ?"

Lahnstein waved his hand. "Let them live, and that drunkard of a steward, too. We don't want to risk a war over this. We aren't carrying a banner, but who knows what rumors folk in the village will spread later. The important thing now is that we get away quickly."

Hagen cleared his throat. "A horse disappeared from outside the castle."

"Faust," hissed Lahnstein. "That fellow is truly in league with the devil. Well, never mind." He practically squeezed the words through his teeth. "As you know, our mission is a different one now."

The raven had arrived at first light. It had been the same raven that had been transferring messages between Rome and Lahnstein for a while now. It was a clever old bird; Lahnstein guessed it came from the pope's famous menagerie. It had carried a tiny folded letter bearing the papal seal, and Lahnstein had wondered how the raven had been able to fly to Tiffauges this fast. If it hadn't come from the pope, Lahnstein would have thought it was sorcery.

But something else had been even more uncanny. The instructions in the letter had been very clear.

Bring Faust's daughter to Rome. She is with child.

How on earth could the Holy Father know that Faust's daughter was pregnant?

Viktor von Lahnstein smiled. At least the girl was eating out of the palm of his hand now. He had been highly convincing, he thought. Faust's daughter would serve them loyally. Perhaps she might really be of use someday.

"What about the other heretics?" asked Hagen.

"We burn them," replied Lahnstein curtly, glad he could focus on practical matters again. "The whole lot. Today, here at the castle. Before the drunk steward figures out what's going on here. We must be far away from Tiffauges before King Francis learns of this. It's not far to the sea from here. By the time Francis finds out, we'll be well on our way to Gibraltar."

"It takes a while to burn more than a dozen people," said Hagen.

"Use dry wood and douse the bastards in oil."

Lahnstein strode away with his head held high. He couldn't satisfy his longing for revenge on Faust, not yet, at least, but those heretics would feel the collective power of his hatred. Oh yes, they would!

And yet he wasn't entirely certain just then if he always served the right side.

~

A few hours later, Greta walked across the courtyard, accompanied by the watchful gaze of Hagen, over to the other tower by the north wall. She still felt a vast
emptiness, beyond anger and despair, even beyond grief. But now a small light
glowed inside her. She touched the amulet around her neck.

God doesn't forsake me!

Since she had accepted Lahnstein's offer to travel to Rome with him, she
was permitted to move freely within the castle, though Hagen always hovered
nearby. Farther back, the Swiss mercenaries stacked up wood and bundles of
brush for the great spectacle that was supposed to take place that evening. The
men laughed and joked about the impending execution. The burning Satanists
would make an imposing image beneath the night sky, and their screams would
be heard for many miles. Just like the screams that had been coming from the
torture chamber all day. Greta felt sick, and she thought about how narrowly
she had escaped the same fate. She felt a surge of pity, but then she remembered
that those people had probably murdered children. They were followers of the
devil and had to pay the price.

She turned away and climbed down the slippery, moss-covered steps that
led to the dungeons where the prisoners awaited their deaths. The castle guards
had been locked up with their steward in another part of the castle, where they
would remain until Lahnstein and his men departed.

Strangely, there was no crying and wailing coming from these prison cells. Greta
heard some voices sing strange-sounding chorales while others laughed hysterically;
one person hurled themselves against their door, shouting: "The lord awaits us! He
will rain fire and brimstone upon you all! Victory is ours! Victory is ours!"

"'Victory is ours,' what a joke. Let's see if they're still so cocky when the
flames lick at them tonight," growled Hagen, walking down the narrow corridor
ahead of Greta. He stopped outside the last door.

"Just until the next stroke of the bell," he said. "Not a moment more. I don't feel like listening to that racket for much longer."

He opened the door with a large key, and Greta entered the cell. A single torch in a bracket on the wall cast some dim light into an unfurnished room with a stone floor strewn with very little straw. A foul-smelling bucket was the only item in the room. Greta was reminded of the similar cell she had been locked in as a young girl in Nuremberg. Johann had saved her back then, but there would be no rescue for the man who sat leaning against the wall in this chamber, not even if he were permitted to leave this cell.

He was his own prisoner.

Behind her, the door banged shut.

"Karl," said Greta softly. "Can you hear me?"

When she had asked Lahnstein permission to visit Karl, he had been unsure at first but eventually granted it. "Maybe you will get him to speak," he'd said. "Although I doubt it. I believe only his body is still on this earth, while his spirit has left him."

When Greta saw her old friend, she couldn't help but agree with Lahnstein. The Karl Wagner in front of her was nothing but a shell. He stared straight ahead like a dead fish, saliva running from the corner of his mouth, and his limbs seemed strangely lifeless and limp, as if his bones had dissolved.

Greta had hoped that Karl had only put on an act for the soldiers—which was why she had asked to enter the cell on her own. But now she saw that Karl truly wasn't in his right mind. Lahnstein had explained to her that it was probably due to the poisonous drink he'd consumed. The poison had rendered him insane, and his spirit had traveled to another world.

Greta doubted it was a nice world.

"I . . . I'm so sorry, Karl," she tried again. "I . . . you . . . we should never have come to Tiffauges. My father has brought us nothing but unhappiness. It was . . . it was our damned love that made us weak, wasn't it? Now look what your love brought you."

Karl didn't respond, still staring straight ahead. Greta noticed then that he was missing all his fingernails. They had pulled them out one by one, but still he hadn't uttered a word. Now she understood why his limbs seemed so lifeless—most likely, they were broken in several places or pulled out of their joints. Crazy or not—Karl would never survive a journey to Rome.

"Karl!" Greta knelt down in front of him and took his bloodied hands in hers. "Where are you, my friend? Wherever you've gone, I am here with you, do you hear me? But . . . but I can't help you. I have to save my child—you understand, don't you? I'm going to Rome, Karl. I will ask Lahnstein to take you to a hospital not far from here so that you can be looked after. He's not a bad man, deep down. He . . . he will listen to me, I'm sure." She nodded with determination as the words gushed out of her. "You're no longer of use to him, unlike me."

Tears streamed down Greta's face, the first ones since the previous night, but she didn't notice. She held Karl's hands tightly. His face was still beautiful, but now it reminded her of a prettily painted ceramic doll.

"I will write to you, Karl. I won't abandon you. But now I must go, to Rome, for my child's sake. We were on the wrong side all along, Karl. I realize that now. I'm returning to God, and God will help you, too, I'm sure of it."

Greta took off her necklace with the amulet. The little alabaster angel had opened her eyes, even if it hadn't managed to protect her. But maybe it would protect Karl—maybe it could stop evil growing in him like it had in her father.

"Here, Karl, take this," she said softly and placed the angel around his neck. "Let it be your guardian angel from now on. If you ever wake up again, this pendant will remind you of me. Of me and of God, who is always there for us, especially during our hours of need." Gently, she stroked his cheek. "I . . . I must go now. My old friend, I love you. I will always love you."

She suppressed a sob, not wishing for Karl to remember her thus. But then she recalled that it was just a puppet sitting in front of her who wouldn't remember anything.

Or was he?

As Greta stood up, she thought she could see the briefest flash in Karl's eyes, as if the fog lifted for a tiny moment. But on second glance there was nothing but emptiness. His head flopped to one side, and a strand of saliva hanging from his mouth reached almost to the ground.

"Farewell, Karl."

She bent down and kissed his hot forehead. Then she knocked against the door and Hagen opened it.

When she climbed up the stairs, Greta breathed in the cool, fresh breeze that greeted her. It tasted of new beginnings.

And with each step she left a little more of her old life behind.

18

UNDER A MOONLESS NIGHT, A LONESOME HORSEMAN arrived at the gates of Amboise. His horse was as pitch black as his coat, so the guards didn't notice more than a shadow. He was riding along the wall, through the watery meadows by the river where the fireflies glowed like will-o'-the-wisps. The smell of rot and sulfur wafted over from the muddy banks. Above the river burned the watch fires of Amboise Castle, rising above the edge of town like a giantess made of stone. The horse took a sharp turn onto the narrow road leading to Cloux behind the castle.

About a quarter of a mile before his destination, Johann dismounted and tied the dripping horse to a tree so that it could graze. Despite the darkness, he had ridden the last few hours at a gallop. His coat stuck to his back, and every muscle in his body ached. But it was a welcome pain, reminding him that his paralysis had indeed vanished.

It had taken Johann eight days and nights to get here from Tiffauges; he had ridden like the devil. He no longer wore the bloodstained robe of the dead priest but a jerkin, trousers, and a black coat with a hood that turned him almost invisible when he rode through the woods. The horse had been a stroke of luck, as its saddlebag had been filled with wine, food, and even a few gold and silver coins—probably loot belonging to a Swiss mercenary. In a dodgy tavern where the landlord didn't care how the strange fellow in the dirty robe had come by his money, Johann had bought his new clothes. He had considered buying a hand cannon also but decided on a set of throwing knives instead. In his youth, knives had always been the weapon he handled best, and throwing knives were more likely to hit their targets at short distances than those awkward guns.

Johann was about a hundred paces away from Château du Cloux now and still saw no lights. The building stood in complete darkness. Perhaps no one resided there now that Leonardo was dead? Hunched over, he crept along the wall. He knew from his walks in the garden that there was a derelict patch that was overgrown with ivy. A pear tree had stretched its branches across the wall there. Cloux wasn't a castle like Tiffauges but an elegant manor house, not designed to keep out intruders. After all, it sat just beneath the royal castle, and that alone afforded some protection.

After searching for some time, Johann finally found the crumbling patch. He tested the tree branches for sturdiness and then started to climb up. It felt so good to use all his muscles again. He had been puzzling for days why the disease had gone and whether it was only temporary. He hoped fervently that it had nothing to do with John Reed's death—that Tonio hadn't accepted him as a sacrifice. But deep down inside, Johann knew that was the case.

He pulled himself up another branch and reached the top of the wall. He gazed into the courtyard and saw that all was silent and deserted, and he could still see no lights. Nearly two months had passed since Leonardo's death; maybe the great artist's friend and helper, Francesco Melzi, had already departed. But what about the two servants? Johann's hand went to his hip, where from a leather belt hung five knives, their sheaths freshly oiled so that the blades slipped out easily. Also hanging from his belt was a satchel holding a lantern and a tinderbox; that was all he had brought for this excursion. He took one more deep breath before jumping onto the shed roof below him. From there he lowered himself into the deserted yard.

Johann looked around searchingly. Where should he start? Until then, his goal had been Cloux. He had returned here because he hoped to find something that was of importance to Tonio. Something that Leonardo had hidden well. Now his plan seemed to him like the proverbial hunt for the needle in the haystack. What had he been thinking? La Meffraye and Henriet had searched for months without finding anything. What could it be? One of Leonardo's inventions, perhaps? Or the philosopher's stone after all? Father Jerome had said that Tonio had tried before to get that something off Leonardo.

What could Leonardo possibly have owned that was of interest to the devil?

The garden spread before him, a black plane in the darkness with trees protruding from it like monsters. Johann decided to try his luck in the manor house first. The main entrance was locked, but the lock was simple enough for Johann to pick with a knife. Inside, he lit his lantern and looked around. Many pieces of furniture had been removed; lighter colored patches on the floor showed where chests and cupboards used to sit. Other pieces of furniture were covered with sheets. Even though Leonardo da Vinci hadn't been dead for long, Johann felt like he was the first visitor in many years.

With his lantern raised, Johann entered Leonardo's atelier. He saw an empty easel, dried-up dishes of paint in the shelves, brushes, and a dead mouse floating in a bucket of murky cleaning water. Johann remembered what the room had looked like when Leonardo was still alive—the many colors, a cage with chirping birds, the painting of the beautiful woman that had been Leonardo's favorite piece—her mysterious smile, as if she knew exactly which secret the master had taken to the grave with him. The library next door that Johann would have loved to browse had been cleared out. Only a few scraps of paper lay strewn on the floor; dust and spiderwebs now filled the shelves.

Johann's steps echoed as he walked over to the dining room where he had often sat with Leonardo and Karl, and from there to the kitchen, where it still smelled of old fat and smoked meat. The house was empty and dead. What was he thinking when he'd expected to find a clue here? There was nothing. He decided to cast a glance belowground, even though his hopes were dashed. Stairs led down into a storage cellar with a broken barrel and empty crates. Here, too, nothing but scraps of paper lay scattered on the ground.

Scraps of paper.

Johann paused.

What were scraps of paper doing in the cellar, where he would have expected to find only foodstuffs? He bent down and picked up several scraps. They were parts of Leonardo's notes and sketches; some pieces contained only one scribbled word. They probably came from books from the library, ripped pages or small notes. When the shelves had been emptied they must have fallen out.

And perhaps then someone carried the boxes of books down here?

In the light of his lantern, Johann continued to search the floor, his heart beating faster. On the right-hand wall that was built from rust-red bricks he made an interesting discovery: one of the scraps was stuck under the wall.

When Johann felt the wall, he could make out joints that formed a high rectangle.

A door.

It wasn't hard to find the opening mechanism. It was behind one of the bricks, which he easily pushed in. The door swung open, and on the other side, secret stairs led into the depths, just like at Tiffauges. Johann briefly wondered if the same architect had built both doors, but soon abandoned the thought. The door at Tiffauges was designed to lock people up, while this one was part of a secret passage—and Johann thought he knew where it led.

To the castle.

It made sense. Leonardo and the king had been close friends, and Francis often visited the genius he admired so much. But since the king didn't want to bring half his court each time, it was much easier to use a secret passageway. Obviously, the documents had been removed from Cloux via this tunnel. Johann remembered the king's words when he had questioned Faust at Chinon.

My scholars sifted through Leonardo's writings, page by page, but they found nothing.

In the passage, too, scraps littered the ground. Johann even found some intact pages, one of them containing an anatomical sketch, the opened torso of a man. The lungs had been removed, making visible the heart, stomach, and intestines. Johann thought about the dissection he had performed with Leonardo and Karl. The precision with which Leonardo had drawn his sketch was truly astounding.

The corridor was supported by ceiling beams every few yards and clad with bricks. As far as Johann could tell, it led in the direction of the castle. He walked faster, the lantern flickering and casting long shadows on the walls. Eventually he came to an iron gate secured by numerous locks.

Johann cursed under his breath. He saw at once that these locks weren't as easy to pick as the one at the entrance. Had he really thought he could simply march into the royal castle? And what did he want at the castle, anyway? Leonardo's documents had surely been taken away a long time ago. Angry and disappointed, he shook the gate. He was about to turn back when he heard a noise in the passageway behind him. At first he thought it was just the echo of the noise he had produced himself. But then he heard it again, low and creeping. It was a shuffling and scraping, as if a huge snake was slithering across the floor.

Someone was walking down the corridor directly toward him.

Johann couldn't detect any light. Whoever or whatever was approaching wasn't carrying a lantern—meaning that Johann was clearly visible, while the other could hide in the darkness. If that other was armed with a crossbow or a hand cannon, they had a decisive advantage.

Johann hesitated, then put out his lantern. Everything around him went black. But at least Johann couldn't be seen. The shuffling stopped for a moment, then started again, faster and louder now. The person was getting very close. Johann involuntarily held his breath. Someone cleared his throat and spat on the ground.

"Nice trick, Doctor," said a low, hoarse voice. "Now we're both as blind as newborn kittens. But still you won't get past me. How do you say at chess? *Remis*, isn't it?"

Johann took a few moments to place the voice. He had heard it just a few times, mostly in muttered words of submission, of humble obedience.

Very well, monsignore. As you wish, monsignore. Dinner is served, would the gentlemen be so kind as to follow me . . .

Now he also remembered the name that the man standing in the darkness before him had used in Leonardo's house. And he remembered the sound of the walking stick when the old butler used to hobble through the rooms of Château du Cloux. It was the same scraping Johann had heard just now.

"Battista!" called out Johann. "Or should I call you Henriet? And how is your friend the cook, dear Madame La Meffraye?"

"I see you're as clever as they say, Doctor. Then I'm sure you have met our Prelati at Tiffauges, or Father Jerome, as he goes by."

"Indeed I have. His corpse is rotting in one of the secret chambers where you used to torture innocent children. His black soul has gone to your lord, where it will hopefully burn for a very long time."

Henriet said nothing. Evidently, this was news to him.

"First Poitou, now Prelati," Johann went on. He strained his eyes but couldn't make out more than the hint of an outline. "Your numbers are dwindling. And I will not rest until the last one of you is dead."

"You'll never succeed, because we are constantly joined by new followers. But I must admit that it saddens me to hear our Prelati is no longer with us. We were a close-knit fellowship, like a family."

"Gilles de Rais, Poitou, the priest Prelati, La Meffraye, and you, Henriet," counted Johann. "How many children have you murdered together? A hundred? Two hundred? A thousand? You've been at it for over a hundred years, after all."

"Every single child is worth it if it buys you eternal life and a place by the master's side," said the voice from the darkness. "The beast will return to earth soon, Faustus! *Homo Deus est!* We are preparing for its arrival, and then the air will be filled with the cries, wails, and screams of those who aren't among its disciples."

"You've tried before, remember?" said Johann. "In Nuremberg. You failed then and you will fail again now."

"We weren't ready then. This time, we are. The master's plan is—I can't help but say—divine. You will understand once he explains it to you. It's not too late, Faustus. Join us." The scraping sound resumed, coming closer, and Johann reached for the knives at his side.

"Did Leonardo tell you what he kept from us so stubbornly?" asked Henriet. "Do you know where the recipe is hidden?"

Johann listened up. Henriet had given away more than he realized. Clearly, the secret wasn't an item but some kind of recipe. Could Tonio del Moravia also be after the *lapis philosophorum*, the philosopher's stone? When Tonio was still called Gilles de Rais, he had frantically tried to produce gold. Was he still searching for a way, and had Leonardo found one? But why would Tonio want to know? He was immortal, at least as long as he quenched his thirst for the blood of children.

What did he need gold for?

Johann decided to string Henriet along for as long as he could.

"I believe you have been looking in the wrong places."

"We turned over every brick in this house and studied every page of his documents. I went so far as to teach myself to read Leonardo's mirror writing. The recipe wasn't anywhere. We searched his dead body, his shroud, all his rings—we even looked inside his mouth. Nothing. And now his body lies cold and stiff at Notre-Dame-en-Grève, even more stubbornly silent than when he was alive. Despite everything the master did for him!" Henriet growled like a dog. "But maybe La Meffraye will still find it. She had another idea, but I don't believe it. It is jinxed!"

"Leonardo might have told me where the recipe is hidden," said Johann. "But why would I tell you?"

"Because the master loves you, Faustus! More than anyone else. And you, deep down inside, love him, too. He wants you by his side—we can still take you to him."

"That's not enough. I want two lives in exchange for mine. Two lives in exchange for my knowledge and me. That's a fair price!"

"Which two lives are you speaking of?" asked Henriet, still nothing but a vague shape in the darkness.

"Those of my assistant and my daughter," replied Johann. "Ensure that nothing happens to them and I will be at your master's service."

More than a week had passed since his escape from Tiffauges. Johann didn't know if Karl and Greta were still alive or if they had fallen victim to Lahnstein and the Inquisition. But he wasn't ready to give up hope. Perhaps this way he would learn something about Karl's and Greta's fates.

Henriet snorted like an ox and then gave a laugh. "You still haven't learned to let go, Faustus. That is the first lesson: free yourself from everything that restricts you—love, first and foremost. We don't care about your assistant, but the master has other plans for your daughter."

Johann caught his breath.

Other plans.

He had thought Greta had fallen into the clutches of the Inquisition at Tiffauges, but could his daughter be with Tonio? Was that what Henriet was trying to say?

"Where is she?" he asked with a trembling voice. "What . . . what have you done with her?"

"Think of the first lesson, Doctor." Henriet laughed mockingly. "Free yourself from love. Your daughter isn't important, just—"

Those words were too much for Johann. With an angry cry he hurled himself at the dark shadow in the corridor. The attack came as a surprise to Henriet. Johann felt a hard and astonishingly muscular body beneath him. On the outside, Henriet looked like a frail old servant, but he possessed the strength of a bull. He twisted his body underneath Johann and soon managed to break out of his grip. The two men grappled in the darkness, Henriet using his stick as a weapon. Johann couldn't see much of his opponent, and Henriet was much stronger than him, but Johann's punches were fueled by boundless fury and hatred.

"What have you done with Greta?" he yelled between blows. "What . . . have . . . you . . . done with her?"

"Easy, Doctor, easy." Henriet laughed and rammed the tip of his walking stick into Johann's stomach, causing Johann to double over and gasp. "I don't want to kill you. The master will tear my head off if I do. You are his favorite, after all. Even if we don't really need you any longer. I will beat you black and blue, bind you like a rabbit, and bring you to the master. Let him decide what to do with you."

Another blow from Henriet's stick sent Johann flying against the wall of the corridor. How could any man be this strong? The devil himself must have given him the power. Johann sat leaning against the wall, blood streaming down his forehead and into his eyes, and he struggled to breathe. When Henriet moved toward him with the stick again, Johann's hand went to his belt. It was a motion he used to be able to do in his sleep, but now it felt awfully slow. Still, he managed to pull out one of his knives.

"Good night, Doctor. Sweet dreams," said Henriet, raising the stick.

Johann threw his knife.

He hit his opponent somewhere in the stomach. Henriet staggered and grunted, the wound not bad enough to make him fall. But at least the stick missed its target. Johann kicked at Henriet's legs, causing the man to trip and fall straight onto Johann. The stick clattered to the ground.

With his last strength, Johann grasped the handle of the blade stuck in Henriet's stomach and pulled it hard from left to right. Henriet groaned and Johann felt warm liquid on his fingers. Then he managed to roll out from underneath the man.

Henriet coughed and spluttered beside him, lying on the floor like a black rock. His voice was but a whisper now.

"You . . . you are so . . . stupid, Faustus! So damned stupid, even though you call yourself wise. The master loves you, and you act like an unruly child. My death changes nothing—nothing! All is prepared." He laughed, but his laugh turned into a rattling gargle. "We . . . we don't really need the recipe, anyhow. It would have been but the crowning stroke in a match that is already won. It . . . it's not crucial. To hell with you . . . With me . . ."

"What have you done with my daughter?" asked Johann. "Where is she?"

But there was no reply.

When he kicked Henriet's body, it tipped to the side. The ensuing silence nearly suffocated Johann. He wasn't sorry about Henriet, but his silence meant that Johann would get no more answers from him. Had Henriet known where Greta was? What had happened to Karl? Or had he been bluffing, just like Johann?

On hands and knees, Johann searched for his lantern and the tinderbox. Once he'd found both items, he lit the lantern with shaking hands. He glanced at Henriet, whose face was wrinkled and hair was gray. He looked like an ancient old man, but underneath the servant's wide clothes had been an incredibly powerful body. Even in death his small black eyes gleamed with evil. The knife still stuck in Henriet's abdomen, and a pool of blood had spread around his body, soaking some of the scraps of paper on the ground.

Johann was about to rush back to the cellar of the manor house when he stepped on something. It was the page with the anatomical sketch he had carried earlier. He leaned down and picked it up. The bloody print of his shoe formed a ghostly frame around the opened torso.

And suddenly Johann knew where the recipe was hidden.

How could I have missed it?

A hoarse laughing fit overcame him. It was so simple! Leonardo had told him on his deathbed. Johann just hadn't listened.

But it wouldn't be easy to retrieve the treasure.

A short while later, Johann stood outside the closed city gate of Amboise. He had ridden as fast as he could in his condition—Henriet had beaten him half to death. He had briefly considered climbing the city wall somewhere, but he was too exhausted and weak. He felt paralyzed, as if Tonio's curse had struck him once more. And so he had tied up his horse near town and now knocked against the small one-man door that was a part of the larger city gate facing the river. After a few moments, a hatch opened and the night watchman stared at him from tired eyes.

"Je suis fatigué et saoul comme un cochon," garbled Johann, trying to appear drunk. He had pulled the hood over his head, hoping the watchman wouldn't notice his beat-up face.

"Vous avez de l'argent?" grumbled the watchman.

Johann pulled out his purse and handed the man a few coins. The man grinned as he pocketed the money, then unlocked the door with a key. Johann walked hunched over and staggered as he entered. It wasn't an act—his whole body ached from Henriet's beating. He knew that drunken men were often allowed in late at night, so long as they had enough money.

"Merci," he mumbled, then vanished into the next alleyway. His destination wasn't far away. Faust would have expected Leonardo to be interred up at the castle, but the old man himself had once told Johann that he didn't wish for a fancy funeral. Henriet had unwittingly told Johann where Leonardo had found his final resting place.

And now his body lies cold and stiff at Notre-Dame-en-Grève, even more stubbornly silent than when he was alive.

Notre-Dame-en-Grève was the small municipal church of Amboise, situated by the city wall. At its rear lay a fenced-in cemetery with a chapel. The church itself was a squat building that looked like it was part of the fortifications. Johann couldn't see a soul around, only a solitary light burned up in the spire. He walked around the church and entered the cemetery, which reminded him of the graveyard in the town where he grew up. The tombstones and wooden crosses, many of them crooked, stood in rows, and at first glance Johann couldn't see any fresh-looking graves.

Where are you, Leonardo?

Johann walked down the rows of tombstones and read the inscriptions by the light of his lantern. He saw that Amboise had a long history, but he found only the names of common burghers and tradesmen. Would one of the most famous men of his time really lie buried in such a plain cemetery? Johann's eyes moved to the chapel; some candles flickered inside. The chapel was circular, with a dome like a byzantine church, and there were no glass windows, just narrow openings to let in some light. On its western side was a low door.

The day's first lark chirped somewhere, and a faint pink veil covered the horizon. Johann guessed that he had less than two hours until sunrise. He walked to the door in the chapel and found that it was unlocked. Inside was a small altar adorned with flowers; a plain wooden cross hung above it, and candles burned on the windowsills.

On a slab of rock in the center sat a sarcophagus.

Johann could tell immediately that it was the sarcophagus of Leonardo da Vinci. Evidently, the old man had chiseled it himself from a block of marble during the last few months of his life. Leonardo's image was carved into the rock, looking so vivid that Johann briefly thought the great artist was merely asleep. The statue wore a wide coat just like the one da Vinci used to wear when he was alive. Each fold in the fabric, each seam, was perfectly worked into the stone. Hair and beard gleamed white in the light of the candles, every strand and every individual hair chiseled to perfection. The hands were folded in prayer, the fingers studded with marble rings. Johann had never before seen such a beautiful and perfect gravestone.

And now he had to defile it.

He guessed the sarcophagus would remain in this chapel until the king returned to Amboise. Francis I would want to give his mentor a worthy send-off, but the difficulties around the election of the German king had kept him away so far.

Lucky for me.

Johann remembered seeing the grave digger's pickaxe and handsaw outside the door. He fetched them and returned to the chapel, forcing the tip of the pick into the slit beneath the grave slab, trying to lever the slab aside. There was a crunching sound and the stone moved backward a tiny bit. Johann walked to the foot end of the slab and pulled with all his might. The marble slab was heavy. Sweat ran down his forehead, and the muscles of his arms felt as though he were being quartered, but eventually he had moved the slab enough to expose roughly a third of the opening. In the light of the candles he saw a plain wooden coffin underneath. It was made of thin spruce planks that would be easy to smash. Johann took a deep breath, preparing himself for the unavoidable stench of decay, and raised the pick.

Forgive me, Leonardo. But it was what you wanted, right? You told me yourself.

The wood splintered loudly—Johann hoped it wasn't too loud. He placed the pieces of wood aside and gazed at the corpse.

What in God's name?

How was this possible?

Leonardo had been dead for nearly two months. Johann had expected to find a stinking, decomposing corpse, but the body lying in this coffin looked fresh and barely smelled. Leonardo's cheeks and lips were full and rosy as if he wore makeup. His eyes were closed, and he was dressed in a snow-white shirt with ruffles and lace.

He looked as if he was sleeping.

Johann had heard of saints whose bodies were perfectly intact even hundreds of years after their deaths. Was it the same with people who'd made a pact with the devil? But perhaps there was another reason for this state. Leonardo had been vain. If he had hoped that Johann would turn up one day to desecrate his corpse, he would have done anything to avoid presenting an image of horror.

Johann bent over the corpse and studied it closely. Now he could make out tiny incisions and stitches on its neck, drops of an acrid-smelling liquid bulging out from the cuts. Leonardo had been a genius unto his death. Somehow he had managed to stop the decomposition process, or at least slow it down.

That only left the question of what the body would look like on the inside.

Johann tried to calm himself. When his hands no longer trembled quite as badly, he pulled one of the sharp knives from his belt. Gently, he unbuttoned Leonardo's shirt, exposing the narrow, sunken chest.

Then he took the knife and placed it on the skin, which parted like parchment.

Johann focused on his work, trying to ignore the thought that he was cutting open the greatest genius of mankind like a common thief. Then he picked up the saw and cut through the ribs until the torso lay in front of him like an open treasure chest.

You clever old man.

When Johann had gazed at the bloodstained parchment with the anatomical sketch down in the tunnel earlier, realization had hit him harder than Henriet's blows. Leonardo da Vinci had practically pushed his nose right up to it, but Johann still hadn't seen. Now he understood why they had conducted this strange dissection on the dead stable boy in the shed of the manor house. Leonardo had shown Johann what he expected of him. And it had been a test to see whether Johann was even capable of performing a dissection in his state. Karl had helped him then, and Leonardo couldn't have foreseen that the younger man would not be with Johann now. Then, on his deathbed, the dying Leonardo da

Vinci had told Johann the secret of the hiding place, speaking in riddles in case Henriet overheard them. What had his final words been?

The greatest secrets lie at the innermost core. The innermost.

La Meffraye and Henriet had searched everywhere—expect for one place.

Inside Leonardo.

Johann closed his eyes for a moment and cleared his mind so he could continue to concentrate. Just like Karl had done in the shed, he removed the lung flaps. They were gray and a little mushy, but still intact. The acrid smell he had noticed earlier was very pungent now. He saw Leonardo's heart, which had stopped beating for good, and below, the stomach sack, which was surprisingly small. Like the rest of the intestines, it was swimming in the sharp-smelling liquid that filled the torso.

It took only a tiny cut to open the stomach.

Something glimmered inside.

Johann placed the knife aside and carefully removed the item. It was the small silver globe, about the size of a marble, that Leonardo had always carried around his neck. The dying man had probably rubbed it with butter or oil and then swallowed it—surely a painful thing to do. But that way Leonardo had managed to literally take his secret to the grave. He had feasted with the devil and outdanced him in the end. Despite the eerie surroundings, Johann couldn't help but smile. What was it Leonardo had said?

He who dances with the devil needs good shoes.

Wherever Leonardo's soul was now, Tonio had not received what he had wanted so badly. The old man had made sure that only Johann learned of the hiding place.

And now he would finally reveal the secret.

With the sleeve of his shirt Johann wiped the blood from the globe.

Just then a cry rang out behind him, sounding like that of a giant bird of prey, and then something was placed around his neck.

A demonic creature pounced on him, screaming shrilly.

Johann reached to his throat and felt a thin leather strap that was tightening relentlessly. Sharp fingernails dug into his skin. He had been so consumed by finally solving the mystery that he had forgotten all about Henriet's words from earlier.

Maybe La Meffraye will still find it. She had another idea.

Johann's eyes bulged as he gasped for air. He went to his knees. It was the same technique the French soldiers had employed in the woods near Chinon—an ancient method of strangulation, simple and effective.

"Little Faustusss," hissed a voice behind him. "You always were a clever boy. But not as clever as La Meffraye!" The creature giggled.

Johann wondered how many children La Meffraye, the barn owl, had murdered in this way, or perhaps only knocked out until Gilles de Rais had his way with them. He felt his strength wane and a blackness spread from the edges of his field of vision. Finally he managed to force a finger between his throat and the strap; he pulled at it and delicious air streamed into his lungs. He rolled to the side, the strap loosened, and La Meffraye now straddled him like an angry harpy.

It was amazing how much the old cook had changed. She still resembled Leonardo's mute servant Matturina, but her true face was showing now. Flashing eyes filled with hatred, a beak-shaped nose, and an insane grin. But within seconds this face could change into a mask of gentleness and motherliness—which had been the downfall of so many children.

Suddenly Johann recognized her.

When he first drank the black potion in the woods near Nördlingen, many years ago, Tonio and Poitou had taken him to a clearing. Many wet tongues had licked him, many greedy fingers had stroked him, and at the end a woman had lowered herself onto him, a creature with long, straggly hair, stinking of sulfur and soil as if she had just emerged from a swamp. She had ridden him like a young stallion, and Tonio had urged her on.

He is yours, Meffraye.

Meffraye's fingers clutched his throat, and toxic saliva dripped onto his face.

"Do you remember, little Faustusss?" she asked. "Why did you run away so soon, back then? The two of us had so much fun together. So much fun!"

Johann was still weakened from the fight with Henriet and the exertion of opening the sarcophagus. He tried to reach his belt with a shaking hand, but Meffraye was sitting right on top of him. She licked her lips and moved her hips back and forth as if making passionate love to him, all the while strangling him like a puppy.

"So much fun," she purred. "Come to La Meffraye, my little one. Let us ride to the master together."

It wasn't even so much La Meffraye's force that nailed Johann to the floor but his horror. Old memories rose up in him, memories from that night near Nördlingen.

Small, twitching bundles in the trees.

Panicked, his hand searched for anything that might serve him as a weapon. Dust, stones, splinters. Suddenly his fingers clasped the handle of the pickaxe. Above him, La Meffraye was grinning and he smelled her rotten breath, breath that came straight from an endlessly deep swamp.

"Kiss me, Little Faustusss." She leaned over his throat and he saw her sharpened teeth. "I will kiss you like no woman has ever kissed you before. Like I used to kiss those sweet little things . . . so much fun, so much—"

Johann screamed as he lifted the pickaxe and swung it hard.

La Meffraye screeched like a bird as her face exploded into a cloud of blood, bone, and brains. For an instant Johann thought he could still see one single eye staring at him.

Then the witch tilted to the side and was finally silent.

Johann just lay there for a long while, listening to his own breathing and the chirping of the birds outside the chapel. The first slanted rays of sunshine fell through the windows. When he finally stood up with shaking knees, he avoided looking at La Meffraye's face, as if he feared the lunatic grimace would still smirk at him. But he knew she was dead. And that there was no more smirk and no more face.

La Meffraye would haunt him only in his nightmares now.

Infinitely tired, feeling more dead than alive, he staggered across the chapel. Poitou, Prelati, Henriet, La Meffraye—he had vanquished them all. Now only Tonio and he were left.

The small silver globe rested by the wall, like a marble some children had left behind after playing. Johann picked it up and slipped it in his pocket.

With his last remaining strength, he pushed the grave slab back in place, put the pickaxe and the saw away, and sat down on the stone steps outside the chapel. With trembling fingers he opened the globe. The sun had risen by now, bathing the cemetery in warm light while the birds tried to outsing one another.

The two halves were as easy to unscrew as if they'd only been waiting for Johann to take a look inside.

At the innermost core of the world.

Inside, folded into a tiny square, lay a flimsy piece of paper. Johann carefully drew it apart and found that it was nearly as long as his forearm, but very narrow. He had to read the scrawled black letters several times in order to decipher the mirror writing. Some words were smudged or simply a mystery to him, but gradually he began to comprehend. Despite the daylight he used his lantern, as his eyes were tired. But eventually he understood what Leonardo da Vinci had invented and what Tonio longed to possess. The last line on the paper sounded like an ominous prophecy.

Death and perdition will befall the world.

And in that moment Johann knew that the master could never get his hands on the tiny document—not for any price in the world.

Not even for the life of his daughter.

A shudder went through Johann's body. He wanted to cry, but no tears came, only hoarse sobs. Too great was his grief.

Greta is lost.

Shaken by cramps, battered, bruised, and at the end of his rope, Johann Georg Faustus collapsed on the steps of the chapel—the most intelligent and the loneliest man in the world.

Act IV

The Whore of Rome

19

SOMETHING CLINKED IN THE BOWL, AND THE BEGGAR IN the dirty torn rags eagerly pulled the vessel closer, hoping to see a coin or at least a piece of stale bread. Karl's mouth watered; he had hardly eaten in days. But when he reached inside, it was just a pebble. Children laughed, and quick little footsteps ran off. Before the beggar could throw the stone at the brats, they had vanished around the nearest corner.

"Dirty riffraff," muttered Karl weakly. "Dirty little riffraff. May God punish you."

The small pebble still in his hand, he leaned back into the shade of the house's wall, where the sun wasn't burning quite as mercilessly. He put the stone into his mouth and sucked on it, easing the worst of his hunger and thirst. A corpulent woad merchant clad entirely in blue strutted past Karl and cast a look of disgust. He kicked at the dented bowl, cussing vociferously in Occitan, apparently because Karl was in his way. Karl lowered his head demurely and made the sign of the cross so that the man wouldn't set the guards on him. Flies buzzed around his head, but he no longer noticed them; they were his constant companions, just like the lice and fleas living in his long shaggy hair and beard.

Toulouse was one of the wealthiest cities in France, having grown prosperous through the trade of woad, a plant that flourished on the calciferous grounds southeast of the city, used to produce precious blue dye for fabric and clothing.

Despite, or perhaps because of, its wealth, the city was full of beggars. They sat on the steps of Saint Étienne Cathedral, hobbled on their crutches across the multitude of market squares near the magnificent city hall, or sent their children pickpocketing in the crowds by the bridges across the Garonne River, which stank of urine and lye. The church preached the donating of alms—those who gave generously shortened their time in purgatory—but that wasn't to say the poor couldn't be treated like cattle.

From the square outside the Basilica of Saint-Sernin sounded the monotonous singsong of the pilgrims and the cries of vendors hawking candied figs and dates; the air smelled of roast mutton and freshly baked bread. Karl felt sick with hunger. Two days ago a kindly pilgrim woman had given him a boiled egg and a crust of black bread, and that had been the last time he had eaten. The only item of clothing he possessed was a filthy tunic that was ripped in so many places that he was practically half-naked. His arms and legs were scabby and thin as sticks; his face was overgrown by a beard and his cheeks sunken, making him look twenty years older.

But at least he knew who he was.

It hadn't always been that way. Karl's memories of the past were blurred, occasionally calling on him like capricious visitors. He had awoken in the austere room of a pauper's hospital at Nantes nearly two years ago. Karl had no idea how he got there. He had known neither his name nor where he had come from, and not even the friendly Benedictine nuns had been able to help him. They had found him outside the gate, dumped like a sack of trash with broken limbs, bleeding fingers, and a high fever, more dead than alive. Very slowly he had regained his strength, and with time, fragments from his childhood and youth had come back to him, like tiny splinters of his previous life. Apparently he came from the German Empire, since he spoke German, and he believed that his name was Karl Wagner. He had probably studied medicine, because a wealth of Latin and Greek terms swirled around in his head. *Clavicula, mandibula, os sacrum, Corpus Hippocraticum.* He had no clue what had brought him to France nor what had happened to him there. He liked to draw, so he used charcoal on scraps of paper to capture the memories that sometime overcame him, even though he didn't know what to make of the resulting images.

A man in a long cloak on a podium. A burning castle. The face of a young woman, wet with tears, her hand reaching out to him. The horned devil, grinning, handing him a goblet.

Karl instinctively touched the pendant that hung from his neck. The little angel was his lifeline whenever the terrible thoughts threatened to get the better of him. The pendant was a simple figurine whittled from alabaster, a token from the time *before*. He couldn't say who had given it to him. His mother, perhaps? Despite the hunger consuming him, he would never sell his talisman; it was the only connection he had left to his old life, like a rope floating in the murky waters of his memory. The pendant felt as warm as if it were alive.

Once Karl had been nursed halfway back to health, the nuns had given him a plain tunic and a staff and wished him good luck in his future travels. They couldn't accommodate him any longer—there were too many like him. Stranded souls, drifting through the country like ghosts and seeking shelter in hospitals and monasteries. For at least one night they would receive a roof over their heads and some watery soup before they returned to the road. Karl had been roaming ever since, but he had no idea where to. He had no compass and no memory; he simply drifted south because it was warmer there and people didn't freeze to death in winter. Along the way he had learned French and some Occitan, the old language of the bards and the people in the south. He begged, and sometimes he managed to sell small pictures that he drew on scraps of paper or tree bark. He knew how to read and write, but his French wasn't good enough to earn a living as a traveling clerk. To most people he was a foreigner and a fool. Only the girls liked him because he had beautiful eyes and a chiseled face, but Karl soon figured out that he wasn't interested in girls. He wondered if his memory loss was God's punishment for his secret longings.

France was a huge country, stretching all the way to the tall peaks of the Pyrenees and from the Atlantic Ocean to the Mediterranean Sea. Thus Karl had traveled to Occitania and eventually arrived in Toulouse. The days crept by slowly, one after the other, all merging into one. He had become accustomed to his missing memory, and he had a hunch that the gaping hole in his recollections used to be filled with something unspeakably awful that his mind didn't want to face.

A horned devil. A black goblet.

Again he could hear shouts and chanting from the square by the basilica, but this time there was also laughter and the clapping of hands. Karl listened. He guessed a troupe of jugglers and minstrels was performing, as he had occasionally seen in other places. The sight of jugglers had always made him strangely happy, though he had no idea why. He decided to abandon his shady spot outside the Dominican monastery and try his luck near the Basilica of Saint-Sernin. The church was one of the most significant pilgrims' destinations in Christendom, accommodating the remains of various apostles. On the square would be many more beggars like him, but also more people who might toss him a scrap of food. People were more generous when they laughed and had a good time.

Karl picked up his rusty bowl and made his way over to the basilica. It was almost noon. Now, in July, the sun blazed so brightly that the brick buildings seemed to glow like red embers. Shimmering heat lay above the square outside the huge church, and Karl wiped the sweat from his eyes. A crowd of pilgrims and burghers had gathered around a shaky podium consisting of a few stacked-up crates. Standing on top of it was an older man in a stained black-and-blue coat who was just about to pull a cackling hen out of his hat. The man swayed, struggling to stay on his feet. Evidently, he'd had too much to drink. His long beard was as ragged as the fur of a mangy dog, his graying black hair matted. He seemed like one of those crazy itinerant preachers who liked to predict doom and gloom and were only tolerated by the church because they made their flock afraid of hell. The flapping animal slipped out of his grip and made a run for it, cheered on by the roaring laughter of the crowd.

"Hey, your supper, wizard!" shouted a man in the front row, the same woad merchant from before. "It's flying away. What will you eat now? Or do you just drink? I'll gladly give you a coin if you can conjure a jug of wine from your hat!"

The man on the podium slowly raised his face to look at the loudmouthed merchant.

Karl froze.

The man's eyes made him dizzy. They were pitch black, sinister, and as deep as wells. Endless grief shimmered at their bottom, and something else that attracted Karl almost magically. Despite his drunken state, the ragged stranger exuded an almost tangible authority. Karl sensed that he knew the man from somewhere. But he had no idea where from or why.

Who are you, stranger?

"I think I will have fried egg," the wizard said with a low, dragging voice. "The egg is the beginning and the end, isn't it? The alpha and the omega." Suddenly he fished an egg from his hat, then another and another. He juggled them, but it wasn't long before one fell to the ground and burst. The two other eggs vanished magically.

"Ha, now you don't even have eggs," jeered the merchant in the bright-blue beret with a velvet ribbon, the sign of his guild. "Or are you going to lick it off the ground like a dog?"

"It's true, I no longer have eggs," replied the man on the podium, his voice very low and yet audible right across the square. "Because you stole them from me."

"What are you talking about, you fool?" growled the merchant, looking around uncertainly. Some of the spectators started to mutter and whistle. "Do you want the city guards to put you in the stocks?"

Karl still stood as if frozen. He was thinking about the image from his memories he had drawn so many times. A man in a long cloak on a podium.

It was as if his drawings had suddenly come to life.

Like a large dark bird, the man jumped down from the crates, staggered but caught himself, then strode toward the merchant with slow steps. He swayed a little but didn't fall.

"And what are you going to do now, you drunk quack?" asked the merchant, jutting out his chin defiantly. "You won't get any hens or eggs from me—but I can give you a kick up the ass."

"Are you sure?" asked the man when he came to a halt in front of the merchant. "No eggs? See for yourself."

With astonishing speed the wizard slapped his flat hand onto the merchant's beret. A yellow mess of egg flowed out from under his hat and down the dumfounded merchant's forehead. The crowd cried out with surprise, and some people laughed.

"You . . . you are going to regret this," exclaimed the merchant, shaking his fists. "Guards! Arrest this man!"

He leaped at the wizard, who, despite his state of intoxication, dodged him with surprising agility. Other citizens rushed to help, but the man in the black-and-blue coat was quicker. He feinted to the left and the right and soon escaped the agitated masses.

Karl followed him.

He knew that he mustn't lose the stranger. He was the key to Karl's old life. If only he had a moment to ponder where he might know the wizard from. But there was no time. And so Karl stuck to the man's heels. The wizard sprinted across the square, tripping several times and catching himself on market stalls, sending them crashing to the ground. Vendors cried out indignantly, geese took off cackling, loaves of bread rolled into the filthy gutter. Karl lost the stranger for a moment, but then spotted him at the narrow entrance to a lane at the right-hand side of the square. The passage was behind one of the stalls, so that no one else had noticed the wizard there. Karl ran, fell on his knees, struggled back to his feet, and continued running. The lane wound its way past several brick buildings and grew increasingly narrow. Finally it ended in a small yard full of trash. Trying to catch his breath, Karl was walking past a stack of barrels when he tripped over a foot. The man in the black-and-blue coat towered above him, a rock in his raised fist. His eyes looked like those of a hunted animal.

"Damned bastard," snarled the stranger. "Leave me alone! Why don't you all leave me—"

"Faustus!" exclaimed Karl.

The name had just popped into his mind, and with the name memories rained down on him like a warm shower. Karl laughed and cried at the same time. The man in front of him was like a messenger from a distant era, an angel come to bring him back to life, waking him from the slumber that had lasted two whole years. The fact that this angel was an unkempt old codger who reeked of schnapps and wine didn't bother him in the least.

"Lord in heaven, it is you. Doctor Johann Georg Faustus! Praise be to God!"

The wizard stepped back as if he'd been struck by a blow. He dropped the rock. Then, with an abrupt movement, he grabbed Karl by the collar and pulled him so close that Karl could smell his alcohol-infused breath.

"How do you know my name? Who told you my name? Who? Someone from the church? A French spy? Speak up, man!"

"No one," gasped Karl. "I know your name because . . ." He faltered. "Because I . . . because I am your assistant. Don't you recognize me? It's me, your loyal Karl. Karl Wagner, the student from Leipzig." He squeezed the talisman around his neck hard. "God Himself must have brought us back together. Finally I remember who I was—who I am. Praise be . . ."

Then he broke off, sobbing, overcome by a flood of tears, longing, and memories.

Karl Wagner had found his master again.

A short while later, two ragged men sat opposite each other in a tavern down by the river. One of the men still cried soundlessly, and the other one was drinking himself into a stupor. Very little light got in through the spiderwebs covering the windows; the hazy outline of the Pyrenees stood on the horizon.

Through a cascade of tears Karl studied the doctor, whom he had recognized by his black eyes and the black-and-blue coat. Faust had aged in the last two years, appearing empty, drained. A long shaggy beard that reminded Karl of a rabbi's covered his face, and Johann's hair was matted. The red veins on his nose told Karl that the doctor was a slave to a very particular devil. A large jug of cheap wine stood between them. Instead of a lordly carriage and numerous crates and chests, Johann's worldly possessions consisted of one old leather sack holding a few items for his magic tricks, and the coat, which he'd probably had made as a sign of his trade. The doctor's hand shook as he lifted the cup to his mouth.

"What a strange coincidence that has brought us back together," he murmured through his beard.

"Coincidence?" Karl shook his head. "I no longer believe in coincidences. This is a miracle—an act of providence."

"Or an act of the devil." Johann laughed dryly. "What happened to the ambitious young scientist who wants to explain everything with reason? Even heaven and hell, if he can?" He paused. "You haven't seen what I have seen. And you don't know what I know."

"What about your illness?" asked Karl. "Your paralysis?" He studied the doctor with the eyes of a physician. "You no longer seem to be burdened by it. If it disappeared, it must have been a miracle. Or did you find a cure in the end?"

"Some . . . something like that."

Karl swallowed and wiped his wet face with his sleeve. He didn't have the impression that Johann was happy to see him. The shabby tavern they were sitting in, not far from the pilgrims' hostel, served as the doctor's accommodation in Toulouse. Evidently he still traveled the lands as a magician, even if he called himself by a different name now and was but a shadow of his former self. To help himself fill the gaps in his memory, Karl had spent the last two hours quizzing the doctor about details. Their journeys through the German Empire with Greta, then Faust's mysterious disease, their escape to France, and their stay at Leonardo da Vinci's. The answers had come haltingly, frequently interrupted by long gulps from the cup of wine that Johann kept refilling. The further Karl progressed in his recollection, the more close-lipped Faust became.

"We were down in the crypt at Tiffauges," continued Karl hesitantly. "You wanted to meet Gilles de Rais. We drank the black potion."

Johann nodded hastily. "That's what must have erased your memory." His eyes became empty and he took another long sip. "Lucky you."

"What happened to John Reed? Did he also come to Tiffauges?"

"He . . . he died fighting Hagen and the other mercenaries in the crypt. God rest his soul." The doctor lowered his gaze, and Karl was surprised at Faust's apparent grief over the death of the red-haired man. Karl, too, felt grief, even though he had half expected that John was dead.

"But at least you managed to escape," Karl went on. "And me?"

"Lahnstein and his men stormed the castle. They had no use for you," suggested Johann. "So they probably left you for dead."

"But then how did I get to Nantes, to the Benedictines? Someone must have cared for me and brought me there."

Karl clasped the small amulet on his neck as if it might give him the answer. Once again it was as warm as if it was made of flesh and blood. Johann noticed the alabaster angel for the first time, and his eyes narrowed.

"Where did you get that?" he asked quietly.

"I don't know," replied Karl. "I remember so much now, but not that part. Can you tell me?"

Johann said nothing for a while, and then he answered. "It . . . it was Greta's. An old midwife in Brittany gave it to her."

Until then they hadn't spoken about what had become of Greta, as if they both feared that there would be no return. Karl saw Johann's face darken, and in the same moment he felt a stab in his heart. He thought of the image he had drawn many times, the crying young woman reaching out for him. It was Greta. She had visited him once after he was poisoned, and she gave him the amulet. Karl focused, allowing the memories to return. In his mind's eye he saw a dungeon, at Tiffauges. Then he remembered a phrase that had been spoken there.

I'm going to Rome, Karl.

"I don't want to talk about Greta," said Johann in a defeated voice as he waved his empty cup at the tavern keeper. "I've said everything there is to say. It will be for the best if we go our separate—"

"So you already know that she went to Rome?" asked Karl abruptly.

"What did you say?"

"I think I remember now. She wanted to go to Rome—she told me so herself."

"To . . . to *Rome*?" The cup slipped from Johann's hands and banged loudly on the ground. "Greta is dead. She burned with the others at Tiffauges—there couldn't have been another way. I . . . I had nothing to bargain with, and so she had to burn with the other heretics."

"She went to Rome." Karl closed his eyes, thinking hard. "I remember now. Lahnstein must have offered her a deal. He needed her alive. I don't know why . . ." He broke off. There was something else Greta had told him down in the dungeons, but Karl couldn't remember for the life of him. Now he clearly saw Greta before him again, extending her arms to him and giving him one last kiss on the forehead.

I'm going to Rome, Karl.

"Greta isn't dead," whispered Johann, more to himself. He gave Karl a pleading look. "Are you certain?"

Karl nodded. "That was what she told me. She was going to Rome, that much I remember. I'm guessing it must have been she who brought me to the Benedictines—"

He stopped when he noticed the doctor was crying.

Tears streamed down his face as he muttered the same words over and over. "Greta is alive. My daughter is alive. I had given up hope."

For the first time, Karl thought he could see the old Johann Georg Faustus behind the shaggy beard.

The man he still loved.

~

Hundreds of miles away, a solitary man was standing on a terrace high above the city the people called Urbs Aeterna.

The Eternal City.

He gazed down on houses several stories high, on churches, crumbling temples, ruins, and newly erected palaces, spreading in all directions. In the haze beyond lay fields, villages, and the Alban Hills; the stinking brown Tiber cut through the city like a knife. In one place the river took a sharp turn to the west, and that was where the man stood atop a mighty round building. Up in this lofty terrace the air was fresh, despite the muggy summer heat, and a light breeze carried the scents of mistletoe and chestnut. The man sniffed and thought he could smell a thunderstorm.

He loved thunderstorms.

The man raised his arms and let the energy flow through his body, the crackling atmosphere that preceded every great storm. The place upon which the building stood was old, ancient; from before the first Roman emperors, yes, even before the shepherds led their goats across the seven hills, this place had been a powerful one, drenched with blood and filled with screams. Perhaps that was why Emperor Hadrian chose it as the site for his tomb. Later, the building was besieged by barbarians, who were struck down by the statues of Roman gods that were flung at them. Now the building served the pope as a place of retreat and domicile. The man chuckled softly when he thought about the name of the building.

Castel Sant'Angelo.

The castle of angels.

A name had never been better chosen.

The man bared his teeth like a wolf, pointing his nose into the wind. Everything was going basically to plan, even if it went much slower than originally anticipated. But what did a few years matter when one could think in eons? They had thrown him from the heavens, but he would come back. Stronger and more powerful than ever, as a ruler over a burning world that had doomed itself. Chaos, not order, was the mother of all that was.

Because everything that is deserves to perish.

Yes, there had been setbacks. Faust hadn't come to him, and the doctor hadn't given him that which he longed for so desperately. But he sensed that the final word hadn't been spoken.

They always had to come voluntarily.

One of them was nearly ready, and Faust, too, would soon return to him. The disease had been nothing but a gentle kiss, a reminder that their pact was still valid. And little Faustus had paid—at least a first installment.

The man on the terrace only had to wait.

Because he had in his control that which the doctor loved the most. And love had always been man's greatest weakness.

Lightning flashed across the sky, and then the first drops of rain fell on the face of the master. He leaned back his head and opened his mouth wide, and there was a hissing noise like from a giant snake.

The bells in the many churches of town chimed for eventide.

~

During the next few days, Johann was torn by impatience and insecurity. He felt like he had been sleeping for years and needed to make up for lost time quickly. How could he have believed that Greta was dead?

He was riding an old donkey because the money hadn't been enough for a horse. Karl Wagner, his former assistant, was walking beside him, occasionally smacking the stubborn beast across the backside with a stick. Both men were freshly shaved and wore new, if poor, clothes and wide-brimmed pilgrims' hats. They looked determined and somewhat transfigured, their faces haggard. The people who passed them thought they were ascetics, pious pilgrims on their way to Rome in search of enlightenment.

And they weren't entirely wrong.

Three days ago Johann and Karl had left Toulouse and headed east. For the first time in a long time Johann felt the wind, the rain, and the sun on his skin. The news that Greta might still be alive had rejuvenated him. The old thirst for action was back, the perpetual restlessness, the eternal dissatisfaction. He needed to get to Rome as fast as humanly possible. Rome was where his daughter's trail had ended, but he would pick it up again. He needed to beg Greta's forgiveness, explain everything to her. Maybe then they could be together again.

For two years Johann had wandered aimlessly through France, like Karl. But while Karl had strived to regain his memory, Johann had tried to forget everything with homemade theriac, potent brandy, wine in copious quantities.

Working under false names and with cheap magic tricks, he had earned a little money and drunk like a fish. It had been the only way to keep the nightmares at bay for a little while, the only way to suppress the guilt he had laden upon himself. Johann didn't know if he could ever bring himself to tell Karl what had really happened at Tiffauges. He had said nothing about almost killing Karl, and had not mentioned brutally stabbing John to death nor that his disease appeared to have vanished because of this horrific sacrifice. Nor had he told Karl about the secret he had been hoarding since then.

The secret of the silver globe.

Johann always carried with him the tiny pendant he had found inside Leonardo da Vinci's stomach. Not around his neck, as he was too afraid it might get stolen from there, but well hidden inside a leather satchel upon which he slept at night and which was now tied to the donkey's neck. Inside the pendant was still the thin tissue paper that Leonardo had hidden so well and that Tonio del Moravia would have loved to possess. In the first few weeks Johann had daily considered destroying the paper, simply burning it and watching the ashes float to the ground. It would have made the world a better place. And yet he didn't do it. He didn't do it for the very same reason that had made him seek the secret in the first place.

It was his pawn in the game with the devil.

Greta or the world? Which is more important?

Johann had pondered this question over and over, but as he had become convinced that Greta was dead, he had kept the globe. And now, it would seem, its contents could still be of use to him.

Greta or the world?

The swaying of the donkey made him slightly seasick; he felt as though he was on a ship far out on a stormy ocean. Johann closed his eyes. In the last two years, he had researched at several libraries and monasteries, had leafed through ancient books and studied pages of brittle parchment and papyrus. And his fears had been confirmed. In the wrong hands, what was written on the tissue paper had the power to throw the world into chaos.

"Do you remember how we escaped from that horrible Hagen at Chinon by a hair's breadth?" asked Karl, tearing Johann from his thoughts.

They were traveling along the Via Tolosana, an old pilgrimage route between Arles and Santiago de Compostela, where the apostle Saint James lay buried. The snow-covered peaks of the Pyrenees lined the horizon behind them. They were passing through a shadowy forest of oaks, offering some shelter from the sun, which burned mercilessly this far south. The air was unbearably muggy. There wasn't a breath of wind, and the woods stood in silence, except for the perpetual chirping of cicadas.

Karl shook his head. "I still can't believe the pope really thought you could make gold." He laughed out loud, which sounded strange in the stillness of the forest. "Did you ever hear from Viktor von Lahnstein or Hagen again? Or the French king? Seems like they gave up chasing after you."

"Seems like it," said Johann.

"Do you think that might have been the reason why Lahnstein took Greta to Rome? Because he was hoping to lure you there?"

Johann said nothing. It wasn't a wholly implausible thought, and it had crossed his mind, too. But then why had Lahnstein never tried to get in contact with him? As far as Johann knew, no one had ever searched for him again—a circumstance he'd found puzzling for a long time. It was as if the papal representative had suddenly lost all interest in him.

"The past no longer matters," he said to Karl eventually. "All that counts is the future. And our future is called Rome."

Johann kicked his heels hard into the donkey's sides. The animal bucked grumpily and then took off at a fast trot toward the sea that lay somewhere ahead of them.

Their journey led them to Carcassonne, the ancient fortress by the river Aude where, three hundred years earlier, the bloody Albigensian Crusade against the Cathars had taken place. Then, many followers of the Cathari beliefs managed to escape, but a few decades later, hundreds of them burned on an enormous pyre at the fortress of Montségur. Johann involuntarily thought of the mass immolation at Tiffauges. There, true heretics had been burned, followers of the devil who, with the aid of gruesome rituals, had somehow managed to prolong their lives. Johann had witnessed the deaths of or killed their most important leaders: Poitou, Henriet, Prelati the priest, and the horrible La Meffraye. But their former master was still somewhere out there. A shiver ran down Johann's spine despite the heat.

Where are you, Tonio?

The many people walking toward them in the lanes beneath the fortress, laughing, chatting, on their way to their business or their loved ones, suddenly appeared unreal to Johann. His eyes turned to the battlements above them, where several ravens and crows circled in the sky. Were Tonio's messengers among them? Sooner or later Johann would have to face up to his old enemy, he didn't doubt it. But not now. He wasn't going to make the same mistake as before.

The only thing that mattered now was his daughter.

From Carcassonne they traveled to Montpellier, where they could already smell the sea, and from there to Arles. Here, the pilgrimage routes to Santiago de Compostela in the west and to Rome in the east met, and consequently, the streets in and around town were bustling with pilgrims. They all wore the typical garb of brown woolen coats and wide hats, so Johann and Karl blended right in. Between the houses stood remains of old Roman palaces and theaters, which the locals used as quarries. Inside the Cathedral of Saint Trophime, the pilgrims knelt before the grave of a former archbishop where several miracles had reportedly occurred. Karl joined the long line in front of the tomb, while Johann waited for him in the shade outside. He hadn't prayed in years. He had forgotten how to, while now his assistant didn't miss any opportunity.

Johann had noticed that Karl was no longer the sensible rationalist he used to be. It seemed as if the years of madness had led him to God. Thankfully, Karl still couldn't remember everything that had happened at Tiffauges, but Johann suspected that somewhere, deep down inside Karl, still resided the images of the horned one, the creature whose presence they had both felt in the well below the church.

The black potion will lead you to him, little Faustus. You are his favorite.

Back then he would have sacrificed Karl without batting an eyelid. Now Johann was glad to have Karl by his side, even if he'd been reluctant at first. He had been alone for so long that he no longer knew what company meant. Johann sensed that Karl loved and needed him more, but the younger man's presence gave him the feeling of leading a seminormal life again. Yes, he was glad Karl was with him. Karl reminded him of the time before Tiffauges, and also a little bit of himself a long time ago.

Something cawed, and Johann looked up. A crow flew past his head and landed on a stone step outside the cathedral.

Johann picked up a stone and threw it at the bird, which rose into the air with a caw and flew away. In the last two years he hadn't paid much attention to ravens and crows—he'd been too busy trying to stay on his feet or sleeping off the booze. But since he'd quit drinking, he noticed the birds again. They seemed to follow him.

Or was he following them, like in the Loire Valley and on their journey to Tiffauges?

Johann had a hunch that Tonio was still closer to him than he'd thought.

When Karl emerged from the cathedral, he gazed pensively at Johann. "I can tell that you're brooding. It's about Tonio again, isn't it? He won't let you go. You're afraid that he is in Rome. With Greta."

"It's nothing," replied Johann, shaking his head, trying to smile. "The sun is burning too hotly, that's all."

It was one of the many small lies he used to once again build up a wall between himself and the world.

20

NEARLY TWO MONTHS LATER THEY FINALLY REACHED THE outskirts of Rome.

Their beards had grown back, the blisters on their feet had healed into hard calluses, and their skin was as brown as tanned leather. Even though their wide-brimmed hats scarcely shielded them from the hot September sun, Johann strode ahead vigorously. They had sold the stubborn donkey a while ago because Johann no longer needed it. His old strength returned with every mile they drew nearer to Rome. The city was surrounded by fields, though many of them were barren and abandoned. Decrepit villas told of wealthy landowners from long ago. Shepherds pushed their goats across the overgrown roads, which used to be wide enough for two carts to pass one another. Now thistles, mint, and rosemary grew in the gaps of the pavers, and the Roman milestones stood crookedly in the ground.

The closer they got to the city, the more ruins they saw in the hills. Some of them looked like ancient heathen temples or mausoleums, while others used to be magnificent summer residences. The houses still seemed to be occupied—not, however, by rich patricians. Women in threadbare, dirty clothing peered out from behind animal hides covering the windows, their men dragging plows across dry, karstic fields where once upon a time luscious gardens and olive groves had flourished. Rising into the sky beyond, like plague boils on the body of an incurably sick man, were the hills of Rome.

Johann tried to imagine how splendid this city must have been once. Urbs Aeterna. The center of the world! But centuries had passed since, many different armies had assaulted the city with sword and fire, and not much was left of its former glory. Still, the sight of the city filled Johann with a deep longing, as if he were returning to a place he'd left behind many lives ago.

Now they could see a high bridge made of stone spanning the landscape. "One of the famous aqueducts," said Johann excitedly to Karl, who was holding up his hand against the blinding sun.

Even though it was nearly October, temperatures were still extremely hot. Johann pointed at the arches of the bridge, which was crumbling in many places even as it stretched across the landscape like a snake.

"Once upon a time, the aqueducts brought water from faraway to the city. There were baths, cold ones as well as warm ones heated with fire in underground stoves. Those baths were huge basins created for the enjoyment of all Romans—poor and rich, men and women. They were called thermal baths." He gave a sigh. "So many things disappeared with the Romans, and it is going take a very long time before those accomplishments return—if ever."

"But those Romans also used to set wild animals on Christians in their circuses," said Karl. "And they loved to watch as gladiators brutally killed each other. Rather barbaric, if you ask me."

Johann nodded. "Man carries both sides within himself—he is angel and demon at once." Quietly he added, "Who'd know better than me?"

They had come down the Via Francigena, the old pilgrimage route that led into the holy city from the north. From Arles their road had led first to Genoa and then to Pisa, then across the Apennine Mountains, which Johann knew from his previous journey through Italy. Back then he had traveled with a troupe of jugglers, performing shows in every city and town. Now, too, war raged in Italy, powerful rulers fighting for predominance in Europe. The German emperor had allied with Pope Leo X and the king of England against France, and Milan was close to falling back to the empire. Many times in recent weeks Johann and Karl had passed refugees carrying their few belongings and dragging along snotty-nosed, whining children.

Johann lifted his head tiredly and looked around. The dusty road had steadily filled with travelers since the morning. Many were clad in pilgrims' garb like he and Karl wore. Some shuffled toward the walls of Rome on their knees and with lowered heads, while others sang loudly or prayed rosaries along the way. Johann listened to the monotonous litanies and emotional pleas; from his time in Venice as a young juggler, he spoke a little Italian. But he also heard a few German voices, Spanish ones, French speakers, and even a few Englishmen. The world still came together in Rome.

They entered the city through a tall old gate made of bronze that hung crookedly on its hinges. Johann instantly struggled with the stink. They had already smelled it out in the fields, hanging above the landscape like a toxic cloud. Now it was so intense that Johann breathed only though his mouth. Once upon a time, the Cloaca Maxima flushed the excrement of thousands of Romans into the Tiber, but that was long ago. These days, trash and feces, as well as human and animal remains, simply stayed in the narrow, winding lanes. Ragged beggars, crippled soldiers, garishly made-up whores, and other dubious figures hung about the corners, hungrily watching the travelers and pilgrims who poured into the city hour after hour. It was a loud and steady stream in which Johann and Karl drifted like corks, past ruins, hastily erected barracks, and derelict temples taken apart for building materials. In between, cattle grazed on overgrown spaces among headless statues. There were monuments everywhere, immortalizing deities whose names had long been forgotten.

The deeper they went into the center of the city, the more they also saw newly built churches, monasteries, and palaces. In the distance they saw a large unfinished structure on the other side of the Tiber. Scaffolding and cranes with pulleys stood on a large square, and several stone arches rose behind them. A mountain of rubble told of a previous building.

"The new Saint Peter's Basilica," said Johann to Karl. "Leo's pride and joy, and perhaps his downfall, too. Pope Julius started the project. Leo wants to complete the basilica as fast as possible as a monument to himself. But now he's lacking the money from the trade with indulgences from the empire." Johann chuckled. "No wonder he's trying to make gold. This Luther truly came at the wrong time for him."

In the last two years, the writings of Martin Luther had spread through the empire like wildfire, and to many Germans, the pope had become the symbol of the Antichrist. In the eyes of those Germans, Rome stood for decadence, whoring, and debauchery. The pope had excommunicated Luther, but the former monk enjoyed the protection of many German rulers, most notably the Saxon prince-elector Friedrich. Only this year Luther had been permitted to defend his theses once more at the diet at Worms, following which the emperor imposed an imperial ban upon him. Since then Luther had vanished, possibly with the aid of Prince-Elector Friedrich.

"I wonder if Pope Leo still wants you as an alchemist and manufacturer of gold?" said Karl.

Johann shrugged. "We should keep a low profile, in any case. We are God-fearing pilgrims, nothing else." He gestured to the east. "I heard that German pilgrims like to take lodgings near the Piazza Navona. There's some kind of German community with craftsmen, taverns, and a newly built German church. I think we should find somewhere to stay there and keep an ear out."

"Keep an ear out for what?" asked Karl. "For news of a German girl named Greta who came to Rome about two years ago? There are probably as many poor German girls in Rome as statues of the Virgin Mary."

"I know," snarled Johann. "But it's a start, isn't it?"

Johann hadn't put much thought into the question of how they were supposed to find Greta in the maze of Roman alleys. Hope alone had brought him this far, but now, among thousands of people, their undertaking seemed utterly foolish. Greta could be anywhere and nowhere. She might not even be in Rome any longer.

Or no longer be alive, thought Johann with a pang.

At least it proved to be easy to merge with the crowd among all the German pilgrims. Around the Piazza Navona a variety of German and Germanic dialects could be heard—like Swabian, Tyrolean, Dutch, and Bavarian. It was as if they were walking through a city in Germany. Johann and Karl took a room at an inn near the square and soon sat in the taproom over a sparse meal. Johann took his wine thinned with water now; during the last two years, he had drunk enough to last a lifetime.

"So, what do we know?" he began, chewing on a piece of salty ewe's cheese and pushing the loaf of bread toward Karl. "Viktor von Lahnstein brought my daughter to Rome with him. Why?"

"If his plan was to lure you to Rome that way, he didn't make much of an effort to let you know," replied Karl.

"'You must return to me of your own free will,'" murmured Johann.

"What did you say?"

"'You must return to me of your own free will,'" repeated Johann. "That was what Tonio told me back at Nuremberg. Remember? It's the only way for the pact to succeed. It's an ancient rule."

"So . . . so you're saying that Tonio is behind all this?" asked Karl with disbelief. "*He* wants to lure you to Rome?"

"I don't know, damn it! But he abducted my daughter before. Maybe he's done it again with the help of Lahnstein? Tonio has a score to settle with me and—" Johann broke off.

"What is it?" asked Karl.

And I own something he desperately wishes to have.

He still hadn't told Karl about the tiny silver globe and its baleful contents—in part because he hadn't made up his mind whether to give the globe to Tonio after all.

In exchange for my daughter.

"I think it's quite enough for God's representative on earth to be involved. The devil doesn't need to be part of it also," said Karl, shaking his head. "No, I believe Lahnstein wanted to strike you where it hurts the most. Greta is his revenge for what you did to him in Bamberg. He takes your daughter, but instead of killing her, he . . ." Karl closed his eyes, trying to focus. "Back at Tiffauges when I saw Greta for the last time, she was no prisoner. In hindsight it seems to me like she went with Lahnstein voluntarily. But why?"

"It's no use." Johann rose. "We must make inquiries. If need be, even among the papal staff. We must find out what became of Lahnstein. Perhaps he's the key to all our questions."

"That means risking attracting the attention of that horrible Hagen again," said Karl. "This is their city, don't forget."

"I haven't forgotten." Johann nodded glumly. "But it's about the life of my daughter and the part I played in getting her here. I must right my wrongs no matter the risk."

It took a few days for Johann to find his bearings in this city. He had been to many large cities before—Nuremberg, Augsburg, Venice—but Rome was different, inspiring and draining at once. Enormous ruins rose at every corner, the imposing Colosseum only one of many. Rome was like a wasteland where thousands of new blossoms sprouted from the earth. Under the rule of the last two popes especially, plentiful new and magnificent churches and palaces had been erected, but in between, the citizens continued to live in foul-smelling hovels. Johann soon noticed that vast parts of the city were barely inhabited. Once he left the larger streets and pilgrimage sites behind, the city became eerily quiet, like a moor or a forest. Since the water supply had broken down, some of the hills the city was built upon were practically deserted, beyond a few beggars and thieves. On the other hand, the quarter on the far bank of the Tiber and the area around Vatican Hill flourished, and a multitude of tradesmen and officials had settled there in the vicinity of the papal palaces.

Karl and Johann soon learned that it was nearly impossible to enter the Mons Vaticanus. It was surrounded by a high wall, and the gates were manned by Swiss guards. Cardinals and other high-ranking dignitaries came and went all the time, so Johann thought it possible that Viktor von Lahnstein, as papal representative, also lived within those walls. But where was Greta? How would they ever find out? The pope himself only rarely appeared in public. The next occasion wouldn't be until All Saints' Day at the start of November—more than four weeks from now.

Karl had taken up drawing again. He used every spare hour to roam the hills and capture with charcoal the many ruins, churches, and statues. In addition, he was working on a map to help them find their way through the labyrinth of Roman lanes. His map showed the city not from the side, as was customary, but from above—a technique Karl had learned from Leonardo da Vinci. During the daytime, they visited the various quarters among the hills, asking people in the streets and at pilgrims' hostels about a blonde German girl named Greta, but without success. In the evening, they would sit over Karl's map in silence, brooding, their hopes fading.

"If Greta went with Lahnstein voluntarily, then he had plans for her," said Karl. "Then it would be likely that she's somewhere near him."

"Which would be on Vatican Hill." Johann groaned and tapped his finger on the map. "It's a huge area and well guarded."

"So were the Nuremberg dungeons, and we still managed to get in," said Karl. "Why shouldn't we do it again?" He smiled. "You're a wizard, remember?"

"I'm afraid my time as a great magician is over," said Johann glumly. "I'm a drunk whose hands shake even doing the simplest card tricks."

Increasingly, they went their separate ways. Karl liked to visit the wealth of churches, admiring the frescoes and altars, many of them created during the reign of the current pope. It was as if Leo X was trying to build not only a new basilica but an entire new city as a monument to himself—a city that was still laced with heathen beliefs.

"This morning, I went past the Mons Palatinus," said Karl one evening as they sat together over bread, olives, and cheese. "There, some commoners still pray to Romulus and Remus." He shook his head. "Allegedly, there are remains of a cave where the two brothers were nursed by a she-wolf. What a ridiculous notion!"

"Really?" Johann smiled. "Weren't those brothers abandoned as infants and washed ashore in a willow basket on the banks of the Tiber? And didn't Romulus kill his brother later on before founding Rome?"

"Yes, I think that's how the story goes." Karl frowned. "Why?"

"Well, Moses was also abandoned in a willow basket on a river, and Cain killed his brother, Abel. So, the one story is a ridiculous notion while the other is true belief? Where is the difference?"

"Debating with you is probably more exhausting than debating that Luther."

"I'm not debating, merely posing questions," replied Johann. "Just like the Greek philosopher Socrates used to do. Questions bring light to the darkness of the world."

Unlike Karl, Johann avoided the churches. They offered no consolation to him; on the contrary. Whenever Johann stood before a crucifix, he thought he could feel the Savior's sad eyes on him. At night, when Karl was asleep, Johann often took out the silver globe, wondering if he oughtn't destroy its contents after all. If Tonio was the one who'd lured him to Rome, then the master would find him.

And with him, the globe.

Following yet another sleepless night, Johann decided to do something he hadn't done since childhood. He made the decision as he stood outside the Santa Maria dell'Anima Church, the German church near the Piazza Navona. It was after sunset, but the church door was still open.

Johann took a deep breath and entered the gloomy building; unlike many other churches in town, it had been built in the old-fashioned German style. Johann headed straight for the confessionals, in the eastern transept. Inside one of them flickered the light of a candle. Johann closed the small door behind him and sat down on the bench. He could vaguely make out the silhouette of a person through the wooden partition.

"*In nomine Patris et Filii et Spiritus Sancti. Amen,*" said Johann, reciting the ancient formula.

"May God, who guides our way, give you true insight of your sins and of His forgiveness," sounded a male voice with a soft Franconian accent.

Johann began haltingly. "Father, I . . . I have sinned. More than most people could imagine."

"God's grace is infinite if you show remorse," said the priest gently. "Relieve your conscience."

"I . . . I only ever thought of myself and . . . and let nobody get in my way."

"Are you saying that you . . . ?"

"That I have killed, yes," said Johann. "Not with evil intent, however—I was . . . I was drugged. The man my daughter loved died by my hand. I wish I could undo it. But that's not all." He swallowed. "Others have died because I chose the wrong path, because I placed knowledge and learning above the commandment of love. Those I loved the most had to suffer. My path is paved with ill luck and pain, Father. With restlessness and discontent. But my intentions were always for the best. The devil is reaching out for me, even now."

"Who else did you kill?" asked the priest.

"Father, I have a question," said Johann quickly. "It is this question which brought me here. What weighs more heavily? The life of one's own child or that of humanity?"

"What sort of a question is that?" sounded the surprised voice of the priest. "Murder is always a deadly sin."

Johann leaned forward until his lips nearly touched the wooden partition. He spoke very quietly now. "May I save my daughter if doing so puts the lives of many others at risk? Imagine—just theoretically—that the devil offers you a pact. Your own daughter or mankind? Jesus died at the cross to save us all. He sacrificed himself for us. Does that mean I must also sacrifice my daughter?"

"That . . . that is blasphemy!" exclaimed the priest. "Watch your tongue, my son!"

"You didn't answer my question."

"Because it cannot be answered. One life weighs as much as any other. Think of the words of Jesus Christ. 'What you did to the least of my brothers, you did to me.'"

Johann said nothing for a few moments. "I . . . I'm sorry," he said after a while. "I shouldn't have come. It was a mistake."

He was about to leave the confessional, but then he sat back down, the words pouring out of him.

"And yet the church sacrifices people. By the thousands! She forces her sheep into so-called holy wars, murdering and looting in order to follow the true path. How many men and women have been burned to death innocently or fallen on the battlefields? How many Christians have been sacrificed for the true faith?" Johann's voice had grown louder and could be heard outside the confessionals now. "The end justifies the means—isn't that what they say? That which holds true for the pope and his followers ought to apply to the belief in reason also, to science. Why can inquisitors like Viktor von Lahnstein elevate themselves above others, kidnapping and murdering in the name of the church, while the common folk aren't permitted to do any of those things? God says nothing about that!"

"You . . . you are confused, son," replied the priest, shuffling uncomfortably on his bench behind the partition. "Stop before you burden yourself with more deadly sins!"

"I have laden so many deadly sins upon myself, one more won't matter. Save your breath, Father. I am the only one who can forgive myself. *Homo Deus est.*"

With those words, Johann stormed out of the confessional, down the nave, and out into the dark street. He was so full of anger. At the same time he cursed himself for his stupidity. How could he have believed that he would find solace and answers in a church, of all places? The church had taken his daughter from him, just like it had done with his beloved years ago. For centuries Christianity had been nothing but a pawn in the hands of power-hungry despots who thought only of their own interests. Pope Leo was just a link in a long chain. The popes had never cared for the people. The individual man was nothing to them.

Only then did Johann realize that he had used the same words in the confessional that Tonio and his men used to say. It had been their motto.

Homo Deus est.

Man is his own god. Johann couldn't expect any help or advice from above. At least that insight had come out of his church visit.

He had to decide for himself what was right and what was wrong.

~

Father Sebastian Keuchlin stayed sitting in the confessional for a long while after the stranger had left. Cold sweat stood on his forehead. Who in God's name had that been? Keuchlin had never experienced such a confession. Usually, God-fearing German pilgrims came to see him because they had broken the commandment of abstinence and spent their money on wine, women, and song instead of donating it to the mother church. Yes, even murderers and thieves had visited him before to confess their sins, but never a sinner like the one who had just been here. The man had sounded like a scholar, practiced in argument, a magister or doctor, perhaps. But something else had resonated from him, almost like a force of evil.

Keuchlin shuddered. And what about those last words? *Homo Deus est.* They sounded like a battle cry. The fellow was not just a murderer but also a heretic.

But something else bothered Keuchlin even more.

The stranger had mentioned Viktor von Lahnstein.

Sebastian Keuchlin wasn't just a plain confessor. He was a member of the brotherhood of Santa Maria dell'Anima, a college of seven chaplains who were responsible for the well-being of the German pilgrims in Rome. In addition, Keuchlin was a close confidant of the papal curia. He had served under Johannes Burckard, the former papal master of ceremonies, who had introduced his young ward Sebastian to the higher circles. Circles also frequented by Viktor von Lahnstein. There weren't many who personally knew the creepy inquisitor—known as "the pope's mastiff" behind his back. In an accident, Lahnstein had lost his nose, making him look somewhat like a dog. Keuchlin shook himself with repulsion. It was kind of fitting for a Dominican—one of the *domini canes*, the dogs of the Lord, as those stern inquisitors were often called.

In the last two years, Lahnstein had vanished almost completely from the scene while at the same time rising to be Leo's personal adjutant—even though no one could say with certainty what it was that he did. And now a crazy stranger turns up and mentions his name. Was it supposed to be a threat?

Sebastian Keuchlin respected the seal of confession, but he also knew what loyalty meant. Santa Maria dell'Anima Church wasn't completed—funds were lacking since that awful Luther preached about the "whore of Rome."

Everything has its price.

Keuchlin wiped the sweat off his forehead once more. The stranger wasn't entirely wrong. The church had to make certain sacrifices for the good of Christianity.

The chaplain squeezed his corpulent body out of the confessional, hurried down the dark nave, and waddled over to the hospice gardens, where his humble abode stood. There, he sat down at his desk and wrote a long letter to His Eminence the papal inquisitor Viktor von Lahnstein.

He felt certain that it wouldn't be to the detriment of the German church in Rome.

21

STEADILY THE CHARCOAL PEN FOLLOWED ITS COURSE, crosshatching here, filling in there, tweaking one line or another. The face of the Mother of God held all the pain in the world, and yet there was solace, too. Mary was holding her grown-up son in her arms like a babe, cradling him, singing him to sleep like an infant. A magical aura seemed to shine from both figures, soothing Karl, as art did for him so often. And this artwork in front of him was the most perfect he had ever seen.

It was the most beautiful sculpture in the world.

With a sigh, Karl put down pen and parchment and focused entirely on the almost life-sized marble pietà before him. He knew that he would never be able to create anything so beautiful, but the act of copying it with a piece of charcoal gave him a deep sense of satisfaction, putting him in a state of contemplation that, he guessed, monks achieved through prayer.

The pietà stood in a side chapel of Saint Peter's, concealed from the eyes of most believers who visited Saint Peter's Square on a daily basis despite the construction work. The tomb of Saint Peter himself lay nearby. A Roman cardinal had commissioned the marble sculpture shortly before his death, requesting the artist create the most beautiful statue in Rome. Not an easy feat considering the large number of outstanding sculptures in the city.

And yet the artist, a certain Michelangelo Buonarroti, had succeeded.

Karl had heard about this Michelangelo before. During the last few years, he had risen to the top of Italian sculptors, just like Raffaello used to be considered the greatest painter in Rome, until he'd died unexpectedly the year before. Leonardo da Vinci had told Karl about Michelangelo and Raffaello. Leonardo's grudging remarks had been tinged with the subtle jealousy typical of old masters faced with talented young apprentices. Looking at Michelangelo's pietà, Karl could understand Leonardo's envy.

For weeks now Karl had been visiting the churches of Rome, drawing anything he laid his eyes on. He would have loved to own a pair of eye glasses like he used to have, but the specially cut pieces of glass were simply too expensive. Even so, drawing helped him to gradually regain his old life. Every day, with every stroke, more memories returned. And it took his mind off the unsolvable task before them.

Greta, where are you? Are you still alive? Do you remember your old friend Karl?

Karl's hand went to the little guardian angel at his neck. Deep down, he had given up hope of ever finding Greta. No one had heard of her—no innkeeper, no pilgrim, not even the whores. Maybe he had been mistaken. Maybe she hadn't traveled to Rome with Lahnstein. In some ways he had doubted the success of their mission since Toulouse, but had followed Johann to Rome nonetheless. Something tied him to the doctor that Karl couldn't explain. Rationally speaking, Faust was too old to be physically attractive to Karl. It was something far greater than sexual attraction—something that went beyond human love.

It was devotion.

Karl still didn't know what, exactly, had happened between him and Faust in the crypt below Tiffauges. It must have been something so terrible that his mind refused to this day to release the memories. As much as Karl loved the doctor, he also sensed that he was harming himself with this love. He had to leave the doctor before he became the end of Karl.

The only question was when.

The church bells started to toll loudly, startling Karl. He had completely forgotten the time. Today was the first of November, All Saints' Day, and therewith the day of the papal procession they had been awaiting for weeks. So far, they hadn't caught a single glimpse of the pope or his inner circle. But today the opportunity would finally arise. In honor of the saints, Leo X had organized a procession with his entire court from Saint Peter's to the Lateran Basilica, where the popes used to reside before their exile at Avignon. Leo was well known for his spectacular processions, and there were rumors that coins would be tossed into the crowds. No wonder the streets along the procession's route had been filled with people since the break of day. Johann and Karl had agreed to meet at the Sant'Angelo Bridge at the stroke of noon, and Karl knew how angry the doctor became when people didn't keep appointments, especially in matters as important as this one.

He quickly packed his drawing utensils into his small leather bag and hurried to the chapel's exit. Outside, people thronged toward the procession in masses; evidently the event had already begun. Karl heard trumpets, drums, and scattered cheers. Cursing, he rushed across the building site, an obstacle course of scaffolds, cranes, sacks of lime, and rocks.

He was about to turn onto the wide street that led down to the Tiber when he heard a soft whirring sound above, followed an instant later by heavy rumbling. Karl looked up. Several bricks in a freshly mortared wall had come loose, and at the same time a cascade of roof tiles came hurtling down from a scaffold higher up. Karl managed to leap aside just before the stones hit his head. A red cloud of clay dust rose up, and then he saw the toppled crane through the haze. It would seem one of the ropes of the pulley had snapped, setting off an avalanche of stone. Breathing heavily, Karl patted the dust from his shirt. He made the sign of the cross and uttered a prayer of thanks. The Lord had decided not to take him today.

But it would seem someone else hadn't been so lucky.

Karl heard high-pitched screams of pain that turned into a mournful whimpering. He looked around and spotted a small figure behind the pile of rubble. He rushed over and saw that it was a boy, no older than twelve, probably one of the many day laborers who lugged heavy sacks of lime in exchange for one warm meal a day. His face was white with dust, blood ran over his forehead, and a heavy beam lay across his chest. The boy's eyes were wide open with fear.

"*Santa Maria,*" he gasped in Italian. "*Che dolore.*"

Karl spoke a little Italian, but it didn't require knowledge of the language to understand that the boy was in severe pain.

"Hang on, I'll help you." Karl grabbed the beam with both hands and pulled, but it was much heavier than he'd expected. As Karl pushed and pulled in turns, the boy repeatedly screamed out in pain. Karl was surprised none of the other laborers had come to their aid yet, but then he remembered that they'd probably all gone to watch the procession.

Finally, Karl was able to pull the beam off the boy's chest. He bent over him, listening and examining the wound like he had learned during his time as a student of medicine. He thought the boy was bleeding internally and certainly had a few broken ribs.

"*L'uccello nero,*" murmured the boy over and over. "*Con le ali nere.*"

"Black bird—black wings? What do you mean?" Karl helplessly dabbed the blood from the boy's forehead.

As Karl used one of his scraps of paper to wipe the boy's face, he gazed down at him. The boy didn't seem to be in his right senses, but he was handsome, with delicate features and long eyelashes, reminding Karl of—

Karl winced.

The boy's face reminded him of the Savior from the pietà he had just drawn.

"*Con le ali nere,*" repeated the boy. "*Con le ali nere.*"

Karl desperately looked around. This injured boy badly needed a physician, a hospital. But the two of them seemed to be all alone; no one rushed to their aid.

Karl reminded himself that he had studied medicine once upon a time. Maybe he could help the boy. But he would need water and wine to wash him and a quiet place to treat him. He could still hear the festive music in the distance, but it was growing fainter. Karl hesitated. He had promised to meet Johann. They wanted to keep their eyes peeled for any sign of Lahnstein or perhaps even Greta. It could be their last chance. But here was a small, fragile person in need of his help.

"*Mamma,*" whimpered the boy. "*Mamma mia.*" Then he closed his eyes and stopped moving.

Karl felt his pulse and found it still beat weakly. He made his decision; he lifted the injured boy; he was astonishingly light. Karl thought of the Mother Mary and how she had cradled her dead son in her lap, immortalized in Michelangelo's pietà. He managed to heave the boy onto his back and carry him through the lanes, which, away from the procession, were all but deserted. The noise and music still sounding in the distance, Karl carried the boy over to the German quarter, pausing every now and again to catch his breath.

After several more breaks, stopping to check if the boy was still alive, Karl finally arrived at the inn near the Piazza Navona. Apart from the half-deaf landlady, no one was in the taproom. Followed by the suspicious looks of the old woman, Karl climbed the stairs with his burden and entered the small chamber he shared with Faust. He gently placed the boy onto the bed and covered him. The boy briefly opened his eyes.

"*Il cielo?*" he murmured.

"You are too young to go to heaven," whispered Karl with a smile. "All will be well. Sleep now."

The boy closed his eyes and lost consciousness again. Karl opened the child's shirt and studied the wound more closely. The rib cage was definitely crushed, and bruises indicated there was internal bleeding. Karl cleaned the boy's chest with brandy nonetheless. The rattling breath suggested that the lungs might be injured.

No physician in the world could help this boy.

Tears welled up in Karl's eyes. The boy's tragic fate suddenly made everything seem pointless—their journey to Rome, the search for Greta, his futile striving for recognition, for the doctor's love. It was as if along with this boy, his hopes were dying.

"Don't go," said Karl softly, stroking the boy's pale cheek. "Stay with me. Don't leave me alone."

Then the boy opened his eyes again and looked straight at Karl. He smiled tiredly.

"*Va bene.* It's all right," he whispered in Italian. "She . . . she told me, back then."

"Who told you what?" asked Karl, fearing the boy would lose consciousness again at any moment. He focused wholly on the words that came across the boy's lips with great difficulty.

"*La donna bianca,*" breathed the boy. "The white woman . . . that time when I had the bad cough from the dust at the construction site. I . . . I asked her if I was dying. 'Not yet,' she said. But I . . . I could tell from her eyes that it would be soon. And now the time has come."

"No one can tell when it is your time to die," said Karl. "Only God."

"Oh, but yes!" The boy smiled. "She knows. Everybody says so. The white woman can tell—she can see it in your hands."

"In . . . in your *hands?*"

Karl's blood ran cold.

La donna bianca . . . The white woman.

"Who are you speaking of?" Karl asked with growing excitement. "Who . . . who is this white woman?"

And the boy told him.

As Karl listened, he noticed once more how similar the boy's face looked to that of the Savior of Michelangelo's pietà.

~

Johann stood in the first row of spectators, wedged in between the crowd of dirty, stinking people, trying hard not to collapse. The shouting, the noise, and the closeness to the rabble repulsed him. Squeezed together tightly, they waited for the pope and his retinue to pass by. From the nearby Tiber, wafts of feces, urine, and rot blew through the lanes. The sky was gray with heavy rain clouds.

Johann had waited a long while for Karl before heading off on his own to find a spot in the front row. He couldn't understand why Karl had failed to turn up. What had happened? Most likely he had simply forgotten the time, engrossed in his drawings, which had happened a lot lately. Johann had decided that he would have to look for Lahnstein by himself. After all, he had practically always done things by himself.

Someone bumped into him, and Johann came close to hitting the perpetrator with his elbow. How he hated this crowd.

"I heard Leo has grown even fatter," sounded a voice right beside his ear. "And the ulcer on his ass pains him so greatly that he can't ride his white horse any longer. That's why he always looks so sour. He hardly leaves the palace anymore, just sits around like a warty toad."

Another man laughed. "Maybe that's why he needs so many jugglers, fools, and minstrels. Whatever the case, his processions are fantastic, just like the fireworks at Castel Sant'Angelo."

"Yes, yes, and in the meantime, the little people starve in the streets. And after their banquets the cardinals toss their golden plates into the river."

"I wouldn't mind if they threw a few golden plates today," said the other one, a burly fellow who towered over Johann by a head and reeked of garlic. "Filled with roast pigeons, too! Ah, I think it's time."

Cheers rang out, announcing the approach of the festive procession. Soon Johann saw the drummers and the musicians. They were followed by a hundred lance-bearing horsemen who gazed down grimly on the common people. Then followed the cardinals' officials in their liveries, and other lower servicemen. Johann craned his neck and watched intently, hoping to spot Greta or

Lahnstein. Other church dignitaries went past, carrying monstrances, smoking incense burners, and statues of saints, followed by the standard bearers carrying the coat of arms of the Medici pope: six balls on a golden background. The smell of the incense somewhat alleviated the stink of the Tiber. Johann frowned. Leo X truly was a master of showmanship. If a procession for All Saints' Day was this spectacular, then the feast for his inauguration must have been incredible. No wonder he had financial difficulties.

Finally, accompanied by loud cheering, the pope arrived.

The Holy Father sat on a gilded throne that was carried by four Moors dressed in golden livery. A baldachin sheltered Leo from possible rain. He wore a flowing robe of white silk, and over it a red coat lined with ermine. A red cap sat slightly crooked on his head.

It was the first time Johann had seen the pope in the flesh—the same man who had searched for Johann for so long across the entire empire and beyond. It was true: Leo embodied everything the new Lutherans despised about Rome. He was incredibly fat, with a huge, spongy head; a short, fleshy neck; a red face; and bulging eyes, making him indeed look a little like a toad. His facial features were soft, like a woman's, and his pale, ring-studded hands looked much too small for the bulky body. With those hands, the pope waved graciously to the crowd.

Striding at his sides were men juggling balls, acrobats performing cartwheels, a muscular giant leading two fully grown panthers on a leash, and a hunchbacked fool. To the delight of the crowd, the fool scaled the backrest of the throne as nimbly as a monkey, peering over the crowd from directly behind Leo. He mimicked Leo's gracious movements as if he were the pope himself. The Holy Father went along with the jest. The two panthers hissed and pulled at their chain as if they wanted to eat the fool alive.

The people laughed and pointed at the hilarious fellow, clad in a red-and-green jerkin with a gugel and a mask with a long nose. It was shows like this one that Leo was famous for. The pope loved any kind of pomp, no matter how ridiculous, expensive, or bizarre. It wasn't entirely inconceivable that someone like Leo truly believed a Doctor Faustus knew how to make gold. But still, Johann wondered who had given him the idea in the first place. Lahnstein? Or someone else?

Like a ship at sea, the pope's throne traveled past the rows of spectators. Now the fool and some of the jugglers tossed copper and silver coins into the crowd, causing people to scream out and raise their hands as if they were catching manna from heaven. The same people who had just been griping about the pope now cheered his name. The big fellow behind Johann gave him a shove, and Johann landed face first in the muck.

"Watch out, you clod!" Johann got to his feet and was about to find a way out of the throngs of people when he caught a glimpse of the papal dignitaries following the throne.

His heart skipped a beat.

One of the men was Viktor von Lahnstein.

In all the chaos, he hadn't noticed the papal representative sooner, partly because Lahnstein wore a wide hood. Johann caught his breath. He hadn't seen Lahnstein in more than two years, but there was no doubt. The same bushy eyebrows, the same piercing look, the same gaunt, tall appearance. Just like during their first encounter at Bamberg, the papal delegate wore the snow-white gown of a Dominican and a large wooden rosary around his neck. As Lahnstein looked up, Johann realized with horror why the man was wearing a hood.

Lahnstein's face was that of a monster, his nose nothing more than a tiny lump with two holes, like the nose of a dog or of one of the panthers Johann had just seen—a beast of prey in the body of a human.

For a brief moment, Johann thought his old nemesis might have recognized him in the crowd. Lahnstein's head jerked to the right, his eyes flashing hatefully, but then he looked straight ahead again. Several other Dominicans walked beside him, praising the Lord in loud voices.

Johann felt enormous rage rise up in him. He wanted to run and throw himself at Lahnstein, the man who had probably abducted his daughter. But then he would never find out what had happened to Greta. And so he let the moment pass, his breathing slowly calming down. He took a few steps back and let the procession pass him by. Then, using the pope's throne as a point of orientation, Johann began following the retinue at a safe distance. They walked to the Lateran Basilica and then all the way back to Saint Peter's. For almost three hours Johann followed them patiently.

When the procession turned toward the construction site near the Tiber, something unexpected happened. The group of Dominicans split from the train and strode toward a big, gloomy building that was surrounded by a wall with four towers.

Castel Sant'Angelo.

A gate opened, and the Dominicans, including Viktor von Lahnstein, disappeared inside as if swallowed by a huge whale.

For a long while Johann remained standing on Sant'Angelo Bridge, which stretched across the Tiber directly in front of the castle. He had found Lahnstein, and yet the man was out of reach. Castel Sant'Angelo was probably the only building in Rome that was even more heavily guarded than the papal palace.

Was Greta inside?

After waiting indecisively for more than a quarter of an hour, Johann hurried across the bridge toward Piazza Navona. During the short walk back to the hostel, Johann couldn't stop thinking about the maimed face of his enemy. Had Karl gone back to the hostel? He couldn't wait to tell him what had happened. They needed a plan—an idea for how they might find out more about Lahnstein. Johann felt the old familiar urgency return, his ambitious need to get to the bottom of things that had brought him so far. His brain worked at full speed.

There must be a way. There always is one!

He was so deeply in thought that he nearly missed the hulk of a man standing in the lane.

The huge fellow was standing opposite Santa Maria dell'Anima Church, talking to one of the priests. The man was so tall that he had to bend down to hear the corpulent clergyman. Johann would have recognized the man anywhere.

It was Hagen.

Johann held his breath.

They had found him.

Johann shoved the door open and stormed into their room at the inn. He was out of breath from racing up the steep stairs to the attic, where, to his relief, he found Karl waiting for him.

"Pack your bags—we must get away—" he began but broke off when he saw that someone else was in the room.

A boy was lying in Karl's bed.

Anger welled up in Johann. "Don't tell me you didn't show up because you were busy amusing yourself. I can't believe you—"

He broke off again when he realized how pale and sad Karl's expression was. He took a closer look at the boy. He was a child of about twelve years—much too young to interest Karl. His skin was the color of marble, and his eyes were closed. His hands lay folded on top of the blanket as if he were praying.

Or as if he were . . .

"My God," breathed Johann, rushing to the bedside and touching the boy's ice-cold hands. "What in God's name happened here?"

"A crane toppled and crushed his rib cage at the construction site of Saint Peter's," said Karl dejectedly. "I was on my way to meet you when it happened. I carried the boy here to care for him, but it was too late." He wiped his eyes. "And yet it was a miracle."

"A miracle? Why on earth would a dead child be a miracle?"

"Because"—Karl paused—"because he might have given us the decisive clue to Greta's whereabouts."

"*Greta's* whereabouts?" Johann stood as if rooted to the spot.

His plan had been to flee immediately. It wouldn't be long until Hagen found them here. But now everything seemed to happen at once.

"What are you saying? He knew Greta?" he asked hoarsely.

"One time, the boy was very ill. A nasty cough, apparently," explained Karl. "He was taken to the Hospital Santo Spirito in Sassia, which is right beneath Vatican Hill—it's the oldest hospital in Italy, if not the world. Even beggars and paupers get treated there, and by trained physicians."

"And what does any of this have to do with Greta?" asked Johann impatiently.

"The brothers working there are assisted by canonesses, nuns wearing white garments. The boy told me about a young sister who can foresee a patient's death in the palms of their hands. She's considered a great healer, and yet she is feared. The poor folks know of her ability and talk about it in whispers." Karl gave a sad smile. "They call her *la donna bianca*, the white woman, and also *la tedesca*, the German one." He paused. "Apparently this young sister has flaxen hair."

"Greta," groaned Johann. "By God, it might truly be Greta. We must go to this hospital immediately!"

"I knew you would say that. But I would like to ask you to help me take this poor boy over to the church first." Karl nodded at the pale child. "He deserves a worthy send-off."

Johann shook his head. "We . . . we can't go in that church. In fact, we should be getting out of the German quarter as fast as we can."

In hasty words he told Karl what had happened in the last few hours, culminating with the sighting of Hagen with a priest right outside their lodging. "I'm guessing it's the same priest I spoke to in confession yesterday. I was so stupid! I never should have gone there, and now it's too late. Hagen might very well be standing outside the inn's door as we speak."

"I won't leave this boy behind without one last prayer," insisted Karl. "We owe him that much." He knelt beside the bed and folded his hands. Johann cursed under his breath and knelt down next to him.

"Domine, exaudi vocem meam. Fiant aures tuae intendentes in vocem deprecationis meae," Karl muttered and said a few more Latin psalms.

Johann felt like he prayed for an eternity. They needed to get away from here! If Hagen found them now, Johann would never see Greta again. It occurred to him that to God, every life was equally precious—Greta's life weighed as much as this poor lad's. Nonetheless, he struggled to hold still.

When Karl had finally finished, he stood up and kissed the boy's cold forehead. "You're in a better place now," whispered Karl. "May God keep your soul."

Only then did he pick up his coat and hat, following Johann downstairs and out into the street.

The Hospital Santo Spirito in Sassia stood by a bend in the Tiber not far from the papal palaces. And yet it seemed like a different world.

Several rotting barges floated on the murky water, which stank worse here than in other places in Rome. The bloated cadaver of a pig slowly drifted by. The hospital itself was a gloomy complex with a church and a campanile at one end. There were two entrances, one of them for carts, and even this late in the afternoon they arrived continuously. On one lay an older man, moaning and thrashing about wildly. A younger man and a woman, probably his relatives, tried to hold him down and spoke soothing words to him. Knights Hospitallers in black habits with the cross of the order hurried past the cart. Next to the gate, several beggars and sick people hoped for alms.

Breathing heavily, Karl glanced back down the street, fearing someone might have followed them. They had come straight from Piazza Navona, having left the inn through the back door to avoid running into Hagen. They'd left behind almost all their belongings in their room, along with the dead boy. Karl had left a few coins for his burial and hoped the innkeeper wouldn't pocket them.

There was a long line of people waiting outside the other, smaller entrance. A cripple with no legs pleaded with a passing monk, who blessed him and gave him a crust of bread. This close to the river, the ground was muddy and covered in filth, and carts struggled to get through the lane. Karl couldn't believe that only a stone's throw away, the pope lived in pomp and splendor.

"So?" he asked quietly. "What do we do now? Line up?"

"We don't have the time. And besides, I'm seriously ill." Faust hunched over and let his right arm hang down limply, just like when he had been struck by Tonio's curse. Saliva drooled from the corner of his mouth. "I think it is the falling sickness. You'll have to hold me up."

Karl couldn't help but smile. It was just like years ago when they used to trick an audience during their acts, only Karl would play the ill man who was healed miraculously by the doctor's homemade theriac. If they really found Greta, perhaps things could go back to the way they used to be.

Johann put his arm around Karl's, and together they limped past the line, causing some of the beggars to complain loudly. In a small hut next to the door sat the gatekeeper, eyeing them suspiciously.

"Dove volete andare?" asked the short man in harsh Italian. "We don't accept any more patients today. Come back tomorrow."

"No physician wants to treat my father," wailed Karl and made the sign of the cross. "They say he is cursed."

"What's wrong with him?" asked the gatekeeper.

"Morbus maledicta," said Karl in a low voice. "When my old man gets angry, he starts swearing profusely and utters curses that sometimes come true." He exchanged a look with Johann. "Holy Mother Mary, it's starting again! Look!"

Johann was twitching violently and began to mutter incomprehensibly, spittle running out of his mouth. He raised a trembling finger toward the gatekeeper, who took a step back. The other people in line also stepped aside fearfully.

"That is awful!" exclaimed the gatekeeper. "Make him take down that finger before something bad happens."

Karl sighed theatrically. "That will only make it worse. The last person my father cursed only had two weeks to live. It started with diarrhea and pus-filled ulcers, and then—"

"Go to the Corsia Sistina and ask for a physician," said the gatekeeper, cutting him off. "Now. Get away from me!"

Karl gave him a nod and led the dribbling and twitching doctor into the huge hospital grounds.

Once they were out of sight, Johann straightened up and grinned. "*Morbus maledicta*—what wonderful nonsense."

Karl blushed. Praise from the doctor was rare. "Sometimes all it takes is a few Latin terms. I learned that at the university." He walked ahead and looked around searchingly. "Getting past the gatekeeper was probably the easiest part. This hospital is enormous."

"Let us find the Corsia Sistina," said Faust. "I gather that's the treatment room. Maybe we can ask patients about a young German nun. If Greta really does work here, someone must know her."

The hospital was a maze of passageways, courtyards, and buildings. Several times they passed Knights Hospitallers in black and canonesses wearing white scapulars and white bonnets.

Donne bianche—white women, thought Karl. *Is Greta one of them?*

Many of the sisters looked very young. Karl knew that canonesses often were daughters from good families who helped in the monasteries without taking vows. He admired them for giving up their comfortable homes in order to dedicate their lives to the poor and the sick. And there were plenty of those here. Long rows of cots lined the corridors, and lying atop them were the most pitiful creatures, scarcely covered with threadbare, stained sheets. Many of the men and women had scabies, their bloodied heads shorn. Some wore bandages saturated with pus, while others coughed or cried out for water. The young sisters leaned over them, soothing them and applying salves or feeding them gruel. In between, men of the order administered clysters and pills.

When Karl and Johann had crossed two more courtyards, they found themselves at the entrance to a larger hall. In his time as a student of medicine, Karl had seen some big hospitals, but never before had he seen a hall that served exclusively for the treatment of the ill. The space actually consisted of two high-ceilinged wings that were connected by an octagonal church room in the middle.

The walls were whitewashed, and evening light streamed in through skylights. Countless beds filled the halls, with narrow walkways in between where canonesses scurried along with busy steps, their billowing scapulars giving them an angelic look. The air stank of disease and excrement and pungent medication. But unlike the hospitals back home, this place didn't remind Karl of a realm of the dead, perhaps because of the fresh white walls but also because of the pretty young sisters, going about their tasks diligently and without complaint.

"Have you registered? Patients aren't permitted to enter the Corsia alone."

Karl jumped. He hadn't noticed the older sister approach them. He could tell by the silver rosary around her neck that she was the mother superior. At least they knew now that they were in the right place.

"Um, we aren't patients," he said.

"You're not?" The mother superior seemed suspicious now, tilting her head to the side like an owl. "Then who are you? You have no business being here."

"We . . . we are looking for my niece," said Johann. "We traveled all the way from the German lands to pay her a visit. Do you know her? She . . ." He paused. "Her name is Greta. Flaxen hair, early twenties. We've been told she is helping here at the hospital."

"Greta?" The old nun raised an eyebrow. "Well, this is rather unusual. Visitors must apply for an appointment first, or else anyone could come along. But since you're already here." She sighed. "Flaxen hair and German, you say?"

Karl and Johann nodded in silence, and Karl saw the doctor trembling and clenching his fists.

The silence stretched and became almost tangible, but finally the nun smiled. "I believe I know who you're looking for."

"Yes?" croaked Johann.

"She works back there." The mother superior gestured toward the far end of the wing they had entered, where the arcades opened into the church room beyond. "You may speak with her briefly. But not for long! Sister Greta is one of our most capable hands, despite her young age. It is nearly time for vespers, and she still has many patients to prepare for the night."

Karl looked in the direction the nun had pointed out.

And then he saw her.

Praise the Lord, he thought, struggling to hide his emotions. *We have found her!*

Like all other sisters in the hall, Greta wore the simple habit of the canonesses, a black robe with a white scapular and a white bonnet. They couldn't actually see much of her face. But Karl recognized her instantly. Several blonde strands of hair had slipped out of the knot and were hanging into her face, her eyes cast downward in concentration. She was bandaging the arm of an old man whose face was disfigured by pockmarks and weeping wounds. Nevertheless, she was smiling—a smile that Karl remembered well. How could he ever forget this smile? He had known Greta since she was fourteen; she had been like a little sister to him when they had traveled the lands alongside the great Doctor Faustus—the happiest time in his life. For two long years he hadn't seen her, and once more the vague memory from their last encounter at Tiffauges Castle came to his mind.

I'm going to Rome, Karl.

Greta hadn't noticed them yet. When Karl glanced at the doctor, he saw that he was shaking heavily, almost as if the accursed disease had flared up again.

"What is the matter?" asked the old nun beside them. "Aren't you pleased to see your niece?"

"I am . . . It's just . . ." Johann's voice was low and husky. "I'm not sure she'll be pleased to see me."

"How do you mean?"

"Things . . . things happened in the last few years." Turning away from the stupefied mother superior, Johann whispered to Karl, "I want you to go to her on your own. Tell her I'm waiting in the church." He jerked his head toward the towerlike building that connected the two halls. "Tell her that . . ." He faltered. "That I am incredibly sorry. That I would like to explain everything to her."

"Explain everything?" Karl frowned. "If you say so."

He gave the nun a grateful nod and started to walk toward Greta—the only woman who truly meant something to him and whom he had missed for so long.

～

Johann's gaze followed him.

Greta still hadn't looked up, entirely absorbed by the task of changing the old man's bandage. Then Karl addressed her. She looked up and gave a small cry as she dropped the copper bowl she had been holding. The clatter echoed through the hall. Thankfully, the mother superior had moved to a different part of the building, so that only a few patients turned their heads. Karl picked up the bowl for Greta, then he embraced her for a long moment. Johann heard his daughter sob. A thick, slimy lump sat in his throat and he was still shaking, his eye welling up. And yet he couldn't cry, nor could he walk over to his daughter.

The sight of her was overwhelming, almost too much for him. She was obviously doing well. The smile on her lips when he'd first beheld her had been real, as if she had found an inner peace that was denied to him. Johann was afraid the smile would disappear if she saw him here at the hospital. That she would call him what he was.

The murderer of her intended.

Would she ever forgive him?

One more time Johann looked at Karl and Greta, still clinging to one another like a shipwrecked couple at sea, and then he walked over to the church and waited. Towering above the altar was a ciborium of colored marble, dedicated to Job, patron saint of those who suffer. Johann remembered the story about the devil challenging God by questioning Job's faith. God tried His follower with numerous harsh blows, and in the end the devil lost the bet. God remained victorious.

Who wins in my story? wondered Johann, kneeling before the altar. *God or the devil?* His head was empty, and he felt incapable of saying a prayer, as much as he would have liked to.

Arcades along the sides of the church opened into the two wings of the Corsia Sistina, so that the patients could glimpse the altar from their beds. From his position on the ground, Johann couldn't see Karl or Greta, and he was glad. He closed his eyes and folded his hands.

Greta, please forgive me. Dear God, forgive me.

Finally he heard footsteps. It was Karl, walking up to him with a pale and serious expression. He knelt down beside Johann and began to pray in silence. A long while passed.

"She told you, didn't she?" asked Johann eventually. "She told you that I killed John Reed and that I nearly killed you, too, down in the crypt of Tiffauges. But did she also tell you that I wasn't in my right mind? The black potion—"

"What happened back then no longer matters," said Karl, his voice break-ing. "What matters is that you kept it from me. Why?"

"I like to deal with things on my own," replied Johann.

"Oh yes, I know that only too well." Karl gave a dry laugh. "And it's always been that way, hasn't it? Then you won't be surprised to learn that you will have to continue to deal with things on your own. Greta doesn't want to see you."

"I could come back tomorrow—"

"Don't you understand?" Karl's voice rose. "She doesn't want to see you ever again. She is happy here, do you hear me? And she doesn't want you to destroy this happiness, too. Viktor von Lahnstein arranged for her place here at the hospital, for whatever reason. Greta has found her calling as a sister and a healer. People appreciate and respect her—treating the sick has lent a purpose to her life that the likes of us are still searching for in books. Accept it, Doctor! Greta is no longer your daughter. She is going her own way now, and that is good. Let her go."

Johann said nothing for a long while. To outsiders it looked as though two men were peacefully praying in front of the altar. But on the inside, Johann was in turmoil. Powerful emotions raged inside him—anger, disappointment, love, grief.

Greta is no longer your daughter.

"I . . . I cannot accept it," he said eventually. "Not like this—not this easily."

He rose tiredly and walked out through the church door into a courtyard, where a cool evening breeze and soft drizzle met his face, but he didn't feel it.

Greta is no longer your daughter.

For the first time in his life, Johann felt much older than he was. Like a decrepit old man awaiting his death without hope and without salvation.

22

VIKTOR VON LAHNSTEIN WAITED IMPATIENTLY OUTSIDE THE double doors of one of the many papal reception chambers. The ceiling of the waiting room was as high as the nave of a church and was decorated with leaf gold, depicting the creation of the world in six days. Lahnstein felt like that was how long he'd been waiting, although it had only been an hour. Still, he had some very important news to share—and had reminded the soldiers of the Swiss guard by the door several times. But they had merely stared in silence at the hole in his face as if he was some kind of strange animal. Lahnstein had grown accustomed to such looks, but they still pained him.

Lahnstein sighed and gazed at the painting on the ceiling to calm his spirit. It had become increasingly difficult in recent months to get through to the Holy Father. Leo seemed to live in his very own world and often retreated into the depths of Castel Sant'Angelo. Even he, Viktor von Lahnstein, the personal representative of the pope, no longer had unlimited access to him, even though people were saying he was Leo's private watchdog, his shadow.

A shadow he likes to walk all over, thought Lahnstein.

Whenever he was annoyed, the wound in his face burned like fire. Things had never been easy with the Medici pope, not even when Leo had first ascended the throne eight years ago. Yes, he was extremely clever and learned, but at the same time he could be as naive as a child. Those ridiculous theater plays and shows he hosted all the time—Leo loved to surround himself with fools, jugglers, and crazy folks. And he was seriously running out of money; the gifts to his favorites alone cost the Vatican eight thousand ducats a month. The fact that the curia pocketed plentiful bribery to appoint cardinals didn't make a difference. If something didn't change soon, then it was only a matter of time before they wouldn't be able to buy candles for the papal palace. The curia already whispered about bankruptcy. A few years ago there had been an attempt on Leo's life. It was prevented in the last moment, and the perpetrator was tortured and executed. But the church's difficulties were still growing. That accursed Luther with his inflammatory speeches. The entire German Empire was on the brink of apostatizing.

Lahnstein shifted nervously on his red-silk upholstered seat. He kept glancing at the closed door. When, a few years ago, Leo had become obsessed by the idea of finding an alchemist who knew how to make gold, Lahnstein had first thought it one of the pope's many harebrained ideas. But then the thought had begun to tempt him, too. Hadn't other great men tried their hand at it and nearly succeeded? Albertus Magnus, Avicenna, and even that heretic Roger Bacon. The question wasn't whether it was possible to make gold. The scriptures definitely stated that it was. Only no alchemist had worked out how to do it yet.

Faust could have been that alchemist, especially since he truly appeared to be in league with the devil, as events at Tiffauges two years ago had shown. They had lost track of him back then, and instead Lahnstein had received the strange order to bring Faust's daughter to Rome. Ever since then, Leo had become more and more absorbed by mysterious books and odd experiments that were supposed to help him find the philosopher's stone.

God moves in mysterious ways, Lahnstein thought. He knew he was completely and utterly at Leo's mercy—too tightly had he interwoven his own career with that of the pope's.

If Leo went down, then so would he.

A gentle bell rang out somewhere, and finally the Swiss guards opened the portal to the reception room. To Lahnstein's astonishment, warm steam came pouring out through the doors. When the fog had lifted a little, he beheld a hall whose ceiling was even higher than the one in the waiting room. Tied up with gold-threaded bands, two panthers were lying in a corner, cleaning themselves like little cats. They were the pope's latest toys and as expensive as everything else his heart desired. The animals had also been part of the procession on All Saints' Day.

In the center of the hall was a huge gilded tub surrounded by antique statues. Sitting in it, amid a sea of bubbles, was the pope. His fat upper body rose out of the foam like a white mountain, and his cheeks were red with heat. His loud laughter echoed out into the corridors.

"Ha, delicious! Too delicious! You must tell me more of those amusing, filthy stories later."

The tub must have been brought to the hall recently. Puddles had formed on the expensive cherrywood parquet, and Lahnstein walked around them as he approached Leo amid several low bows. Behind the tub, half-hidden by the steam, stood another figure. When Lahnstein saw why he had been made to wait for over an hour, he felt sick with rage. No high-ranking cardinal was standing behind the basin, and no foreign dignitary, just the damned jester. The fool jingled his rattle, jutted out his backside, and made a disgusting noise before walking away with one last grimace. Leo wiped tears of laughter from his face and turned toward his personal representative.

"Do you know the joke about Luther riding on a pregnant cow?" he asked Lahnstein.

"I can't say that I do."

"I'm afraid it would be wasted on you." Leo waved with a sigh. "You have no sense of humor, Viktor. That's a character flaw."

Lahnstein bowed, relieved he didn't have to listen to a vulgar joke. "I beg your forgiveness, Holy Father."

"Never mind. That's what I have my jester for." Leo shrugged. "You must excuse me for holding my audiences in the tub, but my fistulas prick like the fork of the devil. It's getting worse." He groaned and lowered himself up to his neck in the water. "Have you heard about Milan?"

Lahnstein nodded. The pope had entered an allegiance with the German emperor a while back, after having previously colluded with France several times. Thanks to the support of a thousand Swiss mercenaries, the city of Milan was very close to falling into the hands of Charles V.

"In return, Charles is going to give me Parma and Piacenza, and maybe even Ferrara. Florence falls under his protection, and the church's territory is growing considerably." Leo smiled. "The alliance with the German emperor is the best thing that could have happened to the church. I want to hold a three-day celebration in Rome, with fireworks atop Castel Sant'Angelo. Will you take care of that, Viktor?"

"Of course, Your Excellency," said Lahnstein, quickly calculating in his head what a spectacle like that would cost the church. And the Swiss mercenaries standing outside Milan hadn't even been paid yet. Lahnstein's look turned to the two panthers that seemed to size him up like possible prey before closing their eyes again.

"But you haven't come to discuss politics with me, have you?" Leo eyed him with curiosity. "So what is it, Viktor? What could be so urgent that you disturb my bath?"

"It's about Doctor Faustus, Holy Father. He has been sighted in Rome with that Karl Wagner. I have it on good authority. He slipped through our fingers at Piazza Navona, but I'm confident we will apprehend him soon."

"Is that right? Faustus?" Leo wiped the foam from his face and seemed to think. "The doctor found his way here after all. Hmm, interesting."

"I assume he is searching for his daughter," replied Lahnstein, a little taken aback by the pope's subdued reaction.

Leo had searched for Faust all through Europe. The letter from the German priest had reached Lahnstein the day before, and he'd immediately sent Hagen to the German quarter, where suspicion had turned into certainty. The man who'd visited the confessional at Santa Maria dell'Anima must have been Faust—too much suggested that he was.

"With your permission, I will have the city searched for the doctor this very day," continued Lahnstein. "It shouldn't take long with a troop of soldiers—"

"You will do no such thing," said Leo, cutting him off. "That would only . . . well, complicate matters."

"I . . . I'm afraid I don't understand," stammered Lahnstein. "The doctor is in Rome and—"

"Not even you have to understand everything, dear Viktor. Believe me, soon everything is going to turn out for the best. It won't be much longer." Leo smiled broadly and scrambled to his feet.

Once more Lahnstein noticed how fat the pope had become in the last few years, a pale, wobbling colossus.

"Soon we will have so much gold that we could line Saint Peter's Basilica with it. I know that you long for revenge, Viktor. Your mangled face truly isn't cause for celebration. But revenge isn't a goal as such. Our goal lies much higher."

"It's not about revenge," said Lahnstein. "The point is that the man you were searching for so desperately is finally within reach. One word from you—"

"Don't worry, we are going to hurt Faust much more than we ever could have on the rack. Patience, Viktor! Focus on the task I set you." Leo leaned forward, looking like a toad that was creeping out of its burrow. He winked at his personal representative. "How is our darling doing?"

Lahnstein nodded. "Couldn't be better. Don't worry. I'm taking care of it."

"Good, that's good. Make sure it stays this way. His life is as precious as gold, one could say." Leo laughed, clapping his fat hands together several times as more water gushed onto the parquet. "Now tell the musicians to enter. I need a little relaxation. The coming night is going be quite"—the pope hesitated—"quite exhausting once again. For body and soul. And, Viktor?"

"Yes, Holy Father?"

"I'll say it once more: leave Faust alone. Don't do anything until I tell you otherwise. Put your mind to the fireworks. And remind Hagen that I need fresh venison for my two little cats. They love venison. That's an order—understood?"

One of the panthers hissed as if lending weight to its master's threat.

"I . . . understand."

Bowing low, his heart filled with insatiable hatred, Lahnstein retreated. His forehead was wet with sweat and the room's hot dampness. He wondered what it was that was going to be so exhausting that night.

He had a certain hunch.

And that hunch wouldn't help him to rest easy.

~

It was two days before Johann spoke again. He had fully withdrawn into himself, seeming to Karl like a walking corpse. Since they couldn't return to the hostel in the German quarter, they sought shelter in one of Rome's more remote districts behind the Palatine Hill. It was a run-down inn filled with day laborers, drunkards, and thieves. At night there was a lot of raucous shouting and fights, and cheap whores looking for customers. When Johann and Karl moved into their room, several pairs of eyes followed them desirously, some belonging to prostitutes and others to thieves. But evidently there was something about Johann that made people leave them alone. It was as if he exuded an infectious disease.

He spent most of those two days walking alone on the overgrown piece of land directly in front of the inn; apparently, the field used to be a gigantic racecourse that the Romans had called Circus Maximus. There were only a few remains left of the stands, and many of the rocks had recently been removed for the rebuilding of Saint Peter's. Here, among the goats and sheep grazing in the tall grass and wild grains, Johann felt as if he were in the country. Now that autumn was moving into Rome, the weather was often rainy, foggy, and cold, so that Karl didn't want to join the doctor on his walks. His former assistant preferred to stay at the inn drawing, waiting for Johann to make a decision.

Should he give up Greta? Should they leave Rome and go their separate ways? Probably, Johann thought. It would be the most sensible thing to do. Leave everything behind and make a fresh start, without Greta, without Karl, and without Tonio, who still followed him like a shadow. Crows circled above the old racetrack.

But it's not over yet, thought Johann. *Not with Greta, and not with Tonio.*

On the morning of the third day he had finally reached his lonesome decision. Before breakfast he left Karl, who was still asleep, and walked along the Tiber until he was back outside the hospital entrance. He was in luck—it was a different gatekeeper than last time.

"What do you want?" asked the man when it was finally Johann's turn. "Are you ill? You don't look it."

"I am a physician from the German Empire and wish to offer my services," he said with a firm voice. "I feel touched by the suffering of the unfortunate."

"Like a pilgrim's pledge, huh?" When Johann made no reply, the gatekeeper asked him to wait. After a short while he returned with a nun. Johann started. It was the mother superior he and Karl had met three days ago.

"I know you," said the older nun. "You are the uncle who came to visit his niece. Our dear Sister Greta. She will be busy all day. We can't allow visitors and idle chat every day. Maybe after vespers—"

"I haven't come for my niece, but because of the sick," said Johann briskly. "I am a physician, a learned doctor from faraway Heidelberg, versed in pharmacology, medicine, and anatomy, and I want to help. God Himself ordered me."

"God Himself, you say?" The mother superior gave a thin smile. "I'm afraid it isn't as easy as you think, *dottore.* The Santo Spirito in Sassia isn't just any hospital, but the oldest and possibly the best in the world. The physicians who work here studied at the most prestigious universities, like Bologna, Padua, and Ferrara. They are the best in their field. Do you have any references?"

"I'm afraid not. I came to Rome as a simple pilgrim."

"Then I am sorry," said the nun and turned away.

"Wait!" called Johann after her.

He studied the first man in line behind him. He was scrawny and older, with sunken cheeks and yellowish eyes, and he was doubling over with pain. Johann looked him up and down for a few moments.

"Passing water is painful for you, isn't it?" he asked loudly enough for the mother superior to hear. "And your urine is slightly red?"

The man gazed at him with wonderment. "*Madre mia*—it's true!"

"They will have to remove a stone from your bladder. Make sure the surgeon gives you a few drops of poppy juice first. And stay in bed for two weeks following the operation, drinking a brew of chamomile blossoms. If you don't, the wound will become infected." Johann stepped to the next patient in line, a narrow-chested youth who was coughing terribly, holding a kerchief to his mouth.

"Is your phlegm red?" Johann asked the young man, who nodded. "That's not a good sign. But we might get your cough under control with an extract of mold and honey. Ask for it at the *spezieria*. If this hospital is truly as outstanding as it claims to be, they will have the elixir. Tell them you're suffering from *la piaga bianca*. The doctors will know what you mean."

Johann slowly made his way down the line, giving advice, gazing into toothless mouths, and palpating broken limbs. He was no physician, but he had read widely and watched plenty of itinerant surgeons in the German Empire. He also knew that sometimes patience and a few kind words achieved more than expensive medicine. Eventually he stopped in front of a small, pale girl who was pressing herself against her mother fearfully. The girl was about five years old and bore dark rings around her eyes. Johann knelt down and looked at her.

"How are you, little one?"

Instead of the girl, the gaunt woman, who could have been the child's mother or grandmother, replied. "She hasn't been eating or drinking. And she sleeps a lot. We can't afford a doctor—the hospital is our last hope!"

"Hmm . . ." Johann hesitated, then he picked up the girl's tiny hand and stroked it gently. He had an inkling, but he wanted to know for certain. And so he did something he hadn't done in years.

He closed his eyes and bent over the hand. He felt a warm throbbing, and dark lines showed on the insides of his eyelids.

The black wings.

And he knew that he hadn't been mistaken.

He took a deep breath before rising with a smile on his face. "I believe your daughter is going to feel much better soon. And about eating." He rubbed his fingers together, snapped them once—and suddenly held a small, wrinkled apple in his hand, and then another one and another. "The food should be sweet, the way children like it. Then they'll eat." Accompanied by the laughter of the girl and the onlookers, he juggled the apples before handing them to the girl with a bow.

"*Grazie,*" breathed the mother, tears of joy in her eyes. "It has been a long time since Clara laughed."

The mother superior came closer. She tried to maintain her stern expression, but Johann could tell that she was touched. "What are you, a physician or a fairground magician?" she asked in an imperious tone.

Johann grinned. "A bit of both, I believe. Aren't good physicians something like magicians?"

"I honestly don't know what to make of you, signore," replied the mother superior with a sigh. "Your show hasn't entirely convinced me, but I am favorably disposed toward you. You may lend a hand to the sisters. Help them wash patients, empty chamber pots, apply dressings, but drop the tricks and juggling. This is a serious place."

"Then . . . then I may work here?" asked Johann.

"Not as a physician, but as a nurse. But beware." The older woman wagged a finger. "If Greta really is your niece—which I doubt—then I don't want you to distract her from her work. We need her here, understood? She gives strength and solace to the sick, which is sometimes more important than medicine."

"You have my word—I won't bother her." Johann nodded. "One more thing, venerable mother." He turned serious and lowered his voice so that no one else could overhear. "The little girl . . ." He faltered. "I'm so sorry, but she . . . she hasn't got long to live. The only thing we can still do for her is to give her a little joy. Please allow me to juggle for her—only for her. I beg you."

"How do you know the Lord will take her soon?" asked the mother superior with a frown.

"I just do. Trust me." Johann smiled sadly. "Like I said—physicians sometimes are magicians."

The following days and weeks were hard. Each morning, Johann left the inn by the old racecourse and walked to the hospital. Karl would often be up already, sitting by the window upstairs, bent over a drawing. Their relationship wasn't the same since Karl had learned what had really happened at Tiffauges. And yet he waited for Johann to decide whether they would stay or leave town.

In the beginning, Karl had shaken his head at Johann's medical ambition. "Why do you do it to yourself?" he had asked. "I know you want to be near your daughter. But do you really believe you're going to win her back like this?"

"I don't know, Karl. All I know is that I thought only of myself for far too long—for my whole life, really." Johann was gazing into the distance, where the Alban Hills were vanishing behind the haze. "I can help people, and that is what I'm doing now."

"And what if Hagen or Lahnstein finds you?" asked Karl. "The hospital isn't far from the papal palaces and Castel Sant'Angelo."

Johann winked at him. "I am nothing, just a nobody who empties latrines and watches at the bedside of the dying. I am just old Johann, not the learned Faustus."

"You will always be Faustus, no matter how hard you try," Karl had replied, and Johann had heard both mockery and pain in his voice.

It was true—Johann did his best to remain in the background at the hospital. He helped wherever necessary, and even though he knew much, he avoided showing off his knowledge. He soon realized how modern the hospital was. There was a hatch for unwanted infants and a foundling wing, a poorhouse, and fresh water from wells and pipes in every hall. The spezieria, the hospital pharmacy, housed any known medicines and even some herbs and spices from the New World. Its wealth of drawers contained small brown beans from overseas that were ground up and served with hot water and ginger, and dried leaves that eased hunger and tiredness. Watching over the spezieria were physicians who didn't often show their faces in the treatment halls of the poor.

Most of the diseases the patients suffered from Johann had seen before. But one particular ailment was new to him; the monks called it *morbo gallico*, the

French disease, allegedly because it had first appeared during the siege of Naples under King Charles VIII. Since then it had spread right across Italy. The victims suffered from fever and rashes, and later extremely painful knots and ulcers appeared, and some patients grew insane and ran screaming through the treatment rooms. They were treated with quicksilver and also with a concoction of a very hard wood from the New World. All that was completely new to Johann, and he was amazed at the vast knowledge in Italy compared to the backward German Empire. Whenever his work permitted, he secretly studied the writs the physicians left on their lecterns.

But most of the time he helped the sisters, occasionally offering some whispered advice. He washed the old people, fed them, carried away their buckets, and cleaned them. Strangely enough, he found this kind of menial work rather satisfying. He barely saw Greta. Whenever he did see her, his heart skipped a beat. She always turned away quickly and continued to go about her work as if she didn't know him. But at least she hadn't asked the mother superior to remove him.

Almost daily Johann sat by the bed of little Clara, juggling for her or showing her some of his magic tricks like he used to do for Greta. The little girl laughed and clapped, but Johann saw she was fading away. She lost weight and grew paler by the day. Her nose bled often, and the knots on her neck were swollen. Johann had no idea what the disease was called, but he knew there was no cure.

He had seen it in Clara's hand. He hadn't used this eerie gift in a long time, the same gift Greta appeared to have inherited from him. Johann could tell when people were going to die. But unlike years ago, the realization no longer upset him as deeply. Everyone had to die, some later and some sooner. Dying was as much a part of life as birth. And so he gave Clara some of the most wonderful hours in her much-too-short life while she steadily grew weaker.

"I dreamed of the dear God," she told him quietly one evening, as if she was sharing a secret. "And of the big black wings. The big black wings will carry me to Him. That's what He said."

"He did?" Johann shaped the corner of the sheet and with soot painted two black eyes on it. "And what about little Hans here? Is he allowed to fly with you?"

Clara smiled as Johann marched the tip of the sheet up and down the edge of the bed like a little soldier. "Yes, little Hans can come. If he is good." Then she turned serious. "Uncle Johann? Does the dear God know how to do magic and juggle like you?"

"Of course He can! He is the best magician there is. You won't believe your eyes when you see what He will conjure up for you. The sweetest fruits, a doll with a head made of cherrywood, a spinning top, and a whole mountain of glass marbles like only the wealthy children have."

Clara fell asleep with a smile on her lips.

The next morning, when Johann saw her again, she was as cold and stiff as a puppet. He had known this day would come, but still he was filled with profound grief—grief like he hadn't felt in a long time.

"I hope the dear Lord performs tricks for you now, little Clara," he murmured. "If God really exists, then He can do magic."

Johann held the hand of the dead girl for a long while. He was squatting beside the bed, quiet and unmoving, when he suddenly heard steps behind him. He knew those steps; they were as familiar to him as the rattling of a juggler's wagon or the drumming of the rain on the canvas.

"Greta," he said softly without turning.

"We need to talk," she said.

"That's what I've wanted all along."

She pulled a stool up to the bed and sat down next to him and the body of Clara. Johann saw her close-up for the first time. She was still his daughter, but her face had become harder. Underneath the white bonnet of the sisters' habit was a grown woman. She seemed much more mature.

And much sadder.

"I've been watching you," she began. "And the other sisters have been telling me about you. They say you're a good man even if they struggle to figure you out. You look after the sick, and apparently you made little Clara very happy, God rest her poor soul." Greta looked at the dead girl with pity and brushed her hand over Clara's face, closing her eyes for good. "Now the worst is behind her and she's in a better place."

"I knew she would die," said Johann. "And so did you, am I right? The black wings . . . That's how we found you. You ought to be more careful with your gift, Greta."

"I am careful. Death can also come as a relief, as suffering finally coming to an end. I give people certainty, but only when they really want to know. You can use this gift for good or bad, and I decided to use it for good." Greta was still looking at the pale, silent child, but suddenly she turned and looked straight at Johann. Her voice was low and decisive. "But I know you're not good, Johann Georg Faustus. You are merely acting, just like you have always acted. Your heart is as black as the walls of hell."

Johann swallowed heavily. "Greta, what happened at Tiffauges—that wasn't me. I was drugged—"

"I know. Karl told me."

"Karl?" Johann looked up with surprise. "You've been speaking with Karl?"

"Yes, we have met several times since you first came here. And I know why you came to Rome. But I will never go with you. Never! My new home is here— a home like you were never able to give me."

It hurt Johann a little to hear that Greta had been meeting Karl.

"I can understand you, Greta. All that has happened can't be undone. I only want . . ." He paused. "I just want you to not think of me as evil. Because I'm not."

"Oh yes, you are." Greta narrowed her eyes. "Lahnstein told me everything."

"Lahnstein?" Johann's knees suddenly felt weak. "You . . . you meet with the papal representative?"

Greta nodded grimly. "Over the last two years, he has been more of a father to me than you ever were. Yes, we used to think Lahnstein was our enemy. But it isn't true. The enemy is you." From beneath her habit she pulled a key ring that hung on a thin leather string around her neck. "Do you see this? Those are the keys to a whole lot of chambers in Castel Sant'Angelo. Viktor von Lahnstein trusts me, and I see him regularly for confession. He led me onto the right path and told me all about you. You are in cahoots with Tonio—with the devil himself. You are but a devil yourself, even if you don't want to know. And I won't allow my child to fall into your hands."

Johann froze. Everything around him suddenly turned blurry.

"Child?" he breathed. "You . . . you have a child?"

Greta frowned. "Karl hasn't told you? I wasn't planning on telling him, but he sensed there was something else. He remembered that I said something along those lines when we'd said goodbye."

Johann felt jealousy flare up again. But he pulled himself together. "Go on," he said through clenched teeth.

"Yes, I have a child, and he is John's son. Little Sebastian is nearly two years old now, and he is growing up somewhere safe. He is doing very well."

Johann closed his eyes. Not only had he taken the man she loved from Greta, but also the father of her child. No wonder she hated him so.

"Where . . . where is your son?" he asked eventually. "Why isn't he with you? Or did you give him to the foundling house?"

"Why do you think he isn't here?" Greta gave a small laugh. "I am leading the life of a nun. I have so much to atone for, do you understand? As much as I try to forget it, I am still your daughter. The daughter of a sorcerer and devil worshipper, cursed with your gifts. Your bad blood flows through my veins, too." She made the sign of the cross. "I don't want my son to grow up like this. I visit him several times a week. In the beginning it was hard to not see him more often, but now I know that it is for the best. He is better off there than here among all the suffering, and better off than at the foundling house, too."

"Where is he, Greta?" urged Johann. "Where?"

"Where do you think?" Greta smiled thinly, and her next words stabbed Johann right in the heart.

"Your grandson is where he is safest from you, at Castel Sant'Angelo. And Viktor von Lahnstein does everything in his power to keep him safe."

23

THE DOOR CRASHED OPEN AND JOHANN STORMED INTO THE small, shabby attic room. Karl looked up, startled. He had been sitting by the window, working on the silhouette of the city in the autumn fog, but now his hand had jerked and an ugly black streak went right across the page.

"You knew!"

"I knew what?"

Johann glowered at him furiously. His whole body was quivering, and he seemed poised to strike Karl. "You knew that Greta had a child by John Reed and that this child lives here in Rome. At Castel Sant'Angelo, with Lahnstein!"

Karl sighed and put the pen aside. "So she told you. I advised her against it. But it seems your daughter wants to hurt you."

He had met up with Greta a few times at a tavern outside the monastery. As canoness, Greta was free to leave Santo Spirito whenever she wanted, but she hardly ever made use of that privilege. The hospital had become her home. Their conversations had been like those of siblings who hadn't seen one another in a long time and who found now that they had become estranged. Greta helped Karl to fill in his remaining memory gaps and told him everything that had happened at Tiffauges. Unlike Greta, Karl didn't consider the doctor an envoy from hell, but Karl's boundless admiration for him was crumbling. Perhaps because, for the first time, Karl saw the man behind the legend.

"I asked Greta not to tell you." Karl raised his hands apologetically. "I knew it would pain you, and it doesn't change anything."

"It changes everything," screamed Johann, his face red with anger. Exhausted, he dropped onto the flea-ridden, moldy bed. "Don't you understand?" he asked, running his hands through his hair. "She trusts him! And Viktor von Lahnstein is holding my grandson hostage, like a pawn!"

"A pawn for what?"

"For . . . for . . ." Faust broke off and waved his hand. "Another time. Believe me—I know that Lahnstein has plans for that child. Or do you really believe he is raising the boy at Castel Sant'Angelo out of the goodness of his heart?"

"Admittedly, it is unusual," said Karl with a shrug. "It's possible that it is some kind of belated revenge on you. And it would be a particularly sweet revenge. Lahnstein couldn't get you, so he takes your daughter and grandson. Instead of hurting Greta, he turns her into a tool of the church. And then he raises her son like his own."

"So you admit that Greta is but a tool?"

Karl sighed deeply. "She has changed, it's true. But the most important thing is that your daughter is well—she and her son, your grandchild. Greta found a new home. You might not like it, but that's the way it is. I beg you: let your daughter go!"

"I know he's got plans for the boy," muttered Johann. "I just know it. Tonio still holds me in his clutches. The pact still stands."

"Tonio? You seriously believe Tonio del Moravia is behind all this?" Karl shook his head. "You were talking about Lahnstein a moment ago and now it's about Tonio?"

"You didn't see what I saw at Tiffauges and thereafter. Evil truly exists. And I can feel that we're very close to it."

"Now you sound like your daughter." Karl gave a tired smile. "Except she believes you are this evil."

Johann closed his eyes as if he was thinking hard. When he started to speak again, he was very calm. "I know you want to leave me, Karl. And you have every reason to. In all these years I've brought you nothing but misfortune."

"That's not true, Doctor," said Karl in protest. "I've learned so much from you."

And I still love you, he added in his mind. *Even if my love is growing weaker by the day.*

Karl had indeed decided to soon part ways with Johann. Their common story had reached its end. Greta would stay here in Rome with her son, and Karl would try to start another course of study. He wanted to travel the empire as an itinerant scholar, sketching, exploring, forever learning. Life as a juggler and quack was over for him. But first he wanted to say farewell to Greta.

"I would only ask you one last favor," said Johann as if reading Karl's mind. "One very last one. Maybe you're right and my grandson is safe. But I have a strong sense of foreboding. Something . . ." He hesitated. "Something is going to happen. Very soon. I can feel it like an impending thunderstorm. Give me one more week. I want us to observe Castel Sant'Angelo for one week. I can't do it on my own—I need your help."

"You want to spy on Lahnstein?" asked Karl, puzzled. "But isn't he the one looking for you?"

Johann smiled. "It's just like chess. Always make the move your opponent least expects. We used to play a lot of chess together. Remember, Karl? Those were good times."

"I almost always lost."

Karl had planned to depart within the next few days. But now that the doctor was sitting there, pleading, he couldn't bring himself to refuse.

"Just this one last favor," said Johann.

Karl nodded. "One week. Not a day longer. If you promise me that afterward, you will finally leave your daughter and her son in peace."

"I promise."

Karl gave him a serious look. "You still talk about your pact with Tonio and about a curse. I never really believed in it, but I've changed my mind."

"So you also believe that Tonio still persecutes me?"

"Oh yes, he does. In here," Karl said, tapping his forehead. "Trust me, Doctor, if you want to vanquish this curse, you have to let go. Of Tonio, of your daughter, of your grandson. As long as you don't learn to forget, Tonio del Moravia will always remain a part of you."

～

The screams of a child echoed through the labyrinthine corridors, long hallways, and remote chambers of Castel Sant'Angelo.

It was the kind of persistent, never-ending screaming that filled one's head and left no room for any other thoughts. The screaming became shriller, like a saw cutting through bone—it sounded like the screams of someone being tortured.

At least, that's how Viktor von Lahnstein perceived it.

He hurried along the corridor, past the guards who grinned furtively. Many of them were fathers and used to such clamor. Unlike a papal representative, who had spent the larger part of his life in monastic austerity.

The screaming came from a room in the eastern wing of the castle, a wing that was reserved for higher-ranking servants and, occasionally, for legates. Lahnstein opened the door just as the noise behind it stopped abruptly. The chamber was clad with silk tapestries but was otherwise rather bare. On a stool in its center sat a plump young woman with healthy red cheeks. Sitting on her lap like a little prince was a baby boy getting spoon-fed. His face was smeared, and porridge was dripping onto the ground. He ate ravenously, as if he hadn't eaten in days, but he looked quite strong. Despite his young age, his hair was full and red.

Like a kobold child, thought Lahnstein with disgust as he averted his eyes.

"What in God's name is going on here?" he thundered. "Is the boy in pain? You know that you vouch with your life for the child's well-being!"

The nursemaid smiled as she pushed another spoonful of porridge into the boy's mouth. After the many months she'd worked here, she was used to the sight of Lahnstein's monstrous face, just as little Sebastian was; the boy gazed at Lahnstein rather blankly, opening his mouth wide. "He is hungry, Your Reverence. That's all."

"And that's why he's making such a racket?"

"That's what children do. Though I must admit that Sebastian has powerful lungs. He's going to be a big and strong man, I'm sure." She brushed the boy's red curls with her hand. "And a handsome one to boot."

Children would always remain a mystery to Lahnstein, partly because he didn't remember much of his own childhood. Since he was a second-born son, his father had placed him at a monastery very early. Small children had only ever struck him as a nuisance, and now he was personally responsible for the life of this squawking brat. Several times a week Lahnstein checked on the boy's well-being, ordering clothing for him and even the occasional toy. He always felt sick in the lead-up to his visits, remembering the smell of baby shit that hit him every time, and the sight of full diapers and spilled porridge on the floor. At first he had found the thought of raising the grandson of the famous Doctor Faustus at Castel Sant'Angelo enticing. He had arranged for the mother to work at the Hospital Santo Spirito—a position she evidently excelled at—and employed a nursemaid whose silence he had bought with a pile of money. He was proud of the fact that Greta believed her father to be the devil incarnate. During long, empathetic conversations he had succeeded in winning over Greta. In the beginning he had thought it was the perfect revenge, but now he found the whole affair abhorrent. Especially now that Faust was in town.

And yet Lahnstein wasn't allowed to arrest the doctor, but instead was forced to look after this screaming child at the express command of the pope. Until now, Leo's intentions had been a mystery to him, though he'd been harboring a growing suspicion. And the previous night, everything had changed.

Down in the dungeons below Castel Sant'Angelo, where only a few select people were allowed to go, the pope had given Lahnstein several very specific orders. And he had put two and two together. The result hadn't been particularly satisfying—rather, deeply frightening.

But at least he thought he understood now why the boy was still here. Lahnstein knew what sort of books were stacked next to the pope's enormous four-poster bed. And he also knew what Leo was doing down in the dungeons at night. Could it be madness or divine providence?

At least we'll soon be rid of the brat.

Lahnstein gazed pensively at little Sebastian, who had stopped eating to defiantly stare at the gaunt man with the maimed face. His eyes were as black as pitch and reminded Lahnstein of the person he loathed the most.

"Man away. Play with Martha," Sebastian said surprisingly loudly as he threw his sticky spoon at the representative's gown. "Man away!"

"Truly a vigorous lad," said Lahnstein with a forced smile. Repulsed, he brushed the splattered porridge off his gown. "With a strong mind and healthy, firm flesh. Make sure he doesn't lose weight."

Then he turned around and left the room.

Only a little more patience.

He would send Hagen right away to fetch the necessary items.

～

"God in heaven!"

With a small cry Greta shot up and paused in her task. The gray-haired man whose stump of a leg she was rebandaging gave her a quizzical look.

"Is everything all right, Sister?" he asked.

"Yes, yes." She tried to smile. "A quick prayer, that's all. I think I'm working too much."

"You certainly are, Sister." The old man grinned with his toothless mouth. "I don't know any other sister in the hospital who cares for the sick as much as you do. Nor do I know a prettier one. I'm sure God will reward you plentifully."

"God already rewards me by lending me comfort and strength every day. You ought to pray for both, too." Greta wrung out the cloth and soaked it in the bowl of warm water. Carefully she dabbed the stump, which was overgrown with blackened flesh and pus. Recently, it happened increasingly often that she was struck by something in the middle of working, as if an invisible force was touching her, trying to shake her awake.

The old man watched her as she went about her task. At least his fever had gone down, which meant the worst days following the operation were probably over. A cart had run over the beggar's leg, and an amputation had been unavoidable. Greta had poured brandy down the wounded man's throat and uttered words of reassurance as the doctor placed the bone saw. Whether the old man would survive the procedure remained to be seen.

Or I could find out right now, thought Greta.

"May I ask you something?" asked the old man, waking Greta from her thoughts.

"What would you like to know?"

"You are young and beautiful. The men lie at your feet, even here at the hospital. Why are you doing this work? I know canonesses usually come from wealthy families. You could long be happily married, to a cloth merchant, a patrician—"

"I am married to God."

"And there never was a man in your life?"

"There . . . there was one. He died too soon. Terrible things happened. God gave me the strength to forget, and that is why I'm here."

The old man nodded, scrutinizing Greta as if he could see right through her bonnet and read what was truly going on inside her. Sometimes she didn't know that herself. More than two years ago she had traveled to Rome with Viktor von Lahnstein. It had been a time of consolation and reflection. Lahnstein had visited her from time to time, speaking with her like a fatherly friend. They had talked about Johann and the fact that he was involved with the devil, that the sin had been transferred onto her and she had to atone for it. When her child had finally been born, his hair had been as red as John's.

But the boy's eyes were those of his grandfather.

Sebastian also carried Johann's burden, the same as she did. The curse had spread across the entire family.

For a few weeks after the birth, Greta had nursed Sebastian, cuddled and kissed him. But Lahnstein had made it clear that her work was elsewhere, and so little Sebastian had moved into Castel Sant'Angelo. He was doing well there; he had a friendly nurse, plenty of toys, and a warm, cozy cradle. Greta was allowed to visit him as often as her duties permitted. Sometimes she felt a pang in her heart, a deep longing, but those moments always passed, and prayer, chanting, and the daily liturgies never failed to calm her. Life had gone on, quiet and peaceful.

Until her father had found her.

Hatred had returned along with Johann, and also the memories of her former life. It had been nice to talk about the old times with Karl, but the appearance of the two men had brought everything back to the surface. Perhaps that was where the strange feeling of being shaken awake was coming from. But Greta didn't want to be awakened.

She sensed that if she did wake, a terrible reality would descend upon her.

"Is it true what they say?" asked the old man after having watched her work for quite some time. "That you can see in someone's hands if they are going to die?"

"Folks talk a lot of nonsense," said Greta, harsher than she had intended. It was true, she had used her gift from time to time. She wanted to give people the opportunity to ready themselves for death, for their last rites. But it had been a mistake, and she had stopped doing so months ago.

"I don't want to know," said the old man. "What sort of a life is it if one waits for death? Counting each day, each breath? I want to enjoy every day as if it were my last. Only God ought to know when we see our loved ones here on earth for the last time."

Greta smiled. "You're right."

She dressed the wound with a fresh bandage and covered the man with a blanket. Suddenly she paused. There it was again, the shaking. This time it was softer, more like a gentle nudge.

Our loved ones.

She stood up and wiped her hands on her apron.

"Where are you off to?" asked the old man.

"I am going to visit someone," said Greta. "I want to make sure he is well."

Longing for her child flooded her heart.

~

The days following the conversation at the inn were the most boring and contemplative in a long time for Karl.

They were also damned cold.

He and Johann had been watching the entrance to Castel Sant'Angelo in turns, hoping for Lahnstein to show, or for anything else to happen that would confirm Johann's hunch. But nothing happened, except that Karl's fingers and toes nearly froze off. It was almost December, and a damp chill had crept into the city and burrowed underneath any layers of clothing. Karl could feel a cold nesting inside him, his nose dripping and his throat scratching. He cursed himself for making Faust a promise instead of leaving as planned.

Castel Sant'Angelo stood opposite Sant'Angelo Bridge, which was one of just two bridges in Rome and accordingly busy. A steady stream of people, wagons and carts, oxen, and horses traveled across it, and so it was easy for Karl to hide in the crowd. He'd heard that years ago the bridge had collapsed, killing hundreds of people. Even now it didn't look particularly stable. Karl had picked a spot at the start of the bridge from where he had the best view of the castle. Yet he knew that their chances were slim. Faust had watched from here all morning and had then rushed over to the papal palaces in the hope of finding Lahnstein there. Karl spent the frosty hours of waiting sitting on a low wall, drawing, eating nuts, and mentally bidding farewell to a time that would soon lie behind him.

His time with the doctor.

Sometimes Karl wondered whether his love for Faust had anything to do with the rejection of his own father. Franz Josef Wagner, renowned chirurgeon from Leipzig, had probably always suspected his son to be a sodomite and had treated him accordingly. Faust, on the other hand, had accepted Karl for who he was right from the beginning, even if he wasn't thrilled about it. But Karl's love had something in common with the obsession that tied the doctor to the creepy Tonio del Moravia.

Karl's eyes turned to Castel Sant'Angelo, a gloomy structure from pre-Christian times that used to serve as a tomb for Roman emperors. Now that winter was moving into town and fog hung above the river, the castle looked even eerier than usual. A tall, square wall with four corner bastions enclosed a towering cylinder. The fortress had nothing airy or angelic about it. A former pope had named it when, during a plague epidemic, he had seen Archangel Michael hovering above it, whereupon the plague vanished from the city like a miracle. Since those times, the castle had been serving as a place of retreat and residence to the popes. Since Leo's reign, regular fireworks took place on the upper terrace. Karl had heard that another such display was scheduled to happen in just a few days. It was part of a three-day-long festival to mark Milan being liberated from the French.

His hands shaking, Karl was about to pull out one of the cheap pieces of paper he had bought off a dealer when he saw someone he knew well meandering along the river toward the castle.

Greta wore her black-and-white habit and kept her eyes lowered. Karl had seen her enter the fortress before in the last few days, and Johann had also spotted his daughter during his watch. But they hadn't spoken to her and made sure she didn't notice them. Karl knew why Greta was visiting Castel Sant'Angelo. It was to see her little son. Greta had found comfort in faith, but her faith was obsessive.

Obsessed by God or by the devil, thought Karl. *By love or by hatred. What is the difference?*

He ducked behind a few passersby so that Greta wouldn't see him. She walked past him without looking up and exchanged a few words with the guards at the gate, who let her through right away. Clearly the men were used to her visits.

More uneventful waiting stretched on. Every now and then an ecclesiastic dignitary would come or go, though Lahnstein wasn't among them.

But someone else appeared.

Karl started from his daydreaming when out of the gate stepped a man who couldn't be overlooked: Hagen.

He towered over the guards by almost two heads. Karl shuddered at the sight of the giant, who was carrying not his longsword but, dangling from his belt, a hunting dagger as long as his forearm. Instead of the colorful garb of the Swiss guard, he was clad in a long brown coat with a hood, making him look like a caricature of an itinerant preacher. Karl remembered with horror how Hagen had hunted them back in France at Chinon Castle. He was a bloodhound who never gave up once he had caught a scent. Karl had been surprised that Hagen hadn't routed them out at their new lodgings near Circus Maximus yet. Was he on his way to find them now?

Karl decided to turn the tables and follow Hagen. That at least seemed more promising than sitting here and freezing his backside off. He might be able to determine how close Hagen was to finding them.

It was easy to keep track of the hulk. He plowed through the crowds on the bridge, and people readily gave way to him. Karl kept a good ten paces between him and Hagen, but this didn't seem necessary, as the tall man didn't look back once. Karl followed him to the east, past the Pantheon, a heathen temple that was now used as a church, and past the crumbling Colosseum, where loud traveling merchants hawked their goods. Then their surroundings became quieter and more sparsely populated. An icy wind swept through the lanes covered in trash and debris. Increasingly often there were overgrown fields between the houses, where poor people tried to find a few last turnips even now, at the end of November. Karl sought cover behind broken remains of walls and ruins, hoping he wouldn't lose Hagen in the thickening evening fog.

After a while they came to an expansive area that seemed to serve as a quarry. Walls and buildings rose in between rectangular holes in the ground lined with Roman cement. It took Karl a few moments to figure out that the holes must have been basins. He was probably looking at one of the former thermal baths Faust had told him about. In ancient times, there must have been enough room here for several hundred people. Now leaves were drifting on foul-smelling puddles. Frogs croaked, and water lilies and swamp plants covered the steps and the fading mosaics in the basins.

What in God's name was Hagen doing here?

For the first time the giant turned around, as if he had heard Karl's thoughts. Karl ducked behind a wall. When he peered back over it, Hagen had vanished.

Damn!

Cursing under his breath, Karl hurried to the spot where he'd last seen Hagen. Dusk had set in, and in the twilight Karl could make out some steps that led down between two crumbling walls. He could hear the echo of voices from below.

Karl hesitated only for a moment before climbing down. At the bottom of the steps was a walkway whose walls were covered in soot and saltpeter—probably part of the old heating system. It ended after just a few steps in front of a rusty iron door that stood ajar. Light streamed from inside, and now Karl could hear the voices clearly. They belonged to Hagen and another man.

"*Porca miseria!* It wasn't easy to find all these things," moaned the other man in Italian. "Especially the bezoar."

"My master pays you well," growled Hagen. "And what about the mandragora? Is it truly from a gallows hill?"

"Very difficult to come by these days, very difficult. But you're in luck. Here it is, freshly harvested from below the swaying remains of a hanged man. And I also managed to find everything else."

"That's good," said Hagen.

"And my payment?" asked the other man. "I had high expenses."

"Oh yes, payment." Hagen laughed softly. "Of course you shall have your payment. The heavens will reward you."

The following sounds made Karl's blood curdle. A blade swooshed out of its scabbard, fabric ripped, then someone gargled and groaned.

"*Gesù e Maria,*" gasped the man.

"You shall meet them shortly. Give them my regards."

A dull crash followed as something heavy fell to the ground. Then something clanked, something shattered, and heavy footsteps crossed the room.

And neared the door.

Karl almost reacted too late. He was running back toward the steps when he realized that he would never make it to the top. Hagen would see him in the light of the moon! At the end of the corridor, near the foot of the stairs, lay a pile of fallen, moss-covered stone blocks. Karl darted behind them and, seconds later, heard Hagen storming up the stairs beside him, and then there was another crashing sound.

God in heaven, please make sure that he hasn't seen me.

Karl's heart was beating in his throat. But the steps faded without slowing, and eventually there was silence. He slowly counted to a hundred before rising and sneaking over to the door, which now stood wide open.

He stepped inside and froze.

A bearded man wearing a black cape was lying in his own blood, his arms stretched out to the sides as if he was crucified. All around him was utter chaos: broken glass, shards of clay, torn scrolls of parchment. This room evidently was an alchemist laboratory, as Karl could tell by the many glass flasks, mortars, and stills that were lined up on the tables and shelves. Once upon a time this room was probably one of the heating rooms for the thermal baths. The walls were black with soot, and a fire flickered in an ancient wall stove.

But that wasn't the only fire.

In oily puddles on the ground, dancing bluish flames were spreading fast, reaching some of the tables and parchment scrolls. Clearly, Hagen wanted to destroy any evidence of his deed. Now the man's cape was catching on fire. Black smoke began to fill the room, making Karl cough.

He quickly stumbled into the room and leaned over the lifeless body. He saw immediately that there was nothing he could do for the stranger. Hagen had slit the man's abdomen from the bottom to the top as if gutting a fish. Puzzled eyes stared at the ceiling of the room. The man was older; broken eye glasses were lying next to him on the ground, and his right hand was clutching a scrap of paper.

Without thinking much about it, Karl wrested the piece of paper from the dead man's fingers. Karl's eyes were watering, and the seam of his own coat was beginning to smolder. It was as hot as inside hell itself! Coughing hard, Karl stormed out into the corridor, which had also filled with smoke, and hurried up the stairs. Behind him one of the larger still flasks exploded with a bang.

When he turned around one last time, he saw a column of fire shooting out of the ground, followed by thick black plumes. It was as if the devil was reaching for him from hell.

Nearly blind and with a smoking coat Karl raced toward the hills of Rome, where solitary lights burned in the darkness like red eyes. His hands clutched the piece of paper as tightly as the dead man had.

Not even half an hour later, Johann and Karl stood together by the dim light of a candle and gazed at the scrap of paper. Karl had run so fast that his heart was still beating heavily, and there was a taste of iron in his mouth. He'd kept looking back the entire time, fearing Hagen might have spotted him. But there hadn't been anyone—only his fears spurring him on. The doctor beside him held his fists clenched and his lips pressed together as he tried to decipher the words on the paper, which was partly burned. Blood spatters told of the terrible crime down in the old Roman thermal bath.

"Mandragora," murmured Johann.

Karl nodded. "I heard that word mentioned."

"*Mandragora* is the Italian word for mandrake," said Johann. "Specifically, it is the root of the mandrake. Infernal stuff, that."

Karl remembered mandrake from lectures at the university. The root often looked like a little man and was therefore associated with witchcraft. It was also highly poisonous and used for abortions. Possession of such roots was punishable by death.

"The stranger was also talking about something called a bezoar," said Karl.

"I've used that before. It's a solidified mass from the stomach of goats and looks like a smooth egg. Bezoar allegedly helps against poisoning, but it's also used in other areas." Johann pointed at the smudged letters with growing agitation, his fingers shaking. "Mandragora, bezoar, amber, *Salamandra salamandra*, sulfur, *dens pistris*."

"Alchemy ingredients," said Karl. "The room below the bath was definitely an alchemist's laboratory. I'm guessing the fellow was conducting some experiments that weren't exactly lawful. There's always someone willing to pay good money for those things. Just like hangmen's ropes or the blood of decapitated people, which is supposed to cure the falling sickness. Perhaps we should have tried it on you back then."

"*Salamandra salamandra*, sulfur, *dens pistris*," repeated Johann. "*Salamandra* . . . Damn it, I know this recipe." He gazed into the distance. "Back at the tower, a long time ago."

"You mean the tower where we once spent a winter?" asked Karl.

"And where I spent a winter as Tonio's apprentice. I read about invocations, some of which Tonio practiced back then. I . . . I remember a pentagram on the floor. Painted with the blood of children." He shook his head as if trying to rid himself of the memory. "In *The Sworn Book of Honorius* is a ritual that requires these ingredients."

"And what ritual is that?" asked Karl warily.

The doctor gave him a grave look and paused for a few heartbeats. "It is one of the most powerful rituals—the ritual to summon the devil."

Karl thought he heard the cawing of a raven outside. A door slammed shut in the distance, a gust of wind swept through the room, and the flame of the candle flickered wildly. Then all was silent.

"Are . . . are you saying that . . . ," stammered Karl.

Johann nodded. "Hagen collected those ingredients for Lahnstein because the dog wants to invoke the devil. This paper is proof." He held the scrap to his eye and squinted. "Unfortunately the bottom part has burned away, or we could see the rest of the list. But even so, I'm fairly certain that I know what's next. I remember it well."

"Which is?" asked Karl, although he had a hunch. He, too, had leafed through *The Sworn Book of Honorius* back at the tower before quickly closing the book again in horror.

"First there follow a few uninteresting ingredients. Ground gold, certain herbs that must be picked under a full moon, the ashes of a cross. But there is one ingredient that is crucial for the success of the ritual. A peculiar juice."

Karl closed his eyes. He remembered what had been written at the bottom of the page in *The Sworn Book*. Merely reading it had made him feel sick.

Quite a peculiar juice is blood.

"A cup filled with the blood of an innocent child," he whispered.

"Have we ever truly asked ourselves who Viktor von Lahnstein really is?" said Johann. "What if Tonio managed to infiltrate the highest echelons of the Vatican? What if the devil is going to be summoned right in the center of his greatest enemy?"

"At . . . at Castel Sant'Angelo?" breathed Karl. "You think Lahnstein might actually be Tonio?"

Back in Nuremberg Karl had met this frightening man once, but there had never been any evidence that he was still at large.

Until the moment Karl had found the piece of paper in the dead alchemist's hand.

Karl no longer knew what to believe, but he had to concede that it was more than strange if Lahnstein's closest confidant murdered an alchemist for a bunch of mysterious sorcery ingredients. Was Lahnstein perhaps more than just a papal delegate?

"This is about the blood of my grandson," said Johann with a trembling voice. "He is supposed to die, and soon. Question is, Where and when precisely? For the ritual, they'll need room for a large pentagram, and there'll be much smoke and noise, but it can't be too conspicuous."

Karl flinched.

Smoke and noise.

"The fireworks," he murmured.

Faust stared at him. "What?"

"There is going to be a fireworks display! Up on the terrace of Castel Sant'Angelo. I heard people talk about it in the streets. The pope is celebrating the victory over France with fire and smoke and spectacle, just the way Leo loves it. Apparently he holds such feasts on a regular basis."

Johann grew pale. "Fireworks would provide the perfect setting. They could conduct the ritual beneath the starry sky and no one would suspect a thing. With the right constellation . . ."

"What is it?" asked Karl.

Johann shook his head. "Something doesn't fit the picture, but I don't have time to mull it over now. I must warn Greta." He was already walking to the door. "She can help us get into Castel Sant'Angelo. Lahnstein trusts her and gave her the keys so she can visit the child whenever she likes."

"It's night," said Karl. "The hospital is closed. Like it or not, we'll have to wait until morning."

"Damn it, you're right." Johann stopped dead, his hand on the doorknob. "I'll use the night to think. We need a plan to stop Lahnstein, and with him, Tonio." Faust's eye gleamed, and Karl thought it looked like it was filled with joyous anticipation.

"The end is near," said Johann. "Finally! I can feel it."

24

JOHANN LEFT FOR THE HOSPITAL BEFORE SUNRISE.

He hadn't slept a wink. Instead, he had sat by the window the whole night and gazed into the fog. He had hardly seen any stars, but even if he'd seen any, it wouldn't have been much good. The stargazing tube he used to own had stayed behind in Bamberg, along with his astronomical notes. But even so, he knew something was wrong.

Back in Nuremberg, Tonio's followers had waited for the arrival of a certain star before attempting to summon the devil. The star had been called Larua, the harbinger of ill fortune, and it returned every seventeen years. But only nine years had passed since its last appearance. And that time, the ritual had been different from the one in *The Sworn Book of Honorius*. If Viktor von Lahnstein truly was Tonio del Moravia, then what was his plan?

Whatever it was, they had to act fast. There was no time—Johann had to save his grandson. And the only way to get inside Castel Sant'Angelo was with the help of Greta.

An icy north wind swept through the lanes, but Johann didn't feel it. He hurried on until he reached the gate of Santo Spirito in the first reddish light of day. Down by the river, beggars huddled around a smoldering fire, but no one was lining up outside the hospital yet. The gatekeeper was just unlocking his little hut. He knew Johann by now and waved him through.

"The good German pilgrim," he droned. "Eager to wipe some more asses. Must have a good deal to atone for."

"More than you can imagine," muttered Johann too quietly for the gate-keeper to hear.

He hurried on and walked through the wealth of corridors and court-yards, which, after all these weeks, were nearly as familiar to him as the halls of Heidelberg University. The few nuns and physicians he passed in the dim light didn't take much notice of him; a deceased man was carried out on a stretcher. Johann searched for his daughter.

He found Greta outside the spezieria, where the apothecary was just hand-ing her a bowl with freshly made pills.

"I must speak with you," said Johann in a low voice behind her.

Greta jumped and almost dropped the bowl.

"Didn't I make it clear that I do not want to speak with you again?" she whispered, trying not to attract the apothecary's attention. "It's bad enough that you're still sneaking about here, frightening me."

"Believe me, if this wasn't about life and death, I wouldn't be here."

She gave him a quizzical look. "Life and death—whose? Yours?"

"It's about the life of Sebastian."

He pulled Greta aside and told her what had happened the night before. He told her about the brutal murder Hagen committed and the list of alchemy ingredients. "It is just as I feared," he finished, waving the scorched piece of paper in front of her face. "Lahnstein is planning something with little Sebastian. There's going to be a ritual, in two days, during the fireworks. They are going to invoke the devil—with the blood of your child."

"And you actually thought I'd believe you?" mocked Greta. "A half-burned scrap of paper? What a pathetic attempt to drive a wedge between me and Lahnstein."

"Please, believe me, Greta." Johann gave her a pleading look. "I didn't make all this up. Karl can confirm it—he saw it with his own eyes."

"Then why isn't Karl here?"

Johann regretted not having brought Karl. But he'd had his reasons. He stepped up close to Greta, touched her shoulders, and suddenly wrapped his arms around her. "Greta, I'm begging you—"

"Don't touch me!" she hissed, and as she recoiled from him, the bowl of pills slipped out of her hands and crashed to the ground, the pills scattering in all directions.

Johann squatted down and started to pick up the pills alongside Greta, under the curious looks of the apothecary. When they were finished, Johann handed her the bowl.

"You will see that I'm right," he said. "Hopefully before it's too late. I love you, Greta. You and my grandson. I won't allow him to fall into Tonio's hands."

Without another word he turned away and walked out of the courtyard, trying his best not to shake.

In his pocket, his fingers clutched cool metal.

She'll notice, he thought. *She must. She'll call for the mother superior at any moment.*

But nothing happened.

Johann hadn't really expected Greta to believe him. He had racked his brain for hours about how he might get into Castel Sant'Angelo without Greta's help. His plan had been nothing but a faint hope, but it had just come true. A long time ago, before Johann became the famous Doctor Faustus, he had been a talented juggler and trickster. Among many other things, Tonio had taught him sleight of hand.

A brief tug at the leather string around Greta's neck was all it had taken. She hadn't noticed because in the same instant, the bowl had slipped out of her hands. Now the ring of keys was safely hidden in Johann's pocket—the same keys Greta had shown him as proof of Lahnstein's trust in her.

The keys that would get him and Karl inside Castel Sant'Angelo.

~

Greta remained standing in the courtyard for a while, clutching the bowl of pills tightly. Tears streamed down her face, tears of anger and confusion. She cursed her father for coming to Rome, for coming and stirring up everything when she had finally found peace—peace with God and with herself. Even with the fact that her son was growing up with a mother who only visited him occasionally because she'd dedicated her life to God. And then her own father appeared and wrecked everything. He sowed doubts. That was how the devil worked. Hadn't he whispered in Jesus's ear, when he was in the desert, that he would make Jesus the ruler of the world?

One had to resist. Pray. Confess.

Nonetheless, Greta could feel her wall of confidence cracking. Partly because of the strange premonitions that continued to hit her out of the blue. Only this morning she'd had another one. She had dreamed of her son, his tiny body pinned to the ground by needles, like a butterfly being studied. Inside a pentagram painted with blood-red paint. He had cried for his mother, but she hadn't been able to hear him. His cries had been silent.

The devil sows doubts. Don't listen to him. Pray, Greta, pray!

Still shaking all over, she wiped the tears from her face and carried the bowl of pills to the treatment hall.

She was deep in thought and didn't notice that there was no leather string around her neck.

~

Johann placed the key ring on the table in their room at the inn, and Karl stared at him in bewilderment.

"How did you come by these so quickly?"

"Once I realized that Greta wasn't going to help us, I spent the morning loitering outside Castel Sant'Angelo. Servants and clerics come and go all day. It wasn't difficult." He grinned. "One nudge, one garbled apology. The keys were on the belt of a papal scribe. He's probably in a cold sweat as we speak, searching for them everywhere."

Johann had thought long and hard about whether to tell Karl where he got the keys from but decided against it. Greta and Karl were close, and Johann didn't know how Karl would take the news. All that mattered now was that they made it inside the castle in time, and to that end he had been gathering information all morning. It felt good to use his mind again. Damn it, he was Doctor Faustus, the cleverest and most cunning wizard in all the lands! How could doors stop him when he needed to save his grandson?

Karl picked up the bunch and studied the individual keys. They were of varying sizes and manufactured with complicated patterns, true masterpieces of blacksmithing. "And you really believe these will get us into the fortress?"

"Of course not! None of those are for the main portal. That is always guarded, and there are bolts, trapdoors, iron gates, and a drawbridge inside. These keys merely unlock a few chambers inside. But which ones, I don't know."

"Then I don't see how your theft helps us at all."

Johann sighed. He hated it when others were slow on the uptake, especially when it was a matter of life and death. Karl was a gifted painter and an intelligent scientist, but sometimes he lacked shrewdness.

"You drew a map of Rome," said Johann. "Bring it here."

Frowning, Karl fished a paper scroll from under his bed and unfolded it on the table. The map had become blotched with wine stains and candle wax but was still legible. Johann pointed at a spot near Castel Sant'Angelo.

"The Passetto di Borgo, the papal escape route," he explained. "It's a corridor that runs aboveground. If an enemy storms the Vatican palaces, the pope can escape to Castel Sant'Angelo via this passage. And the castle has never been conquered."

"And you want to get in through *there*?" asked Karl, surprised. "The passage will be guarded just like the rest of the castle."

"But not nearly as heavily as the main entrance, which is supposed to withstand any attack. I took a look at the tunnel this morning." With his finger, Johann traced the line on the map that led from the Vatican to the fortress. The corridor was about half a mile long—far too long to keep every single yard under surveillance. "Parts of the corridor are completely out in the open," explained Johann, "protected by a wall. If we get across the wall undetected, we aren't quite inside the castle yet but a good deal closer."

"And then?"

"Let that be my concern. Remember how we got into the underground passages of Nuremberg?" Johann winked at Karl. "Back then I had one or two tricks up my sleeve. We still have a day and a half. I am going to make a few purchases that will help us."

Karl gave him a doubtful look. "The way you talk, you make it sound like child's play."

"I am Doctor Faustus—never forget," said Johann, but then his expression darkened. "But this situation is far too serious to be considered child's play. We mustn't waste a minute." He rolled up the map. His hand instinctively went to his trouser pocket, where he was keeping the tiny silver globe these days. Maybe he would soon need it.

"This is about the life of a child—my grandson. And who knows. Maybe it's about much more."

25

To MAKE ALL THE PREPARATIONS JOHANN WANTED TO IN such a short amount of time, he and Karl went to the remotest parts of Rome, to lugubrious dives, dodgy vendors selling their goods at deserted catacombs, goldsmiths, and dyers. The ingredients Johann required were difficult to come by. For the legendary aqua regia, for example, they'd had to visit a silversmith who used the components for the alloying of his knives. After these nonstop errands Johann's savings were completely used up, but the large leather satchel at his side was bulging.

"Aqua regia will help us break through locks," he explained as they strolled across the Campo Vaccino, the so-called cow meadow, in the city's center. It was a field of rubble surrounded by ruins. "If you mix spirits of salt and nitric acid, you end up with a liquid that can eat its way through the thickest metal."

"And through human flesh," said Karl sternly, eyeing the satchel on Johann's shoulder. "And many other utensils in your sack are equally dangerous. You're carrying a highly explosive witch's kitchen on your back."

"That's why we'll only mix the various substances when we need them. Don't fret! Remember the flaming arrows I used to make? In the beginning, the Chinese only used blackpowder as a source of enjoyment. But now we know how deadly the powder can be." Johann grinned. "And anyway, these items are mostly supposed to confuse our enemies—just like back in the Nuremberg underground passages, remember?"

Back then, Johann had filled the corridors with colored smoke. What he wasn't telling Karl was that this time he'd use the ingredients for another purpose. Johann had tossed the idea back and forth for a long time, and eventually he reached the conclusion that it might come in rather useful.

As useful and as destructive as little else in this world, he thought.

It was the afternoon before the great fireworks that launched the celebration of Milan once again being part of the pope's realm. The feast was supposed to last for three days, with music, food, and games, just like in the old times. Crowds had already started to gather around Castel Sant'Angelo, hoping to secure a good spot for the fireworks. The spectacle wouldn't commence until well after sunset, so that the darkness would show off the rockets and firecrackers.

The fireworks had turned out to be a stroke of luck for Johann, as sulfur, saltpeter, and other rare substances had been more readily available than usual—albeit at criminal prices. Johann was glad he hadn't touched his savings in the last couple of years, instead opting for cheap inns. Despite the staggering task ahead of them, he couldn't suppress the thrill of anticipation. The time of waiting was finally coming to an end. What had begun many years ago, when he'd first met the magician Tonio del Moravia, was coming full circle.

You won't get my grandchild, Tonio. No door will hinder me.

Suddenly he stopped. Rising in front of them was Palatine Hill, one of Rome's seven hills.

"Damn it—we forgot something!"

"What?" asked Karl. "We have ground charcoal of alder buckthorn, sulfur from Sicily, saltpeter, even nitric and sulfuric acid. Not to mention all those other ingredients I've never heard of before."

"We're missing a simple picklock!" Johann slapped his hand against his forehead. "I have the clerk's keys, but there are bound to be other locks. And there won't be enough aqua regia for all of them." He patted Karl's shoulder. "You go ahead to the inn and prepare our clothing. Remember, everything must be as dark as the night. I saw a blacksmith up on Palatine Hill who looked like he might produce a picklock without asking too many questions. I'll take a quick detour."

"Do you want me to take the bag for you?"

"And blow yourself up with a wrong movement?" Johann smirked. "The bag stays with me. That's where it's safest. You go find us some rope and hooks so that we're prepared for all eventualities at the Passetto di Borgo."

In truth, Johann didn't want him to take the satchel because he didn't want Karl to ask any more questions about the ingredients.

"I'll be an hour at the most. That'll give us plenty of time."

Johann turned away with one last nod and headed toward the southern end of Campo Vaccino. To the east, the Colosseum jutted into the sky, and directly in front of him stood the Mons Palatinus. With its dilapidated imperial palaces and fortifications, the hill formed the last part of the overgrown grazing lands in the center of the city. The Palatine wasn't a good area; it was considered *disabitato*, abandoned, a place where no honorable citizens lived. Only ruins were left here, and large parts of those had been carried away as building material for the new churches that were springing up everywhere. Lime burners had dug deep pits in between their poor hovels, which looked strangely out of place among the remnants of lordly buildings. Only a few rugged figures moved between the shacks, along with large numbers of stray dogs who barked angrily at Johann.

Johann's eye was caught by a statue standing a little farther on. Evidently, it showed a great Germanic warrior. Johann blinked—for a brief moment he thought the statue had moved, but it was probably just the sun, which hung low on the horizon, blinding him. Despite the sunshine it was miserably cold and, as usual, a damp breeze blew from the north, carrying with it the stink of the Tiber.

Johann continued up the hill, past beggars and vagabonds who eyed him suspiciously. He clutched his satchel tightly. Perhaps it had been a mistake to visit this area by himself. On the other hand, if someone were to rob him, he would simply hurl the aqua regia at them. The screams of a person losing his face certainly would deter anyone else. Once more Johann considered whether he should really go ahead with his plan. He remembered something Leonardo da Vinci had said to him in his garden.

How can we ensure that our ideas don't turn out to be our undoing?

Johann touched the silver pendant he now carried on a chain around his neck—it felt as heavy as the entire world.

An idea that held the power to destroy the world.

There was a cracking sound behind him, followed by the clattering of stone.

A strong hand clutched his neck while a second hand pressed a wet sponge to his mouth. Johann breathed in a pungent, aromatic smell.

A sleeping sponge.

Physicians occasionally used such sponges to sedate patients before surgery. The sponges were saturated with poppy juice and extracts of various plants from the nightshade family. They didn't achieve a complete sedation, but they numbed the mind. This was no weapon of plain thieves and scoundrels.

Johann flailed his arms and kicked his feet, but he could already feel his knees growing weak. His legs gave way as if they were made of straw. He wanted to shout for help but couldn't with the sponge over his mouth and nose.

Then he lost consciousness.

When he came to, his hands and feet were bound, and he'd been gagged. All around him it was black. He could feel solid timber: his legs were pushed up against his chest and he had no room to move. He appeared to be stuck inside some kind of chest. The chest moved and rattled as if it was sitting atop a cart.

Johann desperately tried to focus. He had been abducted. But why and by whom? His head ached as if someone had thumped him with a hammer. This was partly due to the sleeping sponge, but also because of the acrid smells filling the chest.

It was the smells of sulfur, saltpeter, nitric acid, and various other highly toxic substances.

Now Johann felt the leather satchel at his feet. His abductor must have chucked it into the chest with him. With so many poisonous fumes in such a cramped space, he'd be dead soon, from either suffocation or explosion.

Johann wriggled like a fish out of water. Again he tried to call for help, but all he managed was muted croaking. The fumes caused tears to run down his face, and his lungs burned like fire. He needed to get out of there as fast as possible. But the more he struggled, the harder he breathed and the more the fumes affected him. And so he forced himself to calm down, even though his heart was racing.

All of a sudden the cart stopped. He heard muffled voices, then the cart rattled on. The chest was jolted from side to side and Johann hit his head repeatedly, but he barely noticed the pain by then. The acrid fumes were killing him slowly but steadily, breath by breath. He suspected that the tiny flame of a candle would suffice to blow up the chest.

Farewell, Greta. Farewell, grandson I never met.

Again he passed out.

The next time he awoke, he was blinded by glaring light. Was this heaven?

But he felt much too miserable to be in heaven; more likely, he had landed in hell. The chest's lid opened, and someone yanked him out and removed the gag. Johann vomited, then gasped for air. The stink of sulfur and saltpeter still surrounded him, and his skin felt like it was on fire. Only after several long moments did he begin to take in his surroundings.

He was lying on cold, smooth parquet, the dark timber adorned with precious inlays. Johann made out the shapes of several marbles that looked like pills, as well as crossed keys.

The keys of Saint Peter—the symbol of the pope.

Slowly he looked up and beheld two pairs of boots. One pair was dirty and as big as two buckets. The other pair was made of soft, freshly blackened leather and adorned with silver spurs.

"The oh-so-famous Doctor Faustus," sounded a familiar voice. "Nearly drowned in his own vomit. How pathetic! And yet I struggle to feel sorry for a necromancer."

Johann groaned and turned on his back.

Standing in front of him were Hagen and Viktor von Lahnstein. The papal representative, in his white Dominican gown, glared down at Johann with folded arms. Red flaps of skin hung in the place his nose used to be, and above it, two cold eyes gleamed like those of a beast of prey. Johann blinked repeatedly. Perhaps he had landed in hell after all.

"Welcome to Castel Sant'Angelo, Doctor," said Lahnstein. "And so we meet again. I want to ask God in all humility to look away for one moment. I have waited years for this."

With his pointed boots, he kicked the prisoner hard between the legs.

The pain was so intense that Johann passed out once more.

A short while later, Johann was sitting on a chair in the corner of the chamber with his head on his chest.

The room was entirely lined with dark parquet, and at its center stood an antique statue of Hermes. In front of it was a small altar with a cross and one single kneeler for praying. Perhaps this was a private chapel, illuminated by torches in the early hours of the evening.

Johann's clothes were stained all over, and a stinging rash had formed on his skin. His crotch was throbbing with pain, and he felt sick as a dog. To his relief he could still sense the tiny silver globe underneath the fabric of his shirt.

Lahnstein sat in front of him with crossed legs, while Hagen guarded the door in silence. *Overly cautious,* thought Johann. He was far too weak to stand up—and besides, he was tied to the back and legs of the chair with ropes.

"You look terrible, Doctor," remarked Lahnstein, gazing at Johann with obvious disgust. "Like a heretic on his third day of torture."

"That is exactly how I feel," said Johann. The toxic fumes appeared to have affected his airways. Each word was agony.

Lahnstein gestured at the leather satchel lying on the floor beside Hermes. He wrinkled his nonexistent nose in disgust; the room stank of sulfur and other pungent acids. "What kind of witchcraft is in that bag? Tell me, what sort of devilish invocation had you planned this time?"

"Fireworks," gasped Johann.

Lahnstein leaned forward. "I beg your pardon?"

"Fire . . . fireworks in honor of the pope. Isn't that what they do today?" Johann attempted to smile. "Three cheers for Leo, victor over France."

Lahnstein didn't give in to Johann's provocation, waving dismissively. "Whatever it was that you were planning, it nearly cost you your life. It would have been a fitting end for a quack and necromancer like yourself. And yet I am pleased you're alive." He scrutinized Johann coldly. "Did you really think we didn't know where you've been hiding? Hagen has been watching you and your assistant for a while now. Truly an extraordinarily shabby hole you picked out. The wine must be ghastly."

"Better than . . . to drink from the pope's dog dish."

"Is that all you have left? Insults?" Lahnstein smiled, which, on his monstrous face, looked like a bulldog baring its teeth. "You have fallen a long way, Doctor."

"What . . . what are you planning to do with my grandson?"

Lahnstein raised an eyebrow. "How interesting of you to ask. I was about to ask you something very similar."

He shuffled closer with his stool until he was just a hand's breadth away from Johann's face. Johann could smell a sharp-smelling perfume that reminded him of the pine forests of France. He guessed the representative used it to cover up the foul stench of the poorly healed scab.

"Mandragora, bezoar, amber, *Salamandra salamandra,* sulfur, *dens pistris,*" listed Lahnstein quietly, as if he feared they might be overheard. "Do you know this recipe?"

Johann hesitated. Those were precisely the ingredients Hagen had killed the alchemist for. Why was Lahnstein asking? Did he know that Karl had seen Hagen?

"I don't know what you're talking about," Johann said eventually.

"You are the most famous alchemist of the empire and you're trying to tell me you don't know what those ingredients are used for? Are you trying to play me for a fool?" Lahnstein signaled to Hagen, whereupon the giant stepped forward and landed two well-aimed punches in Johann's belly, causing him to cry out in pain. When Johann vomited this time, only green bile came out.

"We need neither rack nor glowing pincers, Doctor," said Lahnstein. "Hagen developed other methods on the battlefields that make stubborn prisoners talk. I will ask you again." He held the list of ingredients in front of Johann's nose. "Mandragora, bezoar, amber, *Salamandra salamandra* . . . What is it about? Is this a recipe to produce the philosopher's stone? Speak up!"

Johann groaned, kept his head down, and thought hard. So far he had believed that Hagen had fetched all those ingredients for Lahnstein, but now it would appear that the papal representative didn't know anything about it. Or was this a trap? Johann decided to take a huge gamble.

"If I tell you, will you give me your word that no harm will come to my grandson?"

Another wave from Lahnstein brought another punch. "I don't care about your grandson, damn it!" snarled Lahnstein. "God alone will decide whether the brat lives or dies. I only want to know what this recipe is about. I questioned every alchemist in Rome, and no one was able to tell me. Spit it out, Doctor! Now. It is important! Does it serve to make gold or not?"

For the first time, Johann noticed a fearful twitch in Lahnstein's eyes.

"It . . . is not for the production of gold," he said.

"But?" persisted Lahnstein.

"The formula is from *The Sworn Book of Honorius*, an old book of sorcery of which only very few copies survive. The recipe serves . . ." Johann paused. "The recipe serves as an invocation. Those ingredients combined with the right spells summon the devil."

"Summon the . . . the devil? Is it true? I knew it, damn it! I knew it all along!" Lahnstein looked at Hagen. "Not a word of what is being said here can ever get out, understood? It would be the end of all of us!"

Hagen nodded in silence and leaned on his longsword.

"And you really believe such a ritual can summon the devil?" Lahnstein asked Johann in a whisper. "Or is it yet more heretic nonsense that the likes of you use to frighten the common people?"

Johann looked at him from red eyes, his skin covered in rashes, his voice as hoarse as a spirit from the underworld. "If you had asked me earlier, I'd have said that it is nonsense, nothing but hocus-pocus and a show for the stage. But now . . ." He coughed blood. "Yes, I believe the devil truly can be summoned with this ritual. Trust me—I've seen him myself. And he is worse than anything you can imagine. Because deep down the devil is a man, too. If we don't stop him, he is going to destroy the world as we know it. And he will laugh as if it were the funniest joke."

Lahnstein said nothing for a long while. Outside, beyond the thick walls of Castel Sant'Angelo, the masses of the eager crowd could be heard. People couldn't wait for the fireworks to begin.

"I always trusted him," muttered Lahnstein eventually, more to himself. "All those years I thought it was just about the philosopher's stone. Not an entirely ludicrous idea, after all. It might have been possible. But lately, he . . . changed. And I believe I know who is responsible." He shook his head. "How could I have been so stupid!"

"Who are you talking about?" asked Johann.

Lahnstein stood up.

"It is not too late. The fireworks haven't started. We might still be able to stop him. Someone has to stop him before this madness drags us all down. Let's go up to the rooftop terrace." Lahnstein turned to the huge mercenary. "Prepare to do the unimaginable in order to save the world."

Without another word he stormed to the door. Hagen shouldered his long-sword and followed.

The door was pushed shut. Johann heard a key turn twice in the lock.

Then he was alone with his pain and his sense of foreboding.

～

Meanwhile, Karl was sitting by the window, staring out into the dusk settling over Rome. Small lights flared up in the hills. Downstairs, in the taproom, a fiddle struck up a tune while a whore laughed loudly as she led a customer into the backyard. There was still no sign of Faust, and Karl was convinced that the doctor wouldn't return.

Perhaps not ever again.

Three hours had passed since they'd separated. Had the doctor been attacked, or murdered, even? Karl had decided to force such thoughts aside for now. Instead he frantically tried to figure out what he could do. He had come to believe that Greta's son was in danger. The list of alchemy ingredients was rather unambiguous, and Lahnstein was certainly after revenge on Faust. So was that his plan? To conduct some sort of gruesome ritual with the blood of the doctor's grandchild? Is that why the boy was being raised at Castel Sant'Angelo?

Just a few days ago, Karl had been ready to say goodbye to Johann for good. Now the doctor was missing—maybe dead—and Karl felt fear and grief consuming him from the inside. He needed to do something. If he couldn't help the doctor, then at least he'd have to warn Greta.

He cast one last glance through the window onto the dark street below, then he put on his coat and hurried down the steps and outside.

Rome received him with noise and laughter, the lanes full of cheerful people heading for Castel Sant'Angelo or searching for a good spot in the hills from which to watch the fireworks. Some citizens carried wine amphoras to keep themselves warm during the cold night. Pope Leo X was well known for his fireworks, and tonight's display was supposed to be the greatest Rome had ever seen.

Karl made his way through the excited crowd along the Tiber until he finally stood outside the hospital. He was out of breath and his heart thumped wildly, but he forced himself to appear calm as he asked the gatekeeper if he could speak with Sister Greta. It was urgent, a family emergency.

"It is evening vespers," said the gatekeeper, waving at the tall campanile rising up behind the hospital. "The nuns are praying in Santo Spirito Church. You'll just have to wait."

Without paying any heed to the stunned gatekeeper, Karl rushed past him and toward the hospital church. He could hear the monotonous chorale of female voices from inside. Karl opened the church door and was hit by the smell of incense. Wafts of smoke drifted through the high-ceilinged building, which was dimly illuminated by a few candelabras. He guessed there were about two dozen sisters singing and praying.

After searching cautiously for a while, Karl finally spotted Greta in a rear pew on the right-hand side. She sat with her eyes closed and her hands folded in prayer. Karl made the sign of the cross and sat down next to her.

"Greta, we need to talk," he whispered. "It's vitally important."

Greta opened her eyes with surprise and turned to look at him. "How dare you disturb me during mass?" she hissed.

"Your son is in grave danger."

"That's what my father said, and I didn't believe him," she replied through clenched teeth.

"But it's the truth, Greta. I swear it by all the saints and the Mother Mary. By the Holy Spirit who gave this church its name."

Karl had spoken loudly enough for some of the nuns to turn their heads. Greta squeezed Karl's hand and nodded at him to leave the church with her. Several indignant pairs of eyes followed them.

"So, what is it you want to tell me?" asked Greta when they stood in the dark lane. "And don't even bother talking to me about some sort of ridiculous devil ceremony like your lord and master, whom, despite everything, you still idolize."

"What your father told you is the truth, Greta. I saw with my own eyes how Hagen collected the ingredients and murdered the alchemist as an unwanted witness. And I also know *The Sworn Book of Honorius*, from which the ritual is taken—a ritual that demands the blood of a child. Whether it is hocus-pocus or not doesn't matter to the poor boy—he is going to be sacrificed either way."

He grabbed Greta by the shoulders and shook her as if trying to wake her.

"Your father went missing today. I believe Lahnstein abducted him or perhaps even killed him because we got too close to the truth. Think, Greta! Your son . . ." He paused as a merry group walked past them. "Your son is Johann's grandchild," he continued in a whisper. "And Lahnstein has a score to settle with Johann. What if Lahnstein really is going to sacrifice your son for an invocation?"

"That . . . that's nonsense," replied Greta, but her resistance was visibly crumbling. "Why should Lahnstein invoke the devil? He is the personal representative of the pope."

"Maybe he is more than that." Karl sighed. "Maybe the devil is very close to the pope. Greta, I don't know! But I have a strong feeling that Sebastian is in danger. Just go to the castle and see for yourself. I'm not asking for more than that."

"Even if I wanted to, I couldn't," replied Greta. "I lost my key ring. Yesterday it was still around my neck. It must have ripped off at work, but I've looked everywhere."

"So that's where he got it," Karl murmured.

Greta gaped at him, and Karl knew he'd said the wrong thing.

"He stole my keys?" Greta slapped her hand against her forehead. "Of course! When I dropped the bowl of pills. He orchestrated everything, as always. That means . . ." She started with fright as she finished her line of thought. "He hasn't been abducted or murdered. He hoodwinked us both. Most likely, he's on his way into Castel Sant'Angelo to steal his grandson. It is *his* revenge, not Lahnstein's! Because he can't have me, he kidnaps Sebastian so that he can teach my son the same way Tonio used to teach my father. He wants to become Sebastian's master!"

Karl wanted to protest, but suddenly his mouth was very dry. Could Greta be right? He'd had a feeling that Johann was keeping something from him. Had the doctor used him once more?

Karl no longer knew what to believe. Just like one of the many Roman statues, he stood outside the church, mute, incapable of making a decision. It was Greta who grabbed him and pulled him along.

"We must go stop my father—now!"

~

Johann listened to the hurried steps of Lahnstein and Hagen fading away. Then he counted to ten in his mind, seeking the tranquility he required to think.

The situation had changed. The papal delegate didn't, in fact, know about the summoning. Until then, Lahnstein had assumed that the pope was desperately trying to produce gold. But now Lahnstein knew that was not the case. What was it the delegate had said about the pope?

But lately, he changed. And I believe I know who is responsible.

And Johann thought he knew, too.

He closed his eyes and focused entirely on his insides. He subdued his shaking and made his body as limp as if his bones were made of cartilage. It was an exercise he had learned during his time as a juggler. Back then, with Peter Nachtigall, Salome, and the other jugglers, they had occasionally performed escape tricks. Salome had taught him how free himself from a tangle of ropes in no time. All it took was a little deftness and inner calm—a serenity that Johann had lacked earlier, in the chest filled with toxic fumes. But now things were different. He twisted and turned his wrists until he felt the ropes gradually loosening. After a while his right arm was free, then his left, and then he hastily untied his feet. Eventually, he stood up, swaying.

Hagen's blows had left their marks; blood was running from his nose, and with every breath his lungs burned from the toxic fumes. Johann grew dizzy and held on to the statue of Hermes to keep from falling. Once he had overcome his urge to vomit, he squatted down and inspected his leather satchel.

In his shock of hearing about the planned invocation of the devil, Lahnstein must have forgotten all about the bag. There was less broken than Johann had feared. Several jars and vials were still intact, and thankfully the small bottle of spirits of salt was among them. Johann rummaged through the satchel and, at its bottom, found the most important thing: Greta's key ring.

He walked to the door and, with unsteady hands, tried one key after the other in the lock.

The fifth key worked.

He exhaled with relief, only now noticing the cold sweat on his forehead. There was a good chance Greta sometimes prayed in this small chapel. Now her belief gave him another chance to avert disaster. He was about to leave the room when he turned around once more to fetch the bag. Some vials were broken, but the rest might still come in useful.

Walking hunched over, he found himself in a dark courtyard. Night had fallen, and Johann heard the occasional cracking and hissing in the distance— the first signs of the impending fireworks. The cheers of the crowds were muted by the castle's walls.

Johann shuddered. Carefully he looked around but saw no guards. From the courtyard, some stairs led to a terrace. He shouldered his bag and headed that way. Through arrow slits in the wall he caught glimpses of Rome, clusters of lights that became more dense the closer they were to Castel Sant'Angelo and Saint Peter.

Johann was about to rush on when he spotted two guards patrolling the round walk, heading straight toward him. This was the wrong way. He ducked, hurried back down the stairs, and decided on a door opposite the chapel. Once again Greta's keys helped him.

The room on the other side was plain, with a tiled stove and a handful of chests. Johann guessed it was servants' quarters. A second exit led him to corridors and more stairs, and he made sure to keep going up, not down. He was hoping to find the terrace Lahnstein had spoken of.

Once more he used Greta's keys to open a door, and twice more guards walked toward him, but each time Johann managed to hide behind a curtain or a door. The soldiers were in high spirits and not particularly alert; they, too, were looking forward to the fireworks.

Johann soon found that Castel Sant'Angelo was a veritable maze. It looked as though, since the days of the Romans, each ruler had added some new walls, stairs, or corridors and barricaded some old ones. The castle was like an anthill with thousands of tunnels. Johann passed through richly decorated deserted halls, and also a high, barred room that was filled with stacked-up iron chests hung with padlocks—probably the papal treasury. Strangely, there were no guards here, either. The higher he climbed, the more forlorn the countless chambers and hallways, erected just for one single person: the pope, God's representative on earth and therewith one of the most powerful men on earth.

After striking several dead ends, Johann finally came to one last steep staircase. A cold breeze was blowing down the steps, and the cries and cheers from outside were clearly audible now.

The upper terrace, thought Johann.

Strangely, there were no guards at the foot of the stairs. Johann's wonder subsided when he realized what that meant.

Clearly, only very few were supposed to know about what was going on up there.

As silently as he could, Johann started up the steps. Now he could make out individual voices coming from the rooftop. Shortly before the top of the stairs, a guards' chamber opened to the left, but it was empty. When Johann reached the top, a heavy iron door stood ajar, and he peered through the crack. He beheld a scene that was so strange and bizarre that for a brief moment he forgot everything else.

The fireworks were about to begin.

But the show was completely different from what Johann had imagined.

26

VIKTOR VON LAHNSTEIN WAS SHAKING.

It wasn't so much because of the biting cold on the rooftop, more than sixty feet above the city. The sky was clear and starry, and the wind tugged at his robe. No, Lahnstein was shaking because he now realized what a horrific nightmare he had helped to create.

Hell on earth.

As soon as Lahnstein had left Faustus, he had hurried to the upper terrace. He'd intended to send the guards downstairs in order to prevent possible witnesses, but he didn't have to. The pope—or perhaps someone else—had already ensured that there was no one to disturb the ceremony.

A ceremony that left no room for doubt about its purpose.

Directly behind Lahnstein was a smaller platform upon which, allegedly, once upon a time had stood an angel, and which doubled as the roof of a small chapel. In front of him, a large pentagram had been painted upon the floor with rust-red paint. At the star's five points stood flaming firepots, and beside each one lay an item that Lahnstein couldn't make out in the dark of night. But even so, he knew what they were.

Mandragora, bezoar, amber, *Salamandra salamandra, dens pistris.*

They were the alchemy ingredients required to summon the devil.

Around the entire pentagram, a tall wooden scaffold had been erected, reminiscent of a multiple-sided gallows on a giant execution site. The framework was filled with dozens of thin tubes of glued cloth with strings protruding from their bottoms—a tangle of fuses that all came together in one thicker string. And this string led to the precise middle of the pentagram, where, beneath a baldachin, stood a throne adorned with gold leaf.

And on the throne sat the pope, the fuse clasped in his fat, ring-studded hand.

The Holy Father had his eyes closed, a blissful smile on his lips. He appeared to listen to the shouts and cheers of the people moving far below him like ants, waiting for the fireworks. Two huge black cats were lying at the pope's feet, dozing. They were the same panthers Lahnstein had seen a few days ago. Evidently, they no longer left Leo's side.

"Do you hear that?" said Leo without opening his eyes. He must have heard Lahnstein and Hagen approach. "The crowds are cheering for me—they are cheering for God. Because we gave them back their faith!"

Lahnstein couldn't help but wonder who the pope meant by *we*. Was he speaking in the majestic plural?

"Faith requires powerful symbols," continued Leo. "Magnificent churches, gilded altars, expensive ceremonies. Otherwise it withers like a flower without water. Just think of ancient Rome! Urbs Aeterna!" The pope opened his eyes and pointed toward the dark outlines of the hills in the night. "Why has this city survived for so long? Because the Romans knew how to create a cult. They revered their emperors as deities, built their temples and mausoleums, venerated the victors and sacrificed the losers. They held costly games, chariot races, gladiator fights. And all to serve just one goal: to consolidate faith." Leo sighed as one of the panthers opened its large, tooth-studded mouth and let off a growl as if the pope's deliberations had disturbed his slumber.

"We must create another eternal Rome, and this time for the glory of Christendom!" exclaimed Leo, patting the big cat's head. "Yes, I was on the right track, building those many new churches and chapels, erecting monuments and palaces. Saint Peter's was going to be my crowning achievement and outshine all other churches. And then this German monk comes along, preaching against indulgences." Leo's voice rose. "Pity Luther didn't follow my invitation to Rome. I would have hosted fireworks in his honor and, for the final spectacle, burned him for the benefit of everyone."

Lahnstein listened in silence. He couldn't tear his eyes off this pope from the famous Medici dynasty, the man he had served for so many years. Leo had always been a little eccentric, preferring his animals over people, but intelligent, learned, and ambitious—and now he had clearly lost his mind.

The representative took a few steps forward, looking around. He had expected to find someone else up here as well, someone he'd been suspecting to be more than he pretended to be for a while now. But evidently the pope was alone.

Lahnstein cleared his throat.

"Holy Father, what are you doing?" he asked in a husky voice.

"Gold is tricky business," said Leo. "Each burns for gold, all turns on gold, isn't that right, Viktor? What haven't I tried? I tortured several dozen quacks in search of the philosopher's stone. I pored over old writings, even over the notes of a mass murderer. I chased after the famous Doctor Faustus, but nothing yielded success. Because I never delved deep enough—because I didn't dare touch the unspeakable. Only he who challenges his enemy can emerge victorious."

"You want to invoke the devil," said Lahnstein matter-of-factly.

"Nonsense! I'm going to *banish* him, you see?" Leo's fleshy lips quivered. "I will summon him and then banish him—vanquish him!" With a sweeping gesture he pointed at the strange construction around him. "He will be trapped inside this pentagram, forced to serve me. And he will ensure that the church receives all the funding that she needs. Satan himself is going to be my philosopher's stone!" Leo held up the fuse. "The moment I light this fuse and the ritual commences, I will step out of the spell zone. All those thousands of people down there are going to witness how the devil serves the church, how I am going to subjugate him, for the good of Christendom! Satan is going to be my slave!"

Viktor von Lahnstein shook his head, incapable of coming up with a reply. He had sacrificed his entire life to the church, had fought against heretics and disbelievers because he was firmly convinced that in this time of new teachings, which placed man and not God in the center, only a strong church could be their salvation. He had gone through hell and high water for this pope, had put up with all his escapades, only to find out now that his master had lost his mind.

The pope was summoning the devil.

Was it insanity or the worst joke the devil had ever thought up?

"You must not do this," said Lahnstein, taking another step toward the pope.

Leo gave him an astonished look. "What did you say?"

"With all due respect, Holy Father, I am not going to allow this. This isn't the church I gave my solemn oath to."

"I am your uppermost master, have you forgotten? I am the ruler of this church."

"My uppermost master is God, and even you are but His servant. I am sorry to say this, Father, but your time is over."

With those words, Lahnstein spun around and strode toward the stairs. He would notify the guards. When they saw what was going on here, they would understand and arrest the pope. It was plain to see that His Holiness had gone insane. Lahnstein couldn't think of any precedents in the history of the church. Popes had murdered their opponents, kept whores, sold their positions, desecrated tombs. But a pope getting involved with the devil?

The representative took long strides and had almost reached the steps. The cardinals would certainly agree with him following a thorough investigation. They would elect a new pope, and Lahnstein would have a new master he could serve loyally. The church would never go down, ever! Not even when the Holy Father himself had sold his soul to the devil. All would be well—

Lahnstein winced when he felt a sharp sting in the back. A moment later, his legs caved in, but he didn't fall.

Strange, he thought.

When he looked down, he saw the blade of a sword protruding from his belly. Blood was dripping off its tip.

My blood.

He wanted to turn around but couldn't move. Instead he felt a deathly cold spreading from the center of his body to the tips of his fingers and toes. The sword twisted several times in his abdomen, then it was pulled back. The pain was indescribable. Only then did Lahnstein fall down the stone steps, tumbling head over heels several times before coming to rest at the bottom of the stairs.

The last thing he saw was the opening at the top of the stairs, illuminated from behind by the glow of the firepots. Standing there was a huge apparition, his sword raised like an avenging angel.

Like the archangel Lucifer, thought Lahnstein, his final thoughts thundering like a storm through his mind. *The light bringer.*

Then he was overwhelmed by darkness.

~

"Did you immobilize him?" asked the pope from his strange throne beneath the baldachin. A small wave was all it had taken to communicate his command.

Hagen nodded. "He has been silenced for good, Holy Father."

"Well done, Hagen," said Leo with a smile. "I knew I could rely on you. I have always been able to rely on you. Now bring me the child."

"Your wish is my command, Holy Father."

Heavy boots trudged past Lahnstein's body, which was already turning cold.

Dust tickled Johann's nose, and his rash burned like fire. He had quickly hidden behind the door to the guards' chamber when Lahnstein had turned around. The last order the pope had issued to Hagen was branded in his mind as if with glowing needles.

Bring me the child.

Johann was shaking with rage and fear. Leo wanted to sacrifice Johann's grandson. Desperately, he racked his brains for ideas. Below him, at the foot of the stairs, lay Lahnstein, his supposed enemy, cut down like an animal by Hagen. Johann had no doubt that the pope's close confidant was dead. Within a matter of moments, nothing seemed the way it was before. Apparently Lahnstein really hadn't known about the plan to invoke the devil. Another was behind all this. Someone Johann knew all too well.

What shape have you taken this time, Tonio?

Tonio was a master of deception, of masquerade, but Johann's eternal enemy hadn't shown himself yet. Sitting enthroned on the platform was a pope who was making common cause with the devil. It must have been Tonio who told Leo about the ritual, just like Tonio must have been the one to put the idée fixe of finding the philosopher's stone in the pope's mind a couple of years ago, resulting in the hunt for Johann.

Where are you, Tonio? What is your plan?

Trembling, Johann stood beside the open door of the guards' chamber. He should have followed Hagen downstairs. But he didn't stand a chance against the giant, and besides, Hagen would bring the boy up here to complete the gruesome ritual.

Johann hesitated for another moment, then he'd made his decision.

The devil could be bartered with. And the pope would be another pawn in the bargain.

Johann stepped onto the terrace, and the wind immediately tore at his clothes. Behind him, the Angel's Chapel with its platform roof formed the rear part of the terrace, and far below him flickered the lights of plentiful torches as if from another world. Johann studied the bizarre wooden construct riddled with rockets, each one ready to go off at any moment. Then he saw that more fuses led across the walls, presumably to more rockets that would be fired from below.

It would truly be a spectacular display.

Johann, still carrying his satchel, walked toward the pentagram.

Leo had closed his eyes again, but the two panthers noticed Johann right away. They pricked up their ears and snarled, pulling at their leash, which was wrapped around the throne. Leo turned, and surprise flashed in his eyes as he recognized the man on the terrace. But he regained his composure in a heartbeat.

"Doctor Faustus," he said with a thin smile and waved for Johann to join him under the baldachin. "What a pleasure. I was told that you were in Rome. Why didn't you notify us? I would have prepared an appropriate welcome."

"I'm sure you would have," replied Johann, his voice still hoarse. He slowly came closer. "A welcome like your most loyal servant just had the pleasure of enjoying."

"Oh, you speak of Monsignore Lahnstein?" Leo sighed. "Viktor disappointed me gravely. I honestly believed he understood how important it is for the church to find gold. If need be, even with the help of the devil. Tough times like these demand unusual methods. Fortunately, I took precautionary measures."

"You mean you won Hagen over," remarked Johann, thinking how cold blooded the mercenary had looked as he murdered his companion of many years from behind.

Leo gave a shrug. "Hagen is my best man within the Swiss guard. And that guard serves the pope—that is what my predecessor, Julius II, decreed. In addition, I have my very own personal bodyguards."

With a wink he gestured at the two panthers, who had settled down peacefully beside the throne. But Johann knew that those beasts could attack him at any time. He guessed a whistle from the pope was all it took to send the shiny black cats flying at him.

"When a Mussulman merchant offered to sell these two beautiful beasts to me, Hagen arranged the purchase. That was when we got to know each other better, because Hagen loves animals almost as much as I do." Leo smiled. "My little ones are from the same litter. I named them Romulus and Remus, in memory of the time of the great Roman emperors, when such panthers chased Christians to death inside the Colosseum. Now they serve the pope. How the times change." He scratched one of the cats behind its ear, and the animal started to purr loudly. "Sadly, my darlings can't cope with noise. I would have liked to have them with me during the summoning. In some cultures they are considered devils, after all. But Hagen will lead them to their cages once he has brought me your grandson."

"All this nonsense here." Johann gestured at the smoking firepots, the pentagram, and the ingredients surrounding them. "Do you truly believe the devil can be invoked like this?"

"Certainly! And you know it, too, Doctor, don't you? You know it because we both learned from the same master. You served him for a long time, but now he serves me. He showed me much during the last few years. He is the greatest wizard in the world—even greater than you. And he has devoted himself to a transcendental power, a power far greater than all worldly empires combined!" Leo pointed at the black outline of the partially built Saint Peter's Basilica. "The power of the church."

"The church?" Johann gave a dry laugh. He took another step toward the throne; so far, the beasts remained still. "Do you honestly believe Tonio del Moravia would ever serve anyone but himself? And where is he, your *servant*?"

"So you call him Tonio del Moravia? I know he has many names, and he uses a different one with me. But why not Tonio?" Leo smirked. "Don't fret, he will come. He promised. He likes to spend his time at Romulus and Remus's place of retreat. That's where he likes to gather his strength. He can be a little, well . . . odd at times. But he's not going to miss the show of the devil dancing to my tune. He loves shows as much as I do."

"It was Tonio who put the idea in your head that I knew how to make gold, wasn't it? And he told you about Gilles de Rais. That was why you wanted me brought to Rome."

"That was shortly after *he* revealed himself to me. And yes, *he* told me about the dark marshal and showed me some of the knight's writs. Admittedly, it took me a while to recognize the jewel God sent me in the shape of your former master. But his disguise was just too good."

So good that not even the pope can tell that Tonio and Gilles are one and the same person, thought Johann. *What is your disguise this time, Tonio? What shell did you slip on?*

Leo gave another shrug. "You managed to escape and couldn't be found. So I needed a new plan, and this one is even better."

"And this plan, too, stems from Tonio," added Johann pensively. "A ritual to invoke the devil."

"Be so kind and tell me how you got here," said Leo. "I had men searching for you for so long—for years—and now you suddenly stand before me. Upon the uppermost terrace of the best-guarded castle in Rome. How did you do it? Can you fly?"

Johann bared his teeth, the skin of his face stinging with rashes. "I am a wizard, remember?"

"You are indeed." Leo snorted with laughter. "The best in the world, they assured me. And therefore I consider it an honor that you will be witnessing my invocation. Especially since your very own grandson is going to be part of it." The pope placed his hand against his ear and winked at Johann. "Ah, do you hear that? It can't be long now."

~

"You really think they'll just let us in?" asked Karl, following Greta through the crowds.

Hundreds of people had gathered outside Castel Sant'Angelo, and hundreds more were standing upon the bridge and lining the far bank of the Tiber. Karl knew that the bridge had collapsed once before and hoped it wouldn't happen a second time tonight.

"I know some of the guards," replied Greta, her arm linked with his. "One or two of them owe me a favor." She glanced at her old friend with a brief smile. "And the way you're looking, you could offer to hear their confessions. You would have made a good priest."

"At least I would have been constantly surrounded by handsome men," grumbled Karl. "Sodomites are common among monks—I know what I'm talking about."

After Karl and Greta's conversation outside the church, they had paid a brief visit to the hospital. Greta had rummaged through the clothes room until she'd found an old monk's habit that Karl had slipped over his clothes. He had insisted on accompanying Greta to ensure little Sebastian's well-being. He couldn't bring himself to believe that Faust had deceived him.

To Karl's surprise, they didn't head toward the main entrance but walked around the fortress until they came to a smaller gate in the eastern wall. It was manned by two soldiers of the Swiss guard. With their halberds, swords on their belts, and grim expressions, they looked like two statues of Mars, the god of war. But when the men recognized Greta, they broke out in friendly smiles.

"Sister Greta!" exclaimed one of them. "My uncle sends his regards. His stomach pains have indeed gone."

"Tell him to continue taking the powder for another five days." Greta raised a finger. "And no meat or fatty foods during Advent."

The watchman grinned. "Old Greedy Guts will find that rather difficult." His eyes turned to Karl with curiosity. "To what do we owe the pleasure of your visit, Father?"

"We would like to check on my son," replied Greta. "Sebastian has been suffering from a nasty cough since yesterday. And Father Rupert is one of the best doctors over at the hospital."

"Better than you? That's hardly possible," said the second watchman, a gaunt fellow with a freshly healed scar on his face. "Your ointments work miracles, Sister. But I understand—a second opinion never hurts." He stepped aside and opened the gate. "I hope your son feels better soon, Sister Greta." He winked at her. "And don't be surprised if some of the guards aren't at their posts tonight. I think a few of them wanted to sneak out to the balustrades to watch the fireworks. They should start at any moment."

Greta gave the guards a nod, and she and Karl walked into the gloomy building.

"I hope God will forgive my small lie," she murmured. She folded back her head scarf so that Karl could see her blonde hair. Her eyes were flashing with the same willfulness he knew from years ago. "I don't even know why I agreed to this charade. My son is perfectly well—you'll see."

"I wish that you're right, Greta," said Karl. "Truly, I wish it with my whole heart. And if you are right, then at least we'll have spent some time together before we go our separate ways for good. I am going to leave Rome soon."

She squeezed his hand. "It was wonderful to see you again, Karl." She turned abruptly. "Now let's go. Before more guards ask stupid questions about the handsome monk in the musty robe."

They were standing inside a narrow corridor that ran between the outer wall and the cylindrical main building. Every ten paces or so stood a firepot, bringing a little light into the night. A larger gate led inside the castle. Here, too, the soldiers let Greta and Karl pass with a nod at Greta.

"You seem to have a lot of friends here," whispered Karl.

"Everyone gets sick sometimes or suffers from one ailment or another. And there are hardly any women at Castel Sant'Angelo—the guards are grateful for any distraction." Greta strode ahead. "But don't forget—this is merely the lower area. The higher up we go, the more heavily guarded you'll find the castle. I don't have access to the upper levels."

As they followed a wide rampart that was shaped like the inside of a snail's shell, Karl had to concede that the papal castle truly was an impregnable fortress. They walked across a trapdoor more than three paces long and as wide as the rampart. In the sides and the ceilings he noticed narrow and deep slits. The walls here seemed to be thicker than some houses, and with no windows or doors. The dim source of light was torches sitting in brackets on the wall at regular intervals.

After a while, Greta took a corridor that turned off to the left. It led them to a small courtyard where young lemon trees grew inside clay tubs; several doors led in all directions. Karl had completely lost his bearings. The moon above him was his only point of orientation, and he faintly heard the cheering crowd outside the walls.

Greta looked around in bewilderment. "There should be guards here," she said, shaking her head. "I guess they wanted to see the fireworks. So long as Martha is still there."

"Who is Martha?"

"Sebastian's nursemaid. She's a kind and caring woman who has raised many children. Sebastian loves her." She paused. "Probably more than his own mother," she added softly.

She walked to a small door in the corner. She was about to push down the handle when she froze. Karl walked up beside her and saw what had made Greta stop short.

The door was ajar, and all was dark on the other side.

"Martha, are you there?" called Greta into the darkness. "It's me, Greta. I know it's late, but—"

She fell silent when Karl touched her by the shoulder. He pointed at the ground. A child-sized shoe was lying in front of the doorstep, and a wet spot gleamed next to it in the light of the moon.

"Wait here," whispered Karl. "Do not go inside without me!"

He hurried across the courtyard, grabbed one of the torches, and returned to Greta, who stared at him from wide eyes. "What is the meaning of this?" she asked quietly. "Where is Martha? Where is Sebastian? Maybe . . . maybe she just took him to the balustrade to watch the fireworks."

"Maybe," murmured Karl.

He shoved the door open and cautiously stepped into the room with the torch in his hand. Flickering light fell onto a table with a bowl of cold porridge. Farther back, Karl made out a plain bed and a cradle beside it.

The cradle was empty.

Karl lowered the torch and saw a child's rattle on the floor, a spinning top, a velvet cushion, a hand.

A hand.

Karl started. Next to him, Greta gave a small cry.

A severed human hand was lying on the floor.

A trail of blood led a few steps to the side, where, in a large pool of blood, lay the body of a woman. Her throat had been almost cut right through, and the stump of her arm was pointed toward the empty cradle as if in silent admonishment. Mercifully, the corner of a sheet covered the upper part of her face.

"Martha!" cried Greta. "Oh God, Martha! Oh God!"

She was holding both hands to her mouth, staring at the dead woman as if she hoped to wake from this nightmare at any moment.

"Where . . . where is Sebastian? Where? Where? *Where?*" Her voice was growing increasingly shrill.

Karl dragged her away from the corpse. It looked as though there had been a struggle between Martha and her murderer. The nursemaid had probably refused to give up the child, whereupon the murderer had first cut off her hand and then killed her with another stroke of his sword.

A stroke of his sword.

Karl's eyes turned to the wooden floor and saw bloody footprints.

Very large footprints.

He grabbed Greta and pulled her to the door. Not far away the first firecrackers exploded, and a solitary rocket painted a red arch above the courtyard.

"Where do the fireworks get lit?" asked Karl breathlessly. He shook Greta, who still seemed in a daze. "Where?"

"Probably upstairs . . . up on the terrace. There'd be enough room. But—"

"Quickly!" ordered Karl. "I think I know where we'll find your son. May God ensure that it isn't too late."

~

The pope reclined in his throne with a smile on his face, like he was expecting a present. Indeed, now Johann heard a crying that quickly became louder.

Someone was coming up the stairs with a child.

"And there he is, the little one!" Leo clapped his hands, and the panthers pricked up their ears. Moments later, Hagen appeared on the terrace with a crying child. The boy was kicking his legs wildly, but Hagen held him in a viselike grip.

Sebastian! thought Johann. *My own flesh and blood.*

It nearly broke Johann's heart to behold his grandson for the first time in this way. Sebastian had his father's hair and perhaps also his stout build, but Johann recognized the child's black eyes immediately.

My eyes.

He took a step toward Sebastian and Hagen, whereupon the giant slowly shook his head.

"Don't even try," said Leo. "The boy will only die sooner. Better enjoy the few moments you have with him. And remember: he is giving his young life for a good cause, the well-being of Christendom. Besides, he is baptized and thus guaranteed a place in heaven. Unlike you." Leo's voice had become malicious and sharp, and Johann wondered how many poor devils had heard this voice as they'd suffered on the rack, deep down below Castel Sant'Angelo.

"Why Sebastian?" asked Johann, not wanting to arouse the pope's suspicions. Johann's expression was blank, but inside, his thoughts were racing. He would only have one attempt—one lousy attempt, but he had to risk it, had to stake everything on one card.

"It was your old master's idea that we use your grandson for the ritual," said Leo. "It could have been any child. But I liked the notion, and to be frank, I thought good old Viktor would also appreciate it. I wanted to give this moment of revenge to him as a gift. Now he's missing it, unfortunately."

Johann closed his eyes and counted down in his mind. It was like during one of their juggling shows years ago, except he hadn't been able to practice this time. It was like a dance on the rope without a net.

Three.

Johann's hand slid into the satchel. Little Sebastian was screaming at the top of his lungs now, his face bright red. Hagen held him by the scruff like a rabbit before slaughter.

Two.

Johann heard a low growl behind his back.

One.

"One wrong movement and my darlings will rip open your throat," said Leo. "They adore Hagen because he always brings them the finest meats. Romulus and Remus would never forgive you if you harm as much as a hair on Hagen's body. You better accept your—"

Now!

At lightning speed, Johann's hand shot out from the satchel and hurled the vial of spirits of salt at Hagen. He had stealthily removed the cork inside the bag, and now the contents of the small bottle were spilling over Hagen's right thigh. Johann would have preferred to hit the bastard right in the face with it, but then he would have risked hurting Sebastian.

But even so, the effect was enormous.

With a hissing noise the liquid ate through Hagen's leather trousers and, roaring with pain, the giant fell to the ground. The child slipped from his grasp.

"My darlings will tear you to pieces for this!" screamed the pope. "Romulus, Remus!"

The beasts hissed and pulled at their leash. Johann darted to one of the firepots, snatched it, and held the flames to one of the many fuses connected to other fuses. There was a soft hiss as the string caught on fire.

"Noooo!" yelled the pope. "The ritual! The ritual isn't complete!"

Thick smoke spread around Johann; there were crackling sounds and blue sparks flying. Then the first rockets howled into the air. Red, green, and blue dots exploded high above the terrace and expanded into star shapes. The deafening noise had precisely the effect Johann had intended.

The panthers went mad with fury, confusion, and pain.

The idea had come to Johann when Leo had raved about his pets earlier.

Sadly, my darlings can't cope with noise.

Beside themselves, the two big cats tore at their ropes, which were wrapped around the throne. The chair crashed to the side, and Leo rolled onto his back like a fat beetle. All around them were thunder, hissing, and cracking as if Judgment Day had arrived. Finally free, the panthers were behaving like a pair of snarling demons. One of them pounced onto the pope while the other prepared to leap in the direction of Johann and Hagen, who was still screaming as he held his leg.

Right between Johann and the panther lay Sebastian.

Once again Johann noticed how much the boy resembled him.

My grandson.

Then the panther pounced.

27

WE HAVE TO GO ALL THE WAY UP TO THE ROOFTOP TERRACE!"
shouted Karl to Greta as the first rockets exploded above them. "The ritual
must take place under the open sky—that's how it's written in *The Sworn Book
of Honorius*."

They ran upstairs, crossed numerous deserted chambers, racing on as Greta's
heart felt like it was going to burst. Fear for her son almost drove her insane.
Until then she had been convinced that the tale about the ritual to summon
the devil was nothing but balderdash—just more lies by her father to lead her
astray. But now dear Martha had been murdered and her son was missing. What
in God's name was going on here?

Greta had never been to the castle's upper levels, as they belonged exclusively
to the pope. But she instinctively found the right way, as if she sensed where
Sebastian was. Outside, they could hear thundering, howling, cracking, and the
shouts of delight of the crowd who'd gathered to admire the fireworks. To her
ears, all the screaming sounded as if the apocalypse had commenced.

The noise led them in the right direction. She and Karl came to the staircase
to the upper terrace, and Greta screamed when she saw Lahnstein lying at the
bottom of the steps in a pool of blood, staring at the ceiling with empty eyes,
his final expression showing shock and also wonder, as if he couldn't believe his
own death. From outside the door, in addition to the noise of the fireworks, they
could hear someone screaming in agony and a growling.

And the crying of a child.

"Sebastian!" shouted Greta. "Sebastian, are you there?"

She had never particularly liked Lahnstein, but he had been a steady companion over the last two years and the person who had smoothed the way for her

here in Rome. The death of the papal representative came as a shock, but she had no time to dwell on it. Her son was up there, and he was in danger. Greta leaped across Lahnstein's corpse and followed Karl up the stairs. The piece of night sky they could see through the rectangular opening was shining in all colors, and still more rockets exploded and traveled across the firmament as bright, flaming arrows. Greta ran out onto the platform.

And stopped as if she'd turned to stone.

What in heaven's name?

A smudged pentagram was on the floor in the center of the terrace, and inside the pentagram lay a throne on its side beneath a baldachin. Groaning and tossing about in a mess of fallen and broken wooden poles was Hagen, the giant mercenary who had always been at Lahnstein's side. Farther back, Greta saw a black panther pinning a man to the ground with its paws, and the man was screaming as if out of his mind.

It was the pope.

The beast had torn the Holy Father's robe, and his fat, pale body was exposed. Leo was bleeding from several wounds. He was shielding his face with his hands as the panther sank its teeth into his shoulder. Greta couldn't help but think of all those poor Christians who, a long time ago, died in this manner at the Roman Colosseum.

"For heaven's sake, get the monster off me!" screeched Leo. "Hagen, do something! Jesus Christ . . . it . . . it is eating me alive!"

The panther took another bite, and the pope screamed like a berserker. Greta remembered a few lines from the Book of Revelation that she'd read just a few days ago.

And the beast which I saw was like unto a leopard, and his feet were as the feet of a bear, and his mouth as the mouth of a lion.

Only now did she notice the second big cat on the terrace. It was prowling toward the balustrade, which was only hip high, forcing a man closer and closer to the abyss. When Greta recognized the man, anger and hatred welled up in her.

It was her father.

In his arms he was holding little Sebastian, who was screaming and squirming and calling for his mother.

"Give me my child, you devil!" yelled Greta.

She was about to rush at Johann, but Karl held her back.

"Don't you see that he's trying to protect your son?" he hissed at her. "One wrong movement and the panther will jump!"

Karl was right; Greta saw now that her father was trying to shield Sebastian from the beast. Without taking his eyes off the cat, Johann gently set Sebastian down and took a step forward, positioning himself between the panther and the boy. Sebastian stood as if rooted to the spot, staring at the animal in fear. The pope's screams had stopped, but the rockets still howled.

"Whatever brought you here, you come just in time," said Johann, panting. He looked terrible—his face was raw with some kind of rash, and his voice sounded hoarse. He didn't take his eyes off the panther, who was snarling and obviously waiting for the right moment to pounce. "I am going to distract this black devil here while you fetch the boy."

From the corner of her eye, Greta saw with horror how the other panther lowered his blood-covered snout into the ripped throat of the pope. Leo's eyes stared lifelessly into the sky; there was no doubt that he was dead, torn apart by his own pet.

Greta struggled to suppress another scream. What in heaven's name was happening? She was trapped inside a nightmare! All that prevented her from going insane was her son and making sure nothing happened to him. Slowly, her whole body shaking, she walked toward Sebastian, who was just waking from his shock. He began staggering toward her, his little arms outstretched.

"Mama!" he whined. "Mama . . . scared . . . bad kitty."

"Oh God, don't move, Sebastian!" implored Greta, trying to keep her eyes on both panthers at once. "Stop where you are! Mama is nearly there."

The panther by the railing seemed indecisive as to which prey was more tempting: the small, easy boy or the man trying to block its way. The animal hissed and growled, shifting its weight from paw to paw, its tail lashing across the stone floor. Johann waved his arms about wildly and roared at the big cat.

"Come on, you devil! You want human flesh? Then come and get mine! I promise you, it is as poisonous as a viper!" Johann also hissed and bared his teeth.

Greta thought it looked as though two equal beasts were facing each other, demons from a dark world that wasn't her own.

"Come and get me!" yelled Faust. "Jump!"

And the panther did.

The beast looked like a black shadow, blacker than the night that was illuminated by countless rockets. For a few seconds, Greta felt like everything happened much more slowly. She saw the panther's muscles tense as it leaped forward, flying toward the balustrade. She watched as Johann dropped to the ground at the very last moment. The cat vaulted right across him.

It seemed to hover in midair for a tiny instant.

And then it was gone, swallowed up by the darkness.

"Go to hell, you filthy cur!" gasped Johann. He got to his feet and peered into the depths beyond the balustrade. "Claws and teeth, but a brain the size of a walnut."

His hands clasped the stone railing as he breathed heavily. Greta was about to rush toward Sebastian and wrap her arms around him when Karl yelled out.

"Greta, watch out! He's right behind you!"

The second panther! thought Greta.

She felt a shove in her back that made her stagger. It was not the panther but Hagen, who was storming past her, reaching for Sebastian. He yanked the screaming boy up by his legs and lifted him into the air head down. In the other hand the giant was holding his bloodstained sword. His leather trousers were torn, showing the gaping wound beneath, but he managed to stay on his feet.

"Not another step," growled Hagen. "Or I'll toss this whining bastard over the edge. I doubt he knows how to fly, even if his grandfather is a sorcerer."

Greta froze. Her son was just a couple of yards away from her, crying and whimpering and calling for his mother. But she couldn't help him—not now. Beside the dead pope lay the second panther, its skull split by Hagen's sword. Leo himself was barely recognizable, his throat ripped, his face a bloody mass.

The devil took the pope, thought Greta.

Cautiously she tried to bring Hagen to his senses. "Give me my son," she said to him. "Please! I don't know what's going on here. I only know that Sebastian is an innocent child who has nothing to do with any of this."

"A child with a certain value," replied Hagen with a smirk, weighing the whimpering bundle as if he were a sack of gold.

"We can't stop you from fleeing," said Karl, who had walked up beside Greta. He seemed shaken but unhurt. "We are unarmed. You don't need the child as a hostage—you can just go."

Hagen raised both eyebrows. "I'm afraid you don't understand. I don't want the child for a hostage. I'm going to bring it to someone who appreciates my work. Someone who is going to pay well for the little one—very well." He bared his teeth. "The high and mighty often make the mistake of underestimating the likes of us. They think we're nothing but dumb soldiers, waving our swords about and incapable of adding two and two. But I figured out long ago who is truly in charge here at Castel Sant'Angelo. It isn't the pope—oh no! Hasn't been for a long time." He laughed. "I think Lahnstein had a hunch. But one must always remain a step ahead, that's what I learned at war. I know where the master is waiting, and I'm going to bring him the boy." Hagen pointed his sword toward the bloody corpse of the pope. "I'll have to find a new master, anyhow. An even more powerful one. Now please excuse me. It's time to disappear before the guards discover this mess."

Without taking his eyes off Greta, Johann, and Karl, Hagen walked to the stairs with the crying and squirming child in his hand. He was limping, dragging his right leg. Slowly he stepped into the corridor and closed the door behind him.

Bolts were pushed across and locks clicked shut. But even through the heavy iron door Greta could hear the cries of her son for a long time, calling for his mother.

They were growing fainter and, eventually, all was quiet.

Greta only noticed now that the rockets had ceased. After all the noise, an eerie silence spread across the terrace.

The fireworks were over.

～

Johann leaned against the balustrade and noticed that his face felt damp and warm. When he brushed his hand across his forehead, it came off wet with blood. Evidently, the panther had still caught him with one of its paws before falling to its death. Johann gazed at the chaos upon the platform. It looked indeed as if they had invoked some kind of demon. Between the charred scaffolding, knocked-over firepots, and shattered vials lay the maimed corpse of the pope, and next to him the black panther.

It could have been worse.

"Sebastian! Sebastian!" Greta's screams startled him. His daughter had run to the closed door and hammered her fists against it.

"Don't bother." Johann stood up with a groan. His body ached all over. When he had saved his grandson from the panther, he had smelled the beast's rotten breath, breath that had come straight from hell. "The guards will be here soon."

"You know what that means, don't you?" Karl looked down and across to Sant'Angelo Bridge, where the crowds of people slowly dispersed. "They will think *we* killed the pope!" Karl gave a desperate laugh. "Doctor Faustus and his two helpers summon the devil, who then comes and takes the pope. Ha! At least we'll go down in Vatican history with this tale. The death penalty for this crime hasn't been invented yet!"

"I don't think they'll want to shout it from the rooftops," remarked Johann tiredly. "I'm guessing the cardinals will try to gloss over the whole affair. They can't afford the story to come to light that the pope tried to invoke the devil. I think they'll say that Leo died very suddenly of illness. And very soon white smoke will rise above Vatican Hill."

"The smoke from our burning flesh is going to rise," snapped Karl. "We won't get away from here. This is the end."

"And my son is lost," breathed Greta. All her strength seemed to have drained from her body. She was cowering at the bottom of the closed door, her face ashen. "It's like a curse," she said to Johann. "With you, evil returned to my life. All those years working at Santo Spirito as a sister—for nothing!" She shook her head. "God is punishing me. But why is He punishing my son?"

"I tried to save your son," murmured Johann, but he could tell that Greta wouldn't hear him now.

They were all lost—Greta, Karl, Johann, and, worst of all, little Sebastian, whom Hagen was taking to Tonio del Moravia at this very moment. Johann still didn't really understand the intended purpose of the ritual on the rooftop. If Tonio was the devil himself—which Johann now assumed—then why would he persuade the pope to invoke him? Leo's ritual had failed, but what good was that if the devil was already in Rome?

Johann felt empty and spent. Surely it wouldn't be long until the guards arrived. What they would find here would change the history of Rome forever. The small silver globe weighed heavily on Johann's chest; he had almost forgotten about it in all the excitement. He still owned this pawn, which he had intended to use to bargain with Tonio.

The globe's contents in exchange for my grandson.

But what use was that when they couldn't get away from here? Johann's eye turned to the mangled body of the pope beneath the baldachin. Miraculously, the shelter had been the only thing to remain intact amid all the chaos. It merely bore a few scorch marks and the fabric was torn at the edges, hanging down like limp wings. What was it Pope Leo had said when he couldn't work out how Johann had made it up here?

Can you fly?

Johann sighed. He wished he could. But it wasn't possible. No man could fly, not even—

He started.

An image appeared before his mind's eye, an image he'd seen a long time ago among Leonardo da Vinci's notes. Back at Château du Cloux, he had been permitted to browse through the library and read the wealth of notes the genius had composed. Leonardo, too, had been fascinated by flying. He had observed the flight of birds closely, studying the movement of their wings. There were images of a flying apparatus with long wings made of wood and linen, and other sketches of types of propellers. But Johann was thinking of yet another image.

The drawing of a man with a large canopy above his head, like a roof.

Almost like a baldachin.

Johann sprang to life.

"Help me!" he shouted at Greta and Karl. "I know how we can get away from here!"

"What's your plan?" asked Karl. "If you're thinking of using the remaining aqua regia to get through the door, I don't think—"

"Quit jabbering—come help me!" Johann had already rushed over to the baldachin.

To make it rain- and wind-resistant, it had been manufactured from solid, reinforced linen that was additionally strengthened by thin wooden sticks. Four poles held up the corners, and strings looped through iron rings held the baldachin to the ground. Johann untied one of the strings and lifted the shelter tentatively. It was amazingly light, and it would be even lighter without the poles.

Karl turned pale. Now he probably also remembered the drawing from Leonardo da Vinci's house.

"Jesus, don't tell me you want to—"

"Can you think of another way?" barked Johann. "We don't have much time! Even if we managed to lower ourselves to one of the levels below, they would only catch us there."

As if to support his words, someone started banging against the door. Angry shouts followed. Johann gave a tired smile.

"At least it looks like Hagen didn't give his key to his comrades. I'm guessing only very few people have access to this terrace. We still have a few minutes until they break through the door."

"Hold on," said Greta. "Are you . . . are you planning to use this thing to . . . ?"

"To fly, yes," sighed Karl as the banging against the door grew louder.

"Eleven by eleven paces. That's how big the canopy ought to be, according to Leonardo's calculations. But I believe he's wrong. A smaller area should work, too."

"But there are three of us!" insisted Karl.

"And we're not trying to cross the Alps but merely to glide to the bottom."

"Glide?" Karl groaned again. "We are going to shatter like rotten apples."

"If it's the only way to get down from here, then so be it," said Greta. "No matter how slim our chances. I would do anything to save my son. Maybe we'll even catch up to Hagen in time." She scrambled to her feet and walked over to Johann, the noise behind the door increasing still. "What do we have to do?"

"Let's remove the four poles and tie the strings into thick ropes." Johann pointed at the thin wooden sticks below the linen. "We tie up the ropes, hold on to those sticks, and jump off the balustrade."

"That's crazy!" shouted Karl.

"Crazier than all that happened on this terrace?" Johann gestured at the dead pope and the equally dead panther, both lying in a pool of blood that was still growing. "At least what I propose is not sorcery or some bizarre ritual, but reasonable science." He winked at Karl. "Isn't that what you always wanted to be? A reasonable scientist?"

Karl hesitated for another moment, but when a powerful thud shook the door, he gave up with a sigh.

"Better to shatter on the ground than burn at the stake, or whatever else they would have done to us."

He helped Johann and Greta to remove the poles and braid the strings into ropes. They worked in silence as the door shuddered on its hinges. Evidently, the guards had fetched something heavy. The top hinge was beginning to come off.

"Faster!" urged Johann.

When the second hinge came off the wall, they had knotted four reasonably strong ropes. Johann tied them together in the middle, leaving three loops. One for each of them.

"Help me carry the baldachin to the balustrade."

Acting on instinct, Johann picked up his satchel full of ingredients and tied it around his hips. Maybe some of it could still come in handy. Then they lifted up the canopy together, and a gust of wind immediately pulled on it, making it bulge like a sail at sea. Still, they managed to carry the baldachin to the edge of the terrace.

"I think a quick prayer wouldn't hurt," said Johann to Greta. "We could really use the Lord's help for once."

"The dear Lord has long since turned away from you," replied Greta.

The third hinge dropped, and half a dozen guards poured onto the platform with raised swords and halberds.

Johann gave a shrug. "No prayer it is."

The canopy billowed.

"Jump!" screamed Johann.

And the baldachin took off.

~

It was no gentle gliding, no elegant flight like that of an eagle, but an abrupt fall.

Karl felt his heart stop for a moment. This was complete madness. Man wasn't made for flying. The ground raced toward him, hard ground, a maze of lanes in between the roofs of the houses right behind Castel Sant'Angelo. Suddenly the baldachin was struck hard by something. It took Karl a moment to realize that it wasn't the impact but another wind gust. It lifted them up and carried them a little distance away from the castle. Karl's hands were cramped around the rope, and beside him Greta was screaming.

And Johann laughed.

It was a throaty laughter that sounded somewhat insane. But the doctor seemed to be the only one who wasn't on the verge of passing out with fear. Instead, he pulled on his loop, causing the baldachin to tumble but also gain height. They started to spin in wild circles. Below them, Sant'Angelo Bridge appeared; the baldachin bulged. Karl heard an ugly sound as the canopy tore.

Then they plunged into the depths.

Karl doubled over in expectation of the hard, inevitably fatal landing. Instead, his feet suddenly struck something cold and wet.

The Tiber! he thought.

The next instant, the water closed over his head. Now, at the start of December, the Tiber was as cold as the kiss of a water witch. Blackness engulfed Karl. He tried to make a few desperate swimming movements when he remembered that he didn't know how to swim. When he had fallen into the moat at Tiffauges, John Reed had saved him. But John was dead.

Just like I am going to be.

Something grabbed him by the collar and pulled him up. Spluttering, he emerged between scraps of linen and broken sticks.

"The bank!" he heard Johann shout. "It isn't far! We can make it!"

The doctor wrapped his arm around Karl's chest and started pulling him through the river. Karl swallowed stinking water, coughed, but Faust didn't let go. Karl's body was pressed against the doctor's. They hadn't been this close since the horrific bath at Tiffauges. Karl was scared for his life, but at the same time he felt strangely secure.

Then they reached the muddy bank. Johann dragged Karl out of the river, where he spewed up water and bile. Trying to catch his breath, Karl looked up and saw that Greta was already waiting for them. Her dress clung to her body and was covered in brown slime, as were her hair, her arms, and her legs. Karl looked down on himself and saw that he was just as filthy.

"We stink like polecats," remarked Johann with a grin and untied the leather satchel from around his waist. He ran his fingers through his black hair, removing leaves and some slimy items that Karl didn't care to inspect more closely. "The Cloaca Maxima drains into the Tiber a little upstream by the Pons Aemilius," explained Johann. "This river truly isn't a violet-infused Roman thermal bath. But at least we flew. How did you like it?"

"How did we *like* it?" Karl thought he must have misheard. "It was awful—horrible! And we didn't fly, we dropped like dead birds!"

"Well, we did fly for a little bit." Johann nodded solemnly. "I believe we are the first persons to prove that Leonardo's flying canopy actually works."

"We might have survived," said Greta, rubbing her arms to warm herself. "But Hagen is long gone with my son." Her eyes grew empty. "I would rather have crashed and died—then I would soon be with Sebastian."

"You mustn't talk like that—" began Johann.

"You can't tell me what I must and must not do!" said Greta harshly. "Was it your idea to summon the devil up on the terrace? Together with the pope or whoever? That's why you stole my key ring! Wherever you go, you spread misery and chaos!"

"That's not what happened."

"He is telling the truth, Greta," said Karl. "He was only trying to protect your son."

Johann nodded. In halting words he described what had happened up on the rooftop. "Tonio is somewhere in town," he concluded. "The ritual failed. But all this can only end once I stand face to face with Tonio. I still don't understand what Tonio tried to achieve with the ritual. If he is the devil himself—"

"I don't care what unfinished business you might have with Tonio or with the devil himself," said Greta, cutting him off. "I want my son back."

"And I my grandson." Johann frowned "Damn it. If only I knew where Tonio was hiding and what shape he has taken on this time. The pope mentioned something earlier on. He said . . ." He closed his eyes and focused. "He said Tonio likes to spend his time at Romulus and Remus's place of retreat."

"The two panthers?" Greta shrugged. "That would be inside Castel Sant'Angelo, in their cage. But why should someone like Tonio spend time inside a cage? It doesn't make sense."

"You're right," said Johann with a sigh. "But those were the pope's words. At—"

"Romulus and Remus's place of retreat, I know," said Greta. "Words spoken by a lunatic. Keeps panthers as pets and names them after the founding fathers of Rome. Even at Santo Spirito the nuns used to whisper about the Holy Father, calling him a fool. How many of the poor and sick could have been helped instead of wasting all that money on fireworks, games, and big cats? It's almost like we're back in ancient Rome."

One last rocket suddenly fired, exploding far above their heads. At the same moment, something exploded inside Karl's mind.

In ancient Rome.

"What did you just say?" Karl looked at Greta with astonishment.

"I said that it's almost like—"

"No, no, before that! You said that Pope Leo named his panthers after the founding fathers of Rome. That's it!" Karl slapped his hand against his forehead, and suddenly he stopped feeling cold. He was still shivering, but with excitement. "Do you get it? It's not about the panthers. It's about the real brothers."

"You mean . . . ?" began Johann.

"Exactly." Karl nodded. "At the place of retreat of Romulus and Remus. That's what the pope said."

"And where is that?" asked Greta.

Karl picked a rotten leaf from his hair and spoke quickly. "Over a month ago I went to the Mons Palatinus to sketch. There's a cave there—I even told you about it. Remember? I told you about a heathen monument."

When Johann said nothing, Karl went on. "It's said that inside the cave, a she-wolf nursed the two brothers after they were washed ashore in a willow basket. Apparently, the cave used to be a well-known place of worship, but now it's partly collapsed. Only very few know where to find its entrance."

"That's right—I remember now! Ha! Why didn't I think of that myself?" The doctor gave Karl a slap on the shoulder that nearly sent him back into the Tiber. "I must be getting old. The Lupercal, the wolf's cave! I've read about it, and indeed, you did tell me about it. One of the many heathen places left in Rome. And it would suit Tonio. He loves the underworld, and inside this cave, he would be right in the center of Rome and yet completely undisturbed. The perfect hideout."

Johann shouldered his bag and started to clamber up the bank toward the lane. He turned around impatiently to Karl and Greta. "What is it? If we want to save my grandson from Tonio's clutches, we mustn't lose any time! Karl must lead us to the Lupercal."

"I have heard of this cave," said Karl. "But to be honest, I don't know where exactly it lies. The entrance is buried beneath rubble."

"Isn't that great," Greta groaned. "The Palatine Hill is the biggest hill of Rome, where one derelict temple follows the next. How are we supposed to find a buried cave?"

"And there's something else," said Karl. "The locals who told me about the cave said it was cursed. They called it *la porta infernale.*"

"The gateway to hell." Johann nodded. "If there were any doubts left that Tonio resided there, they have now been removed. The devil reigns in Rome. And, by God, we are going to find him!"

Act V

Dante's *Inferno*

28

THREE FIGURES IN WET, DIRTY CLOTHES HURRIED TOWARD the Campo Vaccino and past the tall Trajan's Column. It was the middle of the night, and the only people in the streets were vagabonds, thieves, and murderers, but no one bothered the three figures. They stank ten paces against the wind.

Greta bounded ahead of the two men. Near the Sant'Angelo Bridge they had found three torches, left behind from the fireworks display, offering at least a little light against the darkness. Greta ran so fast that the torch was in danger of going out. She couldn't believe how drastically her life had changed in the last few hours. Only the day before she had been firm and unswerving in her faith. Faith had offered her comfort and kept the fear at bay. And now she had joined her old friend Karl Wagner and her father, whom she'd never wanted to see again, to find the man who called himself Tonio del Moravia and who, so her father believed, was the devil.

Greta's heart was racing. Every minute was precious! At least one good thing had come out of the last few hours for her: they had shown her just how much she loved Sebastian, more than anything else on this earth. If she should succeed in rescuing her son, then she would never give him to anyone else again. The last two years seemed like a blurry dream to her now. Despite her fear, she felt strangely clearheaded, liberated. And she knew that she could never return to Santo Spirito. Her life of solitary silence was over once and for all.

They arrived at Campo Vaccino, a field of rubble shrouded in fog and riddled with holes that made for easy traps in the darkness. Twice already Greta had slipped on the wet stones, and both times Karl had managed to catch her before she fell into one of the holes that were probably full of adders and other vermin.

"The Mons Palatinus." Next to her, Johann was pointing at the outline of a tall hill rising into the sky beyond the field. Slung across his shoulder was the leather satchel he had carried with him since their leap with the baldachin. "The Romans also called this hill Palazzo Maggiore, the great palace. Our European palaces originate from here. Many Roman emperors built pompous villas upon this hill. It is the oldest part of Rome and the place where the city was founded."

"You were here yesterday," said Karl as they continued to walk toward the hill. "I don't suppose you saw anything resembling a cave?"

"I didn't have enough time. Hagen overpowered me very quickly and took me to the castle inside a chest." Johann nodded grimly. "Another sign that we've come to the right place. The giant was probably visiting his new master."

Greta turned to Karl. "And what about you? Did you notice anything on Palatine Hill? You drew it, after all."

"There are countless palaces here worth drawing. But the buildings are dilapidated and overgrown—a cave could be anywhere. Like I said, I only heard about it from some vegetable farmers. They sounded like they wanted to warn me about the cursed place, the porta infernale, the gateway to hell."

Johann stopped. He massaged his temples, like he often did when trying to focus. "Let us think. If the cave really was such a sacred place, then the emperors would have used it to glorify themselves." He looked up and gazed at one of the ruins on the hill. "Who is the best-known Roman emperor?"

"Julius Caesar," said Karl.

"Who, as you well know, wasn't an emperor. Only his name served all subsequent emperors as title," said Johann. "And he had no villa on Palatine Hill. Caesar lived down below as *pontifex maximus*. So, who else?"

"Constantine?" suggested Karl. "He was the first emperor to convert to Christianity."

"And cut off the head of old Rome by founding Constantinople?" The doctor gave a snort of derision. "Bah!"

"Augustus?" offered Greta.

"Hmm . . . The first Roman emperor and Caesar's great-nephew." Johann nodded. "Following his death he was declared a god." He gestured toward a large, derelict group of buildings. "That's where his palace used to stand. I once read that Augustus wanted to adopt the name of Romulus."

"Romulus!" exclaimed Greta. "The cave of Romulus and Remus."

"Like Romulus, Augustus wanted to be considered a founding father of Rome." Johann grinned broadly. "So wouldn't it only make sense for Augustus to erect his magnificent domicile in precisely the same place where the first Romulus was suckled by a wolf?"

"Even if you're right—the former palace grounds are still huge." Karl held up his torch, which was already halfway burned down. "And we won't have light for more than an hour or two."

"Then let's hurry up." Greta was striding toward the hill.

Here, on the southeastern side of the hill, steep steps led up its face. Every other step was broken, like a missing tooth, and bushes and weeds grew tall along the edges. Greta felt like she was in the middle of a wilderness. After the noise of the fireworks, this place seemed as still as a graveyard. Somewhere nearby, a raven cawed. Johann stopped.

"What is it?" asked Greta.

"Probably nothing. It could be coincidence, but lately I keep thinking I hear ravens or crows. They are Tonio's messengers."

"And the birds of winter," said Greta. "It doesn't have to mean anything. And besides, if Tonio is the one you think he is, he hardly needs birds to find us."

"His powers are limited in human form. That's what Agrippa told us, remember?"

Johann carried on with a glum expression. Greta glanced at him. Her father seemed much older than he was, emaciated and haunted. He looked like someone who wouldn't rest until he finally faced his old opponent. With his dirty, rash-covered face, his hair matted into a wild tangle, and his torn clothes, he resembled an avenging spirit risen from a musty grave. Greta doubted that Johann was primarily concerned about his grandson.

It has only ever been about you. You and Tonio.

The stairs were steep and treacherous. Once upon a time they might have been wide, elegant steps, but now they were overgrown and so covered in roots that at times it was difficult to find the path. Again a raven called; something fluttered. Greta looked up and saw a black dot move in front of the moon. Something cracked nearby.

"Did you hear that?" asked Karl. "That sounded like—"

Something knocked Greta off her feet.

For a brief moment she thought a monstrous raven was throwing itself at her. But what she'd perceived as wings turned out to be the flaps of a coat, and the pointed beak hacking at her was actually the tip of a sword. A figure that had hidden in the thicket suddenly towered above her. Greta's reflexes from her juggling days still worked. She instinctively rolled to the side, landing in one of the thorny bushes beside the steps. But at least her attacker had missed her. And now she saw who it was.

Hagen was standing in the middle of the steps like Mars, the Roman god of war, his longsword raised above his head. The two-handed weapon was as long as the stairs were wide. Hagen made to take another swing at Greta in the bush, but Karl was faster. Even though he didn't stand a chance against the giant, he rammed his elbow into Hagen's side with all his might.

It was as if he'd hit a tree.

"Run, Greta!" shouted Karl.

Hagen grunted. He grabbed Karl and hurled him away like a pesky insect. Karl screamed as he tumbled down the stairs. Meanwhile, Hagen raised his sword anew and brought it down hard. The blade dug into the ground next to Greta's face, sending lumps of dirt flying. Cursing, Hagen pulled the sword out of the earth, giving Greta just enough time to scramble to her feet and look for a way out. The stairs were lined with dense gorse bushes to the left and right, so the only way was up. She couldn't see her father anywhere.

She started running up the steps and heard Hagen's heavy footsteps behind her. The stairs were becoming even steeper; her muscles were burning and her heart was beating in her throat.

Greta was under the impression that the creature pursuing her was no man but a fierce predator who wouldn't rest until he caught his prey. But when she shot a glance backward, she saw that Hagen was lagging behind. He was limping heavily. Greta remembered that the mercenary had been injured atop the platform on Castel Sant'Angelo. But he wasn't giving up. Slowly but steadily he followed her, his sword dragging loudly across the stones. He didn't utter a word.

When Greta took her next step, a stone broke away and her right foot slipped into a crack. She pulled and tore, but her shoe was stuck. The harder Greta pulled, the more her foot seemed to become lodged. Her ankle started to bleed. She tried to get up but every movement resulted in agony.

Beneath her, the dragging of the sword was accompanied by heavy steps.

Tap, tap, tap.

Greta's dress was laced with thorns, a rivulet of blood ran down her face, and still she tried to pull her foot free. The giant in the long black coat was coming closer and closer, like a larger-than-life wolf on two legs. Yard by yard, step by step.

In her despair, Greta looked searchingly toward where Karl was probably lying with his bones shattered.

Someone was standing at the bottom of the stairs.

Greta blinked. At first she thought it was Karl. But then she recognized her father. He seemed to have appeared out of nowhere, carrying in his hands the leather bag that gave off a strange glow, as if it was shining from the inside.

"Hey!" shouted Johann as he laboriously climbed the steps, raising the bag so that Hagen could see it. "Let my daughter go. It is me you are seeking."

Hagen stopped and looked around. Slowly, he lowered his sword.

"I'm not seeking any of you," he grumbled. "I am merely the guardian. You know the rules, Doctor. You must come of your own free will. And alone. The master wants you and no one else."

"So he told you," said Johann. "You know who you're serving?"

"Oh yes." The giant bared his teeth. "In some ways I have always served him. Since the beginning of time. On the battlefields of the world we sang his song, and when we covered our swords with blood we wrote in his language. The church curses him, and yet she collaborates with him when she sends her sheep to their deaths. But the chaos isn't perfect yet."

Hagen's voice sounded strange, changed somehow, as if someone else was speaking through him.

"Give the master what he desires," Hagen continued in a sonorous bass. "You won't regret it, Faustus!"

"This, you mean? Why not? He can have it."

Johann hurled the satchel at Hagen.

"Catch it and give my regards to your master in hell!"

The bag flew through the air and the mercenary reached out his hand. The moment he caught it, a glowing red mass spilled from inside the sack, and sparks and fire rained onto Hagen.

The giant roared when the fire burned his chest. From there it spread across his entire body, red, blue, and white flames licking in all directions. Hagen dropped the sword and beat at the flames with his hands. But Greta saw to her horror that the movement only made the flames grow faster. Now Hagen's beard and hair had caught fire. He fell to his knees, and his roaring became louder until it turned into beastly screeching as the flames consumed him.

An image from Dante's Inferno, thought Greta.

Never before had she seen such a powerful fire.

Hagen knelt upright as a human torch for a few more heartbeats, then he let off one last long moan. Slowly, he tilted forward and then rolled down the stairs. Faust jumped aside as Hagen hurtled toward the bottom like a burning thornbush.

In the end, the giant was but a ball of fire that burned out in a shower of sparks somewhere on the overgrown tracks of Circus Maximus.

Hell had come to take him.

~

Karl groaned and palpated his limbs like he had learned during his studies of medicine at Leipzig. All his bones seemed to be intact, which bordered on a miracle. After all, Hagen had thrown him headfirst down the stairs, but a protruding tree root had stopped his fall and prevented the worst. When the mercenary had sped past him as a living torch, Karl had quickly sought shelter behind a weathered column. Now he emerged from his cover and looked down. There was no sign of Hagen, but it was obvious that the giant was dead, burned to death like a dry pine tree in the middle of summer.

Karl knew how high-proof alcohol burned, and he knew the effect of black-powder. But this fire had been something else. Something more deadly than anything he had ever seen. It was like the wrathful finger of God had touched Hagen.

Or that of the devil, he thought involuntarily.

He limped up the stone steps until he reached Greta and Johann. Greta sat leaning against one of the steps, her face twisted with pain. Her right foot was stuck in a crack.

"Hold on," said Karl. "The more you move the worse it'll get." He pulled and wiggled the slab until he managed to break it free. Groaning, Greta pulled out her tattered leather shoe.

"Thanks," she said breathlessly and cautiously moved her foot. "I don't think it's broken. The worst part was the fear of being utterly defenseless against that giant."

"At least that is one concern we're rid of," said Johann, slumping down beside Greta and wiping soot from his face. "That bastard will never lie in wait for us again. He is burning in hell, in the truest sense of the word. He didn't have Sebastian, though. I suspect he's already delivered the boy to Tonio."

"Don't you think you owe us an explanation?" asked Karl.

Johann raised an eyebrow. "What do you mean?"

"If I didn't know better, I would believe you had conjured up some sort of hellfire. But I'm guessing it was the contents of your bag, which you lit with your torch just before throwing it." Karl pointed at the flickering stump of a torch that the doctor had stuck into the ground next to him. "So? What was in the bag? I've never seen anything like it before."

"It . . . it's a weapon that no longer exists."

"What are you talking about?" Still visibly in pain, Greta looked at her father. "It's something to do with that accursed alchemy, isn't it? What did you brew up?"

"It . . . it was more of a coincidence. Although I was hoping it might work. I had most of the ingredients, but no time to combine them according to the exact recipe. In all the commotion the various substances must have started to mix and—"

"What recipe are you speaking of?" asked Karl impatiently, sitting down beside the doctor, who was stinking of smoke and sulfur like a veritable demon.

"I'll have to tell you at some point, so why not now?" Johann sighed deeply. "We talked about Constantinople earlier, the city of Emperor Constantine, formerly Byzantium. As far back as the time of the Greeks, a certain knowledge was gathered there which was kept secret from the rest of the world, and for good reason." His jaws clenched. "It is just like Leonardo da Vinci once said. Some knowledge ought to never see the light of day. And yet it happened."

"My son is held captive somewhere around here," urged Greta. "And you are delivering a lecture. If you've got something to tell us, spit it out."

"It is important for you to understand," replied Johann, turning to Greta. "You especially. It's something to do with your son. My grandson." He swallowed hard and continued. "About three hundred years after the founding of

Constantinople by Emperor Constantine, a new power entered the world's stage, a power that swallowed up entire empires. They were fanatic peoples from the deserts of the east who turned up outside the walls of the city. No one had been able to stop them. Not the Sasanians or the Egyptians. It seemed as if all of Europe would soon be under their rule. During those dark times, a Greek inventor by the name of Kallinikos fled to Constantinople. He brought with him an ancient secret, a forbidden recipe, and he refined it. It would be the most terrible weapon the world had ever seen."

"My God," whispered Karl, who suddenly had an inkling what had killed Hagen. "Are you saying—?"

"The Byzantines called this weapon *igró pir*, liquid fire," continued Johann. "The recipe was a state secret and included resin, sulfur, lime, saltpeter, and most importantly, an ingredient that in our climes is more commonly used in healing salves. I am talking about rock oil, or petroleum, as the Greeks call it. The effect is enormous. The Byzantines used pressure pumps, so-called siphons, to shoot igró pir at the ships of the Arabs. The sea turned into an inferno because the flames couldn't be put out. On the contrary, they spread on the water. Thousands of soldiers died in this sea of fire, the ships of the Arabs burned, and the siege of Constantinople was abandoned."

"That's why it didn't matter that the bag was wet," Greta said. "So you found this old recipe and—"

"Impossible!" interrupted Karl. "Igró pir no longer exists. If the recipe had been saved, people would have been using it in war."

"Karl is right. The recipe was lost with the demise of the Byzantine Empire. Until recently no one knew how to make igró pir. Until the day someone invented it anew."

"Leonardo da Vinci," exclaimed Karl. "You got the recipe from Leonardo."

"Yes. He reinvented igró pir. His mixture is probably even deadlier than Kallinikos's original recipe. If it is manufactured correctly, it can even be lit with water and cannot be put out." Johann gave a dry laugh. "Apparently, Leonardo also toyed with the thought of producing an invisible deadly gas. Thankfully, he didn't succeed. But he soon realized that with igró pir he had invented a weapon that had the power to send the world into chaos. In the wrong hands, he knew, Greek fire could topple whole empires and create dark imperia. And that is not all." He paused before he went on, with a grim expression on his face. "Leonardo must have sensed that someone profoundly evil was after his recipe. Someone he couldn't fight. Someone who sent me to Cloux to find the secret for him—without me knowing that I was."

"Tonio del Moravia," said Greta.

Johann nodded. "Now I know that this was his plan. I assume that he black-mailed Agrippa or made a pact with him also, so that Agrippa would send us to Cloux to visit Leonardo. Tonio wanted me to find the recipe for him."

Karl stared at him, feeling a small pang in his heart. "A setup, right from the start?" Once again the doctor hadn't told him a thing; as always, there had been secrets that Faust didn't share with anyone. Not even with Karl.

"I believe that's how it was." Johann wiped his sooty hands on his filthy coat. "Tonio sent me the disease and, through Agrippa, slipped me the clue that only Leonardo could heal me. He knew that I would never have done him such a favor voluntarily! But he was counting on my curiosity and hoped that Leonardo would open up to me, trust me."

"And?" asked Karl. "Did he trust you?"

"Leonardo wanted to ensure that no one else would get their hands on the recipe. But he couldn't bring himself to part with it." Johann sighed. "Inventions can be like a curse that clings to a person. And so Leonardo hid the formula. Inside his own world."

"Inside his own world?" Karl frowned. "What is that supposed to—?"

Johann held up a thin chain he had pulled out from under his shirt. Dangling on the chain was a tiny silver globe.

"The recipe is inside this." Johann rolled the ball between his fingers. "Written in mirror writing, in tiny letters upon tissue paper. Leonardo took every precaution so that only I would find the globe. He wanted me to decide what would happen to his invention." He smiled thinly. "A tempting thought, isn't it? All those wars in Europe, and this weapon could be the decisive fac-tor. Maybe, with the help of this weapon, a unified, peaceful empire could be founded."

"An empire built on terror," said Greta.

"Is that why you kept the recipe?" asked Karl. "Because you haven't decided who to give igró pir to? Hardly to the church, nor to the French king. Let alone the German emperor. They would only cause mass destruction with it."

Johann shook his head with a grin. "Even when they only thought I could make gold, the high and mighty practically bashed each other's heads in. What would happen if they learned of this weapon? No." His expression turned serious. "I kept the recipe because I hoped it would serve me as a pawn. As a pawn in a bargain with Tonio. At first I thought I could use it to win back my daughter. But now it seems I am going to need it for someone else."

Johann looked at Greta.

"For Sebastian. The fate of the world for your son."

~

Somewhere deep below them, in the belly of Palatine Hill, the master bathed in a fountain full of blood. His eyes were closed and he hummed his old song.

Because everything that exists deserves to perish.

This was the oldest place in one of the oldest cities of mankind. The place where everything had begun. The master loved such places, because where there was a beginning, there would always be an end.

Finis terrae. The end of the world.

His great plan had failed. Once again, little Faustus had foiled it. But unlike men, the master had time. Plenty of time.

There was a flutter of wings, and moments later, a raven came flying into the cave and settled on the edge of the well. The bird opened its beak and cawed. If one listened very closely, one could hear a voice that—many, many years ago—might have been human, the voice of a child. The master nodded.

"So he came. And of his own free will. That is good, very good! Prepare everything, Baphomet." He grinned, his fingers stroking the scuffed beak of the raven. "If you fulfill your tasks to my satisfaction, you shall have something especially sweet to eat, my pet. Not salted and dried, but fresh—as fresh as if it was still screaming."

Inside a cage in the corner whimpered a small two-year-old boy.

~

Greta kept staring at the little silver globe, swinging before her eyes like a pendulum.

She had heard what her father had said, but she still struggled to comprehend. If it was true, then contained inside the silver ball were the instructions for a weapon the likes of which mankind could not fathom. Greta had no trouble imagining that someone like Tonio del Moravia was interested in it. He could sell the formula to the highest bidder. Clearly, the pope had been interested. But perhaps also the young German emperor who was locking horns with the French king over Italy, or the English king Henry VIII, who was also considered highly ambitious.

Whoever owns this recipe rules the world, thought Greta. *And they will sow death and fire.*

Tonio had stolen her son because he wanted the igró pir. Sebastian was the hostage in a trade. It had probably been Tonio's plan as far back as her journey to Rome with Lahnstein. They'd only have to hand over the recipe and Sebastian would be free. But then why wasn't Tonio showing himself?

You must come of your own free will.

Evidently this, too, was a part of the sick game between Tonio and her father, a game whose rules Greta neither understood nor wanted to understand. She only wanted her son back.

Even if it means the death of thousands of people on the battlefields of Europe?

The thought was mind boggling. Greta's feet hurt like hell. She had seen unimaginable things at Castel Sant'Angelo, had plunged into the ice-cold Tiber, had run through half of Rome in a wet dress, and had barely managed to escape death—she wouldn't give up, not this close to the goal.

"We have to find this cave," she said eventually.

Johann gave her a hard look. "So you have made your decision?"

"What decision?"

"We give the recipe to Tonio. You know what that means?"

"This is about my son, damn it! How can it be my son's fault if some old men think up horrible things? Why should he pay for it? He is only a child!" She paused. "Even if we destroyed the recipe here and now, who's to say that someone else won't invent something similar, or that the old formula won't reappear? I can only save my son, not the whole world."

"Maybe we'll still find a different solution," said Karl. "But first we need to find the cave." He stood and pointed uphill. "Augustus's palace isn't much farther. Let's start our search there."

Flinching with pain, Greta got to her feet. She was limping, but at least she could walk unaided, albeit slowly. Thus they eventually arrived at the ruins of the imperial palace. Here, too, all was overgrown with weeds. In the light of the moon, Greta saw arches and crumbling walls; in an old courtyard stood a headless statue with a broken sword. She sat down to rest on the remains of a wall at the edge of the courtyard while Johann and Karl set off to find any indications of a cave.

Meanwhile, Greta studied the mosaics on the ground in front of her by the light of her torch. There were birds, fish, and various creatures. She closed her eyes and took a moment to enjoy the stillness. Why couldn't things just go back to the way they'd been a few weeks ago? She had tried to escape her fate, but fate had caught up with her.

Her father had caught up with her.

It seemed like a punishment from God that her love for her child had grown strongest at the very moment he was taken from her. Where had she been for the last two years? With the poor, the sick, and the elderly, with all those people who needed her. But not with her son.

"Nothing. Not a trace."

Greta looked up when Karl returned with his smoking torch. Johann followed close behind.

"We searched everywhere, as well as we could in the darkness," said Karl. "A few rooms are still intact, including some cellars full of trash, but no cave."

"Damn it!" snarled Johann. "The cave is probably some way away from the buildings, somewhere in the gardens of Augustus. But that's a huge area, and it is pitch black. Hagen must have seen Tonio, so the cave is here. But where? Where, in God's name?"

"*Lasciate ogni speranza, voi ch'entrate,*" said Greta softly.

"What did you say?" Johann asked.

"'All hope abandon, ye who enter here.' A fitting sentiment, I find." Greta pointed at the wall she was sitting on. An Italian inscription had been chiseled into the stone. "Even if the phrase doesn't at all go with the little birds, rabbits, and fawns in the mosaics."

Her father hastily brought his torch closer and studied the inscription. Greta now saw that below the words, a square had been etched into the stone. A square with a circle at its center. It looked like a solitary, watchful eye.

"My God," whispered Johann. "Could it be?" He turned to Karl. "Quick! Search the courtyard!"

"But why?"

"Jesus Christ in heaven, do I have to explain everything to you? This phrase is written in Italian, not Latin, so it was added much later. Most importantly, though, it tells us what is to be found here."

Greta read the inscription again, and finally she understood.

All hope abandon.

"It is a quote from Dante's *Divine Comedy*," she exclaimed. "From the *Inferno*."

The monastery of Santo Spirito owned a large library that, of course, included the books of Dante, Italy's most famous poet. About two hundred years ago, Dante Alighieri composed his best-known work, the *Divine Comedy*, in which the poet himself travels through hell, purgatory, and paradise. The description of hell, of the inferno, had gripped Greta strongest of all.

Johann pointed at the letters. "These words are written at the gateway to hell! The porta infernale. Do you understand? It is a sign, perhaps for Tonio's helpers, like Hagen. The entrance must be somewhere very close."

"But we searched everywhere," said Karl dejectedly.

"Then we'll just search again, damn it!"

Karl slowly walked across the courtyard with his torch. "There is nothing here," he said after a while. "Only weeds and rubble."

"Keep looking!"

"What is the meaning of this symbol?" asked Greta, pointing at the square with the circle inside. "It almost looks like an eye."

"Possible." Her father shrugged. "Perhaps it represents the entrance to hell. Or—" He broke off. Then he suddenly gave a hoarse laugh. "Of course, a circle! How could I have missed it!" He stood up and tightened his grip on his torch. "The cave isn't here!" he called out to Karl. "This is just the beginning of our search."

He gestured at the symbol on the stone. "It is the first sign and refers to the first circle of hell. There are ten of those in Dante's *Inferno*. Following the gate are the vestibule of hell and the nine circles representing various sins and crimes. Lust, gluttony, greed, wrath. In the last circle, Lucifer is trapped in a lake of ice." He smiled grimly. "Tonio truly has a sense of humor."

"Does that mean we're not looking for a cave but for another square, this time with two circles?" asked Karl, who was now gazing at the symbol.

Johann nodded. "Then three, then four, and so on. They are markers that will lead us to our destination. To the porta infernale." He raised his torch and marched ahead. "To the devil in his hell."

It wasn't long before they found the second clue, a square with two circles, on a wall a little farther away. From there they followed the third sign, the fourth, and the fifth, gradually getting farther from Augustus's palace until they reached a small wood at the edge of Palatine Hill. There probably used to be flourishing gardens here a long time ago, but now low-hanging branches blocked out the moon, moss hung down in curtains, and the air smelled of rotting leaves and winter. Greta remembered the first lines from Dante's *Inferno*.

In the midway of this our mortal life, I found me in a gloomy wood, astray.

The sentence seemed deeply fitting, as if this poet from long ago had seen right into her heart.

Greta would have loved to bound ahead and search the clues herself, but every time she tried to walk for longer, the pain in her ankle became so great that she was forced to sit for a while. She felt as if someone had tied her up! And somewhere nearby was her son, perhaps already dead. To help her move along a little better, she had found herself a sturdy branch to use as a crutch.

Meanwhile, Johann and Karl had discovered the square with all ten circles and were exploring the surrounding area. The terrain was flat with no rises, and Greta wondered how there should be a cave here. An artificial one, perhaps, but not one in which two infants were suckled by a she-wolf. That was just a myth, nothing more. Just like the story with the gateway to hell was probably no more than the spawn of Johann's imagination.

Greta had been calling out for Sebastian, but the woods swallowed up her voice. Eventually she gave up. The long branch in one hand and the nearly burned-out torch in the other, she hobbled through the woods. Karl had told her to stay put, but she couldn't sit still if her son might be nearby.

"Sebastian!" she called again. "Sebastian, can you hear me? It's me, your mother!"

The silence was oppressive. In the distance she saw two moving lights, the torches of Karl and Johann, still searching for the entrance to the cave. A pale moon shone through the branches; it was bitter cold. Greta's dress had dried, and Karl had given her his coat, but she still shivered as pitifully as if she were somewhere in the Alps, not Rome.

Something cawed.

When Greta looked up, she saw an old raven with blackish-gray feathers sitting upon a branch. It seemed to be eyeing her, and Greta wondered whether her father was right. Could the ruffled bird actually be a messenger from Tonio?

"Nonsense," she murmured. She still thought it was delusional of her father to consider Tonio to be the devil incarnate. Nonetheless, she spoke to the raven. "If you know where my Sebastian is, then tell me. Please!"

Christ, what was she doing? She was talking to an animal! But then she remembered that there were plenty of people who didn't believe that a person's death could be foreseen in the palm of their hand. And yet she could do it.

"Where is my little Sebastian?" asked Greta again, this time even more desperately. "Tell me, please."

The old raven lifted with a caw, flew for a few yards, and landed on another branch. It rubbed its beak on the branch and flapped its wings restlessly. Greta followed it, limping through the undergrowth with her crutch. Again the raven flew for a few paces, just as if it wanted her to follow. Then it came to rest on a branch above a large patch of herbs. The intense fragrance told Greta that it was parsley. She took another step.

And plunged into darkness.

~

Karl gave a start and listened. A high-pitched scream echoed through the grove.

"Greta?" he shouted. "Is that you?"

He and Johann had been searching the area around the tenth sign for a long while now but had found nothing. Despite the tension and the gnawing fear, he was awfully tired, and he was shaking with cold. But the scream made him wide awake.

Another one! It was definitely Greta, and she was crying for help. Was she being attacked? But who by? Karl was briefly overcome by a vision of Hagen, walking through the woods as a burned monster, his skin black and charred and his limbs molten, swinging his sword until Judgment Day.

"I'm coming, Greta!" shouted Karl.

He ran toward the screams, which were growing louder. To his right he could hear quick footsteps. It was Johann, following him with grim determination. They ran until they came to a patch of weeds. The screams seemed to come from inside the knee-high, bushy plants. But where was Greta? Karl was about to walk into the plants, but Johann held him back.

He knelt down and crawled forward on all fours. And still Greta called for help, her voice sounding strangely hollow, as if it came from deep below.

"A hole," said Johann.

Karl went down on his hands and knees, too, and crawled toward a gaping hole in the ground that was almost entirely concealed by the weeds. It was roughly one pace wide, and Karl felt a warm breeze from inside it. When he held his torch into the opening, he saw that Greta was hanging from her crutch right in the middle. The branch had become lodged in the shaft, but it wouldn't be long before it broke. There was a crack, and the crutch moved down a little farther.

"Take my hand!" shouted Karl.

She looked at him with a mix of despair, fear, and spite, then her right arm shot up. For a heartbeat she hung from the crutch only with her left hand—one wrong movement and she'd fall into the depths. But then Karl grasped her hand tightly. He pulled Greta until her upper body was lying on solid ground. Breathing hard, she crawled away from the hole. The stick fell rattling into the darkness.

"That was close. And you found the entrance," Johann said, gesturing at the wild parsley. "This herb is dedicated to Proserpina, a Roman goddess of the underworld. In ancient Rome, parsley was used during funeral ceremonies for the journey to the underworld. Now we know why Karl's vegetable farmers knew of the cave and why they believed it was cursed."

"But this is no cave—it's just a shaft," said Karl.

"Perhaps the entrance used to be at the foot of Palatine Hill, but it collapsed," suggested Faust. "Now there is only this shaft." He sniffed. "Can you smell it?"

Karl took a deep breath. Indeed, he could also smell a waft of rotten eggs. Sulfur.

"The porta infernale," said Johann with a smile. "We have reached our destination."

29

JOHANN CAUTIOUSLY CREPT TO THE EDGE OF THE SHAFT
and peered inside. The hole was pitch black, and yet he thought he could make
out a faint glow far below. The smell of sulfur was becoming stronger. On closer
inspection of the hole's surroundings, he discovered a thin hemp rope that led
down the shaft. It was tied to a nearby tree and practically invisible in the tall
weeds.

"Sebastian!" shouted Greta. "Are you there?"

"Quiet, damn it!" Johann snapped. "Do you want the master to hear us?"

"If your *master* really is down there, he has already heard us."

Greta's pointed remark reminded Johann that he hadn't called Tonio del
Moravia "master" in a long time. Not since Tonio had been his teacher, but
that was nearly thirty years ago. They had made a pact back then, a pact that
would help Johann become the greatest wizard in the world—and also the most
unhappy man, as Johann often thought. He sensed Tonio's presence as if his
former master were a part of him.

My journey is coming to an end. One way or another.

"Hagen probably used this rope to climb down with Sebastian," he said.
"Which means this shaft leads straight to—"

He broke off when they heard something.

A soft whimpering.

"Oh God!" cried Greta. "Sebastian really is down there."

She made to climb into the shaft, but Karl stopped her. "Greta, you're hurt.
If you climb down there, who knows if you'll ever make it back to the surface.
Maybe if just the doctor and I—"

"You expect me to wait here while my child is crying down there, suffering, trapped by a lunatic? Forget it!"

Karl sighed. "I didn't expect anything else."

"I will go first, then Greta, and then Karl," decided Johann. "We have no weapons, but I doubt that weapons would be of any use down there. I only have this to bargain with." He held up the small globe on the chain around his neck. "The deadliest weapon in the world."

Johann picked up the rope, gave it a couple of probing tugs, and started his descent. He held the remainder of his torch between his teeth. It probably would only burn for another few minutes, but Johann felt certain that there would be plenty of light down below.

Hell is brightly lit.

As he slowly climbed down, Johann studied the walls of the shaft. It seemed to be natural and possibly used to serve as the cave's vent. The stink of sulfur was increasing, as was the temperature, so that Johann soon began to sweat. He could also hear the child's crying more clearly.

After a while Johann made out solid ground below. When he arrived at the bottom, he waved his torch to signal the others to follow. While he waited, he inspected his surroundings. He was standing at the end of a low tunnel that led to the west, and that was also where the glow was coming from. The wailing of the child sounded very close now—he couldn't be more than a few paces away.

Then something strange happened. Something that was more unsettling than the crying.

It stopped.

Instead, the child began to chuckle—yes, now he whooped, giggled, and laughed. At the same time, Johann could hear the soft jingle of small bells.

Ding, ding, ding.

And in that moment Johann knew behind which devilish mask Tonio del Moravia had been hiding these past few years.

In some ways the devil has always been a buffoon, he thought. *He laughs at God right in the dour face.*

Greta now heard the laughing, too. She had climbed down the rope next and now stood beside her father. Her heart started to beat faster. The child laughing down the tunnel was definitely her son. But how could that be? Sebastian was being held captive—he had just been crying. Something jingled, and then she heard a faint voice at the end of the tunnel.

"Bumpety, bump, rider. If he falls, he cries out. If into the ditch he falls, he'll get eaten by the crows."

Greta thought of the raven that had led her to the shaft. The old nursery rhyme she herself had sung to Sebastian many times suddenly sounded gruesome and creepy, like the lyrics to an ancient demonic ritual.

"If he falls into the swamp, the rider, he goes plomp," echoed the voice through the corridor.

Sebastian squealed with delight in the way only small children can.

"Who in God's name is that?" whispered Karl, arriving at the bottom of the shaft.

"I believe I know," said Johann grimly. "He's been making a fool out of us, in the truest sense of the word."

Greta could no longer bear it. She hobbled ahead down the tunnel, which took a bend after a few yards and ended in a grotto with a vaulted copper ceiling. The walls were covered in fading mosaics depicting a wolf mother and two infant boys. The center of the verdigris-covered dome was dominated by a large eagle, the symbol of the Roman emperors. In the middle of the grotto stood a stone fountain adorned with small statues of nymphs and fauns.

On its edge sat two crows and an old raven.

It was the same raven Greta had followed through the woods. The room was filled by a strange flickering and glowing whose origin she couldn't make out. Greta squinted and saw another item at the grotto's back wall.

It was a throne made of stone. But upon the throne sat no king, no emperor, and no pope.

On the throne sat a fool.

Greta froze. Viktor von Lahnstein had permitted her to watch some of Pope Leo's spectacles. There had been music, jugglers, dancers, and a court jester. The jester was an ugly, hunchbacked fellow, playing pranks in front of the Holy Father's chair and jingling his bells. Greta never took much notice of him.

Now he was sitting here, bouncing her son on his knee.

"Look who's come to visit," said the fool in a nasal voice. "Uh-oh, it's your mother—now we're both in deep trouble."

The jester smiled a wolfish grin at Greta. The heat inside the cave had made his makeup run like streaks of blood. He was clad in a tight multicolored garment that spanned across the hump on his back. On his head sat a fool's cap with bells that jingled cheerfully.

Sebastian shrieked happily and tried to catch the bells.

"The poor boy was hungry," said the fool in the concerned tone of a nursemaid. "So I gave him something to drink. A very special juice. Now the child is satisfied."

In the dull light Greta thought she could see some red spots around her son's lips.

Red like blood.

"You monster!" she screamed.

She was about to storm up to the fool when he underwent a strange change. He bared his teeth like a wolf and hissed at her, and in the demonic half light it looked as if his body was growing. The shadow against the wall showed a huge horned creature.

"Stay!"

The voice was so deep, loud, and powerful that Greta staggered backward as if she'd run against a wall. Sebastian started to cry again.

"You frightened him," said the fool, rocking the child in his lap, looking like the harmless jester again. "Nasty mummy! Hasn't been looking after poor little Sebastian, only ever thinking of the stern old fellow up in heaven. Tsk, tsk, tsk." The fool shook his head and gave Greta a disapproving look. "He barely recognizes his own mother."

"Of course he recognizes me," said Greta weakly, but the eyes of her son told a different story. Sebastian had only glanced at her before turning back to the funny man in whose lap he was sitting.

"Bumpty bump again," Sebastian called out. "Again!"

"What did you do to him?" screamed Greta. "You . . . you bewitched him!"

"Oh, I didn't need to," said the fool. "A little fun and song was all it took. And, by the way, he was calling for Martha before, not you. He liked good old Martha very much."

A pain shot through Greta's heart as if Hagen had thrust his sword straight through her. Tears streamed down her face, and she was overwhelmed by feelings of guilt. Greta knew that had been the jester's intention but couldn't stop it. "I don't know what you've done to him or what you're doing to me, but . . . but he is my son. I am his mother—"

"What sort of a mother gives her child to a nursemaid and hides inside a nunnery?" The fool chuckled, and the birds on the fountain cawed excitedly, flapping their wings. "An unnatural mother! Kraa! Kraa!" he went, imitating the call of the raven, and his birds joined in. "Kraa! Kraa!"

Greta was crying, her whole body shaking while her son snuggled up to the chest of the villain. She was beginning to feel nauseated from the stink of sulfur, her head thumping. What was going on here?

"Quit the games, Tonio!" sounded Johann's voice from behind her. His hand grasped Greta's shoulder. "Don't listen to him," he whispered to her. "That's what the devil does, tugging and gnawing at that which you hold dearest."

"Bah, you spoilsport!" The fool thumbed his nose at Johann, who was standing behind Greta alongside Karl. Then his pale, painted face began to beam. "How wonderful to see you again, little Faustus! Though we briefly met not long ago. Do you remember?"

"Oh yes, I remember, Tonio del Moravia." Faust nodded. "I remember every single damned moment with you in my life."

~

Every single damned moment.

Johann's thoughts returned to the procession on All Saints' Day a few weeks back. He had seen Tonio then, but his mind had been too preoccupied with his search for Viktor von Lahnstein and Greta to notice. He supposed there had been many people like him in the last few years.

The jester at the court. He is always near, hears all, sees all. No one takes him seriously, and yet he always speaks the truth.

"You walked right past me but you were wearing a mask," said Johann. "And that hump on your back."

"Not bad, for a cheap prop, huh?" The fool Tonio wiggled his head until the little bells jingled. "People love misshapen creatures because it makes them feel superior." He pulled a face, making him truly look like a silly fool. "People are so easily deceived."

"How long has this game been going on for?" asked Johann. "Over two years, isn't that right? You slowly stole the pope's trust."

"Leo loved jesters. It wasn't difficult to get a spot at court." Tonio shrugged. "I can be highly entertaining when I want to, as you know. In addition, dear Leo was extremely quick-tempered—a true Medici. No one dared tell him the truth. No one but his fool." Tonio grinned. "I believe I can say that we almost became something like friends. In the end, I was his most important adviser."

"It was *you* who put the idea in the pope's head that I knew how to make gold," said Johann.

"It was supposed to be a joke, but Leo was so obsessed by the philosopher's stone. He tortured one alchemist after the other and sifted through old documents in the Vatican library. That's where he came across Gilles de Rais and his invocations. All right, I admit I ensured that he found the documents. Gilles always was one of my favorite shells. Forever hungry, never satisfied."

Tonio weighed the child in his arms and stroked his rosy cheeks. Sebastian looked tired; his eyes kept falling shut.

"I thought it might be a good way to bring you to Rome," he continued eventually, looking into Johann's face. "I even traveled to Knittlingen and Bamberg in person to find you. It wasn't easy to justify my absence to Leo. You see, I still haven't given up on you, my little Faustus." Tonio cooed like a dove. "I sent you my curse as a friendly reminder. Later, at Tiffauges, you were just about to return to me voluntarily, but sadly, your daughter and her beloved spoiled the show. Stabbing him to death in your frenzy was a lovely climax, I thought." He laughed. "But now you're finally here. Here with me in my realm. How do you like it?"

Tonio made a sweeping gesture and continued. "I love this place even more than Castel Sant'Angelo. It is ancient! Long before the times of Romulus and Remus, sacrifices were being offered up in this cave. Human sacrifices. The fountain stems from those times, and was later used by the Romans. Later again, baptisms were held here. Oh, if only the Christians had known what the fountain used to hold. Not water—oh no." Sebastian briefly opened his eyes and started to whimper, and Tonio rocked him soothingly. "Hush, hush. Are you hungry again, my darling? Now hush like a good boy while I'm talking to your grandfather."

Johann noticed that the stink of sulfur was growing more intense, and he was beginning to feel dizzy. The fumes were probably rising up from cracks in the earth, and his companions also seemed affected by them. Greta was hanging on to Karl, trembling all over, her face ashen as if she was seeing ghosts.

Or the devil, thought Johann.

"The . . . the French delegate at Bamberg was you, right?" asked Karl now, leaning against the cave's wall, heat and sulfur taking their toll on him, too. "And Greta and I saw you at Metz, below the bridge."

"Hell, I was hungry, and so I became careless." Tonio shrugged. "After Faust's escape from Bamberg, I had to change tack. I was forced to accept the fact that my darling wasn't coming to Rome anytime soon. I would have loved to have him by my side! But I found a way to make Agrippa lure you to France. There was . . . another task awaiting." The master eyed his former apprentice with curiosity. "You know what I'm speaking of?"

"I do," replied Johann reluctantly. The silver globe was hidden underneath his shirt. Johann would hold back the pawn for as long as he could.

The fumes made him see shadows where there could be none, and his head ached from the stink. Little Sebastian was fast asleep in Tonio's lap, the boy's cheeks looking healthy and red—too red. Johann guessed they didn't have much time before the fumes killed them all.

"Did you get what I sent you to Leonardo's for?" growled Tonio, sounding like a large panther.

Johann blinked a few times and tried to focus. "We'll talk about that in a moment. But first there is something I'd like to know."

"Oho!" Tonio spread his arms and smiled. "There is something the clever Doctor Faustus doesn't know? Be my guest."

"You can be so many things—a powerful wizard, an alchemist, even a French marshal. Why in God's name did you become the pope's fool?" Johann shook his head. "All right, you had Leo's attention, were able to weave intrigues and put ideas in his head. Was it about war? Is that what your goal was? To sow discord at the court of one of the world's most powerful men?"

"Think, clever Faustus." Tonio tilted his head. "You are so bright. Why do you think I encouraged the pope to invoke the devil when the devil was already in Rome?"

Johann had asked himself the same question over and over. He still hadn't come up with an answer. Tonio was a master of lies and deception, but he always pursued a particular goal. Something Agrippa once said came to Johann's mind.

The devil appears in all kinds of shapes.

Despite the fumes, Johann tried to arrange his thoughts. In order to walk on earth, the devil needed a shell. That much Agrippa had found out. Gilles de Rais had been one such shell, and later Tonio del Moravia, the sorcerer, and several years ago he, Johann, was supposed to serve as a shell. Back then, in Nuremberg, Tonio's disciples had attempted to bring the true devil to earth. And one detail had been very important.

Johann had to come of his own free will. That was the ancient rule.

And suddenly he understood Tonio's plan.

It was a joke, and it was so good that surely even God in heaven had to acknowledge its ingenuity. Johann struggled not to laugh out loud. The fumes made the terrible suddenly seem funny. It was hilarious!

The devil as pope.

"You wanted to become pope," Johann exclaimed. "That was what the ritual was for. If Leo had managed to summon the devil, you would have been able to slip into his shell. Just like you have done with all the other shells!"

"The devil as God's representative." Tonio clapped his hands as Sebastian slept deeply in his lap. "Bravo, bravissimo! And wouldn't it have been the most beautiful coat for someone like me? Say it, little Faustus. This Martin Luther already called the pope the devil. But what if the pope truly were the devil? Oh, I would have built an empire of terror, of decadence, of gluttony and pomposity. We were well on our way, Leo and me—the coffers were empty, the court was turning into a Circus Maximus, the screams of tortured men echoed through Castel Sant'Angelo. But then you came and once again ruined everything. Bad boy! Bad, bad boy!"

Again Tonio seemed to expand, and his shadow against the wall grew horns, a tail, and long claws that reached for Johann. Johann felt a hot breath of air, as hot as if it came straight from hell.

It's just the fumes, he thought. *Just the fumes. How much longer before I lose consciousness?*

He looked for the cracks the fumes were coming from but couldn't spot any. The glowing at the back of the cave was becoming stronger. It was so hot in here. Johann had heard that in ancient times, heathen priests used such fumes to obtain states of ecstasy, making them see things that weren't there and causing them to speak in riddles. Staggering a little, Johann looked behind him. To his horror, he saw that Karl and Greta had already lost consciousness. He wouldn't last much longer. He had to bring this to an end. His hand moved to the pendant on his neck.

"Tonio, I—" he began.

"You always ruin everything," snarled Tonio. "You never do as you're told." Then his expression changed just as abruptly again, and Tonio looked almost benevolent and kind. "But that's just the way we are. We love chaos."

"We?" asked Johann, his strength fading fast.

"Yes, *we*, little Faustus. Us two." Tonio reached out his hand to him as if he wanted to stroke Johann's head.

"Or have you still not understood who you really are, my son?"

A wagon rattles across the cobblestones of the small town of Knittlingen, the horse lame and the wheels squeaking. In a cage beneath the canopy at the front sit an old raven and two crows, staring maliciously from small red eyes at the children of Knittlingen who run around the wagon, laughing. The magician! The magician is in town! None of the boys and girls know that the birds inside the cage used to be children just like them a long, long time ago.

Sitting upon the box seat, his face concealed beneath a floppy hat with a red feather, sits a man who has seen much: the human sacrifices of the Sumerians, Babylon's arrogance and downfall, the pyramids of Egypt erected with the blood of thousands of slaves; he has watched Rome burn, seen the hordes of horsemen from the East and the demise of Constantinople. He has drunk blood from the skulls of the vanquished, has bitten through throats with his teeth, has raped, murdered, and laughed as he was doing so; he has loved a virgin and at her side liberated the city of Orléans from the English, and then watched her burn at the stake. He was the beginning and he would be the end.

Just then his name is Tonio del Moravia, and he likes it well. But he has borne many different names before: Imhotep, Circe, Judas, Simon Magus, Gilles de Rais.

Name is but sound and smoke.

A pretty young farmer's wife is standing in the window, her breasts full and her cheeks rosy. He smiles at her and doffs his hat. He likes them young, because they smell so fresh, full of life—like freshly butchered lambs, steam still rising from their innards. He takes the girls into the hay, and they come willingly because they can sense the beast in him. Sometimes he lets them go afterward, and other times he slits them open and drinks their blood.

This young farmer's wench will be the next.

They are as easily plucked as sweet, ripe pears. But this one is different, he can tell. A hunger gleams in her eyes, a mischief that he likes. "Take me with you," she says when they lie side by side in the hay. "Anywhere, just away from this world that ends beyond the next brook, beyond the next fence!" He laughs and makes an egg appear for her, and from the egg hatches a warm chick. She pleases him, because he loves adventures and new beginnings. Stagnation is the business of the old man up top.

Because everything that exists deserves to perish.

In a clearing in the woods he finds a cave for them both. He etches his mark into the stone and takes her from behind like an animal. He enjoys it, more than usual. On a whim he lets her live—more than that, he woos her. "I will return," he breathes into her ear, and she smiles. "Take me with you," she whispers. "My dark prince, my wizard."

But he disappears like smoke in the wind. He travels, sowing perdition here, watching a war arise there; he whispers, hisses, slaughters, and kills, always along the new post roads that cross the empire like veins.

Much blood flows in those veins.

When the man passes through Knittlingen again a year later, the farmer's wife has born a child. "Take me with you," she says again. "Me and the child!" But he shakes his head. "Then tell me, at least, what the future holds in store for my son."

He picks up the boy's little hand and sees something astonishing.

The boy is strong, very strong. Born on the day of the prophet.

Name him Faustus, he says. Because he is lucky indeed.

Again the years go by. When he comes to Knittlingen next, he meets the boy who is called Faustus as he had demanded. The boy is a bright fellow with the inquisitive eyes of his mother. The man reads in the boy's hand and finds a puzzle. Even the devil can be amazed.

And the hope grows.

Never before had he fathered a child—it isn't possible—he is not a mortal! But this boy, he senses, is different from all other people. He is never satisfied; he is restless, a renewer, a chaos bringer, a wrecker, a destroyer. He is someone who changes the world.

My son.

And I am his master.

When Johann opened his eyes, he thought the world was ablaze.

Where am I? Is this hell?

It was so hot! Fire licked above him. But then he saw that it was only shadows dancing across the cave ceiling. He was still inside the Lupercal beneath Palatine Hill. But where were the others? Karl, Greta, his grandson? He tried to sit up but was overwhelmed by nausea, and so he sank back down on the ground.

"So you have finally come!"

The voice booming through the cave was deep and familiar. It was the voice of Tonio, and yet it was different.

Much *older*.

"I have been waiting for you for so long," continued the voice. "I have been holding my hand out to you, I have begged, pleaded, and sent you my most special kiss as a greeting. But you never came. Like a stubborn child you kept running away from me for all those years. But now you're finally here. With me."

Johann groaned. He remembered what Tonio had just revealed to him. Strangely, this knowledge didn't fill him with terror, almost as if he had always suspected it.

I am the son of the devil.

Tonio had raised him, had been his mentor. Everything Johann knew—black magic, alchemy, reading the stars, chiromancy, yes, even the gift of foreseeing a person's death—he had inherited from Tonio. Tonio del Moravia had been the man from the west who had visited his mother a long time ago and left her with child. Johann's stepfather, Jörg Gerlach, had told him about this stranger just before Johann had left his hometown of Knittlingen at sixteen. What was it his stepfather had said?

A pale, black-haired fellow carrying a pack full of magic knickknacks. He put a spell on your mother, that's what he did!

All those years Johann had been running from his real father. But now he was here with him.

At home.

Johann was lying on the stone floor at the rear of the cave. The floor was warm, as if blood pulsated beneath it. He turned his head and saw that behind him, at the cave's end, flames licked out from cracks in the rock, about as high as a man's hips, fed by the sulfurous fumes. Now Johann finally knew where the glow and the heat came from. The cave was like a huge, scorching oven, fired by the primeval forces of the earth.

When Johann sat up this time, he saw the beast.

It was so tall that it nearly touched the ceiling with its head, which was as shaggy as that of a prehistoric ox, with two spiraled horns growing from its forehead. Its fur was black, and a long tail whipped through the cave, causing sparks to fly. The beast walked on two legs like a man, but its back was bent, the claws on its fingers reaching almost to the ground.

It's the fumes, thought Johann. *The fumes in the cave are making me hallucinate.*

And at the same time he knew that this was Tonio's true shape—the shape that had come before all the others.

The shape of the devil.

"Where is my daughter?" asked Johann. "Where are Karl and my grandson?"

The beast made a deep droning sound, a kind of sigh.

"What is it to you, Faustus? There is only you and me. When will you finally understand? Nothing else matters."

"That isn't true!" Even though his head was thumping and his limbs felt as soft as honey, Johann managed to get to his feet. "Where are they? Where is . . . where is my family?"

"*I* am your family. Always have been. The others are but embellishments in the story of you and me." The beast gestured behind himself. Now Johann saw some human bundles in the corner, dumped there like pieces of wood. He froze.

"Are they . . . ?" he asked.

"Dead? Not quite, though there isn't much life left in them. The toxic breath rising from the cracks is weakest back there. Shall I let them go? Is that what you want?"

Hope stirred in Johann. "You . . . would let them go?" he asked slowly.

"What am I? A kindly god with a big bushy beard? The silly old fellow?" The beast roared with laughter until several small stones from the mosaics fell from the ceiling. "You weren't particularly obedient, son, and played a fair few tricks on me. Why should I do you a favor? At Nuremberg, when the stars were favorable, I could have returned with your help—in my *true* shape. Instead I am still but a shadow, an outline on the walls of a cave. But all that is going to change soon, very soon!"

The beast leaned over Johann and sniffed him like a deer its newborn fawn. "What will you give me if I let your three little humans go? You know you can trade with me. I love bartering! War, trade, and piracy, they are a trinity indeed, inseparable. What will you give me?"

Trembling, Johann pulled out the little silver globe from beneath his shirt and held it up. He was standing right before the beast now, a small man in front of an enormous, supernatural monstrosity. Carefully he opened the pendant and pulled out the fragile paper.

"Ah, that's how I know the learned man," droned the beast. "Leonardo's formula. The legendary igró pir. I offered him a pact, just like you, but he thought he could play a trick on me and fled to France. As if anyone can flee from *me*!" The beast laughed again, and slaver as caustic as acid dripped to the floor. "So you found the formula. Well done, my son. It will help me to drown this world in chaos even faster. Men are exceptional students of the devil." The beast snarled, its eyes glowing like red embers and its tail whipping across the floor like a furious snake. "But I'm afraid this won't be enough."

"Won't be enough?" Johann withdrew the hand with the paper. "What else do you want?"

The beast leaned down to him until it was very close. Johann felt the hot breath of hell brush over him. "Don't you already know, little Faustus? I want *you*. The two of us are going to rule over this world: father, son, and an unholy ghost."

The beast laughed, stars shining in his eyes, yes, entire galaxies.

"Come back into the arms of your father, and I promise you I'm going to make you even more famous than you already are. I will make you richer than a king and mightier than a pope. Together we will set the world on fire! You must leave everything behind. Love is all that stands in your way!"

Johann slowly took a few steps back. He was very close to the spot where he wanted to be—where the flames were lapping out of the ground. Some of the cracks ran deep into the earth, and Johann had seen a blue-and-red glowing far below.

How far down might those cracks reach? wondered Johann. *All the way to hell?*

"Very well, you may have me!" he declared loudly. "And the formula. If you let the other three go. This is my promise." Carefully he folded the piece of paper again and replaced it inside the globe while the beast waited, visibly impatient. Finally Johann held the small silver pendant up high and said in a loud and firm voice: "This world shall be yours, and I shall be yours until the end of this world. In return, the others walk free."

The beast's claw jerked forward, but Johann pulled back his hand. An angry growl vibrated through the grotto.

"Don't play games with me!" snarled the beast.

"Say it!" demanded Johann. "I want to hear it from your mouth! We both know that words bind you. There are some ancient rules that even you must obey. So say it!" He held up the globe as if he were trying to tempt a bear with a pot of honey. "Say it!"

And the beast spoke the words: "This world shall be mine, and you shall be mine until the end of this world."

"In return you will let my daughter, my grandson Sebastian, and my assistant Karl Wagner walk free and live in peace forevermore. Promise!"

"I promise."

Johann smiled. He really was Tonio's son, a true magician. The greatest magician in the world.

And his final trick would be his best one yet.

With a sudden movement, Johann yanked the chain from his neck and handed the globe to the devil. The silver ball looked like a tiny pearl in the palm of the huge paw. Still, the beast managed to undo the two halves of the globe and take a look inside.

The halves were empty.

And realization dawned in the eyes of the beast.

"This world shall be yours," repeated Johann. "And I shall be yours until the end of this world."

Then he spun around and leaped into the flames.

"Nooooo!" roared the beast. "Stay with me! The two of us will be the rulers of the world! What have you done?"

Seething with rage, hatred, and disappointment, the devil clenched his talon around the small globe, the tiny silver world Johann had just handed him, then hurled the squashed lump against the wall.

You shall be mine until the end of this *world.*

And the devil roared as he realized that Faust had deceived him once more.

~

A loud, angry voice penetrated Karl's innermost consciousness.

It drilled its way through his ear canals and screamed through his head, causing him to wake up. Or was he only dreaming? The sulfurous fumes had made him lose his senses, just like they had with Greta and little Sebastian, who were lying next to him on the cave's floor, unconscious or perhaps dead. So who was screaming? It must have been a dream, a nightmare. Karl lifted his head. At the other end of the cave he saw the doctor disappearing into the glowing earth. For an instant Karl thought Faust was waving in farewell.

Karl squinted. Flames were lapping up from cracks, painting the cave in an otherworldly light. An enormous, hairy monster with horns was standing in front of the flaming hole into which the doctor had vanished. The beast roared, screeched, ranted, raved, and snorted. A hellstorm swirled through the cave, so hot that Karl thought his hair would catch on fire.

Hell! he thought. *This is hell. The pact is coming to an end.*

In that moment Karl knew that this was no dream. He knew the doctor had just left him forever. But it was strange: even though Faust was no longer there, the love for him remained, and Karl was no longer afraid. He felt the love like a warm, glowing gem in his heart. A smile spread on his face.

This is the true philosopher's stone.

The love filled him completely, and Karl knew: no matter how much the beast ranted and raved in this cave, against this force, against the power of love, even the devil was powerless.

Johann was no more—he had gone to hell right before Karl's eyes—and yet he would always be with Karl.

This thought helped Karl to stay sane.

What also helped was that he lost consciousness again.

~

Johann was falling.

He knew that his fall was already taking much longer than the laws of nature permitted. But he also knew that the laws of nature didn't apply to this world. He was surrounded by blazing flames licking at his clothes. Strangely, they were not hot but cold, as if he was tumbling through space. Johann fell, and yet he was weightless, a down feather drifting in the wind, and for the first time in his life he felt something that had been entirely foreign to him until then.

Peace.

No restless pondering and searching, no urge, no thunderstorm of thoughts.

He simply was.

Until just a few moments ago, his thoughts had been spinning. Johann knew the devil couldn't be vanquished. But he could be cheated. Greed blinded the devil, and Leonardo had known it, too. Back in the underground passages below Nuremberg, Johann had also managed to trick the devil, and now he'd done it again.

For the last time.

With a simple sleight of hand—a trick Tonio himself had taught Johann.

With words and gestures Johann had managed to distract the beast for one fleeting moment. Instead of placing the formula on the tissue paper back inside the globe, he had slipped it into the pocket of his trousers. Now, as he fell, he pulled out the paper and let it go. It flared up, turned to ashes, disintegrated, and was gone.

My final magic trick, thought Johann.

The secret of the igró pir would remain secret—at least until someone else set about the task of creating a deadly weapon for mankind. Johann knew the day would come. He himself had chosen a different weapon in his battle against the devil, a weapon that was just as deadly as fire.

Words.

This world shall be mine, and you shall be mine until the end of this world.

Tonio had uttered those words as Johann handed him the globe. And in the moment that the devil destroyed the globe in anger, Johann had been free.

The end of this world.

The devil was bound by his promise, decreed by a law as old as the world itself. Johann laughed, though no sound came out of his mouth. Greta, Karl, and little Sebastian—his grandson—they would live! Perfect happiness flooded through him.

He remembered playing in the hay with Greta's mother as a child, how he performed his first magic tricks for Margarethe, the prefect's daughter; he thought of their first kiss and their secret hours together as they had explored and tasted each other's bodies for the first time. His love for Margarethe, the passion he had felt for exotic performer Salome as a young man, and most of all his love for Greta had carried Johann through life in spite of the unhappy pact with Tonio.

He had laden guilt upon himself and created something good; he had loved and he had sinned, made mistakes and regretted them—in short, he had been human.

Man errs and staggers from his birth.

Yes, he had lived a full life, and he would leave something behind.

A daughter and a grandson.

And a bag full of stories.

And as Johann hurtled toward the great light at the end of the abyss, he thought how well his mother had done to give him this strange name.

Faustus. The lucky one.

He had never felt luckier than in this very moment.

~

Birds were singing, a woodpecker was hammering, and a bell started chiming softly, followed by many other bells. A myriad of other bells!

Karl opened his eyes and looked up at the sky, which was blue and cloudless. Twigs pricked him through his clothes, and he felt bitter cold. It was a crisp and bright December morning.

This isn't hell, thought Karl. *Where am I?*

He sat up awkwardly, his head thumping as if the countless bells were tolling inside his skull. He felt as miserable as if he'd been drinking wine all night. It must have been because of the toxic fumes he—

Karl started, suddenly feeling wide awake.

Toxic fumes!

He looked around. It would seem he was in the small wood at the foot of Palatine Hill, somewhere close to the shaft. Among the barren trees stood remains of walls, broken columns, and stone arches that probably used to belong to the palace of Emperor Augustus. Memories rained down on Karl. He had climbed down into this cave with Johann and Greta, and Tonio had awaited them there with Sebastian on his lap. The doctor had spoken with Tonio, but then everything became blurry. Fragments flashed through Karl's mind that didn't make sense. A huge shaggy beast, a roaring, tongues of fire. Karl frowned. Somehow he had made it out of the cave. He turned around and saw a pile of rocks that looked as if they were freshly collapsed. Beside the rocks lay two figures.

One bigger and one much smaller.

"Oh God, no." Karl scrambled toward them.

Greta was holding little Sebastian in a tight embrace, like the Mother Mary in Michelangelo's pietà. Their eyes were closed and their faces deathly pale. His heart beating heavily, Karl bent over Greta. Her skin was cold, much too cold.

"It cannot be," he sobbed, shaking her. "It just cannot be. Please."

Sebastian began to cry, and moments later, Greta started to grouse.

"How dare you wake me from my deepest—"

She shot up. Her face was soot stained, her hair tangled and full of leaves. "Sebastian!" she gasped and drew her son into her arms. "Where are we? Where is Tonio?"

Karl was so relieved that he couldn't speak for a few moments. The bells of Rome continued to chime, the day was only just beginning, and a cold sun came edging across the eastern end of the city.

"Tonio appears to have vanished, just like your father," said Karl eventually. "Evidently we made it out of the cave. Don't ask me how." He pointed at the pile of rocks. "Perhaps that was the entrance. Now it is sealed for good."

"Sealed?" Greta rocked her son and he soon calmed down. She hoped last night was nothing but a nasty dream in the child's memory. Greta pushed him under her dress, warming him with her body. "And my father?"

"We need to find the shaft." With shaky legs, Karl hurried ahead. It took them a while, but eventually they found the spot where they had climbed down into the cave the night before. By daylight and with the leaves covered in hoarfrost, the green bunches of parsley looked rather pretty. The rope they had used for their descent still hung into the hole, but when Karl went on his knees and peered into the darkness, he gasped with shock.

"The shaft has collapsed," he said. "I can see rubble just a few feet down. Maybe there was an earthquake in the night, or the stones came loose, or—"

"If my father was still down there, then he is dead," said Greta softly but decidedly. "Either he has been struck down by rocks or else the fumes would have killed him by now."

"Maybe . . . maybe he managed to get out, just like us."

"Then why isn't he here?" Greta shook her head, her jaw clenched. "My father is dead. I can feel it. Remember what I saw in his hand a long time ago."

Faust is dead.

Something in Karl refused to accept this thought. *Never.*

"Your father knows every trick in the book," he said. "He is a wizard, remember? And he—"

"He is dead," insisted Greta. "Accept it, Karl. He has been wanting to die since the moment he decided to face up to Tonio. He and Tonio." She paused. "Maybe they both found their grave down there."

"Maybe."

Once more he saw the hairy beast in his mind's eye, a beast with horns, surrounded by blazing flames, and in front of a glowing abyss into which the doctor jumps and vanishes.

Had the devil finally come to take Faust?

"Do you know what's strange?" said Greta as Sebastian tugged at her hand.

The boy wanted to get away from here; he must have been cold and hungry. And yet he didn't cry, almost as if he sensed that his mother was speaking of his grandfather, who had gone forever.

"I truly hated my father," continued Greta. "He killed the father of my child, and he deceived us—yes, all of us, for years. He was in league with evil forces. But now that he is no more . . ." She hesitated, staring at the hole full of rubble. "I believe I have made my peace with him."

Karl nodded. "Me too."

Gradually the realization sank in that Faust might actually have disappeared for good. Left behind was the love Karl had felt for the doctor. Love, but also admiration and respect for the greatest magician of all time.

"I think he will never be forgotten," he said eventually. "They will still remember him in many hundred years. Just like they are going to remember Leonardo da Vinci."

"Who knows, perhaps you're right." Greta's eyes gazed into the distance. "Remember the time in Erfurt when he promised the students he'd conjure up beautiful Helen, and out of the chest came you?"

"Of course!" In spite of himself, Karl started to grin. "Especially the wig. Dyed horsehair down to my hips." He breathed deeply. The memories helped give a home to his grief. "Or the time the doctor held the fireworks at Frankfurt and declared he could fly into the sky on one of the big rockets."

Greta laughed. "And all the while he was already upon the spire and all he had to do was wave. Or remember at Bamberg, when he used the laterna magica to make the prince-bishop and the collective delegates believe they were actually seeing the devil."

"The laterna magica." Karl sighed. "It's a crying shame it was destroyed back then. All those lovely images I painted."

"You could build another one yourself," suggested Greta. "You spent years traveling the empire with the doctor and the laterna magica."

"And why would I do that?" asked Karl. "It was always Faust who thrilled the crowds. I was just the assistant. If the doctor is dead, then . . ."

Greta gave him a questioning look. "What is it?"

"Nothing. I . . . I just had an idea," replied Karl. He frowned as he continued his line of thought.

Faust isn't dead.

"Let me sleep on it," he said after a while. He shook himself and gave Greta and Sebastian an affectionate look. "And what are you two going to do?"

Greta shrugged. "I don't know. I can't go back to Santo Spirito." She brushed Sebastian's red hair from his forehead and squeezed him tight. "I am his mother, that's all that matters for now. I will never leave my son alone again. Everything else will fall into place."

"Everything else will fall into place." Karl nodded and gazed toward the city that stretched in all directions. To the southeast lay the snowcapped Alban Hills. The wide, brown ribbon of the Tiber flowed toward the sea. To the north, fields and meadows stretched as far as the eye could see. If he looked very carefully, he could make out the Via Aurelia, the old Roman road winding its way through the frosty, sugarcoated landscape.

And out into the world.

"This life still has much to offer," said Karl. "Behind every hill a new story awaits."

He stood up and, alongside Greta holding little Sebastian by the hand, walked down the Palatine Hill and toward the bustling, noisy lanes in which every person every day tried in vain to rail against their fate.

In the crystal-clear sky above circled two lonesome crows and a raven.

Epilogue

THE GIANT WORE A LONG AND SHAGGY BEARD THAT REACHED almost to the ground. He was clad in the stained robe of a monk, and his staff was as tall as a fir tree. The scoundrel's head jutted above the crowns of the trees in the forest. A murmur went through the crowd in the hall, and some of the smaller children whined and clung to their mothers with their eyes pinched shut. But most of the spectators stared straight ahead as if spellbound by the sailcloth at the front, which billowed in the draft going through the room, making the giant on the fabric look alive.

"The mighty Rübezahl," intoned the voice of the man standing next to the canvas. "I once met him during my travels through the Giant Mountains. He who mocks Rübezahl or wishes him ill will be met with thunder, lightning, and hailstorms. He who comes as a friend may visit his garden, where the most mysterious herbs grow. One of the herbs has the power to make you fly!"

The man beside the canvas raised his arms inside the wide sleeves of his black-and-blue coat. His face was hidden by a wide-brimmed, floppy hat. The image on the sailcloth changed, showing just that man flying through the clouds like a bird. The audience cried out with surprise.

"I was arguing with Rübezahl over the question of which of us was the most powerful wizard in all the land," the man next to the canvas continued. "When he tried to smite me with his cudgel the size of a tree, I swiftly ate some of those herbs and flew away through the clouds. Then—"

"Pray, honorable Doctor Faustus, what . . . what's it like, flying?" asked a portly older farmer's wife in a trembling voice. "Isn't it rather exhausting, flapping your arms like a bird the whole time?"

The man with the floppy hat gave her a look of impatience through the eye glasses on his nose, something only scholars wore. "That is not necessary, dear. You hover all by yourself. But it isn't particularly, well . . . pleasant." He shook his head as if a memory had just come to him. "Not pleasant at all! But let me go on with my tale. Once I escaped from Rübezahl, I came to the land of the creatures with legs growing straight from their heads and of man-eating panthers."

The image changed again, and now it showed a big black cat ready to pounce. Some in the crowd screamed out with fear, others with excitement and awe. Three days ago, the famous Doctor Johann Georg Faustus had come to their small town, and since then no one spoke of anything else. The old folks told of the doctor's manifold travels, pranks, and adventures; the doctor had visited the town many years earlier with his assistant. Now he had returned, and he looked like he hadn't aged a day—on the contrary, he seemed to have grown younger. It must have been the healing herbs from the garden of Rübezahl, or perhaps the theriac that the doctor sold for three kreuzers a bottle. Doctor Faustus's Original Theriac rejuvenated; helped with ailments of the eyes, constipation, limb pain; and even worked as a stain remover.

The town had given Doctor Faustus the dance hall in the best tavern at the square, and the people pushed together in close rows. This was the third show that day, and the stream of adventures, anecdotes, and tales wasn't slowing. A snowstorm rattled the closed shutters, the wind howling like an animal. These were the weeks of the shortest days and the darkest time of the year, and it was nearly Christmas. People needed thrilling stories as badly as medicine.

"When the panther leaped toward me, I ducked at the last moment," said Faust now, accompanying his tale with wild gestures and grimaces. "As he flew past me, I jumped upon him and rode the beast like a horse!"

Greta was sitting in the first row and smiled. Karl always laid it on rather thickly. He elaborated on true stories, embellished a little here and there, spontaneously added some new monsters, and seasoned the concoction with a few scientific facts. During his presentations, his voice was always a little deeper and rougher than usual. People hung on his every word—he was a born story-teller. Even Greta was so entranced sometimes that she forgot to change the glass image in the laterna magica.

Four-year-old Sebastian on her lap, she was sitting on one of the few chairs in the hall, right beside the wooden box that Karl had built two years ago. Since then they'd been traveling through the German lands and beyond. The laterna wasn't as big as the one her father had constructed once upon a time, but they didn't visit any castles and palaces, either. Their stages were smaller, performing at taverns and inns along the post roads. Karl sold Doctor Faustus's Original Theriac and Greta sometimes juggled a little or balanced on rope above the market square. She was still a talented juggler, but by now she had become an even better healer, and so had Karl. Following their shows the two of them cared for the sick and injured, and especially for those who couldn't afford to see a physician, and there were many of them.

Their biggest attraction was still the laterna magica. In the beam of light streaming from inside the apparatus danced dust particles like tiny animals. Karl called the laterna his "story-weaving machine," and he excelled at continually inventing new stories. Stories that helped to keep the one great tale alive.

The tale of Doctor Johann Georg Faustus.

"In Leipzig, I even flew upon a wine barrel when the tight innkeeper wouldn't let me have it . . . wouldn't let me . . . um . . ."

Greta startled from her reveries when she noticed that Karl had stopped speaking. He was looking at her expectantly. Once again she had forgotten to change the image. Her hands in thin leather gloves, she pulled out the hot glass plate and carefully inserted a new one into the slit. The crate on the floor in front of her contained dozens more glass plates, all neatly sorted, many of them showing figures from German folklore. Others showed animals from faraway countries or comic sketches.

When Doctor Faustus was shown flying through the air astride a barrel, pursued by a visibly furious and very fat, sweaty innkeeper, the laughter was great. Greta and Karl always made sure that each show included not only scary stories but also funny, instructive, and uplifting ones. After all, there were many children among the spectators, and also pious elderly and sometimes even the town priest or other dignitaries. Little Sebastian followed every show with wide eyes, even though he knew most of the tales by heart. Greta hoped ardently that to Sebastian, the encounter with Tonio del Moravia two winters ago was nothing but another nebulous tale. A glass plate whose image was slowly fading.

The cave beneath Palatine Hill.

In the days that had followed, the idea had ripened. At first Greta had been skeptical when Karl told her of his plan.

"We are going to keep the doctor alive," he had told her back in Rome. "Faust is too great to die."

Greta wasn't sure why Karl chose to take this path. He had always been more of a scientist and physician than a juggler. But then she had understood that this was Karl's final proof of love. By becoming Faust, Karl was keeping his love for him alive. It was as if he had ingested the doctor like a sacred wafer. Maybe Karl's never-ending affection had something to do with the letter he had found in an inside pocket of his coat several days after the incident at the cave. It was a letter the doctor must have written shortly before his death. Karl had never told Greta the contents of the letter, but it must have been warm words of comfort. Karl always carried the letter with him, like a treasure.

The most amazing thing about Faust's resurrection was that it had actually worked. During the first year they had avoided places that Faust and Karl had previously visited. But soon such precautions had no longer been necessary. No one ever pointed their finger at Karl and accused him of being a fraud. On the contrary: a few times people had told them about other traveling Fausts, whereupon Karl would declare with outrage that he was the only true Doctor Faustus and all the others impostors who ought to be put in the stocks. The most hair-raising tales were going around about the doctor, leaflets, drawings, and even a small book had been printed, and a bigger one was supposed to follow.

Greta couldn't help but smile.

Faust is too great to die.

Karl had been right—the legend was greater than the man. And she and Karl fed this legend with each new story and with each new glass image that Karl created with paint and brush, often working all through the night.

For two years now they had been traveling thus, and most people probably assumed that Greta was the doctor's wife. She didn't do anything to discourage those assumptions. For a sodomite like Karl, who failed to resist temptation from time to time, it was good to have a woman and a child at his side. It protected him from suspicions. She, too, had enjoyed the occasional fling; her time as a sister of the order was well and truly finished. But she hadn't found the right one. She only needed to look at Sebastian's red shock of hair and the memories of John returned.

Time heals all wounds, thought Greta. *But ugly scars remain.*

"The olifant is a strange creature indeed," said Karl, pointing at the flickering drawing of an elephant on the canvas. This was the scientific part of their show, which Karl loved the most. "It uses its trunk for drinking, but also as a weapon and as an arm to break off branches. The legendary caliph Al Rashid gifted one such olifant to the great emperor Charlemagne. In battle, the enemy would run screaming from this giant beast."

Karl had completed this image not long ago after he found the picture in an old book at a monastery. Meanwhile he had learned that Pope Leo also used to own one such elephant. Greta sometimes thought of the lunatic Medici pope who was killed by his own panthers during the attempt to summon the devil. Her father's prediction had been right: the Vatican had swept the affair under the carpet. Officially, Leo had died very suddenly of a winter flu. His debts had been so extensive that, apparently, there hadn't even been enough money to pay for the candles for his funeral.

Leo's successor, Pope Hadrian VI, a pious man who had wanted to lead the church back onto the path of virtue, had died just a year later. There had been rumors of poison. Now there was another pope from the powerful Medici family on the throne. The Lutherans could no longer be stopped, the church was divided, and in Italy the German emperor and the French king were still at loggerheads. War, envy, and intrigue.

Basically, everything was the same as always.

Sometimes Greta wondered what had become of the igró pir recipe that her father had wanted to give Tonio in exchange for her son. Evidently, they hadn't gone through with the trade. Tonio would have sold the weapon to the highest bidder, or perhaps to all parties at once so that Europe would be reduced to ashes. But Greta increasingly gained the impression that mankind succeeded rather well at killing and tormenting one another without Tonio's help.

Tonio.

A chill ran down her spine as Karl told the audience about his journey through the hot deserts of Africa. They had never heard anything of Tonio del Moravia again. And yet Greta knew that he was still there, somewhere out there. Whether he was dead or alive, he would live on in the tales, just like Faust. Some nights she would wake up screaming because she thought Tonio was leaning over her, feeling her and sniffing her. Ravens and crows frightened her since the events in Rome, and she chased those inquisitive birds away by throwing stones whenever she saw any. Her father's legacy still slumbered inside her, as well as the eerie gift of foretelling death.

She never wanted to use that gift again.

It was too somber, a kind of devilish mark of Cain that reminded her how like her father she was.

I am the daughter of Faust.

Greta looked over to Karl, who was nodding at her. She inserted the final glass plate into the slit. It showed the image of a guardian angel who was standing behind a child with its arms spread. Karl had drawn it especially for Sebastian, and it was the boy's favorite picture. Even now he whooped with joy and pointed his little finger at it. In the background of the image, flames were lapping out of the ground, and the devil writhed with anger because he failed to drag the child down to hell.

The child was protected.

"Good people of this town, may your guardian angel watch over you on your way home and shield you from the devil," said Karl, concluding their final show for the day with a wink. "And don't forget to drop your kreuzers into my hat. As you know, I am Doctor Faustus and I can conjure up demons and worse if I don't get paid!"

Greta hugged Sebastian tightly and gave him a kiss. Whatever might be lurking out there, she would never leave Sebastian again. Evil had no more power over her son or herself or Karl.

They had banished evil into their stories.

Or so Greta hoped.

As the people dropped their coins in Karl's hat and walked out into the cold winter's night, murmuring and laughing, Greta placed the last glass plate into the crate and shut the lid. Enough for today.

But tomorrow, the show would go on.

Johann Georg Faustus would live forever.

Afterword

When I was still in the middle of writing the first book in my Faust saga, *The Master's Apprentice*, and told a friend of mine that there was going to be a second part, he replied promptly: "Well, Goethe's *Faust II* was quite the flop."

I truly hope it will be different with my sequel.

But basically, my friend was right. While Johann Wolfgang von Goethe's *Faust Part I* is perhaps the best-known German play, hardly anyone knows the second part. And to be honest, it isn't easy to get to know because it is rarely performed onstage—not least because it is so darned long. In the year 2000, well-known theater director Peter Stein brought both Faust parts together onstage, and without breaks, it took fifteen hours to stage it! Hardly any theatergoers have that much time. Allegedly, the director himself said later: "When you see the third or fourth showing, you realize that it's rubbish."

I wouldn't go quite that far, but it is true that *Faust Part II* seems a little, well . . . overambitious. Almost as if toward the end of his life, Goethe wanted to show the world one last time what he was made of. The story is brimming with mythological figures and innuendos, and at the same time it is practically impossible to summarize the storyline in a halfway decent manner. Movie producers would say, "Where the f . . . is the plot?" For a good and rather funny overview, I recommend *Faust II to Go* on YouTube, where the entire play is performed in less than twelve minutes by Playmobil figurines. Another option is reading this novel. It takes a little longer but is also quite entertaining.

If you read the first volume, you will know that Doctor Faustus really existed. *The Master's Apprentice* tells the story of how Faust became the restless, egocentric, and yet somehow lovable magician, astrologer, and quack. The second volume describes Faust's (supposed) demise. My version doesn't follow

Goethe's complicated plot (thank God!), but I still tried to accommodate some of his themes. You could say that Goethe is my very own master. And I'd say that isn't the poorest choice for a writer.

Unlike in the first, more personal part, this time the big politics of the time affect the lives of the protagonists. The 1519 election of the German king is easily on par with any current American presidential campaign. Just like in the US today, the candidates needed one thing more than anything else: money, and lots of it. The king of the Germans was elected by the seven German electors. The candidates were the grandson of the late emperor Maximilian, Charles, who had grown up in the Netherlands and Spain and knew the German Empire only from tales; and Maximilian's old opponent, King Francis I of France. With the help of the Fuggers and nearly one million guilders, Charles indeed managed to bribe the German electors and decide the election of the German king in his favor. Nonetheless, it was a close race, and the German Empire almost got a French king. Who knows how our history would have developed then? In any case, Francis sulked following his defeat and retreated to the Loire Valley to work on his castles. In that regard he resembles the Bavarian fairy-tale king whose memory I honor in my historical thriller *The Ludwig Conspiracy*. If you'd like to learn more about the Hollywood-worthy wrestling of the two powerful rulers Charles and Francis, I recommend my novel *The Castle of Kings*.

In Goethe's *Faust Part II*, the emperor's dire need for money leads first to the manufacture of paper money and then to devastating inflation. In my novel, the philosopher's stone takes its place. While the formula to make gold was never discovered, many scientists at the beginning of the sixteenth century considered it not a silly idea but a real possibility. What today we call chemistry was then known as alchemy, a field that the real Doctor Faustus must have been rather good at. I liked the idea of various powerful leaders struggling to extract this secret from Faust—and all the while he doesn't even know it.

Aside from money, war also has a significant role in Goethe's play. In my search for the perfect weapon I happened across ιγρό πιρ, the Greek fire. It was a top-secret incendiary that belonged to the most feared weapons of antiquity and the early Middle Ages. Components of Greek fire are petroleum, sulfur, burnt lime, and several other ingredients. If correctly produced, it can't be put out with water and sets alight anything it touches. I was surprised to learn that this miracle weapon completely vanished after the conquest of Constantinople in 1453, at the latest. In my novel, Leonardo da Vinci succeeds at reproducing igró pir. Consequently, questions arise that are comparable to the questions scientists around five hundred years later must ask themselves on the subjects of nuclear power and genetics: How far may science go? What ethical boundaries are there, and how can we protect those boundaries? And so we arrive at Leonardo da Vinci.

Next to Faust, Leonardo is the hero of this second volume. If you had to define the Renaissance with one person, he is the figure who epitomizes this era. Has there ever been a greater genius? Painter, sculptor, inventor, anatomist, mechanic, architect, musician, and, on top of everything, he was left-handed, a vegetarian, a pacifist, and homosexual. It's easy to become addicted once you start reading about Leonardo da Vinci. For beginners I would recommend Walter Isaacson's gripping biography and Stefan Klein's *Leonardo's Legacy: How Da Vinci Reimagined the World*, a highly entertaining read. Both books have helped me greatly during my research and are as thrilling to read as novels. From those works I borrowed Leonardo's gloomy predictions for the future of mankind. How would Leonardo react to the possibility of genetically manipulating babies? What would he—pacifist and inventor of war machines—say about the atom bomb? Our modern-day scientific way of thinking had its beginnings in the Renaissance.

Leonardo da Vinci left behind around ten thousand sketches and notes, and many of them have now been lost. Who knows, maybe there's a formula for the legendary igró pir among the missing documents? By the way, apparently Leonardo often considered having his anatomical knowledge recorded and bound in a book titled *Figura Umana*. But the master was working on so many projects at once that he never got around to it—only in my novel.

As in every good story, there are not just heroes but also villains. In my research for the first part of my Faust saga, I came across the French knight Gilles de Rais, who lived at the time of the Hundred Years' War and was a close companion of Jeanne d'Arc, the Maid of Orléans. Almost everything I wrote about him is true—as horrible as it seems.

Gilles de Rais became a marshal of France, but he lived beyond his means. After trying to produce gold, he grew enamored of the idea of invoking the devil. To please Satan, but also taking personal pleasure in it, he murdered hundreds of children. He tortured them in the cruelest manner and sometimes even violated their dead bodies. If the devil ever existed in human form, then Gilles de Rais comes very close to it. He was only convicted after many years and hanged alongside two of his companions at Nantes. His helpers in my novel—Henriet, Poitou, La Meffraye, and the priest François Prelati—all existed, just like the castles of Tiffauges, Champtocé, and Machecoul, where many of the children were murdered. Their bodies were burned in the cellars, and their bones tossed into the moat. Gilles de Rais lived on as a symbol of terror in French mythology. The fairy tale "Bluebeard," by Charles Perrault, also told in another form by the Brothers Grimm, is based upon him.

Whenever I wrote a scene involving the devil, in my mind's eye I saw Gustaf Gründgens, the pale-faced, clownish Mephistopheles from the 1960 theatrical film that left such an impression on me as a youth. Gründgens, too, entered into a Faustian pact, namely with the Nazis. This pact is the theme of the novel *Mephisto* by Klaus Mann, which is one of my favorite books. If you haven't read it yet, do—it's worth it.

One cannot write a Faust novel without the devil, nor without science and the urge to reach for the stars, the need to reach further and never be satisfied— that which is called Faustian. Gilles de Rais and Leonardo da Vinci represent the two extremes of this notion. Both show what man is capable of, for good as well as for evil. In that sense, Johann Georg Faustus is very human, standing precisely between the two poles, between God and the devil, not perfectly good and not wholly evil, just like most of us.

Adieu, Johann! You accompanied me for nearly five years of my life. I'm going to miss you!

As always, many people helped to turn a few vague thoughts into a full-fledged novel. Thank you to Jeanne Banizet, from the Metz tourist information, who gave me a good understanding of her town and filled the gaps in my knowledge, and thank you also to the kind archivists at Orléans who supplied me with everything they had on Jeanne d'Arc and Orléans, despite my poor French. In the Loire Valley and later at Tiffauges, there were plenty of helpful people who showed me that the French can be warm and welcoming even if you don't speak their language.

Thank you to my father, who combed the manuscript for medical errors. To my son, Niklas, who contributed with some fantastic ideas and spotted a few mistakes. To Uta Rupprecht, my long-standing editor. To Gerd Schweizer for the books and information on Knittlingen. To the entire team at Ullstein Publishing, who, as always, have been amazingly supportive. Thank you to Barbara Keydel for the Italian translations, Professor Manfred Heim for correcting my dog Latin, and Dr. Irene Balles and Dr. Diarmuid Johnson for the Breton translations. To Claudia, for placing her apartment in Rome at my disposal and supporting me with bicycle, pump, spanner, and much patience; and thank you to the friendly porter at the Hospital Santo Spirito in Sassia. Thank you also to Gerd and Martina from the Rumler Agency and to Christine Rothwinkler, who organizes my book tours with unique dedication (perhaps we could do one to France someday?). And thank you of course to my wife, Katrin, who, as always, trial read this manuscript. You are the best!

Faust for Beginners

Like *The Master's Apprentice*, *The Devil's Pawn* also contains numerous Goethe quotes—this time, of course, from both Faust parts. Did you spot them all?

Faust Part I translations by Charles T. Brooks. *Faust Part II* translations by Lisa Reinhardt.

- Much admired and much scorned. (Faust II, verse 8488)
- Shuddering is man's best quality. (Faust II, verse 6272)
- Each day to this small folk's a feast of fun. (Faust I, verse 2161)
- That's how I know the learned man. (Faust II, verse 4917)
- Am called Magister, Doctor, indeed . . . (Verse 3600)
- These people never smell the old rat, e'en when he has them by the collar. (Faust I, verses 2181 ff)
- Well, art is long! And life is short and fleeting. (Faust I, verse 558)
- My fair young lady . . . (Faust I, verse 2605)
- What you don't feel, you'll never catch by hunting. (Faust I, verse 534)
- I like people who strive for the impossible. (Faust II, verse 7488)
- Quite a peculiar juice is blood. (Faust I, verse 1740)
- Each burns for gold, all turns on gold. (Faust I, verses 2802 ff)
- Name is but sound and smoke. (Faust I, verse 3456)
- War, trade, and piracy, they are a trinity indeed, inseparable! (Faust II, verse 11187)
- Man errs and staggers from his birth. (Faust I, verse 313)

Quotes from Dante's *Divine Comedy* are from the translation by the Rev. H. F. Cary, M.A.

About the Author

Oliver Pötzsch worked for years as a journalist and scriptwriter for Bavarian television. He is the author of seven books in the international bestselling Hangman's Daughter historical series, the children's novel *Knight Kyle and the Magic Silver Lance*, and the Black Musketeers series, including *Book of the Night* and *Sword of Power*. His work has been translated into more than twenty languages. Oliver lives in Munich with his family. For more information, visit www.oliver-poetzsch.de.

About the Translator

Lisa Reinhardt studied English and linguistics at University of Otago and lives with her family on the beautiful West Coast of New Zealand. Her most recent work includes *The Council of Twelve*, the seventh book in Oliver Pötzsch's Hangman's Daughter series.